Margaret P. Kirk was b[...]
lives in Oregon with he[...]
first novel.

MARGARET P. KIRK

Always a Stranger

Futura

A *Futura* Book

ISBN 0 7088 2732 2

Reproduced, printed and bound in Great Britain by
Hazell Watson & Viney Limited,
Member of the BPCC Group,
Aylesbury, Bucks

Futura Publications
A Division of
Macdonald & Co (Publishers) Ltd
Maxwell House
74 Worship Street
London EC2A 2EN
A BPCC plc Company

For Jurek, Jan and Pam

BOOK I

CHAPTER ONE

Warsaw: 1 September, 1939.

It was the uncertainty, he knew that. It shortened tempers, lengthened the days, knotted the mind.

The cadets moved slower this morning, he as slowly as any of them. He made his bed, fudged a little on the required square corners, then climbed into a track suit for the calisthenics that must be endured before breakfast. Complaining, with the others, of the heat, he jogged to the playing field behind the barracks where the gym instructors waited.

He fell in line with his group, one small segment of the Polish Air Force Officers' School, and for almost an hour forced himself through the motions of keeping fit. Knee-bends, jumping-jacks, push-ups — today too many push-ups. The yellow stubble of the September field scratched at his palms, sweat dripped from his hair into the caked ground, instructors growled their orders. And why not? The instructors waited, too. Everything waited. The barracks, the city, all Poland held its breath.

Their training had been intensified and accelerated until now there was time for nothing but learning and eating and sleeping, with but one Sunday afternoon in three off duty. Jan's own Sunday came up in two days. He was already planning which bus to take, what flowers to buy for his mother, what tidbit of military rumour to feed his father —

rumour, at least, was plentiful.

'Cadet Kaliski! Are you with us – or perhaps you'd prefer to take laps in lieu of breakfast?' The nearest instructor scowled, went through the motions of threatening, but the eyes were blank, the threat a matter of habit.

A sudden nudge found Jan's ribs. It was the plump elbow of Roman Kowalewski, friend through elementary and middle school, and now cadet school.

'Watch out for the son of a bitch – if you get detention you can kiss off Sunday.'

'Uh-huh – but it's so damned hot.' He tried to concentrate on a monotonous one hundred toe-touches but the uncertainty stayed with him.

It was during a lull in the shouted commands to 'shape up and snap to' that he heard the throb of engines high above them, coming in from the west. To a man, the cadets and instructors stopped dead. Fifty faces turned up to heaven. Planes! Twenty – no, thirty! in tight formation, black and beautiful against the brassy morning sky. Fifty throats opened in a unanimous cheer.

'*Angielskie, Angielskie!*'

Jan grinned. So one rumour at least had some truth to it. The English were sending help, and not a moment too soon. Above them soared what must be the first batch of planes to supplement Poland's own meagre count of P11s, surely less than adequate to counter the threat of a Germany once again on the move. Roman, wide face alight, seized him in a bear hug and pumped him up and down, bellowing into his ear.

'What did I tell you? It's just what I said. Isn't it just what I said would happen?'

It wasn't, but Jan didn't remind him. All around them cadets whooped and laughed and stomped, stirred up the dry field into a cloud of dust. Relief swept over him, over all of them, as tangible as the dust itself. Poland, trapped between Russia to the east and Germany to the west, had for too many centuries served as a battleground for its warring neighbours, then as the booty to divide up when the wars were over. No more. This time it would be different. France and England were powerful allies, the ink on the treaty barely dry. The huge engines throbbing overhead gave substance to the hope. Poland was not alone. Austria and Czechoslovakia had fallen but Poland, thanks to the flotilla above them and all the others to follow, Poland would stand.

It was Bauman, top student in Aircraft Recognition and resident realist, who pricked the bubble.

'German,' he said flatly. 'Dornier 17s. Range 720 miles. Wingspan 59 feet. Airspeed 255mph at an altitude ...'

'*Nie, nie!*' His litany was quickly submerged under the shouts of men-boys – who desperately wanted him to be wrong. Jan was silent. He made pretty fair marks in Recognition himself and the aircraft, nearer now, had outlines that were vaguely familiar.

A frozen second later all hope shattered, tumbled to earth with the stick-clusters that suddenly extruded like monstrous larvae from the bellies of the Dorniers. Anti-aircraft guns in the adjoining field stuttered into life. If confirmation were needed, this was it.

'Down! Get down!' an instructor yelled. Jan threw himself face down into the brittle grass. Through the crump of exploding bombs and the fussy chatter of the guns he could hear Roman beating his fists against the earth, shouting up at the sky.

'*Cholera*! *Cholera*! What the hell's going on?'

'The war,' Jan said. 'It's started.'

In Warsaw at least, the first two days of war were something of an anticlimax. True, a handful of planes had bombed at random, uniforms appeared on the streets with more frequency, staff cars honked importantly at intersections. But young women still strolled down Nowy Świat in thin summer dresses, old men in their shirt sleeves tossed bread to the pigeons, and the Vistula threaded the streets like a copper ribbon.

The cadets were told they would remain at the school until orders arrived to report to their squadrons. And yes, those with Sunday passes could use them. Jan, pass in hand, was about to leave his stifling room at the barracks for the cool of his parents' home on Morska Street when he heard the cheers from the messroom down the hall. What now? What new rumour could cause such a reaction in a place already saturated with rumour? It was the messroom radio, and this time it was no rumour. England had entered the war.

The news was shouted everywhere, from the tobacconist on the corner to the church-goers passing by, from the bus driver to the passengers, and even – as he stepped from the bus at Morska Street – the flower seller on the pavement gravely explaining to his dog just why the war would end next week, or maybe tonight.

Idiot! Nevertheless Jan grinned as he bought bronze chrysanthemums. In the general euphoria it was hard not to be optimistic. He hurried along the familiar cobblestones looking for signs of bomb damage, but found everything just the same as it always was. Tall apartment buildings shaded him from the sun; pots of geraniums blazed like crimson flags on the balconies; there was the twitch of Mrs Adamski's lace curtain as she logged his arrival. As always, he barely resisted the urge to yell 'Present!' into the froth of lace.

And there was his own front door, the cold of its brass handle surprising him back to reality. Under all the optimism new uncertainties grew and multiplied. The smoke from last night's raid still hung on the air. How long before Morska Street was the casual target?

He stepped into the hall and all at once the known features of the house steadied him. The radio murmured quietly to itself in the living room, with no one there to listen. Dishes clattered in the scullery. From the street the rumble of a horse and cart came in at the open windows, but faintly, everything cushioned by walls built to repel winter blasts sweeping down off the steppes and summer heat-waves rolling in off the vast flat plain.

His mother was stirring an icy borsch in the kitchen, her movements deft and birdlike as she sprinkled dill into the blood red soup. On the sideboard a loaf of rye bread and a slab of butter flanked the waiting bowls. He bent to kiss her and breathed vanilla and lemon and a touch of the cologne Uncle Tadeusz sent every Christmas from Zakopane. Cupping her thin shoulderblades in his palms, it seemed to him she gave off a current, that everything in the house ran on wires powered by this tiny woman. She turned to kiss him, gave a quick tug at his short military haircut as if to make it grow.

'They make you look like a pauper,' she said. 'Tatuš is reading in his room. Go keep him company until I've made the meal. My God, but they're keeping you thin at that place! What are they feeding you, bread and cabbage?'

To look into his mother's face was a long way down. 'Did you hear?' he said. 'England's declared war.'

She shrugged. 'So? Took them long enough. Two days wasted. Pass the sour cream – and don't drag your sleeve through the butter.'

'How's Tatuš taking it – the war, I mean?'

She floated sour cream by spoonfuls onto the soup, small icebergs in a wine-red sea. 'He'll tell you himself – and don't make a noise on the stairs. He may be asleep. Mind you don't make him tired, you hear?'

'How is he …'

'The same.' Her shoulders drooped for an instant, and their eyes met over the soup tureen; his were the first to look away.

Climbing the dark staircase, he stroked the bannister with one hand, read the embossed cherubs like Braille in the wallpaper with the other. For the first time he noticed the distinct levels of wear. The lowest – he must have been five or six then – were about two feet from the risers, with a clear break every few inches thereafter. He'd grown in jumps, his mother said. The rubbed patterns on the wall bore her out.

The curtains in his father's room were drawn. He was not reading after all. He was coughing quietly into a handkerchief and looked up only when Jan moved directly between him and the window. He coughed again, fought for breath, then whispered, as though to use his normal voice was to invite another attack of coughing.

'So they let you come. We didn't think …' The whisper was in French.

Jan stifled a groan. Damn. September, so of course it would be French. After all the earth-shaking events of the weekend, the steady crump of falling bombs, sirens howling in the night, the obscene punctuation of ack-ack, he had not expected he'd be kept to the same dictum under which he'd chafed for the best part of his twenty-one years. A touch defiant, he answered in Polish. 'It's my day off. Naturally they let me come.'

His father, in his gentle way, was stubborn. 'Speak French, please.'

A professor of languages at the university, he'd long since set the pattern – 'for if you don't practise how will you ever learn to be fluent?' Jan had heard it a million times over the years. Polish, French, English and German, a month at a time in strict rotation, then back to the beginning. Again and again, ever since Jan's sixth namesday when he'd eagerly opened his presents to find nothing but language textbooks and a future of halting conversations with his father. And part of the plan worked. He now spoke excellent English and French, passable German. If it were not for Germany's territorial ambitions Jan well knew he'd now be headed for a career in the foreign service. For that, at least, he could be grateful to the Germans. What little he'd heard of diplomatic circles would have bored him to tears, endless papers to shuffle and pass on, round upon round of teas. He was lucky to have escaped, so he could surely afford to humour his father now. He made a special effort to get the pronunciation just right.

'England's in it now, have you heard? Maybe the French too, before tomorrow.'

His father smiled thinly. 'So? Their armies are not ready. Even if they were, they're too far away.'

'Oh, but –'

'But where are the Germans, tell me that?'

'Danzig – but we're holding them off, we're pushing them back.'

His father nodded. 'With cavalry. We're pushing back their tanks with cavalry.' Only another spasm of coughing stopped him from laughing.

'We have the best cavalry in Europe!' Jan protested.

'Maybe, maybe. But against tanks?' He shook his head. 'Listen, son. So they make you a patriot in that school – so that's fine, nothing wrong with that. But watch out they don't make you stupid, huh? You've never been dumb, don't start now.'

'But the Germans are only in Danzig! There's –'

Danzig's just the easiest place to start, that's all. Half the population's German. They'll run to meet the tanks with flowers and smiles, I expect. So don't be disappointed when you hear about it. Expect it, expect anything.'

Jan swallowed. The habit of deferring to his father was strong, but so was his loyalty to the corps. Ever since joining the air force the conversations with his father had followed the same lines, no matter which language they were conducted in. The man was sick, and habit became, in the end, an act of love. What harm to ask, to consult, to pretend the answers were important just because his father uttered them?

'The adjutant was saying yesterday that it might take us six months to get rid of them. What do you think?'

His father surprised him by thinking deeply for a moment, then speaking – whispering – very deliberately. 'It may be over in much less than that. And not so happily as your clever adjutant might think.' He shot an appraising look over the bunched-up handkerchief. 'Look at history. Just look at history.'

Jan knew he was in for a lecture. From habit he closed off his mind, letting the whispers flow over him in a tide of relentless French. Only in moments of extreme emotion would Father break his own rule. It had happened twice that Jan remembered. Years ago he'd fractured his wrist during an English month, and Mother had furiously demanded that her husband stop trying to comfort the child in a language that sounded like a pack of wild dogs. The other time was recent, early last year. The doctor had just left the house and his parents were still down in the hall. From the top of the stairs Jan had heard his mother's voice, unusually thick. His father – at the very start of a German month – had shouted angry, machine-gun Polish at the closed door.

'Busybody! Who does he think he is? God? He had no business –' He pointed suddenly at Mother. '*You* had no business bringing him without telling me.' They'd looked up then, seen Jan, and disappeared into the study. Mother had told Jan later of course, always did, her face turned up to him so he looked straight down into the cleft of her small chin.

'– and don't you dare tell Tatuś I told you, you hear? And if I catch you feeling sorry for him I'll box your ears – and don't think you're too big, either.' As a foretaste she'd punched his arm, packing every one of her ninety-four pounds behind it. Then she sobbed against his chest and he understood that his position in the family had shifted from the pampered only child to the technical head of the household. Mother, of course, was the real head of the household, always had been.

His father's lecture was drawing to its laboured conclusion. '... even if it wants to, a leopard can never change its spots, you see ...' He coughed again, this time a long siege, then: 'Open the curtains. I want to look at you.'

The heavy drapes, peacock blue woven with pale fleur-de-lis, swung open. Sunlight flooded the room, picked out the worn spots on the carpet, poked mellow fingers into the darkest corners, bathed his young-old father with light.

Jan tried not to let the shock show, but it was there, more moving with every visit. Two years ago his father's face had the well-fed look of a gentleman-farmer; now it was melting down, like wax. The eyes, watery blue, were sunk too deep in the bone. And the whisper was coming again, thready, with many pauses.

'You'll do well ...' He breathed in with care. 'You've a head on your shoulders ... always time for the foreign service later, after the war.' He appeared to be looking somewhere over Jan's shoulder. 'I've never told you ... never been able to, quite ... but Janek, don't be brave, eh? Leave it to the heroes ... I'm proud of you now, no need to – well, you know ...'

Jan had to look away from his father. The affection between them, always there but never demonstrated or even acknowledged, seemed about to be, now. And he was acutely uncomfortable. He would have liked to kiss him, but ...

The moment passed. Mother called upstairs that he should come carry up the food, they'd eat in front of the window and watch the Kowalski family (peasants!) start on their evening stroll.

Over dinner she held the conversation within safe boundaries. Aunt Zosia's new husband – did you ever see such a scoundrel! And the price of veal – and even then you had to

16

beg them for it! And had he heard the Helmut Brauns left town? – so many creditors chasing them, and him a professor of economics! All in Polish, of course. No matter what month it was, Mother would have no truck with Tatuś grand plan, so three-way conversations were awkward. She understood everything but refused to answer in kind. Which was why, her husband never failed to point out, her French was a disgrace in an educated woman. And what, she countered, was the use of foreign languages when her entire day was spent shopping and cleaning and making sure the live-in maid-of-all-work (the slut!) remembered to keep the stove lit? The dialogue was as familiar to Jan as the furniture, and as comforting. It wrapped him around like a warm blanket and he was reluctant, in the end, to leave. Mother said she'd walk him to the bus.

On the pavement they were startled when Father's window opened above them and his head appeared over the sill. Of course the effort stirred another spasm of coughing, so they had to wait until it passed before the whisper came floating down, insubstantial as snow on the hot evening air.

'*Uważaj, Janku, uważaj*!' Be careful, Jan, be careful. The head disappeared. The window was closed, blind, full of the evening sun, and Jan knew he'd remember the closed window for as long as he lived.

'Did you hear, Mother? *He spoke in Polish* …'

She sighed, and thrust her hand into the crook of his arm. 'Yes. I know. Listen, there's not much time before the bus. If something happens, if the Germans come – or the Russians – and we can't get word to you … if things get bad, you know? Well, I'll try to get us down to Uncle Tadeusz's place. The mountains should be safer – maybe better for Tatuś. So remember, if you can't find us, you'll know … Look for us in Zakopane.'

'Oh, Mamunia, the Germans can't make it this far, don't even think about it. Three weeks from today I'll be back again and you'll both be here.'

She looked up, held his eyes. 'Yes. But in case. And be careful. Remember what he told you today.'

They both looked up at the closed window. Today. September third. The day Tatuś broke the rule.

Roman was waiting for him on the barracks steps, not only his own bags packed and ready at his feet, but Jan's also, as scores of cadets milled about the notice-board and dozens more streamed from every door and gate in the complex.

'Thank God you're back! I thought I'd have to leave without you. Run to the office and get your train pass – we've orders to make for Lwów and the train leaves in forty-five minutes.'

'Lwów?' Jan said. 'Squadron already?' And he'd just told his mother he'd be back in three weeks!

'Uh-huh. First they said Kraków, then Wilno, right now it's Lwów so let's take off before they change it again – there's a terrific looking girl I know in Lwów.' He shot Jan a lascivious leer and gave him a shove up the steps.

Jan went automatically, the confidence he'd brought back from Morska Street gone in a storm of anxieties. No time now to contact Mamunia, no time to leave a message even. How would they ever know where he was? 'Hurry!' Roman shouted, so he fought to the front of the line, grabbed his pass.

'Kaliski, Jan – yes – Lwów.'

'Who do I report to?'

The clerk passed a hand across his forehead, clearly drowning under a welter of forms, waving hands, shouted questions. 'They'll tell you when you get there – yes, your families will be notified,' he told another cadet, 'and, no, you can't take your bicycle!'

Half an hour later Jan and Roman stood in the confusion of Warsaw station, inundated now with families trying to depart south, other families hoping to meet incoming relatives from the north. No trains had arrived for hours and the few trains already there had the dusty, settled look of having reached home port, never to leave again. There was neither smoke nor steam to ruffle the hot air of the evening. Schedules, it seemed, had been abandoned. When they finally cornered a porter he told them with some satisfaction that there'd been no departures since noon and none expected, but if they wanted they could always try platform six. He shrugged and melted back into the crowd before they realized they were already *on* platform six, and the only thing bearing any resemblance to a train was an ancient first-class carriage labelled 'Bucharest' with lace doilies on the headrests, curtains at the windows – and no sign of an engine to pull it.

The platform was alive with people. Families surrounded by boxes and birdcages and samovars too bulky to pack – even a sewing machine or two – sat patiently on their baggage and fanned themselves against the heat. Children wailed. Mothers scolded. Fathers, worried men with families to protect, acquired stature by their silence. Grandmothers rocked themselves on their bundles and pursed wrinkle-stitched lips at the mêlée. We've seen it all before, their eyes seemed to say. Soldiers and airmen waved passes as though mere squares of cardboard could conjure up a train.

Clearly, Jan thought, something drastic had happened somewhere to disrupt the train service this thoroughly. Doubts thick as summer flies swarmed in his head. All his life he'd been accustomed to the orderly routines of school and home, every July at the same Paris boarding house, every Easter Uncle Tadeusz's visit to Warsaw, and later the even more rigid timetable of the cadet school. What had stopped the trains? The Germans. Or their own cavalry anxious to block an advance route. The Lwów train would be coming from the west – and the west was where the Germans would attack first.

'We should have left five minutes ago,' Roman said, his guileless brown eyes unusually troubled. 'Think they'll give us detention if we're late?'

Jan dragged his thoughts back to the immediate problem. Already he knew that the optimism of the afternoon had been misplaced. There'd be no time for detention, now. Maybe no time for Poland …

'It looks hopeless to wait here,' he said. 'We'll give it another half hour then figure out some other way to get there …' Lwów. The airfield. The Germans had planes, plenty of them. Surely the logical move would be to bomb the military airfields first? And if they did, would there be anything to go to Lwów *for*? But they had their orders.

'*What* other way?' Roman wanted to know.

Jan sighed. As usual, he would have to make the decisions. Roman was a damned good friend, loyal to the point of idiocy, but he had about as much initiative as a lump of coal, comfortable only as a follower.

'Lots of ways,' he said airily. 'We could get lucky and find a car with the keys in, or pick up a couple of farm horses – plenty of farms on the outskirts – and make it to Lwów by the back roads.' The fact that he'd never in his twenty-one years ridden a horse or driven a car seemed of minor importance at the moment.

It was fortunate for both of them that an air force officer, skinny as his swagger-stick, chose that moment to approach, demanding to see their passes, then suggesting they join a half-dozen or so other airmen headed for Lwów. The suggestion came equipped with a steely glance and an undeniable air of authority.

The little group left Warsaw station in orderly fashion, buttons all a-shine, pants creased to a fare-thee-well, scrubbed faces confidently pointed in the general direction of Lwów, no more than 350 kilometers to the south-east.

Ten days later, dirty, tired and discouraged, they were holed up in a farmhouse not fifty kilometers from Warsaw. Travelling by night on backroads dotted with German patrols, they'd made it halfway to Lwów, only to hear, via village rumour and a smattering of radio, that Lwów airfield was no more. A large segment of the Polish Air Force had been pounded to metallic fragments before it could even take to the air, and a German division was outside the city, ready to occupy. The Russians were close, too. Waiting.

Communications were a shambles of conflicting rumours. The war's reverse fortunes had been stunningly swift. On the first day of September they'd been apprehensive but hopeful; on the third, thanks to the Allied entry into the lists, hope had turned to rock solid certainty of victory. But Tatuś the dreamer had, it turned out, known more than the generals and politicians. The French armies *weren't* mobilized yet, the British airforce already beleaguered on the home front. And so in Poland, retreats and advances were ordered faster than shattered radios could report. On the eleventh day communications failed completely.

20

To Jan's relief the senior officer made the decision to return to Warsaw – still, according to rumour, relatively intact. At least he'd get new orders, reliable ones, and there'd be a chance to find his parents, tell them to make for Zakopane quickly. And he'd be able to rest. His shoes were worn through to his socks, his shirt was stiff with sweat. The only bath he'd taken was involuntary, when a little hump-backed bridge gave way and dropped them all into a culvert. Roman had lost a shoe, and one of the other cadets was almost delirious with fever.

From God-knew-where the senior officer procured a farm wagon and two sway-backed nags and the ragged party was on its way back to Warsaw.

They heard it long before they saw it, a steady pounding of mortar fire that went on all night and all day, louder and louder as they neared the city. Conversation in the wagon was sporadic, not a man now sure of anything but his name and serial number.

It was the second night that devastated them all, held every grumbling tongue still.

Topping a small rise they finally saw what before they had only heard. Red rain showered the burning city with metal from every side. The voice of the mortars shook the earth, toppled block on block of warehouses, offices, factories.

'No future there,' the senior officer muttered grimly. 'So it's escape. That's all that's left. We'll hop over the Tatras to Slovakia, then make for France or England – carry on the fight from there.' He tapped Jan smartly on the shoulder. 'Your turn to drive the wagon, Kaliski.'

'Yes sir,' Jan mumbled. But Warsaw! his numbed mind screamed. Where under the ceiling of crimson clouds was Nowy Świat? His school? His church? His street? And inevitably, with the thought of Morska Street came – could no longer be shut out – the fear for Mamunia, for Tatuś. Where, in all that glowing cinder that had once been a city, were his parents?

CHAPTER TWO

Yorkshire, England – 3 September, 1939

'Daddy, where's the thingammy for pruning the roses?' Lallie
Wainwright sat back on her heels and pushed the cloud of
dark hair out of her eyes. What a perfect Sunday morning!
Birds sang, bees hummed, the roses smelled like pure heaven;
Jolly, her best Afghan, chased dream rabbits as he dozed in the
asparagus bed. '*Daddy*!'

Joe Wainwright answered her from the bean rows. 'If you
mean the clippers they're on the hook in the garage where they
belong.' He stood up and rubbed his back. 'I don't know why
you're bothering with that stuff, in any case. Let the gardener
do it tomorrow.'

'Why don't *you* let the gardener do it, then?'

'I like gardening, that's why.'

'So do I.'

'Yes, well … leave something for him to do. I'm not paying
him to gossip with Wilf over the side fence.'

Lallie grinned to herself. He was *so* tickled they'd finally
graduated to a full-time handyman-gardener. Snipping off the
spent blooms, she amused herself imagining just how many
ways he'd manage to spread the word as he downed his pint of
bitter at the Three Nuns tonight. Maybe: I reckon we'll be in
for a rough winter – having my man put down a few extra rows
of spuds and Brussels. Or: I think I'll have to get the new man

to knock me a bit of a shed together – between my big old bus and Lallie's little MG we can hardly get into the garage! For sure he'd aim some such double blast at Major Hartley, retired, who put on airs but had neither an 'old bus' *nor* a little MG, much less a new man to knock a shed together. She knew some of them gossipped about her father – she'd heard the murmurs of '*nouveau riche*' long before she knew what it meant – but she was sure their laughter had a lot of envy behind it. It didn't stop them tapping his sleeve for every little charity in the county, either. And it wasn't as if they were rich. Rich was when you didn't have to work for it, and Wainwright Foundry only did well because Joe Wainwright worked like one of his navvies to make it do so; that he now worked in a business suit instead of overalls didn't make him an idler.

'You and Neil got a date tonight?' he said now, pausing to light his pipe.

'No. His mother's having a group over – the church choir, I think, so Neil's playing host.'

'Think maybe he could do with some help?'

She shook her head. 'Me? No fear! I'd rather curl up with a book than kow-tow to that lot of old fogies.'

'So I'm an old fogey –'

'You are not.'

'Whatever you say.' He looked pleased, then quickly serious. 'Good lad, is Neil. A man who treats his mother properly, well, you know he'll be good to a wife.'

Lallie mimed playing a violin, laughing up at him from the middle of the rose bed. 'Yes, Daddy darling, of course, Daddy dear.'

'Oh, make fun of me if you like, but mark my words! Neil's a young man with a future, Neil is. Not frightened of a bit of hard work, either. I'll likely make him general manager when he's twenty-five, have I mentioned that?'

'Only a thousand times.'

'Yes, well ...' He had the grace to look embarrassed but couldn't quite leave well enough alone. 'I just want you to be sure that you know we approve if ... I mean ... well, you know ...'

'I know. And if there's ever anything to it, you'll be the first

23

one to know.' Really! He was just like a child that's baked its first cake and keeps taking it out of the oven to see if it's done, she thought.

'Joe! Lallie!'

It was Mum, flapping a teatowel from the kitchen window. Jolly was the only one to respond immediately, no doubt sensing scraps. Lallie felt a quick spasm of guilt. She should have been helping her with the breakfast things, but it was much more fun out here with Daddy.

'Oh hell,' he muttered, tapping the pipe out on the fence post. 'What's she on about *now?* She does make such a fuss about nothing at all. Let's go in, lass, we'll get no peace till we do.'

The teatowel flapped again. 'Hurry up! It's the wireless. Chamberlain's coming on in a minute.'

'And there's another bloody fool,' Joe said, scraping his boots on the top step.

Lallie followed suit. 'And here I was thinking you were such a loyal conservative.'

'Only since I've had something to conserve, you cheeky young madam.' He gave her a light slap on the shoulder as Millie appeared once again, framed in the kitchen door.

'Joe!'

'I'm coming, woman, we're both coming ...' But he paused to watch Lallie scrub her hands at the kitchen sink.

He looked at her straight narrow back with intense pleasure. He lied when he said the foundry was the only thing he had worth conserving. If he'd produced nothing else in his life worth crowing about, that girl would have been more than enough. If the foundry went bankrupt tomorrow (God forbid!); if this high falutin' house burned to a cinder this instant (he hoped to God it didn't – cost a pretty penny), if everything he'd achieved over the years went down the spout, why, he'd still consider himself a lucky man. He had Lallie. And come to think about it that's who all the other stuff was for, wasn't it? Without Lallie there'd be no drive to do better. He'd wanted a boy – one with a head on his shoulders, and maybe a girl as pretty as Millie. Who'd have thought – since it turned out they could only have the one – that in Lallie he'd got it all. She had her mother's looks and his savvy – God knew she didn't get *that* from poor Millie ... Well, and he *was* smart, wasn't he? You didn't build a thriving foundry out of a blacksmith's hole-in-the-wall unless you had a bit of grey matter up top, did you?

His wife, pretty as ever in her addle-brained way, darted into the living room and turned the wireless up, seating herself on the couch and patting a cushion for Lallie to sit beside her. Lallie's Afghan threw himself down in front of the empty grate with a sigh.

'It's a special announcement,' Millie said a little defensively. '*Of national importance*, they said.'

Joe's sigh was as deep as Jolly's had been. 'Well, if we all keep quiet maybe we'll be able to hear it.'

Neville Chamberlain's voice, managing to sound tired, apologetic and well-bred all at the same time, crept into the comfortable living room.

'I am speaking to you from the Cabinet Room at 10, Downing Street. This morning the British Ambassador in Berlin handed the German Government ...'

Before the brief announcement was over, Lallie was surprised to feel warm tears tracking down her cheeks. Down her mother's, too, she saw. Daddy looked thoughtful, certainly not surprised – as Lallie was when he got up without a word and poured himself a Scotch and soda, an unheard of indulgence so early in the day. Mixed it with a flourish, too, tilting it to the light, swirling it about in the glass.

'So it's come,' he said. 'Not before time.'

'Daddy!' Oh, sometimes he could be so ... hard.

'Well, the sooner we get on with it the sooner we'll be done with it, won't we? Putting things off never gets it done, does it? They've waited too blasted long as it is. They should have knocked that beggar off his painter's ladder years ago. Now he's armed to the bloody teeth – and us sitting here with nothing ready but good intentions.' He took a speculative sip of the Scotch. 'I wonder if old Fendon's warehouse is still for rent, down behind the foundry ... have to think about expanding now, I shouldn't wonder.'

'How can you possibly think of business at a time like this?

All those people dying, Poland and everywhere ...' Don't be like this, she wanted to say, don't play the big industrialist now ...

'Now, Lallie, it's not your father's fault if people are getting killed, is it?' Mother said from her usual position of confused neutrality. 'I'm sure he'd never ...'

'Well lass,' Daddy said, ignoring his wife, 'some folks have ideals, I suppose – maybe that's *all* they've got. We've got steel, for guns and tanks and bombs and planes –'

'I know that, but –'

'That's all right then, isn't it?' Millie folded her hands.

Mother! Thinking she'd made peace, and happy about it! God! She really was the limit. Turning again to her father, Lallie said, 'But do you have to add up the pounds, shillings and pence in the first five minutes?'

'Now take it easy, please. Nobody's adding up the profits yet – though I don't deny Wainwright's 'll do all right.' He leaned back against the flowered summer cushions of the couch and gave her his cajoling cheeky-boy grin. 'But you must admit it's gratifying to be patriotic and make a shilling or two at the same time.'

'Oh, you ...' But she was melting. 'I still think it's awful.'

'War's always awful. It was last time, will be again.'

She forgave him completely then, remembering the reason for his slight limp, and for the puckered scar on his neck – and damn lucky to have got out alive, he'd told her.

'Settles one problem, anyway,' he said now. 'You'll have to get on the foundry payroll whether you like it or not. You've finished business college, thank God, so you'll be able to help Neil at the office.'

'You know I'm not interested in filing and typing –'

'It's either that or they'll shove you in a munitions factory soon, my girl. Somewhere away from home, likely.'

'I want to breed Afghans. You said –'

'I said when you were twenty-one I'd give you a decent breeding kennels. And that's not for two years, yet. Dog breeding's not a business for wartime, anyway.'

'I hate office work.'

He grunted at her over his glass. 'We're all going to have to

26

make some sacrifices now. What with government paperwork and red tape, Neil's going to need help.' Out of his repertoire of smiles he dusted off the wolfish one, the one she least admired when directed at herself, the one that said everything was going his way. 'There's a war on now, you know, love.'

In the next weeks Lallie worried about her father. War-triggered events in the Wainwright circle moved so fast even Joe seemed to be losing his grip on the lives about him – just when he must have thought them all safe in the niche he had allotted to them. The flood of orders for steel was beyond his most optimistic expectations and staff resources were stretched to the limit; he left the house at first light and seldom arrived home before midnight.

Lallie herself was giving him trouble, and couldn't seem to help it. The stultifying office routine opened her eyes to the way other girls lived, the months of saving a shilling at a time towards a new dress or the latest thing in ankle strap shoes, the tedium of typing invoices, filing, downing innumerable cups of tea and filing again, waiting for marriage to set them free. By comparison her own life was a haven of comfort and parental devotion. But it was a constricted haven, at a time when the whole world seemed on the move.

After a month cooped up in the grimy foundry office she knew there had to be more she could do for the war effort than this. When she begged Neil for something more vital to do he simply looked up from his desk, said, 'Lallie dear, there's a million things to do but nobody has time to teach them to you,' and turned back to his spec sheets.

Stirred by appeals on the radio and unknown to Joe or Neil, she applied to the Land Army, that sturdy band of women who were replacing young farmworkers called into service.

It seemed the perfect answer. She loved the land and gardening, always preferred to be outdoors rather than in. England, long accustomed to importing much of its food, must now depend on its own island soil, for the sea around them was alive with enemy subs and destroyers. The less food to be imported, the better.

She primed herself full of reasons as she waited for her father to get home from the foundry. Mum had gone to bed after the late news, so she was left to herself to rehearse her arguments as to why she couldn't, wouldn't spend the war filing invoices and guzzling tea.

He came in half an hour before midnight, rumpled at the collar and rubbing red-rimmed eyes that widened as he saw she'd waited up.

'Still up, love? What about your beauty sleep – not that you need it.'

'Daddy …' She reached up and kissed him, felt the day's heavy growth prickle her face. He sank into the couch and made no response at all to the carefully thought out reasons she gave, one after another, as to why she didn't want to work in his company. His silence told her how exhausted he was and she was sorry she'd started, but …

'So you do see, Daddy, don't you, why I can't stay at the office? It's just so dull, the work's so useless, and the grime …'

At last he shifted against the couch. 'Just what I said to my father about working in his smithy. Where there's muck there's brass, he said. He was right.'

'But it's a job anybody could do, you'll admit that?'

'Aye, I suppose so. But working on a farm! Why not wait a bit, see how things go?'

She'd hoped he'd ask that, had been saving the answer for a trump card. 'Because if I join something before I have to, I get a choice of where I go, and I told them somewhere around here. They think I'll be sent to Hodgson's Market Garden – both Mr Hodgson's boys joined the navy, you know. So, you see, I'll be able to live at home.'

He rubbed at his eyes and hauled himself to his feet. 'All right, if you must go, you must – though what Neil's going to say about it …'

Encouraged by his almost too easy acceptance of the situation, she dared further.

'That's another thing, Daddy. It's none of Neil's business to say anything about it. I know you think a lot of Neil, so do I –'

'And so you should! He's been like a brother to you, that boy, ever since the day you were born. Why, he came to your first birthday party, I remember. He walked you to school every single day since you were five until the day he came to work for me, and even now he looks after you. I never have a minute's worth of worry when you're out with Neil. Just like a brother he's been.'

'I know he has. That's the trouble. I've never been out with anybody else, have I? Never had the chance.' You've never given me that chance, either of you, she could have said. But it wouldn't have been fair. She'd been a willing captive.

'You've not met somebody else?' She saw the lines creasing the stubble, and rushed in to reassure him.

'No, of course not – but that's just what I mean. How will I know if he's the right one if I never meet anybody else? Oh, don't worry, I'm going to keep on seeing him, it's just ... well, until I'm sure, I don't want you taking anything for granted, do you see? *I really am* fond of Neil, but just –'

'But just in case, you want to try your wings.'

She felt her throat thicken. 'Don't make me feel I'm letting you down, Daddy, please ...'

He pulled her to him then, and she knew it was all right. 'You'll never let me down, love,' he said, tipping up her face. 'I won't let you.'

When Neil took her out to lunch the following week and told her he'd joined the RAF, he seemed even more troubled about telling Joe than she had been herself. His honest brown eyes clouded over with doubt.

'He's done so much for me, you see. I don't know if he's ever told you this – I know I promised him that I wouldn't, and I'm even letting him down on that, now – but when my father died and Joe knew Mother couldn't ... well ... wasn't left too well-off, he offered to see me through university, although you know how he feels about formal education. We couldn't accept, of course, so then he took me into the firm, just like that.' He snapped his blunt, hardworking hands. 'And he's pushed me up the ladder so fast, and now he depends on me. I don't know how he'll manage. Oh, I know it sounds uppish, as if I'm indispensable or something –'

29

'You almost are,' she said gently. 'He could have got you exempted, you know. He's already talked to some people at the Ministry. Your job's certainly essential. So why ...?'

'The same reason as you, I imagine. I just felt I had to be *doing* something.'

'But you are!'

'Yes, but I'm not *in it*! I'm not taking any risks. A nice cushy job on the sidelines, advancing too, when men my age – yes, and a lot of them younger – are getting killed. Do you understand?'

'I do, but will he? He'll feel we're all deserting him –'

'That's what I'm afraid of,' he said, and waited as the waitress served their order of sole. When she'd gone he took Lallie's hands and studied them so carefully she thought he could have written an essay on them. 'You start at the farm next week?'

He knew she did.

'Your hands are going to feel a lot different by the end of the month. Are you sure you want to go ahead?'

'Yes. *Everything's* going to be different from now on,' she said. She'd been waiting for an opening and here it was.

'Us?'

'Not really, but ...'

'But you don't want me to rush you.' He smiled. 'See? I know just what you're thinking.'

'Then –'

'Then I can wait. I'm used to waiting for you, Lallie. I've been waiting for us both to grow up since you were three. I may have been a dumb seven-year-old but I knew you were the prettiest thing I'd seen. Still are. Now eat your lunch, Kendal, or Joe will be accusing me of starving his pride and joy.'

The use of her real name jolted her back to very early childhood. There was a vague memory of their mothers laughing at Neil's stubborn refusal to call her Kendal. 'Lallie' was the closest he ever came, and so she became Lallie to them all. She'd heard her father thank God many times since that young Neil hadn't chosen to call her Kenny.

Joe knew something was up when Neil came into his office after lunch and closed the door.

When the boy told him, he was stunned, but only briefly, then he realized it was what he'd been expecting. Hadn't he done the same thing himself, the last time around?

'I know it puts you in a fix,' Neil finished lamely.

In a fix? Didn't the lad realize he was much more concerned for his safety than the 'fix' into which he'd plunged the Wainwright Foundry? 'I could have got you off, you know ...'

He was almost relieved to see Neil give a decisive shake of the head. 'Thanks, Joe, but no. I'll have about a fortnight, I think, before they send for me, so I'd better get cracking doing what I can between now and then.' At the door, he turned back. 'I appreciate it, you know. Everything you've done, and now accepting this ... I thought you'd fly off the handle.'

Joe forced a smile. 'Just goes to show, you can't be sure of anything these days, can you? I'll tell you one thing, though. I'd have thought less of you if you *hadn't* wanted to go ...' For a long time after the door closed behind him, Joe could see Neil's face in his mind's eye, not really a handsome face, but good-looking in the best way, honest, open, a face in which you could have absolute trust. He shook his head to clear the image, then picked up the phone.

The balance of the year saw the foundry's business explode. A friend at the Ministry of War found a retired army captain with some business experience who was delighted to fill in for Neil, and who was surprisingly helpful – if a little more formal than Joe would have liked.

At dawn every morning – even earlier than Joe, now – Lallie left the house in khaki jodhpurs and shirt, swinging into the MG with her dark hair clouding up about her face and a glow to her she'd never had before, looking, Joe said, like a recruiting poster; coming home every night weary, hungry, and lovelier than ever.

Neil, in a Bomber Command training programme in Lincolnshire, wrote weekly to Joe and almost daily to Lallie.

The letter she received a week before Christmas seemed not so very different from the others:

Lallie dear,

Home for Christmas after all, four days' leave, so get your dancing shoes ready. I'm bringing some friends with me – two Polish chaps training on Wellingtons, like me, except they're already commissioned (they've had a lot more training, were almost done before they left home.) The poor beggars have nowhere to go for Christmas, haven't a clue where their families are, or even if they *have* families any more. Be a love and ask your parents if they'd mind putting one of them up, will you? You know how tiny our place is, and as usual we've got Aunt June and Uncle Charles so we'll be like sardines as it is. You'll like them – they both speak English, one of them as well (to be honest, better!) as we do. They (the Poles) had the devil of a time escaping from Poland, finally got out on skis, over the Tatras. They're mountains – see what the RAF is doing for my geography? Link training coming up in ten minutes, have to go.

Missing you
Neil

PS. Yes, they *do* click heels and kiss hands on meeting a lady. Other than that they're perfectly normal.

'Isn't that just like Neil,' she said, handing the letter to her father after making sure there was nothing romantic about it – he'd have ragged her unmercifully about any 'sloppy stuff', 'to think of bringing his Polish friends home for Christmas? He *is* a lamb.'

'Just what I've been trying to get into your head,' Joe said, scanning the letter. 'Foreigners for Christmas, huh? Well, if we must, we must. Give your mother something to do, at any rate. I expect we'll be talking in sign language all through the holidays.'

'You didn't read what he says! One of them –'

'I know, I can read. I reckon we'll take *that* one then. Your mother has enough trouble talking to strangers as it is – if she has to talk with fingers and thumbs she'll burn the turkey for sure.'

Even Millie herself laughed. Her cooking was a legend.

Sometimes inspired, but vague, as she was herself. At the best of times she was liable to use salt for sugar or vice versa, and with strangers ... well, anything could happen. Lallie quickly promised to help with all of it. It would be exciting, she decided, entertaining somebody completely different, almost as if he came from outer space. Why, she'd barely known where Poland was until the Jerries had marched in. Lallie had never been abroad, never even met a foreigner, unless you could count the Italian who sold ice-cream on the beach every summer at Scarborough. Christmas was going to be fun. Then she read the letter again, the bit about the families of the Poles, and wondered if perhaps they might have preferred *not* to be surrounded by someone else's family this Christmastime.

CHAPTER THREE

Through all the confusion of the last three months, the siege of Warsaw, the escape, the tortuous route to reach England, Jan had never felt so bewildered as he did at this moment.

Beneath him the train's wheels rumbled a siren song of home-for-Christmas, its elderly engine snaking him through fields white under the moon, past blacked-out hamlets, under tunnels thick with smoke.

Within the overcrowded carriage the atmosphere was jovial, redolent of cigars, orange peel, and pine branches, helped along by a tipsy sailor, very young, who roared out chorus after chorus of 'Rose of Tralee', tearfully begging Neil, in the next seat, to join in. Beside Roman in a window seat an army captain alternately snored and whistled, a teddy bear and a potted pine-tree clutched to his chest. A dowager swathed in a purple cloak and enormous dignity uncorked a flask of brandy and passed it around, inviting one and all to 'take a nip, dear, nothing like it for keeping the frost off your chest.'

Jan himself was wedged between the dowager and what must

surely be the world's thinnest man, who kept offering him oranges out of a string bag. 'Have one now, mate, while you've got the chance. They come all the way from Jaffa, they do, there'll be no more when this lot's gone.'

Jan, accepting the brandy – he was cold – and declining the oranges – so were they – was totally bemused. This was his first exposure to the England that lay outside the flying school. What he now saw ran counter to everything he'd heard, and he couldn't believe it. Where was the legendary reserve? The frosty smile? The silence that was supposed to prevail in railway carriages from one end of the United Kingdom to the other? He'd expected a quiet journey with just Roman and Neil, certainly not this barrage of bonhomie that the strangers seemed to feel compelled to shower on him the instant they saw the word 'POLAND' on his shoulder-flash, the one difference from the standard uniform of the RAF officer. It was gratifying – and alarming. He was in no mood for celebration, yet they thrust their goodwill on him in such casual abundance it would have been churlish to turn it back even if he'd known how.

He'd been surprised when Neil invited them home after so short an acquaintance. Now he was not. He had the feeling any one of the strangers in the carriage would have taken him home with them as readily as they'd pick up a stray kitten or tuck a blanket round a sleeping child.

Roman, puffing on a cigar, was practising his English on the army captain with the teddy bear, who was now awake and who seemed to think that if he just spoke loud enough and slow enough there was no reason in the world why Roman shouldn't be able to understand every nuance of idiom. Neil, with the singing sailor on one side and a rosy-cheeked nun on the other, beamed at him across the aisle, anticipation of the holiday in every word he spoke – shouted – for normal speech was impossible.

'Not far now,' he yelled, tapping his watch. 'A few more minutes. Next stop, Sheffield.'

The sailor, perched on the highest note of 'Rose of Tralee', slid gracefully off his seat into the litter of empty cigarette packets on the floor. Neil laughed, picked him up and wedged him securely between an arm-rest and his own wadded-up overcoat. He looked across at Jan and his smile widened. Over the last few days that smile had been a permanent feature of his face. Probably a girl friend at home, Jan thought, with a trace of envy. Learning the ways of an unfamiliar aircraft and the peculiarities of RAF slang had left him neither the time nor the opportunity for meeting girls – though Roman seemed to find the time and had already cut a swath a mile wide through the WAAF population at camp.

The train rattled into the vast chasm of Sheffield's Midland Station in a symphony of grinding brakes, crashing buffers, shouts of 'Merry Christmas' as passengers buttoned their coats and gathered up their bundles.

Neil stared down at the comatose sailor, under whose head his overcoat was wadded. He nudged the sailor's chest.

'Excuse me ... we're here. Sheffield. Isn't that where you want to be?'

No answer.

Neil nudged him again, not so gently. 'Wake up, mate!' he shouted. 'We're here. Wakey wakey!'

Bleary eyes struggled open and closed again, prelude to yet another assault on the 'Rose of Tralee'.

'... *that made me love Ma-a-a-ary, my ro-o-o-ose of Traleeeeee.*' An undulating snore completed the verse.

'Oh hell.' Neil scratched his head. 'The poor bugger'll never get home for Christmas at this rate.' He rummaged in the sailor's pockets, came up with a wallet from which he drew an ID card. 'Good, he lives in Attercliffe Road, not far at all. We'll shove him in a taxi and let the driver pour him into Mother's arms. Catch hold, Roman.'

With Neil on one side and Roman on the other, they hoisted the sailor to his feet and out of the carriage.

'Jan, get our stuff out to the front of the station, will you?' Neil called back. 'Lallie's picking us up, I expect. You can't miss her. She'll be the best looking one there.'

By the time Jan had manhandled three suitcases, three overcoats, and assorted packages of Neil's out of the station, the pavement outside was deserted. Far down the road he could see Neil and Roman conferring with a taxi driver, the sailor slumped against a lampost.

A horn honked, and a large navy blue car tore round the corner and came to a shuddering stop in front of him. A girl in a camel coat with a hood leapt out, and slammed the door. She looked around and, shielding her face with a gloved hand against the near-blizzard, coolly read the Polish flash on his shoulder. She looked up at him.

She had to be the one. The face turned up to his was heart-shaped, its delicacy oddly enhanced by dark, strongly marked brows and a firm, straight nose. Fresh snow dusted the hair that curled in a dark cloud from the hood of the coat. Then she spoke, and he caught the unmistakable ring of silver spoons.

'You must be with Neil,' she said.

'Yes …' His perfect English, so dearly learned, deserted him, and all he could think of to say was, 'He is over there,' pointing to the taxi-stand.

'*Oh no*, he's *not* getting a taxi! He should have *known* I'd be here. I got held up – ran out of petrol. This darned bus of Daddy's simply *eats* it. Every time you look at the gauge it says "empty".' She smiled, showing small teeth, with the eye-teeth tilting slightly inward, which gave her the look, for a moment, of a pretty kitten. 'Except I *did* forget to look at the gauge *at all* – so I had to get a push.' All her sentences were accompanied by gestures, so that her gloved hands were never still. Now she pulled off one of the gloves and stuck out her hand. 'I'm Lallie Wainwright – we live just up the road from Neil. Either you or your friend – I don't know which yet – will be staying with us.'

He hoped it wouldn't be Roman. 'Jan K-Kaliski,' he mumbled, his tongue stumbling even over his own name.

When he took her hand he was aware of an incongruity. To look at, she had that indefinable air of having stepped off the page of a glossy magazine, yet the hand in his was calloused, chapped at the knuckles, the fingernails squared off, with not a trace of polish. The imperfection gave him back his tongue. 'Neil's putting a sailor into a taxi, he'll be –'

'Ah, you've met!' Neil and Roman were crunching towards them through the dirty city snow. There were explanations, introductions, the suitcases piled into the boot, and a

36

light-hearted argument as to who should drive.

'*I* drive,' the girl said firmly, climbing into the driver's seat. 'It's a treat to be sure of a full tank – I'm going to enjoy it. Besides, I get more practise than you do, now. I've been driving Hodgson's tractor all week.'

With Neil beside her, and Jan and Roman in the back, she rammed the car into gear.

'Would you believe this girl's a farmer?' Neil said as the car shot forward, taking the slope from the station like a toboggan. 'She tills, hoes, weeds, milks, and mucks out the pigs.'

There was an undercurrent of something beside banter in Neil's voice, Jan thought. Was it, perhaps, pride? A hint of ownership? He glanced quickly at the girl's hand resting easily on the steering wheel as she shifted gears with the other. No ring. Even later, he remembered grinning to himself then – and feeling guilty about it.

'You don't look like a farmer,' he said. But it explained the roughened hands.

'Haven't been one for long – but I like it.'

They were passing through the city then, and she was silent, weaving the heavy car through massed buses and trams filled with late shoppers. Next to him, Roman yawned.

'God, but I'm tired. I hope it's not far,' he said in Polish. *In Polish*!

Inside the dark car, Jan blushed, embarrassed by his friend's breach of manners. What must she be thinking, the girl?

'Speak English,' he said sharply. 'If you don't practice how are you ever going to learn?' Echoes of Tatuś! Not for the first time since arriving in England he was thankful to his father for his insistence on what had seemed, at the time, like a never-ending punishment.

A voice in the back of his mind elbowed its way to the front. *Where were they, Mamunia and Tatuś?* Don't think, don't think. You've asked the International Red Cross. That's all you can do. When they know they'll tell you. *If* they know, if they ever find out …

He forced the thought back to join the chorus of other thoughts he knew he daren't yet examine. Be grateful you're

37

here, safe, spending Christmas among friends. *They're strangers*, the chorus screamed. Friendly strangers, he answered. Surely they were that?

With Lallie, he entered the cheerful hallway. With Lallie, he stomped the snow from his shoes and helped her off with the camel coat, caught the light flower scent of her hair, the kind of scent you wanted to be closer to, but she moved away.

'Mum and Daddy will be in the living room – we'll go and see them first if you're not too tired, I know they're dying to meet you.'

She threw open a door at the end of the hall and he saw a room not so very different from the living room on Morska Street, deeply cushioned chairs of grey plush, heavily draped windows, a sideboard boasting an ornate silver tea service that probably – like the one on Morska Street – was used seldom if at all. A mother and a father flanked the same tiled fireplace, except this one had an open fire, its flames leaping, wasted, up the chimney, so the room was cool. The reception, by contrast, was almost suffocatingly warm.

Mrs Wainwright, an older, slightly plumper version of Lallie, drew him to the fire while Mr Wainwright poured a hefty Scotch, topping it off with a wedge of lemon and scalding water from the kettle.

'Here lad, get that inside you. I don't often have it hot, but I'll bet that train was a bloody ice-box, they usually are – oh, *do* sit down, Millie, you make a chap feel uncomfortable, dithering about like that.'

'I'm just running to the kitchen – I've got some lovely hot soup ready, chicken, it is, the butcher said he'd none left but when I told him we had a Polish airman coming for Christmas he whipped out a beautiful stewing hen from under the counter, quick as you please.' She turned to Jan, her face wreathed with genuine pleasure, 'You'll have to come and stay with us again,' she said. 'You'll do wonders for the meat ration.'

Here it was again, this open-handed willingness to warm, to feed, to shelter – yet this time there was an added element, perhaps several, that he couldn't quite put a name to, not yet, with the Scotch rising straight to his head and the warmth reaching down to his toes.

'I'll get it, Mum,' Lallie said. 'I'll serve it in here, we can have it by the fire.' With a swing of heather-tweed skirt she was gone. Some of the warmth went with her.

Over the soup and the Scotch and the flaky little sausage rolls, light as air, he fielded questions about the availability of chickens in Warsaw, the kind of food served at flying school, the preparedness of the Polish military. Wasn't it sly, the Jerries and the Ruskies joining forces like that? What was the butter like in France? – you just came from there, didn't you? Ours is shocking lately, they fill it full of salt to make it weigh more, you know. They all, with kindness aforethought, avoided any reference, however remote, to his family.

But he was tired, and it was a relief when Joe Wainwright stood up, knocked out his pipe, and announced it was time they all got to bed.

'This lad's had a full day. Did you put a hot-water bottle in his bed, Millie?'

'Of course – and hot chocolate in a Thermos if he feels like a drink.'

'Well then.'

Burrowing into flannel sheets, lavender scented, he thought about Lallie. Gracious? Certainly. Attractive? Very. Natural? Yes – all of the things a man looked for in a woman and could quite often find. But above all there was an overwhelming sincerity about her; *that* was the most appealing trait. When she'd introduced him to her father, for instance, saying simply: 'I want you to meet my father, Joe Wainwright,' he felt she really *did* want him to meet her father, that it wasn't simply a matter of form, and that she was sure they'd each discover some immediate kinship valuable to both. Which, of course, they had not. As he realized that, he thought he'd also discovered the missing element in the bonhomie. To Jan, Joe Wainwright seemed the typical man of business. Behind the flash of teeth and the hearty handshake he'd felt the hum of machinery, the meshing of gears. There was the impression that Joe Wainwright wasn't really *there*, only some social façade that went through the motions, and that when he went back to his business next week after the holiday he'd have forgotten he'd ever met Jan Kaliski, much less entertained him through a time as intimate as Christmas. That made him remember that tomorrow was Christmas Eve, which he didn't want to think about.

For the first time in years, Joe and Millie almost had 'words' that night ... She practically never disagreed with him on anything, and here she was, going on and on ... Not like her at all.

'Well, *I* thought he was just a lovely young man!'

'Did I say he wasn't?'

'No, but I can tell.'

'You're sharp tonight – must have been in the knife drawer.'

'Oh, Joe ... didn't you notice his manners?'

He sniffed. 'If you like that sort of thing.'

'What sort of thing?'

'All that hand-kissing and stuff.'

'He only did it once! Besides, I liked it, made me feel like a queen. And the flowers he brought me were lovely, didn't you see them? Lallie says he got them at the station shop.'

'We've flowers in the greenhouse – the gardener's got chrysanths in there like bloody cabbages. Anyway, the house looks like a flower shop already.'

'But he went out of his *way* to bring me some.'

'Not *you*!' Joe said. 'He brought them for the hostess, whoever she was. Very likely a custom where he comes from.'

'Well, it was nice. Lovely looking, too, isn't he? Blond hair all wavy like that, really romantic, I thought.'

'Yes, well ...' Damn, but he wished Lallie had thought to bring Neil in for a drink. Just when he thought Millie was asleep she started again.

'I've got my work cut out tomorrow, everything to get ready for the 'do'. There'll be all of us, and five of them from Neil's place. I wonder if that leg of pork's going to be enough ...'

'It'd better be!' he thundered. 'I'll not go kow-towing to that meat merchant for you or anybody else, not on Christmas

Eve, so you'll have to make do with what you've got.'

She was quiet again for a minute, then: 'He'll feel it tomorrow, you know, being all that way away from home. Christmas Eve makes it just that much worse, doesn't it?'

He sighed. 'Oh, I don't know about that, not with you and Lallie dancing attendance on him.'

'Joe!'

'Joe's going to sleep. Joe's tired,' he said.

Long after Millie had fallen asleep Joe lay awake, wondering if it hadn't been a big mistake to let Neil saddle them with this foreigner, even for a day or two.

CHAPTER FOUR

He had the dream again and wasn't quite quick enough, this time, to surface before he saw the face. The mountain rose up white in front of him, seemed to advance. When he tried to back away his feet refused to move. He looked down, saw skis on them, nailed to the snow with bronze chrysanthemums. *But I can't ski*! The mountain turned pink, then red, a glowing coal that finally split into fissures down which Morska Street fell, blazing like a torch, Roman and the senior officer stomping out the flames with skis bigger than his own. They moved away, and out of the ashes a face – He always woke at the same point, terrified of seeing the face, longing to see it. But today, lulled by the warm Wainwright blankets, wrapped in the Christmas-smelling house, he let himself doze again, and the face was waiting …

He heard himself cry out and was instantly awake, relief covering him with a sudden sweat. The tipsy sailor from yesterday's train, opening his mouth for another assault on the 'Rose of Tralee'.

God! He sat up, no more hope of sleep now, and saw it was still dark outside, but from somewhere in the house he could

41

hear getting-up noises, taps opening, drawers closing. How long before he could reasonably appear?

It was Lallie he'd heard, dressing for her morning run to Hodgson's Market Garden, pulling on her work clothes, running a comb through the dark hair, rubbing cream into her face against the bite of frost that waited for her every morning on the open field, running a pink lipstick over her mouth – *What am I doing?* Lipstick for the cowshed? She didn't even use lipstick at breakfast! Tartish, Daddy called it, but still … She paused in front of the mirror, considering. It looked nice, she decided, and left it on.

Lured by the clatter of a cup on a saucer, Jan came down at 5.30. Lallie looked up – did she blush or was it a trick of the light? – and immediately poured a cup of tea for him.

'Couldn't sleep?' she said.

'And you?'

She laughed. 'I'm up every morning at the same time. Technically, Hodgson's is a market garden, just veggies and that kind of thing, but they do have a few beasties on the side. A couple of cows, a pig, chickens, an old nag that should probably have gone to the knackers ages ago. I *hate* the chickens, they are *so* blessed *thick*!'

'But on the morning of Christmas Eve?' He watched her hands, drew pleasure from their constant movement as she spoke.

'Yes indeed.' She stood up. 'Look, don't let me rush you but I have to see to the dogs before I go. I've got the timing down just so.'

'Could I help …?'

She gave him a searching look from grey, black-fringed eyes, apparently assessing his qualifications. 'Fine! If you don't mind?'

In the glassed-in back porch she introduced him to two Afghan hounds and handed him a brush and a smock. 'You can do Silky, I'll take Jolly. They have to be done every day or their coats turn to pure Persian Lamb. *No*, put the smock on first or you'll be covered in it. They shed like mad, you know.'

Jan had never had a dog – not many people at home did – and he could never quite understand why people kept them, but as Silky nudged his hand and then licked it daintily he began to see why. 'She's beautiful,' he murmured, brushing the long, champagne-coloured hair.

'Not really. *This* one's the beauty, aren't you, Jolly? He's already a champion. If I can get a decent kennel started up before he gets too old he'll make *great* breeding stock, won't you, angel? He's got super lines.' She kissed the elegant chocolate muzzle.

Jan laughed, enchanted. 'Well, *I* think Silky's – well – silky.'

'Oh, they're *all* silky, but she's got far too many faults to use her for show, poor lamb. She's just an old love, aren't you poppet?' Now a kiss on the champagne muzzle, the brush constantly working. 'She's all heart and no class, unfortunately – but she earns her keep in devotion, don't you, old girl? Also, she's a wee bit slow up here.' She touched her temple without missing a single stroke of the brush, and her voice dropped to a whisper, as though she didn't want to hurt the dog's feelings. 'Of course, Daddy says *all* Afghans are slow, he says the brain's been bred out to make room for the nose. *That's* because he likes Labs, though. He doesn't really believe it, does he, sweets?' She rubbed both muzzles and was rewarded by profuse kisses and, from Silky, a slightly wall-eyed stare.

Brushes and smocks put away, she stood frowning, suddenly diffident. 'Gosh, I *have* been blathering on – look – I have to do the farm now, and Mum and Daddy won't get up till, oh, eightish – the foundry's closed till Monday … d'you want to, well, read or something till breakfast? I'm awfully late or I'd make you some now.'

He laughed again, falling deeper under the spell of the heart-shaped face and the running stream of chatter. 'I'll probably take a walk.'

Her face cleared. 'Oh well, if you don't mind going out in the cold – and it *is* cold – you can come to work with me, keep me company. We'll be back for breakfast.'

Hodgson's was only half a mile away, she said, '… and not

43

worth getting the car out – besides, the MG'll freeze your ears off,' so they walked, to the accompaniment of more rapid-fire, strangely soothing, chatter. He learned, in the course of the half-mile, that she: *loved* the ballet, *hated* Shakespeare; couldn't *stand* gladiolis, *adored* buttercups; just *knew* they'd win the war – but *when?*; *loathed* the office, *loved* the farm; *worshipped* her father, who was *devoted* to Neil.

Mention of Neil brought him up sharply. What was Neil's connection with this slim bundle of energy striding by his side? Lovers? He thought not. There was an unstudied impulsiveness about her, a naive honesty; if there was a romance there, she would have so indicated – probably couldn't have held it back. Perhaps Neil was simply hopeful, and if he was, who could blame him? Certainly not Jan, who'd had few girl friends at home, and who had never, ever felt anything for a girl that wasn't purely physical. But with Lallie, it was simply a pleasure to be with her, watch her move, listen to her talk, hear her laugh.

'When will you go on ops?' she said suddenly, opening the farm gate.

'Ops? Ah, air-raids! Maybe six months, probably a year.'

'Are you excited? Scared?'

'When I think about it, I'm excited,' he said, 'but I'm not sure how I'll feel when the time comes. I think it will feel more real when more of us get over here; some are coming from France, more every day as they manage to make their way.'

'You won't be flying with Neil?'

She *did* mention Neil often, he thought. A sign? No! 'Oh no, I'll be getting an all-Polish crew and assigned to a Polish squadron. Besides, Neil's going to be a pilot too – we can't both fly the same plane, can we?'

'Don't they have … assistants, or something?'

'I don't think there are enough of us for that yet,' he said gently. How innocent she was! The war hadn't touched her at all. Or any of them, really, except maybe Joe Wainwright, for whom it was a business. No wonder they were calling it the phoney war. Nothing was happening … here.

She banged her temple with the heel of her hand. 'I *am* bonkers! And *I* called *Silky* slow!'

44

'It's still a young war here,' he said. 'You will learn all about it, I'm afraid, later.'

She was quiet for a moment, reaching in her pocket for a lump of sugar, which she gave to the horse that suddenly thrust its head over a stall door. 'Roman?' she said. 'Will he ...'

'A navigator – probably mine. We're friends from kindergarten.'

Her eyes widened. 'Gosh, I hope he's got a sense of direction!'

'Oh, he's learned a lot since then – and there *are* instruments.'

'Bonkers again! Look, here's Bunky.' The square bulk of a cow ambled to meet her. 'Hello old girl, waiting for me, I'll bet.' She turned to Jan, eyes suddenly alight. 'I say, have you *ever* tasted milk still warm from the cow? It's super.'

'No, but ...'

'You shall! Nip into the farmhouse kitchen – the Hodgsons don't mind, I do it every day, they won't be up yet. Make us some toast on the electric fire, the bread's in the bread box and the butter's in the larder. I'll bring the milk when I'm finished with Bunky, alright?'

It was a little disconcerting, stumbling about in a strange kitchen, hunting up bread and butter, but the milk, when it came, was like the company, warm, frothy and delicious.

He waited for her as she tossed the last few pitchforkfuls of straw into the horse's stall. Even knee-deep in straw, some of it sticking to her hair, her riding boots caked in mud, jodhpurs grass-stained at the knee, she still wore that same air of elegance as when he'd first seen her, in the camel coat with the hood. Was it possible that it was only yesterday?

'Home!' she sang out. 'Breakfast. If we don't walk too fast Mum will just about have it ready when we get in.'

Christmas Eve. They were all there in the Wainwright living room, festive now with holly and mistletoe, candles on the tree, the sideboard laden. Roman, on his second drink and laughing a lot, his English broken but uninhibited, had his arms around the shoulders of Neil's mother and his Aunt June, regaling them with the story of the escape from Poland as Jan watched him.

'Snow on top Tatra, yes? Not so deep, October only, we – Jan and me? Jan and I? wiz other cadets. First time on skis, very hard, yes? We fall much times.' He laughed, but a shadow fell briefly on his broad face. 'We think we never find … *gospoda?*' He looked to Jan for help.

'Inn,' he said, remembering. The elusive inn. One thin officer and eight cadets high in the Tatras. Teeth chattering, ankles numb over unfamiliar skis, and night filling the crevasses with purple. No food for two days and no sign yet of the inn they should have come upon that morning. The officer, grey-faced and trembling now, had to fight for every breath of thin mountain air, with none left over for speaking. In the end Jan took the map from him, led them all back on track, and organized a chair lift of crossed arms for the officer to ride. It was already dark when they found the inn.

'Inn, *tak* – yes. Inn of partisan,' Roman said now, giving Neil's mother a confident smile. 'We find partisan and he give us to eat, yes? and beds to sleep. Next day he show us Hungary border and then he leave us, yes? Our captain sick and again must sleep so we rest, and police come, take arms like so.' He made a grab for Aunt June's wrist. 'And they quick give us to prison. All, all to prison. We very …' Again he hunted through his small vocabulary. 'Sad?' Again he turned to Jan.

'Worried,' Jan said. 'It was an internment camp. We expected they'd keep us for the whole war.' The guards had been friendly, but doors were locked, windows were barred. The Polish officer, too weak to negotiate for himself, whispered to Jan that he should try a bribe. Which had worked.

Roman resumed his staggered narrative. 'We money give to guard, yes? He take, he open door, and we quick go!' If Roman's speech was halting his gestures were not. He shot out a fist to indicate the speed with which they'd quit the internment camp and in the process barely missed Aunt June's ample bosom.

Jan caught the fist, steered it to the sideboard, where Lallie filled it with a plate of roast pork and turkey, while Neil supplied the coffee. But Roman, now launched, was not to be stopped.

'Our captain very sick now, very very sick. We must give him to hospital, yes? They keep. We not know what we must do, but Janek – Jan ...' He tapped his temple and bowed to Jan, 'Janek he thinking, much language he know. He make a story, we get papers, ride train to France ...'

How easy Roman made it all sound. Perhaps for him it had seemed so. For Jan it was one long tightrope with traps on every side, some tangible and enemy-induced, some diplomatic and yielding only to folding money.

Their captain's heart was failing. Clearly he could not go on. But the rest of them must, *must*, he told Jan from the hospital bed. 'You have to get them out, Kaliski.' Jan didn't think to ask him 'Why me?' Nor did he ask the cadets who waited, bewildered, for him to emerge from the hospital door. He didn't even ask himself why he, and not one of them, had somehow been elected shepherd. But he – and they – knew he had. Acceptance was automatic and total. He was responsible for them all, his job to guide them to the West. A dozen times he thought they wouldn't make it, thought he'd led them into a trap. They depended on him, and he on the partisans, most of whom were honest, but there were a few who were not. How to tell the difference? How to know which would take their money then turn them over to the police? The wife of a Yugoslav farmer begged them to linger just one more night in the barn. To rest, yes? They must be tired? The others were eager to accept but Jan pushed them forward to the next hamlet, where they discovered that the farmer and his wife turned a brisk trade selling young transients to the authorities. Thus by blind instinct and luck they cleared one hurdle after another.

But the crevasse had almost finished them.

Mountains again. Colder now. Late afternoon shadows already filling up the hollows. One cadet muttering in delirium, another weeping into frostbitten fingers, and as he wept he stumbled, splintered the mountain air with his sudden scream. And disappeared. Jan leaned over the rim and spotted him, stiff with fear, on the ledge below. And almost dark, no

47

time to think, to plan, to weigh alternatives. The others held fast to the rope as Jan hung over the snow-filled crevasse, dangling the spare rope towards the terrified cadet huddled on the ledge. Whose frostbitten fingers missed it once, twice as Roman implored, 'Catch hold, for Christ's sake,' from the rim. The cadet tried, tried too hard, flung himself at the rope and hurtled out into blue-white space. Above, Jan swung on his own rope, saw the cadet's maroon stocking-cap catch on a cedar snag, heard the cadet's last echoing shout of 'Jaaaan ...' as the gorge and the snow swallowed him up.

For months afterwards, Jan had only to close his eyes for the dark red stocking-cap to appear under his eyelids, a malevolent bloom on a field of white.

In the warmth of the Wainwright living-room he shivered, forced his attention back to Roman's triumphant discourse.

'... Jan is knowing French very good, again he is talking, again we are getting papers, and so we come to England, yes?' He lifted his glass. 'And ... we ... are ... here!'

With the exception of Joe Wainwright, who was filling his pipe, all applauded what had surely been Roman's maiden speech in a language he'd been using for three short weeks. Exhausted now by both the effort and the appreciation he sank into the couch and allowed Millie to flutter over him like a solicitous hen.

Jan caught his eye, gave him a look of private congratulation.

Lallie, Millie, Neil's mother and aunt, all began repeating Jan's name, trying to duplicate Roman's inflection.

Yahn. Yan. Yon. Yown.

'You're all right,' he told the four eager faces, 'but not quite. Think of 'yarn' and then take away the 'r' sound.'

Joe Wainwright reached across him and laid a hand on Lallie's shoulder. 'What's all this yawning about? The party's not half started.'

'We're learning to say Jan's name –'

'Yes, well now you've learned why don't you go and help Neil with the gramophone, love, then we can all have a dance?'

Joe and Lallie led off with a tango. Given the age difference, they made a striking couple, well-matched, his iron-grey head contrasting nicely with her dark one. Their faces, not one whit alike, each laughing into the other, seemed to carry the same spirit. With no self-consciousness whatsoever they twirled, chassé'd and dipped, all the while urging the others on to the floor. Jan found himself steering Neil's Aunt June, light on her feet despite her bulk.

'You *will* come to the midnight service with us?' she said. 'Roman's coming. The whole parish has been so looking forward to it – it's not often we get strangers, you know.'

Jan tried to look pleased. 'Yes, of course I'll come.' He'd been hoping to avoid the Christmas Eve mass ... and the memories it carried with it.

'It's not the same, of course,' she said lightly. 'We realize you're probably Catholic, but we *did* want ...'

'I've been looking forward to it,' he lied.

'Marvellous! I'm choir director, you know, have been for, oh, years and years. We've done something a little different this year, cooked up a little surprise –' She gave him an arch smile. 'No! I won't tell, so don't ask me.'

He danced with Millie Wainwright next, then Lallie, encircling her waist with relief at first – she was so light – then with pleasure as the cloud of flower fragrance and dark hair brushed his chin.

'Enjoying yourself?' she said.

'Very much – your mother was just giving me all your childhood history.'

'Oh dear, I *hope* she didn't tell you Daddy spoils me something *fierce*, she tells everybody that and he doesn't at *all*.'

'On the contrary. She was telling me how brilliant you are, how pretty, how thoughtful.'

She groaned. 'That's even worse. I *am* sorry, I really am. Parents can really be the giddy limit.'

'I like your mother very much.'

'D'you really?' She looked surprised. 'She *must* have made an impression. Usually she's a bit shy of new people. And what about Daddy? Now he's *never* shy, not of anybody.'

Jan paused to brush a strand of her hair from his eyes. 'He's very ... confident, I think,' he said at last.

'What an odd thing to say! – but of course, you're right.

That's exactly what he is – but then, he's got a lot to be confident about.'

He sensed he'd put a foot just slightly wrong, and changed the subject. Then the music changed and Neil was tapping his shoulder, whirling Lallie away. Watching them go, Neil's hand steady at her waist, Jan suppressed a quick surge of resentment and turned dutifully to Mrs Armott, who simpered and gave herself stiffly to his arms.

Really, Aunt June *did* have the *most* glorious voice, Lallie thought. Like a violin – no, a cello, rich and plummy, like the brandied fruit cake she gave them every Christmas; it dominated the other voices completely, and so it should. It was the best.

She sneaked a look at Jan and Roman during the sermon, which leaned heavily on the theme of goodwill to all men. The two men it was aimed at were seated not in a pew but in two chairs which managed to face both the lectern and the congregation. She hoped it hadn't embarrassed them, but everyone did *so* want to enjoy them enjoying the surprise. And what a scramble it had been! Last minute rehearsals, everybody mixing up the words, but Aunt June had assured them it would all come together 'on the night'. Well, this was the night.

Jan shifted uncomfortably during the service. It was his first time in any but a Catholic church and he was uncertain of the responses; he felt, too, that he was on show, an exhibit in some national exercise of goodwill. They meant well, but he'd have preferred to be in a pew with the Wainwrights instead of what was the equivalent of centre stage. Roman, it seemed, had no such inhibitions, la-la-ing along to all the carols, spreading his broad smile on minister and congregation alike. Often, now, he found himself envying Roman, who knew exactly where his parents were. His father had died when he was four, and his mother had been in Chicago visiting a sister when the war started. He sighed, tried to ignore the voices in his head, told himself *Mamunia* and *Tatuś* were *all right*, safe in Zakopane with Uncle Tadeusz, enjoying midnight mass in the little church in the mountains. He wished he could make himself believe it.

After what was surely the last carol the congregation of

perhaps forty souls stood, and Jan started to rise also, but was stilled by the hand of the young minister touching his shoulder.

Lights from a dozen candles sprang up, flickered on the smile of Neil's Aunt June. The organ was silent. The entire church and everyone in it seemed to be holding their breath. Looking into the congregation for a hint of what was to come, Jan encountered Lallie's grey eyes resting on him, smiling encouragement. Neil's too, and Millie Wainwright's ... every face in the church was raised to the two men in airforce blue with the foreign insignia on their shoulders.

Aunt June sang the first line alone. Her rich voice, deep with emotion, filled every dark corner with sudden warmth, soared to the arched roof, poured thick and sweet as honey into the ears of the worshippers.

Dzisiaj w Betlejem, Dzisiaj w Betlejem ...

Tenors took up the refrain, then sopranos, baritones.

Dzisiaj w Betlejem, Dzisiaj w Betlejem,
Wesoła Nowina,
Że Panna czysta, że Panna czysta ...

Now the whole congregation was singing. Never mind that the words were almost unrecognizable on their tongues, never mind that a baby somewhere cried, that a dog on the street howled – Jan felt their passion, their desire to bring him joy, was humbled by it.

Roman's hand reached for his, and in their clasp the heartache of months dissolved, drowning him at once with joy and despair and, yes, gratitude. The time they had spent, the caring ...

Aunt June's voice, once again alone and pure in the melting dark, reached out to them, then she was there between them, her plump hands clasping theirs. They stood to face their audience and joined their voices with hers.

Below them, the congregation sighed with pleasure. The work of days was over. They were fulfilled. Lallie, looking up, was fiercely proud of her people, all the friends and neighbours who'd joined to make this moment so infinitely precious.

Her eyes had not left Jan's face during the carol, and on the last note he looked down at her through the flickering candles, smiling. It was, she thought, as though a fine cord stretched

51

between them, gossamer-thin but strong enough already to bear the weight of his grief and despair. Already the contours of his face were etched deep into her memory; now the look in his eyes, at once wistful and sad and ablaze with newborn hope, reached into her heart

It was all different for them after that. They walked home together through crisp new snow, lagging behind Joe and Millie Wainwright despite Joe's backward cries of, 'Hurry, you two. We'll all catch our death.'

CHAPTER FIVE

Lallie was awake well before the alarm rang. She lay there, snug in pink flannel sheets scented with the lavender water Mum sprinkled so liberally on ironing day. A smile curved her lips as she remembered last night, the carol service, the slow walk home, and how he'd looked at her under the Christmas moon. She remembered how she'd felt, still felt, her world suddenly light and irridescent as a bubble and she floating in it with a smile on her face that wouldn't come off, ever.

Wriggling her toes and lifting her arms, she stretched, laughed softly at the new morning as she dressed for her chores at the market garden, and swung open the curtains. Frost prisms etched the window glass and dawn was coming up palest grey, with shadows of deep blue in all the hollows. It had snowed lightly in the night, softening every tree and fencepost with mounds of crystal. Even Hodgson's tumbledown barn in the distance seemed to belong on a Christmas card.

Was he awake yet, she wondered? No, of course not! Why should he be ...

He was waiting for her downstairs in the living room.

The moment she saw him, thin and diffident, profiled against the faint dawn of the bay window, she knew she'd expected him, would have been deeply disappointed had he not been there. He seemed uncertain, his long hands busy with cap and gloves, his overcoat ready on the chair.

'You don't mind if I go with you to the farm?' he said quietly. 'I know that you have work –'

'Mind? I'm *delighted*!' She looked up, smiled straight into his eyes, close enough now to see the fine dark lines with the lighter blue irises. Goodness, if Daddy could hear her he'd say she was being 'forward' and perhaps she was, but the convention of reluctance seemed suddenly out of place. But just in case, to please her sleeping father, she said, 'I *do* get so cold crossing the field in the mornings and if I have somebody to talk to it takes my mind off it.' But that wasn't right either, and not true. 'Not *that* cold,' she said quickly, 'and it's sweet of you to want to.'

It was almost the same as yesterday. The shared pot of tea, the work with the pampered dogs, the crisp walk across the fields, their breath joining in vapour clouds on the freezing air. But there were differences. Yesterday she'd rattled on about anything and everything that came into her head. Today she was quiet, reticent as he, acutely conscious of their steps crunching through the snow, his airforce blue sleeve close to hers. When he talked his words were polite, cautious.

'The day is to be very cold, I think.'

She agreed.

'In Poland the winters are always so.'

'Yes?'

'The cold comes from Siberia, you see.'

She nodded, not wanting to admit that she'd never heard of Siberia, but she made a mental note to get out her old school atlas when they got home and have a look.

He stopped suddenly and took her arm. 'It was very kind last night, the carol ... who thought to arrange it, do you know?'

She felt colour warm her cheeks, heard her own chatter uncoil like a released spring. 'It was a joint effort really. I mentioned to Neil's Aunt June that it might be nice – of course I hadn't a clue how to go about it, but she's *so* efficient and in no time at all she'd found somebody in Sheffield – I think from the cathedral – and it seems they keep heaps and heaps of old music there, foreign and everything. Anyway, she chose the carol and I made copies on the Gestetner at Daddy's office and then the choir, well, we just sort of muddled through. I know we got some of the words wrong, yours is *such* a difficult language, but we thought it might make you feel more at home.'

He nodded gravely. 'It made me very happy. And very sad.'

His eyes clouded and she wanted to reach out and touch him, tell him that one day everything would be as it had always been. When the war is over. But it had barely begun! and Daddy said it would go on for years and years.

'Sad,' she said. 'That's not what we had in mind at all.'

For the first time she saw his real smile, not just the smile of a grateful, well-mannered guest, and it was young and open and began in his eyes. She felt she'd known him for oh! ever.

'I am sorry,' he said. 'Perhaps sad is the wrong word. The carol made me think about my home and I had been trying not to. But I needed to think about it, you see, so it was good after all. If you keep trying not to think about something it is making everything – how do you say? sour? bitter?'

'Both,' she said promptly, and tucked her arm companionably in his. 'Neil was right. Your English is really awfully good.'

And so then she heard all about Tatuś and how he'd patiently taught Jan the languages month after rotating month, about his plans for Jan to enter foreign service and how the war had changed all that. About Mamunia who was less than five feet tall and who ruled her husband and son and the house on Morska Street.

'That's the one thing that gives me hope that they may have escaped somehow,' he said quietly. 'My mother is a strong-minded woman.'

'Then I'm *sure* they got away.' She spoke with more conviction than she could bring herself to feel. The papers had been full of the occupation for months. Change the subject, bring the smile back to those shadowed eyes. 'Mum's not like that at all. I think if Daddy told her to tie herself into a sailor's knot she'd try it.'

But he had turned quiet again and they walked in silence

across Hodgson's five-acre field. It was almost full daylight now. A pale sun reflected dazzlingly off clean, untrodden snow, touching the gaunt elms with a fleeting magic as icicles on the laden branches slowly began to melt. It was as if they were alone in the world, she thought. A new world, filled with mixed new emotions. She, who had never felt shy, found herself groping for words; she'd always felt herself to be pretty enough – didn't Daddy tell her every day? – but she suddenly wanted to be beautiful, irresistable; always confident and secure, she now found herself to be vulnerable, but in the most delicious, exciting way. And very young. And then they were rounding the barn and she saw lights in the farmhouse windows spilling yellow light onto the snow. The figure of Mr Hodgson moved, birdlike, against the fireplace. Damn!

'The Hodgsons are up.'

He looked alarmed. 'Will they mind I am with you?'

'No.' Blast! They *never* got up early anymore, and just when she was getting to know him. 'I just hope you'll be able to understand them,' she muttered.

'They don't speak English?'

'Oh yes. Yorkshire.'

The farmhouse door creaked open and laid a path of gold down the front walk. Standing in silhouette against it, small and bandy-legged, was Mr Hodgson.

'Eh up then, our Lallie,' he bawled. 'How's tha' been, lass? I've seen to Pearl and fed the chickens and milked owd Bunky for thee, seeing as it's Christmas. Who's tha' got there, then?'

Lallie made the introductions.

'How do you do,' Jan said formally.

'Champion, I'm just champion lad, and how's thissen'?'

When Jan looked confused the farmer peered up at him through far-seeing, countryman's eyes. 'Coom thee in and set down, lad. I've got t'kettle on't boil –' He nudged Lallie sharply in the ribs. 'We'll have a spot o' whiskey in t'tea seeing as it's Christmas. Set us up for the day, like.'

Lallie gritted her teeth. The Hodgsons were the *nicest* people, but did they have to choose *this* morning to do her work for her? 'You should have stayed in bed, I could have –'

'Nay luv, not at Christmas. Besides, t'missus has a bit of something for you, for the season, like.'

55

He handed her a parcel hastily bundled with tissue paper and tied with gardener's twine, then opened the door to the staircase behind him and bellowed up the dark alcove. 'She's here, Emmy! Coom on, get yourself down here.' His voice could well have called Bunky in from her pasture. 'Lallie's ready to open it.'

Mrs Hodgson appeared, fully dressed and covered in a capacious green apron, a hair net on waves of corrugated grey, specs thick as plate glass on her putty-blob of a nose. More introductions, Lallie on pins to leave, knowing she must open the package and almost certain what it contained.

She was right. A hand-knitted cardigan of scratchy wool in a peculiarly poisonous shade of mustard. She swallowed hard, kissed Mrs Hodgson, and thanked her.

'Try it on then, lass. I made a right muck up of the neck, had to unravel it twice.'

Lallie was reluctant. If it was anything like the one Mrs Hodgson had given her on her birthday it would be many sizes too big and lacking any shape recognizable as a cardigan. She'd look awful in it, she knew, and just when she wanted to look her absolute best. But many hours had gone into the making so she slipped off her coat and tried on the cardigan. One front failed to match the other by at least an inch; the back hung down below her hips, and the buttonholes could have accommodated small doorknobs.

'It's lovely,' she said firmly. 'Just perfect, and so warm.'

Mrs Hodgson looked delighted. 'I knew you'd like it. Nothing like a nice cardy these mornings. You'll wear it home under your coat luv, keep the cold out.'

Once outside and out of sight of the farmhouse she felt Jan's hand on her sleeve. He was smiling, almost laughing, and she was suddenly furious. With Mrs Hodgson, with herself for feeling ungrateful, with the sweater, with Jan for seeing her in it.

'I don't see what's so funny. It's simply hideous!'

'And you, I think, are very kind. She thought you loved it.'

'Well, what could I do? She's half blind, poor thing, probably spent the entire winter dropping stitches and picking them up again.' It was the waste that angered her. All that effort could have been spent on something that gave Mrs

56

Hodgson herself pleasure, not the piccalilli-coloured horror whose sleeves she tucked as far as they'd go under her own tailored jacket. 'It's also bloody itchy, I can tell you.'

'Yes.'

There was something in his voice, a new confidence and perhaps resolution. They were still. About them was the soft fall of snow from laden boughs, the peck and scatter of the nearby chicken house, the shift and creak of thin ice on the duckpond as it began to melt under the December sun.

'Tomorrow I'll be gone,' he said.

She held her breath but it clouded between them, joining with his as he bent towards her. 'I know.'

He tilted her chin. 'We have not wished each other a happy holiday. At home friends kiss on Christmas.'

She felt herself smiling, the same smile as this morning, the smile that wouldn't ever come off. 'So do we,' she whispered.

His lips were cool and gentle on hers, and too soon gone. He held her away from him, reading her face. 'What about Neil?' he said at last. 'Are you ...'

She shook her head. 'I've known him for ever. He's a good friend, almost a brother.'

Relief blazed in the intense blue of his eyes. 'Then may I write to you Lallie, please?'

The cool formality of his words contrasted oddly with the warmth of his glance, and she smiled. 'Of course.'

'Again you make me very happy.' He inclined his head in what was almost a bow.

Watching them from the window as they came up the walk, Joe Wainwright frowned. They were laughing as they stamped the snow off their shoes on the doormat, and the sound of it through the heavy oak door stirred vague misgivings he was not prepared, at the moment, to pursue. By the time the door swung open his smile was firmly in place and directed in all its bluff heartiness at the foreigner.

'By God you were out early! Lallie I can understand – she *has* to go, but you! You must be a glutton for punishment to turn out on a morning like this.'

'I enjoyed it very much,' Jan said, hanging his overcoat on

the rack in the hall then helping Lallie out of her jacket and the cardigan, which Lallie immediately waved under Joe's nose.

'Got my first Christmas present,' she said, still laughing.

'I'm looking at it. Who could miss it?' He fingered a sleeve, felt its roughness and pushed it quickly away from him. The feel of it, the colour, brought visions of the workhouse, a place he had not thought about since before Lallie was born but which had been an all too vivid prospect once. He shivered in the warm, plushy hall with its burgundy carpet and pink-shaded wall lamps, the wide mirror into which Lallie was smiling as she ran a comb through her hair. There was a glow in her cheeks, her eyes, and for the first time ever the sight of this beautiful child of his brought him no pleasure. The boy was watching her, too. Joe remembered last night, the quick fathoms-deep glance she'd shared with the stranger across the crowded church. Over Jan's shoulder he caught sight of the unopened gifts piled by the living room fireplace, almost all for Lallie. There was a watch, a book on dog breeding, the usual box of linen hankies, an angora twinset in a misty shade of rose, silk stockings, chocolates, perfume, a gold bracelet inscribed 'From Daddy with love'. He, who loathed shopping in its every aspect, had combed the shops with such pleasure. Now a bit of the shine had rubbed off everything, somehow. He must be getting old. The thought came unawares, characteristically followed by a disclaimer. Not bloody likely! He had thirty good years in him yet.

Christmas breakfast was a festive affair at the Wainwrights', prelude to the present-giving to come. The candles on the tree were lit, even though the morning outside was now a dazzle of sun and snow. A green crocheted tea-cosy kept the tea hot within its woolly folds. A bowl of crimson chrysanthemums all but dominated the table until Joe grumbled that nobody could see over them and why weren't the damn things on the sideboard out of the way? There were eggs and ham and potatoes fried to a crusty, glistening gold. And, Millie said, there were kippers if anybody fancied one.

'Jan? Lallie? How about you, Joe? You've always liked a nice kipper.'

'Leave off Millie, will you please?' Joe Wainwright spoke mildly enough, but Jan noticed his plate was barely touched. Lallie's too. She stirred her tea a lot, nibbled at toast with enchanting seed-pearl teeth, answered her parents in a dreamy, far off voice. She looked fresh and innocent in a pale lemon sweater, her hair brushed back but stubbornly clouding forward to frame a face still rosy from the frosty walk home. Would she answer his letters? Looking into her direct grey eyes he thought that she would. He thrust any lingering doubts of Neil firmly away from him.

Gifts were opened to the accompaniment of carols on the radio and coffee with tiny glasses of Benedictine ceremoniously served by Joe, although Jan thought he did it with an abstracted air, as if his mind was somewhere else entirely, probably the factory which supported this slightly ostentatious lifestyle. Remembering his own spartan but intellectual upbringing, Jan felt a surge of pride quickly followed by remorse as his own gift was handed to him. A cashmere scarf so fine as to be almost weightless, its creamy whiteness backed by a lining of red silk.

'It's for flying,' Joe said gruffly.

'We thought it would keep you warm while you were up there.' Millie pointed vaguely at the ceiling. 'The red's for luck.'

Which he would undoubtedly need was the implication. And of course they were right, but he didn't want to be reminded of it. But though showy, the gift was a thoughtful one, and he thanked them. 'Red and white are Poland's national colours,' he said, 'so I can be patriotic and warm at the same time.'

'Then it's doubly lucky,' Lallie said happily. 'Are you going to try it on?' And they both laughed at what was their first private joke.

Jan had not known what to bring or if it would be proper to bring anything at all. At last he'd settled on a porcelain figurine of a dancer, suitable for the house and therefore for them all. It was small but fine, and had cost rather more than he could comfortably manage, but when he saw the delight on Lallie's face he was deeply glad he'd chosen it.

'She's beautiful ...' she whispered.

He wanted to tell her she was beautiful too, but he felt Joe's

59

sharp glance from under the heavy eyebrows, the look of a harried shepherd whose flock required constant vigilance.

Joe came with them to the garden afterwards as they all romped with the dogs and threw snowballs for them to chase, and was with them again when Lallie dug out an old atlas and Jan showed her where his home was – had been – and traced the route of his escape. While Lallie and Millie busied themselves with dinner Joe took him to the Three Nuns and did his hostly duty over a glass of old and mild, introducing him to the regulars as a pal of Neil's who was staying with them just for the holiday. To Jan it sounded very finite and perhaps it was so intended, but then Joe surprised him again by buying drinks all round and toasting 'all our brave young lads' with a proprietary arm across Jan's shoulder.

By the time they got back to Eccles Place it was early afternoon and time for dinner and the King's Christmas message on the radio, to which all the Wainwrights listened with respectful affection. Jan took the opportunity to watch firelight dance across Lallie's face. She was wearing one of her gifts, the rose-pink sweater and cardigan from her father. The colour softened every feature to perfection, and if Joe Wainwright had chosen it then perhaps he was something more than the industrial machine Jan had judged him to be. The selection revealed a sure and loving instinct of what was right for his daughter, who seemed more beautiful every time Jan looked at her. She was like a bud waiting to unfold. Then she smiled at him from across the room, the heavy-lashed grey eyes touching his with warmth.

From his big armchair in the corner Joe puffed on his pipe, watching the scene with the vague feeling that something was missing, or perhaps it was something else. Millie's dinner, most likely. As usual she'd cooked too much food then urged it on them too many times. His irritation increased when Millie, heavy-eyed and drowsy from stuffed goose and port wine, said:

'Why don't you young folks go for a drive or something while Joe and I have forty winks? Derbyshire's nice this time of year. Show Jan some countryside before he has to go back?'

Joe threw her a look that could have splintered glass. 'What would they want to be driving about in the cold for?'

Lallie sprang up. 'Good idea, Mum. We'll be warm enough

if we take your car, Daddy. We can drive in to Castleton and stop at the Cheshire Cheese for a toddy, give Jan a chance to see a real country pub.' Then she turned to Jan and Joe was astonished to see her blush. 'That's if you'd like to come ...'

Jan was already on his feet and they were gone out the door in a flurry of tasselled scarves and laughter, the heavy engine of Joe's car roaring into life not five minutes after Millie's suggestion.

'You're a big help, I must say,' he grumbled.

'What have I done now?'

'You didn't have to tell them to go, did you? Seems as if we've hardly seen her this holiday, what with one thing and another.'

'Well, she's only young once.'

Joe sighed. That's what worried him, that all Lallie's youth and innocence could be squandered on one pointless flirtation that went nowhere, leading to another and another. He'd seen it happen to the daughters of too many. Then he realized what was missing from this Christmas.

'We never got over to Backenthorpe,' he said. 'I've taken her every year since she was three and she hasn't even reminded me this time.'

'Take her next weekend instead.' Millie's eyes, so like her daughter's, had taken on the glaze that preceded sleep.

'Next week'll be New Year, not Christmas,' he pointed out. 'It's not the same.'

'She's growing up pretty fast.' His wife's eyes closed and her face wore the complacent expression that always infuriated him.

'Make up your mind. First she's only young once, then she's growing up fast.'

'Oh Joe, whatever's the matter with you? The goose a bit too greasy, was it?'

'Nowt! Nowt's a matter with me.' He was surprised to hear himself use the broad Yorkshire of his beginnings. Like old Hodgson, he thought, annoyed again.

Millie roused herself with a visible effort and poured him a drink, something she never normally did. Added too much soda, too.

'You'd best have this and take a nap. You're working too hard, that's your trouble.'

She was right. War orders were coming in thicker than he

61

could handle them, and Neil's going had been a big loss.

'Not seen much of Neil this holiday, have we?' he said.

Millie gave him a shrewd, hard look and opened her mouth to say something, changed her mind and said something else. 'Busy I expect, what with all the company they've got over there.'

Half dozing, he let go and allowed himself to drift off.

CHAPTER SIX

The camp was sunk deep in post-holiday doldrums, dismal with dripping bushes and melting slush. Grubby-looking snow lay in heaps beside the runways. From the WAAF quarters across camp the strains of 'White Christmas' came to them, tinny and forlorn, through the last of the daylight.

If Jan needed a reminder of the warmth and comfort of the Wainwright house the contrast was brought home to him with numbing force by the wind which knifed through the cracks of the cheerless little box of a room he shared with Roman. Bare linoleum underfoot; paint flaking off damp walls; heavy blackout curtains at the windows and over them all the smell of petrol and floor polish and Roman's Turkish cigarettes which no amount of airing-out by the batman could quite dispel. A limp bundle of evergreens hung from the naked light fixture – another of the batman's festive efforts come to nothing. A creased map of Warsaw's central district was pinned to the wall, the lone reminder of Poland.

This, such as it was, was their home on the ground. In the air it was L for Lalka, which Jan found considerably more cheerful.

Across the aerodrome a mechanic began to run-up the engine of a Wellington. Roman stirred in the depths of the single armchair as a roar like troubled thunder reached them. 'That one sounds sick,' he said. 'Hope it's from our kite.'

They were all impatient for training to end and operational flights to begin but for Roman who was already cultivating the war-weary ennui of a flyer waiting for a day off any way he could get it. Jan smiled but said nothing. The sick engine now shrieking at maximum pitch was not from L for Lalka. Over the daily practice flights he'd come to know the two engines of his Wellington as well as he knew the hands that controlled them. His engines had been healthy before the holiday and were therefore presumably still healthy. Roman's tentative date with a WAAF notwithstanding, they would fly tomorrow.

He waited for Roman to speak of Lallie. They had been back in camp for over two hours and still her name had not been mentioned – and reticence on the subject of girls was quite unknown to Roman. The train from Sheffield had been crowded, and Neil had been there, but now …

Jan began to unpack, hanging his spare uniform over a chair for the batman to press in the morning and setting his shoes beneath it to await cleaning. He was obscurely pleased to see mud from Hodgson's Market Garden clinging to the insteps. At the bottom of his suitcase was the tissue-wrapped scarf the Wainwrights had given him. As he moved to transfer it to a drawer of the tallboy the scarf slid through its folds of tissue and slipped to the linoleum, lining uppermost, a crimson question mark which Roman could hardly ignore. His moon face creased into plump, troubled folds.

'From the Wainwrights?'

'Yes.'

'Flashy.' He took a deep draw on his cigarette. Constraint hung heavy on the smoky air.

'I like it,' Jan said. 'It's warm.' A mental picture of Millie pointing to the ceiling might have made him smile if he'd been less tense, less filled with the excitement of Lallie.

'You've fallen for her, haven't you?' The words rushed out, as if they'd been held back by a dam whose walls had suddenly given way. 'Neil's girl.' Roman played the dating game to the hilt but he observed all the rules and Jan, apparently, had broken the most important one.

'They're friends.'

'More than that.'

'Did Neil say so?'

'No. His mother did. 'Inseparable' was the word she used.' The single English word leapt out of the surrounding Polish.

'Perhaps she'd like them to be.'

Roman stood up, his stocky frame outlined against the waning light from the window. 'Not just Neil's mother. Neil hardly spoke all the way coming in. You didn't even notice, did you?' He ground out his cigarette in the ashtray and swung to his feet, turned his angry scowl on Jan. 'Out of all the English in camp he's the one that went out of his way to make us welcome –'

'And I appreciate it. I like him. But I also like Lallie and she seems to like me.'

'Her father, his mother, Neil himself, they all seem to think Neil and Lallie –'

'Maybe they should have checked with Lallie before declaring her private property.'

Roman sighed. He could never hold anger for very long. 'It's your life,' he said. 'I'm going to the mess for a drink. You coming?'

'Not now.' He wanted, had been waiting, for a chance to be alone.

On his way out the door Roman again turned brown, troubled eyes on him. 'Be careful, friend. We have enough enemies across the Channel without making our own.'

'Neil –'

'Not Neil. It's not in him to dislike you for something like this. But Joe Wainwright did not love us, I think. He could be a bastard.'

'I don't plan to give him reason.'

Lying on his bed after Roman had gone, Jan knew he would not give Joe Wainwright reason. Clearly Lallie was carefully brought up, the centre of her father's life. Not a girl to take behind a hedge after a few too many drinks at the pub, not a girl to take to London for a quick weekend. This was a girl to marry or to leave alone. Or he could be a friend, like Neil. He shook his head and picked up the scarf. A friend he could not be, not to this girl. Or woman, for surely a woman waited behind the smoke-grey eyes. He remembered the touch of her hands, firm and electric under his fingers, her cheek soft as petals touching his face, lips warm and eager pressed against his own, and again his blood raced at the memory.

Of course it was too soon, but he wrote to her that night, his pen hesitating over every word. Would her parents read it? What were the customs here? Would they expect him to write or would they disapprove? In the end he wrote just what he wanted to say because no amount of thinking could tell him if such a family would ever consider him as anything more than a holiday guest, their welcome little more than a Christmas treat for a temporary refugee.

Then, for the fourth time since leaving Poland, he wrote to the Red Cross. 'Please be aware I am still anxious to know if there is any trace yet of my parents, last seen at 53, Morska Street, Warsaw ...'

He wrote more from habit than hope. In some corner of his mind he knew with numbing certainty that his father was dead, that the frail lungs could not possibly have survived the smoke and dust that hung over Warsaw the last time he'd seen the city. When he thought now of his parents, of where they might be and in what circumstances, only the image of Mamunia sprang to life. She was alone. In writing his enquiry to the Red Cross the desire to find her became an overwhelming need to speak to her, to pour out his doubts, his joy, his confusion, his grief, watch her weigh them all, sift and sort them into truths and certainties, discard the fantasies and hand him back the facts.

'So you've met a girl,' is what she'd say.

'I've met a girl.'

'You've met girls before.'

'Not like this. This is a girl to marry, Mamunia.'

'So marry. What's to wait?'

'In a few months I'll be operational. Bombers get shot down. She could be a widow.'

He could almost feel the impatient slap of her hand on his arm. 'Pooh! Rivers *could* run uphill but they usually don't.'

'Her father would be against it.'

'They always are.'

'Maybe we're too young.'

'Rubbish. You're twenty-one.' Her head would be tipped to

one side, she'd be tapping her fingers on the table by now.

'She's as English as tea and crumpets. Would she be happy in Poland, after the war?'

'Only cretins are happy all the time. She'd get used to it.'

A squadron of Hurricanes from the fighter station nearby shattered the silence as they took off. The tenuous connection with Mamunia was destroyed. He sealed and stamped his letters and walked through a chill drizzle to post them at the officers' mess.

Reading the single closely written sheet, Lallie could feel the weight of her father's stare on her bent head. He had loaded his pipe. He had tamped it. He had lit it. He was now rattling the wooden matches in their yellow Swan Vesta box as he paced closer and closer.

'Didn't take him long to write,' he said at last. 'What's he got to say for himself?'

Lallie felt the blood rush to her cheeks. Would she *ever* be able to control this idiotic blushing! 'He's just thanking us for the holiday. Mostly.'

'That's nice,' Millie murmured, a split second before she switched on the vacuum cleaner and followed it over the red carpet, in the process forcing Joe to move over to the window. Lallie could have hugged her. She threw her a grateful glance and rushed to her room to read her letter in peace. Her parents had never opened her letters, never read them unless invited to, but until now there'd been nothing she was not willing to share with them. This letter she could not, would not, share. She saw it was dated the very day he'd returned to camp.

'... and already I miss you and wonder when I shall see you again. After the time spent with you the camp is very dull and cold but I am thinking of Castleton and so am happy for the first time since I left Poland. In four days it will be 1940. Perhaps everything will be better.

The third Saturday of next month there is to be a special party in the mess. Is it possible you could come? Would your parents approve? If so I can arrange accommodation for you at a hotel as the party will not end until long after the last train. I think you will enjoy yourself and it would make me very proud to present you to my new crew, who have now become more or less my family. There are five of us including Roman. Please write soon and say you will come.

One week ago I did not know Lallie Wainwright and now she fills my thoughts. How can this be?

I send you my wishes and hopes ... Jan Kaliski.'

His stilted yet oddly desolate message crept into her heart and nestled there like a new puppy. No, she would not share this with her father, just as she had not shared the magic of the drive to Castleton in the winter dusk.

The splendid, snow-crowned ruins of Peveril Castle, romantic above the towering cavern, had meshed perfectly with her mood then, as had the quiet bar at the Cheshire Cheese. They whispered, laughed, made silly jokes about his English. She told him how lovely Castleton was in the spring with all the new lambs and he said she must be sure to show him. When they held hands across the little table it seemed natural that they should. Natural, too, when she said, 'You really are most awfully nice,' and he leaned across and kissed the tip of her nose. Inevitable, then, driving home over the dark and silent moors that he should ask her to stop the car. He drew her into his arms for the first real kisses of her life, lovers' kisses, soft and gentle but with torrents raging beneath their quiet surface, his fingers tracing her cheekbones, his lips brushing her eyelids, her hair. Under her cheek she could feel his pilot's wings hard against her skin, swift reminder of his deadly calling which lent sudden urgency to her fingers as she drew his face down to hers.

It was he, finally, who said, 'Your father will be wondering. I think that we must go ...' and she who said, 'But I wish, I wish ...'

And now the mess party next month. A whole weekend to be with him. No, he didn't mean *that* kind of weekend, not for her, but something in her that was treacherous and incredibly delicious wished he did.

She mentioned the weekend at breakfast next morning, tried to work it in casually between Daddy's grumbles about the war news and Mum's clattering of the dishes.

'I'll be going to Lincoln next month,' she said, concentrating hard on getting the marmalade evenly spread on her toast. 'There's a party in the officers' mess and he's asked me to go.'

Her father looked up from the newspaper. 'Lincoln? You must be dreaming. What makes you think we've enough petrol for you to go gallivanting off there? Besides, you're not driving all that way at night, I won't have it.'

'I thought I'd take the train and stay in a hotel for the weekend.'

'A hotel? On your own? I've never heard of such a thing.'

'Oh Daddy! What about that foreman's daughter you've told us about, she goes off all the time, Leeds, London, everywhere, and she's younger than I am.'

'And a fast piece she's turning out to be, have I told you *that*?'

'You said she was self-confident. Independent.' She kept her voice even but her heart hammered in her ears like a drum. 'It's not as if I've never been away from home.' But she knew that weekends at friends' homes or with Aunt Ginny in Chesterfield were not the same thing. In her father's eyes single girls stayed in hotels for only one reason.

It was her mother who came to the rescue, pouring Joe his second cup of tea and giving them her bland, absent-minded smile. 'If the party's in the mess Neil will be there too, won't he? Be a proper treat for him to see Lallie again. If I can get the raisins I'll make a cake to send with you, they'll both like that I reckon.'

Joe's frown eased just a little. 'I was forgetting Neil –'

'And you'll have to have a new dress, Lallie, they've ever such a pretty one in Folsom's window, kind of a burnt almond colour –'

'My God, not brown,' her father interrupted, 'and none of Folsom's rubbish either. If she's going she'll go in style. Show the foreigners what a proper young English lady looks like.'

The implications of the words 'proper' and 'lady' were not

lost on Lallie but her relief was such that she jumped up and hugged both of them, giving Mum's shoulder an extra little squeeze in passing, a gesture that did not escape Joe.

'Don't think I don't know when I'm being manipulated,' he said. 'But maybe it's time you got about a bit, and if Neil's going, well ... you might get him to show you round the cathedral while you're there, it's worth an hour or two.'

And thus the charade was adopted that Lallie would be at the mess party as Neil's guest, with Jan some kind of attendant page. It was a fiction that did not altogether please Lallie but, she thought blithely as she planned her wardrobe, it was better than not going at all. Far better than going against Daddy's wishes. In an excess of gratitude she reminded him that they'd missed their Christmas Day visit to Backenthorpe.

He smiled broadly at them both. 'And here I thought she'd forgot all about it, Millie.'

'Didn't I say at the time that you may as well go on New Year? Same thing really, isn't it?'

Joe always dressed rather carefully for the annual visit to the village in which he'd been born and he saw to it that Lallie did the same. No jodhpurs, boots, headscarves for the daughter of Joe Wainwright, not in the lounge bar of the Black Swan. Quiet and expensive elegance was the order of the day and if Lallie called him a snob for insisting on it – and she did, every year – he simply didn't care. For him the trip was a reminder of how far he'd come from the down-at-heel little cluster of small-holdings; the single shop with the pawn-broker in the back; the stone floor of the Black Swan deeply hollowed by feet whose owners had long since passed to the graveyard, their names already erased from the headstones by wind and rain even as their lethargy lived on in their sons and grandsons. Backenthorpe boasted only one street, lined with one-up-and-one-down cottages whose front doors opened directly onto a cobbled road so narrow that a single parked car created an instant road-block.

The lads Joe had grown up with still sat in their doorways of a summer evening, still drank their ale at the Black Swan on weekends and holidays. It was like going back not just in time but in attitude. In Backenthorpe no one *aspired*. That was their crime.

It was only by a single act of bravado that Joe escaped the same fate. His father had owned the little smithy, and on his death it passed to Joe. Marriage to Millie came too soon. Times were hard when Lallie was born. The smithy had not a single job waiting, and the prospects of none to come. Joe, looking down at his week-old daughter as she lay sleeping in the crib (borrowed from a neighbour) was suddenly seized with such despair he had to turn away so Millie would not see his tears. The baby's clothes were second-hand, as yet there was no pram, winter was coming with no money for coal, and God alone knew where the infant's powdered milk would come from when Millie's supply dried up, as it was already beginning to do.

After the despair came anger, a blind black rage that set him shouting to Millie to iron his good shirt, damnit! and look in her purse while she was at it. He needed sixpence. For the bus to Sheffield. Her look of apology merely fuelled his anger further. She only had threepence left, and she needed it for bread. He took it anyway, knowing he'd have to walk the six miles home. In Sheffield he entered a bank for the first time in his life, was astonished to hear himself asking to see the manager, was even more astonished when the manager took him to his office and closed the door. After Joe poured out his dream of a smithy here in town that the steelworks could come to, the bank manager told him to look around for a decent location and then come back and see him. The interview was concluded with a handshake, at which Joe apologized for the roughness of his hands. It was the last apology he ever made and taught him a good lesson. The banker turned over Joe's young, work-gnarled hands with the grime of the smithy embedded in every crack and said, 'If you'd come in here with lily-whites I'd have shown you the door half an hour ago.'

Three months later they moved from Backenthorpe to the city, lived for four years of Lallie's life in the two rooms directly over the shop. They prospered, but the dirty steel city was no place to send a child to school. Again the banker came

70

to the rescue, and they moved to Eccles Place, a progression somewhat akin to moving from a tenement to a penthouse. They had, as Joe liked to say, never looked back. But he did look back, once every year.

He was well aware that the looking back contained a strong element of showing off, why otherwise would he feel the need to take Lallie with him? Of all he had accomplished she was by far his best evidence. Even when she was only three and long before they could afford a car they'd walk, father and daughter, past winter fields and low limestone walls humped with snow. He'd had to carry her now and then, and usually her Christmas doll too. When they reached Backenthorpe he'd make for the Black Swan. With the little Lallie and her doll safely deposited in the kitchen with the licencee's wife, Joe would order glasses of bitter all round in the taproom and lemonade for Lallie in the kitchen, making very sure that all the customers got a good look at the childish angel-face of his daughter, heard her speak to him in accents far removed from Backenthorpe.

As she grew older he graduated her from lemonade in the pub kitchen to dry sherry in the snug, where he could introduce her to his old schoolmates and even the headmaster, where he'd sit back and watch them goggle at her looks, her clothes, her devastating air of assurance. The morning's outing – among old friends and enemies alike – had become the best part of the holiday. At one stroke he could show off Lallie and his own success. He could buy drinks all round (whisky these days), he could offer jobs to a lucky few. He could bask in their envy and his pride.

Not even Neil had been invited to these outings. They were strictly between himself and Backenthorpe and Lallie, a renewal, a chance to touch the past and make sure the future was secure against a return to it.

Today was no exception, even though it was New Year instead of Christmas. Lallie wore a suit of dove grey suede with matching needle-heeled shoes, pure silk stockings, a silk blouse the colour of lilacs and a glow that came from somewhere behind her eyes, a glow which filled Joe with a deep sense of unease but which also filled him with pride as he

71

sensed the confidence she gave out to these old friends and antagonists.

'By God, but Joe Wainwright's a lucky bugger,' he could hear them thinking as he helped Lallie into her coat and they said their goodbyes.

As usual, they ignored the car for a while and walked across the village green to the scarred bench in its centre, where Joe liked to sit and talk, despite the cold, and simply look at the village and rejoice. To his right was the old smithy, long since tumbled to a picturesque heap of stones covered over with moss. He had the feeling that if he should kick aside one of the stones the smell of poverty would reach out for him, trap him in clammy, suffocating past. But then there was his car, gleaming fat and important and dwarfing the smithy. And by his side his daughter.

He watched her face, open and guileless as a child's. Happy. Thinking about the trip to Lincoln, no doubt. If she were entertaining fantasies of being alone in a hotel room with the Pole, of maybe spending the night with him, such dreams did not show on her face and would in any case be quickly set aside by his next words, just as he intended.

'I've had Neil book you a room,' he said. 'Not in one of the flashy new places. In an old hotel, respectable. The manager will look after you personally, make sure you have everything you need.' He did not add that he'd spoken to the manager himself that morning. He did not have to. Colour rushed to her cheeks.

'Daddy, I'm twenty years old!'

She made it sound like sixty. He smiled. He knew to the year, the day, the hour, how old she was. Five years earlier this subject wouldn't have come up and five years into the future it would no longer matter. Now, on this New Year's Day of 1940, her age was the pivot on which her entire future was balanced. He would not see it squandered in a furtive romp between the sheets.

'I know how old you are. I was that age myself once.'

'You don't trust me,' she cried, 'you think –'

'I think you're not listening. I said I was twenty once. I'm not so ancient I can't remember what it was like.'

72

'I'll bet Mum's father didn't oversee every minute of *her* time!'

He sighed and covered her hand with his. 'No he didn't. Things might have turned out a lot different if he had.' His mind flew back. Warm summer nights in the larches opposite them, young Millie sweet and compliant with the pale moths fluttering about her cloud of dark hair. Then one night the tears, the whispers. 'Oh Joe, it's happened. What am I going to do, whatever am I going to do ...' Entirely typical of Millie that she'd said 'I' and not 'we'. The vessel was hers, as was the shame. They were married within the month. He'd thought many times since that his entire generation had very likely tied the knot for the same reason. But not Lallie, not if he could help it. Not with the Pole or anybody else, not even Neil – but then, he could depend on Neil to treat her with respect. As for foreigners, he wouldn't trust them farther than he could throw them.

'There's things your mother should have told you,' he said now. 'Oh, not the birds and the bees, I'm sure you know all about *that*. But men (and this'll sound old-fashioned), men are funny buggers when it comes to women. They keep wanting what they can't have and they'll say any damn thing to get it. Then when they get it ...' He spread his hands, then saw she was almost laughing, and so he could relax.

'Oh Daddy, not *that* old chestnut!'

'Chestnut my eye! Look at old Henry the Eighth. Do you think he'd have married Anne Boleyn if she'd jumped under the blanket with him the first time he asked her? Not likely. Then we'd have had no Lizzie the One ...'

Her young laugh rang out into the quiet afternoon. 'And you'd be confessing your sins to a little man in a dog collar behind a grille.'

'Not me,' he said, pulling her to her feet. 'I don't sin. I'm your father. I'm perfect.'

'And so humble.' Chuckling, she tucked her arm through his as they walked to the car.

CHAPTER SEVEN

In a corner chair of the camp library Neil Armott was leafing blindly through a magazine when Jan, obviously looking for him, came in. The sight of the Pole, tall and altogether too damned handsome in his officer's uniform, weighted Neil's depression further.

Anybody but Jan, he thought, anybody at all. Yet he couldn't help liking him, that was the hell of it. The younger man folded himself into the easy chair opposite and fixed Neil with a purposeful blue stare.

'I think I should tell you –' he began.

So here it came, as he'd known from that very first meeting that it eventually must. It was when Lallie had picked them all up at the station at Christmas. There'd been just the four of them in the car but even then Neil sensed something else, a tension, perhaps only the sharpened awareness of two people meeting for the first time and finding each other deeply absorbing. Unease had lain dormant in a corner of his mind ever since, until Joe's call yesterday prodded it to life. Now it stared at him, must be faced.

'... I invited Lallie to the party next month,' Jan said.

'I know.' Neil heard the smugness in his own voice and hated himself for it. 'Joe called me, had me book her a room.'

Jan seemed disconcerted for a moment, or perhaps he was simply confused. 'I could have done that – but it was very kind of you.'

'I had no choice, mate. Joe insisted.'

Now Jan really was disconcerted and Neil felt a quick surge of sympathy for this young foreigner who had innocently run afoul of Joe Wainwright's will.

'I don't understand. Why would he ask you?'

Why indeed? Because I'm good old Neil, Daddy's trusted lieutenant. He forced himself to shrug. 'I work for him, remember. Or rather I did – and will again. Maybe I'm the keeper of the morals?'

'I see.' Jan's voice was suddenly cool, a flash of anger in his eyes, an anger Neil knew was not directed at him. He forced down his own bitterness and gave Jan a reassuring thump on the arm.

'Look chum, that's how fathers are – and Joe's not your average father by a long shot.'

He watched the boy absorb what he must surely already have known, watched him swallow, pause, meet Neil's eyes.

'I have to ask you. Perhaps I am – how do you say? – stepping on your toes?'

'No.' You're doing a bloody war dance over everything I've ever hoped for but think nothing of it. You'll never know and she wouldn't care. Not fair, he corrected himself. Remember what you said when Joe called, full of paternal doubts about Lallie seeing the Pole again? Not to worry, Joe, Jan's a grand chap. And Lallie? Hell, they'd both care, but it wouldn't change a damned thing.

'But you are disappointed,' Jan said quietly.

Neil turned back to his magazine. 'She's hardly my personal property, is she? Nothing anybody can do about it. It's just the way things are.'

With a minimum of self-pity Neil Armott had faced many disappointments in his life. He'd had less than one year of university when his father died. After the funeral the lawyer appeared at the house with a long face and a short message. Armott Sr had left them only his chilly, genteel standards – not a penny left to maintain them. So the engineering degree was out, squashed in the bitter knowledge that his mother must somehow be supported. Even if she offered to work (she didn't) she was adept at nothing beyond cutting gladioli from the garden and arranging them stiffly in crystal vases. There were scholarships, yes, for those with quick minds and brilliant prospects. He'd always known he was not of their number. He was a plodder. He did well in school because he kept at it. Concepts grasped in minutes by some might take him hours, but when he had them they were his forever. When Joe Wainwright came to the rescue, offering to see him through university if that's what Neil wanted, he knew he'd have to turn it down. He'd work for his keep, yes, but he couldn't be beholden for five years, couldn't humiliate his mother by accepting; for despite the Wainwright money and his long-time friendship with the family, Agnes Armott treated them with just that degree of condescension her excellent manners would permit. He couldn't put her in the position of tugging at the metaphorical forelock to a family she spoke of (in private) as 'very kind but not quite our sort'.

In time he'd come to love Lallie with a devotion he knew to be dog-like, not far removed from the melting gaze the Afghans turned on her when she appeared with that open-hearted smile calling, 'Anyone for a walk?' and jingling their leashes.

What was more surprising was that he'd come to love Joe Wainwright too. More than he'd ever loved his own father, which made him feel the slightest bit guilty. In Joe's bluff way he'd taught him the business from the ground up. It had been hard, but there was always that appreciative glance from the man he acknowledged to be the boss, and at the end of the week a judgement along with the pay envelope. 'You're coming on nicely, lad. I knew you would.' Working with Joe he could not help seeing how he nurtured the foundry as one might a favoured child. Gratitude became admiration, and admiration love, so that the two most important people in his life now were Lallie Wainwright and her father, his own mother a distant third.

And now this. A small kindness to a likeable foreigner had turned into an explosive charge. The fuse was lit. Jan and Lallie. Lallie and Jan. Whichever way he said it the impact was the same. Shattering. Inevitable. Unless Joe Wainwright did something to stop it. Surely he would try. They were both so heartbreakingly young, made even him feel old. And twenty-four *was* old at OTU. Most of the chaps were in their late teens, eager to fight and heedless of the consequences.

Jan's approach was different. He brought an air of serious study to the bombing exercises. Each day's run must be better, smoother than the day before; each member of his crew was expected to show greater accuracy with every flight. As he'd once explained to Neil, 'If we can't hit the bombing range here where it's calm how will we ever hit the target on an op?' He was a damned good pilot, deft and instinctive, very determined to succeed.

Looking at him now Neil saw what he hadn't seen before. The qualities of the pilot were the qualities of the man.

It *was* the most glorious dress she'd ever worn, after all. Could that really be Lallie Wainwright looking back at her in the heavy old-fashioned cheval glass? The dress shimmered in its own delicate glow and cast the same glow upon her, dimming the hotel room behind her to nothing more than a setting for a fine jewel.

Chiffon the colour of pale, wild primroses fell from a softly draped bodice into long simple drifts of skirt caught at the waist with a narrow belt of soft gold kid. There were evening shoes the same primrose yellow as the dress, and the sheerest of silk stockings. Lovely, lovely, but oh how she'd longed for the black satin strapless and oh how Daddy had thumped his fist on the table and ordered her to take it back by morning or it would go into the fire where it belonged.

She'd been furious at the time. The black had hinted at a certain sultry experience, while the primrose chiffon sang of youth and innocence – just what she *didn't* want to advertise. Yet she had to admit now that this was the prettiest she'd looked in her entire life.

Even her hair was behaving itself today, cloudy dark as ever (not straight and sleek as she's always wanted it) but right, somehow, for the dress, for the evening to come. Just how right she couldn't know until later, weeks and months when the entire evening shone like a beacon against dark clouded nights and dawns pale with anxiety.

She checked her slim gold watch against the hotel clock on the mantel and excitement caught in her throat. Almost time for Jan to come and get her. Doubts rushed in through the open door. A party in the Officers' Mess. A grown-up occasion (rather proper, Jan had told her in letters) with people from simply everywhere who spent their days in casual friendships, their nights in deadly combat. Hodgson's chickens and Bunky the cow seemed a million miles away, the barnyard soaked out of her pores in an hour-long bath of lavender crystals. 'Be a lady,' Daddy said when she modelled the dress for him. 'Be yourself,' was Millie's advice. Whether she could be both was the question. Being Daddy's favourite girl was one thing, making the right impression on sophisticated people was something altogether different. And what was the right impression? A light tap on the open door brought a swift end to the stream of doubts. Jan! No, it was the manager wringing his hands, just as he had when he'd checked her in.

'Flying Officer Kaliski has arrived, madam. I've put him in the front lounge. Whenever you're ready ...'

He seemed inclined to linger and she realized he was waiting to take her downstairs himself. Daddy *must* have been impressive! She picked up Millie's chinchilla coat (on loan with strict instructions not to spill anything on it or leave it in the taxi) and flew downstairs, the manager hurrying behind her but almost forgotten.

From the first landing she could see the top of Jan's head as he waited by a huge overstuffed chair. He was watching the other side of the circular staircase and hadn't seen her yet. She stopped. Looking down, she saw him foreshortened and so not as tall as before, strangely vulnerable in his best dress-uniform with the pants creased just so, the parting in his pale hair regulation straight, brass buttons all ashine as he stood almost to attention. She suddenly felt that he was very self-conscious in the lounge crowded with older men and perfumed women who were assembling for the hotel's dinner dance. Then he looked up and she could wait no longer. She wanted to run down the stairs but forced herself to walk (Be a lady!) in the best Hollywood tradition, Millie's chinchilla trailing the stairs against all the fervent entreaties. Then she was close enough to see his face, the look in his eyes, and could only be herself after all.

The coat forgotten, she ran the last few steps and could truly see nothing else but his sudden smile.

'You look ... no, wonderful is not the right word. Exquisite.'

He took her hands and the same feeling swept through her once again, the one she remembered from Christmas at Castleton. As if she clasped something warm and good and intensely personal.

Then the manager was there again, fussily handing her the coat. 'Your coat, Madam. It was on the stairs. If you would care to wait I shall call a taxi.'

Jan grinned at him, a gleam of the devil lurking in his eyes. 'Thank you. We already have one waiting.'

He helped her into the coat and then they were in the taxi. Except for the back of the driver's neck – which really didn't count – they were alone. *Now* he would kiss her, she hoped. But then her lipstick would smudge and it had gone on so beautifully ...

Instead, he took her hand. 'It is very good to see you again. I have been waiting.'

Don't gush. Be a lady. But she couldn't. 'Oh, so have I! It's been simply ages and ages, I thought today would never come.' His fingers tightened over hers.

'For me also. You are as I remembered.' He touched the soft chiffon of the dress. 'But prettier.'

'Is the dress right? Not too formal or –'

'It's perfect.' Then he did kiss her, but lightly, on the cheek. 'Tonight you will meet my crew. They are anxious to see you.'

She remembered the first letter, when he'd said his new crew was already like a family. 'Are they who you wanted? You like them?'

'Yes, they are good for me. In a few months I think I shall have a second pilot also.' Which would, she knew, mean it would be time to start ops.

'Will you be sent somewhere else when ...'

'Yes.'

'Far away, d'you think?' Please not Scotland, not London,

nowhere so far he couldn't come to Yorkshire on a two-day pass.

'There is no way to know.' The bleakness in his voice echoed her thoughts and they were silent for some minutes as the taxi sped them across the flat farmland of Lincolnshire, then abruptly – no lights to warn her, for the blackout was complete – they were through the main gates of the camp, pulling to a halt before a long low structure. In the dim light of the taxi's open door he smiled into her eyes. 'But tonight we shall have a very fine party, yes?'

'The best,' she said firmly.

No stranger to the term 'an officer and a gentleman' (Mrs Armott's conversation was studded with such pearls), Lallie had expected that the party would be a rather decorous affair, vaguely like the movie version of a court ball. She was not prepared for the mass of shoulder flashes proclaiming servicemen from everywhere under the sun, nor for the hum of voices which met them as Jan ushered her through the door. Music played somewhere but the voices all but eclipsed it.

The accents of Canada and Australia mingled oddly with the slow broad vowels of the Midlands and the clipped, half-strangled whinnies of what Daddy called the Prep School Dainties. A couple of South Africans joked with a Dutchman in Afrikaans. Over immaculate uniforms of airforce blue a trio of white turbans nodded gravely and murmured in Hindustani. A tiny coal-black Abyssinian, his head tipped far back, complained up into the face of a pale Norwegian giant.

And everywhere the Poles. One group here; another by the far door; a larger, noisier group at the bar. They sounded, it seemed to Lallie, like a gathering of trains. Shush! Chick! Shush! Chick! Shush! Chick! Excitable. Arm-waving. Disputing. Laughing even as they argued.

This League of Nations male voice choir was augmented by twitterings (mostly English) from the 'popsies' the crews had managed to gather like wild flowers from the surrounding countryside. (Joe: Just let me catch any of 'em calling *you* a popsie and I'll break their bloody neck.)

There were ladies and tarts and every stripe in between. Long-stemmed ball gowns rubbed shoulders with peasant blouses; thin pointy heels clicked alongside the firm thud of the country ladies' cuban heels. The women were heavily outnumbered, their bright dresses mere sprinkling on a field of airforce blue.

So this was an officers' mess. To Lallie it seemed more like the taproom of the Three Nuns on a rowdy Saturday night. The men were all swigging whisky or Pimms Cup, the women gin or punch.

Jan took her coat. 'I'll put it in the cloakroom upstairs. You'll wait for me here? You won't run away?'

'Now where would I run to?'

'I'm sorry. I wanted too much for you to come and I'm afraid you might vanish.' He left her standing by a long table that ran the length of the room.

As she turned into the room the first face to separate itself from the throng was Neil's, alight with admiration.

'I say, you look absolutely wizard! That dress ...'

She twirled the skirt for him, just the way she had with every new dress since she'd been a tot. 'And Mum lent me her chinchilla, too!'

His face seemed to stiffen. It was as if he'd pulled on a blasé mask that didn't quite fit his features. 'Well, this *is* a big night then, isn't it?' He turned quickly towards the table. 'Let's see if we can tempt the lady.'

There were crusty pork pies, salamis, cheeses, roast turkeys, a magnificent salmon in aspic, bowls of sherry trifle, chocolate tortes, sugared almonds – she *adored* sugared almonds. 'You do yourselves proud. And *I* thought there was a war on.'

'It's not the usual mess-fare – here, let me get you some punch. Highly recommended.'

'By whom?'

'Me. Your father said to be sure to take care of you.'

It struck a slightly wrong note, made her want to tell him, quite sharply, that she could take care of herself. 'I'll wait for Jan if you don't mind – I did arrive with him.'

'So you did.' He turned away and was soon engaging a walrus moustache in animated conversation. Oh dear – but then Jan was at her elbow, watching her stare into the punch bubbles so she wouldn't have to see the hurt in Neil's eyes.

'So you've noticed our punchbowl,' Jan said. 'Different, isn't it? The astrodome of an old kite – Jerry's guns drilled it in just the right places.'

The bowl was enormous, with three neat holes in what was now its base. Somebody had fitted it with coloured lights and bottles of oxygen so that the potent mixture of champagne and liqueurs effervesced with bubbles that ranged the spectrum from palest pear-blossom pink through yellow and chartreuse to the deepest of burgundies. Their reflected light darted like small tropical fish over her primrose dress and bare arms.

It was quite delicious. And heady. When she looked up his eyes were on her face, smiling.

'Perhaps you will drink *brudershaft* with me?'

'But I've barely started the punch!'

He laughed. '*Brudershaft* is a ceremony, not a drink. It means something like brotherhood and it is forever. In Poland we seldom use a person's first name, only if we like them very much and think we will know them for a long time. Then we ask to drink *brudershaft*, like so.' He linked his elbow around hers without spilling a drop from either glass of punch. 'Now we each drink from our own glass at the same time, and after this we are very close, always.'

'It's a kind of pledge?'

He nodded. 'Sometimes much more.'

They were very close as they sipped the punch and she could see herself in his eyes, two tiny Lallies looking back at her, all dark hair and huge, starry eyes against a ground of light, bright blue. 'So now I can call you Jan – which I already do anyway.'

'And now you are always Lallie.'

Over his shoulder she saw Neil. He'd been watching them. He came over immediately, broad smile again in place. 'Jan, you're not feeding the girl. What in the world would Joe say?'

'He's not here and I'm not hungry in the least.' Really, Neil *was* being difficult. What on earth had Daddy said to him? 'Besides, we have to go and meet Jan's crew.' When he flushed she saw she'd been tactless. Neil, though older than Jan, was too new a cadet to have his own crew yet, and it probably rankled a bit. Men could be *such* babies about unimportant things! As they threaded through the crowd to Jan's crew at a table by the bar she felt Neil's eyes follow her, and something in her made her want to turn to him, make him smile at her the way he always had, but Jan's hand was drawing her ahead to the crew of L for Lalka, all laughing and talking among themselves.

Since the first time she'd met him she'd wondered about Jan's crew, trying to picture the life he was living, and with whom. The word 'family' suggested closeness – yet they must have known each other for only a few months. But then, they all depended on each other, most of all on the pilot. If a group of men could ever be a family, who more likely than the crew of a bomber?

Introductions were conducted in a flurry of mess stewards setting two extra places, and it was a second or two before the faces, and the shock, registered. Crewmen? Crew*men*? They were boys, one of them with the down of adolescence still on his cheeks!

Bolek was the rear gunner, a sunny youth with ginger hair and freckles; his only English vocabulary consisted of: I sorry, I no understan', I like England ver' much.

The gangly wireless operator was Lech, with eyes like dark holes. He used his cigarette holder as a baton to orchestrate a private monologue and seemed quite drunk, subsiding quickly into a morose silence. Jan explained to her quietly that there'd been a mistake in today's flight. Lech had given a wrong bearing and upset Roman's navigation. Also his girlfriend had gone off to London with a wing commander for the weekend. 'Tomorrow he will be fine.'

To Lech's right was Kaz, the front gunner, a curly-top with brilliant pink cheeks whose English was unbelievably fast but, as yet, quite incomprehensible unless you knew what he was about to say. Kaz talked all the time and to everyone at once. His arm was around a girl he persisted in calling Linda who, it turned out, was Miranda. She drifted off eventually and did not come back. He scarcely seemed to notice.

And there was Roman, beaming on everyone but especially the Polish WAAF by his side, Janina. She was all cheekbones and liquid eyes and sleek wings of blue-black hair Lallie would have died for.

Her arrival seemed to have a sobering effect on them all. Now

83

they must speak English, and except for Kaz they spent more time hunting for words than speaking them. The more they drank the more they were inclined to give up the battle and one by one fell back to Polish, until only Jan was speaking English. He turned to Lallie.

'They ask your pardon. They are here such a short time. It is very hard for them.'

'Then let's dance and make it easy for them.'

He laughed and reached for her hand. 'Clever girl.'

The lights were low and the music soft, and now she was in his arms, the top of her head resting against his cheek, breathing in the clean talc-and-shaving cream smell of him, feeling his hand, sure and firm, through the primrose chiffon. They did not speak for a long time and she was glad simply to drift across the floor, filled with excitement yet at the same time comfortable, as if she was where she belonged. In a dream yet wide, wide awake; breathless with wonder yet sharply, exquisitely conscious of his lips on her forehead. Impossible that anyone had felt like this before, ever, or the whole world would be mad, delirious with joy, floating with her in the stratosphere somewhere.

When the music stopped he led her to a small table way off in the corner and ordered drinks, held both of her hands in his across the table.

'Like the pub in Castleton, no?'

Castleton? With this hum of languages around them? 'That was a village – this place seems to be a whole world!'

His smile faded. 'A short world. Soon we'll be gone from here, a month or two ...'

No! The dreamworld was fading under a cloud of new, terrifying fears she refused to examine. 'You'll get leave before that?'

'A few days before we're posted to squadron, yes.'

'Where will you go?' She held her breath, watched him over the rim of her glass. 'Where would you *like* to be?'

'Wherever you are.'

'*Oh but you can be*! You can come home to us, I'd love you to come.'

A closed look crept into his eyes and she felt his hand curl, almost clench over hers. 'Perhaps your father ...'

'Daddy wants whatever *I* want.' In that moment she was quite certain of it. 'And Mum would be in heaven, shopping and cooking. Please say you'll come.' She pressed his hand open as if acceptance were hiding in it.

He relaxed suddenly and laughed. 'I'd like to, very much.'

There was a touch at the back of her chair. It was Neil, asking her to dance.

'You and Jan seem to be hitting it off,' he said, halfway through the waltz. His voice was stiff, not like him.

'He's *so* nice!'

'Yes I suppose he is.' The despair in his voice reached out to her, caused sudden tears to gather in her throat. On impulse she reached up and kissed his cheek.

'Oh Neil, I'm sorry, I *am* so sorry. And to think I met him through you.'

He searched her face as if to etch it on his mind, a lopsided grin on his open, honest face. 'That's what friends are for, angel. Scrub round it.' Leave it alone.

Back at the table he aimed a mock punch at Jan's shoulder. 'You've got the prettiest girl in the room hidden away in a corner. Now I ask you, is that fair?'

Jan looked relieved. 'Perhaps not fair, but wise. She could get stolen.'

'Fat chance, chum. Fat bloody chance.'

They left soon after and Lallie was glad. Some of the gaiety had drained out of the evening and left a troubling question in its wake. Waiting for Jan to get her coat she looked at the punchbowl; it had the suffered the same fate. The bubbles had all disappeared, the surface of the punch opaque, uncertainty in its grenadine depths.

In the taxi he reached for her immediately, his lips on her throat, her eyes, his fingers soft on her hair, then hard as he lifted her face to kiss her mouth, a long kiss, not gentle.

'Lallie ...'

'Mmmm ... it was a lovely, lovely evening.'

'So you are lovely also.'

In the gloom of the taxi she could just see his mouth to trace it with her fingers. She wanted to press his head against her

85

breast and hold it there forever, his blond hair crisp under her fingers. She sighed. 'Soon we'll be at the hotel. I wish … I wish you could come up.'

His arms tightened and she felt him tremble, then he put her gently away from him, but kept her hands in his.

'It will not be right for us, I think.'

'But –'

'Everything should be perfect, not to rush, to spoil – how to say it so you will understand? – look, the men in camp, they have a girl for a week, perhaps two, a wonderful time, happy … and then it's over, and soon another girl. It's the war perhaps, the feeling there may not be much time.'

The words chilled her and she pressed closer to him. 'But that's *why* –'

'You are not like those girls, I think. Your life has been … different.'

'But I don't *want* to be different. You sound just like Daddy!' Her father, Neil, now Jan, all protecting her. And she didn't want to be protected, she wanted to live, to love. To love Jan before it was too late, to hold him, know him –

In the dark intimacy of the taxi he cupped her face in his hands. 'Lallie, I think for us there can be more than a few happy weeks together. Do you understand me?'

His words penetrated, expanded, dwarfed the prospect of a heady love affair with a complex, intriguing man, transformed it to a deep awareness that what was between them was serious, inevitable. This was what it was all about. It was as if she were being swept downstream in a fragile craft that must take one fork or another. Suddenly afraid, she wanted to stay exactly where she was –

But here was the hotel with the manager waiting in the lobby, her room key dangling from his hand and in his eyes the clear determination that she would ascend the staircase alone. Like a father. Which was probably what he'd been told to be.

Jan kissed her, whispered that he'd call in the morning.

She swept into the hotel, caught up the keys without speaking.

On the first landing she paused just long enough to shoot the manager a look of withering contempt.

CHAPTER EIGHT

God, he hated Sunday work.

But the men were in – shifts round the clock now and seven days a week, orders for gun castings up to the eyebrows – so what could he do but go in himself? The foundry wouldn't run itself and with Neil gone it was himself or nobody. Who else could he trust?

To make bad worse there'd been another damned silly accident. A winch slipped on an overhead bucket and molten steel splashed all over the shop. Rank incompetence, nothing else. Some daft bugger asleep at the switch. And don't tell *him* it was a miracle there were no casualties! The foreman's office would need a new roof, not to mention all the labour records burnt to ashes. No casualties indeed.

It was already dark when he leaned on the bell at Eccles Place, too tired to bother with his key. And now there was another pill to swallow.

Lallie wasn't home. She should have been in from the Lincoln train at noon.

'So where is she?' he demanded, holding Millie responsible.

'No trouble, Joe. She phoned. She'll be in on the ten o'clock. If you could get a bit of a nap she thought you might drive in and pick her up.'

His anger flared again. 'Like hell I will. She can queue up for a taxi like everybody else. What the devil can she find to do in Lincoln of a Sunday afternoon, I ask you! We should never have let her go.' A nag in the back of his mind whispered that she'd have gone anyway, and if she defied him once she'd defy him again and again, easier every time, then where would he be?

Millie fluttered her hands at him. 'Now don't let's fret. Have a snooze and when you wake up she'll be back, telling us all about it.'

Worn out as he was, he couldn't drop off. He watched the clock go past ten, itched to get the car out and meet her, sorry he'd said he wouldn't. Who knew what kind of riffraff hung about the station of a night looking for young girls? But he'd said what he'd said and he'd stick to it.

Then he heard her key in the door and the light-hearted slam of its closing, her suitcase set down on the stairs. Relief turned back to anger. Nearly eleven o'clock!

'I'm home!' she carolled, humming as she hung her coat in the hall. Then she was in the room, warming her hands at the fire, saying, 'I had the *most* marvellous time *ever*!'

If any one thing could have fuelled his rage further it was the look on her face. Soft. Misty. As if she'd stepped out of a fairy story. Eyes brilliant, cheeks stained a bright pink, mouth curved like a lyre. But her shoulders were set square. Defensive, by God!

'So what kept you?'

'We went out to lunch and the pictures. Mum's favourites, Margaret Lockwood and Anna Neagle.' When he didn't answer she threw him a glance then looked quickly away. So she'd finally sensed it, tension you could cut with a knife.

Millie, disappearing into the kitchen to make them all a snack, went with the air of one glad to escape.

'Neil knows better than to keep you out past time.'

She looked full at him for the first time since she'd opened the door. 'You know I wasn't with Neil. I was with Jan.'

A lump of coal hissed in the fireplace, shot sudden sparks up the chimney. 'Oh? And what did Neil have to say about that? Why didn't he go with you?'

'I think he was on duty or something. Anyway, we didn't ask him.'

One word grabbed him, shook him like a ferret shakes a rabbit. 'We? So it's "we" now is it?'

She picked up an ashtray and put it down again. 'Yes, it's "we".'

So with the one word the truth he'd dodged and ducked for a month was on him, jumped all over him, knocked the ginger out of him. It was a full minute of thunderous silence between them before he could trust himself to speak.

'So you'll drop Neil, a good lad like that, off fighting for king and country. King and country,' he repeated.

'So is Jan.'

He locked into her grey eyes, strength surging back now he'd faced the nature of the maggot that had been eating at him on the sly since Christmas. 'You don't know what you're talking about. They don't even *have* a king.'

'They used to. They used to *elect* theirs.'

'Oh, aren't we the authority now –'

'We're not all ignorant –'

'A month back you had to hunt all over the bloody atlas to find the place, now you know everything there is to know.'

'I know he's fighting for it just as hard as anybody else.'

'Aye, but it's not England he's fighting for, is it? Some tinpot little hamlet in Eastern Europe instead.'

Her chin lifted to a mulish tilt. 'As a matter of fact – you can look it up if you don't believe me – Poland's bigger than England.'

Bigger than England. That she'd failed so completely to understand him, his own daughter! Nowhere was bigger than England. Landmass was nothing; integrity and principle were everything. England was the centre of the universe, the hub around which lesser nations revolved. His faith in that single precept held him rock-solid against what he now acknowledged to be trouble. Bigger than England indeed. There again, she'd been nowhere else, how could she know? He wished now, God how he wished he'd sent her off to that school in France the year she was sixteen. All the arrangements had been made, he'd even gone over there to inspect the place. Once there he'd imagined her leaving Eccles Place to live among foreigners for an entire year and he'd cancelled the plans. And at the time she'd been as relieved as he, that was the thing. He should have sent her – maybe if she'd seen something besides Yorkshire she wouldn't be falling head over tip for the first silver-tongued Romeo to give her the glad-eye.

Now here she was springing to the defence of some godforsaken hole on the Baltic. The location seemed as distant to him as the moon. No, farther than that. He could *see* the moon, knew all its quarters through the seasons of his life. Abroad, as far as he was concerned, was the cluster of countries just across the Channel and maybe, if he wanted to stretch a point, America. Everywhere else was limbo, Africa nothing but a jungle, Asia a treacherous mass of slanted eyes and silkworms, of interest only to Marco Polo, while England … Well, England was this house, Yorkshire, his foundry, stout oaks on the Common under which he'd watched his father play cricket of a Saturday afternoon. It was the Royal Family, Lallie – and now everything was tilted out of place, bearings were slipping …

Millie teetered through the door on her Sunday-high heels with a tray of sandwiches and Bovril and a look of vague distress at what he now realized had been voices raised in anger. He should keep his trap shut, he knew, do some thinking. Plan. The rush of bitterness couldn't be contained. He turned to his wife.

'It seems Flash Harry's been doing some talking to our girl.'

'Our girl' bit into a ham sandwich while the fingers of her left hand beat steadily against the arm of the settee.

Millie sighed. 'Joe, don't call Jan a Flash Harry. He's ever so quiet and polite –'

'– still waters run deep –'

'– and he does seem nice,' Millie finished lamely.

Lallie sprang up, scattering crumbs and consternation into the cosy living room. Her face had gone very pale, her eyes dangerously bright. '*He is very nice*,' she cried. '*I don't care what Daddy says and I'm not going to listen to him*!'

'Lallie Wainwright, tell your father you're sorry this minute!' Millie used her sternest voice in vain.

'I'm *not* sorry. I had the most wonderful time in my entire life and now he's spoiled it.' Then she was at the door, turning back to look at him. 'You may as well know he's spending his next leave here. I invited him.' The door slammed behind her and they could hear her running up the stairs to her room.

Joe looked at his hand clenched round the arm of the chair. It was still shaking with the effort not to strike out at her. Hit Lallie. That's what he'd nearly done. Twenty years of caring for her with never so much as a slap on the hand, and now this. This is what the Pole had brought him to. By God he'd like to beat the bloody daylights out of him.

In the grate the fire spluttered, gave off a sudden violet flame, and settled.

Millie spoke not another word but Joe had known her so well for so long he could read her thoughts as easily from her eyes as anything that came out of her mouth.

Poor Joe, they said now as she reached out to touch his shoulder.

For the first time in many years he did not shrug her off. 'She'll be crying,' he said.

'I'll go up to her.'

He sighed heavily. 'No, I'll go.'

But he didn't, not straight away. Something more than fatigue held him to his chair; it was the knowledge that his girl could be as stuborn as he, would not be deflected by conciliatory words. And what was he to say to her? That this business with the Pole didn't matter? It did matter. Tell her she had to stop seeing him? She wouldn't stop, she'd be all the more set on it. Indecision was a new feeling, one he didn't like. It rendered him helpless just when he needed to act. If it had been a dispute at the foundry he wouldn't think twice. But this was himself and Lallie at a crossroads and God help him if they each took a different path.

Nothing moved in the pretty, lavender-scented bedroom. She was facing the dark side of the room pretending sleep, her face hidden by the pillow and the cloud of dark hair.

'Lall?'

She didn't move.

'Come on lass, I know you're awake. Do sit up and take notice ...'

There was a sniff from the depths of the pillow. 'You don't even know him and you hate him. I know you do –'

'Oh, come on now, I didn't say that.'

'You meant it.'

There she had him. He'd hate anybody that could take her away from him, change the pattern he'd set for her, a pattern he was convinced was right for her. He put a hand to the blanket, felt her shoulder move before he heard the sob.

'I just want you to be happy, love, that's all, among your own people and –' It was as close as he could come to an apology but she wouldn't even let him finish.

'*But what about what I want?*'

She was sitting up and looking at him, tears spiking the thick dark lashes, anger and distress fighting it out on the one face in the world he only wanted to see smile.

'Oh my lass …' but his voice caught in his throat and in a second the blanket was thrown aside and she was hugging him, her tears cool on his face.

'Don't be mad with me,' she whispered. 'I can't stand it when we fight, you know I can't, but I *do* like him and –'

He was helpless. What could he do but smooth the hair out of her eyes and dry her cheeks off with his handkerchief?

'Now stop your crying and get off to sleep. You're still your dad's best lass, you know that.'

Downstairs, he damped down the fire and lit the last pipe of the day, eased by the thought that the problem of the Pole might solve itself. Happen she'd be fed up with him before the winter was out.

CHAPTER NINE

The snow melted early that winter.

By February there were splashes of yellow crocus in the Wainwright lawn. The skies were still quiet over rural England, as if waiting …

By March Lallie was already thinning out Hodgson's tender new lettuce, the mess party a rapturous memory. Joe acquired more storage near the foundry and stocked it to the rafters with iron ingots. There was talk of Jan's crew joining the main body of the Polish Air Force in France but nothing came of it. Millie watched the buds on the cherry tree swell and burst into paper-pink blossom and wondered where in the world she'd find the sugar for jam this year. And little Finland, after three valiant months, fell to the Russian armies.

Early in April Pearl produced eleven piglets as pale and plump as feather pillows, suckled them with beatific smiles and soft maternal rumblings. Germany gobbled up Norway and Denmark and sharpened the knives for France.

And all through the breezy lull of spring, love letters flew swift as homing pigeons between Eccles Place and Jan's camp in Lincolnshire. Dear Jan and Dear Lallie had turned to Dearest, then Darling, and now My Darling. The bundle of letters in Lallie's writing-desk was thick now, and after each day's work at the Hodgsons' she read every line of every letter over again, reassuring herself that Jan Kaliski was real, that his mind had formed these sentences, that his long hands had written these words. To her.

They'd seen each other only once since the party, an afternoon's walk through the greenhouses of the Botanical Gardens. A bitterly cold day, but inside the glass doors of the Tropical Room the lush heat warmed them, wooed them with waving fern fronds and tendrils of vine, all impossibly, improbably green. Their winter-starved lips met and melted under scarlet bougainvillea and sunburst hibiscus, whispered and sighed over great creamy cups of magnolia, counted out the loaves and fishes of the passion flowers, then forgot the count and began again. They saw nothing so clearly as each other, felt nothing so tender as the touch of hand on cheek and throat and hair.

It was almost more than they could bear when he set her gently away from him and took her hands in his.

'It's because of Daddy, isn't it?' she protested.

'Only a little. Mostly it's because of you. It must be right, you see.' But then she kissed him again very slowly, and he had to add, 'And it must be soon.'

'When you get leave in a few weeks –'

93

'We shall talk to your father.'

But weeks! How could they wait for weeks when her heart sang like a thrush, her blood surged and roared through every vein? 'How can you be so calm when –'

'Because I must. I told you, it must be right. It's war, so everything seems so ... urgent – and it is! – but you're not a girl to –'

'You sound like my father!'

'I sound like my mother.' A shadow touched his face. ' "Do whatever you want" she used to tell me, "but do it in style. Don't hide and sneak about." I think she was perhaps right.'

'Oh ...' She didn't understand him, perhaps she never would, but she loved him, she loved him ...

The afternoon was kept a secret from her father but not from Millie, who told Joe where Lallie had gone but not with whom.

'I *hate* keeping secrets from Daddy!'

'Give him time,' Millie counselled. 'He'll get used to the idea, just give him time ...'

Time, time. As if there was oceans of it just waiting for them ...

Jan arrived for his leave a day earlier than expected in a battered Triumph the colour of old rust, zipping into Wainwright's driveway in a cloud of grit and urgent honks of the horn. 'Camouflage,' he laughed to Millie as he swung his suitcase from the battered trunk of the car. 'Under this rusty crust beats the heart of a chariot.'

Millie, flustered and happy to see him and troubled all at the same time, told him Lallie was off to market with old man Hodgson and Joe was down in London for a couple of days. 'A raw material conference or some such,' she bubbled, scurrying into the kitchen to put the kettle on, rattling cups and saucers and pouring milk into a little china pitcher with hand-painted roses on the side. 'Lallie's going to be so excited you're early! She's got a week off from Hodgson's starting tomorrow. Did she tell you?'

'Good show,' he said. 'I knew she was going to try.'

'My word, but you're talking different! – not that you didn't speak just lovely before, but now you sound almost ... well, like one of us.'

She watched him, not sure if he'd take it as a compliment or not, but he just laughed again and she realized nothing she could say to him today would upset him much. Like Lallie, she thought. Head in the clouds for weeks, had to be told everything twice before she heard you.

'I suppose it's just practice. I've even caught myself thinking in English sometimes.'

'That means you feel at home then.' She turned down the oven before she filled his cup, reflecting that things might not be too bad after all. Once Joe faced facts. The last few months had been edgy all round. A good thing he was so busy at the foundry, better still that Lallie and this nice young chap would have a day or two to themselves before Joe got back from London. He had a rough side to his tongue when it suited him, did Joe. Safer to pretend you hadn't heard than to lash back, even if lashing back was in your nature, which thank God it wasn't in hers – she hoped it wasn't in Jan's nature either. Poor Joe had enough grief coming to him as it was. She knew just which well-meant paths had brought him to it – a lifetime's single-minded nurturing – but how could a stranger like this one possibly know? He was tracing the roses on the milk jug with his fingertips now, very likely thinking to himself how Lallie must often have done the same. Oh, she remembered what it was like all right, young and in love and blind to everything else, a beautiful feeling ...

'Help yourself to milk,' she began. 'We've plenty. Nice little jug, isn't it? Joe gave it to me the first year we were married – in a box it was, all wrapped up in tissue paper. It was about the first nice thing we'd ever had.'

'It's very pretty,' he said dreamily.

'Yes, I've always liked it, just because ... well, his family was always poor, you know. So was mine really – we hadn't two ha'pennies to rub together either, but we were happy you see, and it makes a difference. Joe's folks were never happy. His mother was always ailing and no money for doctors, so I suppose it's natural then to blame everything on being poor.'

Millie sighed, remembering. 'Then when his mother died his father got surlier than ever, led young Joe a right old dance, I can tell you. There was no pleasing that old man. To be honest I wasn't sorry when he passed on, he'd have had Joe as crabbed and bitter as he was himself ... and the smithy wasn't a business, not really, just farm-wagon trade – your tea's not too strong, is it lad? – Joe would have been better off at a regular job except there weren't many in those days.' She reached behind her for a tray of herbs she'd been drying over the stove.

'Then Lallie was born and oh my stars! You'd have thought royalty moved in. A real tonic for Joe, I can tell you. Beautiful baby, nothing too good for her to hear *him* talk. His 'bit of sunshine' he called her – he'd just sit watching her sleep for hours at a time! And such a good baby too, not whiney like some. She'd be smiling when she woke up and still at it when she fell asleep. A live wire though, strong-headed as her father. Not perfect of course, who is?, but there's no use telling Joe that. I often think her being such a cheerful little soul was what made him so set-up with her, his folks being such miseries, you know. Only natural, isn't it?'

She crumbled a handful of thyme into a bowl and passed it across to him. 'Lovely sharp smell, thyme, isn't it? Where was I? Yes, well right about when she was born we were having some pretty bad times, not much in the pantry and less in the pocket. One day he just seemed like he'd taken as much as a man can stand. He was holding Lallie, I remember, when he suddenly put her down in her cot and punched his fist right through the wall! "Millie," he said, "I'm sick to death of having nothing but holes in my pockets. I could walk out this minute and rob a bloody bank. This little lass needs clothes, and a garden to play in, decent food in her stomach. When I think she has to grow up in this hole it fair makes my blood boil." We lived in Backenthorpe then, a little bit of a place and the house no better, just one room upstairs and one down. Anyway, next thing I know he's borrowed money from a bank and started a smithy down in Sheffield. My, but I was frightened, all that debt staring us in the face, but he worked, my God did he work! All the hours God sent and a few more besides.'

She looked at Jan over a sprig of tansy. Well, he was still

listening, but was he hearing?

'In no time he bought into the foundry, then before we had time to turn around he'd bought his partner out. Seemed like he couldn't slow down no matter what I said. We never went anywhere together, me and Joe. We still don't. He's never got the time. Not much of a one for pleasure, Joe isn't. His pleasure's all in work, you see.' She paused. 'And Lallie, of course – but you'll have figured that out for yourself, I reckon.'

She glanced at the clock and began clearing the table. 'Just look at the time! You'll be thinking I'm a proper chatterbox – and I am when I get the chance. Now I really must get cracking or we'll have Lallie home and no dinner ready. I've put you in your old room so if you want to go upstairs and unpack … Just make yourself at home.'

Your old room …

Jan, watching this pretty, unexpectedly garrulous woman who was so obviously glad to see him, suddenly *did* feel at home. He felt he knew what moved Joe Wainwright a little better and perhaps this had been Millie's intention. Looking into the guileless grey eyes, so much like Lallie's, he doubted whether she'd had any motive except to entertain her guest until it was time to get dinner.

He felt so much at home that he washed up the tea things over her protests, then went up to *his old room* and changed into civvies, a pair of grey flannels and a black sweater. They were the first clothes he'd worn in a year that didn't carry the faint odour of aviation fuel embedded in the seams. They felt wonderful. *He* felt wonderful, Joe's absence an added bonus, a breathing space in which to be happy before the inevitable clash. How long must they wait? What course would Joe take? Legally, she would need her father's consent until her twenty-first birthday, an impossibly long year away, a year in which he or even she could be killed, never to know each other as they must in the nights, never to wake together in the mornings.

Sheffield was the heartland of this nation's steel production and therefore a prime target for the Luftwaffe, once they had regrouped. Which would certainly be soon. The thought of Lallie's long, elegant body broken in a hail of bombs was a fear he relived with every news bulletin. When France fell (which it must because Tatuš said it must) England would be fighting for her life and the fight would be here in the industrial Midlands as well as in London.

His own future was even more precarious. Very soon now, perhaps next month, he would be operational. Bombing missions would begin, and his own goal would be to visit the same destruction on enemy targets as he anticipated the enemy would wreak on Sheffield. At OTU there were no illusions on the attrition rate of aircrew once the real shooting started. Targets on both sides would be heavily defended. If you were careless or simply unlucky your first mission could be your last. If you were very good, very cautious, very lucky, then you could make your deadly drops many times.

Luck could not last forever, a point Joe Wainwright was sure to raise. 'Is she going to be a widow before she's a woman? Is that what you're proposing?' That's what he'd say, or something very close to it. And the news Jan brought with him would only underline the question.

Thinking about her here in this pleasant, happy house where she'd grown to be so beautiful, so endearing, so ... Lallie, he knew he could not wait for her until the war would be over. Good intentions and the desire to please a father-in-law were like snowflakes before the fire of his need.

Then he heard her voice, young and eager in the hall below. 'Mum? What in the *world* is that parked outside –'

'It's Jan's car –'

'*Jan!*'

Her footsteps running, running up the stairs, her voice running with them on an irresistible crest of excitement. 'But you're *early*. Oh, if only I'd *known*! There's so much to show you I don't know where to begin. Pearl's babies – you'll adore *them* – and there's a new litter of Afghans at the kennels and one is absolute tops and Daddy says ...'

Then youth and lavender and endless energy were in his arms, laughing under his kiss, eyes gazing deeply into his.

'And I have news also,' he was able to say at last.

'If it's good tell me quickly!'

'Some of it's good. Bolek got a letter from the Red Cross.

His parents are safe which means –'

'Which means so are yours!'

'Well, not quite – but they all lived in the same part of Warsaw so –'

'So they're almost *sure* to be all right. Oh darling, I'm so, so happy for you ... if they're safe then there won't be even the tiniest cloud –'

'Except the war, which brings me to –'

'The other news.' Her eyes opened wide, panic in their grey depths. 'You're being sent away, I know you are.'

He laughed and gathered up her hair until it was confined in a soft cloud in his hands. 'No, I'll be closer. I've been posted to Yorkshire. Hempton.'

'But that's only twenty miles! How absolutely, utterly super, you'll be able to come every weekend and I can drive over there –'

'I'm afraid I might be just a little too busy.'

He waited for her to absorb it. No panic now, only a deep, penetrating concern.

'You're starting ops.'

He watched as the blood drained from her cheeks, as tears gathered but did not fall as he'd expected they would. Instead the soft mouth set into a firm, resolute line.

'That settles it,' she said quietly. 'We're not just going to talk to Daddy. Daddy will have to listen.'

Millie switched off the oven and sat for a long time watching the evening fill the kitchen. After a while she measured out a tot of whisky and added a pinch of sugar. In her mind strong drink was either associated with parties or wakes and she did not, in any case, like the flavour, but today she felt its fiery sharpness was somehow fitting.

She'd noticed her daughter's face at the realization Jan was here and could only be thankful that Joe wasn't there to see it too, to know that there was no hope, none whatever, that this affair with the young foreigner would burn itself out.

It burned, oh yes. It burned so bright it hurt your eyes to look.

The next two days were the happiest Jan was ever to know at Eccles Place. With Joe away and Millie at her most unobtrusive it seemed a time set aside just for Lallie and himself. By unspoken agreement, the future and Joe and ops were subjects to be avoided.

Very early in the morning they picked wild mushrooms in Potter's four-acre field, their footprints everywhere in the dewy grass as they rushed like children from one cluster of white buttons to the next, then home again to cook them for breakfast.

He met Pearl's new family. His fondness for the piglets was minimal but Lallie's was a joy to watch. Ignoring squeals from the babies and fretful grunts from their mother she examined all eleven from head to curly tail, checked ears and squinty little eyes, murmured fondly at identical snouts. 'They're just *too* intelligent to *believe*, you know, and just look at that skin, did you ever *see* anything so firm and smooth ...'

To Jan it looked like potential bacon rinds and Pearl nothing more than a gross, malodourous mound.

'But she's a jolly good mother and a splendid porker!' Lallie protested. 'What more can you expect?'

They walked the dogs, let them run free in Little Wood, the wind combing their long silken hair under beeches brilliant with new spring green. She showed him where the tallest, most deeply blue bluebells nodded in dim olive shadows.

'When I was little I used to play May Queen here with Joannie Watt. That log was the throne, we made daisy chains for the crown, we had an old burgundy velvet curtain of Mum's for the train and Daddy gave us sugared almonds – sweetmeats – for the queen and her lady-in-waiting.'

'Need I ask who was the queen?'

'We took turns,' she said, indignant. 'But I *hated* being lady-in-waiting. Joannie ate *all* the almonds and she made me comb her hair. *And* she made me promise not to tell her mother when she said "damn".'

'And you keep your promises?'

'Of course.'

'Then promise me you'll always be like this, that you won't change.'

100

'Be like what?'

Natural, innocent, vibrant, *alive*, he wanted to say. 'Be like yourself,' he said quietly.

She reached up and kissed the tip of his ear. 'Silly! How could I ever be anything else?'

Easily, he thought. The war. Wife of a pilot. Never knowing ... but she'd perched herself on the log with her bouquet of bluebells, slipping effortlessly back into a childhood that never seemed far away.

By comparison, his own city childhood seemed brief indeed, lasting only through kindergarten. Afterwards it was all study, fun confined to holidays and an occasional Saturday afternoon at the theatre with Mamunia and Tatuš, sometimes a *kawiarnia* afterwards for sweet, creamy coffee and little iced cakes. Lallie's childhood never seemed to have ended, even her work at Hodgson's an enchanting playtime with every growing thing, gifts specially for her. Then in the evening he watched her dry the dishes, saw her smile on each painted plate and cup as if she were seeing familiar things for the first time, saw her concentrate on lining up the knives and forks just so in the drawer, her satisfaction in the tidy kitchen when it was all done.

Everything was play to Lallie because she made it so.

Next morning Millie had a Thermos of coffee and a wicker basket of sandwiches and fruit ready for them. 'Perfect day for a picnic,' she said. 'You'll not want to be cooped up indoors.'

Lallie grinned at the determination in her mother's voice. 'Well, if you want to be rid of us we can take a hint.'

'I want you out from under my feet. With your dad coming in I've a lot to do.'

Lallie dressed carefully in a grey suit and a blouse the colour of old roses. She was glad Jan was in civvies again. It felt more comfortable to her somehow, as if the war wasn't even there.

They agreed on Castleton because it was lambing time and she simply *had* to show him. 'I said I would, remember –'

'And you always keep your promises.' He touched her hair, and her heart seemed to stop for a second, then race to catch up. He was *so* dear when he smiled like that, she wanted him to stay looking just that way, the strain smoothed out of his face, eyes filled with laughter.

101

'I shall drive you,' he announced. 'In my car.'

Oh dear. She wasn't sure if the rusty old thing could even get up the hills but he'd been so *proud* when he'd showed it to her.

'You bought a car!'

'A fifth of one to be exact. This is my week.'

'You mean it's shared between all the crew?'

'No, that wouldn't be practical at all. If we were to get shot down – not that we intend to – who would use the car? So the owners are all from different crews. This way, whoever's still around can keep driving it. It's a good arrangement.'

The implication made her catch her breath, but his face was matter-of-fact, closed as he ran his hands over the scarred blue carcass of the car, and she understood that the macabre subject of its ownership was not one he wanted to discuss.

The Triumph started up with a violent tremble, caught its breath, then roared down the drive in a cloud of blue smoke, all its elderly parts aquiver.

They picnicked high on Mam Tor with the dale spread out like a crumpled quilt beneath them, the mellow stone of the village snug as a sleeping cat in its green folds. Bleached fingers of dry-stone walls aspired ever upwards to dizzying summits, only to disappear in puffs of white cloud towards Edale and Hope and Kinderscout.

The lambs she'd promised him at Christmas were sprinkled black-faced and bewildered on the short springy turf, bleating at their new world and nuzzling the ewes against a crisp spring breeze. One of the ewes, more curious than the rest, regarded Jan and Lallie from wide, enigmatic eyes as they sprawled, replete with Cheshire cheese and Hovis and Millie's coffee, on the tartan car-blanket.

'She thinks you're a lazy lump,' Lallie said. 'The ewe.'

'I am, I am,' he laughed, sitting up and propping himself up on his elbows. His eyes followed Winnat's Pass, lingered over the entrance to Blue John Cavern.

'Daddy's pipe-ashtray's made of Blue John stone, quarried right from that cavern there –'

'Specially designed by Mother Nature to fit his pipe?'

Sometimes, just sometimes, she had the slightest suspicion he was laughing at Daddy and what he stood for – but then, he

102

didn't really know him, not yet. 'Silly! They've been mining it for practically ever.'

'Mam Tor?' he mused. 'That doesn't even sound English.'

'But it *was*, a couple of thousand years ago. Mother Mountain.'

'It sounds ageless, like everything here. This is a good place, I think. Permanent,' he said quietly.

She chuckled and tickled his chin with a harebell which, she'd already told him, matched his eyes. 'Permanent! That's what *you* think. The *map* calls it Mam Tor – the people down there call it Shivering Mountain. Every so often chunks keep dropping off.' She laughed as his involuntary fingers clutched at the springy turf. 'Not *that* often! You can relax.'

Yet how could they relax, utterly alone under the great blue bowl of sky, so close she could see the fine net of wrinkles already forming round his eyes. Wrinkles at twenty-one … from too much squinting into the sun, he told her. An overwhelming, yearning tenderness poured over her for this young-old man who was holding her now, his voice a murmur sometimes heard, sometimes stolen by the wind.

'Lallie … I love you, I love you so much sometimes I am frightened … everything was dark and now so bright –'

'And so perfect,' she whispered. 'It's going to *stay* perfect.'

He held her tighter and tighter until she could scarcely breathe, his wool sweater rough against her face, his mouth already as familiar as her own, and so dear … Impossible that four months ago she hadn't known he existed; impossible the hands that touched her so gently daily controlled a great, thunderous plane and the destiny of those within it; impossible he'd been born and grew up without her knowing it in a place that was just a name on a map, alien as the parents he spoke of with such love, such anxiety.

Then somehow her blouse was open and his hands, his lips were on her breasts, a thousand kisses pouring over them until every scintilla of skin tingled, yearned, sprang to life under his mouth, tightened with a sweetness too unbearable to believe – and she suddenly afraid, apologetic, wanting to give him everything in the most glorious abundance, afraid that there could never be enough, enough ... 'They're not very big,' she whispered.

'So smooth ... so perfect ...' A sob, trembling and exultant, seemed to catch in his throat. 'Apples. Pink apples ...'

And over his shoulder there was the clean clear blue across which, at the extreme corner of her splintered vision a speck, black and very high, moved closer and closer until it became a hawk and then a plane. It was a Spitfire, rapier-fast, solitary, gallant, dazzlingly beautiful in the afternoon sky ... She closed her eyes against quick tears that gathered somewhere behind them, surprised that they were already salt on her lips until she saw the tears were his, his heart racing over hers, his voice an urgent, broken murmur.

It was she now who pressed him gently away from her with exquisite, aching regret. She hadn't known – until now she hadn't guessed it would be so ... changing, transforming. Already she was a different person and they hadn't even ... no way to hide a change so incredibly, shatteringly beautiful, no way Daddy wouldn't know. Even now he would know something ... be hurt.

'I suppose you are right,' he murmured later. 'He *would* know. Your face would tell him.'

'We mustn't hurt him ...'

His eyes were impossible to read. 'I love you,' he said. 'To have you I think I must play to his rules.'

'But it's not like that – he's not my keeper!'

He said nothing, just smiled at her gently across the folded blanket.

Joe arrived from the raw materials conference in high fettle, rubbing his hands and grinning at Millie even before he had his jacket off.

'Well, the ball's rolling now, Millie mi lass. Looks as if they'll put Beaverbrook in charge of production. *He'll* yank the idle buggers in Whitehall off their fat arses, see if he doesn't. We'll see some action now!'

Hanging his jacket on the hall-tree, the greatcoat already there snagged his attention, POLAND on its shoulder. So *he* was here. Bloody hell, he'd forgotten all about that.

His mood changed course even before he noticed the look on Millie's face, pleading, appeasing.

'So where is he?'

She folded his scarf and handed him his slippers. 'He went with Lallie into Castleton.'

' "*And everywhere that Mary went ...*" ' he quoted, high-voiced, taking a savage pleasure in the image, the mimickry.

'What are you talking about?'

' "*... the lamb was sure to go*" Is that all he can do, follow her about, making sheep's eyes –'

'Oh Joe ... don't. They're both just young ...'

'Aye, and I want her to keep on being young. He's been around too much for my liking.'

He clumped into the living room and sat, pipe unlit in his hand. Millie stood in front of him, the pleading still on her, a mulish determination hovering just under it.

'It's serious, Joe. It's not going to go away. You'll know when you see her.'

His brain shut off for a minute, nothing but a roar between his temples. 'What are you saying?'

'They'll be wanting to marry I reckon –'

'*Shut up!*'

She didn't shut up, she kept on coming. 'You could make them wait till she's twenty-one but what then? You know how self-willed she can be. Do you think anything will have changed?'

A picture flashed into his mind. Lallie at twelve introducing him to a girl she'd met at her new, high-toned school, hearing the girl say '*The* Joe Wainwright? The blacksmith? My father says you've made pots of money selling scrap iron. Is it true?' Lallie never spoke to her again, not even when the girl was made head-prefect and carried a lot of clout. And at the time he'd thought her loyalty was a virtue!

'Do you think anything will have changed?' Millie persisted.

'No,' he said, weary.

'Then why go against them, love? She'll be first in line at the Registry Office on her birthday, and holding it against you for making them wait. Is that what you want? Or maybe ...' She smoothed her apron over her stomach. The reminder was not lost on Joe. He remembered their own desperate coupling under the larches at Backenthorpe, Millie younger than Lallie was now. Once that tide was on you was there any power on earth could stop it?

'There'll be none of that for Lallie,' he insisted. 'She wouldn't.'

'You know she would if she's set on it. Anyway, sometimes it can't be helped.' Again the hand passed over her apron.

But to throw herself away on a bloody foreigner! The waste of it ... when there's Neil ...

'Foreigner or not, he seems like a good lad to me. And he's not had much to be happy about for a while, I reckon, what with his mother and all. Right fond of her, he is, from the sound of things, and you know the old saying: 'Like son, like husband.' A man good to his mother'll be good to his wife.' Millie folded her hands. 'In any case, what can't be cured must be endured.'

Joe groaned. If there was an old saw handy trust Millie to put her finger on it. She might be right, that was the devil of it. Last year he'd have said there was nothing in Lallie's life he couldn't cure. Christ ...

'Joe, just think. If that boy got killed before they were married she'd never forgive you. Never.'

He put his hands over his eyes. It was minutes before he took them away again. Millie was still there, pity for him welling up in her eyes.

He sighed. 'What's to be done lass, eh? Tell me that.'

Millie was right. One look at Lallie's face when they came in and he knew there was nothing to be done. They came straight at it, first the Pole then Lallie then together, as if they'd rehearsed it.

'But where will you live?' he asked her, knowing it wouldn't be here so what did it matter. The Pole had an answer. Naturally.

'I'm sure I can rent us a place near the camp. One of the married Winco's was just posted away.'

'Aerodromes are going to get hit. A stray bomb –'

'Cities like Sheffield will be hit too, Mr Wainwright. There won't be any safe places soon.'

106

He had an answer for everything, this foreigner. 'Aye, but what's the rush? You say you'll be flying ops come June, so why not wait till after you're done?'

'But that's *why*, Daddy!' Lallie broke in. 'How do we know there'll *be* an after?'

Joe ignored her, played his last good card at the Pole. 'And you'll risk making her a widow then, is that it?' He did not understand the bitter little smile that came to the foreigner's lips so it enraged him afresh.

Jan saw the anger, recognized it for what it was. Frustration. They'd won – or would have when Joe was done going through the motions. Relief brought beads of sweat rushing to his forehead. He could have taken her from her father without Joe's consent, he knew that. But it would have torn her in two, dimmed all that young shimmer. Why was it all so much easier than he'd expected? Where were Joe's Victorian tantrums, blood vessels pounding in the neck, the pacing and thumping of fists? He shot a quick glance at Millie, who appeared relaxed now, happy. Only Lallie, his beautiful girl, still had her eyes fixed on her father as he spoke directly to her.

'Marriage is not something to jump into, love. When the war's over –'

'Daddy! You've said umpteen times that it's going to last for years and years, five at least. We'll be twenty-six then. *We'll be old*!'

Joe bent to knock out his pipe on the bars of the grate, seemed to find in the embers a smile-mask to slip on before he came up. Jan could see the fit was a tight one.

'Isn't this where I'm supposed to ask you what your prospects are … after the war? She's got silk-stocking tastes you know, this girl.' He said it with a touch of pride, as if his daughter's extravagance was a trait he had nurtured with care.

Jan found himself on shaky ground here. The far future was an avenue he had not yet dared to explore. It all depended on Mamunia and Tatuš, if … 'I imagine I could teach languages, or there's always flying, or maybe the foreign service.'

'Where would you settle? You'll want to be near your family –'

'Daddy how can you! That can all be sorted out later – you

know perfectly well Jan doesn't even know if he *has* a family –'

She threw her arms round Jan's neck as if to shield him against blows from any direction, including her own, and Millie was suddenly at his other side, reaching for his hand.

'Now Lallie, don't go begging trouble,' she said, soothing. 'He's going to have two families, aren't you Jan? Us and them. And you're right welcome lad, you are that.' She rubbed at her eyes with her apron. 'Now give us a kiss and I'll make us all some tea. We could stand it, I reckon.'

They had champagne instead, Lallie and Millie as bubbly as the wine, Jan and Joe cautious, each watching the other like boxers meeting as equals for the first time. With the gloves on.

'I'll do my best to make her happy, Mr Wainwright.' Jan wished he didn't sound quite so stiff.

'I'm sure you will,' Joe said just as stiffly, shaking hands.

Millie came between them, clasping both their hands in hers and splashing champagne in the process. 'Now you can start calling each other Jan and Joe,' she said happily.

The men smiled through locked jaws.

CHAPTER TEN

10 May. The evening paper black with headlines.

Chamberlain Resigns: Churchill Takes Over: German Troops in Belgium and Holland.

'You haven't even *looked* at the announcements,' Lallie protested, reading: ' "The parents of Kendal Wainwright are pleased to announce the forthcoming marriage of their daughter to Flight Lieutenant Jan Kaliski of the Polish Air Force." There. In black and white. Oh, I'm so excited I can't *stand* it. Six more weeks and I'll be Mrs Jan Kaliski. *Mrs*!'

Joe scowled over his section of the paper. 'The way the war's going you might be Number Umpity Ump Ump, Prisoner of War by then. The Germans are moving too bloody fast. Thank

God we've got Churchill at the wheel now.'

Lallie hardly heard him. The church was booked, extra tables ordered for the garden, and the little cottage next to Hempton Airfield was already rented in the names of Fl. Lt. and Mrs Kaliski. Like her father she read the war news, but the gravity of it couldn't penetrate the shimmer of anticipation that increasingly gilded every waking moment. Pessimism didn't stand a chance, nor did Daddy's lukewarm response to her excitement. He'd change. Under all that gruff stuff, he was still the cuddly old bear he'd always been. Maybe he wasn't sure about Jan yet because of Neil, but when he really knew him he'd see everything she saw in him. He'd harboured the idea of Neil as a son-in-law for so long it was only natural he'd feel just the least bit crushed.

Poor Neil. Such a dear ... but how could she have known she'd ever feel like this about someone else, as if her whole existence wasn't worth a penny candle if Jan Kaliski were not a part of it? It was disconcerting because she'd never cared much for love stories. Some of them were just silly and some vaguely embarrassing, as if she were peeking into a stranger's most intimate moments. And she'd never really believed them, either.

She believed them now, except they barely skimmed the surface. They went on and on about when the couple were together but never a word about how knowing one person could colour everything else, how every time your thoughts touched his name the dreariest day had a shine to it, how even when you were alone your whole flesh-and-blood turned to a tingling, quivering mass of nerve-endings at the thought of him touching you. Before Jan she'd never really been aware she had needs that Mum's cooking and the daily romps with the dogs didn't fill. Neil had kissed her lots of times, of course, but she'd never hungered for more, never melted at the thought of ...

She remembered how her friend Joannie, when they were six, had told her where babies came from.

Lallie didn't believe her. 'Of course I didn't come from Mum's tummy. How could I ever get out?'

'There's a way,' Joannie said. 'There must be.'

The next year Joannie came by another snippet, about how babies got started. She'd whispered to Lallie in Little Wood one autumn afternoon when they were collecting acorns, repeating what she'd heard in the same graphic, basic terms.

Lallie was shocked. 'You're wrong,' she said firmly. '*My* parents would never do *that*!' As if 'that' were the most inhuman, degrading thing in the world. Then somehow the knowledge was submerged in the annual round of school plays and summer holidays and lacrosse games on the playing field. The girls at school didn't talk about it much. Perhaps they assumed she already knew or perhaps their information was as hazy as hers. It didn't seem to be a subject you discussed at home either, especially when she discovered how many months a woman was pregnant, subtracting her birthday from Mum and Daddy's anniversary and coming up short. No, she certainly couldn't ask them *that*, and besides, what did it matter? It wasn't as if she wasn't *wanted*, they made that plain enough, didn't they?

When she was twelve Mum, blushing and flustered, gave her an illustrated book with which Daddy was less than impressed. 'Facts of Life!' he said. 'Why don't they say what they mean and call it Facts of Sex?' He went on to expound about Life, what it was. 'It's getting up and going to work when some days you feel like hell. It's making damn sure there's a nice cash cushion for the wife and kids if, God forbid, you kick the bucket. It's ... oh hell, there's just no comparison, none at all.'

'Except you couldn't have one without the other,' Millie said quietly.

Lallie read the antiseptic little booklet, found it depressing. Once she'd got the parts sorted out and pictured them all going together it seemed so clinical ... invasive. Why didn't it tell her that when she met the right person she'd ache to be invaded and it wouldn't feel like an invasion at all, she knew it wouldn't.

Poor Mum would probably feel they should 'have a chat' before the wedding but there was nothing she needed to know. She'd long since found out all the facts and if she wanted to know more the girls at school had been only too willing, then, to tell her. In the end she'd known everything. And nothing.

110

Until now. Dear Jan Kaliski. Sweet, darling Jan Kaliski ...

After Daddy was done with the paper she clipped out the wedding announcement and posted it to Jan.

Farther down the long curve of Eccles Place, Agnes Armott clipped out the same announcement and sent it to Neil, who already knew.

Jan, anxious to get the moment over with, had gone looking for Neil immediately after his return from the week with Lallie. He found him in one of the hangars at Hempton, running his hands over the undercarriage of his Wellington, R for Robert, and looking thoughtful.

'Jan! You're back!' He did not look surprised, either that Jan was back or that he'd sought him out so soon. Jan had the distinct impression he'd been expected.

'I wanted to tell you,' he began quickly, his mouth dry, afraid if he stopped he'd never know where to begin again, 'Lallie and I are getting married. The first week in June.' He spoke quietly, urgently, the words coming in quick bursts he neither planned nor wanted. If he could just smooth it over, make it easier – but the colour was already draining from Neil's face. 'I know it's not what you wanted to hear. I – we hope you'll understand.'

He watched Neil's hands spasm around the wheel struts of the Wellington, saw him swallow hard.

'I see.' He seemed to pull the words from far away, as if some interior magnet made a quick pass over scattered pieces, gathered them up and gave them back. 'Well, congratulations old boy. All the best –'

'Do you want to come? We'll understand if you don't –'

Neil blinked once, very fast. 'I was there when she started school, I gave her her first driving lesson, took her to her first dance – of course I'll be at her wedding.' He thrust out his hand to clasp Jan's. 'You're a lucky dog, you know that.'

Jan nodded, his throat tight. 'I know. If you hadn't invited me at Christmas –'

Neil's quick gesture thrust away what had begun to be an apology. 'I hope you'll be happy.'

'I wish you could be happy also,' Jan said quietly, but Neil had turned away.

'Right. Not to worry. Got to run now. We'll hop into York some night and celebrate properly, right?'

'Right,' Jan said, but he doubted if they would. There was a distance between them now that couldn't soon be bridged.

Jan made his way slowly to the mess common-room, tried to write to Lallie and found he could not, today, find the words. So many images crowded his mind he set aside the pen and covered his eyes.

The way it should have been, running up the steps of the house on Morska Street with the potted geraniums on the balcony, running to tell Mamunia and Tatuś he'd met a girl, *the* girl, Lallie Wainwright, that soon he'd be a married man ... But the walls of this room, anonymous, given over to brief recountings of destruction, already saturated with unspecific loss, were too pervasive for the fragile image of his parents to be long sustained. The mental picture of them faded, replaced by childish, futile anger. Soon I am to marry. This thing I should share with you and where are you? *Where are you?* Your names go into the void and nothing comes back. Echoes. Why don't you answer, why don't I hear *something* ... already ten months since we talked, months of escape and fear and learning to love – and *where are you?* Mamunia? Tatuś? I am twenty-one. Answer before I am old, answer ...

Neil tapped at the open door behind which his senior officer was carefully gluing strips of wood to the model of a Whitley with the aid of eyebrow tweezers. Even the pale unpainted wood failed to lend grace to the bomber. The squadron leader looked up, gestured casually to the only other chair in the cubbyhole.

'Sit down, old top.' He turned his genial grin back to the model and deftly tapped home a strut. 'Clumsy looking sod, isn't she?' The tip of his tongue roved over his upper lip until it encountered the well-tended moustache, then drew in abruptly. 'What's up?'

Neil, who'd joined Squaddie in many a beer at the Horse

and Rider, felt his throat seize up in unexpected embarrassment and wished – almost – that he hadn't come.

'I know it's a hell of a thing to ask this close to ops but …
would it be possible to get me posted? To another station?'

The tweezers clattered to the desk. 'From Hempton? We've
only just arrived! What d'you want a bloody posting for, old
chap? Home away from home, Hempton is. Besides, your
crew's all assigned.' He lit a Gold Flake and studied Neil
through the smoke. 'Got anywhere particular in mind?'

'Anywhere but here.'

'Ah.' Squaddie dipped his head and resumed his finicky
work on the model. 'Girl friend giving you trouble?'

Neil shrugged. 'There's a girl – she's a friend.'

'And that's the trouble.'

'I was expecting more than I had a right to, that's all.' It was
easier to talk to the top of Squaddie's head than to his face, and
he found himself telling about Joe and Lallie and Jan.

'Ah-ha! One of the Poles. Romantic buggers, aren't they?'

'Jan's a decent sort. It's not his fault.'

Squaddie tipped his chair perilously far back. 'You should
have popped the question first, old boy. Too late now.'

Neil sighed. 'She seemed so young –'

'Not if they're over thirteen, that's my motto.'

'– and when the war started it hardly seemed fair. Besides, I
don't think she'd have had me. If I could just go to another airfield … they'll be living in the village here after the wedding,
you see.'

'And you won't want to keep running into them, I suppose.'
Squaddie shook his head. 'Sorry, old chap. No posting. If we
moved you we'd have to send your whole ruddy crew along,
too. It's just not on, is it?' He disappeared behind a battered
filing cabinet, clattered about a bit, and came up with a pair of
hefty pink gins. 'Bottoms up.'

Neil barely tasted the drink as it spread slowly over a field of
dead hopes, stirred into life doubts he hadn't, until now,
acknowledged.

'It's not just the disappointment,' he reasoned. 'If I thought
they were right for each other –'

'*They* must think so. I thought you liked him!'

113

'I do … but Lallie's – well, she's what her father's made her. Me too, I suppose. She's used to a man's whole concentration – worship, even! And she gives it all back, loyal as the devil, she is. If something happened, hell, I think –'

'I think you're over-thinking, that's what I think. Have another snort, old top, get your mind off her.'

'Easier said than done. She's like moss, is Lallie. Grows on you.'

'She must have grown on the Pole the same way then, right?'

'Ah, but he's different, isn't he? Not nationality, I don't just mean that – he's different from other Poles, too. He's deep, got all kinds of priorities that haven't a thing to do with Lallie. You've seen how he leans on the mechanics – have they checked this, that, and the other? He's the same with his crew –'

'Nothing wrong with that, is there? That's what makes him a good pilot. I've heard no complaints –'

'Oh, you won't! They worship him, aircrew and groundcrew alike, makes them feel safe as houses –'

'Because he does his homework.' Squaddie topped up both glasses and squinted over the top of his own. 'Again I say, what's wrong with that?'

Nothing at all, but he couldn't help wondering how much would be left over for Lallie in the crunch, just where she'd be on the list of priorities. Kaliski was driven, seemed pulled in a dozen different directions …

Squaddie laid a heavy hand on his shoulder. 'Look sport, you may not like to admit it – hell, you wanted her yourself – but they'll probably be happy as turtledoves, the pair of 'em. Now, what d'you say we toddle over to the Horse and Rider? Tie one on?'

For the first and only time in his life, Neil Armott drank himself into oblivion. When the post arrived next morning he threw away the clipping his mother had sent, swallowed a couple of aspirins, then wrote to Lallie. It was a generous, light-hearted letter filled with good wishes for her future with Jan and barely brushed the surface of his own desolation.

'… and if you need anything, anything at all, just remember

114

I'm here – not that I'll let you forget. Jack-of-all-trades, that's Neil. I mend fuses, stop leaks, train dogs, trim trees – hell, I'll even have a shot at being godfather when the time comes if you ask me nicely. But of course you will ...'

She read the lines once, then between them many times more, guessed what it had cost him to write at all. The hurt was meticulously covered over with a warmth far more wrenching than any reproach could have been. What in the world could she answer that wouldn't hurt him more? Wouldn't scratch the salt deeper in the wound? She tore up many drafts before settling on the truth.

Darling Neil:
What can I say? I love you in the nicest, warmest possible way and wish wish wish I could do something to make you happy again. I can't, of course. No use saying I'd like things to be different because I wouldn't. I'm so happy it frightens me. I'm glad you'll be here to see me off – it wouldn't be the same without you.
                                        Lallie

The letter dropped into the postbox at the corner of Eccles Place with a soft thud, signal for the perplexed and helpless tears that had been gathering in her heart for Neil Armott since the day he'd brought Jan Kaliski to meet her.

Almost unnoticed in the bustle of wedding plans, Jan was assigned a second pilot.
Emil Bura.
He could have been an actor posing for a recruiting poster. Young and golden and fresh-faced, clear of skin and eye, every feature an artist's dream. The small scissor-shaped scar on his jaw only emphasized the perfection of its surroundings. His credentials were impeccable: son of a distinguished general in the army, kid brother to the captain of a frigate.
At the controls of L for Lalka, Emil Bura was competent. Perhaps a shade too obsessed with the gauges – but that was

probably the stress of flying under the eyes of his captain for the first time.

Squaddie was waiting for Jan when they landed.

'Bura work out all right, mate?'

Jan hesitated just a fraction before he said, 'He'll do,' and wondered afterwards why he'd hesitated at all. But then Roman, who was taking his duties as best man all too seriously, hurried in with more questions about flowers for the bridesmaids, how much should the vicar get, who was ordering the photographer and did they or did they not have to ask Emil Bura to the wedding?

'Why not?' Jan said. 'He's a member of the crew.'

'He's a glamour boy,' Roman grumbled.

'Invite him. Not his fault he's pretty, is it? Remind me to drop a note to Lallie's mother about the extra guest.'

Any lingering uncertainty about Emil Bura evaporated in the stink of aviation fuel and the thunder of nearby engines.

At Eccles Place Millie heard Churchill on the radio warning of a possible invasion as soon as the situation in France 'stabilized'.

'He means when they get licked,' Joe said glumly. 'And they will. Jerry's over 'em like ants over jam.'

Millie wrapped up the best china in shredded paper and hid her tins of hoarded hams and peaches in the cupboard under the stairs, then remembered about the wedding and got them all out again. 'Invasion my eye,' she said. 'I'll not set a table with potted meat and cheap cups, not for Lall's wedding reception.'

Over at the market garden Mrs Hodgson sewed herself a mud-brown dress for the wedding and Lallie pinned up the hem as the farmer's wife revolved slowly atop the kitchen table like a figure on a music box, warning Lallie not to get it too short. 'We don't want to show a lot of leg, do we?'

Mr Hodgson was to provide all the dairy and garden produce for the reception and every day dropped elephantine hints about a special surprise 'on the day'. Lallie hoped it wasn't to be a suckling pig but didn't know quite how to ask;

116

the worry simmered gently under the euphoria of a white wedding dress hanging in her wardrobe and a going-away outfit of the palest, gentlest apple green.

She had no doubts at all until the very eve of the wedding itself. All around her was the quiet living room, with Daddy beside her puffing on his pipe by the fireplace, Mum's companionable clatter from the kitchen as she glazed pastry, the deep couch and Jolly and Silky snoring softly at her feet. Home. This was home, and after tomorrow it wouldn't be, ever again. Home would be the cottage in Hempton, fresh now with new curtains and paint and cheerful rugs on the linoleum floors. Home, but strange just the same. As Hempton was strange. A little village straining at the seams with airmen, nearly all foreign. *Jan's foreign ... yes, but you love Jan ...* There were the others, unquestionably foreign, who from tomorrow on would be almost like family. There would be neighbours certainly, but nothing like the people she had grown up with, not like the Hodgsons who were so reluctantly letting her go – 'Eee lass, if it mun be then it mun be, but you'll be sore missed.' She shifted against the cushions and Joe, alert to her smallest move, reached for her hand.

'It's not too late to change your mind, love. Been done before, plenty of times.'

'It's not that. It's just ... leaving everything. I hadn't really thought about it till now. But I do want to marry him, Daddy. There couldn't be anybody else, not now.'

'Aye, that's what I thought. But we'll be here, your mother and me. We're not going anywhere. You'll come back any time you've a mind to. It's your home.'

No, her home would be with Jan. 'I wish you liked him more,' she said.

He sighed. 'I was hoping you'd go for Neil ...'

'But I love Jan.'

'Happen I'll get used to it, in time. Can't help being disappointed though, can I? Just so you know we're here, no matter how it turns out.'

His voice was heavy despite the comfort of his fingers patting the back of her hand, and she suddenly felt a surge of impatience for tomorrow, for it all to be over with so she could get on with her new life.

'Wartime's rotten for getting married,' he went on, determined, it seemed, to hold the moment. 'And to a bomber boy at that –'

'*Neil's* a bomber boy!' Unspoken between was the knowledge that Neil would have considered all the possibilities and waited until the last all-clear before taking her to the altar. And with Neil she'd have been content to wait. Content. That's what life would have been with Neil. With Jan …?

'Poor Neil,' she said.

Joe sighed again as she sprang up from the couch and ran lightly up the stairs to try on her wedding dress. Again. Poor Neil indeed. Poor Lallie, more like. On the top stair she paused, the ceiling light touching her with silver. Joe remembered a fishing trip back when he was a lad, all the young salmon rocketing upstream, heedless of the falls to be leapt over, ignorant of the rocks, the pike, the nets in the shadows.

Oh, my lass …

CHAPTER ELEVEN

'And to think it all started with our little Christmas carol.' Neil's Aunt June sighed happily as she sniffed a bowl of carnations and sweet peas. 'A truly lovely wedding, Millie. Such a beautiful couple, they just glow, don't they? And how clever of *you* to find marzipan. It's one of my weaknesses, I'm afraid.' She nibbled delicately at her piece of wedding cake. 'Scrumptious!'

Millie beamed. 'Considering there's a war on …' She added more sausage rolls to a depleted plate on the guests' table and made vague excuses about refilling the cream jugs, to drift off bathed in the afterglow of June Armott's praise. People had been such a help – fancy old man Hodgson coming up with a whole wheel of Cheddar. Everything was going off champion, just champion. The rain had held off and the church! well, she'd never seen such flowers, every garden in Eccles Place must have been gathered in.

'Millie!' It was Joe, a pink carnation in the buttonhole of his dark suit, a public smile pasted firmly on his face. 'What the devil are you playing about with milk jugs for? Leave it for the caterers, damn it, come and be mother-of-the-bride.'

She smoothed blue watered-silk over her hips. 'Where are they? Lallie downstairs yet?'

He nodded towards the lawn ablaze with the gardener's best efforts. Tubs of blue delphinium and purple lupin flanked the tables, clumps of daisies and pale columbine nodded in the borders, and the trellis was a cloud of pink and white roses. Lallie and Jan were the centre of a smiling group, the airforce blue and Polish shoulder flashes of the crew sprinkled among the dark suits and summer dresses of the locals.

'If only his Mum and Dad could have been here,' Millie sighed. 'Still, he *does* look happy. I'm ever so thrilled for them, Joe ...'

He grunted under the smile. 'Of course he looks happy, my God, getting a girl like Lallie. Any man'd look happy.'

'They're *both* happy –'

Joc cut her off with a quick gesture. The smile was beginning to slip. 'Hell, I wish I could be sure he'd treat her right, but how can you tell? God, just look at them. Did you notice their hands? Manicured, Millie! I'll bet not one of 'em ever had a bit of honest muck under his fingernails. And cigarette-holders – what kind of men use cigarette-holders, tell me that?'

'I expect they're just used to them.'

'Listen to them! All jabbering away in their own lingo, not even trying to fit in.'

'They just haven't had time to learn yet – and of course they fit in. Jan's the bridegroom and they're speaking his language, what could be fairer than that?'

He rested his smile behind his champagne glass. 'That's just it. Different language, different customs, different way of looking at things. It's what I've said all along. She's throwing herself away. They're not like us, can't be, never will be.'

'Oh, folks are pretty much of a muchness, I reckon. Just because they talk different doesn't mean –'

'It means they think different. And when all this lot's over with, what then?'

'I suppose it depends if his parents are alive, poor lad. From what I've heard it sounds to me as if they'll be staying here.'

'That's what they say now, but just wait. He'll want to go back where he belongs, only natural isn't it? And he'll take her with him. We'll never see her …'

'We don't *know* that, and we might have a few grandchildren by then. Anyway, they've this lot to get through first and what with his flying an' all … I do think they might have given him more than forty-eight hours for a honeymoon though –'

Neil approached them, his smile more believable than Joe's.

'They're about ready to go. Coming to wave them off?'

Millie watched them, Joe and Neil, as they paused on the fringe of the laughing group. A flicker of regret went through her. Poor Neil. She'd seen his face as Lallie walked down the aisle. Bleak, it was, all his nature crushed under the radiant smile of her daughter. But he rallied, bless him, for the reception. Put a good face on it for Lallie's sake. He wouldn't spoil her day with his own troubles, not Neil. Lallie had made her choice and he accepted it. As she had. A pity Joe couldn't do the same.

He couldn't. He was trying, God knew, but it was a far cry from what he'd planned for her. The knowledge pressed him down, drained at his spirit as she looked up at him, tender as spring grass in her apple-green going-away outfit.

Going away … She was young and dewy and filled with hope and he loved her, so he elbowed through the group, hugged her to him and it all came rushing back, Lallie baby-plump at three, shrieking 'Higher, Dada, higher' as he pushed her on the park swing; Lallie happy and eager for her first day at school, handing her over to Neil at the garden gate and at the last second a tear trickling down her cheek and him wanting to take her up and rush her back home where she belonged, safe under his hand; and at twelve, a rosebud on a slender stem, defying the ugly school uniform of striped tie and mannish white shirt. God, how could he stand it, all his hopes and plans swept away, and by a sober-sided foreigner whose hand was even now tugging at her sleeve –

'Daddy! Not so hard, you're squashing my suit, my lovely new suit!'

'We'll get you another,' the Pole said, so Joe had to hug her again to hide the scowl he couldn't seem to smile away. Then he felt her cool young lips on his cheek in a last, private kiss.

'You're past due for a proper hug, my lass, so don't complain if your suit gets rumpled.' He would have said more, made some rough wish for her happiness, but his throat had shut and it was a moment or two before he turned, wedding smile firmly back in place, to his daughter's new husband.

'Look after her now, lad, or you'll have me to answer to –'

Neil pulled the sting, booming, 'And me!' as he delivered a friendly slap at Jan's shoulder. 'The best, the very best to you both.'

And by God, he meant it! Joe shook his head, puzzled at an attitude he could not understand.

There was a constraint between them in the train, two strangers who suddenly found themselves man and wife and didn't quite know how to move within the circle of the wedding band.

For a moment Jan wished there were other passengers in the compartment, but when an elderly woman climbed aboard at the last second he could have knocked her flower-pot hat off her head. Lallie winked at him, an impish smile lifting the corners of her mouth.

'Going to Scarborough, love?' the woman asked her. When Lallie nodded the woman became garrulous, clearly set for a chatty journey. 'Me, I live there. Just been visiting my brother's family in Sheffield and damn glad I am to get away, what with the traffic and all. Give me the seaside every time.'

'Oh, we're just going for the weekend, aren't we darling?' Lallie shot Jan a look that curled his hair, flashed the too-new wedding ring at the woman, who immediately looked up at the equally new luggage on the rack. Disapproval tightened her wafer-thin lips.

'Very nice this time of year, Scarborough. A bit nippy –'

'Oh *we* don't care about the weather, do we dear?' Jan was treated to another sultry look from his wife.

The woman sniffed, and sniffed again as Lallie straightened Jan's tie and kissed him, leaving the merest tell-tale of lipstick, which she rubbed off with a giggle and another look at the woman.

The response was a rustle of a peppermint wrapper. 'Attracts a nice class of people, Scarborough does –' she paused just long enough, '– generally.' Rheumy eyes darted from the ring to the luggage to the POLAND on Jan's shoulders.

Lallie nudged him, smiled sweetly at the woman. 'But with the war on I expect you're glad of any tourist trade you can get.'

The woman's lips disappeared altogether, then Jan reached for a cigarette and she suddenly gathered up her string bags and struggled with the door. 'I'm moving,' she said huffily, 'smoke doesn't agree with me, doesn't agree at all.'

Confused, Jan opened the door for her and she staggered off down the corridor, umbrage in every step.

The woman's brief visit had melted the constraint between them and Jan was able to slip his arm about his wife naturally. 'And what was all that about? Some old English ritual I haven't learned yet?'

Laughing, Lallie sat on his lap. 'We shocked her. She thinks I'm off on a dirty weekend, Woolworths wedding ring and all. *And* with a foreigner.'

She smelled delicious, of lavender water and soap and her special shampoo. 'It's not Woolworths! And what's a dirty weekend?'

'You know … not married.'

'But we are.'

'She doesn't *know* that, *silly*. She thinks I'm a wicked wanton woman and she'll have a perfectly lovely journey, shocked to the bone and asking everybody she sees whatever are young women coming to these days.'

'It wasn't the cigarette?'

'*No!*'

'Well then, since she won't be back …' He tipped up her face and kissed her, but she spoiled it by giggling in the middle.

'Wife! Wife! I can't believe it – I simply don't feel any different at all!'

He nibbled at her ear. 'That can be repaired.'

'Fixed.'

'That can be fixed.'

She giggled again. 'Now?'

'*On the train?*'

'Well ...'

'You *are* a wicked wanton young woman.'

'Wife,' she corrected him. 'Wicken wanton wife.'

They were saved from indiscretion by the sudden appearance of the conductor, who punched their tickets and who also noticed the new luggage – and perhaps the speck of confetti on Jan's collar.

'Just married?' he asked gravely.

'Yes!' they said together.

'Well, the best of luck to you then. You'll need it.' He sighed heavily. 'What with the blasted war, I don't know why anybody bothers.' And to Jan, 'You a pilot, are you?'

'Yes. Bombers.'

'Oh aye.' He rubbed his hip. 'My oldest lad was a pilot. Fighters. A Hurricane it was, poor beggar. I've often thought as how he might have lasted a bit longer if he'd been in a Spit. Oh well. It's all mad, isn't it? Bloody crazy world we're living in.'

His visit soberd them. For Jan, who'd seldom thought of the fighting to come with anything but excitement, the prospect of sudden death took on a new, graver aspect. Lallie a wife, young and vital, was one thing. Lallie a widow, rent by grief, was another. His father-in-law's doubts took on new significance. The weight of his new marriage began to settle, lightly as yet, on his shoulders.

The promenade was still bright with seashine but already blackout curtains darkened every window of the hotel. Barbed wire crisscrossed the beach, the now familiar wartime features of sandbags and fire-buckets lined the colonnaded steps, and a news banner blowing in the gutter bore the headline: *They're Home from Dunkirk!*

Inside, the war – the world – did not exist.

The hotel was small and very quiet, an establishment that, before the war, catered exclusively to public figures whose main concern was for plush and comfortable privacy. Once inside the lobby the iodine smell of salt and seaweed was tempered with suggestions of brandy and beeswax and huge hothouse gardenias. The chandeliers were small but very fine, the upholstery muted greys and blues vaguely stained with rose. Casement windows opened only on the ocean, never on the street; firelight and dim wall sconces glowed softly through lobby and lounge and dining room. Velvet curtains quieted every whisper, heavy Persian carpets softened every footfall. In the Eagleshead Arms never a maid rattled crockery, never a housekeeper jingled keys; the wine steward pulled corks with so discreet a pop you might have thought you were drinking Chablis if the bubbles had not tickled your nose.

An island of peace, perfect for two people with only forty-eight hours in which to discover each other and join their lives before war would once again engulf them.

'Isn't it terribly ... *grand*?' she whispered across ecru table linen and a starburst of crystal prisms, eggshell china on which slivers of roast lamb nestled close to minted peas and tiny new potatoes glistening in butter sauce.

'Nothing is too good for Joe Wainwright's daughter on her honeymoon.' He smiled when he said it but she felt the barb, resented it for Daddy's sake. Suddenly he seemed to gather himself, push whatever he was thinking aside, and said, '*And* for my wife,' kissing the palm of her hand across the shadowed table, shielded by potted palms and a copper urn of late tulips.

She was deeply impressed when he conferred with the waiter in rapid French as to the selection of Mrs Kaliski's dessert. Mrs Kaliski! *That's me*! she wanted to shout to the other decorous, whispering guests, then Mr Kaliski said, 'I've ordered us cheese and fruit in our suite if that suits you ...'

In our suite. For the first time she felt out of her depth. At home they'd wanted for nothing, but *in our suite*? A suite with the same hushed grandeur as here, a glowing fire and candles, blue velvet couches, burgundy drapes drawn against the sea, the night, the sirens, the air-raid shelters. She thought of the double bed under its canopy of pink brocade and took in a ragged, excited breath.

His hand covered hers. 'You don't have to be afraid.'

'Afraid? Oh no, I *want* ...' She looked around at the waiters and the maids, the other guests all confident in their maturity, 'I think I'm intimidated.'

'By this place? It *is* grand, I wanted it to be.' His mouth softened, curved into a smile touched with sadness. 'I want us to remember this place. Who knows what is waiting for us, after this?'

'But we're the youngest people here – they probably think we're children!'

His smile widened. 'If they do I'm sure they wish they were children also. You look ...'

'Fetching?' she offered. 'Mr Hodgson says I'm "fetching".'

'You look like my wife, my very beautiful, very innocent wife.'

She swallowed hard as she felt the blush starting at her toes and working its way up. 'In all the books I've ever read I'm supposed to go up first and, you know ... undress.'

He laughed softly, with the same breathless quality as that day on Mam Tor. 'You have a husband now,' he said. 'There are some things you need not do for yourself.'

It was better when they closed the door of their suite behind them and he took her in his arms. The handsome stranger across the dinner table disappeared and he was her Jan again, young and not quite as assured as he looked, kissing her, murmuring, 'Lallie, Lallie, don't be afraid darling,' as he unbuttoned the apple-green wool, unhooked her bra, ran his lips over her neck, her arms, her shoulders, her breasts. Then lowering her to the chaise to kiss her again and again, until every last bit of her yearned upwards to meet his hands as they touched here and here with an aching mixture of reverence and passion.

His lips were everywhere, tracing the long curve of her hips, the flat plane of her stomach, the satiny inside of her thighs as she yearned, ached, whimpered to be taken up to some glistening, pulsating plateau known only to the two of them. A quick, sharp pain, unbearable in its sweetness as if some fragile

125

rampart surrendered, then the fierce, penetrating surge into the very centre of her being. She cried out, felt his tremulous young mouth on hers. For an earthshaking instant the world stopped, shuddered and exulted and ached before coming to a last, sighing stop ... She felt suspended, rocked on a gentle sea, afloat in love and wonder. She'd loved him before, but surely not like this, as if she were now and forever part of him and he of her, belonging to each other as they always would, knowing each other, really *knowing* ...

'And I didn't even wear my pretty new nightgown – Mum gave me her own clothing coupons to get it.'

'Wear it tomorrow,' he whispered, his lips gentle on her cheek, breathing in the lavender and innocence of her. Still innocent. Always would be in her own fey fashion.

'So tell me, Lallie Kaliski. This thing that was so frightening ... I think you enjoyed, yes?'

'Enjoyed? It was absolutely the *most* sensational thing that ever happened to me! How could I have known it would be so ... magical?' She snuggled deeper into the crook of his arm, scattered little nibbling kisses across his chest, ran her fingertips over his stomach. 'I imagine it's a bit like swimming, the more you practise the better and better it becomes.'

She sounded so exactly like a child who hopes to be offered a second cookie that he couldn't help laughing.

'It's really not that simple, darling. A little rest ...'

'Oh no, really! I feel just wonderful –'

'Not you. Him.' He pointed.

'Hmm. I see.' She propped herself up on an elbow and stared hard. 'Do you realize I've never seen anyone like him before?'

'Was he such a shock?'

'Well, he was a bit of a surprise,' she admitted. 'I didn't see how everything could possibly fit together. He looks harmless enough now of course – like an endearing overfed worm – but before, well my goodness, all in a flash –'

'Flash Harry, that's our man.'

Suspicion dawned in the grey eyes. 'Where did you get that expression?'

126

'Oh, from the camp I suppose. Why?'

'D'you know what a *real* Flash Harry is?'

'I think so ...' He really did not, but the expression had intrigued him, one of many he was discovering each day he was in England.

'A Flash Harry is a bit like what's-his-name, your new co-pilot –'

'Emil Bura.'

'Yes. Mr Perfect. A bit too good-looking, a bit too heroic, a bit too charming to the girls – did you *see* the bridesmaids lapping it up? Poor Kaz was quite neglected and he *is* so sweet, Roman too of course – Mum really loved them I could tell ...'

Then her attention was caught by a stir from their own Flash Harry, and talk of the wedding and the crew evaporated into the brocaded canopy of the bed.

She slept like a child, her fist curled under her cheek, dark hair spilling over the pillow, her lashes dark-fringed crescents against her cheeks, mouth curved with fulfillment.

It was the first time he'd seen her asleep and he watched for a long time. She looked so happy, in love not just with him but with all of life, had no concept of what it would soon become. Very soon. Next month at the latest, probably much sooner. Did she think about his flying? He thought not. It was just something he did when he could not be with her. Could she grow up fast enough? He searched the guileless face then remembered Millie saying how her father used to watch her sleep 'for hours at a time'.

The parallel disturbed him. He drew the blankets gently across her shoulders and put out the light, but still he could not sleep. He lit a cigarette and stepped out onto the balcony.

The moon was dazzling. It hung full and pure in a clear night sky, laying a brilliant path onto the black and shifting sea. A Bomber's Moon they called it. The term was chillingly ambiguous. What bomber pilot wants such clarity? He wants a cloud or two in which to hide from the fighters, the flak, the searchlights; he wants only an occasional glimpse of the ground to spot the landmarks, the target ...

He shivered.

In a few short months responsibilities had crowded in on him, multiplying with alarming speed. A year ago his only pressing burden had been his father's health, with perhaps the problem of lining up a Saturday-night date a very distant second.

Even the escape from Poland had begun under the wing of a senior officer.

Now there was the crew of the Wellington, a casual obstreperous bunch, yes, but he was their captain, his job to lead them over hostile skies and bring them back to base alive.

And finally a wife. And such a wife. Sheltered, innocent, passionate. Lallie was the lightest, yet the heaviest burden of all. Had she any idea of her future? The waiting hours, listening for him to take off, listening more carefully for him to come back – or perhaps not to come back, or to come back maimed? Until today he had given little thought to the prospect of dying, but the knowledge of the young girl asleep in the room behind him made him want, very much, to live. His shoulders drooped with the weight of it all as he flicked his spent cigarette into the dark sea rolling below him.

Mamunia, your Janek grows old so fast, so fast ... and still sometimes he is afraid of the dark.

She groped through layers of sleep to reach his voice.

'... we must leave, darling,' he was saying, shaking her gently under the pink brocade canopy.

'But we still have another whole day!' she protested.

'Not now.' He read from the War Office telegram propped against the coffee pot on the breakfast tray. ' "Report by 16:00 hours Sunday. Urgent." I'm sorry, darling, I'm so very sorry. I wanted – planned for this time to be ours, an island ...'

It should have been forty-eight hours! How could they? They'd promised. Was it so much to ask? She packed with clenched teeth.

The shores of their island were shrinking, closing in on them ... The taxi sped them through deserted morning streets to the station. Bare masts of sailboats toothpicked the sky, their sails furled for the duration.

'I am so sorry,' he said again, his lips on her wrist.

She forced herself to smile as she ruffled his hair, her hand trembling just the least bit. 'I don't know why you're apologizing. I can't wait to get to our cottage, there's just so much to *do*!'

CHAPTER TWELVE

Jan sat quietly through the briefing and listened to the indignation of the assembled crews.

'A lousy paper drop?'

'A year's training and all we get to drop on them is damn pamphlets?'

The briefing officer gave them a bland smile. 'Propaganda pamphlets. An important weapon or so I'm told.'

Hoots, jeers, whistles of derision. A horse-laugh from Kaz. Roman thumped his wide fist on the arm of his chair: 'They use them for toilet paper!'

Again the genial smile. 'We hear rumours. Just make sure you cut the strings. Some clever buggers have been known to chuck out entire bales. Pretend you're throwing confetti at a wedding.' The smile became sympathetic, was directed at Jan now, who nodded and fumbled with the envelope of flight orders.

Of course the men were furious. For months they'd trained, waited for a chance to clobber the enemy – only to be sent forth to sprinkle bits of paper over the German countryside. But it was what he'd expected. They were to be broken in gently for the first raid, dropping pamphlets over an unimportant, lightly-defended target. Tonight was no more than a curtain raiser, a sensible one, to ease green crews into the hazards of searchlights and flak and perhaps a hostile fighter or two. He glanced round the spartan briefing room at his crew.

Kaz grumbled at top speed to his neighbour, a Canadian, who looked puzzled but commiserative as the stream of fractured English rolled over him. Lech had his cheeks sucked in, more cadaverous even than usual. Roman and Bolek scowled behind billows of cigarette smoke. Emil Bura (Jan smiled as he mentally substituted Mr Perfect) was not present. The too-good-looking co-pilot was in sick bay, probably green with nausea, hanging his handsome head over a kidney-bowl. He'd been taken ill an hour before take-off time, presumably from the veal in the mess dining room.

Emil ill. The rest of them frustrated, unhappy at the prospect of a paper-run instead of the bombing raid they had been gearing up for. Suppose they'd been called away from a honeymoon, as he had?

The train from Scarboroush had been late, barely time enough to share a quick meal with Lallie at the cottage before sprinting to the briefing room, Roman's note spurring him on:

'We fly. Finally. Don't be late.'

Lallie read the note, her eyes huge. 'Oh, Jan ...'

All through the tender, anxious hours of the train journey he'd dodged the subject of his sudden recall but now it could be avoided no longer.

'We have to start sometime,' he said gently. 'That's why we're here, isn't it? They've not trained us for months just so we can sit here and eat egg and chips – not that they're not delicious.' They were not, in fact, delicious. Lallie had not inherited her mother's skill in the kitchen.

As yet, there was nothing to disturb the country quiet of the evening. The roofs of hangars scalloped a fading lemon-coloured sky; above the perimeter road woolpack clouds drifted grey behind control-tower and flight office. Perhaps if the clouds thickened up they'd scrub the flight altogether – or perhaps they wanted cloud? She wished she knew more, she should have asked – then perversely didn't want to know. The more you knew the more you had to worry about. The very last thing he'd said was, 'Just sleep, darling. By the time you wake up I'll be back here again.'

'When will you take off?' she persisted.

'Probably at first dark – we won't know for sure until the briefing.'

'And you'll be back –?'

'By dawn.' His voice was firmly cheerful, so the words that were forming in her throat had to be held back. Instead she said, 'That long? All those hours in the air with no sleep?'

'I'll sleep tomorrow,' he'd said, very sure.

The evening was peculiarly still, that eerie interval after the birds fall silent and before the night things rustle and creep. Far across the airfield a solitary engine roared briefly then shut off. A moth fluttered past her on its way from elm to oak and back again. The clock on the church steeple in the village struck nine. What time was first dark and why had she never noticed?Whereacrossthatsaggingfencewasthebriefingroom?To what target were they sending him? Why did she feel so utterly alone?

She shivered despite the warm evening, and went into the cottage to wash the dishes. The task only used up ten minutes, even after she'd cleaned the sink and stove and set the tea-tray for later. If only the dogs were with her – but Daddy said the noise of the airfield would be likely to drive the daft Afghans stark raving mad, so Jolly and Silky were still at home. Her parents' home.

At ten she called Eccles Place. Her mother answered. No, her father wasn't back from the foundry yet and she herself had just been out pinching back dahlias while the light lasted.

'It looks like being a good year for blooms – and what are you doing with yourself?'

'Nothing much.'

'Isn't Jan there?'

'No.' Lallie had seen enough careless-talk-costs-lives posters not to say where he was, and Millie also knew better than to ask.

'Well love,' she said, 'you'll just have to find something to keep you occupied these nights, won't you?'

'But I don't know anyone yet …' There was Mrs Roscoe who owned the cottage, but she lived a mile down the road.

After she hung up she didn't even consider going to bed, not until she heard what she was waiting for.

It came a moment or two before dark, the first rumble of what was to become a thunder of engines, shattering the evening peace as, one by one, they began to warm up. She ran into the garden to look over at the starlit airfield and there they were, great black shapes rolling sedately down the runways, the moon glinting off polished windscreens, dimly lit cockpits with helmets moving busily inside. They all look alike! she thought in sudden panic. How will I ever know which is his?

The first Wellington rose like a great black bat, massive over the tiny cottage. The roar of its two Rolls Royce engines rattled the door in its frame, rustled every leaf on the trees under its wings. A second plane joined it, and a third. More and more yet. She knew she must count carefully. Twelve planes to a squadron, he'd said. Twelve to take off, probably. The same number to return.

At dawn.

After the long months of training Lalka's first operational flight was almost anti-climactic; only the distant enemy territory lent spice and tension to what was otherwise a familiar routine. Their early training had been without a co-pilot, so even Bura's absence enhanced the feeling of continuity – Jan didn't need him, was more comfortable without him.

Somewhere below, occasionally hidden by cloud but mostly gleaming under the moon, the North Sea rolled sloe-black on every side. Roman was behind him, peering at the Mercator map in a narrow cone of light. At the wireless operator's station Lech frowned over his direction-finder as he beamed from one radio beacon to another, constantly taking bearings. Kaz and Bolek, both twenty and the babies of the crew, were out of sight at their gun stations, but squabbled amiably over the intercom.

Crossing the German coast, thin pencils of light groped for them through scattered clouds, just too low to reach the Wellington. Then the mouth of the Elbe was below them. All they had to do was fly down its throat and they were on target.

132

There it was, child's play to pinpoint, already brightly lit by flares dropped by the lead plane.

'Are you in position, Roman?'

A muffled 'Yes,' came to him. Roman was flat on his stomach peering down the sights, only his legs visible as Jań glanced over his shoulder.

'The bales are undone?'

'Hell, yes.'

Assorted raspberries from the rest of the crew came over the intercom. 'Chuck 'em out whole, put a lump on their noggins!'

'Any chance of paper exploding?'

'Okay, let's get the damn things dropped and be off. I'm going in. Say when.'

They droned on. More searchlights now as they passed the fringes of the city and aimed straight for the cluster of flares.

'Steady,' Roman panted, 'keep steady, steady ... Okay! Bombs away, such as they are.'

A thump under their feet, then the whole plane lurched noticably upward, the weight of paper gone to a fluttering cloud of confetti upon the city. Kaz sang about sending a letter to his love '... and on the way I dropped it.'

'All right,' Jan said. 'Let's go home.'

Below and above them flak was bursting in sudden yellow blooms, but L for Lalka was left alone. All the way home they sang to keep awake, were still singing as the dawn came up just as they touched down on the familiar runway of Hempton.

After debriefing Jan felt obliged to visit sick-bay.

Emil Bura did indeed look ill, his perfect complexion a waxen beige with brilliant pink circles on his cheeks. Like a doll, Jan thought. A pretty, celluloid doll.

'Sorry I couldn't make it,' he was saying. 'Some damn thing I ate, I suppose ... how was it?'

Jan grinned. 'Do you want me to shoot a line or would you rather hear the truth?'

'Whatever.' The little scissor-shaped scar was livid white.

'It was money for old rope. The searchlights never came near us and the flak was either too high or too low. I didn't even have to weave. The highlight of the trip was Roman spilling coffee into his lap when we hit a patch of rough air. Bloody boring, if you want to know the truth.'

Bura closed his eyes. 'Too bad,' he said.

The night had been the longest Lallie could ever remember. She'd intended to go to bed the instant the night sky swallowed up the squadron but her mind was too busy, busy …

He's gone. He's gone over Germany in a clattering machine that's nothing but big engines and canvas stretched over strips of metal –'

It's a perfect flying machine, he said so, light and strong –

He said that to make you feel better. What's to stop them shooting him down –

Stop that. Pretend he's a night-worker like Dad's foundrymen. He'll be home in the morning –

Maybe –

I said stop that! The very last thing he needs is a worrying, whining ninny for a wife –

Wife! I've been a wife since *yesterday morning* – this is the second night of our honeymoon and I'm here and he's over there. *It's not fair* …

Are you going to dither about all night feeling sorry for yourself? You know what your father would say about that –

So she unpacked their things, stacked underwear neatly in the single chest of drawers, hung his shirts in the wardrobe next to her wedding dress and apple-green going-way outfit. When it was all done she dug out familiar jodhpurs and silk shirt and walked through deserted moonlit lanes, past Hempton's little post office, the butcher, the Horse and Rider pub, the village green with its trees and bench – very like Backenthorpe in its woolly lethargy.

But Hempton was small, quickly measured and understood. Its few narrow streets and alleys took no time at all to explore and she was back at the cottage before the night was half through. Only 2.30, silly to go to bed to lie sleepless in the dark room. She dug out a packing case from the garage, found her book on Afghans, mentally designed her breeding kennel, planned runs and bloodlines, longed to feel Jolly's silky coat under her fingers – and none of it was any good at all, not with a war going on and her Jan somewhere over enemy territory being shot at and hounded –

Stop thinking like that! You don't know. Bad thoughts bring bad things – but dog-breeding seems a bloody frivolous occupation with all this other going on, day after day, with Jan –

The nightmare had begun. She'd known it had to start sometime, but if it just hadn't started so soon ...

When the first bombers droned in from the coast she began her count, easier this time because she could see them, heavy yet oddly beautiful against the pale morning sky, coming in widely separated, now two, now five, now a single craft arrowing in towards the airfield, then three bunched together. Eleven. Where's the last one, where is the last –

And here it came, lovely beautiful Wellington. All were home. With relief came fatigue like a sudden, comforting weight. He was home. After debriefing he'd be here.

She watched him cross the perimeter road, duck through the fence, saw the tiredness in his shoulders the same moment she heard his cheerful whistle.

By the time the door opened she had tea brewed and a bowl of cereal ready next to a jug of buttercups she'd picked at first light from the meadow behind the cottage.

'You're up already?' he said, lifting her chin and rubbing it against his morning stubble. 'Couldn't you sleep?'

'I'm used to being up early.' His mouth was cool over hers. Tired. 'Did you ... how did it go?'

He kissed her again, sighed as he stroked her hair. 'It was bad only because I wanted to be with you instead. Apart from that it was a piece of cake.'

'Did you ... drop bombs?'

'You could say that. I brought one back for you.' He fished out a pamphlet from his tunic pocket. It was printed in German and a cartoon picture of a jack-booted stormtrooper marched across its cover. 'Doesn't look very lethal, does it?'

She caught her breath. It was so much less than she had imagined – 'When will you have to go again?'

'Maybe next week, next month, maybe tomorrow. It doesn't

matter darling, not yet. We're still on honeymoon, remember?'

He looked at the pillows, tested her side of the bed. 'Feels cold. Are you sure you slept?'

'I'm sure you're back. I'm sure I missed you.'

'Are you sure I love you?'

'Yes.'

'Then be sure I'm not going to get shot up. There's too much to live for.' His fingers found the little pearl buttons of her shirt.

Easy to believe him then, his breath warm on her skin.

CHAPTER THIRTEEN

It was a good month for roses, that June.

The *Charlotte Armstrong* at Eccles Place lifted great pink blooms to a brilliant sun. In the cottage garden at Hempton a trellissed *Peace* scattered its first yellow petals over the flagstones by the gate.

The war did not stand still for roses.

France surrendered. Italy belatedly declared war on what was left of the Allies. On the radio the evening news was now preceded by the national anthems of those conquered nations whose governments-in-exile had taken up phantom residence in London. It made a grim parade, much like the casualty lists in the morning papers, a roster of ever increasing dead. Abyssinia. Belgium. Czechoslovakia. Denmark. France. Holland. Luxembourg. Norway. Poland. It was expected that Greece and Yugoslavia would soon join the cortege. Churchill had a chilling, challenging message for the Commons and the country.

'We shall fight on the beaches … in the streets, in the hills … we shall never surrender.'

'That's telling 'em,' Joe Wainwright said, grimly satisfied

with his bulldog leader. 'If they come over here we'll be ready for the buggers.'

'Oh dear, it surely won't come to that, will it?' Millie's butter knife froze over a plate of scones.

'It damned well could. We're really going to get it now, you'll see. I just wish Lallie would come home, get away out of it. They'll be hitting the airfields now, no place for her, not when she could be safe here.'

'Oh Joe ...' If he could just accept it. He'd been like a bear with a sore head since the wedding, yet when she suggested running down to Hempton to visit the newlyweds he grumbled about petrol rationing and not wanting to take time off from the foundry. The truth was, he just didn't want to see them together, not as happy as Lallie sounded every time she phoned, bubbling over with 'Jan and I' this and 'Jan and I' that and 'Of *course* I can't come back home to live! I'm married now ...'

Jan and Lallie were enjoying an unexpected respite. In the afternoon there'd been a routine test flight in Lalka. Emil Bura was back in the crew, released by the Group doctor as fit to fly. He was eager to get back into action, he said, even going so far as to stay behind to talk to the fitters about the condition of the engines, which were running well.

That night, when the rest of the squadron was sent to Bremen, Lalka was grounded. According to the ground crew one of the engines was unserviceable.

'She can't be US,' Jan protested. 'Everything was fine this afternoon.'

'Listen to this!' The fitter ran up the starboard engine and they heard a random, metallic clatter.

While the rest of the squadron headed east Lalka's crew had to stand idle as the fitters disassembled the engine, found and removed a strip of copper wire no longer than a pencil-lead.

The sergeant-fitter scratched his head. 'What the –'

Jan turned on his ground crew. 'How did that get there? Damn, there's just no excuse –'

The fitter shrugged. 'There was no problem this morning,

sir, and we haven't touched her since you took her up this afternoon.'

'The wire didn't get there on its own.'

The fitter, a wizened little veteran unintimidated by rank, said: 'Look at it this way, sir. You'll miss one op. Plenty more where that came from. We'll have her like new by morning.'

Jan was puzzled for a moment, troubled by more than just a missed op. The ground crews were meticulous. There was no way they could have missed a thing like that. However, the aircrew behind him were already making plans to seize the moment and go out on the town, and he suddenly grinned.

He had a night off! He was happy, glad of another night with Lallie, glad of her warmth and vitality.

'What shall we do with it?' he asked her. 'The others are on a pub crawl, and it's not my week for the car.'

She laughed, an anticipatory gleam in the grey eyes. 'What do you mean, what shall we do with it? What do we always do with a night off?'

At first he'd been surprised, was now entranced at the delight with which she approached what must certainly have been the mystery – and perhaps the apprehensions – of sex. Given her upbringing, as narrow and rigid as Joe Wainwright could reasonably make it, she might easily have been shy, even frigid. Instead she'd taken to sex as naturally as a lark to singing. She brought to the marriage bed a zest, a devastating honesty that enchanted even as it aroused. Her responses were immediate and generous. No coy evasions, no games. 'Oh rats!' she said once, almost in tears. 'In a couple of weeks I'll have uncles-and-cousins, *you know*, my period.'

'Yes?'

'We won't be able to make love!'

It seemed a good time to bring up precautions. He was for them, she was against.

'But we *want* babies,' she insisted.

'But do we want them *now*,' he said, thinking of flak and Messerschmitts and going down in flames.

'Why ever not?'

It was not really at issue. She enjoyed sex for its own sake, separate and apart from the love between them. 'Even if you

138

were not so good at it,' she told him one night by the open window, the scent of honeysuckle a mist around them, 'I'd love you just as much but oh! what a difference it makes.'

'How do you know I'm so good at it?'

'Why, you *must* be! How else would I enjoy it so much? Joannie – she's married to a sailor, did I tell you? – she doesn't like it *at all* so you *know* he must be going about it all *wrong*.'

Thus he gained confidence, not only in the bedroom but in the briefing room, the cockpit, in encounters with subordinates. Through the prism of Lallie's energy and innocence he saw the world afresh and it was a more light-hearted, yet more logical place than it had been before, a world in which decisions could be made quickly when necessary or could be held in limbo, depending ...

Without this new confidence he would have agonized endlessly over the problem, been intimidated by the Bura family's military tradition. As it was, he knew exactly what he must do if the time came.

The next night their orders were for Essen. A groan went up in the briefing room. Essen. The Ruhr. That Cracker Alley of Krupp's armament factories. The most heavily defended of all the targets.

Bura was pale under the harsh lights.

'You don't feel well,' Jan said. 'Why don't you run over to sick-bay, see if you're fit to fly?'

Bura gave a forced smile, little beads of sweat glistening on the sculptured nose. 'I'll be fine. Just a bit under the weather still, that's all.'

Under Jan's eye he seemed to gather himself together, muster all his willpower into one resolute effort.

'You can take off if you like,' Jan said slyly, knowing he wouldn't. 'Or handle the controls over the target?'

'No ... I'll take her when we're coming home like the rest of the dickey pilots, okay?'

That wasn't quite how it was supposed to be. Other than take-off and landing and when actually over the target the co-pilot was supposed to share the routine flying. But at least he was coming, which meant something.

Essen was no paper-run. Lalka's belly was heavy with

hardware and they'd been warned to expect a hot welcome from ground defences.

Cloud cover stretched from Hempton all the way to the enemy coast so they flew blind, Roman and Lech straining every second just to stay on course. In the rear turret Bolek sulked over a fickle girl friend so Kaz had the intercom to himself, singing softly against the monotonous surge of the engines.

Emil Bura sat stiff as a cardboard cutout in the dickey-seat, spoke not a word until Roman said:

'We should cross the coast in five minutes.'

Bura's gloved hand jerked in his lap. 'Five minutes!'

Jan glanced at him in the dim glow of the instrument panel but very little showed under helmet and oxygen mask except the eyes, which stared straight ahead.

'Do you have your oxygen on, Emil? We're at nineteen thousand.'

Again the jerk. 'Yes.'

Scared. Not enough to do. 'Check the petrol, okay?'

He could have been an inept robot checking the gauge and when he at last gave the reading it was minus the reserve tanks. Then from up front Kaz shouted, 'Break in cloud to port!' and there was no time left to bother with Bura.

'See anything?'

Now he could see it too, a thread of silver that was the Rhine.

The next instant they were in the thick of it. Fingers of light hunted them through the scattered cloud. The master searchlight held them pinned, lit up the aircraft as a dozen lesser beams were drawn in like moths.

The cockpit was sharp with black shadow and white light as Jan threw the plane violently into a weaving pattern to escape the web. They broke free just in time as burst after burst of flak shot up through the cone of lights. Safe again in the darkness, the intercom sputtered with life.

'That was close.'

'Christ, they're quick with the lights.'

And from Roman a quiet, 'Nice flying, pal.'

Nothing at all from Bura, who was now slumped back, his

140

arm flung over his eyes. Between his feet a telltale shine.

Less than an hour to target. A quiet hour. The clouds closed again, tight as lambswool below them, then slowly began to turn pink over the city, where fires were already raging. As predicted, the welcome was warm, but again they were lucky. Only once did Jan ask for help from Bura and when none came he cursed briefly and reached for the lever himself. The bomb doors closed and they were headed home, Jan in a cold fury that no amount of compassion could soften.

After the others dispersed he took Squaddie aside.

'About my new Second.'

Squaddie laughed. 'Bura? Handsome beast, isn't he? He's got the WAAFs twittering like a flock of starlings –'

'I want him off my crew.'

'Off … What the hell for? Too old-school military for you? He can't help it, man. Runs in the blood. You must have heard about his family, heroes all?'

'He's LMF.'

'Jesus, are you sure?'

Jan filled him in on Emil's performance, starting with the copper wire, ending with the pool of urine on the Wellington's deck. 'He's a liability. I can't afford him on the crew.'

'But LMF! It's going to look God-awful on his service record.'

It would. Lacking Moral Fibre. 'Does it have to go on?'

'Of course it does, how else can I justify grounding a pilot? There aren't enough to go around as it is.'

'He's not fit to fly. With anybody.'

Squaddie made a notation on his clip-board. 'I don't have another Second to give you.'

'We can do without. If I got shot up Roman could bring us in, no problem.'

The next afternoon Bura, son of a general, brother of a navy hero, was posted to a distant station and assigned a desk job. Before he left he tracked Jan down in the deserted hangar.

'Kaliski, you lousy bastard –'

'Emil, I'm sorry …'

'How the hell do you think it's going to look when it gets back to the family?'

141

'It's nothing personal –'

'Not to you, you bloody iceberg –'

'Look, it's not your fault, happens all the time.'

'*Not in my family.*'

'I've got the rest of the crew to think about. That wire was a stupid trick, what could it serve? Keep us down for one night? If we hadn't found it you could have killed off the whole damn crew.'

'You're riding high now, aren't you? Top dog with your stupid crew, married into a rich family, everybody's blue-eyed boy – but you'll get yours, Kaliski … my God, if I ever get the chance I'll nail your fucking balls to the wall –'

Bura's beautiful hands were curled into fists Jan knew would never throw a punch, and tears had sprung into the furious eyes. Jan walked away from him, sorry for the boy, the situation, the war which had flushed out the flaw in his nature. The poor, craven bastard.

And what was wrong with his captain, Jan Kaliski, that he couldn't help the one crew member that needed propping up? Had the LMF report to Squaddie been *that* urgent, that vital? But there were the others. Kaz, Roman, Bolek, Lech. Keen as the devil, all of them, but just as young, just as vulnerable as Bura. And trusting him.

They were never given another co-pilot. Raids were more frequent, more costly to aircraft and crew. By summer's end pilots were spread thinner than margarine on the mess toast.

Jan looked tired all the time now. Lallie hid her concern under spurts of domestic zeal. The cottage shone, her cooking improved, and every second spent with Jan was a jewel to be treasured and relived when he wasn't with her. Mornings when he slept very late after a raid she shopped in the village, finding much of it as familiar as Eccles Place, the same groups of little girls skipping rope to the same nonsensical chant:

Cups and saucers, plates and dishes.

Our old lass wears calico britches.

Red-cheeked little boys, evacuees from London, knelt bare-legged on the butcher's front steps to swap marbles; in the cemetery the vicar's dog chased the postwoman's cat over the gravestones and up the chestnut tree; the district nurse and the village bobby pedalled bumpily over the cobbles and called: 'Good morning, lovely brisk day,' to each other and anyone else they happened to meet.

In the last few months Hempton had sustained several air-raids. A cluster of bombs meant for the aerodrome had fallen on the milking sheds of the local dairy, resulting for some time in a glut of under-the-counter beef and a shortage of milk. The runways were hit twice, producing the bonanza of a few days' leave each time as they were being repaired, days spent at Eccles Place with Daddy complaining that she looked tired and thin (she didn't) and Mum saying the same about Jan, who did. Lallie was growing up in ways her father could surely never have envisioned, and she sensed he didn't like it, although he said little beyond the occasional dig about her language, now liberally sprinkled with RAF slang.

A giant stride was taken when she noticed the absence of Emil Bura from gatherings in the mess and at the cottage.

'He's posted,' Jan said. 'I had to put him in for LMF.'

'Goodness! He *must* have been brave,' she said.

'It's not a decoration, darling.' He told her about Emil, and although she had not liked him she was sorry in a way she could not then have expressed. At the same time she saw her husband more clearly, his determination, his responsibility for those he judged to be in his care – and saw his peril in a clearer, more chilling light than before.

As flying schedules became more taxing and the entertainment in town palled, some of the crew took to dropping in at the cottage on evenings they were not 'working', and so for her as well as for Jan the young airmen became like a second family. Neil too, who now seemed resigned to the marriage, came often, bringing his own crew.

There was an intensity in all of them now that rubbed off on Lallie, a closeness born of the knowledge that each time they drank beer by the fire, sang songs around the battered cottage piano or made untidy attempts at Polish dishes together in the kitchen it might all be for the last time. They were flying two or three ops a week now, sometimes more. Their young faces –

143

even Roman's fleshy smile – all had the drawn razor-edge look of too many long nights, too many close calls. Fully two-thirds of the original twelve crews had 'gone for a Burton', either over the target or in failing to nurse a crippled Wellington over the long homeward hazard of the North Sea. The missing aircraft and crews were quickly replaced, their tenure in the squadron sometimes so brief there wasn't time to learn their names before they too were on the lists of the missing, sometimes to be reported later as prisoners of war, sometimes to be declared officially dead. After a while Lallie consciously avoided meeting the new ones. Except in the abstract, you couldn't agonize over those you didn't know. It was easier that way.

Men from other crews told her that L for Lalka led a charmed life. Lucky L, they said. Lalka's crew told a different story. They were still around because Jan was cautious, cool in a crisis. Over the target he did not simply dive in, dump his load, and rocket out again. He flew higher, scouted about a bit, looked for gaps in the patterns of flak and searchlight; when he found one he went for it calmly, with a minimum of shouting over the intercom, no panic at the sudden approach of fighters because he could depend on Kaz and Bolek fore and aft to keep their eyes peeled. And thus they continued to survive, dependent one on the other.

The night before the final flight of their first tour they had a party, to celebrate not only a break in tension but also their survival of the night before.

It intrigued Lallie that the Poles never threw, organized or gave a party. They *made* one with all the frenetic energy of children playing their last game of hide-and-seek before being called home to bed. In vain she reminded them there was to be a party in the mess at the weekend for the whole squadron. Well of course, but they must make their own party also for the Poles, of which there were ten. At the cottage, naturally. Jan shrugged and then laughed. Why not – this was the closest thing they had to home.

They assembled a set of drums, balloons, a gramophone, a case of vodka, three tins of Vienna sausages and assorted popsies.

It was a gay evening, bright with the prospect of just one more raid then two blissful weeks' leave.

Inevitably the case of vodka was hit hard. At the height of the party Bolek leapt onto the table to propose a toast to his new girl friend Brenda, to General Anders, to Haile Selassie and to the station cat, a one-eyed grey tom called Casanova. He was quickly followed by the pilot of the other crew who called for silence. He had something to say. The last time his crew made a foray into London a well-known socialite – quite a pretty thing, he admitted – had given him a present, a dose of the clap. He thumped his chest at the outrage and asked them all if that was not a most unpatriotic gift? Yes! they roared. Therefore, in the interests of those to come after –

His navigator produced a thunderous roll on the drums.

– he announced her name.

His rear-gunner made an involuntary pass at the front of his pants, muttered 'Bloody Hell', and poured himself another vodka. Lech's face, more gaunt than ever, turned pale. Their more selective friends laughed uproariously and proposed a toast to the lady in question.

When Lallie retired to the kitchen to heat up yet another batch of Vienna sausages she was closely followed by Kaz, who had been unusually quiet all evening. His cheeks were a flaming pink with rare embarrassment and his curly hair stood on end from repeated comb-throughs of his fingers. He touched her shoulder and swallowed. He too had something to say. But first he made an odd little bow and brought forth from behind his back a little silver tankard, much dented and in need of polishing.

'I something to give Janek's wife, no? I glad very much you marry wiz him, you make listen to me and I thinking you onnerstand me. This cup my great grandfather give my grandfather. He Kazimir, my father Kazimir, I Kazimir also, *prawda*? My grandfather he bury cup into ground when war come – not this war, but far, far before.' His arm swung behind him to indicate some long-distant conflict. 'Onnerstand? Is very old, maybe four hundred years. Only one thing left so I want give you to keep for me, no? When I after go again to Poland maybe you give me back if you want. If you no want, you keep for babies, *nie?* You onnerstand?'

Oh yes. He was telling her something he could not bring himself to say in any language, that if he were killed he wanted her to have it, if not for herself then for her children. She was touched. To hide the knowledge of what he meant she took the tankard, still warm from his hands, between her fingers and felt the pattern of its rim, acorns and wild rose embossed on a narrow copper band. There was a worn coat of arms, dimpled and scratched from four hundred years of his family's history.

She reached forward and kissed his hot pink cheek. 'Of course I'll take care of it for you,' she said. 'When you go back home it will be waiting for you, but in the meantime I'll enjoy using it.' His cheek still had the faint bloom of down on it, making her feel very mature and wise for a moment.

She was still holding it after he went back to rejoin the party, and when Jan came in to get the sausages she showed it to him. 'Wasn't it sweet of him?' she said.

He put his arm around her and kissed the back of her neck. 'It's you who are sweet. You made him happy by taking care of it. Tonight you make all my friends happy.'

'And you? You're happy?'

'How could I not be? Every day there is more reason. You were naive and I loved you for that. Now you are growing up and I love you more. Imagine how I'll love you when you're fifty!' His hands moved down the slim curve of her hips.

'What time d'you think they'll leave?' she whispered.

He laughed softly into her hair. 'You're still impatient and I love you for that also, but first we must feed our guests. *Bardzo dziękuję*, Pani Kaliska.' Thank you, Mrs Kaliski. A quick kiss on her forehead and he was gone, platter of sausages and cheese held aloft.

Waiting for the coffee to perk she reflected that he was right. A year ago she'd barely heard of Poland, knew nothing of bombers, flak, ration cards, had never expected to live on a seesaw of anxiety and ecstasy. Setting cups and saucers on a tray she chuckled to herself and blushed. Gosh, a year ago she hadn't even heard of the *clap*!

Then he was back again, not touching her, not seeing her, sitting at the kitchen table with a dazed look in his blue eyes.

'What is it?' she said, sensing his rapid change of mood.

'The Triumph. We've been so busy I've just realized – I told you Luckner didn't come back last night? Well, he was the last one. The car's ours.' He lowered his head and a shudder seemed to go through him. What a way to ... oh, Christ ...'

'Oh darling –' She took his head between her hands as if to squeeze out the images that must be crowding it. 'After tomorrow night we can forget all that for a while ...'

CHAPTER FOURTEEN

After tomorrow night.

It was Essen again. Even before they were over the target the trip had become a disaster. Crossing the coast at Rotterdam they took flak in the starboard wing and some more they couldn't see in the tail section. The sky was alive with flung hardware. The engines wouldn't hold them at twenty thousand feet and when they finally levelled off they were at eleven thousand. The plane handled like a slug. He could have turned for home. Legitimately.

Afterwards he was to wish he had – but the rest of the squadron were all about him, pressing on to the target. Essen. Christ, it would have to be Essen!

A frantic sky, enough searchlights to be high noon instead of midnight, enough traffic aloft for rush-hour in Piccadilly Circus. A hundred Wellingtons at least, some Lancasters, and God alone knew how many Jerry fighters. Their own squadron strength was down to eight, the briefing officer's last words before take-off: 'Above all, get home. No heroics. We're short on kites.'

And here was Lalka all wrong, stubborn as stone. Already his arms ached from holding her against a distinct list to starboard, and they were practically over the target now, no time to check the systems.

Below them Essen was a smoky glow, around them the sky, an arena of hurtling metal bodies, flak coming and coming, no end to it, yellow starbursts on every side, then a sudden blaze to his left, a Wellington screaming earthwards with a tail of fire, its impact, fireworks as the load of bombs explode all at once. No time now to wonder who it was, the intercom suddenly alive in his ear, Roman's voice no longer a lazy drawl.

'Christ, can't you get us up a bit? We're sitting ducks!'

'No chance. She won't go. We'll go straight in, make the drop, and get the hell home. Are you set?'

'Yes. Okay, easy now, easy ... left a bit, a bit more ... okay, whenever you're ready.'

'Now!'

A rumble somewhere deep underneath him.

'Bombs gone!'

The plane, her load lightened, lifted slightly. He pulled the lever that closed the bomb doors, waited for the jolt of their closing.

And waited.

And waited.

And now everything happening at once, flak sure as hellfire bursting all around them, Jan leaning hard on the wheel, feeling as if only his own brute strength turned her to port. Then they were headed for home – but not before another burst got them aft on the fuselage, a hole in the geodetic frame so big he could have stuck his head through it. Patterings like pebbles on a tin can against their underside. He called to the crew to check in, was interrupted by Kaz up in the front turret. Excited.

'Fighter at one o'clock high. Coming fast. Weave, *weave*!'

A burst of gunfire from the Me-109. Tracers streaked by to port. A tremendous jolt through the control column ... an answering squirt from Kaz's guns ... a shout from behind, Bolek yelling of another fighter on their tail as he opened up on it, and all the time Lalka lurching like a drunk across a sky gone mad, slow to respond, slow to turn, quick to drop if he let up even for a second on the stick.

Christ, his arms ached.

'Got him!' Kaz screamed as the fighter in front flamed and vanished.

'Lost mine,' Bolek said. 'Shit.'

Then they were pulling away from trouble. Slowly. Time now for a quick look at the gauges.

No revs on the starboard engine. He adjusted trims. So okay, they could make it home on one engine. Be a bit late, that's all, but Lallie fretting … and still the worry of not hearing, not feeling the bomb doors shut.

One other thing. A disturbing absence on the intercom. There was Roman's slow drawl to Lech, Lech grunting figures back at Roman, Bolek reporting no hostiles behind them.

One voice missing.

'Kaz? Kaz? You there, chatterbox?'

Nothing. Only the breathing of the others.

'Roman, get me a bearing then get up front to the nose, see what's keeping Kaz quiet. And hurry back.' For the first time he wished he had a second pilot (not Bura!), another pair of hands to give his own a rest.

Follow the course, press on for home, hope to God you don't meet much stuff crossing the coast because Lalka's weaving days were over, as much as he could do now to keep her halfway level, even with the trims set to the limits. His wrists were numb from holding her, his eyes grainy from peering at dimly lighted instruments. And where was Kaz's voice?

Then Roman tapping his shoulder, his voice tight.

'*He's hit. Kaz is hit.*'

'Bad?'

'I don't know. He's not talking. There's a lot of blood.'

No, not Kaz. Not curlytop with his stream of incomprehensible English as fast and staccato as his guns. Jan's throat closed against the sob rising in it.

With the Rhine a thread behind them he called Roman. 'Hold her steady and keep your eyes open. I'm going up front.'

Kaz was slumped over the guns. Moonlight streamed in through the dome, turned leather helmet to silver, thickened blood on the forehead to a deep, glistening blue. Jan touched his hand. Not cold yet, but cooling. He unfastened the helmet and eased back the head, the curls a springy mat under his fingers except where the wet started at the temple. The face was untouched, still young, still laughing. But not the eyes.

He fought to keep down the gall rising bitter in his throat and scrambled back to the cockpit. Roman moved over.

'How is he?'

'He got the chop.' The words quiet, controlled.

'*Jesus*!'

So Kaz was the first to go. But there was no time, yet, to grieve. A cloud of apprehension formed, pushed the memory of Kaz's dead face into the background. Airspeed was dangerously low, even accounting for the dead engine.

'Roman, check around in the bomb-sight. See if you can spot the doors. I didn't hear them shut.'

Roman's eyes flickered. 'Hell, now you mention it ...'

'It would account for the airspeed ...'

'Bloody hell – but we could try the manual –'

Jan forced his voice to stay even. 'If the doors are open we've probably lost the hydraulic system.'

'So?'

'So no flaps, no lock on the undercarriage.'

'*Sweet Jesus*!' Roman's wide face tightened, then cleared again. 'There's the manual for that –'

'We're hit all over the bloody place. What makes you think the manual will work, you stupid bugger?'

Understanding dawned. 'Oh shit! Shit-shit-shit. I'll check.'

A long wait before he reported back. He'd seen nothing from the bomb-sight. But he'd felt a draft. Good God ...

To the east the sky was tinged with morning ... miles more of it to stumble through before they crossed the English coast to safety.

Dawn ready to break through the cottage window and still he wasn't back. Eight planes had left, only five were back.

Lalka not among them.

Standing at the open door, afraid to breathe, afraid to make the smallest sound that might muffle the drone of home-coming planes, she forced down hysteria that rose in a swarm of doubts whenever she stopped talking to herself. He was a good pilot. Hadn't they all told her that? A responsible pilot who'd get them back through anything? Neil: Safe as the

Bank of England, Jan is. Kaz: Jan careful, yes? – you be no worry, Lallie. Squaddie: Saves us a fortune in kites, that husband of yours.

So where was he, that husband? Why no call from Froggie in Control to say Jan was on his way? Was delayed due to headwinds, storms, *anything* … anything but flak … fighters … flames … Alliteration smashed through her own control, sent her sobbing suddenly to the hall, to her coat – But he's told you, over and over, not to go bothering Control when he's a bit late – but he *wasn't* a bit late, he was hours and hours late –

Running, she left the cottage door swinging on its hinges, tore through the gap in the hedge, heels clicking on the long concrete walk, fists pounding on the Control Room's door –

And there was Froggie coming at her, routine smile firmly in place, making soothing noises as he led her to a chair, ordered up tea as he patted her hand, told her quietly, oh so smoothly that Jan hadn't called in yet, it was just a matter of time, of patience, patience before he called in …

Then why the tense faces of the WAAFs as they moved counters across maps, logging in returnees from here, there and everywhere – so where in all that neatly organized sky was Jan Kaliski? … where was he? … where was he?

When tea came she sipped it politely because they'd gone out of their way – and they were busy – so how could she tell them it didn't help, sympathy didn't help either, nothing helped because he was so late, late, and while they calmly went about their business of tracking and logging, her husband was dead or captured or burning, his blue eyes closed forever to her … to everything –

Then a familiar-sounding crackle from the maze of wires attached to a WAAF's head, Froggie running, taking the wires from the WAAF, speaking –

'Come in Lalka! What the hell kept you?'

Her chair seemed to buckle. Hot, sweet tea spilled to a floor which didn't want to keep still, kept shifting –

Froggie's voice came in clear and strong over the laboured thunder of the port engine. What had kept him? Where to begin?

151

He looked up, saw Lallie's picture smiling at him, young, ingenuous, happy. Hell, she'd be in the Control Room by now, even though he'd told her and told her … When she heard about Kaz … he was her favourite. Naive Lallie, who until now had believed all the bullshit bandied about in the Horse and Rider, all the daft chatter about pranging, going for a Burton, getting the chop. Shop talk. Defensive flimflam because if you wrapped up death in your own special slang it hurt less, made you part of an exclusive club, one with an extra-heavy turnover in membership. If death came in euphemisms you could pretend, at least in public, that the whole thing was a bit of a lark. Your sweating was done in private.

'Is Lallie down there with you, Froggie? Can she hear?'

'Yes and yes.'

Thank God it was Froggie, the one Pole in Control. He switched to Polish, gave Froggie their position as far as he knew it, and the condition of the plane. And Kaz. 'No need to panic Lallie yet – make her go to the cottage, okay? Tell her I'm starving or something. Pull rank. I think we'll be coming in on the belly.'

'*Christ!*' A break in transmission, then he was on again. 'Roger, she's gone, after a bit of arm-twisting. How much petrol –'

'Not much. Can you see us yet?'

'No.' Another delay as they crept close enough to the drome to be spotted. 'Okay, Lalka, we see you.'

'Do you see the bomb doors?' Jan held his breath.

'Hell, yes. They're open. Sorry about that.'

'Not half as sorry as –'

'And your undercarriage is trailing. Have you tried the manual –'

'Of course we bloody well have. Okay, you know what to do …'

'Roger. Good luck.'

L for Lalka circled the field. Jan's arms were numb, his face stiff with cold. Cold. Don't think about Kaz. No time. Try the undercart one more time. Limp as lettuce.

'We're still not locking,' he told the crew over the intercom. 'You know the drill. I'm aiming for grass. Get ready to jump.'

A quick intake of breath from the others. Lech and Bolek checking harnesses, shouting 'See you! Luck!' and jumping, their 'chutes billowing out into the morning.

Roman leaned to watch them as they drifted towards green fields. 'Pretty,' he said.

'I ordered everybody to jump. That includes you.'

'I don't hear well. The bombs must have deafened me.'

Jan threw him a savage grin. 'If you're staying, get off your arse and give me a hand.'

Fire-tenders crawled into position below. Ambulances idled between perimeter road and farm track. Figures with hoses ran hither and yon, more figures bearing stretchers erupted from the meat wagons. Frantic as ants from up here.

Roman squirmed in his seat. 'God, I could do with a pee.'

'Too late. We're going in.'

He took Lalka in easy, just fast enough not to stall, fought to keep the nose up, braced for impact as the village church swept under them, the common, the cottage, the dairy. They skimmed the fence, ploughed a shallow furrow as the belly touched down, bounced, settled back. Then the nose tipped in. Tons of metal juddered through summer grass thick with buttercups until dust blinded them to everything but Lalka's nose rammed in the earth, her tail angled up.

They jumped clear and stood, dazed, as the meat wagon rushed in. Men swarmed into Lalka, reappeared with Kaz, passed his limp body onto a stretcher and took it away. Jan blinked, swallowed hard as the wagon disappeared.

Exhaustion swept over him. There was grit under his eyelids, dust in his mouth … and a wrenching ache he was too tired to face. He touched Roman's shoulder and turned away. Debriefing still to face, make the report, then the final entry in Kaz's log book …

When it was all done he slowly passed through the hole in the fence, reluctant to see her this soon. He needed time.

She was in slacks and shirt, her jaw rigid, her hands making half-hearted attempts to trim the rind off rashers of bacon. 'You're so late,' she said quickly. 'I thought … then they made me come back here, said you'd be hungry –' Then she saw the blood on his tunic and shirt, the dry brown flakes of it on his

153

hands. 'You're hurt!'

'No. It's Kaz. He's dead.' His voice was stiff, drained, and he wished he could have prepared her in some way. After the months of careful evasions, little lies about the risks involved, this seemed too brutal an introduction into life as it was and would be for as long as he was flying, but just at the moment he had nothing to give her, not sympathy, not tenderness, not love.

She didn't cry. She just turned away from him for a second and when she turned back her face was composed again, but pale. She eased off his tunic and shirt and got to work with a bowl of vinegar and water, soaking out the stains.

'It should be lemon juice,' she said flatly, 'but there are no lemons. Vinegar will have to do.'

'Don't worry about it – the batman will get it out, he knows all about bloodstains.'

'By then it'll be set.'

She poured him a large Scotch and he drained it and held out the glass for a refill.

'Shouldn't you go to bed?' she said. 'I'll bring your breakfast upstairs.'

'I'm really not hungry, or tired.'

'But you'll rest better there.'

So he lay on the bed sipping whisky and after a long time he realized her arm was around his shoulders, had been for hours. 'You'll have a cramp,' he whispered.

'I'm fine. Try to sleep.'

And she *was* fine, he thought. Joe Wainwright's little girl was just fine. The tears he'd anticipated were his own, trickling down his face all unnoticed until she took his head to her shoulder and rocked him until he drifted off to sleep, Kaz's voice going with him, trusting him ... even in nightmare still trusting him.

'*Get us the hell home, Janek, get us home ...*'

He is here.

He is with you, hold onto that. He's back. Whole.

Forget the waiting, forget the watching, the counting. He's

here, asleep on your shoulder, warm and oblivious. He's all right, his sad, tired whisky breath warm on your cheek. He's back, brave and young and resting except for a muscle in his jaw that twitches every now and then, a network of fine blue veins on flickering eyelids, flecks of salt drying on his cheeks. For Kaz.

Sociable little Kaz with the bounce and confidence to speak so fast, so badly, and never stop to wonder if anyone understood him. Kaz, who just yesterday gave her his little speech, his trust, his family cup still warm from the heat of his hands. All that life gone to – God, where do they put them when they come back dead and why don't I know? Do they give them a funeral and if they do who will there be to go except the crew? Oh Kaz ... no, don't cry because if you start you'll never stop, and when Jan wakes up he'll need every bit of strength you can give him. He'll blame himself for Kaz once the shock has worn off. There's enough, too much, on his mind without a wife who has to be petted, propped up, smoothed over at every crisis. He already thought she was spoiled (sheltered, he called it) because of Daddy but – oh dear, Daddy! He was expecting them at Eccles Place this evening to start the two-week leave.

No way to go yet. There'd be the funeral first and in any case he shouldn't have to face up to Daddy just yet. Daddy was so ... gung-ho about the war and it would be some time before Jan would be gung-ho about anything. He needed solitude, somewhere the sun could get to the new wounds.

He woke much too soon, reached out to her with a cry.

'You're here ... thank God you're here, I need you, I need you so much ...' he murmured against her mouth.

For the first time their lovemaking was not a slow stream of delight. It was a raging river, a desperation to join flesh, to shut out last night, to hold back the future and the casual slaughter of innocents like Kaz, to affirm they were not alone in a murderous world.

When it was over they clung to each other, gazed into each other's eyes as into their own souls, bathed in each other's sweat, hardly breathing, not speaking. There was nothing to say. Their joining had said it for them. They were comforted.

155

He slept again and she got up. She should have been packing for what was to have been a relaxing fortnight at Eccles Place. A holiday. It could hardly be that now, but looking at his worn, sleeping face she knew it must be a healing time. A year since he left his home; doubt over the fate of his parents; the three-month tension of trips over enemy territory and more to come. And now Kaz. It was too much. She touched his hair and it came to her that their marriage had come of age. He had let her see his anguish and it had become her own. The phrase 'man and wife' took on a new meaning. Now she was truly a wife, not just a lover with a license.

In the cupboard she found a tin of silver polish and spent a diligent hour on Kaz's tankard. She buffed up the wild rose and acorn border, rubbed at the scratches and hollows of four hundred years, and she thought of his great grandfather (or was it his grandfather?) who must have turned the cup in his hands, considering, before digging a hole and burying it deep in the Polish soil, out of reach of some advancing enemy. What had he thought, that long-dead stranger, deciding the fate of this useless, pretty trinket that was nevertheless something to pass on to the son and the son's son ...?

And now the last son was dead.

On impulse she filled it with deep blue forget-me-nots and a mist of white babies'-breath, set it on the window-sill where the late September sun danced off all the points of the family crest, filled the dents with light.

When she looked up Jan was watching her from the doorway, his hair rumpled with sleep, a sad little smile at the corner of his mouth.

'I thought you'd want to bury it with him ...'

'No,' she said, very definite. 'It's been underground long enough. Besides, I said I'd keep it for him and if ... if he didn't come back I was to give it to our babies. I think he'd like to know it was here, that we were looking at it.'

'I'll ask his father about it. Today I must write to his parents.'

'Won't the Air Ministry do that?'

'They'll send them a telegram, not that they'll get it. Probably won't get my letter either, but I have to write it, in case, let them know how …'

'First you'll have some breakfast,' she insisted, tossing the forgotten rashers of bacon into a pan.

'First I kiss you. You were very good for me before … I didn't want to upset you but –'

He was apologizing for his tears, trying to. Really, *men*! 'You're my husband,' she said quietly. 'We share.'

CHAPTER FIFTEEN

To Lallie's surprise her parents arrived for the funeral. They drove up as the small group of mourners waited on the church steps for the hearse.

Mum emerged from the car all in black, formal in hat and veil and long kid gloves. Daddy wore a dark suit and tie, was conspicuously civilian among the mass of airforce blue; the moment he spotted Neil he led him off to the side and could be heard talking steel.

'How on earth did you get him to come?' Lallie asked Millie.

Her mother gave her a look that seemed to draw Lallie into some mysterious conspiracy. Poor Mum. Of such small triumphs …

'I reminded him what you said at the wedding, about the crew being like family. You married into it, didn't you? So how could he refuse? Besides, the lad should have some parents here to see him off – if not his own, then somebody's. And I liked him.'

By the time she'd followed the zigzag path of her mother's logic, Lalka's crew was shouldering the burden of Kaz's coffin up the church steps. Jan looked pale but somehow in control, and she realized with a shock that at twenty-one he was the oldest pallbearer.

Today he looked it. Despite the adjutant's offer to make all the arrangements Jan had insisted on attending to every sad detail himself. At some point grief had hardened to anger, a process which seemed to have begun with the matter of a flag to drape over the coffin. The RAF had provided a Union Jack, which Jan instantly rejected.

'Kaz is – was – a Pole. If there is to be a flag it should be the Polish Flag.'

Calls to the authorities in London failed to turn up a single Polish flag. He called every Polish unit from the south coast to the northern tip of Scotland. As the negative answers built up, so, it seemed, did his anger.

'It's a disgrace! There must be thousands of Poles here now, all services. A lot must have died already. Must they all be buried with a lie?'

She thought he was overreacting, and said gently, 'Why not use the Union Jack, darling? What difference can it make?'

'Everything must be right! I must tell his family how he was buried –'

'You don't even know his family!'

'I know they're Polish, that's enough. To them there will be *much* difference whether he is covered with his own flag or some strange –'

Strange? The Union Jack strange? 'You're in England now, Kaz will be buried *here*.'

'It was Poland he was fighting for!'

His eyes blazed with a cold blue passion and she backed off, intimidated by its power. She'd never given much thought to nationalism. Daddy considered that to be British was to be privileged and often said so; since she'd always believed him there was nothing to get defensive about.

'You're overtired,' she said. 'You'll see it differently when you're rested.'

His mouth set in a line so firm it seemed impossible it could ever have said *I love you* against hers.

In the end he'd bullied silk from the draper's shop in the High Street, hunted up the village seamstress and stood over her as she stitched the simple red and white rectangle. In the same single-minded fashion he'd tried to talk the other crews into coming to the funeral. They were reluctant. Most of them

158

had barely known Kaz. Men were killed every day now; the fact that this one's remains came back to Hempton instead of falling over Germany made little difference. Besides, it was their leave-time. They wanted to be away, far from the roar of engines. Some wanted bright lights, some wanted time with families. None wanted to be reminded of the fate that might be waiting for them when they came back.

'Callous bastards,' he raged to Lallie at the cottage.

'They're tired, darling,' she murmured, seeing the burning strain in his eyes.

The strain was there now, Jan could feel the heat of it scratching his eyes like sand as the minister droned through the eulogy. A little man, the minister, very English with his red cheeks and twinkly little eyes, very obviously bored to be conducting a service for a boy he had not known. Jan had met him only yesterday, disliked him on sight, perhaps only because of his response to Jan's request that a few words in Polish be said over the dead airman.

'*Polish?*' The twinkly eyes had all but laughed. 'If you'd said French I could have obliged, or maybe a bit of Spanish ...' He spread clean, fat little hands over camphorated vestments.

'I can speak for him myself,' Jan offered.

The twinkle faded. 'But you're not ordained!'

Jan kept his voice even. 'Perhaps under the circumstances?'

Dimpled hands closed plumply over a blue prayer book. 'I'd like to accommodate you but it would be setting a precedent, you see. Anyway, he wouldn't hear you, would he?'

No, you sanctimonious little hypocrite, but the others would hear me; they'd know that if they die here or some other strange place there might at least be something familiar about their going, before the earth closes over them ... It was no use. The man was immovable, and as he mumbled now over Kaz's coffin Jan only half-listened.

'... this young man so far from his earthly home ... gone to that Heavenly rest for which we all yearn ...'

Rest? Speak for yourself, foreigner. The very last thing Kaz ever yearned for was rest. He was young. He wanted to do, to be.

'... and so we join together to mourn with his comrades ...'

Jan looked up. Lallie was watching, smiling at him across the pews. He felt the edge of his anger begin to soften and exhaustion creep in to replace it.

'... and consign this our brother to His peace –'

The shriek of a siren cut the minister's mumble. He gave a shrug and brought the service to a quick finish. As Kaz was lowered into the brown earth of England a dog-fight began in the heavens above them.

Back at the cottage Jan's anger began to return as they served tea to Joe and Millie and Neil. Joe, it seemed to him, could scarcely wait to brush Kaz's dust out of the way before launching into a spirited plea that they spend the rest of Jan's leave at Eccles Place and that Lallie remain there afterwards. The dogs were missing her something fierce; the vicinity of the airfield was clearly too risky for his daughter – witness the dog-fight still going on and the distant crump of bombs; and surely Jan would be able to concentrate on his flying much better without the worry of a wife on the ground who could be bombed out of her bed before he arrived home from work?

Work? Joe equated what the bombers did over Germany with work? As in a foundry? As in bigger orders? As in reaping bigger profits? But Lallie seemed to be handling her father nicely and Jan was glad to turn his attention to Millie. Today he felt more drawn to his mother-in-law than to any of the others, even to Lallie, and he took Millie into the garden to show her the last of the roses.

She touched his arm. 'I *am* sorry about your friend, love. He seemed like such a nice lad when he came to the wedding. Makes you think, doesn't it? A young fella like him ... never hardly got started before he was done for. His Mum and Dad must be in such a stew, poor things.'

'It may be some time before they find out,' he said quietly.

'That's a blessing then, isn't it? My Gran used to say, if there's one thing keeps better than salt cod it's bad news ...' She pulled at a few faded leaves with surprisingly graceful fingers. 'You've heard nothing about your family yet, I suppose?'

'Not yet ... I keep writing but ...'

She sighed. 'Aye ... but you'll hear someday, love, never fear.'

The funeral had upset Lallie more than she'd allowed the others to see, and it was a relief when Daddy and Neil took a walk around the village and left her alone to wash the tea things, Jan and Mum just visible through the kitchen window.

It wasn't only the image of the box being lowered into the grave and the thought that it could so easily have been Jan in it instead of Kaz – though the thought had been there, and very strongly, always would be, now. But it was also the minister, the whole paraphernalia of death, the church … Her religious views had always been ambiguous, alternately fogged up by certainties and doubts. Her parents never bothered much with church, but when Lallie was very small Mum had taken her by the hand every Sunday afternoon and deposited her, starcard in hand, at the Sunday School entrance. The starcard looked a little like a bankbook, and Lallie felt vaguely that goodness would somehow accrue in it as surely as interest accrued in the bank account Daddy had opened for her with the first profits from the foundry. The starcard was the most important part of Sunday School. You could earn three possible stars each week. Just for showing up they gave you a green star; for sitting quiet during the lesson and not chattering to your neighbour you got a silver star; if, in addition to being there and keeping quiet, you were able to impress the teacher with what he perceived to be a reverent and spiritual nature, then you got a pat on the head and a gold star that he personally licked and stuck in the appropriate square.

Lallie never got the gold, or even silver, just a neat row of green stars for being there. Perhaps Daddy was the reason. He always came to get her when class was over, and his greeting never varied as they hurried down the church steps and up the hill to Eccles Place.

'Well, what rubbish did they stuff you up with today?'

One Sunday Lallie was sent home early with a sore throat. As she ran into the house she was astonished to find the living room and kitchen empty and the fire banked up as if the house was to be empty for hours. Panic-stricken, she rushed upstairs, only to find her parents' bedroom door not only shut but *locked*, incomprehensible noises coming from the other side. Her small fists hammered on the polished door and there was a sudden scuffle from inside, her mother exclaiming '*Oh, my stars*!' as she tied her dressing gown cord and hurried Lallie into the kitchen where she gave her orange juice and aspirin, flitting all hot and flustered about the stove as Lallie obediently drank.

The Sunday School class eventually died of inertia, and she was at least twelve before she again went to church with any regularity. At some point (perhaps connected with the facts-of-life book Mum gave her) they decided her time should be occupied with something other than hop-scotch and skiprope and unsupervised walks in the park.

'Who knows what riffraff you could get mixed up with,' Daddy said. So once again she was encouraged to attend church, specifically the choir.

'She'll meet a nice class of young people,' her mother reasoned.

'She couldn't come to much harm, anyway,' her father admitted.

Lallie had a good voice, light but true, and she enjoyed singing, so she became a regular at choir practice. Neil was also in the choir, for reasons more profound than her own. Neil had faith in a way she did not. He never questioned his. The difference came to the surface every now and then, as it had today at the funeral. Seeing him now gravely pacing Hempton High Street with her father she felt that Neil Armott may well have been the only one in the congregation to respond to the death of Kaz the way the church seemed to intend. His head had been bowed in grief at first, but then, at the clergyman's words of affirmation, the promise that Kaz was with God, gone to that Heavenly rest, Neil's eyes had lifted to the altar, visibly comforted. Yes, Neil believed.

Mum believed of course, her faith homespun, vaguely glued together with the precept that Gentle Jesus Meek and Mild watched over little children; God looked after everyone else, though not quite so well. And Daddy, if he'd had a God at all (not that he would!), would have created Him in Joe Wainwright's image, a Yorkshireman and a foundry owner who took care of his own. Bright-eyed boys like Kaz dying too soon, and all that concerned Daddy was Mum and herself –

and probably Neil. Were other people any different? She thought not.

And Jan? In four months of marriage the subject had barely been raised, didn't seem important. She knew he'd been brought up a Catholic of course, and Catholic friends had hinted (not in Daddy's hearing) that in time she might want to 'take instruction'. They made it sound like a dose of medicine.

Stacking the clean saucers in the cupboard she decided it wasn't the divisions of religion that disturbed her, it was religion itself. It would be comforting to believe, but in whose God? And what did it all stand for? Loving one another as she'd been led to believe? or killing one another as she was beginning to suspect? If God was the loving creature of Mum's comfy expectations, why was quick little Kaz slowly rotting in the cemetery down the street?

Millie and Joe were staying over so they could go to the mess party tomorrow night. Millie appeared to have reservations about it, but Joe knew he wouldn't hear them until they were in bed and he was just about to drop off. He was correct.

'It doesn't seem right,' she said. 'A party right after that poor lad ... well, you know.'

'I don't know any such thing. Men are killed every day at these places. Where would they all be if they wailed and whined for months on end? You have to be realistic. The world doesn't stop spinning because one lad snuffs it.'

'Well, it should!' Millie said with some vigour, turning away and pulling the covers over her ears. A minute or two went by, then: 'They seem happy, don't they?'

Joe groaned. He didn't want to talk and he especially didn't want to talk about that! 'I've no idea whether they are or not. I do know I don't like her living in this place. It's a proper pleck. Lino on the floors, nothing but a two-ring gas stove to cook on, and this bed's like a bloody board.'

'You're forgetting about our first place over the smithy, I reckon. Compared to that, this is a palace.'

'Aye, but we'd never known any better, had we? It's different for Lallie, poor lass.'

'She doesn't seem to mind. I doubt she even sees it. They were lucky to get it, Lall said he hunted high and low –'

'Well, he found one and it's low. I don't know how she stands it.'

'She's in love,' Millie said, the slight flag of challenge in her voice.

'So you keep telling me,' he said with some weight. 'Let's wait and see if she's in love in six more months, living here – if she's alive.'

'Now, now Joe, you know fine and well we get as many sirens as they get down here. It's six of one and half a dozen of the other. You'll not get her back like that. She's happy.'

'But will she be happy next year, that's what worries me.'

'She will if somebody minds his own business.' The covers were once again over her head, this time for good. Even when he laid a tentative hand on her hip there was no response.

Jan ached to be away from Hempton, the roar of the aerodrome, the drab camouflage of its buildings, the talk in the mess, the party. For him it was a weary affair, lit only by Lallie, a fragile flower in dusty rose, and by Millie, who'd insisted on black.

Lech, Roman and Bolek were at a nearby table for four, the empty chair a shrieking reminder of Kaz. A new front gunner was already assigned, a quiet youngster named Leon, who was from Kalisz. That was as much as Jan knew of him, or wanted to know. Easier not to know them at all, then if they came a cropper ... The others must have felt the same, for the new man was not at the party. Joe, of course, was. And must be entertained.

On being introduced to Squaddie, then in turn to the wing commander and the mess sec., not forgetting the barman and sundry others in their progress across the crowded mess, Joe's greeting hardly varied.

'Wainwright, that's right, Wainwright Foundry ... Lallie's father, you'll have met her ... that's right, in pink ... well, of course *I* think so, but then I'm partial, I'm her father. Business? It's bloody booming, naturally, must keep you lads in hardware, you know – *and* my little girl there in pretty frocks ...'

It was as if he saw none of the faces he spoke to, was merely bent on impressing them with his connection to Lallie. He might as well have hung a label on her: JOE WAINWRIGHT'S PROPERTY – HANDLE WITH CARE. Had Jan been less tired he would have been furious, would have reacted in some way. As it was he smiled the right smile, danced with the right ladies in the right order, ordered the right drinks and waited for Lallie's signal, which came earlier than he could have hoped.

'I think we should call it a day,' she said to her father. 'I'm tired and I'm sure Mum must be – and you've a long drive home.'

Millie agreed, picked up her handbag and they were out – but not before Joe remembered he hadn't said goodnight to Neil.

When their hooded tail-lights winked a final goodbye and turned into the main road Lallie reached up and kissed him, enveloping him in the light, lovely fragrance that seemed to belong only to her. 'Tomorrow we'll be gone too, just the two of us.'

'Am I to know where?'

'Why don't we just drive until we come to somewhere perfect?'

Somewhere perfect – but where in all of summer-sweet England was perfect now?

With Jan asleep beside her she drove west and still farther west, all the way to the sea. Isolated villages slipped by; red flags of hollyhock and climbing roses still bloomed on whitewashed cottage walls; scents, now of fresh-cut meadows, now of sea and salt and marsh grasses, drifted in the open windows. Occasional glimpses of ocean, wrinkled by distance, sequined by sun, yellow sands and hot, brassy sky all ran by them – except barbed wire now latticed the beaches and barrage balloons like tethered whales floated in the afternoon sky. Reminders were everywhere. Road signs painted out or removed, schoolboys with gas-masks slung on straps around their necks, and every few miles another public air-raid shelter. Above them planes endlessly patrolled the coast.

She glanced at the sleeping face beside her. So worn ... there *must* be a place, but where? Even as the thought formed she knew where, a place so sleepy even war could not possibly have shaken its stupor. She turned back inland.

The resort was an old one, a little gone to seed since that distant summer Mum brought her here to shake off a stubborn bout with bronchitis. Small chalets, much in need of paint, ringed a lake not very much bigger than Hodgson's duckpond, but willows fringed its cool green water, dappled trout hid under its banks. In spring there were violets and wild iris – but it was late summer now, no flowers, no people, no cars. For one dejected moment she thought this place, like many another, was closed for the duration of the war and she was about to back out of the cracked driveway when she spotted the sign in the window of the lodge. OPEN.

There was movement on the seat beside her. He stirred and sat up, brushed his hand across the nape of her neck.

'Are we here?'

'We're somewhere. Whether you'll want to stay –'

'I do.'

'You haven't even looked!'

'I've looked at you. For the next ten days that's all I want to see.' Already he was beginning to look rested, the blue eyes tender, less strained, his mouth softer as he looked at her. 'You're beautiful.'

The odd note in his voice made her smile. 'You sound surprised!'

'I think I'd forgotten ...'

The knot of anxiety she'd been carrying for oh ... months and months began to melt. It would all be all right now ... must be.

The door of the lodge swung open and a woman in a coarse apron clumped towards them, a couple of terriers worrying at her heels.

'Off with you – get away inside!' She waited until the dogs retreated to the porch before she approached the car. Lallie asked if there was a chalet vacant and was surprised at the bitterness in the woman's answering laugh. 'Vacant is *all* we are since the war. Pick whichever one you want,' she muttered.

Before Lallie had a chance to speak Jan said, 'The quietest.'

The quietest was down the lane and out of sight, in amongst a stand of sycamores. There was a rowing-boat they could use and a small dock, and they could get tea and toast of a morning if they had a mind, '– but no meals! I don't bother with them these days.' Which meant they'd have to go down to the White Swan for lunch and dinner. Lallie was about to demur – a holiday with no meals available? – but Jan quickly told the woman the chalet would be perfect, just perfect.

It was just a little shabbier than she remembered. A double bed with a faded counterpane, a small table and two chairs, a worn moss-green carpet and a bathroom no bigger than a clothes closet. One large window, but it looked out onto the circular lake, a plate of beaten gold now in the sunset, gently lapping at the shore.

The instant they were alone he stretched himself on the bed and pulled her towards him, his cheek against her hair, his lips brushing her forehead. '... I thought it would never happen, that we'd finally have some time ...' His voice was husky, heavy with import, and she thought to lighten the moment.

'Silly, we've had ages and ages!'

'We've had almost nothing yet,' he murmured, barely moving, kissing each of her fingers very slowly, his lips lingering over palm and knuckle and wrist as if to eke out the seconds, spend the minutes carefully, like a child warming pennies in his palm until the very last moment, then counting them down slowly, one after the other. 'Since we started ops ... each time I've looked at you, kissed you, each time we've cooked a meal, made love, taken a walk or a drive, always at the back of my mind I've had the thought that it could all be for the last time ... and now we've got days and days and days ...'

She reached up to loosen his tie but he stayed her hand. 'No, not yet. I want to tell you. So many times when you waved to me through the hedge as I went to briefing, the picture of you stayed in my head all the way ... you can't imagine how often I wanted to turn back, do a Bura ... you know, find some small fault with the engines or the gauges, some excuse, *anything* so I could turn back, crawl into our warm, safe bed –'

'You'd never do that,' she whispered, filled with pride, 'no matter how much you wanted to.' She tried to see into his eyes but he'd turned his head to the open window.

'If I'd done that on the last raid – I could have, you know, we got shot up pretty badly over the coast – if I'd turned back then, Kaz might still be alive.'

'You couldn't have known.'

'Yes I could. I knew we weren't getting enough altitude, I knew it would be dicey over the target, difficult to get home.' His fingers tightened over hers. 'If I'd just taken us in higher, we were so damned *low* –'

'But you couldn't!'

'I knew that, knew the risks, and I still kept on going ...'

He turned to her then, reached up and drew her cheek against the fine gold hair of his chest and it was as if she were breathing him in, as if there was nothing anywhere but the lake and the willows and the two of them who, slowly and sadly and filled with love, became one. But not like before, not anything like before. Now there was no urgency, no desperation, nothing to think about except each other, except fingers softly touching skin and healing as they touched, lips touching lips, lips touching cheek and breast and hair and thigh, cool and smooth in the twilight, then warm and liquid as the breeze quickened the lapping of the waves.

The days passed like dragonflies on the lake, darting quick as fish one moment, hovering endlessly the next. They loved, rowed on the water, loved, swam to cool themselves and loved again, fished lazily and unsuccessfully in the early evenings, ate spartan dinners at the White Swan and forgot, by the time they reached the chalet, what it was they'd eaten. The tiny hot-water cistern could produce only enough for one bath so they shared, soaped each other with tenderness, and loved again. It was as if they had only the one body constantly aching to give itself pleasure. He watched her, smiling, as she brushed her hair; she watched him, utterly absorbed, as he shaved, feeling the rasp of blade on flesh as acutely as if it were her own cheek. Never had they been so close and never – one morning near the end of their stay – so far apart.

He rowed them to the other side of the lake, their favourite spot under an old sycamore with its carpet of moss spread seemingly just for their pleasure in its shade. He murmured, as he had a dozen times before, about how clever she'd been to find them just this perfect place. They were nibbling sprigs of watercress that grew down in the rushes, lying idly on their backs looking up into a sky of perfect, cloudless blue when a Sterling, quite low and obviously damaged, roared over their heads. His face changed on the instant, suddenly as taut and strained as when they'd arrived. To divert him she told him how she and Mum came to be here before, how Daddy worried so about her persistent cough. So perhaps she *did* go on about Daddy just a wee bit, about him calling in first one doctor and then another, but just to take Jan's mind off the plane, that's all, not noticing his eyes darken until she was saying:

'– and so Mum finally brought me here, so you see I'm not so smart as you think. I knew the lake was here all the time,' and then looking up at him, seeing the set of his mouth, feeling the chill.

'You mean your father actually let you out of his sight?'

'They were busy at the foundry. He couldn't get away.'

'Yes of course, I forgot. He had to keep his pretty daughter in all those "expensive frocks".' He mimicked Daddy's tone so perfectly that at any other time she would have laughed. She should have laughed now but the words came out before she could think, before she could stop them.

'I *knew* you minded when he said that in the mess, I just *knew*!'

'He wasn't very tactful – or truthful. He knows perfectly well I can keep you in frocks –'

'But that's just Daddy's *way*! He doesn't *mean* anything by it –'

'Then why say it?'

'Oh, I don't know, and what does it matter?'

'He says it to impress.'

'Daddy doesn't *have* to impress *anybody*!'

'But he tries, how he does try.'

'Are you saying he's a show-off? My father?'

'Yes.'

If she'd just let the word lie there, pretend she hadn't heard it, but the silence was stretching between them and she was so *angry*!

'You're jealous. You're jealous of my own father.'

'*He's* jealous of *me*. He can't stand the thought of you being married, not being his personal property any more.'

'*That's not true*!' she cried. 'That's not true at all – he was simply dying for me to marry Neil –'

'Neil, yes. Then you'd still be Daddy's girl.'

'I *am* still Daddy's girl. I'm his daughter. I love him.' The next words flew off her tongue quick as knives. 'You'd be singing a different song if it was *your* father bragging about *you* – oh no! how *could* I have said that, pretend I didn't say that … I'm so *sorry*, darling, so terribly sorry …' Too late she put her hands to his ears, too late she covered his face with kisses as sycamore leaves trembled above them, dry as old love letters with summer's ending.

Then he was kissing her too, cupping her face in his hands. 'I'm sorry, too. We must not fight. It's not your fault about my parents … and perhaps I *am* a little jealous of your father, I'm jealous of anybody who's known you all your life.'

'Oh, not Neil, you couldn't possibly –'

He laughed then. 'No, not Neil, I'm sorry for Neil. He lost you.'

She wanted to say Daddy had lost her too, but she knew it wasn't and wouldn't ever be true. Daddy would never lose her.

CHAPTER SIXTEEN

The threatened invasion had not come. The Luftwaffe, having failed to knock out the airfields, set its sights on bigger targets. Newsreels punched home the crippling raids on London; the King gravely inspected new ruins; the Queen, with sombre dress and motherly smile, stepped daintily through the rubble.

To the north Joe's foundry was still intact, as was most of Sheffield, unaccountably left alone for the moment except for regular nuisance-raids of a bomber or two – not enough to inflict much damage, just enough to sound the alert, get people out of warm beds and into damp shelters.

Life at Hempton was balanced on the knife-edge of tension and relief. Cologne ... Essen ... Hamburg ... Emden ... names as familiar now as London, as Warsaw. Lalka's crew still led a charmed life, although Lalka herself was now Lalka III – her predecessors long since riddled beyond repair and melted down for scrap.

Jan was all angles and sharp edges; Lallie thin-drawn, flinty with everyone but him. From her count of the landings she knew exactly how many crews did not return, but she no longer asked who they were. She no longer went to the mess to see the new faces, nor did she let herself speculate on old faces not there. Blinkered, like a racehorse taking the curves, it was possible to go on. She knew, now, how to receive Jan when he came home in the early mornings. The set of his mouth told her if the raid had been a bad one or just routine, told her whether to offer him breakfast and some kittenish reference to Flash Harry or simply to pour him a large Scotch and hold him until he slept. Sometimes he slept heavily until twilight; more often he tossed and turned, bathed in sweat, muttered of Mamunia or flak or trains or oranges or Kaz ... As he slept again she'd wonder about the oranges, remember their pitted, aromatic peel with sudden thirst. Had it been so long? Oranges were for babies only now, and not many even for them. Then she'd think about babies, of wanting one, so that if (not that it would happen, or course) but if one morning he didn't come back she'd have something of him to keep for herself, the way she had Kaz's silver cup. Then he'd wake again, automatically reach for her hand as she towelled off his face and sweat-darkened hair, the pillow damp under his head.

'I keep seeing –'

'Don't think about it, darling.'

He shook his head. 'I keep having this dream. I'm looking into a window and I can't see through it – it's crimson, I think

171

with sun – and then somehow I'm on skis, probably in the Tatras, and this hole opens up in the snow and there's a face in it ...'

'Yes?'

'That's just it. Up to that point it's more or less always the same, but I don't ever want to see the face and I feel myself struggling to wake up ...'

'So you never see who it is?'

'Oh yes, if I can't wake up fast enough, but it's always a different person. Sometimes it's you, sometimes your father, once it was a face I met on a train ... but the point is I'm so *relieved* that it's not someone else, and I don't even know who it is I'm afraid of seeing.'

The eyes would close, a tracery of thin blue veins on transluscent eyelids, impossibly delicate when she remembered the weight of the Wellington and the void between earth and sky. Sometimes she'd catch him watching her when he thought she wasn't looking. His mouth would be straight, his eyes an intense, burning blue. Out of a silence he'd ask odd, unconnected questions.

'Could the crew come to Eccles Place for Christmas?'

'Of course, if they don't mind doubling up.'

'Will the choir remember *Dzisiaj w Betlejem*?'

'Sure to,' she lied.

'You *do* remember where the cheque book's kept?'

'In the desk drawer, where else?'

'I've sent them your photograph, did I tell you?'

Three times, to her certain knowledge, he'd sent copies of the wedding pictures to his parents' old address. 'You told me.'

'They'll still want to see you, you know, even if ...'

'They'll see both of us,' she said, and changed the subject.

Neil was a help. Too much night-flying had brought on a vision problem, and he was grounded until it abated. He saw them often now, ostensibly to pass the time but always watching for cracks in the shell Lallie seemed to be forming about herself.

It was too much, he thought. Too much for Jan, too much for Lallie. There'd been too many ops. He'd flown continuously except for that ten-day break about which they'd

172

both been so secretive, from which Lallie had returned looking so heartbreakingly happy. She didn't look happy now, not to Neil. She smiled a lot, yes, and even laughed, but it was brittle laughter, the kind that could give way in an instant to tears or to crack-up. In his weekly letter to Joe he was careful to mention only that Lallie looked beautiful as ever; she did, but in a distant, abstracted way, as though part of her listened to you, smiled at you, while another part trembled on a hidden precipice, waiting ... To tell that to Joe would surely bring on another round of the circular argument that Lallie return to Eccles Place. Which could be disaster. The difference between Lalka's crew and those shot down in flames or captured was the steadiness of Lalka's pilot. And what held Lalka's pilot steady was Lallie Wainwright (even now he could not bring himself to think of her as Lallie Kaliski).

He went often to the cottage, sometimes to take Jan fishing when bad weather precluded flying, sometimes to play Monopoly with Lallie after the squadron roared eastwards to Germany. At least it kept her mind off the counting, he thought.

... four ... five ... six ...

Only half of the squadron taking off? No. There went the other six. Not to Essen, don't let it be Essen, not since Kaz –

And now over the thunder of the engines Neil was trying to say something.

'What?' she said. 'I missed –'

'You're on Bond Street. Aren't you buying? You've already passed up Park Lane and Mayfair.'

'Yes, yes all right.' She dragged her mind back to the gameboard. Neil was shaking the dice irritatingly loud and long; by the time he'd done, the squadron was nothing more than a distant drone.

'It's not Essen, Neil? Just tell me that and I won't ask –'

'It's not Essen, and you still owe the bank for Bond Street.'

'Bremen?'

He held up his hand. 'They won't be back until at least four o'clock and it's not even midnight yet. Can we get on with the

173

game? I'm buying King's Cross Station, so watch your step.'

It was the coming back that was the worst. Had they really been on target? How to tell with the whole thing under pink smoke? Was Lallie asleep yet? – of course she wasn't. Where the hell was the German coast? Once through that he could sit back, switch to autopilot. Damn it, they should *be* there by now ...

'Here she comes,' Roman said at his shoulder. 'And a nice warm welcome by the look of it.'

They were almost through it when one late burst of flak ripped into the middle of the fuselage. Oh hell, not the undercart again! The plane rocked, lurched, filled with smoke. The oxygen system. Out of the corner of his eye a sudden bright flash. *Christ!*

'Get the damn fire out!'

Roman was already ripping off his Mae West jacket to smother it –

Too late.

For just long enough they made a perfect target. Every flak-battery on that stretch of coast zeroed in ...

Lallie was winning. She now owned Pall Mall and Mayfair and Trafalgar Square, all crowded with little green houses and red hotels. Despite glancing at her watch every few minutes under cover of the tablecloth, despite not caring if Neil landed on the utilities (when had she bought those?), despite not hearing a word he said to her all night, her pile of money kept on growing. Not for the first time, it crossed her mind that Neil just might be cheating against himself, but if he were, did it matter?

Every hour or so he piled more coal on the fire, and at two o'clock he made her eat a poached egg on toast because, he said, if she were not careful she'd be airborne herself. At that weight, just one good breeze –

'And if *you're* not careful you'll turn into a fussy old woman,' she told him, sorry as soon as she'd said it. It wasn't Neil's fault he was safe down here while Jan was somewhere up there.

174

The first plane came limping in just after 4.00 a.m., a thin whine then a troubled roar. Nothing, then, for some time, then suddenly a queue of them, one after the other. Under the table her fingers kept score. Six down already, and the drone of others waiting their turn at the runway. How many others? Sometimes – not often – they all got back. If Neil would just *shut up*!

'You're taking the skin off me tonight,' he said, moving his old-shoe token into JAIL. 'I'll have to mortgage the Old Kent Road. Now you get three free shakes.'

Another Wellington taxied in, its engines purring to a stop. How many was that? Eight? No, seven –

Neil pushed the dice toward her. 'Are we playing or not? Shake, girl, shake!'

I am shaking, I am shaking ... but here was another and now another. 'I think that's nine,' she said.

'At least. And there's debriefing so it'll be some time yet. I'll pour us a drink while you count up your winnings.'

Did he have to make such a clatter with the bottles and glasses? Must he slam the cupboard door like that? He'd have it off its hinges ... *oh, come on the other three* ...

'I can't hear any more of them, can you Neil?'

The shrug didn't sit well on him. 'There's always some who drag their feet coming back, you know that.'

Half past four. Fifteen men still not home.

Against Neil's protest that it was bloody freezing she opened the window. Chill dampness drifted into the cottage. A quiet chill. Nothing in the sky but stars. No lanky figure in Mae West and flying boots ducking through the gap in the hedge ...

Her arm brushed against Kaz's cup on the sill. She shivered. Something was happening to her jaw. Her teeth were trying to chatter and she bit down hard, tasted blood on her tongue. And who was that mewling and whimpering in her head? Stop it! Go out and look for him, he'll be talking targets or weather with Squaddie, stooging about when he could be ...

She already had her coat on when Neil caught at her arm.

'I'll go,' he said quietly. 'You know how they are at Control about civilians butting in. You promised, remember?'

'Hurry then, just hurry.'

She knew, even as she stood at the cottage door watching Neil fumble through the gap in the hedge, that there was no hurry. The night was too quiet, too far gone. A leaf from the apple tree rustled down onto dying chrysanthemums. The first frost of winter glinted off the ruts in the lane. Against the fence, the shadows of flowerpots left over from summer began to blur with morning. Mist over the airfield, no longer churned by propellers, hung in unmoving clouds. No ambulances waited on the perimeter road, and as she watched, the lights of the flarepath winked off.

No more planes were expected home.

She waited in a straight-backed chair at the table. After a long time she flung her Monopoly token at the fire but it missed, and the little flat iron clinked into the hearth. If Neil wasn't back in another half hour she'd go ... but ever since Kaz died she'd promised Jan she'd stay away from Control. At the time, she'd been glad to agree. The very walls reeked of tension, the WAAF at the board listening only to the signals, her eyes staring straight ahead at the blackboard, at the names still not checked off. Lallie especially didn't want to go now, reluctant to face the eyes of the returned crews, that quick flicker of relief (*I'm* all right, Jack) before they blinked it away with decent pity. She knew how it was, had felt the same way herself, sorry somebody was missing but fiercely glad that Jan was not.

And now he was. Had to be.

It was ages before Neil came back, at least an hour, and then he just stood in the doorway looking helpless, not *telling* her anything, why wasn't he *telling* her?

'Now don't cry, love, please don't start crying ...'

From nowhere, anger crept in and saved her. 'I'm not crying – just *tell* me!'

'They don't know anything for sure, yet ... hell, I'm sorry, love, I'm sorry, but Squaddie definitely saw them go down over the coast, said it was like bloody daylight what with the moon and the searchlights. He tried to follow them down to watch for 'chutes but then he got hit himself and his navigator got the chop, and about then Watson's kite exploded right in front of him and it was all just the devil of a mess ...' He floundered and tried again, his face pink with the effort. 'Anyway, the last Squaddie saw, he said it looked like Jan was trying to level off. Look love, he's probably wolfing down a plate of Wiener schnitzel in some cozy POW camp.'

'When will I know?' She could hardly believe it was her own voice. So cool, so remote ... 'How long before they tell me?'

'A day or so, maybe a week – it all has to go through channels. Just be patient ...'

It was the word 'patient' that almost did it, that brought her hand up to within an inch of his face, an inch away from all that loving concern, all that devotion. She hated him as he stood there, hated the faithful brown eyes that kept him on the ground while Jan was ... God, she'd have hated anybody in this minute. *Daddy, why didn't you tell me it would be like this?*

'I'm staying here until I know,' she said, very firm.

'You'd be more comfortable at home.'

'I *am* home.' She lied. The cottage was home only when Jan was in it.

'Maybe the minister from the village would be a help ...'

'No! He's a crêpe-hanger. I don't want him, I don't want anybody.'

'I'll have to call Joe, he'd never forgive me if –'

'I'll call him myself.' Her fingers flew furiously over the dial, as she prayed that her father answered. If Mum knew, no power on earth would keep her off the next train.

It was Daddy, grumpy with sleep. 'Thundering Heeley! D'you know what time it is?'

'Daddy, Jan's missing.' She told him the details quickly, in far fewer words than Neil had told her. '... and don't tell Mum yet, all right? She'll only get in a lather and –'

'Right.' An odd silence hung between them for a minute, then he said, 'I can be down there in two ticks if you want me –'

'No, really. I'm better on my own.'

'Aye. Well, you know where I am.'

'I know.'

He asked to talk to Neil then, and she walked out into the morning, glad of the cold which suited her feelings exactly. Neil caught up with her by the perimeter fence.

'Look Lallie, if there's anything I can do ...'

177

'There is. Badger the people at Records for his new address, it has to be Stalag something-or-other. I want it quickly.' Her voice was cold, imperious, one she wouldn't even have used on a delivery boy, yet she couldn't seem to change it, was afraid to change it. From some frozen corner of her mind came the realization she was incurring a debt that would have to be paid back someday; he looked wounded but resolute, and for the first time she knew what moved some people to kick out at a faithful dog when nothing else was handy.

'Look love,' he pressed, 'you'll have to consider all the possibilities. He *could* be a prisoner but then again …'

She looked over his shoulder into the mist. '*If he was dead I'd know.*'

In the days that followed it became her article of faith. If she assumed Jan was alive, he was. If, on waking in the too-quiet cottage, she felt the most timorous of doubts nibble at the edge of her thoughts, she spoke to them severely (and sometimes quite loudly) until they went away.

She tried to ignore the doorbell and the telephone, but could not escape the telegram from the Air Ministry telling her what she already knew:

… REGRET YOUR HUSBAND FLT.LT. KALISKI … REPORTED MISSING … ENQUIRIES … INTERNATIONAL RED CROSS … AWAIT FURTHER INFORMATION …

She creased the slip of buff-coloured paper into its original folds and pushed it under the dresser. Just as methodically she fended off fears that crept, sometimes little spiders, sometimes crouching tigers with blood on their teeth, through the days and the nights. There were things to do! His dress uniform to sponge and press, his civvies to take to the cleaners (he'd need them in a month or so), shirt-buttons to sew on, Kaz's cup to polish, the Triumph to wash, the cottage to clean, sixty minutes of every hour to fill. And when it was all done there were places she had to go, to see, to remember. Under that elm (it had been in spring leaf then) he'd kissed her. On that park bench they'd bickered gently about her monthly cheque from Daddy. 'We don't need it,' he said. 'He's just trying to help,' she answered. In this field they'd picked mushrooms, in that

178

one she'd hung a daisy-chain round his neck and dared him to wear it to Hamburg.

One evening she went alone to the Horse and Rider, sipped dry sherry in the snug and forced herself to picture him sitting opposite her.

He looked wonderful.

He looked alive.

Even then she didn't let herself cry – if she began now how could she ever stop?

It was eight days before the delivery boy came cycling down the lane with the second telegram from the post office. He seemed curious, inclined to linger in the warm kitchen. She hurried him off with a tip that widened his eyes and brought a surprised grin to his face.

Here it was, address-side up on the table.

She watched her hand inch towards it, then pull away at the last second. So sure it would hold good news but ... She turned her back, hardly breathing as she walked to the window and waited for the buff-coloured tiger to spring at her from its crouch. Daring it, she lifted Kaz's cup from the sill and ran her fingertips over its cool hollows, drew from its battered surface the courage to turn round and pick up the envelope. Wartime paper, processed and reprocessed, still warm from the delivery boy's pocket. The instinct to call her father, have him here when she opened it, was almost overpowering. Such a comfort to lean on him ... no! You've made it this far on your own ... Daddy's girl ... but the news wasn't here then ...

She ripped open the envelope, waited for the teeth.

... YOUR HUSBAND FLT. LT. JAN KALISKI ... REPORTED TO BE PRISONER OF WAR ...

Now she wept.

She wept for Jan, restless Jan behind bars, but *alive*. For little Kaz, who was not. For the unknown Watson's exploded crew, for all the nameless others she hadn't allowed herself to know. When the storm was over she called Eccles Place.

'Daddy? Jan's a POW. It's going to be all right! I'm coming home to wait ...'

CHAPTER SEVENTEEN

If Joe didn't see the change in his daughter, Millie did, each day a little more. The carefree girl who'd left on her honeymoon, all orange blossoms and innocence and sudden, impulsive gestures, was disappearing. The Lallie who'd come home to wait for war's end and her husband's release was quieter, given to long silences and walks across winter fields, her grey eyes waiting ...

Her life had a new centre. It wasn't the dogs any more, though God knew she loved them, kissed their pointy Afghan noses every chance she got; it wasn't the market garden, though she was over there every morning before the sun came up; it wasn't even Joe – not that he'd ever admit it, even if he knew. The single focus of Lallie's life now was Jan Kaliski. His letters, read a dozen times and answered the day they arrived, at length and in private. His clothes, brushed and aired to a rigid schedule. His parents, whose whereabouts she now made systematic efforts, through the Red Cross, to discover.

'She's wasting her time,' Joe said, smartly cracking his egg ration – one, boiled for three minutes, let stand for two – with the back of a spoon. 'From what I hear there's not much still standing over there.'

Millie passed him the salt, thinking how handsome he looked, full of life again now Lallie was back. 'She can but try. Your egg's not too hard, is it? Be a nice coming-home present for Jan though, wouldn't it, if she had some news ...'

'Coming home to where?'

'Here of course, when the war's over in a few months –'

'Months? You're off your rocker, woman. Years, more like. Look at this!' He passed her the morning paper. 'See the pounding they just gave to Birmingham? Last week it was Coventry. Before long it'll be us. Jerry's hardly got started.'

Oh dear, she was glad Lallie was at Hodgson's and couldn't hear him, or there'd be 'words' for sure. That her daughter would have to wait months to see her husband again was bad enough; she wouldn't tolerate even the suggestion that it might be much, much longer. 'Poor things,' she said, 'hardly seems fair, does it?'

Joe spooned up the last of the egg and spread marmalade on his muffin, tilting in his chair and stretching his legs. 'You never know, Millie. Being penned up like that might be the best thing that could have happened –'

'Oh Joe!'

'No, think about it. If he'd kept on flying he'd have snuffed it pretty quick I'm thinking.'

'No!'

He shrugged. 'Luck doesn't last for ever, does it? As it is, he's safe now for a year or two. He'll have time to think, and Lallie the same.'

'I can't see what –'

'Because you're a dreamer. You believe all the sloppy old sayings you were brought up on. "Absence makes the heart grow fonder." Not bloody likely. It sets it looking round for something nearer. Changes come fast in wartime.'

She thought back, remembering the urgency of everything then.

'No,' Joe went on, 'by the time he comes back they'll both see they've made a mistake.' He gave her an odd look, speculative. Wondering how far he could go? 'When the dust settles she can think about a nice quiet divorce ...'

Divorce? He was thinking divorce? The word knocked her speechless. Lallie *loved* Jan, really loved him, surely Joe could see that? Oh, he could put blinkers on when it suited him, could Joe! Why, even if Lallie *hadn't* loved her husband, she'd never ... people like them never even thought the word divorce, never considered it. Nobody they knew had ever ... Of course, Wallace Simpson a year or so back – but she was American so that didn't count – and a right old mess *that* made at the time. Joe would say she was thinking like Backenthorpe again, but how could she help it? She was Backenthorpe's product as Joe somehow never had been. Old ways were best. What couldn't be cured must be endured – and marriage wasn't a condition subject to cure. Whatever bed you made you had perforce to lie upon. You cut your coat according to your cloth and if it didn't fit you wore it anyway. But divorce – that was just Joe's wishful thinking. He was like one of those dolls you couldn't knock down. He was riding for another fall if he was thinking divorce. If there was one thing she was sure of it was Lallie's loyalty. Oh, that Joe! She couldn't believe he was glad Jan was a POW, no, she'd never accuse him of that, but he had perked up a treat since Lallie came home, whistled 'Bless 'Em All' again as he shaved, and even arrived from the foundry early enough to eat her dinners as she served them, not warmed up between two plates in the oven at midnight. No, he'd see nothing amiss in making hay while the sun shone, her Joe.

'I don't know,' she said, perplexed. 'I can't see Lallie wanting a divorce, no matter how long he's gone.'

'Not now you can't, but just wait. She's a sight happier now he's gone than she was the last time we saw her, you have to admit that.'

'The last time we saw her was at a funeral! And I'm not sure she's happy at all – I think she's just relieved Jan's all right.'

'She looks fine to me,' he said, spreading margarine on another muffin. 'Where's the butter? This stuff tastes like candle-fat.'

'I put the butter ration into a shortbread for Lallie. Needs the flesh, if you ask me. She's stretched a mite tight over the bone for my liking.'

He sighed, exasperated. 'You're never going to make a carthorse out of a thoroughbred no matter what you feed her.'

Millie tried to remember if he'd ever called *her* a thoroughbred – she was built on the same lines as Lallie – but the nicest thing he'd ever called her, even in his more tender moments, was 'a decent-looking lass, not run to seed like some'. A rare flicker of resentment stung just long enough to let her say, 'Divorce? That'd set some tongues aclacking.'

'Who cares?' The last of the muffin disappeared, followed by sweet tea and a sigh of satisfaction. 'Some folks never have enough to talk about. Time hangs heavy for 'em, I reckon.'

For Jan, the first days were depressingly long. The shock of capture had quickly given way to a tedium of barbed wire and leaden winter skies, turnip soup and slabs of coarse black bread, endless walks around the compound under the eye of armed guards high in their wooden towers, their mounted machine-guns trained on the prisoners below.

Around him, bored officers slouched in a motley assortment of clothing. The uniforms in which they'd been captured (Jan's was only marginally cleaner than most) were augmented by grey, prison-issue blankets and anything else that could conceivably be clutched about the shoulders to blunt the biting winds. Propaganda newspapers supplied by the captors were carefully folded under jackets and pants until too worn to deflect the cold; only then were they torn into squares and threaded on string for use in the latrines. Men of a dozen nations and numberless professions, all levelled down to rags and hunger and perpetual cold, each with his individual dream of normality. Roman, as he told Jan and the others almost every day, dreamed of potatoes fried in butter and sprinkled with dill, Janina across the table and a pitcher of buttermilk between them. Lech, taciturn as ever, wanted just one more night between clean sheets in a London hotel, popsies optional. The new front gunner, with several teeth broken in the crash-landing, bemoaned the lack of a dentist. Bolek swore he'd be a happy man if he just had the goosedown *pierzyna* he'd dragged all the way from Poland to England; it enraged him to think it was likely spread, light as air and warm as August, on the bed of some stranger at Hempton.

For himself, Jan yearned for hot showers and clean, dry towels and Lallie's elegant body, but mostly he needed to see the optimism in her wide grey eyes. Her letters tried hard, but with night and the silence of the camp all her determined cheerfulness crumbled to the naivety of a young girl trying to please her love.

'... *very* soon, darling, and you'll be home. Meantime I keep busy. Went to see the Red Cross people again last week. The woman was *so* nice I'm absolutely sure she'll be able to help. Mrs Hodgson's knitting you a sweater. It's the colour of pea-soup and has cable-stitch up the front except I think she's got it a wee bit wrong ...'

Inside the locked hut filled with the snores and grunts of sleeping men, the only item in her letter in which he could truly have faith was Mrs Hodgson's efforts with the knitting needles. Without the light of Lallie's eyes to fire him he could no more believe her estimate of a quick end to the war than he could convince himself of eventual reunion with his parents. No matter how well-meaning the woman in the Red Cross office, she could not locate people who no longer existed. With him in the camp were a handful of Polish airmen who'd left Poland well after the German occupation began. They all told the same story. The total devastation of Jan's old neighbourhood, fires that burned and smouldered for weeks under the onslaught of incendiary bombs and relentless shelling. Total breakdown of services. Thousands dead in the streets, thousands more trapped and dying under heaps of rubble. No water except what could be carried from the river, and that contaminated now. No supplies, no food, stories of shelled horses butchered even as they died, by men desperate for food to take to their families. How could his sick father and tiny mother have survived such destruction?

Now even Lallie's safety was in question. The camp radio, hidden under the floorboards of the kitchen and tuned to the BBC, told of increasing raids on the industrial centres of Northern England, of more and more civilians killed. In the darkness of the hut his fears for her grew as he remembered the casual satisfaction of a crew (any crew) hearing 'Bombs gone!', turning for home with no more than a passing thought as to where it was the bombs had gone. His Lallie, so carefree when first he'd met her, so untried ... Now the bitter pills of Joe Wainwright's worst predictions were coming true one by one. Himself a prisoner for the duration, her own little corner of

184

England threatened …

The familiar ache to hold and comfort her as she had comforted him was punctuated by the sudden snarl of one of the guard-dogs that nightly patrolled the compound, trained to bring down any prisoner who dared step out of the hut after dark.

There was no comfort anywhere, for any of them.

Except for the anxiety of never quite knowing how his captors were treating him, except for missing him as she would miss the loss of one of her own limbs, Lallie was not unhappy at Eccles Place in the first months of Jan's imprisonment. Once his absence was accepted she could admit to herself that she was relieved. No more ops, no more counting the take-offs and landings. Under all the tensions of Hempton the premonition had lurked, not too far back in her mind, that some night he would be killed, that one time he would go through the gap in the hedge and be lost to her forever. Now he was safe. No more combat for Jan Kaliski. His imprisonment became, in her eyes, their salvation. Perfect happiness had not been snatched away, it was simply in abeyance until after the war. He was safe and she was safe, and one day soon they'd be together again.

For now, being back at Eccles Place was a return to the womb, warm and familiar after the cold terrors of Hempton. She was back to drinking the water in which Mum had boiled Brussels sprouts on the vague premise that drinking the bile-coloured liquid was good for the complexion. Back to protesting that it tasted vile but drinking it anyway, back to Mum's vindication: 'You've never had so much as a pimple!'

Daddy was being an utter treasure. He stole time from the foundry and lunched her at the Grand, dinner-danced her at Cutler's Hall, and once drove her down to Hempton to pick up the last of the china and linens stored at the cottage. Neil was there, flying ops again now but making time to help them pack, and taking them to lunch at the Horse and Rider. The comfort of looking about her in the pub dining-room and seeing not one familiar face – except for the licencee, who seemed to share her vague sense of water having passed safely under a dangerous bridge. 'At least you know where he is,' he said, after he'd asked about Jan.

Then back to Eccles Place, to brushing and walking the dogs, working at Hodgson's in the mornings, the welcoming snort from Pearl, a plaintive moo from Bunky, then home to Mum and Daddy for breakfast.

It was only a few days after they'd been down to Hempton that the phone rang very early, just as she came in from the farm. Daddy picked it up in the hall.

'Yes,' she heard him say, 'of course it's Joe, Agnes. Who else would it be?' as she went into the warm kitchen and closed the door, not wanting to hear. He was always so impatient with Mrs Armott – not that she didn't deserve it!

When he followed her into the kitchen several minutes later he was as upset as she'd ever seen him. His fist shook around his pipe-stem and his mouth was tight and very pale, all the blood drained away.

'It was Agnes,' he said. 'Agnes Armott. Neil's had an accident. Crash landed coming in off a raid ...'

Oh Neil, poor Neil ... she tried to remember the last private words she'd said to him, when Jan was shot down, but the confusion of the night blanked them out. What she did remember was the tone in which she'd uttered them, cold and superior, weighted down with bitterness. 'How bad is it?'

His hands flew in the air in a rare gesture of helplessness. 'You know Agnes – too bloody well-bred to talk at all! His leg's smashed up – I got that much out of her – then she said something about his face and a fire ...'

No, not his face, all that patience and devotion she'd hated so much when – 'Where is he now?'

'A hospital near London, Agnes gave me the address. Finally. I thought I'd have a run down this afternoon.'

'I'll come with you.'

Mum was against it. 'Oh, I shouldn't if I were you, Lall. You know how he is about you. He'll be upset enough as it is, and if he looks ... well, you know ... not himself, he wouldn't want you to see him like that, love. He's had enough to put up with, God knows.'

186

Lallie sighed. Really, Mum's kindly light did shine off a dim bulb sometimes. Neil would *love* to see her, Daddy said so. 'Just what he needs!' he said. 'Cheer him up. We'll both go.'

The volunteer at the hospital brightened as soon as they told her who they'd come to see. 'Ah, Flying Officer Armott. What a lovely man! Makes you really believe the word 'patient' if you know what I mean ... such a favourite with the nurses already, they'd do anything for him, anything at all, and so good-looking.'

Good-looking? Neil? She'd never really thought of him as that, but perhaps if she hadn't practically grown up with him ... Then she realized what the nurse was implying, that he was *still* good-looking, had not been disfigured the way so many boys had. Again she found herself sending up a tentative prayer ...

His leg was in a cast and suspended on a pulley arrangement; a bandage covered one side of his neck and jaw, and the part of his face she could see was scratched and bruised, but his eyes lit up as they walked into the room.

As usual when he was in a sickroom, Daddy's approach was hearty.

'By God, you've really done it now, lad. You look as if you've gone fourteen rounds with Joe Louis.'

Neil grinned around the bruises, his smile as open as ever. 'They tell me I'll be gorgeous again in a week or two, when the swelling's down. There'll be a spot of grafting to do on the old neck – would you believe they're going to take the skin off my backside?'

Daddy's laugh boomed round the sterile white walls. 'That should get you up off your arse pretty sharpish, I'm thinking.'

A frown flickered for a moment, then was lost in the gauze. 'It's the knee that's the problem. They're talking about putting stainless pins in it ...'

'You see? Joe's never wrong.' He slapped the bedrail with a vigorous hand. 'I always told you your future was in steel.'

'But I'll have a bit of a limp, they'll not want me in the airforce now.'

'Their loss is Wainwrights gain, then. God knows there's plenty of work for you at the foundry. You'd best hurry up and

187

get back to the office where you belong.'

Watching them both, Lallie felt a quick surge of admiration for her father. Sympathy would have embarrassed Neil, as would obvious kindness; the bluff expectation that he'd be back at his desk in no time – and was needed there – was exactly the right tack.

'Don't listen to him, Neil,' she said. 'He's a slave driver.'

As they left him, Neil thought he'd never seen anything lovelier than the expression on Lallie's face as she looked at her father. Pride. He'd seen it there before and it always gave him a feeling of kinship. He was proud to know Joe Wainwright too, proud to have his respect. Mother, who'd left just before the Wainwright's arrived, had predicted Joe would expect him back at the office quickly. She had resented it in advance.

'A thoughtless man,' she said. 'But then, there are people in this world who take the last slice of meat off the plate without a second thought; then there are others, gentlemen, who would rather die. Your father was one of the latter.'

Who died, Neil thought. Died without ever giving me the least sign I meant anything more to him than his collection of first editions. To my father I was not a person. To Joe I always have been. A person with potential.

During the weeks of recovery, Joe Wainwright visited him often, though not again with Lallie. Neil's disappointment at her absence, though keen, was tempered by relief; she was not a witness to his clumsy first efforts at controlling the unfamiliar action of his knee. With time, and much excruciating practice in the hospital corridors, he could at last walk and turn with only a minimal limp. The bruises on his face were gone. When they finally allowed him to wear a shirt and tie he was pleased that the collar covered the skingraft on his neck almost entirely. Now he felt able to face Lallie again. For although he had long since accepted her marriage to Jan, some stubborn core in him could not give up wanting to always appear at his best for Lallie Wainwright. To him that would always be her name.

CHAPTER EIGHTEEN

'And how was London?' Lallie kissed her father's cheek as they manoeuvered through the surging crowds of the railway station. 'I thought you'd *never* get in!'

'Sorry love. The train stopped here there and everywhere. And crowded! Like bloody sardines, we were ...'

She hugged his Harris Tweed sleeve to her face, glad to escape the smiles of young women meeting their men in uniform. There was comfort in the tweed, the heather and tobacco smell of it as it scrubbed at her cheek. 'We'll soon be home,' she said. 'I'm parked right in front.'

'Good lass. No letter from Germany today?'

'How did you guess? Got two yesterday, though ...'

'Feast or famine, feast or famine. And how is he?'

'Ready to come back.'

They emerged into a brilliant night. Over factory roofs and a regiment of billboards the full moon rode serene in its scattering of stars. A stage set for lovers. A wave of loneliness poured over her, and she held tighter to her father's arm. How much longer would it go on?

Joe squinted up at the moon. 'Bright,' he said.

Lallie shivered, not from the cold. Such a night brought it all back, all the waiting in the dark bedroom of the cottage for the steady drone of returning Wellingtons ... how many would make it? ... seeing him caught in a web of lights ... She gave herself a mental shake. That worry, at least, was over.

'Did you look in on Neil?' she asked her father.

'Aye, last night. He's healing up a treat, might be home for good at the weekend, thank God.' He settled into the passenger seat with a grunt of relief. 'You drive, lass. I'm fair done in. Mum home?'

'You *must* be tired. It's Thursday, remember? She's taken Neil's mum to the Lyceum. She must have told you.'

'Oh aye. She told me something else, too.' He scrubbed at his eyes like an elderly, irritated child as his voice sharpened, anger lying just under the fatigue.

Here it came. 'Are you very cross with me, then?' she said.

He sighed and thumped his thigh with a large, gloved fist. 'I called home last night.'

'Mum said you had.'

'You were out,' he said.

'That's right.'

Silence for a second as she pulled away from the kerb, as he closed his eyes, Patience on a monument. She glanced at him under her lashes, waiting for his eyes to open.

'So where were you?' he said through clenched teeth.

'Mum told you where. I went into town and signed up for the ambulance service.'

'Oh, God save us! I told you to stay close to home! One of these nights there'll be such a bloody bust-up downtown.'

'Maybe so. That's what the Auxiliary's for, surely? They'll need every driver they can get if there's a blitz –'

'*If? If?* We're turning out steel hand over fist down there. Of course there'll be a blitz, no ifs about it. They'll have to clout us soon –'

'They already do –'

'Not like they will, you mark my words.'

'Then they'll need ambulance drivers, right?'

'You don't have to be one of 'em!'

'Somebody has to be – and I can drive,' she said reasonably.

He sighed, slumped again into his seat. 'I should never have got you a car, never. You know you're giving me grey hairs?'

'Oh, Daddy! Look, I promise I'll be careful –'

'And a fat lot of good careful's going to be when the big bombs come down –'

'I'll only be on duty at the weekends, except in emergencies.'

'Fine,' he said. 'I'll tell Hitler. Maybe he'll oblige us with a five day week – give his air force the weekends off.'

'Oh, now ...' Daddy *was* a grump tonight, she thought, swinging the heavy car into the Intake Road. 'Ministry got on your nerves, did it?'

He grunted. 'A pack of chinless wonders, the lot of 'em. Badgering me for more stuff – they think I wave a bloody wand and steel stacks up in the sheds all on its own. They've got requisitions and projections and communiques – and no more sense than old Hodgson's pig.'

'Pearl is a *very* clever pig –'

'Compared to that lot in London, I expect she is.'

Good. She'd got him away from the subject of ambulances. For now. Tomorrow he'd come back to it. 'Mum's left us a stew to warm up and she's bringing some sally-lunns from town. She said to be sure you didn't fill up on biscuits.'

He sighed. 'I sometimes wonder how Millie would occupy her mind if she didn't have food to think about.'

'Somebody has to think about it,' she said sharply. Just because Mum didn't keep up with the latest war news –

'You don't have to jump down my throat,' he said. 'I'm only saying she's a homebody. Anything wrong with that?'

Yes. What he implied, what she knew he thought, was that Mum was ... well, not too bright. And she wasn't, Lallie thought with a pang of guilt. In twenty-one years of marriage Mum hadn't changed one jot, while Daddy went from strength to strength. I'll not do that, she promised herself. I'll keep up. But her spirits lifted at the prospect of an evening at home with just Daddy. She loved having him to herself sometimes, batting the day around without Mum constantly pouring oil over waters that were not troubled, only bracing.

By the time they reached Eccles Place and he opened the garage door for her, they were laughing. A glass of sherry shared over the stove restored him completely.

'Now aren't you glad Mum thinks about food?' she said, ladling a second helping of stew onto his plate.

'It's not bad,' he admitted, 'not bad at all,' dipping his bread into the saucepan to get the last of the gravy before stretching himself out on the settee in front of the fire. 'Wake me up for the nine o'clock news, love,' he mumbled, and was instantly asleep.

She covered him with a tartan rug and settled the dogs for the night before writing to Jan, always the best part of the day, the closest she could get to talking to him. The sheets of creamy notepaper had an almost sensual quality as she imagined his long hands unfolding them, his thoughts eased away from barbed wire and shouted commands. That her words were read by censors was inhibiting – she sometimes wondered how much was left after both sides had run their pencils through – but the contact was renewed as she recounted everything she'd done since her last letter. She told him about her day at the farm, the horse's colic and Mr Hodgson's sciatica.

'... signed up to drive an ambulance. Daddy's miffed of course, but I doubt there'll be much for me to do. Only one visit from Jerry this week, dropped their load in Bush Park by mistake, killed off a park bench and the north wall of the gents' loo ...'

She nibbled at the end of her pen. Shouldn't have mentioned Jerry. They'd ex it out for sure.

'... Mum's at the theatre and Daddy's snoring on the settee, just back from London. He saw Neil down there, who sends his best and says he'll write you soon. His graft's raw still, and he limps a bit but Daddy thinks he'll be home for good soon – I just wish *you* ... but no, not that way. A lovely clear night. I look at the sky a lot and imagine you under the same stars. Do you have windows, I wonder, or just bars? I *hope* it's windows – it's *very* cold. I'm in front of a huge fire and the big green easy chair is empty and waiting for you. So am I. What idiot coined the phrase 'Out of sight, out of mind', I wonder?'

She sealed the letter and held it to her face for a moment before putting it out for the post and washing the dishes.

Nine o'clock came and went. She did not wake her father, had never intended to. His notion that the war effort would come to a sudden stop if Joe Wainwright missed a single news bulletin was just silly. Instead, she turned on the gramophone very low and listened to Vera Lynn, ached sweetly to 'We'll Meet Again' and 'Silver Wings in the Moonlight'.

Once she thought she heard a distant siren but when she opened the door everything was quiet. She closed it again quickly and made up the fire. Mum's play wouldn't finish for an hour yet, then the long chilly walk to the bus, unless she took a taxi – as if she would! Lallie shook her head and set a tray with her mother's favourite cup, the white china with a painted rose in the bottom.

Millie Wainwright entered into the world of the theatre with the same ingenuous pleasure as when she'd been a small girl watching the Punch and Judy show on Attercliffe Common from the perch of her father's shoulder. The lights, the costumes, the heavy theatrical make-up all opened up a world her own imagination could never have invented. Sitting in a cloud of Coty and cigar smoke and the rich smell of boxed chocolates, she relaxed into the red plush seat next to Agnes Armott and waited for the curtain to descend on the second act.

She'd seen the play twice before, so the happy ending was a pleasure all the greater for being deferred, and the interval, in any case, was an important part of her enjoyment of the evening. Rose velvet curtains closed on a flurry of applause, the signal for silver trays bearing pots of coffee, plates of wafer-thin cucumber sandwiches, sponge cakes dusted with icing sugar and filled with cream – well, mock cream, but that was just the war. Everything about the theatre seemed to whisper, very discreetly, that Millie Wainwright was somebody, was no longer the little millgirl from Backenthorpe who'd married an out-of-work blacksmith with not a hope in the world they'd ever have two shillings to rub together. The chinchilla Joe gave her last birthday (now hanging in the cloakroom next to a Persian lamb and a champagne mink) confirmed her station. She'd been scandalized at the cost, of course, and told Joe as much, but she stroked its dove-grey fur every morning with the same guilty pleasure as when she counted the tins of black market ham and salmon on the pantry shelf, or squeezed a hard-to-get lemon over a nice bit of Dover sole – though God knew when they'd ever see sole again now Jerry was sinking the trawlers. And lemons, well, pure gold they were.

'A lovely play,' Agnes was saying over the rim of her coffee cup. 'So kind of you to invite me.'

Millie sighed. Joe had Agnes down pat, her upper-crust accent and the slightly resentful quality of her gratitude. Eccles Place's monument to genteel poverty, Joe called her, although he did admit she'd done a good job with Neil. She was speaking again, eyes gone suddenly distant. 'I do miss not having a season ticket – we always used to until ...'

Until Mr Armott passed away. Millie suppressed a flash of irritation. Agnes' husband had been dead all of ten years, yet from her voice it could have been last week. 'Agnes,' she said, a little more briskly than she intended, 'I'm just glad you can keep me company. I don't like coming into town on my own and Joe can't abide the theatre, and as for doing the shops ...'

'Oh, the shops,' Agnes said faintly, as if shopping were not a subject she cared to think about very much. Millie could guess why. All that fancy schooling and then the poor dab had to make do with scrag-end of mutton for Sunday dinner, all tarted up with curry and raisins and a damn silly name like Lamb Calcutta. It didn't bear thinking about. Rationing was bad enough, but to be posh-poor into the bargain ... just thinking on it depressed her. She edged her foot under the seat until it encountered her shopping bag. She felt better, hearing the crackle of bakery wrappings that enclosed Joe's sally-lunns. If there was one thing Joe liked with his bedtime cup of tea it was a fresh sally-lunn, and you couldn't seem to get them much nowadays. She'd been lucky to get these, what with Agnes hanging about the art gallery oohing and aahing over this picture and that, and then the queue at Martindales'. It had been all they could do to get to the front of the line before the shop closed. She only hoped the icing wasn't melting off the tops.

'I wonder if Joe got home all right,' she said. 'I hear tell they're bombing the trains something fierce. Watch for the tracks, I expect. Wicked, they are.'

'I'm sure Mr Wainwright will be able to take care of himself,' Agnes said with a touch of asperity. 'A most capable man.'

'I suppose so,' Millie said, guilty again. Here she was fretting over nothing ... If she could only be like Agnes, who held all her worries inside where they didn't show, who sat calmly sipping coffee as if she loved it – and her boy in hospital waiting for his skin to grow back on. As always when she was with Agnes, the old mix of envy and regret swept over her, compounded now as the older woman's worn cuff brushed against her wrist. Though Agnes was too well-bred to admit she'd been hurt, Millie knew it stung when Lallie rejected Neil in favour of Jan. 'A foreigner,' Agnes had murmured when Millie broke the news of the engagement. 'Well, I'm sure I hope they'll be very happy.' And that was *all* she'd said about it, ever. If there had been any way of helping Agnes without also giving offence Millie would gladly have done it, felt the better for it. Less guilty. Poverty was humbling, who should know better than Millie herself? Thank God those days were over. Maybe if she got Agnes a nice leg of lamb for when Neil came home ... food *was* the staff of life, didn't the Bible say so somewhere? Even if Joe called the Bible a fairy tale for the weak and simple, *she* liked to believe there was something after all this. Otherwise it all seemed a bit pointless, didn't it?

The last-act curtain rose on a drawing room warm with amber light, and Millie slipped back effortlessly into the action of the play.

The ending was lovely, all smiles and tears and the girl melting into the arms of the hero; Millie, who remembered the curtain-line, mouthed it along with the girl, and when the hero kissed her it was as if he was kissing Millie herself.

Outside, the women buttoned their coats, Millie with a surreptitious stroke of the chinchilla, Agnes with a longing glance at a cruising taxi.

'If we miss the bus we'll get one,' Millie promised, clasping her elbow, 'but they're robbers, the way they charge. We shouldn't encourage them.'

Down the High Street, past the post office, whose clock said they had only a minute left –

'It's fast,' Millie gasped, 'always has been. Keep going, Agnes, we'll make it.'

They stumbled over the cobblestones on Spital Hill, past newstands whose cold headlines flapped in the piercing wind. The 101 bus was already revving up, the conductress's thumb on the bell.

'Come on Agnes, put a spurt on –'

When they finally collapsed into their seats they were speechless with the effort. The bus was loud and gaseous, its windows steamed and runnelled with the breath of munitions workers headed home after the late shift. Millie, still warm from the glow of the theatre, the chinchilla, and her triumph over rapacious taxi-drivers, chatted amiably with Agnes as the red and white double-decker shifted and changed and stopped and started at mean streets and city pubs. Even its engine seemed to sigh with relief when at last it flashed hooded tail-lights at the final straggle of council houses and turned towards the plush darkness of Norton's open fields. The conductress punched extra hard on the bell, her signal to the driver to get a move on. One last hill, approached with rattles and groans and a new influx of diesel fumes.

Agnes drew on her black kid gloves with the palms uppermost, but Millie had already noticed the broken seams on the backs and was careful to turn away. In the seat behind them a soldier sang 'I've Got Sixpence' in a slightly tipsy monotone. Three steelworkers and a couple of WAAFS took up the chorus ... *tuppence to spend and tuppence to lend* ...

Agnes sat in ladylike silence but Millie couldn't resist beating time on her handbag, mouthing ... *and tuppence to take home to my wife*.

The labouring engine and the voices and the bell quite drowned out the voice that came suddenly from above them. It was only at the last moment she heard it, too late to do anything but reach a protective hand across the sally-lunns.

It was after eleven when Lallie switched off the gramophone and lit the gas under the kettle. Mum should have been home ten minutes ago; the bus must be running late. She'd wait until she heard the brakes squeal at the corner before she brewed up – if there was one thing Mum couldn't stand it was stewed tea. Her father still snored gently on the settee, sleep and firelight softening his mouth until it looked almost, well ... tender. She poked up the fire and added a lump of coal very quietly so she'd be sure to hear the bus when it stopped.

The abrupt ring of the doorbell surprised her because she still hadn't heard the bus. She fumbled with the latch and thought for the briefest moment that Mum must have taken a taxi. *'What? And waste all that money?'* Lallie could practically hear her say.

It was the local bobby, grey and hollowed, whom she'd known all her life. He clutched a large brown paper bag in one hand and a hooded flashlight in the other, stamping his feet on the doormat against the cold.

'Lallie? Your dad home?'

'Oh dear, have we got a light showing again?'

'Nay, your blackout's fine, love. It's Joe I have to see. Is he in?'

After eleven at night for goodness sake? 'He's resting,' she said firmly. 'Some trouble at the foundry?'

The constable said nothing. She looked up into his face and felt the first flicker of real anxiety. Even in the gloom of the front porch the distress in his eyes reached out and trapped her. Layers of awareness spasmed and shut off, but from some small unguarded corner of her mind she heard Mum's voice. *'You'll have tea ready for me, won't you love?'*

'Daddy!' she called out on a note of rising panic. 'Daddy?'

He stood in the living-room doorway, rumpled with sleep, looking at first vexed and then troubled as he saw the bobby.

'I thought I heard the bell,' he said. 'What the hell is it? Come in, man, come in and shut the door –'

The constable stepped in, juggling paper sack and flashlight and his hard black hat. 'Christ, Joe, I'd give anything if it were somebody else ... I never ... I mean ... I wasn't even supposed to be on duty really but they were shorthanded so I said I'd go in and –'

'What the hell are you on about, man? Get on with it, do.'

197

Lallie looked from her father to the constable, watched narrow features settle into the patterns of condolence. His lips were working but nothing was coming out. Then Joe, too, was quiet, and Lallie felt the walls reach in, heard a roaring that blocked the constable's next words but she knew them anyway, had known when she'd looked into his eyes.

The bus. Of course.

'… hit the Arbourthorne bus, Joe. A Spitfire it was, shot up and trying to get back to the aerodrome. The conductress says it just fell down on 'em out of nowhere. One minute they were all singing, and the next –' He shook his head.

'Millie. Where's Millie?'

The constable's chin crumpled. 'I'm sorry Joe …'

'Bloody hell.'

Dazed, Lallie heard her own voice from a long way away, thready and childlike. 'But she *has* to come home, her tea's ready!' Then she was pulled into Daddy's rough tweeds and pipe tobacco and the midnight moisture on his cheek. She clung to him tight, tighter than she ever had before, afraid to be alone. *Oh Jan, Mum's dead and where are you, where* … The first sob tore at her throat.

'I know lass, I know,' Joe said over and over, while the constable stared at the toes of his boots. At last he coughed.

'I have to be going, Joe. There'll be arrangements to see to –'

'Bugger off, will you? Just bugger off.' His voice was harsher than she'd ever heard it. The poor bobby, and him only the messenger …

'Daddy, he's just doing –'

'– his job. Aye, his job. And now he's done it so he can push off.' A shuddering sigh shook the frame that held her. 'Where've you put her then?' to the constable.

God yes, where was she, was she warm? Such a cold night, where had they put her? The constable knew, of course. Bobbies always knew.

'She's at City General, for now.' Looking infinitely helpless, he set the paper sack on the burgundy carpet as if it were a bag of newlaid eggs. 'Her things. I thought as I'd bring 'em with me …'

Her father became painfully formal, very un-Joe. 'Thank you, constable, I'm much obliged. I'll call the station in the morning. Now if you don't mind ...'

So the sad messenger left and they were alone, Lallie and her father, in the quiet, Millie-warmed rooms gone so quickly cold. The hall clock that Millie had got from her grandmother, the clock she had wound every day of her life, ticked steadfastly behind them as Lallie let her father lead her into the living-room.

'What's this?' he said, puzzled, stubbing his toe on the paper sack as if he'd never seen it before. 'What the hell's this?'

'He told you. It's her things. Purse ... shopping bag, I suppose.'

A sack with Martindales' Bakery printed on it fell out onto the carpet. The sight of it seemed to pull her father together. Close to his chest she felt him fill with ... sadness? grief? Neither, it seemed.

'*Jesus Christ, she had to go! She had to go!* Running up to Sheffield for the shopping. She couldn't stay at home where she was safe, oh no, she had to go to town.' Veins appeared, blue and prominent, at his temples. '*She had to go to town, couldn't keep out of the shops, hunting up food when we've enough to feed a bloody battalion right on the pantry shelf –*'

'No! She wanted to see the play, too – you know how she liked to watch the actors ...'

He was gone, the bathroom door slamming behind him.

She sank onto the settee, the tartan rug still warm from his nap, still warm from before ... before the doorbell rang. It was the play, Mum wanted to see the play Jan, that's all, she just went into town to see the play and she didn't come back and she won't ever come back and *I need you, I need somebody here* ...

Her father was there again, his eyes red but dry, a glass in his hand.

'Here. Get this down you, love. It'll make you sleep.'

Raw Scotch burned her throat and she pushed it back at him. 'It's too strong, I don't want –'

'Do as you're told, there's a good lass.'

Like a child, she thought, like a child he talks to me, but she drank it down, recoiling from the strength of it. 'Don't be

199

vexed with her, Daddy ...'

His large hands opened and closed, then rubbed at his eyes. 'I don't know, Lall, I just don't know. God!' Bewilderment spread between them, gathered them in. 'You should be in bed ...'

Not the bedroom. It was empty. 'Not yet,' she said, 'I'm better down here with you.'

He tucked the tartan rug about her legs and pulled her head to his shoulder, rubbed her cheek with cold fingers. 'You're lucky,' he said suddenly. 'You got her looks.' And they held each other and cried. At some point she wondered dimly about Agnes Armott ... poor Neil ... then it was just all too much to take in, and she reached for the glass.

She woke hours later, cramped and cold. Her father's arm still held her but he stared stone-faced into the dying fire. It was true then. She touched his arm.

'Daddy ...'

He nodded. 'Aye. She's gone. There's just me and you now ...'

She wanted to remind him that there was also Jan, but Germany seemed very far away.

CHAPTER NINETEEN

Millie Wainwright was buried on a cold Thursday morning, among the sunken graves of Backenthorpe cemetery and close by the mossed-over stones of her gran and her great-gran.

By nine that night Sheffield was in flames, deep in its first true blitz. Joe was trapped in his foundry, all exit roads pocked by craters big enough to hide a truck in. His calls to the house, all his attempts to tell Lallie to stay home, went unanswered.

She was behind the wheel of an ambulance, the first time she'd been called to duty during an actual raid. An emergency. And she was frightened. Not of the bombs – she'd discovered in the last two hours that hovering death from above was not nearly so terrifying as the moaning heaps she was helping pull from the rubble and rush to hospital. At first she'd watched from the depot, stunned, as wave after wave of enemy bombers slogged across a brilliantly clear sky. The first intruders rained fire-bombs high in the hills which circled the city. Within seconds, trickles of flame were running down the folds of the hills, bright arrows pointing towards the heart of the city. So this was what they called a 'baptism of fire', she thought wryly, not yet afraid, secure in the sturdy vehicle around her, grateful for the duty nurse, Flo, who sat calm and solid beside her. Flo had done this before. She would know what to do.

The real horror started just as Flo squinted up at the surrounding hills and said, 'By gum, them fires are taking hold quick, aren't they?'

They were, and into the superbly lit arena the succeeding bombers thundered, black with menace and low enough to see the painted swastikas on their tails. Lallie's unit was ordered to the High Street, and from then on there was no time to think of anything but steering the ambulance through an obstacle course of overturned cars and dustbins, sheets of plateglass, downed lamp-posts twisted into surrealistic snakes.

They made it to the High Street just as the first heavy bombs crumped down on the familiar wide avenue of shops and restaurants, just as the city's largest department store toppled its treasures, floor by laden floor, into the street below. Silken scarves and leather gloves spilled among tweed coats and rolls of Axminster carpet. Brussels lace and a bolt of robin's-egg satin swathed a stout cabin-trunk that would not now sail the world in an ocean liner. Czech stemware and German figurines splintered democratically with Chinese porcelains and Wedgewood rose-bowls. The blast from a dozen bombs shattered Spode and Royal Doulton; caught up silver candlesticks and chafing dishes; hurled them into plateglass windows already buckling under the heat of fires that suddenly bloomed everywhere.

The next hours passed in a daze for Lallie. Gas mains exploded into enormous crimson blooms, lighting the target ever more brightly. With a full load of injured (and one who

201

died even as they loaded him onto the stretcher) they were on their way to the nearest hospital when a bomb fell directly in their path, picking up the ambulance and depositing it, right side up, on the sidewalk. When the dust cleared and Lallie once again had the steering under control, an elderly woman suddenly staggered out of a burning house, her flannel nightgown blazing about spindly shanks. Flo wrestled her to the ground as Lallie pressed a blanket around the flames, shocked when Flo asked for a hand in unloading the dead patient from the ambulance.

'Whatever for?' she said, numbed, her mind a blank.

'We've no room for him now, love,' Flo said. 'Got to take the old girl instead. The living have to come first. Pick up that end of the stretcher, there's a love.'

'We can't just leave him in the street!' Lallie protested, knowing there was nothing else they could do. Why hadn't they told her it would be like this? her head screamed as her hands steered the vehicle around overturned buses, their wheels still spinning. Button Lane was a sheet of flame. Behind the tea-urn of a workers' cafeteria in the Wicker, a young couple in evening clothes sat up stiffly in their Vauxhall sedan, their dead faces faintly surprised at being killed in so commonplace a seting. A jeweller's shop in Change Alley spilled melted gold into gutters already running with blood.

'How many trips have we made?' she said once, heading out of the hospital grounds.

'Six so far,' Flo said, giving her a shrewd glance which took in her tiny gold watch, the hand-tailored slacks now stained with blood and soot. 'All this is a bit of an eye-opener for you, I reckon. I'm surprised your family lets you do it.' There was a touch of patronage in the nurse's tone, and it stung.

'My father's at work,' Lallie said, 'my husband's a POW and my mother was buried this morning.'

Flo's hand patted her knee. 'Oops! I put my foot in it, didn't I? Sorry love.'

The easy sympathy jarred, but she said nothing. Hours ago she'd known that without Flo she would have been helpless. Flo shut off feeling and could therefore function. And because she was there Lallie could also function, though with nothing like the brisk cheerfulness of the professional. How could she? She'd never seen anyone dead until Kaz, and he'd been prettied up by the undertaker. Daddy hadn't even let her see Mum's body. Better remember her as she was had been his advice. Now suddenly there were dead everywhere. Avenues of fine homes and alleys of tiny row-houses all came to the same thing – bricks and sticks through which frantic fingers, some jewelled and some calloused, scratched and scrabbled in a desperate search for family and pets, and over it all the smell of molten metal, smoke, burning rubber, scream of bombs falling, now and then the chatter of machine guns as firemen on roofs were gunned down by diving bombers. Yes, she was grateful for Flo. How else could she have steeled herself to pick up a severed arm and lay it beside its unconscious owner on the stretcher – though she still wasn't sure why she'd done it. Just as numbly receive a newborn straight from the womb of a young woman whose two other children looked on, wide-eyed, as their mother gave birth and died in the middle of their school playground. Reach out and catch a black and white terrier running in crazy yelping circles on three legs, the fourth swinging to and fro under its open belly, gather it all up into a pillowcase and hand it to a fireman who mercifully bashed its head in with a fallen brick.

Without Flo or someone like Flo she'd be running in circles herself by now, as crazed and mindless as the black and white dog. As it was she operated like a robot, not quite believing any of it until a sustained and raucous whine from overhead filled her ears and the nurse's mouth was shouting at her to '*Get down! Get down!*'

It was almost daylight by the time Joe, eyes red-rimmed with smoke and fatigue, made it home from the foundry. His feet in their business shoes were blistered and God alone knew where his car was – he'd abandoned it on the lip of the first crater he'd come to, stumbling then through six miles of flying debris to get to Eccles Place and relative peace. The house was empty, Lallie not back yet. God. Millie buried not twenty-four hours. Lallie still in that hell downtown.

He called the number she'd given him (Only for *real* emergencies, Daddy!). They were a long time answering, a longer time still finding out that Lallie's ambulance was 'out of commission'. His daughter? Yes, she'd called in, they were sending a vehicle to get her when they had one free –

'I'll get her myself, dammit, if you'll just tell me where –'

They'd hung up, likely to answer another frantic call. And what car could he take, anyway? Hers would be down at the depot. Torn between wanting to go find her and wanting to be home when she got here, torn – oh hell, the whole bloody world was falling in.

The emptiness, the silence of the house, ashes cold as charity in the grate, a hall clock which had somehow stopped because nobody remembered to wind it – they all pressed in on him, drove him outside to the deserted street to pace up and down, up and down until he'd numbed that desolate thing in his chest. Lallie was safe, that was something. The house was still here, waiting for her, for them both. The street was still here, untouched except for smoke drifting up from town. No car in the doctor's drive – likely he'd been ordered to town, like Lallie. The lawyer's place looked ship-shape, considering. Trust them buggers. The Oaks was looking seedy, front lawn knee-high in weeds – but then, they'd just lost their lad, hadn't they? Who worries about dandelions at a time like that? The Archers' place was empty again and on the market, but on the whole the street had changed little since the day Joe had brought his pretty, overwhelmed young wife and small daughter to the wide, curving avenue lined with massive sycamores and expansive country houses.

Millie, on first seeing it, had whispered, 'Oh Joe, it's ever so posh – are you sure we want to live here?' and even young Joe had to swallow hard and long before he walked past the parade of houses that had 'grounds' instead of gardens, names instead of numbers.

Millie traipsed through the gracious, carpeted rooms of Number 8 in a trance. 'Whatever are we going to call it?' she wanted to know, still in that intimidated Backenthorpe voice, her threadbare coat practically a capital offence to the elegant room in which she stood. 'We'll have to give it a name, Joe.'

She gazed out at the expanse of lawn tastefully laid out with silver birches. 'We can't call it The Birches, that's taken already, so's The –'

'The deed says Number 8 and Number 8 it'll be. If them bloody snobs don't like it they can lump it.'

'Oh Joe, they're not our sort of folks at all.'

But in the end they'd been accepted, Millie less readily than he because Millie couldn't bluff her way through a cobweb. But money talked, now't truer than that. The day came when one of the majors (Coldstream Guards, retired) lost his shirt in the stock market. Joe heard the house was going on the block and bought it on the quiet, rented it back to the major – which allowed him to keep his military stuff upper lip. The major was most grateful. The major's wife invited Millie to afternoon tea.

'Whatever shall I talk about?' Millie asked Joe.

'Lallie, what else? They'd give their eye teeth for one like her. They've no kids, they've now't at all now, nobbut his pension and the bloody fool's lucky to have that –'

'But Joe, their house is so … grand. They've got tables from India and I don't know what all –'

'Oh, have done, woman! We own the shingles over their bloody heads, can't you get that through your noggin? It's ours, and a pretty penny it's costing me an' all. And don't go feeling sorry for 'em, neither. I'm not making a profit …'

And he hadn't – not until he sold it ten years later at a very tidy gain. Even before that he'd never regretted its price. The graititude of the major's wife was Millie's ticket into Eccles Place, and as such it was a bargain. He'd never told her that, had he? He'd never told her a lot of things he should have. He'd never told her how he waited to see her face when he got home from Manchester or The Smoke. She'd thought Manchester was passing posh and London was where the nobs hung out so why would a man want to rush back to a homebody like her? She thought he hurried home for Lallie – well, he had, hadn't he? But Millie was there too, in the picture he called home. Maybe she was fussing and dusting and baking and getting on his nerves, but she was there.

And wasn't anymore.

He shut his eyes against the bitter wind off the Derbyshire

moors, told himself it was the wind making his eyes run, the bloody rotten lousy thieving wind that cut him to the bone but oh Millie lass, Millie, Millie, Millie ...

It was not yet daylight, and all was quiet except for the wind. It came out of the east, penetrating every gap in the walls of the hut, moaning down the tin chimney-pipe, slicing easily through the thin prison blanket. Half awake, Jan traced its path on the map of his memory. Down from the Siberian plateau in a bitter sweep, gathering momentum over the plains, whipping to a frenzy over the Urals, racing across the onion-domed heart of Moscow but saving its iciest blast for Warsaw and Morksa Street before crossing the German frontier and the stand of pines that circled the camp, their reedy trunks no match for the chill bite of the wind.

This early morning he could almost shrug off the weather. Yesterday the first Red Cross parcels had arrived. His contained a can of milk, hot chocolate, Vienna sausages, and a packet of tea. More warming still was Lallie's letter. Written only a week ago its news was more current than usual, so fresh he felt he could almost feel the touch of her fingers on the pages.

He pictured her writing it. Joe asleep on the settee, Millie at the theatre with Neil's mother, and Lallie alone, warm and beautiful and missing him. Safe at Eccles Place. Her grey eyes clouded perhaps, but troubled by only little griefs. Mr Hodgson's sciatica and his horse's colic, no meat for the Afghans and no petrol to drive to Castleton for a nostalgic trip at Christmas. But safe. He frowned, remembering she'd mentioned joining the ambulance service – but 'Daddy was miffed' and could be depended on not to let his girl take risks. Not Joe. Much as he disliked his father-in-law, he knew there could be no better custodian of Lallie's safety than Joe Wainwright. In the beginning he'd almost wished she'd stayed at the cottage alone instead of going back to Eccles Place, yet he could see it was for the best. 'Just think of all the rent we'll save,' she'd written at the time, 'and there's all your officer's pay piling up in the bank – why, we'll be rich as Croesus when

206

you come home!' He smiled in the dark, remembering. How innocent she was! Just one of the little trinkets Joe showered on her would be more than his service pay for a month. After the war he could take care of her himself, but under the circumstances he was glad Joe and Millie were there with her now. If not completely happy, she was at least secure. He thought of her sitting by the fire, then of Millie arriving home from the theatre. They'd have tea, Millie bustling between kitchen and living room as Joe harangued and cajoled Lallie out of driving an ambulance during the air raids. Angry but convinced – he hoped – Lallie would run upstairs to her room, sit on the edge of the bed in her nightgown and brush her hair with the tortoise-shell hairbursh ... he slipped back into sleep with the memory of her dark hair touching him, enveloping him in a cloud of benediction with lavender and love at its heart, her ingenuous smile, kittenish and subtly alluring, her smooth length of thigh and hip firm under his hand, the slim slope of shoulder, the sweetness of her eager, pointed little breasts, like apples ...

'*Appell*! '*Raus*! *Appell*! *Appell*!'
  'I hear, I hear ...' Aching in every limb from the hard mattress stuffed with wood-shavings, the unending cold which pierced to the bone, he struggled awake and gave the wall over Roman's and Bolek's bunk a few hard thumps. '*Appell*! Get up!' He aimed an extra poke at Roman's fleshy shoulder. 'Hurry.'
  No need to rouse Lech. He was wide awake, staring at the paint-flaked ceiling. His eyes in their deep sockets burned with an anger Jan could neither reach nor understand. Always taciturn, given to deep depressions and sudden, inexplicable bouts of savage celebration, since they'd been shot down Lech had become almost mute. He spoke only when spoken to – not always then, preferring to pace his days endlessly by the warning wire that ran some distance inside the main fences. Yesterday, with the arrival of the food parcels, close on two thousand men rejoiced as they lined up at Distribution. Not Lech. Jan had to search him out and insist he line up with the

others. And he was so thin! The little food he ate seemed to fuel only his hostile spirit, with nothing left over for the man.

'Come on, Lech. Don't let's have trouble.' Not again. One man missing from roll call meant endless waiting for the others as the guards counted heads and counted again, all in the bitter blast that knifed through the pines, sharpened itself on the barbed wire. Last night a fiesty little Cockney had told Jan: 'If that lanky Lech bastard's late again a few of us will be paying him a visit.'

At last it was Roman, angry at having to get up himself, who pulled Lech from his bunk and marched him outside. 'You're too patient with him,' he told Jan over his shoulder. 'He's an inconsiderate, sullen *chłtop*.'

Yet Jan felt sorry for the moody crewman who was being frog-marched into line. A lonely man, Lech, one who seemed to seek out loneliness despite the popsies who'd flocked around him at Hempton and in London. Well, there were no women here. Perhaps that was his problem.

Outside, the lines of disgruntled men shuffled feet to keep warm, jogged in place, hugged threadbare blankets to thin chests, blew onto numb fingers.

'*Achtung!*' the guards shouted in vain. '*Achtung! Appell!*'

Roll call took two hours, hours of cold feet and hot tempers, empty stomachs and numbing boredom. The movements to keep warm inevitably shifted lines, and the count began again. And again. Nothing to do but stare at each other or the warning wire, which was separated from the main fences by a no-man's-land of carefully raked, untrodden sand some thirty feet wide whose surface concealed buried microphones so sensitive the lightest footfall would set off the klaxons.

Both the main fences were nine feet high and ran five feet apart, formidable barriers of close-meshed barbed wire, the space between so densely packed with still more wire that the stunted pines on the other side were no more than vague shadows shrouded in morning mist. The sentries in their towers stood out clear enough, machine guns primed and aimed at the compound.

The warning wire was only knee-high. A man could step over it without breaking stride. None did. Not intentionally. A man had fallen over it once. When the guns finally fell silent the prisoners were marched past the remains.

A warning.

Appell was as close as the *stalag* came to a social hour. Here you heard the latest news from the hidden radio. Here you talked with other crews. Jokes were exchanged and embroidered, mail was distributed, deals were made. A tin of Klim for a pack of gum, a stub of pencil for a tin of Players, a penknife for a pair of gloves. Although the Red Cross parcels had only just begun to arrive, somebody had already cornered the market on raisins.

'Lomanski's bought up every damn raisin,' Roman whispered. 'He's making wine for Christmas, God knows how.'

At last the numbers of shivering men jibed with the printed lists. The mailbags appeared, the long wait as letters were sorted, distributed.

'Kaliski.'

Two letters.

Nothing from Lallie – but still he raced back to the deserted hut, his heart pumping loud and hot with conflicting surges of hope and dread. He dodged through shuffling groups of prisoners, leapt over piles of empty cans, scattered chessmen as the two players cursed his fleeing back.

On his bunk, he turned to the wall and stared at the letter from the Red Cross. One way or another this would be final. After this, no more doubts. They were found – or they were lost forever. The answer he'd sought for over two years lay in his palm. And he was afraid to read it, to know, to make the jump from hopeful ignorance to certain knowledge. He felt his life was a ledge jutting out over a deep abyss, the depths filled with snow ... He took in a ragged breath as his fingers eased open the flap, withdrew a trembling sheet of paper.

'*We regret –*'

The letters blurred, shifted, ran one into another. The wind in the chimney-pipe screamed their names. Mamunia ... Tatuś ... '*But you knew!*' it shrieked. '*You always knew!*'

They were sorry. While none of the dead could be positively identified at this time, the devastation was such that it seemed

209

logical to accept –'

Logical! Mamunia and Tatuś dead and I should be logical?
They were not old, were in their forties ... Were. Were. See
how logically you accept? Tatuś, Tatuś I accept, he was sick.
But Mamunia! So little, but quick, quick. And strong. Her
heart must beat forever ... What had she said at the last? Yes,
that's it, she was making plans, *plans*! to go to Zakopane.
Nothing could kill her, not all the tanks, the cannons, the
armies ... but she was five feet tall, less than a hundred pounds
of energy and strong opinions. A convulsive heave in his chest
and the sobs started, deep, wrenching, no tears to ease their
passage, sobs that opened the crevasse of his nightmares,
showed the face in the snow, the one he'd been afraid to see.
Mamunia ...

The ledge in his mind creaked as a chunk of granite – not a
large chunk, less than a hundred pounds – snapped off and
tumbled to the snow.

Somehow he got himself out of the hut before the others
could return, to lean as far over the warning wire as he dared,
to stare through the barbed-wire and the pines towards
Poland. Fifty miles to the east, miles of snow-covered fields
and forests, all frozen under the heel of a winter that would not
end ... Once, it had always been summer, shining on the warm
bricks of Warsaw, the flower sellers' gaudy stands on street
corners, Mamunia in thin silks and a picture hat with flowers
under the brim. He was very small and they'd been to the
circus, and after that to the *kawiarnia* for coffee and little cakes.
He remembered crying at the table because he'd lost his circus
programme in the crush.

'Do stop snivelling, *kochany*,' she'd said. 'You want to make
me ashamed, a great boy of five mewling like a kitten?'

'But there were horses on the front! They had their knees up
and their hair was blowing and the necks all curved –'

'Pooh! That's just the circus.' With one quick motion she
brushed off a crumb and a fairytale. 'In real life they pull
turnip-wagons and make *kaku* on the street. These *faworki* are
delicious. Do have one of those with lemon-cream on top,
they're your father's favourite cake.'

It was a long time before he could bring himself to open the other letter, from Neil. He always wrote in such cheerful vein, and Jan was not ready for cheer, however well meant. The first words caught him completely off guard and he had to read them several times before they penetrated the sudden rush of blood to his head.

'... don't worry if Lallie isn't quite up to writing for a day or two. Bad news, I'm afraid. Millie is dead. She and Mother were on their way home from the theatre when a lame Spit crashed into their bus. I'm sorry. I know you were fond of her – we all were. Joe and Lallie are taking it as well as can be expected but of course they're shattered. Thank God they have each other. Lallie's driving an ambulance now, which will help take her mind off Millie. Joe's against it, of course, but at the moment he doesn't seem to have the heart to make a fuss. My mother came out of the whole thing with nothing more than a sprained wrist and a scratch or two ... Don't worry about Lallie, I'll try to help. I'm home now for a day or two and by next month I'll be home for good. Sorry to be the one to tell you, old man. Just wish the damn war would be done with so we all go back to normal ...'

Written a week ago. Millie dead for a week and he hadn't known. Sweet Millie, so kind to him always, trying to smooth his path with Joe, pulling her little strings when she could and closing her ears when she couldn't. He remembered her crumbling herbs, warning him about Joe. All that softness and sympathy gone, and with it another piece of the ledge tumbling into the crevasse, disappearing in blue-shadowed snow. Millie Wainwright dead ... while stupid, genteel Agnes Armott simply sprained her wrist.

Hard on the heels of grief came guilt. Lallie needed him now and he wasn't there, as he had not been there when she had counted off the bombers, had not been there while she waited to hear if she was a wife or a widow. And now this. A woman loses her mother, her husband should be there to hold her, tell her the world has not ended, stroke her hair. Don't worry, Neil said. He was doing what he could, and there was always Joe. Oh yes, she had Joe. Thank God they had each other. Well, maybe Neil was right.

Through the haze of bitterness and loss he felt a tug at the blanket that draped his shoulder. It was Bolek, frowning and perplexed behind the cloud of vapour that issued, this freezing morning, from his young mouth.

'You rushed off without hearing the news.'

'What news?' Jan said dully. He'd had enough news this morning to last a lifetime.

'Sheffield had two big raids this week ...' He paused, stared down at the toes of his flying boots scuffing the ice-crusted sand. 'Made a bloody mess of the place, according to the radio. Roman said not to tell you, but –'

And Lallie driving an ambulance.

It was enough. Too much. The weight in his mind exploded into fragments that propelled him around the circuit of the warning-wire until he could run no more, and must stare up, exhausted, at the sentries bundled warm behind their guns.

Later, lying mindless on his bunk, he was not even surprised at the rattle of machine guns.

Roman ran to the window, turned back white-faced into the room.

'*Lech went over the wire. They've shot him.*'

No. No.

The day was a sharp lesson. He learned that the purgatory of not knowing was safer than the hell of knowing. Mamunia and Tatuš in limbo could be thought about; reunion, however tentative, could be imagined, new pictures spun from old memories. Now there was no hope, none at all. They'd moved out of limbo. Out of his life. *It was logical to accept ...*

And Lallie now as bereft as he, Mille gone and no husband to give comfort, to hold ... just Joe and Neil ...

Now Lech, survivor of all the murderous raids, had found the one, the only way out of Stalag Luft III ... solid ground everywhere crumbling, pebbling off bit by bit, no ledge anywhere strong enough to bear the weight of hopes, plans. Nothing was safe, no one ...

Except maybe Bura, secure behind his desk.

CHAPTER TWENTY

So far so good.

Daddy said she was doing well: 'Thank God you've kept an even keel, not whined and whinnied like some would have.' Neil made it a point to pat her shoulder every chance he got and murmur, 'Good girl, Lallie, you'll do,' which set off a quick surge of anger, as quickly damped down. They meant to praise her, but succeeded only in building a dam of resentment that filled up a little more each day.

No need to listen at keyholes to chart the drift of their huddled conversations in the living room when she was safely out of earshot. Yes, poor Lall was having a rough go of it, what with being a grass widow and losing her mother into the bargain, and after all that misery down at Hempton. And the raids, yes, let's not forget the raids! They tutted and they patted, thought up this little treat and that, and it was all so damn useless she could have hit them. And patronizing! Childish! As if she was still in rompers and had just had her tonsils out, for Heaven's sake! Because they meant well she contained her anger behind a brisk wall of efficiency. Looking forward helped. And keeping busy. When time hung heavy (not often) she had the sensation of bracing herself against a downhill slide to water that boiled and raged beneath her, holding herself together in the frantic round of market garden and animals and ambulances. Her days were full. There were the doggedly cheerful letters to Jan, the thousand and one things to do around the house now Mum wasn't there to do them – not that she did them half as well, but racing from one task to the next kept her head up and her mind busy.

Just the same, it was a relief to be out of it, immune behind the wheel of the ambulance – which had stalled on and off all evening, and finally died on the top of Brincliffe Edge. Something thunked in the gearbox, metal gouged metal, and the whole decrepit heap settled its bald tyres to the kerb with a final asthmatic gasp. No amount of gentling could get its stubborn carcass moving again. Blast!

The duty nurse (not Flo tonight) said, 'Look on the bright side, hinny. Now I get the night off. I can nip home and see what my husband looks like for a change! Nothing much doing here, anyway.' In no time she was on her way in a whirl of black cape and the clip-clop of sensible shoes, leaving Lallie stuck on top of the hill to wait for the tow. When she called headquarters from the pub on the corner the dispatcher told her it could be a long wait. Not that it mattered. Unlike the duty nurse, she had no husband to go home to. The landlord of the pub said why didn't she wait in the bar, out of the cold? One look at the jovial faces behind pints of old-and-mild and she opted for the cool moonlight of Brincliffe Edge – she didn't care much to be around people anymore. They tended to gather in pairs, she noticed, and resolutely stopped the next thought with a slam of the pub door.

Frost already rimmed the hood of the ambulance. Its worn leather seat struck shivers through her thin jacket, and in the end she paced the top of the hill to keep warm. The moon was starkly brilliant, impossible to ignore. Perhaps it was that – or what it revealed. She hadn't noticed it for months, not since Jan stopped flying, but tonight it hung like a great white lantern over the city, throwing buildings and telephone poles into sharp relief against the deep violet of the sky, silvering barrage balloons with unearthly light.

And tonight there was time to look at it all, really look.

Sheffield from the top of a hill. Not that it had been a pretty city; it was industrial, and industry wasn't pretty. Some people called it The Muck and they were not wrong – but it was *her* city, *her* Muck, washed now with moonlight, all its new scars laid bare, robbed of dignity like so many of the wounded she'd carted off to City General. The wasteland of bricks and tortured street lamps over there used to be The Moor, shoppers' Heaven, where Mum took her every season to hunt for new school clothes, rubbed winter woollens and summer cottons between thumb and forefinger, tutt-tutted over poor quality and frowned upon the 'good stuff'. 'Oh the prices, Lallie! A scandal they are – but Joe'll skin me alive if I dress you in rubbish.'

Buried in among the craters of Angel Street was a restaurant with chandeliers and blinding white tableclothes, a string quartet sawing away behind potted palms as Mum weighed the iodine benefits of grilled halibut against the dark mysteries of shepherd's pie. 'Who knows what they put in it?' she'd whisper when the waiter was out of hearing.

Somewhere in the burned-out skeletons of Eccleshall Road, a twisted *barre* and shattered mirrors were all that remained of Madame Olga's School of Ballet and Tap (Acrobatics Optional), where Lallie was drilled every Saturday morning for six years, loving it even as she winced at over-stretched muscles. At the time, her regimen ruffled the always-prevailing calm at Eccles Place.

'It's not natural,' Mum said. 'Twisting her in knots like that – fifth position and fourth, arabesque this and grand jetty that!'

'*Jeté*!' cried the little Lallie. 'If Madame hears you say 'jetty' I'll die, *I'll just die* ...' knowing even at that age just what she was doing.

'You see?' Daddy demanded, point made. 'Think of the polish, the edge it'll give her – not that she needs it. If it's good enough for Shaeffer's girl and Warton's poor dumpling –' ringing in his competitors' offspring '– I reckon it's good enough for Lallie. Besides, she likes it.' That was that. She'd shot her mother a look of pure triumph and Daddy roared with laughter, lifting her to his shoulder and galloping her round the living room until she bumped her head on the ceiling and was allowed to stay up till all hours in case of concussion.

Looking now on battered Eccleshall Road, the shame of remembered triumph stung, burned, sizzled to sudden fury at the sight of a dozen solid old places rich with her childhood. Nothing now but cement and shards of glass. All gone, and thousands more besides. Street after broken street stirred a river of anger she hadn't known was there. Just as Jan must have felt, watching his Warsaw burn ... worse for him, his parents were in it, and now ...

Oh God ...

Joe waited for her to come home.

He seemed to do a lot of that lately. Every time the sirens sounded she was off into it again, coming back all blood and dust, a look on her that creased him across the chest. Once she set her mind ... he smiled, grudgingly aware that at the core she was very much like himself, would not be talked out of it no matter what arguments he raised. He should have nipped it in the bud, but what with losing Millie ... By the time he was thinking straight, Lallie's driving an ambulance was part of her life, like mornings over at Hodgson's, afternoons writing to the Pole and walking the dogs.

A different kind of girl would have filled Millie's place and been content, cooking and shopping and such like. Not Lallie. 'Which is why,' he grumbled aloud to the cluttered kitchen, 'I'm brewing tea and washing the dinner things.' And no help to be had now at any price. Women made too much in the munition shops. Time was, he could have got some old body to live in and do it all for bed and board and a pound a week in wages – yes, and damn glad of the job! Right away, Mr Wainwright. Certainly, Mr Wainwright. Stand still and I'll kiss your feet, Mr Wainwright. Them days were gone, more's the pity. Even the gardener had gone to greener pastures, a trail of weeds and seedy cabbages in his wake.

A good thing Neil was back. He not only lightened the load at the foundry but he also stopped by the house a lot these days, talked on this and that, filled up the time and some of the emptiness left by Millie.

Ever since primary school she'd been there; he'd never looked farther afield than Millie. What for? She was the best looking thing ever to come out of Backenthorpe, and a worker besides. There'd been a time he thought himself lucky to have her … funny how you stopped noticing the woman you lived with. Until she was gone. It was the little things. Coming in out of the winter to no fire and nothing on the stove. His socks all snaked up in the drawer instead of paired and rolled. The empty pillow on the other side of the bed. Oh, there were plenty who'd grab at the chance to fill her place – by God, even Agnes Armott simpered at him these days, the daft ha'porth. But there'd be nobody else. He had his foundry and he had his lass.

Who came in grumbling.

'You forgot to give Silky her drops! I know you did, the bottle's in exactly the same place I left it.'

Oh, but she was a lovely thing to see. In uniform now and not a whit the plainer for it. All that marvellous hair, eyes to bring a bird right off the branch. Like Millie. But had Millie ever looked like this, angry and sad and beautiful all at once? He thought not. Millie never had Lall's confidence, never had the background that could have given it to her. She'd never have asked him to tend the dogs, let alone complain if he forgot. 'Sorry love, it slipped my mind.'

'The vet said four times a day!'

As she fought the losing battle for Silky's sight, Joe made her a bite of supper, watching her face and buttering the back of his hand in the process. Something had rubbed her wrong, and it wasn't the dog's eyes.

'A bad night?' he said, spilling a few drops of soup as he set the tray in front of the settee.

She shrugged. 'Quiet, just a nuisance raid. The ambulance broke down again.'

'No damage?' he pressed.

'The bandstand at Fannington Park, that's all. Where Jolly won Best of Show before the war, remember?'

So it wasn't that. 'So what's the matter then?'

She took her time answering, staring into the fire with blank eyes and set jaw. 'What isn't? It's just rotten, everything …'

'I'm listening.'

She started to say one thing then changed it to something else. 'Jan's letter this morning sounded … *down* … *fed up* …'

His anger flared. 'He could keep it to himself, couldn't he? Does he have to load you with every little upset? What –'

Her eyes, suddenly flint in the firelight, were steady over the bowl of the spoon. 'I'm his wife. Who else would he tell?'

'Still and all –'

She shook her head as if to clear it. 'It's not just – oh, to hell with it! I'm tired, that's all. I'm going to bed.'

Her spine was rigid as she mounted the stairs, the barrier still in place. He sighed. Tears he could handle, but this ... Millie could likely have detoured around it, but that wasn't his way. He didn't know where to start.

Christmas was on them before they were ready for it. From habit they drove to Backenthorpe, a dispiriting trip during which neither spoke more than a word or two. They hung about the Black Swan until the landlord's shout of 'Time gentlemen, please!' thrust them outdoors to fields dismal with half-melted snow, every hedge and stile laced with dead leaves and old cobwebs. North or south made no difference. Every path they took brought them back to the cobbled main street and the waiting car.

'We may as well go home, lass,' he said at last, the prospect even bleaker than the sodden fields.

'I suppose.' She turned mechanically towards the car, her face almost hidden by the mohair scarf wound about her neck, but the angle of her shoulders told their own tale. She knew as well as he why they were killing time. He squeezed her arm in its heavy woollen sleeve, thinking if he could just squeeze away the last of this awful year –

'It's not much of a holiday, lass, but in time ...'

The house waited for them. No blue hyacinths scenting up the hall this year, no chrysanthemums blazing on the Christmas table. The fire in the grate was a heap of smoking coals, and the duckling they drew out of the oven was beige, rubbery, and obviously still raw.

'Happen it wants another hour to crisp up,' he said.

That's *all* he said, but she turned on him like a wildcat, her eyes much too bright. 'How do *I* know what it wants? I've

218

never cooked one before, have I? If you're not satisfied you should have had Agnes Armott over to help. She offered!'

He tried to laugh it off. 'God, Aggie's a worse cook than you,' but it didn't seem to help. Calling Neil's mother Aggie (which for Neil's sake he would never have said to her face) did nothing to fill the empty kichen. He no more wanted Agnes in Millie's kitchen than Lallie did. Neither wanted to hear her continually bleat about Millie having 'passed over' – as if poor Millie just took it into her head one night to sprout wings and drift up to some gentle heaven on a whim. Instead of which – oh, Christ, don't start down that blind alley.

'Tell you what,' he said, sliding the pan back into the oven and turning the switch to Full. 'I'm going to make you a good stiff drink – yes, that I *can* do – and by the time we're ready this pathetic little bugger will be a nice, crozzled brown.'

'It's not just that!' she said wildly. 'We're supposed to have things *with* it, potatoes and greens and gravy, we're –'

'Now take it easy, just calm –'

'How *can* I calm down? I've a dozen things to think about and –'

And they had nothing to do with Christmas dinner. 'Oh lass ...' but she was fumbling with a paring knife and a bag of potatoes. 'Just leave them be, we'll manage –'

'Oh yes, we'll manage!' Potato peelings flew in thick, angry ribbons to the draining board. 'We'll manage. We'll *all* manage. If there's anybody left to manage! There's just no end to it. You pick them up out of the streets, out of their beds! Old men and women. Babies who never hurt anybody ... it's *all such a waste*. The lists in the paper, longer every day.' She threw down the knife and reached for a cigarette – another new habit he didn't like. 'Mum ... Kaz ... Lech ... Neil with a cane ... Jan caged up like an animal –'

'I warned you when you got married. That's war –'

She shot him a furious glance through the haze of smoke. '*I know it's war*! *And the foundry makes money on it hand over fist.*'

By God, she cut deep. 'Steel has to come from somewhere – and *you* don't want for much. Whatever you need you've only to say –'

Her shoulders slumped and a wave of her hand absolved

219

him. 'I know, I know that, but what I want money can't buy –'

If he could just have touched her, taken her up as he had when she was little, held her until the storm raged itself out … but there was a shell on her these days, and it wasn't just the Pole, it wasn't even just Millie –

'*I want it done with*!' she cried. 'It just makes me so *mad* I could … but there's nothing *to* do! Oh Daddy …' Her mouth, firm for too long, began to quiver just as the smell of burning flesh eddied between them. '*Oh no! now we've burned the damn duckling*!' She flew to the oven and dragged out the smoking remains of Christmas Dinner. When she looked up at him her cheeks were flushed, her lashes spiked and shining.

The tears started and he was helpless now to stop them, helpless to hold her back as she dashed blindly upstairs to her room and shut the door. Worse, a tightness gathered in his own throat, thickened the bitterness he carried like a bag of coal on his back. All these years, slaving so the foundry might succeed. And by God, succeed it had! Thanks to the war, the wife-stealing, child-stealing war.

He threw the duckling into the fire, poked its black little carcass deep into smouldering coals and sat back on his heels, grimly eased by the resulting crackle of strong new flames.

She turned down her bed and washed her face, pressing the cool facecloth to her burning cheeks. It hadn't been fair to take it out on Daddy. Such a silly thing to set the match to her anger. It wasn't the first meal she'd burned and wouldn't be the last, but the sight of it was symptomatic of everything around her … It was exactly the way it had been years ago when she'd built the most perfect sandcastle on the beach at Bournemouth and a stranger tromped through it – except then Mum had dried her tears and promised her a ride on the donkeys to make up for it … Oh Mum … Mum …

She turned to the dresser for her hairbrush, but minefields of hurt lay everywhere she looked today. Kaz's cup, full of snowdrops, was there. She reached for it often, as she did again now, tracing the scars and hollows of its pitted surface, touching it to her cheek. In some mysterious way the cool metal gave her comfort. Its scars mirrored the sadness, its hollows echoed the emptiness of her days, *but it had endured ...* After the war it would have to go back to Kaz's family, but it wouldn't matter then. She'd have Jan. But when, when ...?

She brushed her hair in front of Jan's photograph in its silver frame, knowing the exact shade of his hair and eyes, the shape of his firm mouth that could soften in an instant over hers. Harder to remember was his touch, his hands, his lips, the strong urgent body needing hers. All she knew for sure was her own hunger, a deep river which surged and thundered through her nights, on and on and on, her life running away from her ...

In the quiet room the tears squeezed again through her lashes, ran warmly, slowly into the pillow. Weak tears she was ashamed of, but they ran just the same ... and when would they ever stop ...?

Where is there an end to it?

BOOK II

CHAPTER TWENTY-ONE

Plump white clouds scudded across blue skies. Union Jacks snapped in the breeze. Thousands had danced all last night through the streets and were said to be still at it this morning.

It was May, 1945. The boys were coming home.

Lallie moved from one room to the next, now fluffing cushions in the living room, now smoothing the folds of a new pink suit which hung, pressed and ready, in her wardrobe. She'd washed her hair and done her nails, charmed a pre-war bottle of Chanel No 5 from the locked-up hoard at the chemist's shop on the corner; a small suitcase was packed with overnight things; the MG's engine was tuned, it's tank full of petrol.

Everything waited on Jan's phone call from wherever in England the government chose to land him. 'You may as well relax,' Daddy had told her as he left for the foundry. 'It might be weeks before they let him out.' But how to relax? How to pass by the phone without picking it up to make sure it still worked? How to look at his picture without the panic rising? Four years of prison camp. They'd worn slowly for her. How much more slowly for him? Common sense told her he would have changed, but in what way? *She* had changed. The values of twenty-one were not those of twenty-five. The world had turned upside down in the interim. Abundance had become scarcity. Security was a night of no sirens and a letter from Jan in the morning mail. Permanence was an entire month in which no one she knew got killed. Passion, greatest of all luxuries and too long denied, was frosted over with numbing routine. She was no longer sure if her memories of him were grounded in fact or fantasy. What did she really know about him? Everything, she told herself. Wasn't the dressing table packed with his shirts and socks, her writing desk crammed with four years of his letters. But how many people wrote the truth? *She* hadn't, not about the raids … Oh, she was being silly, silly. All these years and not a moment's doubt until this week. 'And no doubts now,' she said aloud to the quiet rooms. 'Stop moping and take Jolly for a walk,' remembering as she reached for the leash that she hadn't even told Jan that Silky, his favourite, had died – at the time it seemed an unnecessary load to add to all the others.

Jolly was frisky this morning, glad to snag her attention. Poor Jolly! She *had* neglected him this week.

In Little Wood she sat on the May Queen log and let him off the leash to run, ignoring his look of surprise when she didn't join him. 'I'm tired,' she said firmly, slapping his chocolate rump to get him going. Tired? Her nerves were electric wires that jumped and sparked and crackled, never the same twice.

When she saw the stranger in the dark blue suit watching her from the dappled shade of the beeches she panicked, scrambled to her feet. Where was Jolly? Why hadn't he barked? Then she saw why. Jolly was right there, his long muzzle under the stranger's hand, pink tongue lolling, happy as when he laid a stick at her feet.

Blond hair longer than she remembered it, eyes the same piercing blue, straight mouth already curving as he looked at her.

The May Queen log under her seemed to tilt. Bright leaves blurred to liquid green as her heart gave a slow roll, then raced, raced as she forgot to breathe. Something in her, frozen for a long time, began to melt as he moved towards her, tentative at first, then with a sudden rush as if all the time in the world would never be enough to make up for what they'd lost.

'*Jan*! *Oh Jan* …'

He stooped and touched her hair and he hadn't changed at all, not the least bit! Oh, he was thinner, older, and there were lines around his eyes that hadn't been there – but his lips kissed the same, tasted the same, his arms held her the same, gently at first then tight, tighter until she was fighting for air.

'I thought you'd call!' she gasped. 'You're home so fast – I was coming to pick you up – and you're in civvies! Oh, and I was going to be all dressed up and –' burying her face in his shirt-front until he tilted her chin and searched her eyes.

'I thought I remembered but really I didn't …'

And his voice was the same, quiet but tense, as if torrents raged just under its calm surface, the accent still there but fainter now. 'You had my photograph,' she said.

'Someone stole it.'

'Those rotten Germans –'

'No, a prisoner took it. I can't blame him. You're still my lovely girl.' Long fingers traced her eyebrows, cheekbones, her suddenly trembling lips. She drew slightly away as the years stretched between them, as tears gathered in her throat. She tried to tell him that she couldn't believe he was really home but little sobs of relief kept getting in the way.

'And you weren't sure either,' he murmured softly, holding her tight against the tears. 'Don't cry, don't cry … it's over …'

Then Jolly was pushing between them with a stick in his mouth, his tail a brown pennant feathering the breeze.

'*Jolly*!' they said together, then they were all laughing, Jolly prancing between them through daisy-sprinkled fields and hedgerows thick with primroses.

Soon they were in the hall at Eccles Place, where the phone stopped ringing just as she reached out towards it.

'Probably Daddy. I'll call him back and tell him you're here.'

He looked at her for a long moment, then shook his head. 'Leave a note. Tell him we'll call him in a day or two.'

'But where …? I thought you'd want a little time at home before we took a holiday.'

'A honeymoon,' he said gently. 'And then we have to *find* a home, darling, *our own home*. Make plans.'

She wanted to say there was lots of room here and that they were more than welcome, remind him that Daddy would be alone if they moved away, but something in his face stopped her, caused a momentary disquiet which soon melted away under his kiss. He was back. That was enough.

'We'll talk about it later,' he said. 'Maybe Castleton …?'

Joe brought Neil back for dinner, only to find her fly-away note propped against the tea-caddy, every word underlined with black, rapturous strokes.

Jan's home! Back in a few days!

'Christ, will you look at that!' He threw the note across the kitchen table to Neil. 'Gone off. Just gone. No whys or wherefores, not a bloody thought for *us*! He hasn't been back half a damn day and already he's got her gallivanting who-knows-where.'

He slumped into his easy chair and waited for Neil to fix their drinks. So it was starting already. Four years he'd watched for cracks, four years of buying theatre tickets and being called away at the last minute so she'd have to go with Neil. When that failed he'd flirted steelmen in front of her, cutlers' sons, even the junior partner his lawyer had just taken on, good solid fellows with steady livings behind them and decent prospects in front of them. But no … she never gave them a second thought. And now it was starting up again.

Neil handed him his Scotch, said mildly that it was only to be expected. They'd been apart a long time, naturally they'd want some time to themselves. 'They'll have to get to know each other again, I expect.'

'She knows all she needs know,' he grumbled. 'And us with no dinner ready. I told her I was bringing you –'

'She'll have forgotten, that's only natural.'

He looked at Neil, amazed as always by his calm acceptance. If he'd just got off the mark when he had the chance – but as always, irritation with Neil turned to approval. The lad's dogged determination to make the best of things was a quality he admired in others. He sighed. 'God alone knows what they'll do. There's no future for a foreigner, I reckon, and him not trained for anything useful.'

Again Neil showed his generosity. 'You could always take him into the works …'

Neil was General Manager now. The prospect of the owner's

228

son-in-law easing him out must surely have crossed his mind. Not that it would happen. Joe wouldn't let it, but … The desire to keep Lallie by his side battled with reluctance to have the Pole underfoot. He shifted his weight in the big easy chair and gave a sharp laugh. 'What? *Him at Wainwright's?* What makes you think he'll want to get his hands dirty?'

Neil gave him an odd glance, one Joe couldn't read. 'He could start in the office …'

'Not bloody likely! You know my motto. Whoever comes in starts from scratch. It's the only way to learn, isn't it? You've only to look at yourself, eh?'

'Yes, well …' Neil finished his drink. 'Do you want another or shall we nip over to the Three Nuns for a mousetrap sandwich?'

'Oh God, bread and cheese. We can have *that* here –'

'All right. I'll fix it, don't get up.'

He watched Neil potter about the kitchen, heard him put the kettle to the gas, rattle cups and saucers onto a tray. In some odd way Neil reminded him of Millie, the way he filled in, made things comfortable. Joe sighed again, poured them both another drink and waited for his cheese sandwich. From the tawny depths of an otherwise good Scotch a face insisted on rising to the top. The Pole.

The reality of her was sweeter than the most lilting of memories.

In all the long winter nights of the *stalag* he'd warmed himself at the fire of old joys. At first memories were sharp and thoughts of her had driven him half mad with wanting her, but as the years passed the picture of her in his mind dimmed; it became an effort of will, a long journey back in time, to recapture her touch on his skin, her breathless voice under his mouth. Towards the end he was filled with doubts. Could she, could any woman, be as perfect as he remembered her, as delicate, as quick to respond to his lightest touch? As fragile, yet her need for him as strong? Ego was the first casualty of imprisonment. One day a pilot, immaculately uniformed, in command of aircraft and crew; the next day a shuffling number with no rights, no function beyond staying alive until the next food parcel. On the worst days he'd wondered how a woman like his Lallie could possibly care for a blanket-huddled nonentity such as he'd become. It was a perilously close step to conclude that perhaps she did not, perhaps she kept writing only because she was sorry for him, too soft-hearted to tell him the truth until he came back. Uncertainty was a never-ending epidemic which infected them all. Doubts bred more doubts – all of which receded in the euphoria of victory, of release to creature comforts they'd almost forgotten about, hot baths and good food, clothes that carried no taint of the delousing chamber.

But doubt had not truly died until he saw the joyshine pour like spilled silver when her eyes met his in Little Wood. He wanted to hold that look to himself, to marvel at, to gloat over, to drown in, before exposing its fragile beauty to the deprecating glance of his father-in-law.

It was for this he had brought her to Castleton – and to cement, if he could, the path of their future without benefit of Joe's one-sided advice.

And to wake within sight of Mam Tor.

Mother Mountain.

Half its heart already scooped out, crumbled into the valley. Within the confines of the *stalag* the mountain's finite rim had increasingly become his own precarious ledge. There was the memory of Lallie telling him, on their first picnic, that the mountain was not as permanent as he seemed to think. 'The *map* calls it Mam Tor – the people down *there* call it Shivering Mountain! Every so often chunks keep dropping off.' After that, it seemed no time at all before the people in his life began dropping off ... Kaz ... Millie ... Lech ... Tatuš ...

Mamunia.

The hotel was old, respectable, with heavy panelling and views of folded hills from every casement window. Joe would approve, he thought wryly. No sooner had they checked in than the owner (who quizzed Lallie to discover that Jan was fresh from Germany) sent up a bottle of burgundy and a bowl of oranges.

'How utterly sweet of him,' she said, peeling an orange with

230

long, delicate fingers. 'I haven't *seen* them for years, and you ... well, I don't imagine you ...' She popped orange slices into his mouth and her own as he poured wine into heavy crystal goblets with ruby stems. His fingers shook, spilling a few drops onto the embossed silver tray.

'Jan,' she whispered, 'look at me please?'

The leaves in the elm outside the window quivered in the slight breeze. The moment he'd ached for – and dreaded – was here. It had been a long time. Suppose he couldn't ... suppose it wasn't right?

He met eyes the colour of dark smoke, huge, black-fringed, brimming with quick-sprung tears. 'You haven't touched me ... have I changed so ... grown so old ...'

Old! At twenty-five! And so beautiful he was afraid to draw breath lest she fade like so many of the dreams. Still his hand seemed frozen in the task of pouring the wine. She reached towards him. Orange-scented lips, warm and alive, touched his. The smell of lavender rose from her hair and soft pink skin. Over the sudden roar that filled his ears he heard her whisper.

'I've waited, too ...'

Somewhere a man's voice, thick with tears, groaned her name again and again. 'Lallie, oh Lallie ...'

The barrier of years parted. Fingers – who knew who's – tore at buttons and zips and hooks. Warm skin melted to warm skin, ignited sparks and old, well-travelled dreams. Sparks bred flames, licking and yearning to bridge the years, the wasted years. Years which could never, no matter how hard he thrust against them, be regained.

He took her awkwardly, like a young boy, the learned finesse of old times forgotten in the surge to belong again to this tremulous miracle from another sphere who was magically, incredibly, his wife. *And who still wanted him*!

She gave a little cry, arched against him, and all the dear familiarity came rushing back as her fingertips pressed deep into his shoulders, as over and over again she sighed his name ...

The room was quiet. Only the leaves moved, and the soft rise and fall of her breast. 'Such a wonderful idea to come here,'

231

she murmured, her breath warm and sweet on his throat. 'At home it wouldn't have been quite the same ...'

At home. The reality of Joe hovered between them, a presence that must be dealt with. Perhaps he should begin now – but already she was drowsy with love, her lashes brushing his lips as she settled lightly into sleep. Later, when she woke ... She stirred, a small tremor touching her lips.

'You're not cold?' he whispered. 'I can close the window.'

She smiled in half-sleep, her hand curled under her cheek, her hair a dark cloud on the pillow, and shook her head.

He took in a deep, grateful breath as the afternoon breeze billowed sprigged muslin into the room. No warning wire here. Could he ever breathe his fill? The air came to him pure, unfiltered by stunted pines and barbed wire, untouched by men's shouts, unmenaced by guns.

It was moist peat and new bracken scooped from the windswept top of Kinderscout. It was short, springy grass tumbling over limestone walls, running down crumpled green hills. It was lazy smoke from the vllage chimneys. It was dales dotted with black-faced sheep and the bleating of spring lambs. It was village sounds of cart-horses and farmers' wives and children just out of school, their voices drifting in like bells from Winnat's Pass and Hollins Cross.

It was innocence.

It was freedom.

It was hope.

And it was Lallie, more beautiful even than before. The tiny lines about her mouth told him what her letters had not. He'd left behind an untried girl whose greatest challenge had been to break free of her father's benevolent tyranny. He'd come back to a woman who'd seen the face of death many times over. Her smile was open still, but frayed edges of knowledge lurked under its sunny surface.

What now? she'd be asking soon, when the first flush of reunion was over. What to tell her when he was not yet sure himself – except on one point. But how far from her father could she be drawn?

He kissed a slender finger tip and noticed the nails for the first time, long and polished, delicate as sea shells. At least she was free of the market garden now, with Mr Hodgson gone. He remembered the line in her letter: 'Dear Mr H, just sitting on the milking stool – Mrs H thought he was nodding off but he'd *died*, can you imagine? On *the* most beautiful morning. Poor Mrs H.'

His lovely, ingenuous wife. Whom he would keep. The one facet of his life that could not, must not, fall away.

He dressed quickly, then hesitated, torn between the mountain and the woman – but the woman slept and the mountain beckoned, drew him inexorably to her bleak summit.

After four years, a steering wheel felt strange under his hands. The wind, as he took the long hill to Mam Tor, drew the little MG close to the mountain's rim, but the feel of steering came back to him, enticing after years of controlling nothing more demanding than a safety razor. He drove to the limits of the old road and parked at its precipitate end, where a barrier spared the unwary driver the same fate as the rest of the road, long since fallen to the scooped out face of Mam Tor. He pulled on the hand-brake and saw with some surprise that his fingers were trembling.

Wind tore at his new demob suit and raced through his hair, bringing with it all the elements he'd felt at the hotel, but more concentrated up here, where everything began. Peat and bracken and clear waters were here, but something else, enigmatic and at the same time familiar, not a tree, not a shrub to break its insidious pull. The place he'd lain with Lallie so long ago must surely be higher, up over scree and boulders and the wild, tufted grass. He climbed higher, his breathing ragged in the thin air of late afternoon, his eyes watering as they swept the smooth curve of the summit, hunting for the spot where they'd shared Millie's picnic basket of sandwiches and fruit, where he'd touched Lallie's sweet breasts for the first time, and been enslaved.

The rim was here, under his feet in their new government-issue shoes – but was it the *same* rim, unbroken in the years of the *stalag*? It looked the same, sharp on its edge, and green, falling to brown and dun hollows farther down the slope. He walked at the very edge – in the end he ran – pausing to run his hands across a boulder, willing it to be the one over which the black-faced ewe had gazed at them.

At the centre of the summit's curve he threw himself to the resilient grass, its moisture cooling his face. It was no use. There was no way to tell if the mother mountain had crumbled in his absence. One rock was like another, this hillock the same as that. Beads of sweat gathered on his forehead and dripped into the gorge, the heart of the mountain open to the wind. Open yes, yet there was something oddly secretive in her bland, blighted face. Cloud-driven shadows fingered rock strata and moved on, leaving unexpected concentrations of light that played tricks with his eyes. One shadow flew faster than the rest, so like a Spitfire he could have sworn – but it was a lone swallow sailing the updraft. Inches from his eyes a black beetle burrowed into the gritty soil. From behind him there was a cry, plaintive and childlike. He turned, but it was only a lamb bleating for its mother, who came on the run, shooting Jan a look of outrage before nudging her young to safety, well away from the sheer drop and the intruder to their territory.

He walked slowly back to the car, took the downhill curves thoughtfully. Lallie was dressed when he opened their door, turning her open smile full on him.

'You've been on Mam Tor,' she said.

'I wanted to see if it was still the same.'

'Is it?'

Through the window he saw the long, broken ridge, then looked back to Lallie's wide grey eyes.

Was it the same? In the *stalag* the image of Mam Tor had come to him often, bringing its enigma with it. Through long nights waiting for morning, this mountain's scarred rim had come to parallel his life, the fallen shards at its foot everything he had lost. Tatuś was there, Poland was there, the wallpaper cherubs from Morska Street were there ... but Mamunia ... was *she* there? Logic said yes she was there, of course yes – but a thing with no name denied it, urged him to deny it too. If the mountain had not broken while he was away he could keep on denying it. The mountain's permission to hope. *But was it the same? He couldn't tell ...*

'Well? *Is* it the same?' Lallie asked again.

'Close enough,' he said, handing her a few harebells he'd picked on the summit. From her delighted laugh they could have been pearls from the Orient.

After dinner she insisted they stroll through the village. 'At least until we can go back to bed without shocking the hotel staff *too* much,' she said, and he remembered that first mess party, with the paternal hedge of Neil and a hand-picked hotel-manager to guard the virtue of Joe Wainwright's daughter. 'You realize,' she went on, 'that at home we could have stayed in our room as long as we wanted ...'

He took a deep breath and steered her towards a bench within sight of the darkening mountain. 'That's what we have to talk about,' he said, slipping an arm around her shoulders. 'Home. Somewhere to live.'

A troubled look came into her face. 'Oh dear, I was afraid you were coming to that. I thought ... I hoped you'd want to live at h- – well, you know.'

'That's a pretty poor start for a marriage, darling.'

'But it *could* work if –'

If his father-in-law and he had the least shred of liking for one another, he thought. Not once, in all the years of the *stalag*, had Joe sent him so much as a postcard.

'Look,' he said. 'We were on our own at Hempton and we were happy, weren't we?' He kissed the tip of her nose, and a passing matron turned her head indignantly. Such goings on in the village nowadays! Lallie hadn't noticed. The corners of her mouth were down and her brow was still perplexed.

'But Mum was alive when we were at Hempton, you see. We're the only family Daddy has now. Just us.'

Us. Half of Joe Wainwright's only living family a bloody Pole? He could imagine what Joe would say to that! 'He'll get used to it, darling. In time he might even marry again.'

'Never! How could he, after Mum?'

'Men do,' he said mildly.

'Not Daddy.' She sounded so sure – and so proud as her fingers pleated the edge of her sleeve. At last she said, 'How far away would we be?'

'It depends on where I work ...'

'You still want to fly? With the airlines?'

'It's what I'd like,' he said, immediately uncertain. Before he was ten his father had aimed him at the diplomatic service. The war had aimed him at the airforce. In prison camp the most challenging decision he'd faced was whether to jog or to walk the daily circuit of the warning wire. Everything else had been decided for him. The thought of working at something he chose himself, something that allowed Lallie to live as she always had, wanting for nothing, was an uncomfortable one. The prisoners were warned, on their release, that such doubts would arise, but at the time he'd laughed, eager to be out, to be living his own life. Now he had to decide what his life was. For both of them.

'There are lots of things I could do,' he said, with more confidence than he felt. 'I could teach languages …'

'I … er … thought you might … you know, consider the foundry.'

'Whatever made you think that?' He was genuinely surprised. What could *he* do in a foundry?

'Neil sort of hinted … and you know he'd show you the ropes!'

Work for Joe Wainwright? 'Oh no, I'd be terrible at it darling, really. I'm just not cut out for business – never been involved in it, you see. No, it'll be either flying or teaching.'

'No foreign service?'

He shrugged. 'That would have to be in Poland, and there's no knowing how things will go there, is there?' And what a fuss your Daddy would kick up then, my Lallie.

Nothing more was said about it then. After a nightcap at the Cheshire Cheese they walked back to the hotel and an infinity of love-making in the fresh, muslin-sprigged room.

'It's as if you'd never been gone,' she said dreamily, her eyes smoky, fulfilled, happy, seeding a line of feathery kisses across his chest. 'At first it was *so* awful, your not being there when I went to sleep, but after a while I made myself … not think about it … you know?'

'I know.' He pressed her cheek against his shoulder and breathed in the scent of her hair. Two days ago Germany, weary, waiting with the others like sheep for the endless war to end. 'I thought it would never be over … I can't believe I'm

236

back …'

She made a sympathetic little moue, her eyes already heavy with sleep. 'You're back where you belong,' she murmured. 'In England … with me …'

Just when he thought she was sound asleep her eyelids fluttered, dark crescents against her flushed cheeks.

'So long as we don't go *too* far away …'

CHAPTER TWENTY-TWO

After much searching they found a flat to rent in the city. It was tiny, rundown, and cost twice what it was worth, but the bombs had reduced the housing stock and they were lucky to get it.

Against Joe's will they dragged him down to see it on a rainy Saturday morning when he should have been at the foundry.

'About what I expected,' he grunted, looking around the two poky little rooms. 'You can't say I didn't warn you.'

'Daddy, *please* don't grump. All it needs is a spot of paint and some nice rugs, and I thought we'd bring in the bedroom suite from my room and perhaps that comfy ch –' She stopped, hand to her mouth, and looked at the Pole. 'But no, they'd be too big, I expect. We'll find something smaller in the shops.'

Ay, and gimcrack stuff it'll be, Joe thought. 'It's daft, the whole idea. God knows what you want to move for, there's room for ten at home.'

'The deposit's paid,' Jan said. 'We're moving in next week.'

Joe looked for a fireplace to knock out his pipe, but there was only a gas fire and a shilling-meter. Not even a kitchen, just gas-ring and sink behind a faded curtain. He leaned his hands on the sooty windowsill and looked out on rooftops and alleyways, railway lines and other people's dustbins. Not a tree in sight. The one patch of smudged green turned out to be mould on a factory's tin roof. My God, Lallie living down here … even Backenthorpe beat this.

237

'Well,' he said at last, 'I hope they're not charging for the view. It's not exactly Plush Park –'

'Lallie!' Jan interrupted. 'You were going to check if that shop on the corner sold shelf-paper.'

She turned big eyes on them both and ran obediently downstairs and out the front door.

So! Joe thought, invigorated at last. We're going to have a set-to. And not before time. It had been building for a month, them taking off flat-hunting every morning, coming back to Eccles Place with a lost look on Lallie and the Pole with a stubborn set to his mouth that Joe was coming to know all too well. And he was aiming straight at it, by damn!

'Look, Joe,' he began. 'I know this is not what you want for Lallie – it's not what *I* want either, but right now it's all we can find –'

'All the more reason to stop at home. I can't for the life of me see why you have to bring her to this dump.'

Blue eyes locked onto his, flinty with purpose. 'You know why. We both know.'

Jesus, he was a cocky bugger! He needed taking down a peg, he did that. 'Now you listen to me, young fella. My girl's lived all her life with the best that money can buy. A decent house in a respectable neighbourhood, good fresh air and open country. She's not used to this –'

'Neither am I, but it's all we can find at the moment.'

'To think I slaved, yes *slaved* down here in The Muck so she'd never have to live in it –'

'I see. The Muck is good enough to make money in but not good enough to live in.'

'Right first time! You're learning –'

'I'm learning a lot of things since I came back, Joe. I'm learning it was all right to fight here, night after night in the damn bombers, but it's a different story looking for a place to live, a job to work at.'

'Airlines turn you down, did they?'

A flash of anxiety crossed his son-in-law's face. 'They're not set up yet, naturally. It's too soon, but –'

'There's a lot of English lads can fly too, you know. You'll not get in there.'

'Well, I'll have to wait till I do,' Jan said.

'And what are you going to live on while you're waiting, may I ask? Lallie's not used to cutting corners, you know. She's never had to.'

'So you keep telling me, in one way or another.'

'What's that supposed to mean?'

'It means I'd appreciate it if you didn't keep buying her clothes, for one thing. I'm her husband. I can pay for them.'

'Hoho! That's what you think. She's never looked at a price tag in her life.'

'I'm beginning to realize that,' Jan said, 'but we'll live within our means.'

'Which are?'

'You're forgetting,' Jan said bitterly. 'I've four years back pay.'

Joe almost felt sorry for him. 'Service pay? Lallie'll go through that like a knife through butter!'

'We'll manage.'

'For the time being, yes.'

Again their eyes held. 'Just the same, Joe, I'd appreciate it if you stopped giving her money. Please?'

Damn, he'd *told* Lallie to keep it to herself –

'No, *she* didn't tell me, but it had to be coming from somewhere ...' Jan sighed as he folded himself into the only chair, a stained leftover from the previous tenants. 'I just want to make it clear that I intend to make her happy. I can, you know, and in my own way – but it would be a lot easier if you didn't keep "helping out".'

Joe walked over to the window, torn between loving his daughter and wanting to give the Pole a kick in the arse.

Smoking chimneys belched up at him. A cat in the alley had its grey head in a sardine tin, and down behind the dustbins two little lads giggled as they puffed on a fag-end. The door of the corner shop opened and there was Lallie, rolls of shelf-paper clutched to her cashmere coat, her calfskin dress-shoes picking their way through gutters clogged with sodden newsprint and God alone knew what else.

Christ!

It cost every scrap of self-control he possessed to turn back

239

to his son-in-law.

'I'll tell you what I'll do,' he said. 'If nothing else turns up I expect I can make a place for you at the foundry.'

The Pole flushed, whether from embarrassment or anger was not clear. His answer was a long time coming, and when it came Joe didn't know whether to be glad or sorry.

'Thank you Joe, but I don't think your foundry's quite what I want.'

While Jan explored job possibilities, Lallie shopped for the flat. Daddy always said she had an eye for quality. Now she could exercise it on something other than clothes, sallying forth every morning with lists and swatches and boundless enthusiasm. As she reminded Jan many time in the next weeks, they weren't buying for just the flat in Attercliffe – not that it wasn't just darling now it had been painted – but they had to consider the house they'd have next year or the year after. Short-term bargains were simply wasted money, weren't they? She discovered the loveliest bedroom suite – 'Darling, *do* look at the *workmanship*! It'll last a lifetime.' With a bit of diplomacy she persuaded him to accept a couple of chairs and sundry vases and silverware from Eccles Place and was able to swear: 'Honestly, they haven't been used for years and years!' At Ridley, Phipps and Saunders she discovered some exquisite pre-war French brocade and had Mrs Hodgson run up curtains and a bedspread for the flat, and in the process solved a problem that had nagged at her ever since she'd agreed they should have their own place. She got Daddy to take on Mrs H as housekeeper. To live in. 'It's the perfect answer, Daddy. Somebody has to look after you and Mrs H isn't exactly a stranger, is she? Besides, she's old enough that people won't *talk*, if that's what's worrying you.'

Life was shimmeringly perfect – except perhaps for the business of the living-room rug. They needed one, they really did, the floor was so bare, cold ....

After looking all over town she found exactly what she had in mind. It was Chinese, with graceful herons and apple trees on a ground of the mistiest, softest blue. She ordered it on the spot, confident that when it arrived Jan would love it too. He did, but pointed out that the cost (exactly half their entire bank balance) was outrageous. 'You're right,' she said quickly, 'you're right. I'll call the store and have it taken back.' It was the *most* humiliating call, and when she finally made the salesman understand that no, they couldn't keep it and no, none of the others appealed to her, she hung up close to tears and Jan put his arms around her and kissed the top of her head.

'I'm so sorry, darling,' she said into his sweater. 'I've never done it before and oh … I should have known, I should have thought!'

'The rug is perfect,' he said, 'it's just that we have to be careful until I get a job – and even then it will be a long time before we can have such things.' He tipped up her chin and made her look at him. 'Do you mind *very* much?'

'No! No I don't,' she said, too quickly. But when she saw the sad set of his mouth and rushed to soften it with kisses she realized she didn't mind so very much after all.

After they drew the French brocade curtains against the dreary afternoon street, after they put a shilling in the gas fire for warmth and made love on the misty blue carpet with its herons and apple trees, she tried to explain.

'I don't mind not having the rug – well, not much, we'll get one someday – it was having to call and tell them. I felt so … *mortified*.'

'People probably do it all the time,' he said gently, running long fingers over her stomach and following them with kisses.

'I don't know,' she said. She did know she'd never be able to walk in that store again, ever.

Even if the flat wasn't quite what she'd envisioned, she was happy. Sometimes, when he came through the door with a smile for her or a bunch of violets for Kaz's cup, happiness struck her such a sharp blow she wanted to freeze time, keep everything as perfect as the moment.

'I don't know how you stand living in that poky hole,' Daddy said sometimes when they were alone.

'I hardly notice the flat. I've got Jan,' she was able to answer with complete honesty.

241

The primitive cooking arrangements didn't bother her in the least. She wasn't fond of cooking and they dined at home with Daddy at least three times a week, anyway, and Mrs Hodgson was a smashing cook. Jan said they went to Eccles Place far too often, but for her it wasn't often enough. She *did* miss Daddy, not to mention Jolly, poor darling, who greeted her every visit with mad barks and frenetic circles round the cherry tree.

She also missed her car, but she wouldn't for the world have told Jan, who said they couldn't really afford to run it anyway. They hadn't been in the flat a week before someone etched vulgar words into the MG's red paintwork. Daddy was absolutely livid and insisted it be kept at home in the garage in future, well away from the riffraff in Lallie's new neighbourhood.

Lallie thought he was being a bit of a snob but had to admit the neighbours were not very friendly. She distinctly heard the man downstairs say 'Well, if it isn't Mrs La-di-dah,' when Lallie passed him in the hall. And right after she'd lent him a shilling for the gas! She didn't mind for herself, but she did mind when the man's wife told her to 'tell that effing foreigner not to whistle on the stairs of a morning. Who the 'ell does he think he is, the bleedin' Prince of Wales?' Their son Maurice, (a change-of-life baby, the woman had confided,) lurked about the hallways a lot, a giant with a pale, vacant face and unreliable coordination. Lallie always felt he was waiting to speak to her, but instead he'd blink his moist, slow eyes and lurch into the alley. She didn't tell Jan this, either. She did mention it to Neil, who said, 'Ignore them, sweetheart. They're jealous. It enrages them to see people happy, that's all. Just be sure to keep your door locked,' – though what that had to do with it she couldn't imagine. The doors at Eccles Place were never locked until bedtime, and not always then.

This new neighbourhood was a place of 'moonlight flits' in which tenants, late with the rent, moved in the middle of the night, everything they owned piled on a handcart to avoid the landlord and the law. The bobby on the beat was not Constable Curtain, who always had a biscuit for Jolly in his tunic pocket; here, the law was enforced by a nameless uniform who peered into every face on the street, shone his flashlight not just behind the dustbins but inside them too, to Lallie's utter bewilderment.

Jan had more to worry him than the neighbours, although he'd overheard enough of the men's remarks about Lallie to make the hunt for a job and thus a new neighbourhood doubly urgent. It was unnecessary for Joe to tell him that Lallie should not be alone at the flat after dark, though Joe *did* tell him, quite often. When interviews took Jan out of town overnight, Lallie slept at Eccles Place. The arrangement did not please him, but he could see the wisdom of it.

The job search was not going well. The airlines, gearing up for commercial service once again, already had more pilots than were needed, all English. The discovery that he did not, in any case, have nearly enough flying hours to his credit was a bitter pill. Not enough? All those tense hours over Germany not enough? Heads shook in sad amusement. 'Last week we had to turn down an ex-Wingco with double your hours.' Only as he was walking out the door did they give the whip a last gratuitous flick. 'A pity ... he was a local lad, too ...' It took less than a month to be turned down by every commercial line based in England.

Which left teaching, a prospect that did not excite and was unlikely to offer quite the life Lallie was used to. But he answered ads for language teachers anyway, sent resumés, went on endless interviews. Already he was wishing he'd joined the Polish Resettlement Corps, a stop-gap measure for returning servicemen. The PRC would have given him a breathing space, but in his haste to put the war behind him and be Lallie's full-time husband he'd signed away the option as lightly as he'd signed a mess chit in the old days.

'No, you were right,' Neil said when Jan admitted his regrets in the saloon bar of the Three Nuns. 'Best to make a clean break. You'll find something. You have a lot to offer.'

'Sure,' Jan said, bitterly aware of his age. 'Like thousands of others I can fly a bomber.' In a month he'd be twenty-eight, with no more idea of what to do with his life than he'd had at ten.

Neil wagged a finger. 'Aha, but *you* can fly in four languages, mate! Makes a difference,' he said, chuckling into his beer.

'Seriously though, I don't see why you don't come to the foundry. When markets settle down we'll be exporting like mad. We'll need a chap with your language background, and by then you'll know the ropes.'

'No,' Jan said quietly.

'Why? Joe told me he'd offered.'

'The way he'd throw a bone to a mongrel.'

'Oh, that's just Joe's way. He means well, but he couldn't be diplomatic if he tried.'

'He didn't try.'

To Jan's relief the subject turned to next week's soccer match. With Neil he could discuss his worries honestly, as he could not bring himself to do with Lallie, but the subject of Joe Wainwright was best avoided with both of them.

In September Roman and his new wife Genia visited them, their first real dinner guests to the flat. Stationed in Lincolnshire, the newlyweds were both with the PRC but planned, according to Roman's last letter, to return to Poland 'as soon as we know what the hell's happening there'.

Jan was oddly excited at the prospect of their visit. In all the months since leaving the airforce he'd spoken with not a single Pole. For a long time now he had thought almost entirely in English. It began in the airforce. At the *stalag*, surrounded by British, the habit was reinforced, and gradually the mental translation of each sentence before he spoke became less and less a conscious process. Let him hit his thumb with a hammer or cut his chin shaving, the 'DAMN!' instinctively called forth surprised him more than the small mishap. *Cholera*, it should have been, or *O Boże* ... but damn? At such moments he had the nagging suspicion that he had translated *himself* into English, that only in sleep was there anything left of Jan Kaliski, Pole. Waking from dreams, the fresh-dredged words clung to the surface of his mind, familiar yet foreign, words belonging to someone else. Even as he touched the cloud of Lallie's hair on the pillow beside him for reassurance, his mind would finger the known contours of the words, draw from them a bewildering mix of pain and comfort.

Góra. Yes, mountain ... and *lato*, summer ... *kwiaty*, flowers ... and *las*, forest ...

244

That his dreams always featured mountains and forests did not surprise him, nor that it was always summer and Mamunia wore a wide straw hat, cornflowers on the brim. But the word that floated alone, apparently unconnected to the dream's substance, was *kraj*. Country. Pronounced so like the English word 'cry' that it came laden with its own sorrowing reservoir. The country that had given him being, identity, was herself now defenceless, once again under the heavy-handed paw of Russia. In near-sleep he pressed his fists into the pillow, its down plucked from the breasts of English geese, and wondered if there was anywhere in the world he truly belonged – except in the slim arms reaching out to him.

'Having a bad dream, darling?' she'd murmur.

'I don't know,' was his invariable answer.

And he did not know.

The day Roman and his wife were expected, Jan had an interview at a private boys' school in Leeds for the post of language master. He saw himself, a few hours into the future, sitting across the dinner table, telling Lallie and his oldest friend that he had a job. Perhaps today, sunny and mellow for late September, would be lucky.

The moment he was shown into the headmaster's study his mood began to shift from vaguely optimistic to wishing he'd never come. Beige walls, brown curtains, ironwood desk and cupboards, leather-covered chairs icy to the touch. The room brooded under dark paintings depicting the battles of Trafalgar and Jutland and Waterloo. Grim-faced Victorians posed on croquet lawns, stiff and respectable in high collars and button-shoes. Facing him, its lip as extravagantly curved as its antlers, a stag's head gazed stoically at the visitor's chair.

The entire room seemed designed to intimidate, as no doubt it did. He shuddered at the image of small boys sitting here, exaggerating some small infraction of the rules as they waited for the headmaster's cane.

In the centre of the ironwood desk lay his application, its margins black with pencilled notations. He was tempted to read them, but the open door, the ancient heroes, the stag's lip, all argued against it.

He was made to wait half an hour exactly before the

headmaster entered, a middle-aged man with a set smile that seemed to be pinned up on the sharp points of his moustache. After a perfunctory greeting, in which he mangled 'Kaliski' out of all recognition, Mr Arbuthnot came straight to the point.

'Your qualifications are somewhat … irregular.' A complaint Jan had heard before. 'Exams not taken here, I see.'

'No, the University of Warsaw, but I think you'll find their standards comparable.'

'Well now, the University of Warsaw.' Mr. Arbuthnot's brow creased at the concept. 'Warsaw …' It might have been Mars.

'It's listed in the appropriate registers,' Jan said, his voice level.

'Quite … quite.' Pale fingertips almost met above the details of Jan's private life as set forth in the application. 'I see you are married. English, I presume? One stresses the point because our masters' families all live in the village. They tend to be a rather … close-knit group.'

Jan forced a calm breath. 'I'm sure she'd fit in.' Fit in? If this specimen was the norm, she'd dazzle them blind.

'Née Wainwright … a local girl, then?' In Mr Arbuthnot's tone lay the conviction that no well-brought-up girl would join in matrimony with a foreigner.

Jan stared at the carefully waxed moustache, the weak mouth under it, and wanted to laugh. Joe Wainwright brushed off Arbuthnots like bits of lint! 'Wainwright Foundry,' he said, very distinctly, and regretted it immediately. If they offered him the job now, it would be on Lallie's qualifications rather than his own.

'Indeed.' Respect dawned briefly, followed by a closer examination of the resumé and appropriate wrinkling of the brow. 'We'd have to let you know, of course. *So* many applications … but one can't help wondering how you'd get on with our people. We're rather … set in our ways up here, you know. Some might even say provincial.' His smile made it clear that *he* wouldn't say so, and that there were worse fates, anyhow, than to be English, provincial, and safely ensconced behind a desk. 'Do you follow me, Mr Kaliski?'

Jan looked directly into the smile, smug under its canopy,

and was immensely gratified to see a fair-sized cavity on the right incisor.

'Do you follow me?' the smile said again.

'I think I'm ahead of you, Mr Arbuthnot.'

He stood up. With the vague promise to call him soon the headmaster showed him out. By the time he reached the station, grey now under a sudden downpour, he was seething. *Do you follow me, Mr Kaliski?* Condescension – from a mediocre little school without a single claim to any kind of quality!

He missed his train by minutes. An hour to wait for the next one, barely enough time to make it to the flat before Roman got there – and Lallie with everything to do, and worrying if he'd got the job.

Lallie was having a simply marvellous day! That morning she'd taken the bus to Eccles Place to get Mrs Hodgson's advice on the dinner – she did so want it to be just perfect. The housekeeper did better, gave her a choice of a steak-and-kidney pie already made, or the roast chicken now browning in the oven; artichoke hearts or kidney beans – 'And you might as well take these poached pears and a cheese flan because me and your dad can't eat everything ...'

Oh dear, Jan would be so cross if she took it – but it *was* a special occasion and with food still rationed – not that Daddy seemed to have any trouble, and Mrs H was so used to cooking for a husband and two grown boys she couldn't seem to prepare *small* anything. The question decided, they had great fun rummaging in the attic amongst the 'best' things Mum had hardly ever even brought downstairs. Silver napkin-rings or brass? The matching candlesticks, of course! Brussels lace or pre-war Irish linen? And for the centrepiece asters, or pink roses from the rambler under the eaves?

So blissfully happy she hardly noticed the descent from airy Eccles Place to the closed-in grime of Attercliffe, she staggered off the bus laden with flowers and boxes of food to spend a few humming hours getting everything ready. She arranged the table and filled Kaz's cup with pink roses and babies'-breath, first giving the silver an affectionate rub with a soft cloth until

247

the bumps and hollows gleamed back at her just right. Oh, everything looked perfect, Jan would be so pleased – he was late, of course, but if he'd got the job there'd be all kinds of things to arrange …

The doorbell rang when she was bathed and ready, except for the dress Daddy gave her at Christmas, ivory silk with a thin gold belt and shoes to match. She shrugged into her kimono and ran to the door, hoping it was just Jan and *not* their guests before she was even dressed –

It was Maurice from downstairs, giving her his slightly unstable smile and shuffling from one foot to the other.

She stepped back in surprise, and he leaned in just far enough so she couldn't close the door without hitting him, an empty toffee-tin in his hand.

'It's mi mother,' he stammered. 'She says could you oblige her with a quarter of tea until the rations come out?'

She hesitated, wanting to give him the tea to get rid of him – but they borrowed all the time, money and rations, and nothing of it ever came back. She compromised. 'I can let you have a little, that's all. I'm short myself just now.'

She was in the kitchen spooning tea into the tin when she heard Maurice lurch after her, the smell of old beer and cigarettes preceding him. Turning quickly, she stared right into the knot of his greasy red tie. A dab of spittle ran off his chin.

'You're nice,' he was saying. 'Pretty. Maurice has been watching you.'

She set the toffee tin firmly against his chest and pushed. Don't let him see he makes you nervous, pretend he's a child – which he is, an old, backward child. 'You'd better hurry. Your mother's waiting for her tea.'

He laughed, and a look of sly daring flickered in his eyes. 'She's not in, mi dad neither. They over at the pub.'

'But she sent you –'

'Nah!' He laughed again, delighted at his own deceit.

Now she really was frightened, didn't stop to think before she whispered, 'Get out! Go home this minute!' reaching behind her for the paring knife on the counter.

He took in the flash of steel and shook his head, confused for a moment, hurt, his loose mouth in a pout. 'You don't

248

want to talk to Maurice like that … Maurice fancies you, he does.' His large fingers squeezed her wrist and the knife clattered into the sink. 'Ooh, soft,' he said. 'Soft skin. It smells nice …'

He leered down at her, and she had the sensation of moist, sick dreams closing in, his breathing loud and laboured on her forehead. She didn't move, not a muscle, as the fingers crept up her arm, the wide thumb stroking her neck. Think. What would he be afraid of?

'The police are coming soon, Maurice. You don't want them to find you, do you? There, do you hear them on the stairs?'

Again the over-large head swung from side to side. 'Police?' He answered himself in the mindless argot of the back streets. 'Police? Mi dad says they're fifty to t'dozen, police.' He laughed at his own joke. 'Mi dad says you're a bad 'un, you are. You let foreigners do *that* to you …'

'Do …?'

'You know,' he said, cunning. 'What Jesus says you shouldn't do.'

She daren't look down, but she sensed his hips were slowly moving back and forth.

Over his shoulder there was a flash of movement, but she couldn't seem to look away from the slack mouth until Jan's voice slipped between them, soothing, shaking only slightly.

'Come on, Maurice. Time to go. You can visit us another time, when we're not so busy.' At Maurice's puzzled frown he added: 'Jesus wants you to go, Maurice. He's waiting downstairs.'

Maurice stamped his foot, petulant, but with Jan's arm companionably guiding him to the door he left meekly enough, Jan talking, talking all the way down the stairs. Maurice safely behind his own front door, Jan raced back to the flat, his mind a chaos of relief and fear, anger and shame waiting in the wings. Suppose the train had been late, suppose he'd stopped for a newspaper at the corner shop? And Maurice! No wonder his parents filled him up with Jesus – God, what else could they do? They had no control any more, their monster-baby bigger than either of them, and healthy, except for his head. And he'd brought Lallie to this …

249

He closed the door of the flat behind him, noticing the pretty table, the flowers and candles for the first time, the smell of roast chicken and roses, the residual smell of Maurice lingering over everything.

He found Lallie in the tiny bathroom, scrubbing at her arms as if she'd never, ever get them clean. He held her and stroked her face, brushed her dishevelled hair as she poured out the broken story of Maurice and the quarter-pound of tea.

'To frighten you like that … oh Lallie, I'm so … sorry.' And responsible. And guilty.

'I was silly – really, he didn't *do* anything …' She grinned up at him but her cleaner-than-clean hands still trembled as she towelled them dry. 'A poor simpleton like Maurice, but he did seem to … *loom*, you know?'

He knew. Looming and sniggering, that poor simpleton would have raped her with the same childish pleasure he took in skewering worms on a stick. Jan had seen him often enough doing just that in the alley.

The flat was suddenly suffocating, its wretched space made human only by what had been brought from Eccles Place. Below them a train flashed by. Have-to-get-out, have-to-get-out, have-to-get-out it thundered, whizzing to the greener pastures of the countryside. This was what he'd brought Lallie to. Oh, she didn't complain, even said she liked the little rooms. Cosy, she said – but he couldn't help noticing that she never called it home. Home was Eccles Place. Why don't we go home to see Daddy? Or Jolly? Or Mrs H? Because she knew they couldn't afford it she never asked to go dancing or to the theatre either, not since she began to understand their situation, but she studied playbills at the Lyceum and the Empire as if she were taking an exam on them.

At least she hadn't asked him about his job in Leeds yet, but she would. He remembered Arbuthnot's satisfied smile. The bastard. The smug, self-important little snob …

And now Maurice. Pride was a nice thing to have, but it was becoming one more luxury they couldn't afford.

Then Lallie emerged smiling from the bedroom, radiant in the ivory silk dress, looking as pure and untouched as the day he met her. The only residue of the afternoon was the way she

250

subconsciously fretted at her arms, the touch of apprehension that flickered somewhere deep in her grey eyes. His lovely dream – one he now shared with Maurice. And how many others?

After the episode of Maurice the little dinner party had the calming effect of warm slippers and a good fire.

Roman's smile was as wide as ever, his voice as boomingly hearty. Jan didn't realize just how much he'd missed hearing Polish until he heard its amiable thunder coming up the stairs, Genia's quiet twitter in the background. They came bearing vodka and chocolates and a potted plant that had not travelled well. They, however, had, and their laughing account of the trip (accompanied by a sample of the vodka) eased the strain of the afternoon as perhaps nothing else could. Jan gave them a wicked imitation of Arbuthnot's 'Are you with me, Mr Kaliski' and Roman, on hearing Lallie recount Maurice's words, grabbed her arm and covered it with wet, smacking kisses, slobbering, 'Soft ... ooh, soft ... Roman fancies you, he does,' while Genia blushed and shushed and told him not to make fun of a poor thing like Maurice.

The women went to bed early, which left Jan and Roman in the living room with the remains of the chicken and the vodka, which they drank Polish fashion, in single gulps from shot glasses, the gas fire a quiet hiss in the background.

The years rolled back as they reminisced about schooldays, friends from their cadet unit, the bombing raids which had become high adventure and fun now they were over. They talked of marriage; the scandal of the Yalta Conference with its crushing implications for the future of Poland; the changes they saw in post-war England, the return of the old insularity and suspicion of foreigners; Polish clubs springing up everywhere (news to Jan) where Poles gathered for *kietlbasa* and *kiszka* made by Polish butchers and *babki* baked in the back rooms of new little bakeries springing up in the suburbs.

'Remember how we used to feel sorry for them, the peasants, back in Poland?' Roman said. 'All they knew was how to grow crops and cook food, when *we* could fly planes?' He laughed and shook his head. 'Big heroes, eh? They've got the laugh on

251

us now, lucky devils.' He told Jan of a butcher, right here in Sheffield, who supplied half the Poles in Northern England with groceries. Jan made a note of the name and promised himself, the minute he got a job, to go there for the biggest grocery order he could imagine. When he got a job ... yet the worry of even that was eased, chatting in Polish again, his old friend opposite him, Lallie sleeping safely in the bedroom. Of course they thoroughly dissected the scene with Maurice, and even easy-going Roman frowned at the possibilities.

'God, man, if that fool had really –'

'He didn't.'

'But *if*, friend ... If he ever does you're going to be one sorry Pole, to say nothing of what her father –'

'We're not telling him. We've already decided.'

'Smart.'

'But we have to get out, we *have* to – but we can't afford to move and even if we could ... hell, there's nowhere to move *to*, unless we buy something, which is out of the question.'

Roman's wide fist punched him lightly on the arm. 'Cheer up, you'll just keep your eye on her, that's all, until something turns up. You don't really have a choice, do you?'

But Jan knew there *was* a choice, one he didn't want to think about, much less discuss. 'She's so damned *innocent*! I wouldn't put it past her to give him a bar of chocolate or something tomorrow, just to show there's no ill feeling.'

The mention of chocolate made Roman dip into the box he'd brought, then he poured them each another shot of vodka as the talk turned to famous drinkers they'd known at the mess.

'Even little Kaz could do his share,' Roman laughed, his broad thumb rubbing the acorns on the rim of the silver cup. 'And Lech ...'

They were quiet for a long time, watching the blue flames of the gas-fire flicker in and out, but the future pulled them back, an aching tooth that drew their tongues like a magnet.

'What about Poland,' Roman said at last. 'Thought of going there? I hear Bura went back. Genia wants to, eventually. Misses her family.'

'No,' Jan said, meaning it. 'Poland's out.'

'I'm with you. I'm damned if I'll work for the commies.

Bloody Yalta. Bolek found himself a good job –'

'Where? What?'

Roman held up his hand, laughing. 'Argentina, would you believe. Flying! No, that's all I know about it, but some of the others signed up too. Worth thinking about.'

'Now you tell me.' His mind raced, spun, danced. God, to fly again, in peaceful skies ... But would she go? There was Joe ...

Like an echo, Roman said: 'Lallie wouldn't want to go that far, with her father here.'

'She's not married to her father.' But it would crush her to leave him ... and what do *you* know about Argentina? Nothing. They had llamas – or was that Peru? And in any case, how could he take her away? She was like the roses in Kaz's cup, the parent plant firmly rooted in the soil of Eccles Place. Already the roses on the table were drooping, while those still on the tree would be radiant as ever tomorrow morning.

'It makes you think,' Roman said comfortably, gnawing on a chicken wing.

It did indeed.

He seemed different after Roman and Genia's visit. Lallie sensed it in the way he read the want-ads, still checking off 'possibles' with a red pen, still mailing his carefully written letters to box numbers which seldom answered – but there was no anticipation now, as if he'd passed a fatalistic milestone only he knew was there. He no longer drew utopian plans for the home they'd build at the coast or up in the Lake District. The future was a closed subject. When he thought she wasn't watching him she could see the contours of defeat etch themselves ever more deeply into his features. She longed to smooth them away but he seemed closed to her also, spending long hours with books whose pages never seemed to turn.

It took such a little thing to change it all. He'd gone to the library to hunt through the out-of-town papers and she was restless, pacing the tiny flat and debating whether to splurge on haddock for dinner or settle for macaroni and cheese, when she glimpsed her reflecton in the window and turned back for another look. Gosh, and she thought *Jan* had changed! Her hair ... it looked, well ... positively unkempt! It was long of course, she'd always worn it long, but until lately Charles of Merton's had trimmed it every six weeks of her life, something to do with keeping the ends healthy, they said. It looked as if they were right. She was definitely overdue for an appointment. But Merton's ... She'd never seen the bills (Daddy's secretary took care of all that), but they were unquestionably high. And Jan working all last evening with the cheque book and a stub of pencil! Well, she'd learned to scrub floors and clean windows, hadn't she? And she'd watched Charles often enough.

Comb in one hand and scissors in the other, she set her goal at two inches. Three would have been more like it, but just to be on the safe side ...

She began. Once she got the feel of the scissors it was so *easy* she couldn't imagine why she hadn't done it before. Starting at the right, she worked her way carefully round to the other side. Somewhere in the middle she caught the cheerful snip-snip rhythm and worked faster, hair falling like dark rain to the linoleum underfoot.

There. It was done. All it needed was a comb through – but no matter how many times she combed it the sides didn't seem to match. She picked up the scissors and snipped a little more here, a little more there, then more again ...

It seemed hours before she was finally satisfied that the two sides were even. It was *much* shorter than she'd intended of course – even the longest bits only came to her shoulder now, but at least it was passable. As an afterthought she reached for a handmirror to check the back. No! She couldn't have, she just could not have done that! At some point in all that happy snipping she'd lopped off a swath to within an inch of her scalp – and at centre back, where it showed the most! How *could* she ... and what would Daddy say? And Jan? He *loved* her hair, always had, even from the very first night they were married he'd wanted to brush it and brush it until it became a nightly ritual, she picking up the brush and he taking it from her. 'Let me ...' Perhaps if she curled it ...

'Why?' he said, standing at the door and taking in the pile of clippings and her new curls. 'Why did you do it?'

She'd forced herself not to cry but now she saw the look in his eyes, sad and so kind, she couldn't stop herself.

'I thought you'd be furious,' she sobbed. 'I made such a mess of it ...'

His hands gripped her shoulders and he made her look up at him. 'Just tell me why you did it.' Then his mouth seemed to crumple and his hands dropped to his sides. 'No, you don't have to tell me. I know.'

He brought a dustpan and swept the dark cloud of her hair into a bag. 'I'll keep this,' he said grimly. 'It will be a good reminder.'

It was Jan who switched the light off when they made love, and for the first and only time she had to ask him, in the dark storm of passion, please not to hurt her.

CHAPTER TWENTY-THREE

Joe puffed on his pipe and waited. He'd made the offer once, couldn't speak fairer than that, and what did he get thrown back in his face? A bloody cocky answer, that's what. 'Thank you Joe, but your foundry's not what I want.' You spent a lifetime building up a business only to have some young pup look down his nose at it? Well, the shoe was on the other foot now. He'd be damned if he'd make it easy – but it was gratifying, just the same. There was a thing Millie used to say, something about casting your bread on the waters ... aye, and it was finally coming back, not a day too soon for Lallie's sake either, poor lass.

The day was nippy for October, but Mrs Hodgson had a nice bit of fire blazing in the grate. She was banging about the kitchen now, whipping up a gooseberry fool or some such, mumbling as she dusted flour off her specs. Lallie was out on the common with her dog, thank heaven. Opposite him across the living-room hearth was the Pole. His long hands looked folded, but Joe knew better; they were clenched as tight as his teeth – if the muscle jumping in his jaw was anything to go by. Joe fancied he could see sentences being formed and shuffled and re-formed under the pale, foreign-looking hair of his son-in-law. He wouldn't crawl. Joe gave him credit for that. He put the Dunhill lighter to his pipe again and watched the fresh smoke drawn lazily, inevitably up the chimney. His son-in-law seemed to have made up his mind, clearing his throat and looking straight into the fire.

'You offered me a job a few months ago, Joe. Is it still open? Not that I know the first thing about a foundry ...'

Joe poked at the fire and picked up the tongs, added a few lumps of coal and watched the new coal-dust give off cerise and violet flames before he allowed himself to sit back and look directly at Lallie's husband.

'Had a few doors slammed in your face, have you?'

The face in question flushed and hardened. 'Not slammed, no. That's not the English way, is it? Doors are closed quietly here.'

Doors are closed quietly here. God, he talked like a bloody book. He'd mastered the language though, there was that to be said for him. 'I suppose you're skint,' Joe said.

'Skint?' The Pole frowned, lost, as Joe knew he would be, in the idiomatic jungle.

'Financially embarrassed, I expect you'd call it.'

'We shall be soon, but it's not just that. We can't go on living down there. Lallie ... it's just no place for her.'

'I told you that. I also told you, if I remember right, that you could live here anytime you've a mind to. Glad to have you. I miss my lass, as if you didn't know. You don't have to work for me if you don't want to.'

The Pole gave him a twisted, painful smile. 'Yes I do. We don't want charity – I think I told *you* that before.'

Joe's opinion of the young man opposite soared another few notches, so much so that he found himself wanting to use his name – oh, not Jan yet, he couldn't get his tongue round that! – but he came close enough to feel he'd taken a giant step. John.

'Well, John,' he said. 'If that's what you want – you'll have to start at the bottom, mind! From the foundry floor and work up from there, like everybody else. It's not going to be easy. You'll have a bit of muck under your fingernails before you're done.'

'I'm prepared for that.'

Joe doubted that, but it showed willing. 'One thing – just so there's no misunderstanding. It's Neil. He's got every reason to think he'll be in my spot someday. He will be.'

His son-in-law smiled at last. 'I'm sure he should be. There's something else – "just so there's no misunderstanding". I'm asking for a *job*, not a career. Nothing permanent. Eventually I'll want to fly ... or teach ... or something.'

Joe forced himself to smile back. A cool young sod, this. Hard-headed. Had to flex his muscles even while you were doing him a favour! Well, he'd need every bit of muscle he could scrape up once he got on that foundry floor with Congreave as his gang foreman. 'You never know, lad,' he said heartily. 'You just might like it.'

They shook hands awkwardly and Joe poured drinks to seal the bargain – not that he knew quite what the bargain was. They touched glasses and drank, staring side by side out of the window. Across the common he could see Lallie walking the Afghan. By God, but she was a picture. She'd be pleased, he knew that. He said as much, touching the young man's arm in a gesture that did not come easily. 'She'll be fair chuffed when we tell her.'

'I expect she will,' was the less than enthusiastic answer.

Joe looked at the set face and experienced a sudden ache of compassion. Why, if the lad had been English, he wouldn't be surprised he could even have really taken to him!

'Never mind, John,' he said. 'Things'll start looking up now. Who knows, in a few years we'll likely have made a real Yorkshireman of you.'

Blue eyes suddenly stared into his, a fire in them that Joe neither expected nor understood.

'*Jan*,' said the tight voice. 'Not John. Do you think you can remember that, Joe? *My name is Jan.*'

257

Lallie was ecstatic. Every secret, wonderful thing she'd yearned for over the last months was happening – and so fast!

Jan was back to being himself – not enjoying the foundry much yet, that would come later – but he walked with his head up; he brought strange foods home from the Polish shop in town and had Mrs Hodgson cook them for him; he bought books and Chopin records and listened with such pleasure that only now did she realize what it had cost him to forgo them. He built shelves for the little suite they'd devised for themselves upstairs. They took their meals downstairs for the suite was small, just a sitting-room, bedroom and bathroom, but they were on their own, a lock on the door and a view of the common from every window.

She'd insisted on those rooms, knew they had to have some place where Jan could relax after work without Daddy always in view.

That was her one cross. With so much in common, she couldn't for the life of her see why they didn't get along better. All that strength of character, that stubborn pride in their roots. She said that to Neil once, and he roared with laughter.

'Sweetheart, that's just the trouble!' he said. 'Their roots are too damn different, aren't they? Like plum pudding and *kietlbasa*. Besides – I'll let you in on a secret – they *love* their arguments.'

She didn't. It was like living between two volcanos, either of which could erupt at the drop of an ill-chosen word. Let Jan say something the least bit favourable about the government and Daddy was sure to grumble that Whitehall was a bloody comic opera that only dreamy idealists had any faith in. Let Daddy gloat over a new reconstruction order and Jan couldn't seem to resist a crack about double profits. 'Wainwrights knock them down and Wainwrights build them back.' But it was only over dinner they clashed and, in any case, Mrs Hodgson kept mealtimes far too busy to leave much room for arguments. With 'a real family' to cook for again she was in her element, myopically rolling out pie crusts, mixing up cut-and-come-again cakes and Thursday dumplings, crumbling the daylights out of suet crust for her silverside pie. Her eyesight a life-long affliction, she'd long since learned to 'feel' the texture of what she stirred and kneaded and whipped. The results were superb.

Lallie was delighted to leave her to it. It left her free to concentrate on the kennels. The very first week they were back home Daddy had swept her off to Surrey to look at a couple of litters he'd heard about. They brought back two gangly pups with promise and a year-old bitch, Suleika, who had the most exquisite lines Lallie had ever seen.

'You're always busy,' Jan said, slightly miffed at the time she spent planning and supervising the construction of new runs.

'But darling, now we've *got* the dogs we need somewhere to *put* them! When Suka gives us our very own litter you'll see it's worth it. We'll have the best breeding stock in the north.'

There was a sticky moment when the registration arrived. Daddy's secretary took care of the paperwork so the kennel's registered name was something of a surprise. Jolallie Afghan Kennels.

'Oh dear,' she said, showing Jan the certificate. 'I *am* sorry. I suppose Daddy just … wasn't thinking.'

'On the contrary,' he said, his eyes unreadable. 'He's thinking like a businessman. Kaliski Kennels wouldn't have sold many dogs, not in this country.'

'You *do* mind, I can tell! And it doesn't *mean* anything –'

He pulled her to him so fiercely she could feel his heartbeat. 'Are you happy?' he whispered, 'really happy?'

'Of course I am, I can't even begin to take it all in!' Life was utterly, shimmeringly heaven. Jan and Daddy and all her *own* people close by, the kennels to run and these lovely familiar rooms to come home to. She didn't have to pretend any more, pretend she liked the flat, pretend it didn't matter when he came back defeated from an interview, pretend she *liked* riding the bus, counting pennies and shillings … 'There isn't a single thing I want that I don't have.' She nuzzled his ear, his shoulder, his chest. 'Except maybe …'

'Yes?'

He sounded so intent, so *listening* that she laughed in the evening hush of Eccles Place. 'A baby, of course!'

'We don't seem to be having much luck –'

'We will, we will! We just have to keep trying.'

Then they were both laughing as they sank to the thick burgundy carpet.

Afterwards, the distant bells at Martinswood ringing for evensong, he said, 'If we ever *are* lucky and it's a boy, just remember my father's name was Stefan, not Joe.'

'You *do* mind, *you do*!' she cried, pretending to pummel his chest.

'No,' he said smiling. 'If you're happy I don't mind anything.'

And he didn't seem to. Eyes closed, he lay on the settee listening to Chopin's Polonaise over and over until Lallie knew every note by heart, but the name of the breeding kennel was not mentioned again.

Every shift was an assault on the senses. The stink of spitting-hot metal seared nasal tissue; thick ribbons of liquid alloy, white and blinding, lingered on the retina long after their flow narrowed to silver-gold threads; winches screamed vats of molten metal across mammoth overhead tracks; in the shadows of the foundry floor gang-bosses postured and bellowed up at crane operators, directing the hazardous loads to waiting moulds.

Jan was on Congreave's team, quenching red-hot ingots in great tubs of water, closing his eyes against hissing gouts of steam, the tongs he wielded growing heavier as each shift wore on. As the muscles in his arms swelled and hardened, as blisters on his long hands matured to callouses, so did a grudging respect for Joe Wainwright take form. Not liking, not even admiration, but a man who started with nothing except a smithy in the country and turned it into this ... well, he deserved respect. How many gallons of sweat had he dripped onto this floor in the early days of the company? How many seven-day weeks, eighteen-hour days? That Jan felt it was done from greed and ego in no way minimized the effort spent.

Although nothing in Jan's experience had prepared him for such gruelling labour he was surprised to discover, with time, a certain satisfaction in the swing of the tongs and the hammer, the letting of sweat. Dirty and monotonous as it was, it was a

260

relief to return to after the hostilities of the tea-breaks.

From the beginning he was the outsider. His gang (no word could have been more apt) consisted of twenty labourers under the supervision of a foreman. Jan had always thought Joe Wainwright narrow and insular; the gang was a hundred times more so. Joe's boundaries spanned the length and breadth of Britain and possibly, on a magnanimous day, the Colonies. The gang's boundaries were no wider than Tinsley and Rotherham, with occasional Saturday afternoon forays to Sheffield for a football match.

In the naive hope they'd accept him at face value he told no one in the gang that he was in any way related to Joe Wainwright. When questioned, he simply said he'd applied for a job and they'd given him one. That was all. But even then:

'Don't mind us, we're not used to foreigners.'

'You talk like a bloody bank manager, mate. What were you 'afore this? Chancellor of the Exchequer?'

'You're lucky they took you on chum, with English lads lined up at t' Labour Exchange – them as aren't on the bleedin' dole. There should be a law against it.'

'My brother can't get a job – and he lost a leg at Dunkirk!'

There were a few of them who, in different circumstances, he could have enjoyed. Eddie the errand lad, who dispensed tea and highly personal weather reports each morning at ten. 'My mother's in her woolly knickers this morning, lads. Snow on the way!' 'Everything's thawing, even my wife!' There was Fat Percy, who worked a furnace some of the time and a betting shop all of the time, taking wagers on cricket or soccer, wrestling or push-ha'penny, on any two spiders walking across the ceiling. Congreave the foreman, barrel-chested and bandy-legged, made friendly overtures only when the gang was not around. For the most part, Jan was not allowed to forget that he was better-dressed and better-educated. He was tolerated, but resentfully.

He'd been at the foundry three months when it became known that he was married to Joe Wainwright's daughter. Friendly smiles turned to sullen nods. 'How's tricks, mate?' turned to cautious requests that he pass the hammer, please, or the tongs – but never the time of day. Ritual gripes about management and working conditions stopped cold. Let him get within ten feet of any group of navvies and tongues were instantly stilled. How could he blame them? Their position was impossible.

And so was his.

One payday, what little goodwill remaining was blown to smithereens. Jan happened to be away from the gang when the girl from Wages delivered the weekly packets of crackling, instantly-spendable cash – no cheques for hourly workers at Wainwrights. Envelope flaps were never sealed, just folded over. Jan returned to find a burly navvy, bolder than most, counting out Jan's pound notes and reading the accompanying time card. Jan tapped him on the shoulder.

'I think that's mine, Arthur.'

Arthur looked angry and prudent by turns as he stuffed the money into the envelope and handed it over. At the last moment anger beat prudence by a hair. 'It's bloody well not *mine*, mate! They paid you the telephone number by mistake.'

He'd exaggerated of course, but his point was made and quickly broadcast. Mistrust hardened overnight into silent, venomous hatred.

'It's so stupid!' Jan raged to Lallie. 'I'd no *idea* they made so little – what on earth was Joe thinking about?'

'But you're in the family, of course he'd pay you more, it's only natural.'

'It's humiliating. No wonder they hate me. I feel like a … a prostitute.'

'But you work so hard,' she said, genuinely perplexed. 'You deserve –'

'– no more than the rest of the gang. I get almost twice as much. Arthur has three children, one of the others has six!'

He tackled Joe over Mrs Hodgson's apple turnovers.

'Damn it, Joe, I do less work than they do – they're bullocks, some of them – it's not fair!'

Joe shook his head in wonder. 'There's just no pleasing you, is there? I try to make things easier for you –'

'But I'm not earning it – and we don't need it!'

'Maybe you think you don't – wait till you see the bill for the new dog coming next week –'

'We don't need that either!'

'*Jan*!' Lallie chimed in. 'We *have* to have that dog. Jolly's getting a bit past it and we have to breed with Suka if we want –'

The economics of a breeding kennel were not at issue here and he told her so, rather more sharply than he intended. She threw down her napkin and ran from the room.

'Now look what you've done,' Joe said, calmly slicing off a wedge of Cheddar.

'It's still not fair,' Jan persisted.

'Life's not fair, that's why you have to look after your own, isn't it? Nobody else will.'

'But don't you see the position it puts me in –'

'I see I'm having my dinner. At home. I don't talk business at home.'

'But the men –'

'If the men don't like the way I run my business they can go elsewhere. There's hundreds more where they came from. Mrs H!' he shouted to the kitchen. 'What about some more tea?' He turned back to Jan. 'Of course, if it bothers you that much I could move you to Purchasing. You've been on the floor about long enough, I reckon.'

Jan shook his head. 'To move now would only make it worse. I'll stay where I am.'

Joe leaned forward. 'Suit yourself, but remember this. *She* doesn't go without, not while she's under this roof, is that clear? If *I* give her what she's used to you complain, so it has to come from you – and navvy wages don't cover it, not by a long shot.'

Jan remembered the little wad of Lallie's hair tucked in a corner of the dresser, and kept quiet. Then she was back in the room, bending to kiss his forehead and ruffle his hair. 'I *am* sorry, darling. Silly to flounce out like that, and of course you were right. And *you*, Daddy –' wagging her finger at Joe '– are not very tactful.' But she moved round the table and kissed her father too, trailing her delicate fragrance and her sweetness between them.

He was in a velvet vise with no permanent way out except the want ads, which he continued to scrutinize with no better

263

results than before. When the vise became too tight, as it sometimes did, he found sanctuary at the shop of Henryk Ryba.

To step over the threshold was to step back in time. From the very first day the long, narrow shop seemed like a microcosm of the Poland he'd grown up in. Baskets of rye bread and honey cakes lined the counter; *polędwica* and *Krakowska* hung from the ceiling on long, swinging hooks, their smoked skins a rich, gleaming brown; *kietlbasa* rings were strung like bracelets on a string and fat rolls of *salceson* always flanked the slicer, ready for the sample Henryk offered anyone who stepped through the door. 'Makes sales,' he shrugged when his wife grumbled at the waste. On the shelves were boxes of herring, freshly smoked and sent up from London twice a week. There was dried mushrooms and Vienna sausages; stringy bunches of dill and tiny packets of saffron powder; a giant barrel in which gherkins floated and bobbed in a murky green brine. And the thing that brought him back every week without fail, a Polish newsletter printed in London and sent up with the Saturday herrings.

When Lallie went to the shop with him, Anna Ryba invited them up to the flat above to take tea, pinching Lallie's cheek and telling Jan in rapid Polish that she was '*jak lalka, nie?*' Like a doll, a pretty doll, tweaking Lallie's chin and touching her hair. 'No,' Jan said quickly, repeating Lallie's name very clearly so the woman would understand, yet not quite sure why it was important to him that she make the distinction. Perhaps because the other Lalka was a wreck somewhere off the German coast, her flame-licked body riddled with bullets? He knew the parallel disturbed him, brought back memories of a ledge from which he was quick to step back.

The Rybas' flat delighted and grieved him, so like the flat in Morska Street it seemed an injustice that Mamunia was not in it, 'making' her household accounts and offering terse judgements on family and friends. Heavy curtains shielded them from the street, faded old rugs muffled their steps and the wallpaper was thickly embossed. He saw Lallie's grey eyes take in the massive furniture as she settled herself gingerly on the smallest chair – just as she would have entered Morska Street, uncertain and on her very best behaviour. He was amused and thought perhaps she'd gone a little too far when she invited the Rybas to dinner at Eccles Place the following Saturday. What would Joe say about *that*?

'He'll be pleased,' she said firmly as they drove home, the MG open to spring breezes. 'It's time we started asking friends in. It's our home too, and Mrs Hodgson will have a marvellous time cooking.' They were putting the car in the garage when she said, 'It's a pity they don't speak more English though – you can't very well translate the whole evening.'

'You could learn a little Polish …' he said, not for a moment thinking she would. At Hempton she'd made a start, but their time there was too brief for anything more than a few halting phrases, awkwardly learned and soon forgotten.

'That's exactly what I'll do! For the whole week don't let me speak a single word of English!'

When Joe heard her efforts he was quick to comment. 'What do you want to waste your time with that for?'

'Why shouldn't she?' Jan demanded, furious Joe had so swiftly stepped on her enthusiasm.

'Why should she? It's not as if you're ever going back.'

The certainty in Joe's voice enraged him further. 'How do you know? We might want to –'

'You can't though, can you?' A touch of triumph was added to the certainty, and Jan lost his temper.

'We could if you hadn't given Poland away at Yalta!'

'Oh, come on! If it wasn't for us you'd be singing Heil Hitler now.'

'Is the 'Volga Boatman' any better?'

'*Oh you men,*' Lallie cried. 'Couldn't we have *one* evening, just one without an argument?'

'Honestly,' she said later, when they were upstairs. 'You're like two little boys. I wish, I just wish you'd both …' Her voice broke up into little sobs, the second time in as many days. He was contrite – and mystified. The argument had been no worse, and much shorter, than usual.

'I'm sorry darling, I didn't think it upset you –'

'*Of course it upsets me*! *It's just a tug of war all the time –*'

'I'm sorry,' he said again.

'— *and I'm the rope!*'

He pulled her into his lap and smoothed her hair, wondering if perhaps ...

'You've been on edge lately —'

'So have you!'

How could he deny it? 'You're not ...?'

She shook her head, the scent of her hair clouding its sweet mantle over them as she sighed against his neck. 'No. I wish I were, oh I do wish ... every day ... I keep thinking we wouldn't have all this friction if you just had something to *share* with him.'

They sat for a long time in the darkening room. At last he said, 'Look, Roman's still writing about people going to Argentina to fly. I could look into it if ...' His voice trailed off, waiting for her quick rejection — which did not come.

Instead she drew in a tremulous breath and whispered, 'Perhaps you'd better,' very slowly. She didn't speak again until they were in bed and he thought she was asleep in the circle of his arm.

'It's not that I *want* to go, you know. He'll have no one, will he? But I love you both so much and you're tearing me up and there's nothing I can do ...'

'Sleep,' he whispered, his lips on her hair. 'We'll talk about it tomorrow.'

He knew they wouldn't. How could they when it hurt her so?

TWENTY-FOUR

On the pretext of tending the dogs Lallie came to spend more and more of the dinner hour at the kennels, less and less at the contentious dinner table in the house. In the kennels she could relax. The dogs were high-spirited; they barked and yipped and occasionally snarled, but their hostilities were short-lived

266

and decisive. One dog conceded, another dog won, and within minutes there was peace.

The two men in the house seemed incapable of the smallest concession. One pushed and the other pushed back. The more Daddy strove to turn Jan into an Englishman the more Polish Jan became.

If Daddy wanted them to go to the races Jan would find a foreign film they just could not miss even if it meant driving fifty miles to see it. Gilbert and Sullivan on the radio was the signal for Chopin records upstairs. If Daddy asked Neil and his mother to come for dinner, Jan would invite the Rybas – whom Daddy did not like and said so.

'You don't like Agnes Armott either,' Jan said.

'At least she speaks English.'

'So do Henryk and Anna.'

'You call that English? I don't see why you have to kiss her hand when she comes in, either. I thought you'd outgrown –'

'I've outgrown nothing. She's married and she's Polish. It's expected. She'd be offended if I didn't. If we can't bring our friends –'

'Why don't you make some English friends?'

'Where? At the foundry?'

It was so petty! Listening to the hairs split, she wanted to scream. Daddy hadn't changed and never would; if he was blunter to Jan now it was because they knew each other better and he could be more open. But Jan *was* changed, in ways that troubled her thoughts and even intruded on the private time they had together.

Every mention of Poland in the papers was cut out and filed. The newsletter from London was read and read again, its every paragraph translated for her over the evening glass of wine. Letters to the editor; bleak personals with their desperate pleas for news of relatives; inflammatory rumours on conditions in Poland. Poland was a prison. People were living in the streets. They were starving. No news could get out. Useless for her to argue that if no news got out how could the writers of the newsletter *know* what it was like inside Poland. The iron curtain *had* come down with a crash, and that was all she was sure of. Perhaps it's all based on rumour, she tried to suggest. If so, it was rumour he was prepared to believe. What had seemed to be no more than natural interest was, in her eyes, becoming an obsession. Old bones that should have been forgotten were dug up and worried at again and again, the scars pointed out to Daddy and then to her.

The victory parade in London, right at the end of the war: Crews from every other country in the fighting were invited to join in the fly-past. But was there a Polish crew? A Polish squadron ...

'Even when we came home from the damn *stalag* there were flags waving all over the place – but was there a Polish flag? No! God, we couldn't find one for Kaz, remember?'

'Why can't you just forget?' she asked him.

'Because I can't forgive!'

'But the war's over now. You belong here with us in England. With me. If you'd just look forward ...'

'You've been listening to your father,' he said bitterly. 'I should become an Englishman, that's what you're trying to say, isn't it? Another legal, loyal subject of the King? I swear by Almighty God to bear true allegiance?'

'It wouldn't do any harm,' she said gently. 'You must admit it would help you get the kind of job you want –'

'You make it sound like joining the Norton Garden Club! What I am is *important* to me, damn it! You want me to throw it away, just so I can join the club?'

'Please don't, darling. Don't be cross. I love *you* –'

'In spite of my nationality!'

'That has nothing to do with it. I married you, not your nationality –'

'*That's just the point*! I *am* my nationality. Do you think I'd be the same person I am now if I'd been born here?'

If only you had been, she thought wearily. Then they could live in peace – but no, that was disloyal, not fair to him ...

Much as she liked them, the Rybas were no help. With them Jan was different, more relaxed, but when he came home from the shop it was as if he'd been to Poland and liked it and wanted to stay. It was easier with Roman and Genia. They were younger, more flexible, and Roman seemed to understand Jan's depression and could lift him out of it – but they were a hundred miles away. The Rybas were here in town. He seemed to be using them as surrogate parents, their living room transformed, because he was unhappy, into the living room in Morska Street, which no longer existed. She lied now when Jan asked her if she was happy. How could she be, when he was so obviously not? And no sign yet of the baby she was certain would solve everything.

Emigration still hung like a question mark between them, often mentioned but never acted upon. The United States had quotas and long waiting-lists. Australia was more accessible but would he be any more welcome there than here? He said not. Which left South America, a prospect which appealed to him but not to her, but then again, if he'd be happier ...

After a particularly rancorous argument between the men over something so meaningless she couldn't remember what started it, her temper, so long controlled, finally snapped.

'For God's sake let's go somewhere, anywhere!' she cried in desperation. 'Anything would be better than this ... this *limbo*!'

He stood very still, and she suddenly realized that it was she and not he who'd raised the subject of leaving Eccles Place. A first, but she was too angry to back down.

'Do you mean it?' he said quietly.

'*Yes!*' she cried. '*Yes, yes, yes!*'

She recovered herself to insist they at least discuss it with Daddy first. 'I owe him that.'

'Tell, not discuss,' he said firmly. 'It's our life, not his.'

They 'wanted a word with him', sprung it on him out of nowhere, hardly even gave him a chance to settle in his chair and unravel a bit.

'Hang on a minute,' he said. 'Let me get in the house before you come at me – God, what a day! Where's my drink?'

Lallie ran to get it as he eased into his chair and lit his pipe, the problems of the foundry pressing on him still. Business was good but the unions were clamouring for the moon again ... easy to demand this that and the other when somebody else had to provide it. Tea breaks and holidays with pay – it would be Turkish baths and feather beds next, he wouldn't wonder.

'Thanks, love.' The first twinge of anxiety came when he

accepted his glass and saw her eyes looking at him over its rim. Bigger, darker than usual, with that smudged look as if she'd been crying for a long time. And her mouth looked different, too pink and not quite steady round the edges as she spoke. Even when she was a baby he always knew when she'd been having a weep – sometimes before Millie noticed. What was it the Pole said a while back? 'I can make her happy, Joe, I can.' And a fine job he was making of it by the look of things ...

Joe hardly noticed what she was saying until an unexpected word jumped out and showed its teeth.

'... to South America, Daddy. I know it's far, but –'

'But a lot of Poles are going,' Jan said. 'Doing well from what I hear –'

' – and we can come back for holidays or whenever you want us to, Daddy?'

He tried to find his voice but it was off somewhere, shouting down the corridors of the past. *Come on hinny, smile for Daddy ... Give your Da a kiss then, and another ... Wait till you see what he brought you – Christ! don't squeeze it, it's pedigree's longer than yours ... She's gone love, Millie's dead so there's just us ...'*

Going away ... away ... South America ... Lallie in South America ...

'Things aren't working out very well, Joe,' the Pole was saying, the young smooth look of him making Joe want to smash him, knock away the possessive hand on Lallie's shoulder. The face blurred in front of him and he heard himself shouting.

'What d'you mean, not working out? You've got a nice home, haven't you? A job? By God, if I'd had this at your age I'd have thought I was in clover!'

'But you don't get on together, Daddy,' Lallie said, her eyes pleading.

'I get on with him fine, fine! Is it my fault if he can't get on with me?'

'Oh Daddy ...'

'The point is,' the Pole cut in quickly, 'we've decided. There are opportunities. In Brazil or Argentina I can fly –'

'*You*, yes – but what's *she* going to do on the other side of the world. *And why there?*'

The Pole's eyes lit up as if he'd been waiting, hoping for the

270

question. 'Because we're welcome, that's why.' There was bitterness in the words, but Joe caught the ring of triumph, too. '*We're welcome.*'

'*Welcome?*' he roared. 'Every bloody Nazi in the world's welcome, too – they're running like rats to a hole. Some countries take anybody, anybody!' He knew he was making it worse, proving their point, but the thought of Lallie – 'You'd take my lass all that way? To live with foreigners?'

'No, Joe. Lallie will be the foreigner, the way I am here.'

The concept shocked him to silence for a moment. Lallie the outsider, whispered about, pointed at, dark eyes touching her, darker thoughts moving over her. 'She'll have nobody ...'

'She'll have me.' Jan stood up, suddenly looming large over him. 'I know it's been a shock, but it does seem to be for the best.'

Best for the Pole, aye, but what about her?

'What about you, love?' he said, turning and shutting out his son-in-law. 'You wouldn't have the dogs – poor old Jolly with nobody but Mrs H, and Suka ready to whelp next month ...' And Joe, what about Joe, his head thundered? What about me?

Then she was on his lap, her cheek wet against his, the silk of her blouse cool to his face. 'We're not going *tomorrow* Daddy,' she whispered. 'It'll take months and months ...'

They rocked in the chair for a long time and he made her take a sip of his Scotch. When he looked up the Pole was gone. After a moment a tide of Chopin came rippling down the stairs and into the room, surrounding them with quiet persistence.

In April, after preliminary papers for Argentina had already been filed (and when the cherry tree at Eccles Place was a cloud of organdy, when Suka produced five squirming but nevertheless patrician puppies, when Lallie clearly didn't want to leave any of it), they drove to Ryba's shop for a ring of *kietlbasa* and a bag of honey cakes. And the weekly newsletter, which he read as Lallie drove. It was a shoestring affair, four pages of news and opinion with the last page reserved for personals and ads, easily read, even to the accompaniment of Lallie's chatter about Mrs Ryba's new permanent wave and

271

that simply *horrid* pike they'd had in a basket on the counter –

'All those *wicked* teeth! Jan, *why* would anyone want to eat something so *ugly*? Oh, and we really ought to stop at the greengrocer. Mrs H said specially she needed some watercress and parsley ...'

Her voice ran over him like water music, no answers expected and none given. Now a start had been made on their plans to leave England, it was as if she felt compelled to fill every small silence with idle chatter, leaving no chink for talk of Argentina to creep in. Books he'd brought home from the library on South American countries and customs were left untouched on her bedside table; questions as to whether they should sail or fly were answered with a vague 'We'll decide when the time comes, darling.' Most ominous of all, she'd planted a lilac hedge in front of the greenhouse. 'They make the *loveliest* screen – oh, they won't do much *next* season, but in two or three years they'll be heaven ...'

Joe, it seemed to Jan, was mellowing. He could actually be seen to bite his tongue, and dinner-table harangues were a thing of the past. But Joe, no more than Lallie, could be drawn into talk of a future that did not place her squarely at Eccles Place. Jan was disturbed but not deterred, convinced that once the tie was loosened they would all breathe easier. Doggedly, he made plans and job contacts in Buenos Aires, and meantime kept up with Polish affairs here.

Hard news was easier to come by and more reliable than either Joe or Lallie believed. He'd seen her wordless signals to her father that said, plainer than words, 'Humour him, it's just a phase.' They thought it paranoia founded on rumour when he talked about Poland's condition, the treacheries of the war compounded by deliberate silence after it. It was useless to expect them to believe, with no knowledge of Poland's past and no apparent curiosity. How could they understand, their lives spent in a stable country whose only border was the sea? The sea moved by the moon's edict alone. He had friends, some from childhood, who started the war as Poles, had by turns become German and now Russian, all by edicts handed down by committee, by foreign leaders with no higher aim than to make the bed neatly, mitre the corners and sweep the dust as far underneath as it would go. In the peaceful English countryside through which they now drove the evidence of war was already fading. Soon it would be gone, taking its nightmares with it. People wanted to forget. Reminders like the newsletter were uncomfortable, better ignored.

Lallie was heading the MG into the garage, still chattering about nothing, when his own name leapt out at him from the last page of the newsletter.

It was one line, buried in the personals.

Jan Kaliski, ex-airforce, contact Piotr Bauman.

She waited for him to help her out with the shopping. When he made no move to get out of the car she looked into his face, saw surprise turn to bewilderment then to an expression she couldn't fathom, as if a spring inside him wound tighter and tighter. It was that damn paper again …

'Darling, what *is* it?' She tried to keep the impatience out of her voice but she heard it just the same. Oh dear …

He translated the item in a flat, tight voice. '… and there's a London phone number.'

The message was odd, certainly, but not alarming. If he just wouldn't take everything so *seriously*! 'I know what it is,' she said, nudging him in the ribs and hoping for a smile. 'It's your wicked past coming back to haunt you. A long lost love you jilted somewhere …' No smile, just that tight look to his mouth, the muscles of his jaw working. 'I *am* sorry, darling, I shouldn't tease. It's probably some old airforce crony wanting to borrow a pound or two. Go in and call.'

She gave him a little push and watched him walk slowly into the house, feeling again the tug of sympathy and the enormous gulf between her own life and his. Much as she tried, she couldn't begin to imagine how it must feel to be stateless, no family, no country, nothing left of your past but memories and griefs and that terrible, corrosive anger.

He was on the phone for a long time. When he came to her in the living room he seemed to sway on the threshold, uncertain where to go, his face a sick, deathly grey. His long fingers opened and closed as if on strings, and when she spoke to him he just stood there dazed, shaking his head.

Shock. He'd had some terrible shock … but what?

Instinctively she pushed him into Daddy's chair and chafed his hands, cold and damp, in hers. She'd seen this numbed, unblinking state before, in the blitz. He was so still. His lips, moving to no purpose, were tight and bloodless. Only the eyes lived, a burning blue, electric in the dead pallor of his face.

Oh God, he was ill, desperately ill ... or mad ... He *looked* mad ... but the flaccid hands in hers suddenly jerked to life, clutched at her fingers with the strength of a fanatic, bruising her skin.

'Darling, what *is* it? Tell me, please ...'

His mouth moved. '*Mamunia.*'

As she watched, the entire structure of his face seemed to alter. Hard lines softened, ran together; straight lips trembled and crumpled; the startling blue of his eyes was suddenly dimmed, awash with tears. A long, painful sob was wrenched from his chest. He began to speak in Polish then stopped, began again in English.

'It's my mother. She's been in Auschwitz ... she's alive ...'

Then it was she struggling and failing to absorb it. That damned newsletter ... it was some sick sadistic joke ... it was a mistake ... it was –

'No,' he said, 'no, it's true. Bauman – he was with me in cadet school – he lives in Switzerland. His uncle works for one of those relief groups ... They see all the lists ... she was sent back to Poland in an ambulance ...'

Oh, the cruelty, to stir up such hope! 'Don't, don't *hope*, darling. Somebody would have *told* you –'

'Somebody did. Bauman.' He stared over her shoulder into the past. 'It's funny. I never liked Bauman, he was ... too clever, always made top marks –'

'Not him, somebody *official* would have told you!'

'They will, eventually.' His lips twisted. 'They'll tell when every name's been confirmed, every T crossed. He – Bauman, says they've thousands to trace, find next of kin ... It can take years ... He saw her name, remembered me ... when he came to London he advertised, hoping I'd see it –'

'Why didn't he call you direct?' she said, latching on to the irrelevant because everything else was shifting, uncertain.

'How would he find my number? The phone is listed under Wainwright.'

She had no answer for that. 'Did he say where she was?'

'In Poland.'

'Where in Poland? Exactly?'

'He didn't know ... just that she'd been sent. A hospital, probably ...'

She didn't know what to say to him. If it were true she should say she was happy for him – and she *was, she was*! But if it turned out to be a mistake ...

'Why don't you wait, darling, until you hear officially ...'

He suddenly looked very tired. 'She's not a young woman ... five years in Auschwitz ...'

And sent back to Poland in an ambulance. She saw what he was thinking and she hated Piòtr Bauman, *hated* him for raising hope where none existed, none at all. It was cruel, cruel ...

'I have to go of course,' he said. 'I have to find her.'

'I'll go with you –'

'No!'

TWENTY-FIVE

His mood swung wildly between jubilation and foreboding.

Mamunia was *alive*, tapping impatient fingers, waiting for him to come for her, wondering where he was – even if he'd survived the war.

But Mamunia in a concentration camp, all her pride (some had called it arrogance) crushed by degradation. What had they done to her? Why had she been sent back in an ambulance? Like everyone else he'd seen the newsreels, flinched and closed his eyes against the skeletal heaps that moved. Barely.

One moment he was tempted to rush to Poland and find her, the hell with entry visas and passports and permits – the next he knew without question that he'd never get past the border. So he filed application forms and waited.

Not for an instant did he doubt Bauman's story. Lallie, although she begged to come with him, obviously did. But she did not say so, and was unbelievably tender in the first dream-racked nights when he wrestled with the news, fought frantically to adjust. The hours of trying to *think*, to imagine, with no sleep possible, and sleep, when it finally came, so filled with terror he struggled to wake. Mamunia bundled in her best winter coat, dark green wool with a sable collar and matching hat, picking her way across the cobbles to the bakery which became, as she walked into it, a vast oven ... Himself in pilot's uniform, pouring wine into a silver cup with acorns on its rim, passing the cup to fingers which had no flesh, were bones from whose rattle he fought to wake ... Tatuš and Millie walking through a field of wild thyme, not seeing the warning wire until it was too late –

'Wake up, darling, wake up!' Lallie's soft kisses on his cheek, hands holding him tight to firm young breasts under which a heartbeat fluttered quick as birds' wings.

'You know I have to go? You understand?' he whispered.

'But I want to go with you,' she persisted.

'You can't. It's a different country now – I can't be sure what it's like under the new regime.'

'But still ...'

'It's too risky.'

'And not for you?'

Patiently he explained that he spoke the language, knew his way around. 'I'm Polish. From their point of view I belong there. I'll be able to move around, make enquiries, find her and get her out – or at least see if she's all right.'

'Yes, but –'

'It's better I go alone.'

On that if on nothing else, Joe Wainwright agreed with him. But as to the purpose of the trip, he seemed sceptical. They discussed it in the warmth and privacy of the greenhouse, surrounded by vegetable seedlings and flowers and tomato plants heavy with green, pungent fruit.

'If you ask me it'll be nothing but a wild goose chase. Somebody's pulling your leg, lad.'

'I don't think so. There was never any kind of proof that she'd died … I just assumed, from everything I'd heard.'

'Aye, but even if it's true I don't see why you have to go tearing off – I mean, you'll find out eventually, and in the meantime you know she's being looked after –'

'If she is, it's by strangers. *She's my mother, Joe*! And from Auschwitz! God knows what her health must be like –'

'Auschwitz!' Joe said, exasperated. 'Why the hell would they have put her there? Doesn't make sense. She's not Jewish, is she?'

Jan passed a hand across his eyes. 'No, Joe …'

'Well then!'

'You didn't have to be Jewish. The Nazis were liberal. They took in millions. Poles, Belgians, Dutch …'

'What reason would they have?'

'Reason didn't enter into it,' he said wearily. 'I know I have to go, that's all.'

'And if it turns out to be a cock-and-bull story?'

Jan met his father-in-law's eyes and found real concern looking back at him. 'Then I'll come back, nothing lost,' he said. Nothing but Mamunia. Again. 'You know Lallie wants to go with me?'

Joe sighed. 'Aye, so she tells me. She's not used to roughing it –'

'Before the war we lived as civilized as you do!'

'Before maybe, but this is *after*.'

'I know. I've thought about it. Warsaw was a shambles and there hasn't been time to rebuild … I'm not even sure the hotels are open, so you don't have to worry. I can't take her. Besides, there's no need. I'll be back in a few weeks.'

'I wouldn't be so sure about that. It might be a long search.' Joe looked uneasy, rubbing a leaf between finger and thumb, releasing the smell of summer and fresh tomatoes into the steamy heat of the greenhouse. 'What sort of welcome do you expect, then? In Poland?'

Jan's temper rose at the implication. 'It's my country! Of course I'll be welcome,' he said defensively.

'What about the lads that have gone back to live? What do they say?'

It was Jan's turn to be uneasy. He hadn't heard from any of them, not one. He shrugged. 'You know what the mail's like, so it's hard to tell. Maybe they're too busy to write.'

Joe seemed unusually thoughtful as he looked down on the tender new green of lettuce seedlings. To Jan's astonishment his father-in-law reached out and laid a hand on his shoulder. 'You'll not rest until you've found out for sure, will you lad?'

'No.'

He shook his head. 'You're a stubborn young devil and no mistake. Well, we'll just have to hope for the best, won't we?'

Jan had never felt closer to Joe Wainwright than he did at that moment in the warm, moist air and the heavy scent of tomatoes and Easter lilies.

As they walked across the lawn to the house, Joe stopped. 'What about South America then?' he said carefully.

Jan had to reach back in his mind … South America! That was before Bauman's message. The reasons for wanting to go there seemed so petty now that he laughed. By comparison, the prospect of finding his mother dwarfed everything else. How could he think about the future until he knew if Mamunia would be in it? But she would be, of course she would.

'We'll have to wait and see,' he said, not quite ready to let Joe off the hook yet despite the new feeling of cautious warmth between them.

Permission to enter Poland arrived sooner than he'd dared hope.

'You see?' he said to Lallie, kissing her jubilantly by the open window and smiling as the crisp breeze ruffled her hair – which was once again elegantly cut and shaped by Charles of Merton's. 'If I'd listened to you and Joe, taken out citizenship, it might have been months – *years* before they let me in.'

'But why?' she said, genuinely puzzled.

Untravelled, she had not the faintest notion of the complexities of a post-war journey. Her assumption, typically British, was that a man could go wherever he chose, no question asked. A short month ago her ignorance of such things had irritated him; now, the exhilaration of the moment made him indulgent.

'Because, my innocent, Jan Kaliski-British subject would

278

have been a foreigner, would probably not have been allowed in at all!'

'That's silly. You can prove you were born there.'

'Aha, but it's a 'people's government' now – or so they claim. And the British are imperialists –'

'They are not!'

'That depends on where you're standing.' He picked her up and swung her around, narrowly avoiding a jug of bluebells and beech leaves on the window sill. 'You see?'

'Oh ... you!' She kissed him in full view of the village constable, who was pedalling serenely by the house and waving to them through the open window. 'I know exactly what you're up to. You're trying to make me forget you're deserting me.'

'Only for a few weeks –'

Her grey eyes clouded for a moment. 'I'm not sure I like it, just the same. All on your own in a strange country.'

'It's my *own* country, how many times ... Listen, there are no tigers hiding in the bushes, no bandits to cut me off at the pass, no quicksands, no typhoons, not even a desert I can get lost in. It's just a place of streets and houses, like this, and the people are all exactly like myself –'

'Impossible –'

'And like you – not as beautiful, of course, but then, I'm prejudiced.'

'I should hope so.' Mollified, she chattered on about the arrangements she and Mrs Hodgson were making. They were going to do up the downstairs study for Mamunia. '... she might not want to be climbing stairs for a while, and Mrs H is going to help me with the wallpapering – Daddy says we should get a man in but I think it's much *nicer* if we do it all ourselves, then she'll know she's really *wanted* ... and Neil's giving us his spare radio so if she feels like listening to some music or news on her *own* sometimes ... the poor darling's had such a *terrible* time she might want to be alone ...'

Useless – and unkind – to point out that Mamunia wouldn't understand the news or very much of anything in England for a very long time. He remembered how stubbornly she'd resisted Tatuš' efforts to make them a multi-lingual family.

'... *so* lucky that we've got Mrs H. They'll be wonderful

279

company for each other ...'

Not if Mamunia treated the Yorkshirewoman as she used to treat the little live-in maids that came in a constant stream from the country, who scrubbed and mopped and dusted only until they found themselves a husband. Oh yes, there would be problems ahead – but he could handle them, could handle anything now, even Joe, who was being so unexpectedly cooperative now it was established that Lallie was not coming with him.

'... and just think how she'll enjoy the garden! The roses will be blooming nineteen-to-the-dozen by the time you get back. I thought we'd have that comfy old garden chair re-covered and –'

'Look, don't go to a lot of trouble,' he said, the cool breath of superstition at his neck. Suppose Mamunia didn't want to come here? Not for a moment did he entertain the thought that he might not find her. 'You really don't have to –'

'Yes I do,' she said, very serious, looking away then directly into his eyes. 'When you first told me I wasn't very – well, understanding, was I? Pestering you to take me and not quite believing any of it. But then it hit me. If someone told me that Mum was alive I'd do anything, simply anything at all to get her back.' Tears trembled on thick lashes, to be quickly scrubbed away before they could fall. 'Anyway, I'm sorry.'

'You've been wonderful, there's nothing to be sorry for.'

The eyes turned to his were those of a contrite, devastatingly honest woman he realized it would be very difficult, now, to leave, even for a short time.

'No ... I didn't *rejoice* enough, inside. But if I'd known her ... and you really haven't talked about her very much, you see ...'

He hadn't. Before it had been too painful; now it was too difficult. Mamunia's life had been full of changes, cruel changes. She could not help but be different. 'When we come back you'll get to know her. She'll love you.'

The last days were a flurry of packing and unpacking. Lallie insisted on helping him, and crammed two large suitcases with 'essentials'. Six shirts, two suits, four sweaters, a dozen pairs of socks, a spare pair of shoes, aftershave, needle and thread, house slippers, shoe polish, notepaper, an assortment of magazines, spare buttons ... When he saw her squash a travel-iron into one of his shoes he took over.

'Darling, I'm *not* going to Cannes for the season. I'm going to Poland to look for my mother. A *small* case, a change of underwear, socks and toothpaste.'

Joe looked in, laughing at Lallie's idea of essentials. 'Women! They think we're just like them!'

'Since you both know so much,' she said, 'you pack! I'll be at the kennels.'

'What belt are you taking?' Joe asked when she'd gone.

'This – I'll be wearing it.' Jan said, mystified.

'A trick I learned in the first world war. You unpick a few stitches, slip in some money and sew it back up again. They never check belts.'

'What on earth would I want to hide money for?'

Joe squinted at him through pungent pipe smoke. 'You never know. That's the idea, isn't it?'

'I'll have money in my wallet!'

'If you're smart you'll have some more where they can't find it. Money talks.' He shrugged. 'But suit yourself.'

Jan shook his head as he watched him leave. How typical of Joe to think money was the answer to everything!

The day before he was to sail Neil insisted on taking him to the Three Nuns for a goodbye drink. The regulars, reserved since Jan's return to Eccles Place, warmed to him again when they heard where he was going and why.

'You've more stomach than me,' said one. 'You wouldn't catch me going to a country that's gone commie, not for anybody! I don't trust 'em ...'

A few weeks ago Jan would have retorted that Poland hadn't 'gone' communist, she'd been pushed. He'd have told them by whom, given chapter and verse of the country's recent past – but today the pervasive goodwill of the crowd won him over. They clapped him on the shoulder, sent drinks and their warmest smiles to the little table he shared with Neil.

Only Neil seemed untouched by the general bonhomie. 'It could be dicey, this trip. Have you thought, old chap?'

Jan nodded. 'Of course – but what choice do I have?'

'None.' He lit a cigarette and stared at the glowing tip, clearly embarrassed. 'You've been back from Germany a year, right? Not a very good year, either – oh, I don't mean with Lallie, thank God that seems to be going well – but the foundry … I know it's been rotten, but if you'd gone into Purchasing when Joe offered –'

'I couldn't. By then –'

Neil nodded. 'Yes, I know. When you come back we'll talk. Joe seems to be mellowing out and – well, I could use some help at my end. We're getting orders from Europe now, we could use somebody to travel for us. I'm sure I could pave the way with Joe if you'd just … you know …'

'Try to fit in?'

Neil flushed. 'God, but you can be an obstinate devil. Between you and Joe … it's like wrestling with two hedgehogs.'

'We've each got our own ideas,' Jan said stiffly.

'All I'm saying is when you come back, let's see if we can't all get squared away – you're not still thinking of South America, are you?'

'Probably,' he said, instantly defensive. 'Joe –'

'Forget Joe. What about Lallie? Yes, I know she's your wife and I've no right – but damn it man, you must know she wouldn't be happy away from here.'

If he hadn't liked Neil so much he might very well have thrown a punch at the kindly, well-meaning face, but Neil's distress was so patent, the distaste for what he had forced himself to say so obvious, that Jan had no answer for him.

'As I say, it's none of my business and I've a damned nerve bringing it up but … well, I do want Lallie to be happy.' Happier than you've made her this year, he clearly meant. 'Think about what I've said, anyway. You'll have time on the boat …'

Back at the house Neil's mother and Aunt June, visiting from Doncaster, were waiting to wish him bon voyage. Agnes Armott was standing in the hall, very composed with her hat just so and not a hair out of place, easing on black suede gloves finger by ladylike finger.

'I trust you'll find your mother well and happy,' she said

formally. He might have been embarking on a courtesy call to some distant relative taking the waters at Leamington Spa!

Aunt June was warm and matronly, a little plumper each time Jan saw her but graceful as a dolphin in her grey silk dress, her rounded arms floating out to him. 'Such a lovely thing, to find your mother,' she murmured.

'I haven't found her yet.'

'You will, you will.' She gave a deep comfortable sigh, and the scent of her face powder danced between them. 'So many changes since that first Christmas ... I'll never forget it, you know, you and Lallie.' She laughed softly. 'I'm a romantic old fool, I know, but I've thought it was the only time I've actually *seen* two people fall in love ... Lallie does *glow* so, doesn't she? She's a bit anxious now, naturally, but when you bring your mother back ... she *needs* a mother, you know, every girl does. And a husband, of course. So hurry back, won't you? You *will* be careful?' She dispelled the somber touch with her liquid, trilling laugh and Jan, hearing it, was carried back on the notes of the old carol, her voice pouring over him like a miracle. How young he must have been, to believe in miracles ...

In the evening Mrs H left to spend a few hours with her sister at Nether Edge, and Neil carried Daddy off to an industry dinner at which Daddy, by some sleight-of-hand known only to Neil, turned out to be the featured speaker.

'Sorry Joe, I should have mentioned it but it slipped my mind,' Neil was explaining as he hurried Daddy into the car, pausing only to give Lallie a wave and a wink. Really, Neil *was* such a dear and she was sure she didn't appreciate him nearly enough.'

Jan's packing (such as it was) was all done, and the new pups were snuggled up with Suka for the night, leaving only Jolly to share the last lazy evening with them. They agreed it was far too perfect an evening to be indoors, carrying lawn chairs and blanket and egg and watercress sandwiches out to the arbor, its trellis heavy with the year's first roses just waiting to burst into creamy-white bloom. To the west a pale sun retired discreetly behind the larches just as the moon came up in the east, a luminous scimitar in the mauve and apricot streaks of early evening.

All of spring seemed to be trapped in the arbor, so very beautiful the familiar lump rose in her throat. Mum used to sit here to shell the year's first boiling of garden peas; Daddy still worked the crossword puzzles here every Sunday morning ... Could anywhere be more perfect than Eccles Place in spring, the sycamores rampant with new green and the winey scent of last autumn's apples wafting from the storage shed at the bottom of the garden? How could he bear to leave it?

In the half-dark she could see the outline of his face as he lay on the blanket next to her, could feel the coiled tension in his fingers as they stroked her wrist.

'You're too quiet,' he said softly. 'You really don't want me to go, do you?'

She caught her breath. How should she tell him about the flicker of apprehension at the back of her mind? It had lain there festering since the day the news came about his mother – jealousy she was sure, a wormy little canker, niggardly when set against his errand. Only a few weeks, he said. What were a few weeks when they had a lifetime? And the business of South America seemed to have been pushed aside – surely that was compensation enough. But it wasn't.

'It's just that you ... seem so happy to be going – oh, not just about your mother, of course I can understand that, but you seem glad just to be going to Poland, leaving me ...'

He squeezed her wrist. 'How could I be glad to leave you? You're the only reason I stay here ... but yes, you're right, I *do* want to go home, I want *very much* to see –'

'Your country. I know.'

'And it hurts you?'

'Yes,' she admitted. 'It does. In lots of ways I'm just like Daddy. I can't imagine anywhere could be more perfect than here.' She knew what he was thinking, that she'd never *been* anywhere else – but she didn't want to, had never wanted to. 'I know it's provincial and I'm sorry but –'

'I wouldn't want you to change,' he said slowly. 'You belong here ...'

'And you think you don't?'

She heard him take in a deep breath as he gathered her into his arms. 'When I come back I'll *make* myself belong,' he said fiercely. 'I know I've been difficult –'

'No!' she lied.

'– but it's been a difficult time. Once I get Mamunia –'

'Then you won't feel so cut off,' she said, tracing the tight line of his jaw with her thumb. The treacherous doubts would not be still. 'I'm just worried things might not be what you expect, that something might happen …'

'There you go again! What a pack of savages you must think we are,' he laughed.

'You *really* think you'll be back in a few weeks?' she couldn't help saying.

He sighed. 'If I can find a government office to tell me where she is, yes. If not, then I'll have to make the rounds of the hospitals – but we're a small country, there can't be that many.' He leaned over her and she caught the fresh scent of his shaving lotion. 'Lallie, listen to me. Why should I stay away longer than I must? I love you. Without you I have nothing. We must be sure of each other, we *must*!'

Under the spell of the soft spring night she *was* sure, the glow-worms shining their tiny green candle-flames in the grass, Jolly snapping at an occasional moth, the laburnums almost ready to flower. In less than a month they'd be weeping their golden tears into the lawn –

'You'll miss it all,' she said sadly.

'There will be other years.'

His lips lay against her closed eyes, sealing in the picture of this perfect night. They were quiet for a long time, then she felt his shoulder move restlessly under her hand. And just when she thought he was about to suggest they go upstairs!

He tipped up her chin. 'Let's go out,' he said, his voice urgent. 'I'll drive.'

'But we *are* out – and it's dark!'

'And mountains are still mountains …'

'If that's what you want,' she said, puzzled.

How to explain to her the insistent need to feel the great bulk of Mam Tor at his back before he went away, its black mass screening the picture-perfect moon? To her, he was simply off to Poland to gather up Mamunia, much as she collected Joe from Victoria Station when he'd been to London on business. How could she know – he didn't *want* her to know! – the thousand uncertainties ahead. The system was changed, and despite his reading he had no way of knowing how much. Would he be allowed to go looking for his mother? Would he find her? And would she be alive? Would she come back with him? The mountain had answered him once and he had not understood the answer, not until Bauman's news. The face of the mountain had not fallen away while his back was turned in the *stalag* and perhaps it had not fallen yet.

'But it's dark,' she said again, her hair flying in his face as he whipped the MG up moorland roads and headed down to the village of Hope, so perfectly named, gateway to Castleton and Mam Tor. How to explain that darkness and light were relative, that the mountain, even in sleep, lived and moved in its own light?

'It's chilly,' she murmured, snuggling into the jacket he'd thrown over her shoulders in a fever to be away from Eccles Place and all its associations. Joe with his job and his gruff charity, the house that was a monument to the foundry and a plush prison to Lallie, the staunch northern values he wanted to embrace and could not. 'Your jacket's *so* English,' she said, nuzzling the rough weave. 'Tweedy, heathery ... and *you* chose it – that means you *do* belong here, at heart ...'

At heart, yes, because she clasped that just as firmly as she clasped his jacket to her sweet young breasts – but heart was *not* soul. Heart was something that happened, a new friend takes you home for Christmas and from that moment on everything changes. Soul never changed. It came with your mother's milk, the room in which you woke every day of your childhood life, the cobbles under your toddling feet, the small-time fur trader who brought rabbit skins every Monday on the corner and had to beat off the neighbourhood dogs with a stick, the Vistula threading through the streets, the schools, the faces, the voices. All waiting for you tomorrow.

Tomorrow.

The wire wheels of the car devoured the miles, but fleet as they were they couldn't get him there fast enough, the road a curled grey ribbon between dark hills whose valley pointed straight to the heart of knowledge, he the supplicant to what had become, in some deep recess of his mind, the oracle.

He stopped the car in the shadow of Mam Tor and looked up into the storm-battered heart. The moon cast its eerie light on spring turf and fissure alike, enigma shining on silver enigma. He stood frozen, disappointment bitter to his tongue. If answers were here they were locked away, deep inside that eroded dish.

'Jan! What is it? Are you all right ... you look strange ...'

He shook his head to clear it, kissed with love and sudden inexplicable anger the kitten-face turned up to his. Where was the answer? In the mountain – or in the lips under his, warm and giving and dewy with love?

'Jan ...'

He sank into the spring grass and pulled her down, trembling at the fragrant silk that brushed his face. His fingers opened the tiny buttons at her breast; his lips drank at all the tender buds of her body, tasting lavender and jasmine and sweet juices that flowed straight from the heart. There were voices, hers and his and the soughing sighs of a mountain besieged. *I need you, I need you, I need you*, its rhythm driving into the rock beneath him and above him, Lallie the frail conduit trapped between. Again and again she cried out his name as he stormed defences that resisted then parted before him, tender and innocent – but the answer always lay just beyond his reach until he was held, locked, the blood surge deafening to his ears.

The spring grass was cool, moist with dew and a recent rain. Over the dark and fragrant cloud of her hair he looked up into the face of Mam Tor, enigmatic, open to moonlight and scudding clouds, closed to the foreigner on its rim.

'You'll be home soon?' pleaded Joe Wainwright's daughter.

'I'll be home soon,' answered Mamunia's son.

CHAPTER TWENTY-SIX

Sky.

That was the first overwhelming impression of Warsaw. There was so *much* of it, sky on every side, limitless stretches of pale blue with fast clouds racing.

Where were the buildings, great structures that had risen, soared, focused the eye? There were chimneys and girders yes, entire streets of shop fronts, but the shops had no back, the windows no glass.

Now the eye was drawn downwards to neat piles of rubble, tightly spaced and compact, all that was left of theatres, churches, office blocks. He'd expected devastation, been prepared for it – but here was total ruin, impossible to absorb. Without the street signs: Marszatkowska, Nowy Świat, Putawska, he could have been anywhere in the world where civilization had flourished and was now dead.

This was Warsaw?

'*Tak*,' the driver nodded, mournful behind his grille and the smoke from a Sport cigarette. 'But we breathe, we eat ...' A small smile, knowing and cautiously bitter, lurked under his drooping moustache. '*Smutno* ...'

Sad indeed, but Jan Kaliski would not let himself be drawn. He turned again to the window of the van and peered through its barred window at the darkening street. An old woman with a rush broom endlessly swept her small section of pavement. A youth with ginger hair and freckles glugged vodka from a green bottle. Battered streetcars clogged the square, their

288

interiors packed solid with homeward-bound workers; still more workers outside, precariously clinging to any handhold that offered itself as the streetcar lurched across the intersection.

The driver spoke again. 'Like bees on the comb, *nie?* A miracle they don't drop off. You're lucky you're in the van.'

Jan doubted it. Four days since he stepped off the boat and he had still not been allowed to officially 'enter' Poland, to walk the streets, mingle with the people. At the docks there had been a processing centre, draughty sheds with broken windows and armed guards, a clutter of desks staffed by officious but strangely ineffective clerks. He was housed in a converted hotel that was long on forms to be filled out, short on bed linen and food. When they handed him his bowl of cabbage soup the first day, he refused it. A couple more hours and he'd be able to go outside, buy a decent meal. The second day, assured he would be released that afternoon, he refused again. For the last time. Now he ate what he was given and was glad of it, black bread and the ubiquitous soup, with a cup of what was described as coffee on the side.

This morning when they issued him a stamped official-looking document he assumed he was free to go, but no. It was simply a transfer to another processing centre in Warsaw. He was to be driven there by van.

'Train service is not yet ideal,' he was told. 'So much rolling stock destroyed, *rozumiesz?* The van will be more comfortable.'

He could see the logic of it, but he would have felt more comfortable if the windows of the van had not been barred, if its door had not been locked, if he were not separated from the driver by a battered, rusty grille.

The van inched slowly through taffic-clotted streets. He tapped on the grille for the driver's attention.

'How long is all this processing supposed to take?' He'd asked before, many times, and each person gave a different answer.

Hands lifted from the steering in an expansive shrug. 'You're coming on a bad day. Tomorrow is Friday, *prawda?*'

'So?'

'So tomorrow you will have to be admitted. There is all the

paperwork – well, you know, from the port. Then there'll be a medical exam –'

'They gave me one at the port centre!'

'Ah, but that was back there.' He thumbed vaguely towards the port. 'You'll have to have one for *this* jurisdiction here. By then it will be afternoon … the office staff goes home on weekends.'

So it would be Monday before anything was accomplished! He'd have been here a week, and no start yet on finding Mamunia.

'I can't believe this!' he raged through the grille. 'I could be about my business –'

'But without the correct papers how could you get about? You'll need travel permits, ration coupons, hotel vouchers …' He reeled off the names of a dozen permits, most of them incomprehensible. 'This way everything is orderly, *nie?* Just wait. You'll be surprised. The new system is very thorough.'

Not to say sluggish. 'It's like a different country!'

'It's Poland.'

'I wouldn't know,' Jan said bitterly. 'I haven't even *seen* Poland yet.' All he'd seen were dismal sheds, this rusted van, and a bureaucracy gone mad.

When the van stopped it was already dark. They were in a courtyard surrounded by what seemed to be barracks, an impression fortified by barbed wire atop the gate and a dimly lit guardroom bristling with rifles. The driver gave Jan a slow, sardonic smile, incongruous on his lumpish features.

'*Welcome to People's Poland,*' he said as he handed Jan his single small suitcase.

More waiting in the guardroom as he was processed as a 'temporary' and given a card that proved he had the right to legally stay where he was until tomorrow, at which time 'We can begin final processing, sir. Sorry for the delay,' the clerk said, shamefaced, turning him over to an orderly who escorted him across the courtyard to his room.

There were twelve beds in it, about half of which were occupied by snoring bundles. Of the rest, Jan chose the best of a poor lot, a bunk by the window and close to the door, which he noticed the orderly locked on his way out, muttering something about security precautions as he did so.

The mattress was a straw pad encased in holey ticking. Two blankets, thin as matzos, and no pillow, no sheets. The washing arrangements consisted of a large cracked pitcher half-filled with cold water.

'No exactly the Grand Hotel,' he muttered, stowing his case under the bunk. 'Bloody barracks!'

Opposite, a figure disengaged itself from the blankets and came over. He was a whippy little chap with a gold front tooth and eyes like a terrier.

'Barracks?' he said. 'We should be so lucky. Barracks you can get out of. See the guards on the gate?'

'Yes.'

'Thick as fleas on a dog, they are. Where are you in from?'

'England.' He lay back on the bunk, tired after a day with no food. 'I'll be out by Monday, thank God.'

'Good luck. That's what they told me last week. Stocki there is on his second week, Kalina on his fourth.'

For the first time Jan allowed real fear to brush the edge of his fatigue. 'Why don't you go out? What are you waiting for?'

'Passes. Documents. You can't move a mile now without a fistful of papers. It's the new Poland. No paper for the toilets; reams for crossing the street.'

'It's like a prison!'

'Oh no,' said Gold Tooth, whose name turned out to be Kowalski. 'They mean no harm. This place for instance – they call it a hostel. The reason we're kept, they say, is because without all the papers they maintain we need, *we'd be arrested on the outside within the first two days*!'

'That's crazy –'

'But true. They've got everybody pegged, labelled, sorted and blood-tested. Takes time, *prawda*. You damn near need a permit to take a pee.' He rummaged under his own bunk and came up with a small paper bag. 'They didn't feed you, I'll bet. Want a bit of bread? I bribed one of the guards for it.'

Jan looked at the lump of dark bread, saliva rushing to his tongue. 'Thanks.' It was dry and hard but it filled a corner of his stomach. He chewed slowly, trying not to think of the bedtime snacks at Eccles Place, Mrs H's home-baked crusty

291

bread lavished with butter, wedges of Cheddar and Caerphilly, slices of York ham, fresh tea in china cups, Lallie pouring it, bathed in firelight. 'Has anybody been allowed to leave since you got here?' he asked the friendly Kowalski and held his breath for the answer.

'Bless you yes! Some of 'em after just a couple of days. It's the red-tape, see? It does move, slowly, but once it gets a knot in it ...' He held up his hands. 'What passport are you on?'

'Polish,' he said simply. 'That's what I am.'

'Mmm. Pity. If you had a British passport you could thump the desks and demand they call the embassy, couldn't you mate?'

How you would smile, Joe Wainwright – but Lallie had urged him down the same road and he'd refused her, too. On many things. Wait until they let you know officially, she'd said. He was beginning to wish he'd listened. What would she be doing now? Urgently papering Mamunia's room, probably ... Thank God he hadn't brought her! He tried to picture her in a locked van being driven to some holding-hostel, being offered cabbage soup in a chipped enamel bowl. His imagination stalled.

Friday went pretty much as the van driver had predicted. A breakfast of bread and margarine, served with the drink they called coffee. It was brewed, he was told, from roasted grain and chicory – and they were lucky to have it. On the outside it was rationed – if you could find it. After breakfast women doctors weighed and measured him, drew blood from his arm, listened to his chest and tapped his knees with rubber hammers. The process took less than half an hour. The waiting ate up the best part of a day.

Just when he'd despaired of starting the paperwork that would spring him from the seedy protection of the 'hostel' he was taken to a shed with 'Bureau of Documentation' over the door and patched linoleum on the floor. At least the bureaucrats did not do themselves well, he thought. And that was the best that could be said for them. A young woman, alone in the office, had a sheaf of blank forms for him.

'Have these filled out ready for your interview next week, all right?'

She turned back to a stack of papers under which the cover of a magazine was just visible.

He spoke a little louder than he intended. 'My interview *will* be on Monday, right?'

She sighed and turned to face him, ticking off each point on a stubby finger as she made it. 'Monday morning there's a meeting of management at headquarters. Afternoon is Staff Review. Tuesday is Doctrinal Discussion led by the Commandant. That's all day. Wednesday there's ... they may see you in the afternoon.' She waited for him to go.

'But I have to get out of here! Already a week wasted –'

Her shoulder moved a fraction. '*Naturalnie*. Everyone wants to leave, of course. *Nie?* You are the latest arrival, Pan Kaliski. There are others before you. You will have patience, yes?'

He looked at her bored, placid face and the week's frustrations exploded. 'I've *been* patient! Now I want you to get on the phone *this minute*, call whoever you have to call *even if it's Joe Stalin*, and get my interview set for Monday, understand? *Monday morning!*'

She cast a furtive glance around the room. 'The phone?' she whispered.

Something besides the fear in her voice snagged his memory. He'd seen plenty of desks this week, and heaven knew plenty of documents, but ... 'No phone?' he said.

She shook her head. 'The local system's been down for weeks.' The brown eyes grew reproachful. 'This is not England, Pan Kaliski. It may be hard for you to understand but there was much damage here. The telephone system is old. There are waiting lists, even for parts. In any case, only top officials ... Sorry.'

Realization hit him like a truck. There went his best, quickest means of finding Mamunia when he got to the outside. He'd planned on checking into the closest hotel and spending as long as it took to call every hospital in the country. He found himself explaining about Mamunia and that he'd come to find her. He leaned across the desk to make her understand.

She softened and reached for yet another form. 'In that case you'd better fill this out too. It's for the Missing Persons Bureau. I'm sure the government will find her much quicker than you could yourself.'

She wished him good luck and turned back to her magazine as he left to get in line for supper. Potato soup.

Lying on his bunk, he felt as if everything he'd every believed in was sifting to dust, piling up like the fragmented heaps of stone on the pavements outside. Poland had come to this, a shambles of inefficiency and shortages. The girl in the office scared out of her wits because he'd mentioned Stalin's name. The snail's pace of even the simplest undertaking.

He wrote Lallie a note explaining, as cautiously as he could manage, the delays facing him and telling her he loved and missed her. Then he asked Kowalski how you went about buying postage stamps. The gold tooth flashed in a grin.

'From the Post Office, where else?'

Which of course was *on the outside*. Wouldn't the orderlies bring some in, for a price?

'What would you use for currency?'

Exactly. On disembarking from the ship he'd tried to change English pounds to zlotys, was told it could be done only in a state bank. *On the outside*.

When the orderly trundled in a water barrel to top up the pitchers, Jan motioned him over.

'I wondered if you'd post a letter for me?' He casually leafed through his wallet, making sure the orderly saw the fan of English money, crisp and new.

He saw it – and jumped back as if he'd been shot. He spoke in a whisper, very fast.

'We can't take anything from the guests, sir. Anything at all. If I was to be caught with foreign currency – oh no, sir. It's more than my job's worth.' He scuttled out, locking the door behind him.

'Better wait until you're out,' Kowalski said. 'It shouldn't be too long.'

Jan didn't answer. He could picture Lallie standing at their bedroom window as she listened for the postman to come whistling up the walk.

CHAPTER TWENTY-SEVEN

Eccles Place, Yorkshire, 1946

'You're *quite* sure this is all?' she said, riffling through the handful of mail. Bills, circulars, registrations of pedigree, a past-due notice on the South American books from the library. Nothing from Poland – and it had been a whole month!

The postman looked sympathetic. 'Aye, lass. Sorry. There's now't from foreign parts.' He pronounced it very long, 'furrrin paaahts', which at any other time would have delighted her. But a month was *such* a long time to wait, and just now she was waiting for so many things ...

'Never mind, lass.' It was Mrs Hodgson at her elbow. 'Like your dad says, he'll be back with his mother before you can turn round.'

'I don't *want* to turn round, I want a letter.' A letter with news and messages, I-love-you-and-miss-you messages. 'Oh, Mrs Hodgson ...'

'Aye, oh Mrs Hodgson's right, dead right! We've not finished the old girl's room yet and her expected any minute, *any minute*!'

Dear Mrs H, squinting at the front door as if Jan might indeed lead his mother through it any minute. And perhaps he might. Mamunia's room should have been finished weeks ago but she'd been feeling so lazy, on account of Jan's being away, she supposed – that and all the waiting. If he didn't hurry up

295

he was going to miss the whole spring! Already he'd missed so much – the tulips done blooming and ragged, *and* the narcissus, which had smelled simply heavenly. Two more weeks and the laburnums would be over too – such a shame because they were right outside the window that would be his mother's.

'All right, let's get on with it,' she said.

The wallpaper she'd chosen for Mamunia's room was flowery, white daisies on a field of sunny yellow. 'You're sure it looks really peaceful, aren't you, Mrs Hodgson? We don't want anything frantic – or depressing.' She stood back, surveying the three walls already done.

Mrs Hodgson blinked behind her thick lenses. 'You're asking the wrong one, lass. To me, *everything* looks peaceful. Fuzzy, you might say. I sometimes used to think that if my eyes got one good shock they might clear up, but nothing of the sort. Even butcher stripes look blurry to me and I *know* they're not.'

Lallie pasted a new length of paper with wide sweeps of the brush. 'All right now. Hold the ladder. We'll have it up in a jiffy.'

But at the top of the ladder, the wallpaper heavy with paste, she began to feel, well … squiffy, as if she'd had a glass of champagne or a guzzle of Daddy's Scotch. Daisy petals began to spread, white wavering into yellow, the tiny green leaves disappearing altogether. There was the overpowering smell of paste, gluey and nauseating, as the length of paper slipped from her hands. Mrs Hodgson's voice from a long way away …

'Lallie? Lallie girl? Are you all right up there?'

Her head was clearing and she gripped the sticky top of the step-ladder. 'Yes … I think so.' She backed down slowly, oddly light-headed, and sat on the bottom step as Mrs Hodgson reached down, pressing the back of her head and pushing.

'Get your head between your knees, love. Feeling a bit giddy, are you?'

The blood rushed to her head and her vision cleared. 'Just a touch of dizziness, that's all –'

'I told you you should have had some breakfast. You young

women, you've no idea of looking after yourselves, none at all.' She bustled into the kitchen and hurriedly made tea and poached egg on toast.

The tea tasted delicious. As soon as she began to sip it Lallie began to feel herself again and thought about going back up the step ladder just as soon as she'd had some breakfast. Then Mrs H brought the poached egg, normally the favourite Eccles Place breakfast, and Lallie was ravenous, she really was. She picked up her fork and regarded the egg, firm and white, sitting on the slice of toast. 'Looks perfect, Mrs H,' she said, nicking the membrane with her fork and watching the yolk trickle out.

The next second she was racing for the bathroom and after that the bedroom, from which she emerged in coat and gloves, calling over her shoulder to a mystified Mrs Hodgson left standing in the hall.

'Back in a jiffy ...' and she was away, headed for the MG.

She caught Dr Waithe just as he was setting out on his rounds, swinging her car neatly behind his, blocking his escape route down the drive.

'What the ... Lord, Lallie, what's got *you* in such a tizzy? Nothing wrong, I hope?'

'No! Something right, absolutely marvellously right! I hope.'

Ten minutes later she was in his office, hardly daring to breathe as he slowly filled his pipe, tamped it and lit it.

'Well?' she said, as he proceeded to scribble at some length on her chart. Really, he could be so maddening!

'You've missed just the one, then?'

'Yes, but I put that down to being so worried about Jan – I missed *three* when he was shot down, remember?'

'Mmm ... noticed any tenderness around the breasts?'

She blushed, which was silly. Dr Waithe had nursed her through every childhood illness since she was four. 'As a matter of fact, I have ...'

He wrote again, scrupulously dotting I's and crossing T's. When he looked up he was smiling. 'It's a bit soon to tell but from the symptoms I'd say yes, you very likely are.'

On the way home she stopped the car and sat in the park for

a little while, pressing her hands to her stomach. So it was true then, at last. For the past two weeks she'd suspected, hardly letting the hope form in case it should be crushed. She'd been disappointed before – but this time she'd known. Almost. Oh, he'd be *so* happy! If only he were here. Now she *really* couldn't wait for him to come home. For all these last tense months to end like this, everything falling into place at the perfect time. It was a miracle – and how wonderful they'd be able to share it with Mamunia. A small shadow edged over her happiness; Mum would have been so delighted – but there was Daddy, he'd be simply over the moon when he heard. Jan should be the first to know, of *course* he should, but he wasn't *here*, and how long could she hug it to herself? Jan was right, she was *so* impatient. No sooner had she promised herself that she would, *must* hold the news until Jan came home than she spotted Mrs Hodgson trotting towards the park, her short legs pumping remarkably fast for her age.

'Lallie! Whyever did you have to go tearing off?'

Poor darling, so anxious, of course *she'd* have to know. Jumping up from the bench she caught the housekeeper by the waist and danced her past the duck-pond. 'I'm pregnant, I'm pregnant! Isn't it the most amazing thing you've ever heard?'

After that, of course, there was no stopping it. She only hoped she could manage to tell Daddy before the neighbours beat her to it. They all knew before lunch. By mid-afternoon Constable Curtain had it from the district nurse, who'd got it from the greengrocer, who'd got it from the doctor's wife, who wouldn't have dreamed of breaking a confidence except she'd known Lallie since she was a tot ...

She did surprise Daddy, who surprised her back by weeping – and in front of Mrs Hodgson, too!

'Ee, mi lass,' he said, holding her so tight she could scarcely breathe. 'If only Millie ... oh love, you couldn't have given me a better ... to think, a grandson –'

'It might be a girl!'

'No, it'll be a little lad, you'll see.'

He held her away from him, beaming and laughing and ignoring the tears on his cheeks. 'Oh, but you're a fine one, you are right enough!'

Nothing would do now but he must open a bottle of champagne, call Neil to come over and drink the baby's health. 'And yours,' he told Lallie sternly. 'You'll take proper care of yourself now, no more sitting up until all hours waiting for pups to get born –'

'Oh, Daddy!'

'I mean it. You'll look after that grandson of mine.'

Neil arrived amid popping corks and the smell of Mrs Hodgson's cheese straws fresh out of the oven.

'To go with the bubbly,' she said happily.

Daddy raised his glass. 'To mother and child!'

'And the lucky father,' Neil added, giving Lallie a warm smile over the rim of his glass. 'You haven't heard yet, I suppose?'

'No.'

'Well, he did say the post was unreliable, didn't he?'

'Yes, but I wish –'

'Oh, you worry too much,' Daddy said. 'Very likely he's visiting all his old haunts, living it up on vodka and that sausage stuff he's so partial to.'

She looked across at Neil. Hadn't *he* said something very much like that, the night Jan was shot down? But now Daddy was opening another bottle to 'wet the baby's head' and Neil was telling him he was a bit too soon. You didn't do that until it was born.

'Then we'll do it all over again,' Daddy said, lifting his glass again. 'To Lallie's son. Just think, by the time he's thirty he'll have the foundry!'

'Daddy …'

'Oh, I expect I'll be long under the sod by then, but Neil will keep it going for him, won't you lad?'

'Of course –'

'But only think!' Daddy exulted. 'Another Wainwright for Wainwright's foundry!'

Lallie started to speak, then stopped. She couldn't ever remember Daddy looking so happy. Now wasn't the time to remind him that her baby, boy or girl, would be a Kaliski.

There'd be plenty of time for that later, when Jan got home.

CHAPTER TWENTY-EIGHT

Warsaw, 1946

Six weeks, and nothing had changed but the 'guest' roster posted on the door of the hut. One by one the original inmates had been released and new arrivals had taken their place, which should have offered some hope that his turn was coming. It did not. This morning four of the most recent arrivals had been issued travel passes and sent on their way, while Jan's only progress was a succession of interviews with officials of steadily ascending rank but not, apparently, of power. The departments involved each questioned him at length but at no point did their functions seem to converge.

There was the Resettlement Department, singularly ill-equipped to deal with one who did not wish to settle. They were polite.

'At which address do you plan to live?'

'None. I plan to leave as soon as I can.'

'How then can we issue a resident's permit?'

'Issue what you want, just let me go.'

Concerned bafflement. 'Excuse the question, Pan Kaliski, but you did request a visa to enter this country.'

'For a short stay, that's all.'

They looked at him with embarrassment, hosts caught unprepared by an unexpected guest. 'You must appreciate our position, please. Post-war recovery is not yet complete ... we

300

have not the facilities for tourists, this is why we do not offer tourist visas.'

'Which is why I had to take the only visa you offered.'

'We are in a difficult position ...'

'Give me a pass out of here and solve your problem.'

'Without an address to send you to it is not possible.'

On impulse, he gave the address in Morska Street. There were relieved smiles as they turned to reference books at their backs. Then a pained silence.

'This address no longer exists. Please do not make joke.'

Jan leaned forward, fists on the desk. 'I will sleep on the trains! I am here only to see my mother!'

'Her address, if you please?'

'*I don't know*!'

Again, relieved smiles all round. 'Ah, then you first need the Department of Missing Persons. Perhaps they can help you.'

'I already *have* seen them.'

'In that case, you must simply be patient, *prawda*?'

Another week waiting for the second interview with Missing Persons. Who greeted him with raised eyebrows.

'Such things cannot be resolved overnight, *rozumie* Pan?'

'No I *don't* understand! Your records seem to be very complete – surely you know she entered the country!'

'Thousands and thousands entered from the death camps, sir. They are scattered all over by now. It will take time ...'

'If you would let me out I could look for her myself!'

'Then how would we know where *you* were?'

'I would tell you.'

Heads shook at his innocence. 'At all times we must know where each person is, *dobrze*? How else could you receive your entitlements? Ration coupons, pension, etc ... Believe us, life is easier within the system. How else can there be order ...?'

'But you say *you* don't know where she is!'

That was just a temporary measure. They were trying. They would locate her, but the paperwork, the channels ... Excuse piled on excuse until at last it was Jan who terminated the interview, rising so suddenly that his chair slammed into the wall behind him.

'My God, what is this? What are you doing to this country?

301

It used to be a man could go where he wanted, *when* he wanted – now it's nothing but a haven for incompetent clerks!'

He stormed out, but not before he saw consternation on two of the faces as the third was lowered to a ledger, a pen dipping into an inkwell.

If the Department of Missing Persons was staffed by incompetent clerks it was soon made clear to him that the Department of Records was not. There were surface similarities, yes, but ...

He was ordered to report to the office very early one morning, which meant passing up the mess of gruel that was ladled into his bowl promptly at seven.

An orderly came to escort him, but he was quite unlike the others who carried water and pushed brooms. This one was neatly, if poorly dressed. The eyes were clear and he marched at a fast clip, so that Jan was almost running to keep up with him.

'What department is this?' Jan said, panting after him.

'Records.' Voice crisp, no subservience in it.

'What is its function?'

The orderly stopped, looked straight into his face. 'They coordinate.'

'Coordinate what?'

'Everything.'

They hurried through a maze of corridors deep in the actual barracks, a solid stone affair that seemed to have come through the bombing remarkably unscathed. They passed dozens of doors, all closed. Stone steps echoed under their feet. The office to which he was led was on a corner of the top floor. He was told to wait in the anteroom, little more than a cubicle furnished with a small table and a chair. An easy chair! The first he'd seen since he left Eccles Place. Well, so perhaps he was getting somewhere. If they coordinated *everything* perhaps his papers were at last ready ... perhaps they'd even found Mamunia –

A buzzer brought him to his feet.

'Come in please.' The voice was bland, almost bored.

The room was incredibly dark, due perhaps to a cracked window patched with cardboard. On the centre table a desk lamp glowed mellow in the pervading gloom, softening the figure of the officer who was just opening a thick file, meticulously smoothing the papers. He was spare, grey of hair and skin, and he had an air of fatigue which Jan saw was caused by unusually heavy eyelids. He spoke very quietly, almost in a whisper. He was Major Wajda, he said, and had the pleasure of finalizing Jan's 'case'.

'There have been ... difficulties, I understand?'

'One major difficulty. I'm still here – after eight weeks.'

'And of course you are impatient to be on your way ...' He nodded, smiling gently. 'This I can understand ... we are all at the mercy of ...' He paused and looked pointedly at the file. '... of incompetent clerks, *nie*?' One military man to another.

Jan flushed, ashamed that his flash of temper with the Missing Persons people had been brought to the attention of this mild, well-mannered officer. 'I am sometimes very frustrated, yes. So much time wasted – I have not even been able to write to my wife! She will be frantic –'

Major Wajda nodded again. 'It is inexcusable, I agree. You understand the problems, of course. Once we let orderlies accept money ...' His grey, tired hands fluttered and his voice dropped even lower. 'We must guard against corruption, you see. Once the seed falls, roots are sure to follow.' He turned suddenly, and spoke over his shoulder. 'Sasha, can we find a cup of coffee for Lt Kaliski?'

'I'm a civilian now,' Jan said quickly as a figure rose out of an armchair he'd thought empty. Sasha moved behind a curtain in the dim recesses of the room and emerged with coffee, *real* coffee. And in a china cup – two lumps of sugar in the saucer! *Two* He wondered if he dared put them in his pocket for later.

Major Wajda laughed indulgently. 'Yes, I'm afraid our cuisine has not impressed you so far. Don't worry, your ordeal will soon be over. Our commandant has taken a personal interest in your case. He was a pilot also. I'm sure he will be understanding.'

'When ...' God, but the coffee was *good*! 'When do you expect I'll be able to leave?'

The major smiled apologetically. 'Our clerks really *are*

303

incompetent. They spend so much time and still the formalities are not quite completed. There is one more document needed – one can't imagine how it could have been overlooked. Sasha? Ah yes, we have it all ready. Let us know as soon as you've completed it and we'll talk again.'

'But …?' This, after all the sweet talk, the sweeter coffee!

'I know, I know. It's impossibly maddening but –' He handed Jan four stapled pages of closely printed questions. 'This is positively the last – you have my personal assurance.'

Jan swallowed hard and looked directly into the heavy-lidded eyes. 'I'm sure I can depend on you, Major.'

The escort was waiting. Jan followed, fuming, down the echoing corridors, in a fever to fill out yet another form. But perhaps this really *was* the last. Wajda seemed so … civilized. And he had a name, which must mean something.

The questions on the new form were different, requiring the most miniscule details not only about his own life but about Lallie's too, and Joe's and Millie's.

Where was Millie born? She's been dead five years, he wrote.

The date of Joe's service in WW1? How could he know?

Joe's first business address? He drew a question mark.

The nature of the first business? Smithy.

Current business? Foundry.

Joe's place of birth? Angrily he scrawled *Buckingham Palace?* on the cheap paper.

He was forced to leave many blanks but nevertheless asked for a meeting with Major Wajda the next day. The orderly came for him an hour later, surely a good sign. Not so good was the two-hour wait in the anteroom, presumably while they looked over his angry answers on the new form.

Today Major Wajda was at a side desk, his function apparently that of onlooker. Sasha, whom Jan had hardly noticed yesterday, was at the centre table. He was exceedingly fat, small brown eyes almost buried in cushions of doughy flesh. Where the major was grey, Sasha gave off nothing but shades of brown. Biscuit-coloured skin peppered with darker freckles, a chocolate-brown civilian suit of conservative cut, ox-blood shoes very well polished, and sparse rusty hair that had perhaps once been curly. His fingers, heavily stained with nicotine, leafed through the stapled questionnaire.

'You don't know where your mother-in-law was born?'

'No, and as I said, she's been dead several years.'

'Father-in-law? Foundry owner, yes? Well then.' He made a notation on the form and muttered, 'Industrialist,' under his breath.

'I wouldn't say that! He has a business, that's all.'

'He's engaged in manufacture, *nie*?' Fat fingers spread. His speaking voice was not much louder than the major's had been yesterday, but it was infinitely stronger. 'This ... foundry. What does it manufacture?'

Jan paused, caution signals sounding in his head. 'Castings, what else?'

'Castings for what?'

Jan stretched against the back of the chair, gave himself time to think, assess the new implications. Until now the problem had been bureaucracy. Was it still? He was no longer sure.

'Castings for what?' Louder this time.

'When I left we were doing bathtubs,' he said lightly.

Brown eyes squinted, disappeared into fat. 'And during the war?'

Aha. *Now* he was sure. Industrialist had translated to imperialist. Joe's wartime business had flushed out the paranoia inherent in the system. What were they up to? Where was this going? The possibilities stopped his mind, one word ringing through the barrier. Lallie ... Lallie ... my God!

'And?' prompted Sasha. 'During the war?'

Careful. Step softly. 'I wouldn't know. I was otherwise engaged.' He pointed to his military record on the desk with every other form he'd filled out since he'd arrived.

The eyes opposite closed again. To indicate patience being expended, Jan wondered? Then the heavy head turned, beckoned to the major, who advanced with a dusty, dog-eared book that looked like a directory, riffling through its pages with slow, tired fingers.

'Ah yes, I have it. Wainwright Foundry, Sheffield, Yorks. Castings for tank parts, anti-aircraft guns, aircraft engines.'

If they'd known, why did they ask?

'Withholding information is a serious matter, Pan Kaliski.'

'Why – since you already have it!' he retorted.

'Nevertheless ...'

The word hung between them, its message suddenly clear. Now he knew why he was afraid, knew the source of the paranoia. Production capacity geared down to bathtubs could be geared back up again, turned against the new regime. Christ! He looked towards the major, who turned away and studied a chart on the wall. The chart was in Russian, which shouldn't have been surprising, but it was. And frightening. No, don't let them –

'My mother,' he said boldly. 'What progress have you made?'

'None. We told you, they're scattered from one end of Poland to the other. It will take time.' Sasha lifted a fat wrist. 'Exercise period is just beginning.'

Jan didn't move. 'I don't feel like exercise today.'

The eyes didn't even flicker as Sasha heaved his huge bulk upright and walked quickly to the door. He flung it open and there was the orderly, waiting. Sasha smiled. 'Come, Pan Kaliski. Here we follow routine. It makes everything easier in the long run. We'll see you again.'

For the next hour Jan stretched and bent and jogged and jumped. They knew what they were doing, he thought bitterly. Between the exercise and the diet there was little strength for making trouble.

For hours afterwards only his thoughts were active, running this way and that like captured mice. His prospects were worse every day. Why? Others were released, why not him? And Lallie would be going mad, mad. A few weeks, he'd told her. Now it *was* a few weeks and he was no nearer to going back, no nearer to Mamunia. If he'd just listened, taken citizenship – or not come at all, waited prudently for official word. But how could he, with Mamunia lost somewhere in this bureaucratic madhouse that had once been a nation ... He forced his thoughts to slow down, down, and *think* ...

There was a reason why this was happening, there had to be. Something Wajda said yesterday, something he'd missed while the major laved him with sweet words and coffee. 'Our

commandant ... a pilot also ... personal interest in your case
... he will be understanding ...'

Again why, *for what reason?* Smoothly working machinery
behind his forehead, the pieces that sorted, meshed, made
careful, rational choices suddenly missed a cog. They were
trying to drive him mad ... Blood surged in his ears, blinded
his eyes with a red tide of fury.

He was not conscious of making a decision, only of running,
running across the courtyard, of pounding on the door of the
guardhouse and then of beating his fists on the chest of the
guard who opened it, a guard too astonished to reach for his
gun.

'*The commandant!*' Jan gasped. '*I demand to see him, I demand!*'

He was on his knees on the guardhouse floor, great gulping
sobs tearing at his chest, a circle of guards looking down.

It seemed to him that he was there for a long time, dimly
aware of running feet fading away and coming back, of
whispers over his head, hurried discussions. Hands on the back
of his collar hauled him up, pushed him towards a chair, and
the sergeant of the guard was looking at him with puzzled,
dawning respect, speaking to him in cautiously deferential
tones, advising him to comb his hair and calm himself.

'God knows why, but Major Bura says he'll see you.'

CHAPTER TWENTY-NINE

Eccles Place, Yorkshire, 1946

He'd been gone for two months when the visas for South
America arrived. She pushed them far to the back of the desk
and stood looking at the closed drawer for a long time.

Two months later still all but the hardiest summer flowers
were faded and wind-torn in the beds; flocks of starlings
headed south, more and more of them every day.

Still he was not back.

She'd given up waiting for the postman. She hid from him now, as she hid from Constable Curtain and Agnes Armott and all the other enquirers, well-meaning or not, who looked from her face to the small bulge under her smock and then to her face again. Some of them asked if she'd heard any news yet; others, thinking to be more delicate, asked nothing. Nevertheless she caught the downward sweep of their glance, the swiftly veiled pity. At first she'd stared them down, thrown bright smiles and brighter greetings like dust into their puzzled eyes. But as the weeks crept by and the smile didn't always hold its shape she retreated to the little suite upstairs.

He had not left her.

There was a reasonable explanation if only she could find it, if only she knew where to look.

'Come on lass, *do* buck up,' Daddy said, bringing her a bottle of perfume or tickets for the theatre or a maternity dress so cunningly cut that nothing showed at all. 'Moping won't remedy owt, now will it? I'm *talking* to you, so perk up and listen!'

'I listened when you told me not to go with him –'

'*He* told you the same thing!'

'– and look what's happened.'

'Nothing's happened, he's just later than he expected, that's all. Maybe the old girl's too sickly to travel, maybe –'

'Maybe I should have gone with him and be damned to both of you!'

'A place like that's not for you, love. At least we both agreed on that.'

'I should never have listened to you, either of you. I'm tired and I just wish you'd leave me alone, that's all.'

When he tiptoed away she would lock the door behind him and polish Kaz's cup – though with weaker and weaker strokes. Jan should have taken it. Why hadn't he? 'Because I can't take time to find *his* family, too!' he said, and she believed him. But why wasn't he back? Why didn't he write, *why*? Useless to tell herself there was no mail from behind the Iron Curtain. Roman and Genia got letters, '... but not *all* of them, Lallie, and they're always so late ...' Just last week Henryk Ryba got a letter from his brother complaining of short rations and long food lines and no fuel in sight for the winter – but the letter *came*.

So why nothing from Jan? Why wasn't he here to lie beside her and touch the bulge that was their baby, feel its warmth against his hand?

Their suite was her haven and her prison, a two-room limbo of anxiety and despair through which she endlessly paced. One day led inexorably to the next and the next. She forced herself not to listen for the postman's step on the front path, kept the pillow pressed tight to her ears until it was much too late for Mrs Hodgson to blunder up the stairs with anything more vital than a breakfast tray – and even on that reminders lay like ticking clocks.

'Now finish up your tomatoes, Lallie, they're the last we'll get from the garden.' Or:

'See you drink up that good summer milk – the dairy's gone to winter feed already.' Or:

'*Do* have that blackberry jam on your toast, love. There's me with scratches up to mi shoulder-blades and you not even tasting it!'

Someone (Daddy or Mrs H) ordered baby clothes 'on approval' from Waymans, fleecy jackets and smocked rompers, crib gowns and woolly bonnets, receiving blankets and bootees, silk-and-wool vests and liberty bodices. But what was the point? A baby had a mother and a father. When its father came home was time enough to think about a layette.

The months all ran together, a grey river with no certain direction, becalmed, waiting for Jan to come home and chart the course, correct the drift.

Bells were ringing over at Martinswood. Well. So it must be Sunday. Not that it mattered. No mail came on Sundays, the one day some secret spring inside her could relax. There was nothing to wait for on Sundays.

Through the long nights when she couldn't close them off, the tensions and frictions of the past year replayed themselves over and over. That seedy flat in Attercliffe. Maurice and all he represented. The fruitless, discouraging interviews for jobs which never materialized. The calluses, physical and mental, of the foundry. Could it have been too much? Back in Poland, among all that was familiar, had his life *here* seemed just too much of an uphill grind? The arguments with Daddy ... and yes, with her, towards the end. But he *loved* her, she knew he did ... Perhaps it had all been too much for his pride? She said as much to Neil when he came over one night and insisted on walking her across the common and back because she wasn't getting enough exercise. Because it was dark she agreed to go, but she couldn't help gnawing on the same bone.

'He's just so proud, Neil. Maybe we – everything just chipped away at it until –'

'Rubbish. He's got more pride than any ten men I've ever met. No, he's just hung up somewhere ... It's a different world over there, especially now with the new government and everything. If you'd just start taking better care of yourself – you're nothing but bones and a bump, girl! What he'll say when he sees you like that I can't imagine. And do you realize what it's doing to Joe, seeing you like this day after day? And there's the baby to think about –'

'I'm doing everything I'm supposed to do for it!'

'Except enjoying it –'

'How am I *supposed* to enjoy – oh, you don't understand, nobody does!'

Joe thought he understood all right, but he wasn't about to share his thoughts with Lallie, not in her state. The bastard had left her, that's what he'd done, found somebody over there that he fancied – but God, what man could want anybody else after Lallie? It didn't bear thinking about but he couldn't seem to think about much else. Her face was the first thing he looked for every night when he came home. Maybe today there'd been word from the Pole and she'd be smiling again, playing with the dogs instead of sitting in front of the fire pretending to read. He knew it was a futile hope. If there'd been a letter she'd have called him at the office.

He badgered Bob Waithe. Surely there were pills he could give her to spark her up a bit, make her take notice? Some miracle drug – they discovered new nostrums every time you

310

turned round these days, why wasn't there something for this? And all the old quack could do was spread his hands, like some damn conjurer proving he had nothing up his sleeves.

'Only two remedies, Joe. If her husband comes back there's nothing to worry about.'

'And if he doesn't?'

'The usual bromide. Time. Eventually ...'

'Eventually my arse! More than four months pregnant and she weighs less than she did last year, man!'

Even to Bob Waithe he couldn't bring himself to mention the one overriding fear. It was the look in her eyes that kept him awake nights. Not just confusion, defeat ... Like the doctor said, sooner or later that would mend itself. It was something else, a detachment, as if she was backing away from everything, curling in on herself, not quite all there when he talked to her. His lass, going off her rocker ... God!

'Brandy Tsar's breeder called me,' he said to her just last week. 'He's keen on putting him to Suka. Pick of the litter and no fee. What about that then?' Brandy Tsar was the best in his class, they'd been angling for him for months and here he was on a plate!

'Oh, there's time ...' she said, looking over his shoulder at the wall.

'Like hell there is! The dog's getting no younger and the bitch comes into heat next month. We'll not get a chance like this again.'

She sighed, pulled her attention back to his face. 'Well,' she said, 'I keep telling Mrs Hodgson. She just doesn't listen ...' and drifted off upstairs again, stopping halfway up as if she'd forgotten where she was going or why.

At such times – and they seemed to come more and more often – he'd slip a leash on one of the dogs and walk until he couldn't walk any more. Where to turn? Millie would have known. In her simple, feather-headed way she'd known more about what went on in Lallie's head than he'd ever know. Which didn't seem right, considering his lass was the centre of his life. Millie's life hadn't had a centre; she'd spread her affection all over everybody. God, she'd even liked the Pole. Right now she'd have been wringing her hands and worrying where the poor lad had got to, hoping he hadn't come to any harm. By Christ, if he ever showed his face at Eccles Place again he'd come to some harm! There'd be a pair of fists waiting for him right enough!

When the load of helpless rage got too much for him he carried it to Neil, the only one who understood it.

'Neil lad, I'll crucify that sod if I ever get my hands on him. He never *meant* to come back, the bastard! He's just dropped her, as if she were some slut he'd picked up on a street corner. Our Lallie! A girl like that – oh, mi blood fair boils when I think on it. I *hate* the swine – leaving her like this *on purpose* –'

Neil shook his head. 'I don't think it's that, Joe. You had your differences, I know, but he loves Lallie. I'm sure of that.'

'Then why doesn't he come back –'

'I don't know. If there was something we could do …'

Poor Neil. He didn't even have the satisfaction of hatred. It wasn't in him. He'd look for reasons and then for solutions. Revenge would never occur to him.

'Didn't I read somewhere about that ministry pal of yours moving to the Foreign Office?' he said now. 'Maybe he could tell us something. It would mean a lot to Lallie, give her something to hang onto.'

So he called his crony at the Foreign Office and told him the tale, not without embarrassment. The likelihood that his daughter had been abandoned was bad enough; confessing as much to business acquaintance was infinitely worse.

'We could make enquiries,' the pal said. 'No promises of course. I'll need a few details, his passport number – I take it he *does* have a British passport?'

'No.' Joe burned at remembered words bandied across the dinner table. 'He has principles instead, or so he led me to believe.'

A long silence on the line. 'Oh dear. If he's carrying Polish documents our hands are tied. He's their property, isn't he? Principles and all. Nothing we can do, officially *or* under the table. It's sewn up tight as a drum over there.'

'Hell.'

'Sorry. Winston did warn us, didn't he?'

'A pity someone didn't warn my lass.'

Since Lallie knew he was calling the Foreign Office he had to tell her the outcome, or some of it. She was playing records upstairs, her head tipped to one side as if waiting for a particular note. He had to say her name twice to catch her attention. As he repeated an edited version of what he'd just been told she kept her eyes on the record sleeve that dangled from her thin fingers. '… but they'll keep their ears to the ground, just in case,' he lied.

'That's nice,' she said. 'Thanks for calling him, anyway.' She took the Polonaise off the turntable and slid it carefully into its sleeve. 'It's a pretty piece, isn't it?' When she turned back to him her eyes were brimming. For the first time in months she didn't try to back away when he gathered her to him and pulled her on his lap in the armchair.

'Don't you think I'm getting a bit big for this?' She patted her smock, her voice pitched precariously between laughter and tears. 'Sitting on your lap at twenty-seven?'

'Nay love, not to me. You're just my lass,' her shoulder blades sharp to his hands. 'Just my thin little lass …'

'Oh Daddy …'

He sighed. 'I just wish you could be happy love, that's all I want.'

A sob tore up through her throat and shook them both. 'So do I, Daddy …'

She wept then, quietly and for a long time, and he rocked her until she fell asleep.

He covered her with the old tartan rug and remembered that he'd done this before, the night Millie died.

CHAPTER THIRTY

Warsaw

Bura. Emil Bura.

Memory groped back to before the *stalag*, touched torment and recoiled.

Emil Bura, LMF. His famous family, his pretty face, his urine a puddle on the floor of the Wellington.

'... *you bloody iceberg ... I'll nail your fucking balls to the wall ...*'

He was to wait for the aide. No mere orderly to conduct him into the presence of the commandant. 'Commandant of what?' he asked the sergeant. 'This way-station for returning civilians?' Oh no! he was told. This barracks was just a tiny part of the battalion's strength, a part which was usually ignored.

'You travellers have to be housed somewhere, *nie*? Just our luck that we had the space. Major Bura never comes here, *rozumiesz*? You are to be taken to his office in the city.' Clearly, the sergeant was impressed, and waxed expansive. 'He was a war hero, you know, flying from England. More decorations than a Christmas tree.'

Bura a hero? From behind a desk? But then, who would know, here? With an honest face and the right connections a man could say anything he wanted.

The aide's car arrived and the sergeant snapped to, saluted, and wheeled away. Jan was left with a driver, armed, and the fussy, chatty aide who rubbed his hands briskly as he hustled Jan into the car.

'We go, Pan Kaliski! Not so far, but with the traffic ... just look at the lines for streetcars! Why don't they walk and take the pressure off the city services? Lazy, lazy. Cigarette? No?' He tutt-tutted and snapped his fingers at the driver, who obliged with a match. 'You are very honoured, you know. Major Bura never sees anyone on weekends – unless of course they are ladies, ha ha.'

They were driving through Stare Miasto, the oldest part of the city on the banks of the Vistula. Stately old buildings lay in ruins; what was left was heaped into the usual tidy piles. 'See?' The aide waved at a level patch. 'In three months the original building will be back. Did you hear me, the *original* house! Yes, complete with the mosaic on the outer wall. Oh, we have been industrious! As I speak the bits are being pieced together; soon the mosaics will be back where they belong. Yes, we are very industrious in the new Poland.'

Jan looked at the carefully tended fingernails. Not much

industry had come from those nicely polished tips, he thought vaguely, too preoccupied to care very much. When had Bura found out he was here? Today? Or from the very beginning? Probably sometime between the two. Now that he knew, what did it mean? Help? Or a vendetta? Certainly not a cosy chat about the good old days – yet there had been some of those, before Jan threw him off the crew. Bura knew Lallie and had seemed to like her; perhaps that might smooth the path? From somewhere the expression 'Flash Harry' surfaced and Jan's genitals instinctively stirred …

The staff-car swept through wrought-iron gates and up the long drive of what had once been an impressive townhouse. Chestnut trees lined the drive and gardeners stooped over immaculate flowerbeds.

Bura's office? Or his home? One thing was sure. With quarters like these he was in good standing with the party.

The room was spacious, with high ceilings and intricately parqueted floors; velvet at the elegant windows and park-like grounds beyond them. By the fireplace a canary trilled and warbled within its ornate cage.

Bura did not get up.

He sat posed in a blue wing-back chair, smoke curling from a cigarette, brandy in a snifter at his elbow. The perfect features were young as ever, the eyes just as clear. Seven years, and not one of them showed.

But he was harder, smoother, no lingering trace of vulnerability to soften the sculpted mouth; not a scintilla of emotion in the deep, brilliant blue of his eyes. His uniform was tailored to the nub, resplendent with the badges of rank. Not bad, for pushing a pencil through the war. The aide hovered between them, making introductions neither of them acknowledged.

'Wait in the hall,' Bura told him quietly. 'Close the door.' He waved Jan towards a chair and crossed one leg carefully over the other, a smile flickering above the scissor-shaped scar on his jaw.

Jan waited. Social? Was that the way it would be played?

'So! Jan Kaliski! You're looking well – and how is the pretty wife?'

'Waiting for me to come home, I imagine.'

Bura seemed not to hear. 'And her father, bastion of British industry? How is he? Is he waiting also?' His laugh stretched the scar on his chin. 'I think not.'

Jan swallowed, determined to keep this civil if he could. 'I'm just here temporarily Bura, that's all.'

A delighted laugh – Jan wouldn't have been surprised if Bura had clapped his beautiful hands. 'Temporarily! We're *all* temporary *somewhere*, Kaliski, *nie?*'

'Which means?' Jan held his breath.

Bura sipped his brandy and looked about the handsome room. 'Whatever we take it to mean; one place is pretty much like another.'

'You seem to have done well for yourself.'

Bura shrugged. 'The usual story. It helps to know the right people.' He fitted a fresh cigarette into an ivory holder and lit it, watching Jan over the flare of the match. 'Of course, it doesn't help at all to know the wrong people.' The voice was far calmer now than it had been in the hangar at Hempton, and why not? The man behind it held all the cards. But he was not happier, Jan surmised. There was a brooding, dissatisfied air about him, as if he'd tried everything and nothing came up to expectations. 'They tell me you're looking for your mother. Auschwitz, was it?'

'So I hear.'

He sighed. 'Problems ... paperwork ...' In a gesture at once reflective and insulting he polished one of his medals on the sleeve of his tunic.

Jan couldn't resist. 'And you must know all about paperwork.'

A pink tide crept over the classic features. 'Still an arrogant bastard, aren't you? I thought the Germans might have knocked that out of you in the *stalag*. Oh yes, I kept track. Pity about Kaz. And Lech – though I gather he just cracked. Couldn't take it.' He waited, the invitation wide open, but Jan wouldn't be drawn again. He'd made one mistake already, perhaps one too many. He drove to the centre.

'Look, I have to get home – finish what I came to do and *get home* ... tell me how to go about it, Emil –'

The fine mouth smiled a reproach. 'You want to leave us already? But you've only just arrived.'

'Weeks ago –'

'We're not making you welcome enough, is that it?' His voice, pitched low until this moment, rose slightly. 'What's the problem? No brass bands? No big parade for one of our conquering heroes? Is that what's bothering you?'

Jan felt the blood rush hot to his temples, the curl of his fists aching to smash the pretty face. 'I didn't expect a welcome, no, nor did I expect to be locked up. You can't keep me –'

'*Sit down!*' Two words, whips cutting across the space between them, telling Jan exactly where he stood. 'Sit down and listen.'

Jan blocked off the host of fears that Bura's voice conjured up and sat, tense with waiting, on the edge of the chair.

'That's better. If you listen you might learn something. Rule number one. Don't tell me what we can and cannot do. We can do what the hell is best for the country. If it's best to lock somebody up –'

'But why? What could it possibly serve? Just because *we* have – *did have* – a personal –'

'Don't flatter yourself, Kaliski. Don't imagine you're a special case just because I've taken a personal interest. You're not, not by a long chalk. They come rolling back covered in glory and mildewed medals (you're not wearing yours, by the way – Cross of Valor, wasn't it?) Well, that's beside the point. Yes, back they come to good old Poland, think they're going to take over, think they've earned a special place because they've got a few decorations, a pre-war education ... Leaders of men –' He laughed, and he didn't look pretty anymore. 'They've got opinions, too, every damned one of 'em. They cause trouble, ask questions, stir things up. They're a bloody nuisance, that's all. We've things to do in this country now. If we listened to every jumped-up hero with an opinion we'd get nothing done, would we? So they have to be re-educated, don't they? Put somewhere safe until they've learned some sense –'

No, they wouldn't do that – '*You can't do that, I have to get back* –' God, Lallie waiting at home ... 'Emil, listen to me –'

'Major Bura to you. In a year it'll be Colonel Bura.'

Smooth him down, flatter him, anything ... 'Congratulations. I really mean that, Emil. You've done well ...'

He seemed pleased with that, buffed his nails and his two gold rings on the sleeve of his tunic, smiled into the pink pads of his fingers. God, had cowardice tilted him towards insanity? Instability, certainly – but then, he'd always been rash – the copper wire, the sudden illnesses ... 'You've done *very* well, Emil ...'

'Not bad, in the circumstances.' Complacent. Gratified. But then it all clouded over. 'No thanks to you, you bastard. You still think I'm pathetic, don't you? I failed your goddamn code somewhere, didn't I? That makes me flawed and you perfect. Upstanding. Honourable. Responsible for everything you touch. It rules you, Kaliski, your lousy code.' He reached for the brandy and drained it, filled the glass again from the decanter. 'Well, I'm not like you, thank God. Which is why *I'm* where *I* am and why *you're* where *you* are. In the shit. And you deserve it. Who the hell are you anyway? God?'

'Oh, Emil ...' It was useless to talk to him, he could see that, useless ... but he had the answers, did Major Bura, somewhere this man had the answers. He swallowed the hard lump of his pride. 'Emil, if you know where my mother is – I think you do – please tell me. Please. I have to find her, take her back ...' To Lallie, to the sane haven of Eccles Place.

'Don't beg, Kaliski. It doesn't suit you. You don't have to, anyway. Of course I know where she is. I've got connections – or hadn't you noticed? She's in Zakopane ...'

Of course. Zakopane. Just where she said she'd be. We'll try to get to Zakopane, to Uncle Tadeusz ... Of course. 'Emil, thank you. I can't tell you ...'

'How grateful you are? Music to the ears, that. The great Kaliski humbled at last.'

Humour him, placate him. He'd done this before somewhere ... for Lallie ... Maurice, yes Maurice, with his large head and dangerous brain ... so be careful. This Bura could fix everything – if he wanted to. 'How soon do you think

I'll be able to get my mother, take her back?'

'Ah yes, that's the question. How soon ...'

He felt like a mouse, tossed between the cats-paws of Bura's pride and Bura's problem. 'Please, Emil ... It's my mother, my family –'

'*Family? Family?*' Bura reached for the brandy again, a nerve Jan hadn't noticed before throbbing in the classic column of neck. 'What would *you* know about family, Kaliski? What were they, your family? Teachers, that's all. Teachers. Grandfather a maths teacher, father a language teacher ... *Some family*!' Bura closed his eyes, pressed fingertips to temples. In the beautiful room only silence, broken now and then by the canary, who alternately sang from his perch then scratched busily in the grit at the bottom of the cage. 'Family ...'

Then Bura was on his feet, towering over him ... and outside, a guard at the door.

'Do you have any idea what you did,' he whispered, 'you with your lousy LMF? Your dutiful report?'

'I had no choice, you know that –'

'So you said. So you explained, very noble and correct.' The pink of his cheeks turned to red, then to a dangerous magenta as he thrust an exquisitely manicured hand into his pocket. 'Explain this, then!' He threw a faded envelope into Jan's lap. 'Go on, read it! My father's last letter to his beloved son. Read it.'

Jan made no move. 'You know I had no choice, Emil.'

'I'd have got over it.'

'If we lived that long. I couldn't risk it. It would have been stupid to –'

Bura made a sudden move and the wing-chair crashed behind him. 'Stupid? That was the *kindest* thing my father called me. Weak, yes. Craven, yes. Gutless. Pathetic. After that, stupid was almost a compliment.'

'Emil –'

But Emil was looking past Jan, past the elegant windows and manicured lawns. 'That letter wasn't just from my father, Kaliski. It was from my idol, my ideal. He was everything *I* wanted to be, *had been born to be, would have been*! He was proud of me, that man – and you *killed* it and went off to bed with the new wife! You didn't give a damn.' He turned away and rapped sharply on the canary's cage with the back of his open hand. 'He wrote that letter from Monte Casino. A week later he was dead.' Then he was standing over Jan's chair again, his curled fists working at his sides.

Jan wanted to reach out, tell him that a man can only be what he is – but reticence got in the way. 'And your brother?' he said instead.

'Torpedoed off North Africa.'

'I'm sorry.'

Bura stared down at him, lips twisted. 'I'm afraid 'sorry' doesn't quite cover it. Here – if you're too squeamish to read it for yourself –' The single sheet of paper rustled in his fingers. 'It's very brief.'

You are a disgrace. To me, to your name, and to your country. You are not my son.

He thrust the letter into the flames and watched it burn. When he turned back to Jan his face was as cold as the marble mantelpiece. 'They died disgusted with me, both of them. Because of you.'

'You saved the note …'

Bura nodded. 'Until now.'

He touched a button on the desk and the aide appeared, twittering brightly.

Jan stood up, his legs weak as all the ramifications of this meeting scurried like mice in his head.

'I guess I'll be seeing you again,' he said bitterly.

The mask gave him a distant smile. 'Afraid not, old chap. We're both moving on. I've been promoted … again.'

'And?'

'And you? Come now, Kaliski. I'm a busy man.' He gestured to the aide. 'Get him out of my sight.'

The aide's prattle flowed over him in a thin syrup all the way back to the barracks, an irritating counterpoint to the questions that now surged in faster than he could deal with them. 'We're both moving on'. So he was to go somewhere … but where? Out? Or further in, smothered in red tape?

However, Bura had spilled the acid that ate at his heart. Perhaps now they'd let him go – but if they didn't where was the recourse?

At the barracks still more confusing signals were waiting for him. The remaining inmates of the hut had gone, their bunks stripped and their enamel plates clean, stacked on the table. The orderly came whistling in with Jan's dinner, a heel of bread and a mess of turnip and potato.

'All gone,' he said cheerfully, filling Jan's chipped cup with coffee substitute. 'Maybe they'll get to you now.'

'Where did they go?' Jan said, suspicions worming in.

'Released! Just like that! Papers all in order, everything neat and tidy. It's bound to be your turn next. We're closing down this unit so they'll have to put you somewhere else.'

For a week they left him where he was, a week in which he was permitted contact with no one at all. Major Wajda was on leave, he was told, and Sasha was in Moscow for orientation – whatever that was. His every demand for action was sidestepped or evaded or ignored, but with a new deference he found vaguely encouraging.

Then he was told to pack. 'Gather up your things, you'll be out of here by evening.'

It was true. He was getting out. Any minute now clerks would issue him permits and coupons and passes, all the bits of paper deemed so necessary to life in the new Poland. He packed his few belongings and waited, tense as a sprinter poised for the starting gun. By tonight he'd be in the real Poland, check into a real hotel, place a call to Lallie if he could and write to her if he could not; he'd eat a real meal, sleep in a real bed (were they still made of feathers? he wondered), and tomorrow he'd begin his search. Who knew, he might find Mamunia within a couple of days and be heading for England within the week. And Lallie. By now she must be frantic, watching the mails, running to the phone ... Poor Bura, how empty his life must have been to keep his father's cruel judgement for so long, souring power and position and beautiful surroundings. By comparison, how blessed *he* was, a wife who loved him and a mother soon to be restored ... even Joe Wainwright, from this distance, seemed not so heavy a

321

cross, his faults springing only from devotion to his daughter. Who was Jan Kaliski – who loved her also – to argue with that?

It was dark when they came for him.

Tyres squealed outside the hut. Doors slammed. Feet pounded on the cobbles and then on the wooden floor by his bunk. Uniforms and blank businesslike faces. Hard hands jerking him to his feet as he tried to ask where they were taking him. He asked again, louder. His arms were jerked over his head, knuckles slammed into his jaw and the floor swung up to meet him.

When he came to there were wheels rumbling beneath him, racing him through traffic that seemed to advance and retreat with his senses. In brief periods of consciousness he made out three men in the van ... another van? ... moonlight glinted off weapons and off the metal grille separating them from the driver. Smells of metal and cigarette ash and old urine swirled around him on the floor of the van. He struggled to sit up, barely stifling a scream as his arm buckled under him and pain roared up the arm and rammed his shoulder. Darkness again, the long slide away from pain, gratitude in every ragged breath ... The next time he came to he was more cautious, gingerly exploring his shoulders with his good hand. He touched them again and then again, from one side to the other, unwilling to believe what his fingertips told him.

His shoulders did not match. The left side was there but what should have been his right shoulderblade was ... was not there! His fingers inched farther back, found the lump. He knew what it was, what must be done, and done quickly.

'My shoulder's dislocated ...' he gasped. 'Please ...'

Three faces, pale in the moonlight, glanced down. One of them laughed but another, punching the laugher's arm, said, '*Nie, nie,*' and bent down, roughly checking what Jan already knew. Through the new spasms of pain surging through him with every smallest movement he heard their brief discussion. The laugher seemed to be subordinate; the fingers exploring his shoulder cavity seemed to belong to the leader, whom the others called Adam. None of them knew what to do but the

322

laugher was being blamed for the injury.

'Look,' Jan whispered, afraid to move lest another surge of pain slide him down the hill again. 'You take my arm, brace your foot in my side, and pull ...' Just the thought of it brought mist swirling back but he set his teeth. 'Pull hard ... you'll hear it go in.'

Adam was not sure. He'd never done anything like –

'*Please*! *Do it*!'

Adam was tentative but strong. Bone grated on bone. The arm slipped back, the thud reverberating through every nerve in his body. He could breathe again.

'I'm sorry,' Adam said. 'It should not have happened. We had no instructions ...'

'What *were* your instructions? And where are you taking me?'

'To pick you up, take you to –'

'Yes?'

'I'm sorry. I can't say. But you were not to be hurt.'

'On whose orders?'

'*Przepraszam* ...'

But Jan would *not* excuse him, kept pressing, insisting, and at the end of half an hour knew little more than he had when they grabbed him from the barracks.

'This is how you treat your own countrymen when they come back?'

'Sorry sir, but no. Your case must be ... different.'

'How different? Because it involves Bura?'

No answer.

'How far are we going?'

'To the country ... a farm.'

'Farm?'

'Work farm ...'

'Why?'

He shrugged. '*Nie wiem*.' He didn't know.

He didn't know but he *did* seem to care, a little – which encouraged Jan to press harder. 'Is it a punishment, a sentence?'

'*Nie wiem* ... everything is different now. The laws change ... it's hard to say why.' He glanced over his shoulder in what seemed to be a purely reflex action. 'I am sure it is for the best.'

'How could it be? I don't choose to go to a work farm, I –'

'Please sir ... better don't talk, eh?' He turned away.

Jan was dimly aware of barbed wire and what looked in the darkness as if they might be towers. He was hustled to an office, his single suitcase searched and handed back.

'Am I under arrest?' he asked the guard. 'On what charge?'

The guard shrugged. 'The usual. Crimes against the state.'

'What crime?'

A grubby finger followed a line on a chart. 'Vagrancy.'

'I'm a traveller!'

'Documentation?'

He patted his pocket for the little wad of authorizations issued him at the embassy in London. It was gone! His pockets were quite empty; not even a comb had been left to him. But when ...? In the van, of course. Adam – or the laugher? And what difference did it make? Without identification, without money ... he felt stripped, remembered Joe Wainwright's quaint idea of a money belt and wished he'd listened. A bribe might have just –

If the room at the barracks had been a shed, what they now led him to was unequivocally a cell. Dirt floor, one wall of bars, three of mildewed cement. A bench, a bunk, a tin plate and a malodorous bucket, all lit by a single electric bulb hanging far above his head. *A work camp?* This was a prison –

As if in direct confirmation there was a snuffling on the other side of the bars. Three dogs roaming the corridors.

A welter of emotions collided in his brain. Anger at Emil Bura and the incident that had brought him to this pass. Fear for what would now become of him. Aching frustration for Lallie so far away, innocently waiting for his return. Wrenching anxiety over Mamunia – was she really in Zakopane? Who was taking care of her? Was *anyone* taking care ...

He rattled the tin plate across the bars. His answer was a disgruntled shout from farther down the corridor and the muzzle of a German Shepherd lifting as it ran to the cell to stand snarling at him through the bars.

He threw himself to the straw pallet, flung his arms across his eyes to shut out the naked light and the desperation washing over him in waves. The pain of his shoulder came and went with movement; despair was a constant weight, pressing him to the hard straw.

It could not be happening. It was a nightmare from which he'd surely wake to hear Mrs Hodgson rattling about in the kitchen, Lallie humming as she dressed for the kennels, Joe revving up the car for the trip to the foundry ...

There was a sensation, oddly familiar, on his neck. A faint movement on his arm. He opened his eyes.

They were crawling through the pale hair of his forearm, scores of them come to feast off the new blood.

Lice.

Again.

Another *stalag*, worse than the last. *That* had been in enemy territory. This one was at home ... home ... home ...

In another room a guard switched on the radio for the news. The traditional notes of the Polonaise preceded it, desolate and haunting in the autumn night.

The light in Cell Block Four shone down on the new arrival, on tears that squeezed in slow diamonds through his lashes.

CHAPTER THIRTY-ONE

Eccles Place, Yorkshire, 1946

Afterwards she remembered that morning as a kind of distant beacon, not a very bright one yet because it *was* so far away and the brooding reality of Jan's absence was very close, obscuring the light.

Her pleasure in the coming baby had been little more than a tender seedling when fears for its father began to spring up around it, absorbing all her thoughts and all her days. Jan was not there so how could she take pleasure in anything else? Her pregnancy, which recurring nausea forced her to notice, had seemed little more than a medical term like mumps or tonsilitis, a swollen condition with a predetermined outcome – but in the future, when Jan came home.

Until now.

At first it seemed like nothing at all, the merest trembling of a leaf under her flowered smock.

She held her breath but it did not come again until hours later as she lowered herself into a warm bath. This time the sensation was just as delicate, but prolonged, tendrils curling and relaxing under the gentle movement of the water. In the fragrant mists of shampoo and bath salts the water seemed to tilt, lap gently at breast and thigh, and she thought for a moment that she was about to faint. Instinctively her hands went to the smooth roundness of her belly, covering, protecting. And the feeling came again, more vigorous, the faintest pressure under her palm. Ever so gently something was turning and stretching inside her. The thing she'd referred to, even in her thoughts, as the Bump became a baby, her baby, hers and Jan's. A person. A little creature of their own making that they – and no one else – were responsible for. And in Jan's absence she, and no one else …

Other people had always been responsible for *her*, Mum and Jan and sometimes Neil – *always* Daddy. She'd been pampered and protected, sheltered and shielded from every conceivable ill. Now for the first time there was someone for *her* to protect, a tiny stirring human that would learn to love and to cry, to hope and despair … and for the first time she was not alone in waiting for Jan.

'He'll be here soon,' she whispered to the child in her womb. 'When he comes home we'll go walking on the common, we'll go to the seaside and you'll build sandcastles and run with the dogs … he'll carry you on his shoulder and you'll clap your hands …'

And suppose Jan wasn't back …? 'Then I'll find him for us, you'll see. But I expect he'll be back any day, d'you hear me? Any day now you'll have a Daddy.'

She shopped for a baby carriage and a cot and called Waymans to send the layette for her to look at again. In the crisp autumn mornings she even began walking the dogs on the common again. In daylight. While she didn't exactly go out of her way to greet people she didn't avoid them either. When they enquired if she'd heard anything from Jan yet she was able to look them in the eye and say fairly cheerfully: 'No, but it's just a matter of time. Communications are difficult.' She had Charles do her hair again – because Jan might call at any minute and she must be ready to go to the airport for him. 'I'll wear the lavender wool coat,' she told the baby inside her, 'it's *just* big enough for both of us and he always liked me in that – but he'd better come soon or we're not going to fit into it!'

To Joe, the change came not a moment too soon.

'By God it's a relief!' he said to Mrs Hodgson when Lallie was persuaded to go into town with Neil to see *Outward Bound* at the Lyceum. 'I was beginning to think she was ... you know, going off her head a bit. All that moping about and not speaking to anybody.' he shifted a box of tiny flannel nightgowns from his armchair and sat down. 'No good for her, you know. No good at all, spending all that time on her own. Always been a one for company, Lallie has. I reckon she's looking better – though what made the difference I don't know –'

'She felt life I expect,' Mrs Hodgson said, matter-of-fact. 'Nothing like it for showing you what's what. I remember with my first, it never really hit 'til I, well –' She flushed and made quite a business of folding the flannel gowns back into their box. 'And she's eating better, if you notice. Could do with a mite of flesh on her, I'm thinking. Of course, I never had *that* problem!' She patted her ample hips and sailed off trailing tissue paper and flannel and cardboard boxes.

Who knew? thought Joe, sipping his Scotch and stretching his legs towards the fire. Was the bugger coming back or wasn't he? He'd bet a pound to a penny they never saw hide nor hair of him again – but there was his lass, dusting the mother's room every morning and airing the bed, chrysanthemums in the jug as if the old girl would totter in any minute. Oh well, once she got the baby she wouldn't bother about the Pole much then, he reckoned. Between himself and Neil they could fill in the gaps so she'd hardly notice he wasn't here. Happen Bob Waithe was right, and time would fix everything ...

He was less sanguine the following week when Lallie announced she was off to London.

'What the flaming Heeley are you going there for? I told you what they said at the Foreign Office – there's nothing they can do.'

'Not there! I'm going to the Polish Consulate. They're bound to know something.' She blushed and turned away.

She was keeping something back, he'd swear to it. The thought set alarm bells ringing in his head. What now? Was there no end to it? Then Neil walked in like a saviour. Thank God Neil had some sense, *he'd* talk to her. 'She wants to go to the bloody consulate, what d'you say to that?'

'She *is* going!' Lallie turned on them both, her eyes blazing.

Neil stood between the two of them, looking thoughtful. 'I'm not sure they'll be able to tell you much but –'

'She can't go in her condition!' Joe spluttered. 'Driving all that way –'

'I'm taking the train. I've already got the ticket. I'm not an invalid, you know. I've three months to go yet.'

'If you go I'm going with you!'

'I'm going on my own and that's that!'

'*You're not going.*'

'*Try and stop me*! *I'll be on the ten o'clock train tomorrow*!'

Joe was at a loss. Three months ago he'd have given anything to see that determination on her face. Well, it was back now, and with a vengeance. 'You've plenty to do here. We've Brandy Tsar coming tomorrow in case you've forgotten –'

'I can take care of that if you like,' Neil put in.

Oh, it was too much! Just when she was getting back to herself she had to go looking for another disappointment. Goaded beyond caring, he said, 'Has it occurred to you, have you stopped to think that he just might –'

'Joe!' There was warning in Neil's tone, and just in time too. He turned his comfortable smile on Lallie. 'I'll see to the dogs, love. I'll be over first thing so you can get an early start.'

'Oh Neil, you really are a gem!'

So then he had to stand there while Lallie threw her arms round Neil and kissed him. When she'd left he turned all his helpless anger on Neil.

'A great help *you* turned out to be! Encouraging her to –'

'I'm not encouraging her but you were really going to *flatten* her. You were going to tell her he'd left her, weren't you?'

'I think it's time she started being realistic.'

'*I* think she should be left to find the truth out for herself, whatever it is. She'll get nowhere in London, we both know that –'

'Then what's the point of her going?'

Neil sighed. 'Joe, she has to be let do something for herself. It'll keep her going, help her along.'

'And all this time I thought you loved my lass ...'

And then Neil was looking at him as he never had before, as if *he, Joe Wainwright* was a fractious child he was tired, at the moment, of humouring. 'I do love her – but not enough to smother her. Or maybe too much to smother her. I know this is hard for *you*, but nothing like it is for her. If Jan's *not* coming back she'll know eventually, and by then she'll be able to accept it. She couldn't accept it now, Joe.'

For the first time in his life Joe knew he'd been well and truly reproached. And by Neil Armott!

So lovely to be in a train again, and marvellous they had a carriage to themselves so she didn't have to talk to anyone but the baby. She patted her lavender coat and felt the answering thrust of a heel – or a fist – from the other side.

'They'll know something in London, baby. Maybe they're even holding a message for us and can't find our address. I know he'll get word to us if he can, if he hasn't been hurt or anything ... and of *course* he hasn't. Poor Daddy (*my* Daddy, not yours) thinks Jan's not coming back to us, that he doesn't want us. He very nearly said so yesterday, didn't he? But Jan *is* coming back, precious ... and if he doesn't we'll just have to go to Poland and find him, won't we? We'll ask them for papers – not that we can go until you're born of course – but after that we'll think of something ... '

She liked talking to Stefan – or Rose. It kept her mind busy so the other thoughts couldn't get in quite so much. It *was* Stefan she was fairly sure, but in case it wasn't she'd decided on

Rose, which had been Mum's middle name. Stephanie Kaliski sounded, well, long, and Rose Kaliski was just right. But somehow she was sure it was Stefan in there and addressed him as such.

'We're going to be very calm when we talk to them, too. They're Jan's people and we want to make a good impression so they'll let us go to Poland later if we have – if we want to.'

She'd only ever been to London once and that was with Jan. Except for the fact that he'd been with her she hadn't liked it. It was a bustling place, strange, and the people seemed to look right through you. Some of the buildings were lovely of course, but there were so many of them and they seemed remote, far too big to ever feel one belonged in them. She knew every corridor of Sheffield's Town Hall and library, had been in every shop and restaurant in its High Street – but who could ever say that about London?

'Don't worry, we won't get lost,' she told the baby as she hunted through the enormous phone book for the consulate's address.

Just to be sure she took a taxi and the driver seemed to go a very long way around – she was sure they'd been down that street at least once – but when he finally stopped at the address she'd given him she wished they could have driven a few more unnecessary miles.

The building looked so ... grey, so *closed*. A façade of massive stones; brooding windows behind which she could see nothing at all. The door wasn't open and she had to ring the bell, which surprised her. Somehow she'd thought a consulate was a public building where one could come and go at will. A little man who was polishing a brass plate by the door spoke to her in rapid Polish. Seeing her expression he sighed and tsssk'd through his front teeth. 'Appointmen'? You 'ave appointmen'?'

'No ... I want to speak to the consul.'

Jak się nazywa pani?

'I'm sorry ...'

'Name! Name!' he said, shaking out his polishing cloth.

'Mrs Kaliski.'

He opened a flap and said something into a speaking tube. All she could catch was 'Pani Kaliska' several times, then he resumed his polishing and she was left to wait, feeling more and more foolish as the seconds dragged on. Just when she was about to remind him again she heard footsteps on the other side of the heavy door. A key turned and the door inched open.

'You have no appointment?' a voice asked.

'I want to see the consul,' she said firmly.

A consultation on the other side, the voices young and uncertain, then the door opened a crack more.

'What is your business?'

'It's about my husband.'

'Aha. *Chwileczke* … a moment, please.'

The door closed again but at least the key did not turn.

Another wait before it was opened fully by a young man with very thin lips and a wary smile who led her down a long dark hall, its highly burnished floor reflecting heavy furniture and thick, depressing hangings. The smell of Mansion polish was incredibly strong, as if the people had no other function than to polish the several squat tables and straight-back chairs.

'The consul is not in,' the young man said smoothly, 'but the vice-consul can give you a few minutes.'

She was put to wait in a gloomy room with bars on the window, a desk (again thickly polished) and two small hard chairs.

She felt very small and unimportant. Perhaps she should have let Daddy come with her after all – but oh dear, by now there'd be thunder in the halls; he couldn't bear to be kept waiting … 'and we don't want them getting cross, do we?' She slid her hand under the lavender wool but there was no answering pressure. Asleep again. Perhaps just as well … Except for the language, which she'd heard often enough at Hempton, it was so very foreign here. No feeling of Jan at all and she'd thought – hoped – that she'd feel closer to him here somehow.

But she warmed to the vice-consul immediately. He was bald and pink and twinkly, with hard little hands that he rubbed together very fast as if he were in a simply tearing hurry to get somewhere. He heard her out patiently with a minimum of prompting. Then he offered her tea, but since he glanced at his watch in the process, she declined.

'But of course.' He twinkled some more and rubbed his

fingertips together. 'All I can tell you – not that I *should* – is that your husband applied for a visa –'

'But I *know* that! And I wanted to go with him but he – *and* my father said I'd better not –'

'I see.' He looked down at the so very empty desk and ran his fingertips across its high shine. 'We don't keep records as you see, so there's really nothing I can tell you …'

He was very nice, she thought, very nice indeed, and it was with some effort that she ignored the pink kindliness and the obvious expectation that she would now leave. Jan had talked enough about the new system for her to know she would have to press.

'In that case I'd like to apply for a visa – not to leave *now* of course,' indicating the bulge under her coat, 'but for later. For myself and … you *do* have papers I can fill out? Just in case my husband isn't back in a few months?'

The twinkle didn't quite go out but it faded perceptibly. 'A visa for permanent residence?'

'Well …' She hadn't thought that far *yet*, my goodness!

'In that case.' He opened a drawer and withdrew a form, scribbled her name hurriedly. Her age? How long had they been married? Her present address? To which countries had she travelled previously? With whom in Poland did she wish to live?

'My husband.'

'And his address in Poland?'

'I don't know.'

He sighed and set down the pencil very precisely across the form. 'Pani Kaliska … we can issue no permanent visa if – Where would you *go*?'

'I would look for him! *He* didn't have an address and you gave *him* a visa!'

'But of course, he is a Polish citizen.'

'And I'm his wife!'

He studied the form again very closely before he looked up. 'Tell me, Pani Kaliska. Do you speak any Polish at all?'

She shook her head.

The hard little hands spread wide. 'I'm sorry …'

'I'll take a tourist visa,' she said quickly.

332

The vice-consul looked devastated, crushed. 'At the present time it is not possible, so sorry. The war ... there is not enough accommodation for our own people, you understand? First we must rebuild, then we will be happy to see such a charming tourist ...' He wadded up the incomplete application and tossed it into the wastepaper basket.

The walls seemed to close in around her. 'But what can I do?' she cried. 'There must be something!'

The vice-consul stood up. A look of compassion flitted across his face briefly. 'Please understand ... it has been a very long war for our people. Very long. Our country is in ruins – but it is our home, *prawda*?' At the door he stood for a moment, the hard little hands rubbing together. 'At home I have a daughter like you, not so tall but as pretty, yes ... as pretty. I tell you what I would tell her. *Better to wait for your husband here, with people who care for you.* Please stay here – someone will show you out.'

And he was gone.

She didn't know what made her pick up the crumpled application from the wastepaper basket, unless it was to stop herself thinking about what the vice-consul had said.

Only her name was entered. In all the other spaces he'd drawn little hearts with broken lines across them.

CHAPTER THIRTY-TWO

Poland, November, 1946

The new camp was more – and less – than he expected.

In that they cleaned bricks and stacked them on trucks to be carted away for Warsaw's reconstruction, the place was a work camp.

In that there were armed guards at the single exit and

identity cards required for anyone coming or going, it was a prison. There were cells and guard dogs and sentry towers. And of course the lice – perhaps they came with the blankets, as they had in the *stalag*.

Sensibly, the food was an improvement over the hostel. Here the inmates worked and must therefore be fuelled. Occasional bits of meat floated in the soup and sometimes there was a spoonful of jam or fruit compote with the evening meal. And lots of bread, dark indeterminate hunks whose composition was a mystery; the texture hinted at sawdust, the weight at powdered rock.

Jan had little now with which to barter but he managed to exchange his extra shirt for a postage stamp he hoped would get a letter to Lallie.

Darling Lallie:

So much has happened I don't know where to begin, or even if I should ... Months since I left and nothing accomplished, nothing ... I did find out where Mamunia is ... I think ... Nothing is sure here, except that I can't seem to leave and perhaps won't be able to for some time. Go with your father to the authorities, tell them I'm being held – I'm not sure just where – see if the Foreign Office can put pressure on, Joe will know how. He's been right about so many things. Tell him that. I must get out, must get back to you, must get my mother from here, must plan ...

Be patient, darling, please be patient. I think of you all the time, want you ... am sorry I ever came, sorry for giving you this burden, sorry for Mamunia, for so many, many things I am sorry. Try not to worry. I am well, just not free – but I shall be. I know I shall. When you receive this ... *if* you receive this. If you don't I think I shall go mad.

But no matter what, don't even think of coming here. I beg you, don't even think ... you cannot imagine, but your father, I think, can. Listen to him. Wait for me. I love you.

Jan

For the price of a pair of socks one of the guards agreed to post it for him.

Grimly determined now to get out of here any way he could and as soon as he could, he quizzed the other detainees. Were they serving specific sentences? And for what?

'For opening my mouth.'

'For stealing eggs.'

'For getting drunk.'

'For punching a party member.'

'For selling my ration book.'

'For buying black market sugar.'

A picture emerged. There was much reconstruction work to be done and men must be found to do it. But for how long? No man knew the exact length of his sentence and few seemed to care. They'd been in the wrong place at the wrong time and passively accepted the consequences. Most seemed to be drifters, well aware of the housing shortage on the outside – 'And at least we're fed, *prawda*?' When the 'emergency' was over, why then, they'd be released ... None, it seemed, had families to go to – and perhaps that was why they were here.

What safer hole could Bura have found to wreak his petty vengeance? Yet even as he raged Jan knew that, to Emil Bura, what had happened at Hempton was not petty. To a man raised in a military family, fed on its tradition, steeped in its past, cowardice – LMF, white feathers ... every war spawned a new phrase – was anathema.

But Lallie was waiting, trusting ... and Mamunia, who did not yet know that a different life was open to her, she waited also, in Zakopane.

One day Jan spotted a familiar face among a group of new arrivals. It was middle-aged, grey with worry.

'Haven't I – weren't you in Fighter Command during the war?' Jan asked him.

The man shook his head as if to clear it. 'Yes, yes I was.'

'What are you doing here then?'

'I wish to God I knew. I came back six months ago. To stay, I thought, to get back to the family's law practice. Since then I've been shuffled from camp to camp. This is the fifth. I don't know what to do, I just don't know ... If I could get word out. ... '

No wonder he'd seemed familiar. A group captain who'd commanded a good chunk of their fighter strength during the war – now a shuffling bundle of uncertainties. Bura's voice came back. ... *You're not a special case, Kaliski ... they come back ... decorations, pre-war education ... leaders of men ... they ask questions, cause trouble, stir things up.* Oh yes, it all fit. The new regime couldn't afford men like these – '*covered in glory and mildewed medals.*' That had been Bura's envy speaking. The man in front of him now was covered in bewilderment, bitterness perhaps. Not glory.

A prisoner the others called Pogo drew Jan aside and gave him the facts of life as they referred to Cell Block Four.

First, Jan was asking far too many questions. They'd think he wanted to escape.

'But of course I do!' Jan retorted.

Pogo sighed. He wore his skin like a big brother's suit, sagging and empty in unexpected places. He explained patiently that spies were planted among the prisoners, that things were seldom what they seemed. Better to wait and watch, *nie*? Besides, even if he got out it was winter. Winter. What would he eat? What would he wear? And Jan had no papers.

Jan had told no one that his authorization to be in Poland was stolen on the way here. 'How do you know?' he demanded.

Pogo laughed. '*Everybody*'s papers are stolen on the way in! They're worth money, *gold* on the outside. Of course you have no papers. And the letter? You surely didn't expect the guard to post it? He'd be a prisoner himself if they caught him – and all the mail is censored anyway, so what's the point?

He had to get out.

Wait and watch, Pogo said.

He spent every free minute of the first month watching the exit from behind various casual-seeming vantage points. Who went out and came in, at what time and what they wore. The staff was not large but it was depressingly regular. None of them seemed to get sick or take holidays; the few who fraternized with the prisoners were close-mouthed.

He knew he was in the countryside surrounding Warsaw, but it was an area not familiar to him from before the war and he could not expect to recognize any landmarks even if such were still standing. Through the wire there was little to be seen but fields under flat untrodden snow and a few sparse and distant trees. If he was going to get out it would have to be at night. Because of the snow and the footprints he would leave he must go via the main gate and the one cleared road or else wait until the snow melted – at least three months, which didn't bear thinking about. By then he'd have been in Poland almost a year!

With some thought to Pogo's warnings he began to hoard bread and to consider the biggest problem, clothing. With no money and without identification of any kind he would have to make the search for Mamunia on foot, at least until he could somehow get hold of papers. Once again, the weather was the most problematic hurdle. Away from farms and houses he would quickly freeze to death in the clothes he had with him. Wanting to travel light, he'd laughed Lallie out of packing his heavy overcoat and had brought instead a light raincoat – far too clean and new for his purpose now – and no hat. The civilian staff of the camp and the other prisoners all wore clothes of pre-war cut, a polyglot collection of Russian and German army overcoats no doubt taken from the dead. Heads were swathed in woollen scarves or knitted balaclava helmets against the biting cold. To walk out of here bare-headed would be to invite immediate questions from even the most unsuspecting civilian. Not to mention frost-bitten ears and nose.

Thanks to his scorn over Lallie's extravagant packing he had little with which to barter. What he could have done, now, with all those sweaters and shirts and socks she had so carefully packed! He tired to shut out the picture of her diligently bending to the task, her hair so fine and fragrant in his face as he said, 'Darling, I'm *not* going to Cannes for the season!' Here, no one had *anything* to spare, not a hat or a coat or even a comb. But in the surrounding farms … he knew the Polish peasants, well used to pillaging troops. They buried anything they could until the hordes had rampaged on past. If he could just get out, get to one of those farms …

He watched the movements of the civilian staff, noted at what times they arrived through the gates, what times they left and with whom, paying special attention to a carpenter who seemed about Jan's height and colouring and was often alone. From a distance ...

Christmas would be the best time, with the guards relaxed and the civilians hurrying to their homes outside.

CHAPTER THIRTY-THREE

Eccles Place, Yorkshire, December, 1946

She looked well enough – pink-cheeked from the daily walks, nourished according to Dr Waithe's precise instructions – but Neil was not deceived. That she was desperately unhappy and too proud to say so was obvious, but it was what she was *not* that troubled him.

She, who had cared about everyone, was now interested in no one but the coming baby. She went out, she attended to the business of the kennel, she shopped and gardened as much as her expanding girth allowed – but there was no spark, no involvement with anything but the process going on inside her. She put on a very good act. If he didn't love her so much, ache to ease her burden in some small way, he would have been fooled like the rest of them – all but Joe, but Joe was saying little these days, at least to Neil. The old affection was still there and when they talked the conversations were easy. But very brief. It was as if Joe could only think and care about Lallie, and Lallie felt only for the child.

The change had set in when she came back from London with an odd, bright smile and no news at all. 'Oh, they were nice, very nice,' she'd said at the station when they met her, 'but they're *dim*, didn't know a thing!' Then she went into a long catalogue of complaints about London and the people and the traffic and the train, which was too slow, too dirty, too crowded. Listening to her, Neil didn't know her – or he didn't know the façade she was showing them.

She no longer mentioned Jan at all. When Roman and Genia came to visit she was polite and changed the subject the instant they showed any anxiety about Jan. Last month Mrs Hodgson had been laid up with bronchitis for a week; Lallie made no attempt to take up the slack as she would have done before, didn't even pretend to cook and serve the meals. She simply drifted through the days with her smile and her baby.

When he had the chance Neil quizzed Roman:

'Why on earth doesn't he *write*?'

But Roman was as puzzled as he. 'Even if he couldn't for some reason, why doesn't he get something through the underground – I keep watching the little newsheet, but there's nothing, nothing out of Poland at all ... It's not like him, but ...'

'But what?'

'Homesickness. It's a funny thing. Take Genia – she *knows* what it's like in Poland now, gets letters from her family complaining of this and that, but she still nags me to go back. Misses it ...'

'You think that's it? That he just wants to stay there?'

Roman looked around at the comfortable living room, the bright fire, a tray of expensive chocolates on the sideboard. 'If he *did* want to stay there, I doubt if he'd consider taking Lallie away from this. They don't even have *space* – Genia's family is living seven to a room, *one room*! Just think ...'

'Then why would *he* want to stay?'

'I don't think he would ... but then I remember what a patriotic cuss he turned out to be and I can't help wondering.'

'But the baby –'

And Roman reminded him that Jan didn't know about the baby, a little detail *he*, who could see it growing every day, had forgotten.

The room that had been intended for Mamunia slowly reverted back to a study. Books began to pile up on the bedside table and Joe began to do his accounts at the old desk. As Christmas approached they needed space for boxes and decorations and Mamunia's bed was first shoved into a corner out of the way, then as the boxes piled higher the bed was moved to the attic to make space. Slowly but surely, Eccles Place was becoming the house it had been ten years earlier. Lallie still slept in the suite upstairs but a few key items found their way downstairs, where she once again did most of her living. Kaz's cup, the one thing that seemed to keep its place in her life, was now on the sideboard downstairs. The little living room upstairs, her refuge with Jan during the last bitter year before he left for Poland, was to be the nursery. That way the baby would be close to her at night'...

Lallie knew herself to be hanging on.

Since the trip to the consulate she'd built her defences brick by slow brick, knowing she must build and for whom.

'Oh, baby, your mother *is* a bit of a ninny, not firing on all cylinders, you know? Grandad's right, you really *can't* trust everybody and it's safer to duck behind the wall sometimes, especially when the guns start up ... but you won't remember the blitz ... you had to keep your head down then, I can tell you! Your grandmother never knew that but we know, don't we? We keep ourselves to ourselves and nobody but us knows what's happening, right?'

She heard herself say the words from some distance, one half of herself forever listening to the other half and frightened at what she heard – but quite incapable of stopping the voice. Most of the time the frightened, lucid half knew exactly what was happening, could look at the other woman with a critical, appraising eye. What she saw were little globules of sanity leaching out, propelled by daily and sometimes extraordinary pressures, shifting the delicate balance of hurt and compensatory salve. What could she – they? – do but dig in, hang on tooth and claw an inch above the pit, cling to tussocks of comfort on the downslide and wait for an upswing that was too long coming. At times the temptation to let go was almost overwhelming, but then the baby would kick or turn or fling out a fist and she knew she could hang on forever if need be. She felt like a turtle paddling blindly through a tidal wave, only the rock-solid carapace to shield the fragile being inside. At such times she longed to be a little girl again, safe with her Daddy and her Mum, with no plans – firm or half-formed – beyond next week's school play or a trip to the seaside. But Lallie was a big girl now, had been 'through the mill' as they said in certain parts of town, and if a lad chose to look the other way, why then, what else was there to do but look everybody straight in the eye and keep on keeping on ...?

Less than a week to Christmas and Ina Hodgson was beset with decisions nobody else seemed inclined to make. Turkey or leg-o'-pork? Chestnut stuffing or parsley and thyme? Or maybe sage and onion, which seemed to go with everything. Were they decorating or weren't they, and if not, why not? It wasn't as if they'd had a funeral, by God! It was all too much for her. Too many rooms to get to, that poor lass upstairs in no state to help overmuch, and Joe Wainwright walking about with a face like a wet weekend.

Her stays – God! they were killing her. Whalebone and laces, laces and whalebone, why she even bothered ... At last the pots were washed and tea trays all set up for morning. She lumbered up to her room and took off her shoes, wiggling chubby toes deep into the Wilton. Oh, the comfort. Lovely it was, best time of the day. She let out a gusty sigh as she unhooked her corsets and indulged in a satisfying scratch at whalebone welts and stretch marks from the two boys. Just as she licked at the froth from her glass of Guinness –

'Mrs Hodgson! Mrs H Come quickly!'

Oh lord! – here it came, a month too soon by her reckoning, which owed nothing to medical science and everything to phases of the moon.

Joe was there before her, wringing his hands over his daughter who was speaking to him in a voice nobody had heard for quite some time, downright impatient it was:

'Daddy, *don't* go on so, it's not exactly a surprise! Just call the doctor and alert the hospital –'

'I'm against that, I've always been against it! Your Mum had you in her own bed and –'

'And the arrangements are already made. Either call them or let *me* do it!'

341

'You're not moving off that bed until they come with the stretcher and that's that!'

In the end it was Mrs Hodgson who made the calls, poured Joe a quick drink and pushed him into his armchair downstairs to wait. 'Call Neil!' he shouted to her as she went back upstairs.

Inside of ten minutes they were all gone and she had the house to herself. Not that it mattered; the glass of Guinness would be flat by now.

They told Joe to go home but of course he didn't and neither did Neil, who insisted on talking ... talking, when there was nothing to say except, 'God, let it be over soon, let it be over soon.' You saved your pennies all your life, you made plans, you worked your socks off – all for one lovely lass, and when she was hurting what did it all come down to? He was helpless. Seven hours and all the damned nurse could say was, 'We're coming along, we're coming along ...'

The night staff went home and the day staff took over and still she was in the delivery room, not a sound coming out of it – but now the new day nurse was walking up, looking down at them with lifted eyebrows.

'The father?'

'I am,' Joe said, jumping up.

She seemed flustered, but only for a second. 'Well, we're coming along nicely, about another half hour then doctor will be out to see you, Mr Kaliski.'

'Wainwright.'

Again she paused, blushed and recovered some of her frosty cool. 'Just have a seat then, as soon as your baby's born –'

'No,' he said, rubbing at his eyes. 'I'm *her* father. The patient's.'

Warmth returned. 'And the baby's father?' She looked expectantly at Neil.

'Its father's away,' Joe said flatly. 'When can I see my daughter?'

'The patient –'

'Patient? No wonder you call 'em patient, they *have* to be

342

bloody patient in here –'

'Now, Joe.' Neil was patting his shoulder. 'It's not the nurse's fault.'

She flashed Neil a smile and brought them cups of tea from the nurses' station down the hall, then Bob Waithe was joining them, tired but smiling.

'A boy,' he said. 'A bit premature but otherwise fine –'

'And Lallie –'

'Fine, fine. Tired out, naturally, but she'll sleep and you can see her this afternoon.'

'What's he like then?'

The doctor beamed and punched Joe lightly on the arm. 'A baby, what did you expect?'

Stefan.

Pink and pale gold, wrapped in talc and blue flannelette and the perpetual enigma of newborn life.

She held him – and the defences of months began to crumble.

Stefan – except he was Jan, just a new, tiny Jan. Hair the colour of early wheat, unbelievably fine; on his forehead an echoing spiral, silver-white above the unfocused blue of his eyes. It was his mouth that stamped him indelibly as Jan Kaliski's son; the new-baby rosebud was already firm and well-shaped; it would smile and it would cry, but nature seemed not to have designed it to pout. A thin baby (long for a preemie, they told her) who was destined to be a tall boy.

Stefan.

He was perfect and beautiful and she was filled with wonder – but so like Jan that the loss of him engulfed her afresh, and delight in the child became inextricably tangled with an aching sadness for its father.

If he could just see the baby he'd come back, she knew he would. How could he stay away from this child conceived in the shadow of Mam Tor unless … So close to new life, her thoughts drew her towards death, Jan's death, for how else could he bear to stay away from them now. Surely his savage urgency on Mam Tor meant something – a buried knowledge

343

that he would never come back and must plant his seed in the shadow of the mountain, the one corner of England he had seemed to treasure? For too many months she'd closed her mind to it, erected walls, stratagems, tunnels of pretense and pride, wandered through them with closed eyes and a stubborn heart. All began to dissolve in the piercing blue of the baby's eyes.

They gave him to her to feed. Baby lips fastened to her nipple. Under the tiny knuckles kneading her breast her heart seemed to expand, burst, re-form into chambers too vast, too mysterious, now, to explore ...

CHAPTER THIRTY-FOUR

Poland, 1946

Pogo followed him into the warming shed, one hand held out to the glowing brazier while the other went through the ritual of scratching at something under his coat collar.

'You're going through the gate?' he said quietly.

'Why should you think that?' God, he'd been so careful!

'I keep my eyes open. Don't say I didn't warn you, that's all. If they catch you it's Block Ten. Solitary. No work, nothing. That's where they put the incorrigibles. You could be stuck there for years.'

'And if I stay here they'll let me out tomorrow, I suppose? With a good-conduct medal?' Jan spoke through lips cracked with cold.

'Here you never know. In Block Ten you *know*!'

Their glance met over the brazier. Jan thought he saw a flicker of envy in the other's eyes, but if he did it was quickly submerged in the lethargy that hung over the camp like a melancholy mist. Next week they'd be let go ... or next month

... or sometime. For now there was a roof over their heads and food – so it was *bad* food, but who knew if there was *any* food on the outside, who knew anything for sure ...? So their thoughts and mutterings ran, one day sliding into the next. Perhaps they truly had nowhere to go, no concept of life outside the gate now that the party made the rules, no amibition to go there, to start living again. He did. He had people to live with and to live for. Emil Bura's sick vengeance would not stop him.

Pogo looked away and sighed. 'Well, good luck ...' His loose skin seemed to hang even looser as he shambled for the door, turning to give Jan his crooked grin as an icy blast from the open fields swept between them. 'And Merry Christmas!'

Over the last weeks Jan had mounted a careful watch on the carpenter.

A man of regular and solitary habits, he stopped off at the same latrine after every shift before walking purposefully to the gate, where he flashed his ID at the guard and hurried out into the night.

Jan was afraid Christmas Eve might make for deviation in the pattern – a holiday drink at the carpenter's hut, perhaps – but here he came, buttoning his coat as he crossed the compound for the latrine, a dark grey figure under the lowering shadows of early evening. Tonight there was even a ground mist, surely a good omen.

Jan waited behind the window of the deserted latrine, teeth chattering with the cold. He had his bundle of bread and as many of his belongings as he could tie up in the square of canvas he'd ripped from his matress. The suitcase he'd discarded as too conspicuous. As he watched the carpenter stopped, set his tool-bag down in the snow ... No, don't let him change his pattern, not tonight, not when he'd waited so long – The man was tying his shoelaces. Now he was standing up, rubbing his back, reaching for the tool-bag, making for the latrine, the vapour clouds of his breath preceding him.

Jan tensed and held his own breath – God! if just breathing were to give him away now ... He flexed the muscles so laboriously built up in Joe Wainwright's foundry and now toned daily at the brick-yard. Since the inexpert sparring of his

High School days he'd hit no one, had never needed to – except once when he'd knocked Roman down just seconds before his friend aimed a punch at a Hempton MP after too many gins at the Horse and Rider. He was anxious now, afraid he might hit the carpenter too hard, crack his innocent skull on the latrine's concrete floor.

It was almost too easy.

The man's mouth gaped in astonishment, his arms slack as he made not the slightest attempt to avoid the fist that came crashing into his jaw. He sagged against the wall, semiconscious and unresisting as Jan switched coats, pulled the scratchy wool of the balaclava helmet off the carpenter's head and onto his own. A quick riffle through the overcoat pockets and yes, the ID for Zawacki, Carpenter, was his, together with a ration book and a handful of zlotys.

Bread and clothing safely in the tool bag, he hurried towards the brightly lit gate, the carpenter's ID ready to flash at the guardhouse window.

But he was going too fast!

He forced himself to a measured stride, kept his head averted as if adjusting his coat collar against the howling wind.

A vague wave of the ID card and he was through! Out!

He was out, walking down the long drive, breathing easier –

'Zawacki! *Czekaj*! Wait – come back! You forgot the captain's present. Vodka! Come back!'

His heart stopped but his legs kept moving, moving. '*Jutro!*' he shouted back. Tomorrow he'd stop for the vodka, tomorrow …

'Zawacki! *Czekaj*!' Then feet were pounding behind him, a guard with a tumbler of vodka and a wide holiday smile –

'What the –'

The smile disappeared, quickly replaced by a revolver which came crashing down …

Images came and went, each more bizarre than the last. Lallie gazing into a punchbowl while tropical fish darted across a soft dress the colour of singing canaries … Joe Wainwright glowering over a red and white scarf ... Mamunia stirring creamy ice-bergs into a blood-red soup.

Slowly the images gave way to reality ... a cold grey room in an endless grey corridor, a large 10 in black letters on a grey door, pain and anger exploding scarlet and white in his head.

CHAPTER THIRTY-FIVE

Eccles Place, Yorkshire, 1947

Stefan's arrival turned the routines of Eccles Place upside-down.

Nappies billowed on the clothes-line. Lights were turned on at all sorts of odd hours and Lallie or Mrs H or even Joe Wainwright could be seen at the kitchen sink, testing formula on a wrist or walking a bundle of blankets up and down the hall. A high-sprung pram gleamed daily at the front door, an elderly Jolly standing guard; in its way the pram's almond-coloured coachwork was as elegant as the chocolate-and-cream Afghan. On clear spring days the pram was wheeled under the cherry tree and dimpled fingers waved at pink blossoms blowing on a blue sky.

Spring slipped into summer, and under the fruited boughs a blond baby sat on a tartan rug, watching gravely as a young woman schooled one dog or another to turn, to gait, to present. Tall and unusually slim, she moved with an abstracted air, concentrating now on the dogs, now on the cooing child; sometimes she just stood, focused on nothing in particular.

To her father, driving in from the foundry, the picture was irresistible. What more could a man want than this – except maybe Millie fluttering in the doorway with his paper in her hand and his slippers ready on the hearth?

'And how's mi little old Grandlad today?' he shouted, jumping out of the car.

The baby's sudden smile was enough to make Joe run the last few steps, lift the child to his broad shoulder and gallop him around the lawn, singing as he went. 'O, tantivy-tantivy-tantivy, a hunting we will go –'

'You're distracting the dogs, Daddy,' his daughter reminded him mildly. 'How can I get them ready for the ring with you jigging about all over their pattern?'

'Sorry, love. Got carried away a bit – I signed the papers today. We're Wainwright and Associates now, the associates being not just you and Neil but *this* little fellow-me-lad.' He tickled the baby gently in the ribs.

'The new associate's teething,' Lallie warned. 'Until now he's been grumpy all day and he's getting sleepy.'

'Not him!' Joe settled himself on the tartan rug, the baby facing him. A wakeful baby. His cries were as rare as his smiles, but from the first he seemed to take in everything, and rare as the smile was it was always ready for Joe Wainwright. Much as he resembled his father, the smile was Lallie's entirely. But a contrary little bugger even now, ignoring Joe's extended finger and reaching beyond, twisting the buttons on Joe's waistcoat.

'Independent little devil, young Stephen.'

'Stefan,' Lallie said automatically, 'Stefan.'

'He's Stephen to me.'

He ignored Lallie's frown and pulled the child closer to him, burying his nose in the fragrant silvery hair. What a grand little chap he was, this grandson! The difference he made! Another reason for keeping the wheels turning downtown, for coming home of a night. It was just like when Lallie was little – more so now that he had both of them to work for. When Lallie was this age the wolf (not that *she* ever saw it) was seldom far from the front steps. Nowadays he could and did buy whatever he fancied for the child, with no thought of indulging anyone but himself. 'You'll spoil him,' Lallie said every other day, but she was wrong. Toys never spoiled children, comfort neither. Lallie had had whatever she wanted and it hadn't spoiled her – as soon as she was old enough for kittens and puppies she'd never asked for much else. This little fella would be the same, once he settled on what pleased him. No, it was neglect that spoiled children, families that didn't care, didn't touch. *He* touched by God, couldn't help himself. And why should he? The bairn needed a man about – between himself and Neil the lad wouldn't want for men ... Dark thoughts of the Pole brushed the back of his mind but he ignored them. If the damn fool wanted to give up a beautiful wife and perfect son, well then, that was his loss. And my gain, he thought, planting a moist kiss on the baby's cheek.

'Neil's eating with us,' he said to Lallie.

'Again?'

'Aye, Agnes has her bridge women coming, or some such. I thought I'd bring a bottle or two of champagne up – celebrate with the new associates.'

'Not Stefan,' she said, taking up the baby. 'He's going to celebrate with a bath and a bottle of milk, aren't you, poppet? You'll put the dogs away, Daddy? And bring in the blanket?'

He watched them go with reluctance, but he was satisfied. Lallie was bucking up nicely, even Neil admitted it. More like her old self, just a bit quieter ... As if to prove it she paused at the door and waved Stefan's fist for him. 'Say goodnight to Gramps,' she said, turning to the house and calling towards the kitchen.

'An extra place for dinner Mrs Hodgson. Sorry!'

Really, Daddy could never find enough excuses to get Neil over for the evening! Between them they clucked over her like two broody hens over a sick chick – yet irritating as they could be, she knew she'd be in sorry straits without them. Who else would have put up with her in the year and a half since Jan left? She hadn't exactly been Little Miss Sunshine around the house, still wasn't – perhaps never would be. Her moods still lurched from wild hope to despair, but the hopes didn't fly so high and the troughs of despair were not so deep. Yet no matter what she happened to be doing there was still a corner of her that couldn't forget, couldn't quite stop waiting. When the phone or the doorbell rang, when the mail dropped through the slot there was always that moment when everything stopped, when hopes rose to the surface like bubbles on a lake – but time was passing and the moments were shorter each day, the bubbles smaller.

It was Stefan, of course. In the most innocent possible way

his dimpled elbows were edging his father out. The wild plans of a year ago to get to Poland with the baby and somehow find Jan became more preposterous with every news item she read – and she now scoured the papers daily. The more unpopular the new regime became, the more repressive were the measures to quell the unrest. As Henryk Ryba said, it was a closed camp with deprivation the only certainty. In passing, Henryk dropped a small bomb that turned her blood to ice. Under Polish law the child of a Pole was considered Polish, would be subject to their laws. And there was the memory of the vice-consul: *Better you wait for your husband here, with people who care for you.*

Sometimes she'd look at Jan's photograph smiling up at her and she'd know beyond doubt that he was dead; the husband she loved had loved her, would never have stayed away for so long. Then one day she overheard Daddy talking to Neil, saying what she'd never, until then, allowed herself even to think:

'God alone knows what laws they've got, if any. He's likely divorced her on the sly.'

She wanted to rush downstairs and *hit* him, hit him *hard*, but the impulse died as quickly as it came. Wasn't that what *everybody* must be thinking? And wasn't there a possibility that everybody was right?

There were times she wanted him so desperately she punched at her pillow before crying herself to sleep in its muffling feathers, but then Stefan would wake and she'd take him up from his cot, cradle him in the crook of her arm, and the hungers of months were appeased as his warm little body snuggled close to her.

The heat of summer faded and the last of the roses wilted in Kaz's cup on the nursery windowsill.

A week before Stefan's first birthday Daddy came home with three tickets for a dinner dance at the Assembly Rooms. She didn't want to go, was reluctant to face the memories such an evening would surely conjure up – Jan had taken her there often in the year before he left, as much to escape the frictions of the dinner table at Eccles Place as to enjoy the dancing.

Daddy was insistent. It was time she started to get out and about. She wasn't chained to the nursery and the kennels, and it wasn't as if Mrs Hodgson didn't love the baby as she would her own grandchild. 'Besides,' he said, playing his trump card, 'it's a steel "do" and now you're part of the business you should show your face sometimes.' Neil was encouraging too. 'I wish you'd come,' he said. 'Otherwise I'll be stuck dancing with the shop foremens' wives all night. I'd rather dance with you.'

So she found herself dressing up again, pulling on sheer silk stockings and stepping into black chiffon of vaguely Grecian cut. Charles came to the house to do her hair, pulled it back into a cloudy chignon with soft tendrils escaping here and there.

'Isn't it a bit sophisticated for me?' she said.

'You *are* sophisticated now,' he said through a mouthful of hairpins.

The dance was the annual steel industry gala, the Wainwright table prominently placed as befitted the size and clout of what the foundry had become.

Even with Daddy on one side and Neil on the other, Lallie was self-conscious at first. What were they thinking, all the business cronies of Daddy's, stiff in their boiled shirts and middle-class values? Where had Joe's lass *been* all this time? Hadn't she married a foreigner – and if she had, where was he?

'Do they know …?' she asked Daddy, uncertain how to phrase the subject she'd so long avoided.

'They know just what I tell 'em and I tell 'em nowt! It's none of their damn business anyway and –'

But she'd stopped listening. The band had started the first waltz and young couples were drifting onto the floor, girls looking up into the faces of young men, murmuring and smiling as they revolved under soft pink lights. Just so had she murmured to Jan. 'You're not supposed to kiss on the dance floor –'

'We used to at Hempton … You didn't mind then.'

'That was in the war. Things were different then.' But of course he didn't stop and of course she didn't mind.

Then there was a spot dance, with prizes for whichever couple was caught in the random silver disc of light that roved among the couples. It took her back to a time before the *stalag*, right after their wedding in fact, when they'd won the prize, a wrinkled orange that had somehow run the U-boat blockade. 'All the way from sunny California,' the announcer boomed, presenting it to them in the flurry of applause from surrounding crowds. They'd taken it home to Millie, who agonized over whether to share it between them all or put it into an orange sponge. 'We can, you know – I've saved this week's egg ration,' and Daddy saying, 'Good God woman, it's a damn orange, not the bloody crown jewels. Cut it up and let's have it!'

Daddy seemed hardly to have changed at all since then. A little greyer perhaps, his face a little more … worn, but as impatient now as he'd been then. He was standing up, his fingers worrying at his stiff collar as he asked her to dance – if 'ask' was the right word.

'Come on, flower! On your feet – I didn't bring you just for decoration, you know!'

She danced with Daddy and then with Neil, then with sundry young men who were 'on their way up' as Daddy so pointedly put it, but really she preferred to be an onlooker. Watching the young couples in their early twenties she suddenly felt old, much too experienced for their company. As the evening wore on it was the young who stayed on the dance floor; the older ones, business men and their wives, drifted over to the bar.

Lallie was content to sit, to look, to take in the new fashions that somehow seemed to have passed her by …

To Neil, watching her from the other side of the table, she was the most stunning woman in the room. From being a vivacious, extremely pretty girl she had become a luminous beauty, the kind of woman who could dress in severe black, sit utterly still, and draw every masculine eye in the room. It was as if grief, by quieting the once active features, had enhanced them, much as a pale moth was loveliest at rest. Her eyes, once grey brilliants darting with life, were now reflecting pools that mirrored hard-won tranquillity.

When Joe wandered off to badger a supplier about late

deliveries, Neil was left alone with her.

'Would you like to dance, sweetheart?'

She shook her head, smiling. 'Not really.'

'It hurts you, all this?' He gestured at the dancers, the couples whispering to each other on discreet couches behind palms and pillars. She'd been here often with Jan, he knew. He'd been at Eccles Place sometimes when they came home, their eyes so full of each other that he and Joe might never have been there. 'Perhaps we should have left you to yourself ...'

'No,' she said thoughtfully. 'I *thought* it would hurt, but in an odd way the memories all seem ... well, happy. I'm enjoying myself ...'

He hesitated, afraid to shatter the moment, to be (as Joe would say) too previous. 'In May he'll have been away two years – Jan, I mean.'

'Yes.' Her voice was guarded but warm.

'It's a long time ...'

'I know.'

She looked so vulnerable in the black dress, pale and fragile as the tapers they lit in church, that perhaps he should have left it there. But he'd waited a long time ...

'You don't think it might be time to ... make a decision?'

The tranquil smile faded slightly, its edges blurred by uncertainty, and although she spoke gently her voice was a door closing quietly in his face.

'If it ever *is* time, I'll know,' she said.

CHAPTER THIRTY-SIX

Poland, 1948

If he'd had a bit of paper he could have written to Lallie – if he'd had a stub of pencil, if he'd had a stamp, if he'd had someone to post it for him, if he'd had the energy to do more than watch the seasons go by.

There was the nonsense rhyme from wartime Yorkshire that Joe Wainwright had delighted in reciting over breakfast: 'If we had any ham we could have ham and eggs, but we've got no eggs!' Jan had not found it funny at the time but the ludicrous logic as it applied to him now made him laugh, a hollow sound which bounced off the damp stone walls and went racketting down the hall to fetch up on the grey door with its painted 10.

The single window high in the wall of his cell let in as much of the seasons as twelve square inches of glass could record. A year ago the square had been grey, heavy low clouds leaden with snow and more snow. A few more months and the grey gave way to pale blue touched with a water sun, then to brassy skies of summer, heat reaching down, filling the small cell with light that seemed to last all day, disturbing his sleep. And now the square was leaden again, Christmas again.

His mood had changed with the square of glass. Rage could not last for ever. It had turned, in stages, to ill-temper, to self-pity, to lethargy. The desire to sleep was overwhelming, especially in the summer. He slept fifteen to sixteen hours a day then, and would have slept more if he could, hibernating because there was nothing in the world to wake up for. Not the scenery, the routine, the food, the company.

The scenery was the bit of sky. Once its colours had been explored it held no interest. The routine was two meals a day, a tiny bowl of cold water to wash in once in the mornings, and an exercise period of fifteen minutes in the yard surrounded by a ten foot wall and nothing but space. He was not permitted to see other prisoners now; attacking the carpenter put him in a special category, much as a rogue elephant is segregated from its fellows. The food was standard prison fare which never varied except in the quantities, which seemed to shrink week by week. As for the company, there was none. A silent guard stood in the yard as he exercised; another one, just as tight-lipped, slid his food under the grille; the old man who collected his bucket every morning seemed to be genuinely deaf.

In the beginning he'd thought exclusively of Lallie, replaying their special times together behind his eyes to shut out the bleak and hopeless present, seeing again and again the smooth play of sunshine on muscles, veins, feeling again the warm, sweet echoes of their union. As month piled on month, as rations shrank and lethargy took over, the pleasantest thing of all was sleep. To be unconscious, oblivious to the sights and sounds around him, blind to the pictures in his head that seemed more and more like fantasies …

Sometimes he heard the voices of other prisoners but from a long way away. The walls were thick and he was in isolation. The suspicion grew that not only had Emil Bura forgotten about him but the system had forgotten also.

As he weakened his thoughts became a nightmare carousel ride and he was glad, in the end, to slip off and roll into the shadows.

And then one day – he wasn't sure of the exact month, but there'd been snow on the window for several weeks – guards marched down the corridors opening cells and shepherding a ragged little group across the field to a transit building. They were told to stand in line behind a desk. They waited a long time. One man fainted and after that the rest of them sat down on the wooden boards and no one told them to stand up.

When they looked around the guards had all disappeared, and there were only the harassed clerks behind the desk, frantically filling out forms and issuing papers.

'Where are we going?' Jan said when his turn came.

'Out,' said a clerk. 'Where are you headed?'

'Zakopane,' Jan said dully, with no thought but to give *some* answer, to oblige.

'Right. Board the bus outside. It will take you to Warsaw. Here's your ticket to Zakopane, your ration book, subsistence allowance. ID card – you did say Kaliski?'

He nodded.

'Next!'

But Jan had to ask. '*Przepraszam*. Why? Why are we to be let out?'

The clerk looked up, annoyed at the delay. 'Nothing to feed you. The rations didn't arrive. *Next!*'

From the bus driver he learned that it was 10 January, 1949.

There were only five other passengers, one of them very talkative but the others as silent as Jan. Perhaps, like him, they'd given up hope and could not now grasp their astounding good fortune! Good fortune! He did some arithmetic. January, 1949. Over two and a half years since he left England! Lallie! Mamunia? Was she still alive or had it been a hoax? His mind spun in ever-shrinking circles as his hand fingered the small wad of zlotys he'd been given. When they pulled into the depot in Warsaw the driver simply got out and walked across the street to a cafeteria. It was some time before anyone got up to follow him. Jan was somehow waiting for another guard to climb into the bus ... when the truth dawned they all tried to get off the bus at the same time, and the man who'd fainted earlier did it again.

Jan helped him up and together they staggered after the bus driver, ordered broth and sausage and fried potatoes in the cafeteria and waited for it to arrive, suspicious still that it was all a trick. But the food came, fragrant and substantial. After that Jan bought an apple from a vendor on the pavement. It was a winter apple, hard and sour, and it hurt his teeth, but he persevered and bought another for later in the day.

He was free.

Free.

For some time he sat on a park bench, dazed thoughts clearing slowly after the first solid meal in two years. He knew vaguely that he was dirty and ragged and all of his teeth were loose – when had he stopped noticing such things? In a sudden panic he wolfed down the other apple and bought two more; dipped his filthy handkerchief in pavement snow and scrubbed at his face; desperately struggled to order his chaotic thoughts.

First, get word to Lallie. The British Consulate. Tell them he was here, ask them to send a message ... perhaps they'd let him use the phone ... if there were still phones. What had that girl said, the one in the first camp? Before he saw Bura? 'Phones? This is not England, Pan Kaliski ... our phone system is old, suffered much damage ... only top officials ...' He looked around him, not a phone kiosk in sight. A post office then, there'd always been public phones there.

There was, and an officious clerk who placed the calls.

'Where to?' she said.

He said the first name on his tongue. 'Eccles Place ...'

'What?'

'Sorry, *pani*. England.'

She smiled, humouring him. 'No sir, I have no time for jokes. Where to?'

'I told you. England.'

She frowned. 'You not make joke at me?'

'No! I want to call ... I have to call ...'

She nodded, accepting. In that case he must go to a 'government building, fill out an application. 'There's a waiting list, of course. Many weeks, I understand, while they process the forms, check records ...'

Oh yes, check records. He understood. Forms, papers ... '*At all times we must know where each person is. How else can there be order?*' And Bura waiting somewhere for Kaliski's name to appear on a list.

Where was he? What had he planned to do? Ah yes, the embassy ... He walked, tried to find his bearings in this new Warsaw whose streets he was seeing for the first time. Landmarks were gone or changed beyond recognition. A few hastily built apartment blocks, gimcrack and already shabby, replaced the dignified old buildings of before the war, but blank spaces by far outnumbered the ugly new blocks. The banks of the Vistula were the only permanent feature. Its bleak winter ribbon told him roughly where he was, and he turned towards the district of diplomats and embassies. Even if there were no phones, surely embassy mail would be sacrosanct?

He approached the once-rich district with bitterness, shouldering aside a score of drunks as he stumbled to reach his goal. From under what rocks had they crawled, all these drunks? He remembered the group captain at the work-camp telling him how generous was the government's subsidy on vodka, how it was now in every man's reach. 'The party's not so stupid, *tak*? In the long run drunks make less trouble than people like us.' Drunks asked no questions, didn't wonder why there was so little food, why they couldn't do better, be freer, why this year's hopes were out of reach until next year, or the next or the next …

Then he saw Embassy Row and realized something himself, that hope might be a more potent drug than alcohol after all. It was here his father brought him every Saturday afternoon of his childhood, flirting the foreign service before his child's eyes like a promise. Squat, expensive cars had lined the kerbs then, leisured diplomats had strolled the streets, rolled umbrellas and foreign newspapers in hand. It was for this Tatuś had drilled him mercilessly in one language after another. And look at it now! Scarred buildings, half the windows boarded up. Armed police paced the pavement, checked every visitor's credentials and turned away most of them.

As he watched from across the street a middle-aged woman waved papers in the face of an armed guard, threatened him with a frail fist behind which could only be desperation. Within seconds a van appeared (where did they *come* from, all these vans?) and the woman was talked to, leaned upon, surrounded, finally hustled into the van and sped away.

It was over in a moment. But he'd seen it, knew there was nothing for him there but the chance of a gun to his back, another ride in a van, another work-camp. Ignoring a sudden weakness in his legs he turned away, forcing himself to move before they approached him, one of these too-curious militia with the flat, expressionless faces.

They'd fought, so many of them and for so long, for this? Cities bombarded to dust, a third of the population dead or displaced – for this? A hopeless experiment sanctified by the stroke of a pen at Yalta? He moved south through darkening streets filled with men in cloth caps and the same wide assortment of overcoats as the guards and prisoners he'd just left; women, stout in thick black coats and wool babushkas, were lined up with empty shopping bags at a dozen little stalls, waiting their turn to buy beets and potatoes and slabs of rye bread cut from enormous wheel-shaped loaves. No, don't think of your stomach, that chasm was already empty again, already growling. Don't think of Lallie serving Cheshire cheese and Mrs Hodgson's good bread at the dining table of Eccles Place, her lovely face inviting him. 'Cheese, darling? A bit of apple tart? Or me?' her small, even teeth laughing at him, grey eyes alight with love … with giving.

Think. What next? Not going back, don't even think of going back yet – you came here for a reason, and how would you get back anyway, yet? No passport, no travel permit except to Zakopane, no money for a ticket even supposing he'd be allowed to buy one … and there was Mamunia … wasn't that why he'd come? Yes, Mamunia.

Exhaustion swept over him. Cold knifed through his worn jacket, and the prison longing for endless sleep tried to creep in on him again. To fend off its insidious pull, to keep his blood moving, he turned towards the train station. Get to Zakopane. Find Mamunia, find Uncle Tadeusz. Uncle Tad would know the ropes, if there were ropes to know, if he was still alive. He'd been old when Jan was in his teens – but everyone seemed old then – and Mamunia would be in the town somewhere. *If Bura hadn't lied*.

'Zakopane?' The clerk in the booking office stared back at him, her face bored, tired. He'd just missed the afternoon train. Nothing else until close to midnight. Did he want to book? Yes. 'But you can't wait in here,' she said, handing him a confirmation.

Of course. It was warm in the booking office.

Weak, half delirious with hunger, his legs made the decision where to go. Morska Street. Home. As fast as the word rose up a sob rose with it. Where *was* his home? Did he have one? Joe Wainwright's home? Yes, if Lallie was in it. Not Morska Street, not anymore. Nevertheless, his legs took him to where it should have been.

It wasn't there. Nothing was there. Without the new street sign he wouldn't have known where it began and ended. Not a wall, not a stick to break the smoothly raked expanse of empty land. No piles of rubble even, through which he might have sifted for a fragment of stove tile or a shred of peacock blue from the heavy drapes in Tatuś' room, an old doorknob or a scrap of cherub wallpaper from the staircase – some small thing from his childhood. There was nothing but low winter skies scudding fast on the bitter wind from the east. The cobblestones of the street remained, broken now with patches of tamped earth, craters hurriedly filled and left to settle.

And a few patches of colour so out of place in the ruins around him that he could not, at first, think of anything else.

Flowers.

Cut flowers – in January. Chrysanthemums in bronze and yellow, orange montbretias, gladioli of every colour in the spectrum.

Neat bunches just as they came from the florist, placed at random on the raked earth. The people queuing for food, accommodation at a premium – and hot-house flowers tossed in the street?

As he stood there a woman rounded the street sign, black-coated and stout like all the others, but this one was old, very old, and she picked her way carefully over the broken cobbles. She carried something very bright that glowed in the dusk with almost a luminous quality. She came closer and he saw she carried more chrysanthemums, two dazzling white and one a vivid, blood-red crimson.

As she passed him she glanced up briefly before hurrying on. Something in her face tugged at him, pulled him after her. The walk was familiar, one he'd seen many a morning as he sped off to school late, always late, hurrying past slow-poke Mrs Adamski who always seemed to be around somewhere, if not in the street then behind her lace curtain, checking the comings

360

and goings of every family on the block.

He could see nothing about the spot to which she so purposefully walked that marked it as in any way different from the rest of the dirt, but having reached it she laid down the flowers carefully and backed off a step or two, her small old mouth moving silently as she crossed herself.

'Mrs Adamski?'

She stared, blinked, and stared again. 'No! No, it can't be! Janek Kaliski!'

He nodded and she came bobbing up to him, offering her hand to be kissed. The skin was tissue-thin under his lips and smelled of anise and cooked beets. 'Quick,' she said. 'Quick tell me! Where've you been and what's happened to you and what are you doing here? – God knows there's nothing to come here for now, eh?'

He asked her about the flowers and her eyes watered in the wind. Didn't he know? 'They're for the dead of course, what else? Mr Adamski's about here –' she pointed at the red chrysanthemum. 'And my sister, rest her soul, is where the white ones are. No graves, oh *my* no! Not with everything else blown sky high, how could there be? We tried, oh yes, but where to find an undertaker when the whole world's on fire, huh? You wouldn't have believed ... do you know, with my own eyes I saw ... The horses! You would never believe, not for a minute. They were getting shot *first*, and who knew who shot them, eh? The Germans, everybody *said* – but all I know is I saw people slicing steak from the poor things before they even hit the ground! Can you imagine? No food to be bought, not a nibble, so how could you blame them, eh? I'll tell you, between the dead horses and bodies all over we thought we were in hell, eh? You can't imagine how long – weeks – before they came and took care of it, just piled everything together and sprayed quicklime on it, what else could they do? Then they brought machines and rolled it all under.' She sighed and pulled her babushka tighter under her chin.

'Mrs Adamski ... my parents, I'm trying to find out –'

'Oh, your father! Yes, he'd be somewhere about there –' She pointed vaguely to her right as Jan closed his eyes. *But he'd known about Tatuś, of course he'd known.* 'But it was a blessing,' the garrulous old voice went on. 'Your poor mother, how she –'

'What happened, tell me what happened!' He wanted to shake the silly, addled old head until the brain spilled out for him to read but he hung on to his patience – prison taught you that if nothing else.

'Your father ... all that smoke and dust on his poor lungs – well, you remember, *prawda*? And your mother down the street looking for somebody to bury him before the Germans got here ... Oh, Janek, everything was insane, *nie*? Who could she have found, I ask you, and the soldiers coming down the street, herding people like cattle, eh? The last I saw she was arguing with an officer ... Terrible, terrible ... Auschwitz, I heard tell, but maybe Treblinka ... I forget –'

'You've heard nothing since?'

Weak tears gathered in her eyes. '*Przepreszam dziecko*, I nothing know ...' She dabbed at her eyes with a corner of the babushka and began to rock herself back and forth, back and forth. '*Przepraszam dziecko* ...'

Sorry, child. Child! He was thirty years old, his life never more unsettled than now, and still she called him a child. However, he'd got confirmation, such as it was, that Mamunia had been taken somewhere, not simply shot and left in the street. Like Tatuš. So Bura *had* told the truth.

He peered into the dusk to see where Mrs Adamski had pointed but the light had almost gone and he saw nothing but the smooth earth, hospitable to the last. *Tatuś* ...

'Come back with me, Janek. I'll give you *herbata*, eh?'

But he was already away, his legs once again making the decision. What did he need with tea when his father lay under a pile of rubble, unmarked and unmourned?

He combed the streets for a shop which was still open and finally found a lean-to in the shelter of one of the thousand barricades that veiled the ruins from public view. He bought the few flowers the old man had left, three stiff spikes of yellow gladioli, and laid them roughly in the spot Mrs Adamski had pointed out, saw in his mind his father's gentle, melted-down face, heard his whispering, careful voice the first day of the war – and the last time he'd seen him:

'*Don't be brave. First things first. Be practical. If I'm not here when*

362

you get back, take care of Mamunia ... family ... take care of family. Countries can look after themselves, but family ...'

'*You'll be here, Tatuś.*' Neither of them believing it.

'*Just in case ... be practical.*'

What would that practical man say if he could see him now? 'A hole in your stomach and you buy flowers? Better you buy meat, son.'

He'd known nothing, that cocky, ignorant boy. Nothing. But how could he have known, how could anyone?

Family, take care of family ...

His mother.

But wasn't Lallie family, too? Yes – well cared for by Joe, while Mamunia, who was caring for her? From what he'd seen of this nurturing new Poland, perhaps no one. Lallie would understand – who better than a woman who adored her own father? The argument went around and around, no stopping it.

Perhaps a true realist would find the quickest way out of here, shake Poland's blood-soaked earth from his feet. But *this* patch of earth looked up at him, its yellow flowers pointing the way.

Sustained by the remaining apples (his teeth already seemed firmer in his gums) he boarded the train for Zakopane at midnight. The knowledge that soon he'd see Mamunia, would have done everything that humanly *could* be done, warmed him through the long, cold journey.

The train was slow. It was morning before it pulled into the little country station, the chalets and pines white under a new fall of snow. The war seemed to have missed Zakopane entirely. It was the same mountain resort it had always been. The streets had not moved while his back was turned, the Tatras still held the community in the palm of its wooded green hand. Uncle's villa was quite a distance out of town, and it was noon under an invigorating sun before he spotted the old chalet from the road, smoke curling from its chimney into the pale winter sky.

CHAPTER THIRTY-SEVEN

Yorkshire, England, 1949

Lallie frowned at the table. Had she forgotten anything? There was hot chocolate for the children, the silver tea service and Mum's best china laid out for the mothers, plates of tiny sandwiches and Mrs H's richest madeira cake …

How had she *ever* let herself be talked into the Pony Club for goodness sake! And why the kick-off meeting here, not at someone else's house? Oh, that Daddy! It wasn't enough to give Stefan a Shetland pony, to buy the neighbour's two acres to graze it on, to sign Stefan up for riding lessons, Pony Club *and* and the spring gymkhana. He had to get *her* involved in it too – when he knew perfectly well she was uneasy among all the young matrons.

She enjoyed the children well enough, and their mothers were very nice as long as they talked about ponies and dogs and the kindergarten teacher, but of course it never stopped there. Sooner or later the talk always turned to husbands, and she never knew quite what to say.

Her status was so … fuzzy.

Early in the year Daddy had sent a lawyer to talk to her.

'You don't have to decide anything, love. Just hear him out, okay? He knows his business and there's no harm listening, is there? You can leave things where they are or … and you could always cancel later, if you wanted to.'

She'd been ready to scream at him until she saw his face, strained and oddly pleading. Daddy, pleading! Then she realized. He wasn't a young man any more, pretty soon he wouldn't even be middle-aged. He was worried about her.

The lawyer was very patient. 'You see, Mrs Kaliski, as long as you do nothing it leaves matters very ambiguous ... untidy, if you know what I mean. It's not just your personal situation, you see. It's all tied up with the business. And of course, as long as you're ... encumbered, as it were, not free –'

'There's nothing I want to be free *for*!' she cried.

'Not now, perhaps, but if such a time arises ...'

'I've not even *thought* about divorce.'

'Oh, divorce ... it drags *on* so, doesn't it? I was thinking more in terms of annulment.'

'But I have a baby!' Even then she noticed she'd said *I* have a baby, not *we*.

The lawyer's fingertips steepled in the professional manner. 'I think it could be arranged. There are mitigating circumstances. No, it shouldn't be too much fuss, I think – and it would be handled discreetly, of course. Nothing would be changed – you could continue to use the name – or not – as you prefer –'

'But if he should come back!'

'In that happy event there'd be ... remedies. In law there are remedies for everything.' A murmur of Latin as he made judicious notes on a yellow pad. He stood up. 'I take it, then, that I can proceed with the preliminaries? I'm sure your father mentioned that it can all be cancelled right up to the last moment.' His voice was so soothing, like the man who sold them insurance on the kennels. 'Not that you'll ever need it, of course, but in case ...'

She felt drained after the lawyer took his briefcase and his umbrella down the drive. Divorce ... Annulment ... The words were a foreign language to her, one used by other people maybe but not by the Wainwrights and their friends – though Daddy did keep saying that marriage wasn't the life sentence it had been before the war. Ending it ... such a big step. Final. Admitting that he'd never come back.

Yet what, really, had she done that couldn't be stopped?

Nothing. However, the feeling of guilt followed her upstairs, went with her as she ran her hand across his suits in the wardrobe, touched his ties hanging on the rack. Was it guilt – or regret? What did she have to feel guilty about? It was *he* who'd gone off, just left … She picked up his picture, but reassurance didn't come, hadn't for a long time. In its place there was a core of anger, of outrage. It grew each time she explained to Stefan why his Daddy wasn't here, because the explanation wore thinner and thinner and thinner with each telling. 'He loves us very much and he'll be back just as soon as –' Stefan would turn away then, pick up a crayon from Kaz's cup and draw his scribbles of the traditional house with smoke coming out of the chimney, a long haired dog in front and two tall stick-figures with a small stick-figure between them. She'd feel very angry with Jan then, very angry indeed, and feeling angry somehow eased the hurt.

Nevertheless her position was still – as the lawyer said – ambiguous. She'd heard nothing more from him, and as the months went on she stopped dwelling on it quite so much. Daddy never mentioned it either, but then, they were so caught up with the kennels (which were now showing a profit) and the new pony, and all Stefan's little affairs, that they didn't have the long talks they'd once had – which was probably how she'd got herself roped into the Pony Club tea!

It was a decorous afternoon. The children – six of them – behaved nicely, although the youngest *would* keep pulling Jolly's tail. The mothers, taken up with choosing ribbons and awards for the gymkhana, managed to stay off the subject of husbands until almost the end of the afternoon. One had just started complaining about how Derek – or Phillip – could never remember to pick up her *Home Chat* at the newsagents, when the doorbell rang out in the hall.

It was Neil.

He was white about the mouth and trembling, and his hands seemed to be doing disconnected things at his sides, patting his pockets as if he'd mislaid something absolutely vital. It was a second before she realized he still had on the grey smock he wore over his suit any time he had to go to the factory floor.

'Get your coat, love –'

'But I've got all these women –'

'Hurry love, do hurry – we have to go ... I'll tell you in the car –'

He reached for her coat from the hall stand, bundled her into it. It was about Jan, it must be, he'd heard something – but he could have called –

He shouted for Mrs Hodgson who ran out from the kitchen drying her hands on a teatowel. 'Could you get rid of the hen party, Mrs H? And look after Stefan? We have to leave –'

'Whatever's happened?' she said, flustered.

'It's Joe ... there's been an accident.'

No. Not Daddy, please not Daddy, don't let it be Daddy –

She didn't remember getting into the car. The drive to the hospital was a blur. Neil always drove so carefully, but he was going through traffic lights and stop signs as if they were not there.

'If you'll just tell me ...' But she was afraid to hear.

'One of the vats slipped – Christ, we've told them and we've *told* them to check before they pour – some of the men were caught underneath, got splashed. All that molten ... God, the screams ...'

'*Daddy's burned, he* ...' She felt her own scream rising –

'No, no. He's not – by the time we'd run down to the floor most of the men had been pulled clear, but Bert Dales – you won't know him – couldn't seem to move, his legs were in it and he was screaming. We started pulling on his arms and as we got him clear Joe just seemed to ... collapse. He was holding his chest and oh, Lall, he did look poorly. I wish I could tell you different but I'd be lying.' His hand reached for hers across the seat. 'I'm sorry, sweetheart. I should have told you better, helped you, but Joe ... God, Joe ... I didn't know whether to go with him or come for you –'

'You could have called ...'

'Oh no – I didn't want you driving, all upset – I wanted to be there, you know.' His voice thickened and there were tears on his cheeks. 'Besides, I needed you ...'

The catch in his voice reached out to her. Neil Armott *needing* anyone – calm, steady Neil who was there for everybody to lean on, who never made demands. Neil crumbling ... It

367

came to her dimly that the two of them were probably the only people in the world who knew the best side of Joe Wainwright – there was Stefan too, of course, lighting up for his Gramps, but it would be years before a child could understand just how *big*, how uncritical Daddy's heart could be for those he loved. People thought he was so hard, when really …

'He may be all right, Neil,' she said quietly. 'He can be obstinate when he wants –'

She couldn't go on. They drove in silence, each on his own little island of foreboding despite their touching fingers.

'*Everybody* liked Mum,' she said once, not quite knowing why.

The emergency room was a nightmare.

Extra staff were everywhere, moving from one stretcher to another with their carts and clipboards. But of course … it was a real emergency. All those Wainwright men … she'd forgotten.

A young doctor hurried towards them, led them to a small sitting room and closed the door against moaning bedlam outside. He looked far too young – why hadn't they called Bob Waithe?

'Your father's doctor's with him now – he asked me to have you wait in here.'

'But how's …'

The intern held up his hand. 'He's … we're supposed to say "resting comfortably".' He blushed and fingered the stethoscope dangling from his pocket. It looked very new. 'Actually he's in some pain, but your own doctor will tell you more.' And he was gone, shutting them in.

'Oh Neil …'

'Aye.' He sighed. 'He's always been such a flinty bugger.'

Neil sounded just like Daddy these days – odd she hadn't noticed it before. He used to sound a little … well, stuffy, like his mother, but the Joe-isms had crept in without her even noticing.

'You know,' he said, 'if I didn't have Joe I'm not sure I could –'

'You could! Of course you could, he's always had such confidence in you.'

'Oh, not the foundry, that's not it. I can handle that. It's the idea of him not being there. He's been like my dad, a lot more than my dad ever was! He's stuck with me, pushed me and chivvied me, made something of me I'd never have been. The first conference he sent me to – I was supposed to give a talk on castings or some such – I was frightened to death, all those faces looking up at me, waiting – and big nobs in the steel trade, the lot of 'em. It was my first time and I felt like *nothing* standing up there. "I'm scared," I said to Joe – he was next to me on the dais, "I'm bloody petrified." He just grinned at me, you know how he does, cocky? "Everybody's scared, mate," he said. "Everybody's scared their whole flaming lives. That lot down there, dolled up like a dog's dinner, you think they're not scared? They're scared they'll go bankrupt, they're scared somebody *thinks* they're going bankrupt, they're scared of their wives, their mothers, their kids. They're scared they've got a bit of spinach on their front teeth and they're scared to rub it off in case somebody's watching 'em." Oh, he really got to me, I'm telling you. But you know, when I looked at all those faces again, they looked like different people. They *were* different people – they were just like me.'

'I know ...' If only Jan had understood Daddy, but he never really had, never even liked him. It would have made all the difference ...

Sometime in the long wait they were brought tea, which neither of them touched. They watched the door and it seemed a terribly long time before it opened.

Bob Waithe looked harried and tired but he didn't have those folds in his face that meant –

'How *is* he?' she said, knowing just by the doctor's eyes that Daddy was alive. 'What happened?'

'A heart attack, Lall. It's been coming on, you know.' He sat down on one of the spindly chairs. 'I'm going to be frank. It's in the balance. He drives himself too hard, always has. I've told him ... He's had warning signs – didn't he tell you?'

'No!' But of course he wouldn't, not Daddy. She remembered his face when he told her he was sending the lawyer to see her. And he'd been so busy with lawyers lately. Settling up the business, of course. Just in case. *Everybody's scared* ... 'When can we see him?'

'Normally I'd say not for a few days – but with Joe ... well, you can go in for a minute – one at a time. Just smooth him down, you know what I mean. We don't want another one, do we?'

She went in first, was shocked at Daddy's pallor. *Smooth him down.* 'Well, a nice scare you gave us! And me in the middle of that damn Pony Club tea you let me in for.' She bent to kiss him (gosh, he needed a shave) and his cheek was moist, so was his forehead ... 'Daddy ... just don't worry about anything, please? We can manage everything, honestly we can. You just get better –'

'The men. How are the men?'

'They're being attended to now –'

'That bloody foreman, I've told him –'

'If you don't stop that I'm leaving. Neil can handle everything until you're on your feet.' She laid her head on his chest and his hand came up and smoothed her hair. She tried to feel his heart beating under her cheek but of course she couldn't ...

'Ee, lass, we're in a right pickle now I reckon.'

'Not if you behave. You should have told us –'

'Oh, you've enough on your mind.'

'Nothing as important as you.' She kissed his forehead.

He sighed heavily and she felt the sweat break out afresh under her lips, salty and warm. 'There's the little lad –'

'He's fine – but he'll be a sight finer if you're around.'

'Aye. He's a grand 'un, isn't he though? Who'd have thought ...'

'They'll not let me stay long –'

'That's the trouble with doctors. They get a bit of authority and it goes to their heads.'

'You're incorrigible.'

'I know.' A weak grin broke through the pallor.

'But really, you have to stop worrying about everybody. Just pamper yourself a bit ... when you're better maybe we'll go on a holiday with Stefan. But you have to relax.'

The grin faded. 'I'd be easier in my mind if you were settled, lass.'

'I *am* settled. I'm happy.'

'And I'm King Arthur of the Round Table.'

The doctor was waiting for her in the hall. 'Well?'

'He's ... cheerful.'

'But he's ill, Lallie. Don't let him kid you. If he takes care of himself he could outlive me – but you should know his heart's in poor shape. Don't take anything for granted.'

'No.'

They watched Neil go into Daddy's room and then Bob Waithe pulled her aside. 'Look, I didn't say anything to Neil, he's upset enough now, but somebody should go and talk to the families of the men. They're all out in the waiting room now.'

'How are they, the men I mean?'

'A couple of them are in a bad way. Johnson and Dales I think they are. Their wives are here.'

'I'll talk to them.'

And say what? she thought. Mrs Dales was elderly, quite fat, and her hair was in curlers. Mrs Johnson was very thin and very pregnant. They stood apart from the others, whispering to one another as though they were already at the funerals. But Bob Waithe was right, they were Wainwright people and deserved comfort from a Wainwright.

They seemed dazed as she led them to a couch, and afraid of more than the condition of their husbands. Mrs Johnson, the pregnant one, said what was on her mind. 'I don't know what we'll do if Jack can't work – I've three at home besides this one.' She laid her hand on her too fruitful belly. 'I just can't think ...'

She knew exactly what Daddy would say and said it for him. 'I don't think you need worry. Wainwright's will take care of everything. Just concentrate on getting your husband better.' Then she was embarrassed, remembering all too clearly what Jan said once in one of his rages against Daddy. 'Joe's so damn *patronizing*!' But Daddy took care of his own.

Then a doctor – not Bob Waithe – was bending over Mrs Dales. 'I'm sorry,' Lallie heard him say. 'We did everything we could.'

The heavy woman lumbered to her feet. She looked around

her at the crowded waiting room, rocked for a second, then opened her mouth in a keening wail that brought nurses running from every direction. Her eye fell on Lallie and the wailing stopped abruptly, replaced by a look of pure, impotent hatred.

'Look at Mrs Gracious there! It's easy for the likes of *you*, isn't it? Don't come telling *me* you're sorry, patting me on the back. *You don't know what trouble is, your sort don't.*'

Nurses persuaded the woman to lie on a cot and they brought her sedatives and tea. 'I'm sorry, madam. She's hysterical,' one of them murmured to Lallie.

She asked Neil on the way home: 'Who was it Daddy was pulling out of the steel when he had his heart attack?'

'Bert Dales.'

'Yes, that's what I thought.'

Stefan was bathed and ready for bed – 'But he's waiting up for his granddad,' Mrs Hodgson whispered as they went in.

Lallie looked at Stefan's intent frown. He was playing with his blocks, the pink tip of his tongue poking out as he single-mindedly stacked one brick on another in a structure remarkably complex for a boy his age. 'It's a hangar for my daddy's bomber,' he said, 'and when Gramps gets home he's going to play RAF with me.'

'Not tonight, darling.'

'But he promised!' The eyes turned up to her were speedwell blue, and the look in them was highly indignant.

She picked him up and buried her nose in the clean silver silk of his hair. 'Gramps can't make it tonight, love. He's been called away for a week or two.' She was numbly conscious she'd said almost those same words to him, many times over. Only the name had changed. 'Neil and I will play RAF with you.'

'No, thank you.' He wriggled from her grasp and began to put the blocks in their box. 'But you could read to me, if you like.'

Across the top of his head she caught Neil's eye and in spite of the horrendous afternoon they exchanged wry smiles. No matter what games they played with Stefan, no matter how many times they pushed him on the swing, supervised his rides on Muff the pony, they were always given the distinct impression they were somehow being catered to.

'*Just So* or *Pooh*?' she said.

He considered. '*Just so. The Elephant's Child*, I think.'

They were on their way upstairs, Stefan riding on Neil's shoulder, when he said, 'Where did you say Gramps went?'

Daddy was still listed 'critical' when Roman and Genia stopped in at Eccles Place. They'd come to say goodbye. They were leaving for Poland in a week or two.

'England very nice but I want go my family,' Genia explained.

Lallie gave them tea and they all managed to talk of old times while carefully avoiding direct mention of Jan. It was a tightrope performance for everyone and Lallie was relieved when they got up to leave. Since Jan had left she sensed they came only out of politeness and a certain curiosity. She'd liked them, still did, but they belonged to a world that seemed to recede more and more each day as immediate pressures closed in and filled the space. Roman looked ill at ease but finally, as they stood at the door, he said what Lallie suspected he'd come to say all along.

'If I see Jan – I don't expect to, we're not *such* a small country – but in case, do you have a message maybe?'

Something in her froze. 'You won't see him. I think perhaps he's ... not alive.'

'But if I do?'

'If you do, it means he doesn't want us, doesn't it?'

'He can't know about Stefan. Perhaps that would make a difference, yes?'

There was distress in his wide face and she took his hand, but she couldn't give him the answer he so clearly wanted.

'If I'm not enough to come back to for myself, perhaps it's better he stays where he is.'

'But –'

'Thank you, Roman, but no. There's no message.'

373

When they'd disappeared down the drive she switched on the lights and closed the curtains against the night.

CHAPTER THIRTY-EIGHT

Zakopane, Poland, 1949

Uncle Tadeusz was home.

'Yes yes I'm home, where else would an old man be but in his home, eh?' between kisses on the cheek and sudden darting hugs and smile, old old smiles that transformed his walnut face into a wizened little sun.

But his sister, where was she? Where was Mamunia?

The smile flickered but Jan was caught up in another hug. 'In Zakopane of course – I see her every evening when the weather's fine ...'

Jan heard nothing else. His uncle's voice faded into a mist. The weight of months – years – lifted, leaving him suddenly light-headed and he had to sit quickly in the chair by the fire. She was here. 'Here?' he said through veils that might have been tears or perhaps steam from the kettle on the hearth.

Uncle Tadeusz, thin and stooped, remarkably spry between table and hearth, poured tea into glasses. 'No lemon, sorry ... Your mother *here? At the villa?*' He looked reproachful. 'Janek, how could that be? She is very sick.' He tapped first his knees and then his temple with a knarled finger. 'She's in town – not so far in good weather – a convalescent home for people from the camps.'

Convalescent. 'Then she's getting better?'

Uncle Tadeusz turned away, busy with black bread and a bowl of cream cheese. 'Not to say better, no,' he said carefully. 'They did something to her legs, experiments – the ideas that Mengele had, inhuman, *nie?* She can't walk – or if she could

374

she won't. Nobody knows. The doctors wanted to try operations but you know her, a mule she is, gives them more trouble at the home than a dozen patients.'

His quick mother, confined to a bed. 'And her mind?' he said, afraid of the answer.

'Sharp as vinegar. Leads the nurses a fine old mazurka, believe you me. Won't let her bed be moved, never wants to eat – and *me, she won't talk to me at all*! *Her own brother, can you imagine?* All I tried to do was persuade her to have the operations! She said she'd never speak to me again if I didn't stop it. Of course I couldn't stop, how could I? So now she won't talk to me.' His shoulders moved in an exasperated shrug. 'A rock, she is. A rock. But she'll talk to you.'

Jan let out a long relieved breath. Every surface in the large rustic home took on new lustre. Dust motes danced in the pure light from the windows. The warmth of the fire crept over him, a comforting blanket. Rock or not, *he would move her*. To England, to Lallie, to the little study that was now her bedroom – yes, even to Joe. He'd get papers, plane tickets, the hell with the system! There was nothing he couldn't do now.

Uncle Tadeusz pushed a plate of bread and cheese at him. '*Jedz*! Eat! You'll need all the strength you've got to handle that baby sister of mine – she'd try the patience of a saint. How we ever came from the same father ...'

But not the same mother, there was the difference. Uncle Tadeusz was Mamunia's half-brother, courtesy of an earlier war. Twenty years her senior, he treated her more as a daughter than a sister. The family's pampered little terror, Mamunia.

'*Jedz!*' his uncle said again. 'They won't let you see her for two hours – they're strict as a convent about visiting hours – so you might as well eat. And look at you! I've seen fatter scarecrows – and cleaner. You'll wash and I'll find you some clothes. The good God knows what she'll say when she sees you like that ...' He sighed and laid his dry hand over Jan's. 'You'll be a shock, boy. She's had a bad time – her heart I can't answer for.' He made fluttering motions in the air and a new gravity settled over both of them. 'You'll be careful, *tak*?'

'I'll be careful.'

She was asleep.

'She sleeps a lot,' the nurse whispered.

He understood. Prisoners did sleep a lot – and in this narrow room on the cot she was a prisoner just as surely as he had been.

The nurse left. He approached the bed and looked down on the mother he had not seen for ten years.

Surely there'd been some mistake ...

It wasn't the same woman – couldn't be! This one was ancient. His mind reeled, scrabbled back in time, counted years and then counted again. Mamunia was fifty. The woman on the bed looked eighty, looked dead!

Slim she'd always been – but now she was skin stretched on bone, her closed eyes too deep in their sockets, cheekbones much too prominent for the small face. Her hair, once the colour of thick dark honey, was white and baby-fine, thin too, the scalp showing through fragile as an eggshell.

He touched her hand gently, the skin dry and powdery under his, and waited.

At last the hooded lids fluttered and her eyes, when she opened them, were Mamunia's eyes, dark and bright as a monkey's, then awash with tears that tracked through the netted wrinkles of her cheeks. Sunken lips moved, silently at first, and she touched his face with wonder.

'Mój synku ... mój synku ... mój synku, ty żyjesz ...'

My son, my son, my son ... you live!

He couldn't see, couldn't think, couldn't speak. All he could do was gather up the nothing weight of her, cradle her to him as she wept and kissed his face, touched his eyes and his hair and said his name over and over again, 'Janek, my Janek, my Janek, my Janek,' as if it were a prayer she was reciting.

Hearing her, holding her, he knew how close he'd come to giving up the search ... If the ticket they'd given him had been anywhere but Zakopane ... The prison, the long separation from Lallie, *everything* was worth this moment, was worth the joy blazing from her dark eyes, the spirit that even now began to reassert itself as they talked, questioned, filled in the gaps of ten years.

376

A nurse brought them tea and propped Mamunia up on her pillows, but still the voice did not pause for a moment. About her legs:

'Pain? Well, it's over, *prawda*? I think they were looking for ways to fix the soldiers' kneecaps after they were shot ... who knows? And what does it matter now, eh? I'd think to myself – it made me feel better – that they were not human to do such things, *rozumiesz*? But they were, Janek. Yes they were ... they had children at home like everybody else. And *they* had nothing either, you know. One of them, a nurse, her boy had pneumonia and she had no medicine for him. She cried to me one day, and I could see ... I watched her eyes, Janek, I saw her decide to steal my medicine.' She lay back, pleating the threadbare sleeve of her robe. 'How could I blame her? I'd have done the same for you ... I suppose they must have caught her, I never saw her again ... she used to bring me tea sometimes, her own tea, saved from lunch. So you see ...'

He told her about Lallie and about the *stalag* and about Lallie and about the prison here –

'You've been gone nearly three years?' She frowned, pulled at her lip. 'And she's young, *co*? Best you go back, son. Best you go quick.'

'I'm taking you with me.' Even through the elation of finding her the problems surfaced. Here he had no legality at all, his only sure record that of criminal, a prisoner who'd attacked a guard. And under the surface Emil Bura's twisted spirit waiting ... 'I'm getting out and you're going with me,' he said firmly.

Her hand crept into his. 'This is my place, son. I go nowhere.' Her voice was gentle. Her eyes, rivetted to his, were steel.

'We'll talk tomorrow,' he said as the nurse appeared again, looking pointedly at her watch.

At the villa he worried at it with Uncle Tadeusz.

'She'll never go, Janek.'

'She has to! I'll apply for visas –'

'And if you don't get them?'

'We'll find a way to get over the border –'

'With her on your back? Through East Germany?'

'There's a way, there must be.' If he couldn't get out legally he'd go the other way, alone if need be, get back to England and take citizenship, return here with a passport they couldn't touch, fly Mamunia to Eccles Place, *make her go*! Meantime, 'I *must* get word to England, Uncle. How bad is the censorship?'

Uncle Tadeusz set another log on the fire and poked it fussily into place. 'Who knows?' He turned back, caution in his face. 'There's no glue on the envelopes anymore … maybe there's a shortage of glue? It wouldn't surprise me.'

'*But what do you think?*'

He shrugged. 'The older I get the less I think.' He leaned forward, whispering. 'One thing I *know*. The government keeps lists. Many, many lists …'

CHAPTER THIRTY-NINE

England. Winter, 1949

Daddy was a fractious patient, but obedient once the doctor let him come home. 'It's too soon, Lallie, but the nursing staff's driving him round the bend. He's better off at home if he behaves himself, and he swears he will.'

His pallor was still frightening and the bottle of little white pills was always kept close to hand, but there was a steady improvement. He baulked at being packed off upstairs 'with the linens' and so Lallie had a day bed put by the fire in the living room where the life of the house could circulate about him.

'And glad I am for that, Lallie,' Mrs Hodgson said. 'My legs couldn't have stood much more of that chasing up and down stairs every time he shouts.'

He shouted often. For his paper, his specs, his tea-without-milk and his meals-without-salt – and shouted again when he got them. 'Has that Bob Waithe *tasted* a soft-boiled egg without salt?' he rumbled. 'It's dead, which I'll be if they keep this up.'

'Now, Daddy –'

'Aye, well –' He whacked the top off the eggshell and stared into its bland interior. 'Breakfast. Christ!'

But if he was impossible about little things he accepted his absence from the foundry with singular equinamity. Neil came in each evening to give his report and Joe listened quietly, offering his opinion only when asked.

'I don't believe it,' Neil said to Lallie. 'I thought he'd be checking on me at every touch and turn.'

'Be thankful,' she told him. But she wondered herself. The business was Daddy's baby and, as she knew herself by now, one's baby came before everything else.

'How d'you think Neil's doing, then?' she asked him one afternoon.

He fingered the empty bowl of his pipe (tobacco was another pleasure now denied) and puffed out his lips in thought. 'He's doing well, damned well. That's the only good thing about being laid up. I'm getting a preview of what'll happen when I shuffle off for good, not that I'm planning on *that*. I always knew Neil had it up here.' He rapped his waxy forehead with an equally pale knuckle. 'But clever's not always smart, is it? Theory gets you nowhere when you've got shop stewards stirring the pot and work piling up in the yards. Aye, I'm right satisfied with him.' He sucked a moment on the cold stem of his pipe before laying it back on the stand. 'He'll be there, will Neil.'

He shot her a look of such complicity she suddenly wanted to escape but he was adept, now, at playing the invalid.

'Sit with me a bit,' he said. 'The house is too flaming quiet with the lad at kindergarten. I've been wanting a bit of a talk with you, ever since I've been laid up – no, don't go telling me I'll live to be a hundred. Happen I will and happen I won't, you know about as much as I do – and we both know as much as the doctors.'

'If you'd just take care –'

'Be quiet and listen. I *am* taking care, I've plenty to live for,

379

haven't I? It's you I want to talk about now, not me. You'll admit I've not badgered you and I'm not going to. You've run a rough road but you've come through –'

'I can't see I had any choice.'

'You could have gone flying off in all directions – for a while there I thought – but you're bull-headed like the rest of the Wainwrights. What I'm telling you is this. Neil's not bull-headed. He's patient, too patient for his own good. He's a smart lad, but where you're concerned he's daft. He lets you use him – so make sure you use him right. Don't play cat and mouse with him, do you hear? I know I can be an interfering old sod, but you'll do as you like no matter what I say. Just be fair with him, that's all I'm saying.'

She nodded, sure now that he'd heard her take the call from the lawyer yesterday. Now he'd bring up Jan's name. He didn't. He shifted against the pillow and stared at the ceiling. 'You know, I sometimes used to think Millie was a mite thick between the ears (thank God I never told her!) but now I think she might have been a sight cannier than we are. She never worried over much, did she? never made plans – so how could she be disappointed when they didn't work out?' He sighed. 'Isn't it about time you went to fetch Stephen?'

'Not for another hour.'

'God, the afternoon does drag with him out.'

'That posh little school was your idea,' she reminded him.

'Well, he's got a head on him, hasn't he? With the right background there won't be a door he can't open.'

'He might not reach for the foundry door, you know.' She ought not to have said that, he wasn't supposed to be upset – but he was chuckling!

'You know what the young scamp asked me yesterday? He wanted to know if we had any books down at The Muck. I said we had ledgers and trade manuals and such like, and he gave me that old-fashioned look, you know how he does? "Not *those*, Gramps," says he, "I mean *real* books with *real* things in." Like I told him, just try picking up a Wainwright casting and you'll know it's real enough.'

By the time winter set in Joe was well enough to take Stefan back and forth to school. The doctor said no driving yet, so they'd walk down the path every noon, Joe at a measured pace and Stefan trotting along beside him, holding onto his grandfather's hand except when the now matronly Suka tangled her lead around an ankle. Lallie would watch from the front window then keep her eye on the corner of the street until Daddy and Suka reappeared.

Bob Waithe still stopped by each morning on his rounds but his visits to his most difficult patient were shorter now. 'He's coming on nicely,' he told Lallie, 'but he's not out of the wood and never will be. I don't want him to go back to the foundry and to tell the truth I'm not sure he wants to.'

He was right. Joe had switched his priorities.

After the first fractious month of bedrest he'd come to miss the foundry less and less. For the first time in his life he was free to do whatever he liked. From Backenthorpe on he'd faced every day like a battle to won, always that urgency driving him to build, to expand what he'd built and expand again, all so he could give Lallie a life better than his own, but the goal somehow got lost in the quest. Her life was as padded now as money could make it, and if it was still half empty she'd have to fill it up herself. The lad helped. He helped them both, and what more could a man ask? The foundry was big enough now so that they could all lean on it the rest of their days no matter if he slaved at it or not. Good times or bad, it was only the little man that stood on the edge of the crater; if management was sound the big boys were never at risk. And a sounder man than Neil Armott he'd never find.

It was as if he'd stepped off a treadmill. Windy days he took the lad to fly his kite on the common; on dog-show weekends they watched Lall's Afghans prance off with ribbon after ribbon; come a frosty night and he'd have Stefan on his lap in front of the fire, listen to him pick out words from the page of a book. As year's end rolled around he took the bus to town and spent leisurely hours shopping. Electric trains, toy sailboats, a tricycle. The shops were full again now and it was a pleasure to pick out this dress for Lallie, that scarf, a bolt of fire wool she could take to the dressmaker. Again she was a joy to look at. A touch of the old sparkle had gone and her nature wasn't as soft as it used to be, but a bit of reserve towards

381

strangers was no bad thing to his mind. Looking at her, you wouldn't say she was a happy woman – and she'd been such a happy girl – but thank God she'd lost that waiting look that knifed at him every time he saw it. Oh aye, that was behind them. It was the little lad's doing, he reckoned. An engaging chap and no getting away from it, from the minute he came downstairs every morning, prying Joe's eyes open with careful but determined fingers, 'You waked up yet, Gramps?' to the minute he went to bed, all pink and clean with his teddy bear and his book. He'd brought a pattern back into their lives, the boy had.

At Christmas Lallie drove them over to Backenthorpe, and while he and Lall nursed their drinks in the snug (his was brandy now, very long on soda) the boy stayed in the pub kitchen with the publican's wife, who fed him mince pies and milk and tales of how his mother used to sit in that very same chair with her doll and her pretty little face. Afterwards they walked over the fields and sat on the bench by the green. Watching his daughter and grandson pick their way across the cobbles and touch the mossed stones of the old smithy he realized that for the first time in a very long while he was happy, that he no longer feared the spasms that still came sometimes to his chest. They pressed a bit softer than they used to and his blood pressure didn't shoot up now when he thought about the unions or the Pole. The one was in Neil's hands and the other, well, likely it was a closed chapter.

'Come on then, you two,' he called across the green. 'Let's have you – there's a nice leg of roast pork waiting at home.' And turkey salad for Joe, damn it!

It was the most reluctant spring ever. Clouds wherever she looked and not a snip of blue in sight. Plying the grooming brush on such days she wondered why, *why* she'd fallen in love with Afghans. 'Because you were too young to know better,' she muttered, her mind adroit now at blocking the next, inevitable thought. 'Keep still, Goldie, there's my lovely girl.' Brushed and clean, she *was* lovely; bedraggled as she was now after a run across the field, she had all the appeal of a worn-out kitchen mop.

She'd finished Jolly's Golden Girl and was starting on Ivan

Tzarevich – known (not always with affection) as Ivan the Terrible – when a small shadow appeared at the kennel fence. It was Stefan, with Neil and Daddy a long way behind.

'We went on the common,' he announced, hopping up and down, twanging the steel wires of the fence. 'And guess what?'

'What darling?' She smiled at him over Ivan's foolish, aristocratic head but kept a wary eye on the dog. Ivan was given to sudden affectionate lunges that had knocked her down more than once.

'You know that old tree near the bandstand where my kite always gets stuck?'

'The beech? It's *not* finally got leaves?' She looked with pleasure at Stefan's winter-pink cheeks and pale hair. Ivan seized the moment to sweep his tongue across the back of her neck.

'No,' Stefan said, knowing the game. 'Try again.'

'It fell down?'

'No.' His chest swelled under the fawn cardigan. '*I climbed it*! *My very own self*!'

'Well ...' She thought of its knobby, rheumatic branches, all of twenty feet tall.

'On my own, too – Uncle Neil gave me a leg up, but *then* I was on my own all the way up!'

Her heart stopped, then galloped ahead. 'To the top?'

He flushed. 'Well, halfway – but I could see the village hall and the church and the postman digging his garden –'

'And don't forget the bird's nest.' It was Neil arriving with Daddy.

Was it her imagination or was that a touch of defiance lurking under Neil's grin? Yes, it was! 'I can see you've all had an exciting morning,' she said. 'Stef, why don't you and Gramps go in for a slice of cake? Mrs Hodgson's just taken a date-and-walnut out of the oven.'

'Uncle Neil likes date and –'

'Uncle Neil and I have to talk,' she said firmly.

Joe chuckled and rubbed the top of Stefan's head. 'Come on, laddo, they don't want us and we'll not stop where we're not wanted.'

Stefan scampered off with Joe in his wake. Neil took Ivan's

brush from her and fell quickly into the steady rhythm of grooming. 'That beech – it's quite a small tree.'

'He's quite a small boy.'

'Better he tries it when I'm there and not when he's on his own then, isn't it?'

'He's not allowed on the common on his own.'

Neil sighed. 'That's another thing, isn't it? You're being over-protective, love.'

'That's not it at all!' she cried, louder than usual because she knew he was probably right – but she couldn't help it, she was terrified of something – anything happening which could conceivably take Stefan from her. 'I like to be careful, is there anything wrong with that?'

'You're going to make him a mummy's boy.'

'He *is* Mummy's boy! He's mine!'

'You know what I mean. You give him swimming lessons in town and then you won't let him go in the water at the seaside.'

'The waves –'

'You're even scared when he rides Muff – I've watched you – and Muff's about as risky as Joe's rocking chair. You even tell him to slow down on his tricycle –'

'But he could fall off!'

'Boys usually do, all the time. He's desperate to play with the Paulsen boys and you won't allow that, either. And they're nice kids.'

'The eldest's twice Stefan's age!'

'That's why he wants to play with them.' Ivan tried to get in a loving lick and was immediately quelled by a light tap from Neil's palm. 'You behave. We're talking.'

'No, *you're* talking,' she said, angry all over again because he even handled the difficult Ivan better than she did. 'And you're interfering.'

He stood up and hung the grooming brush on its nail. 'I expect I am, but you can't keep him in a glass bubble, sweetheart, it's not fair –'

'And it's not your business.' And *that* wasn't fair either, she knew it wasn't. *He'll let you use him, Neil will, he's daft where you're concerned.* But he was changing. Since Daddy's illness he'd become more ... assured, even forceful about some things. Not

384

that he was bossy, but in the nicest possible way he did seem to take charge. Even Daddy had mentioned it, something about a man changing when he had absolute authority, the way Neil did at the foundry, otherwise people would jump all over him. It was Neil, now, who came home with tickets for this and that, who made sure Daddy walked every day and maintained his diet, who encouraged her to handle her own dogs at the shows and not depend on a professional handler. And now he was telling her she was making mistakes with Stefan – and that *really* wasn't his affair, even if he just might be right.

'I know it's not my business,' he said now, his hands on her shoulders as he forced her to look at him, his brown eyes calm but determined. 'But I want to make it my business. I've waited a long time.'

'I know you have.'

'There's never been anybody else –'

She forced herself to smile. 'Oh no? What about that blonde secretary you had last year? And the librarian? And –'

'No, you're not going to sidetrack me this time. None of that was serious, and you know it.'

He crushed her to him and kissed her and it wasn't like the other times at all. His lips were hard and demanding, first on her mouth, then her neck, and through their thin summer clothes she could feel his heart beating – or was it her own? Her arms seemed to go around him of their own volition and she felt some hard core of ice begin to melt under the warmth of his mouth. It was he, not she, who stood away at last, breathing hard.

'I'm not a chunk of Wainwright steel, love. I've got a breaking point.'

'And you wouldn't want ...' She wasn't sure quite how to say it but he knew perfectly well what she meant.

'No, I wouldn't. Not with you. It's marriage or nothing. I want to look after you. And Stefan. You *can't* still think Jan's coming back –'

She stiffened. 'You know I don't want to talk about that.'

'It's high time. Arithmetic's never been your strong point so I'm going to do some for you. You've been married ten years. You've had a husband for less than two. You had a year at the

A.S.—18

385

beginning and a year when he came back from Germany. That's all.'

'No –'

'Yes! A husband's somebody who's there day after day, good times and bad, somebody you can depend on and who depends on you. "As long as you both shall live," isn't that the way it goes?'

'It wasn't his fault he was a prisoner of war –'

'But *now*. What about now? There's you with half a life, there's Stefan with no father. And there's me, thirty-four next month. I'm tired of waiting, Lallie.'

'Is this an ultimatum?' She was suddenly very frightened, the prospect of life without Neil Armott a bleak, real possibility. *But he'd always been there …*

'Call it what you want, but I'm not a beggar. I'll not ask again. It's up to you now.'

He walked away very fast, and for the first time in a very long while she noticed the slight limp he fought so hard to conceal and the dear, determined set of his shoulders.

Walking away from her. Neil walking away from her.

Everything in her wanted to run to him, tell him – but the back door opened and Stefan was running to him instead, waving the scaled down cricket bat Daddy had given him.

'Uncle Neil! Could we have a game, *please* Uncle Neil?'

It looked for a moment as if Neil might walk past him. But of course he didn't. He set up wickets and bails and spent a painstaking half hour sending down balls so slow and easy that even a child Stefan's age missed very few.

CHAPTER FORTY

Poland, Spring, 1949

Each day he went to see Mamunia and each day he waited for the mail.

He waited for Lallie's letter – he'd written a dozen times now, mostly postcards they wouldn't have to open to censor, so surely she knew his new address, would start some wheels turning somewhere. He also waited for visas. Two months since he'd filled out the necessary emigration papers and still no word from Warsaw, not even an acknowledgement.

'I'll have to go to Warsaw,' he said at last to Uncle Tadeusz. 'I'll *ram* the damned paperwork through!'

'A lot you know about the system if you think –'

'I know people are too blasted patient. If they'd just *insist*!'

'So go to Warsaw and insist – but tell your mother. And eat some breakfast before you go. You're beginning to look human.'

It was true. At Uncle Tadeusz's country table his strength had come back; his teeth were firm in his mouth again; his mind was clear, impatient. Of the lethargy of the prison nothing remained. Now he was in a fever to get to England; with the return to strength had come renewed longing for Lallie and the life they could have now that all desire to live in Poland was dead. But there was still Mamunia to persuade.

Her bed was in its usual place, steadfastly turned against the

387

window. She was sitting up today, reading from a tattered book. Her right hand, an ivory claw, clutched at her robe. Her voice seemed stronger this morning and a touch of colour tinged the cheek she presented for his kiss.

'They tell me you ate your breakfast, which is good,' he said. 'But you're still in bed, which is bad. After all we've said – and we turned Zakopane upside-down to find that wheelchair.'

She shrugged. 'I told you I didn't want it. And Mr Krzyczkowski loves it, has his poor silly sister trundling him all over the grounds in it.'

He started to argue and as usual her eyes closed, her fingers moving over the coverlet like a nun telling her beads. 'I was thinking about Tazienki ... remember how we'd go on Saturday afternoons? You'd feed the swans while Tatuš read the paper, then off to that little *kawiarnia* for tea ... they had those little rum cakes with the almonds on top and –'

'Mamunia! If you won't try the chair then try to walk, *try*! They say it's possible you could learn ...'

'Maybe I could. You never saw Basia Stolp ... had the same operation they gave me. She learned to walk, yes, and if there'd been a carnival left to hire her she'd have made a fortune.' She laughed, but it was harsh laughter and he was glad when she stopped. 'Crabs walk better!'

'*Stuchaj, Mamus*...' She *had* to listen.

'*Nie.*' Her lips folded shut.

'Please.' He took her hand. 'If you'd try, look forward ... We could go to England together, we can manage. Today I'm going to Warsaw, I'll get papers –'

'Enough.' She sighed and leaned back against the pillow. 'Try to understand, *kochany*. In that butcher's shop at the camp, when they were doing ... well, you know – I didn't want to think about what they were doing so I thought of Zakopane instead. I got so good at it I could smell the pine trees, and I told myself then that if ever I could come back here I'd never leave. I *am* back.'

Frustration and tenderness washed over him. 'You don't even *look* at the pine trees.'

'I don't have to. I know they're there, you see. And I don't have to make a spectacle of myself staggering about on crumpled legs. What I need I have here. I'm not going anywhere.'

'How can I leave you behind?'

'*Go*! I want you to go, you should never have come back –'

'I came to find *you*.'

'You found me.' She looked down at legs that made barely a ripple under the coverlet. 'A broken doll, *prawda*?' She leaned forward. 'Listen to me. You think to make me happy when you come every day to see me? You make me sad … and angry!' Her chin began to quiver and she turned to the wall. '*You were safe, Janku, safe. You had a life*!'

'I still do,' he said quietly. 'But I also have a wife. I want to be with her. I want to care for you.'

'You want it all.'

'Look,' he said, on his knees by the bed. 'Perhaps I can bring her here – though God knows – but she'd come, I know she'd come.' Jesus, Lallie here, to *this* life? She'd go mad.

Mamunia spoke patiently, as if to a child. 'There is nothing for you here, nothing for anybody but the old too set in their minds to leave. Like me. Look, my robe is worn out, *nie*? It's torn, like me.' The claw clutched ever more fiercely at the worn blue fabric. 'Why do you think I hold it together like so? I'll tell you why. *Because in all Zakopane there is not so much as a needle to cobble it together*! Not even a needle, can you imagine?'

'So there are shortages. It's a new system, things will get better –'

She wasn't listening. 'Once there were tailors on every street, bolts of woollens … silks to the ceiling. And now not a needle. And you think to bring an *Angielka* to *this*?' The claw relaxed and the ripped wool opened to a chest of bones and powdery skin quickly covered by scrabbling fingers. 'Here is nothing.'

'It's still Poland –'

'Poland! You sound like the rest. Poland's not fields, monuments, stones. It was Tatuš, it was me, it was Morska Street. All finished, eh? If you stay here you'll be finished too.' Her fingers plucked at the coverlet. 'I said it doesn't make me happy to see you. So I lied – I have the privilege. You make me very happy.' She nodded. 'Yes. But it would make me happier if you'd go. Then I'll know everything is not over.'

'Mamunia …' Every day the same arguments, where was the end to them?

'Go.'

'I'm going to Warsaw, that's all.'

When she saw the documents, cast-iron crowbars that would prise them out of here, she'd change her mind.

'Go.'

'And try the damn wheelchair while I'm gone!'

Warsaw was warm under the spring sun; young girls wore summer dresses and light cardigans; plum trees bloomed pink and red in the parks. It was possible, walking down the wide boulevards, to believe there was hope.

He faced the reception clerk in the government office.

'I applied for visas.' He passed her copies of the forms. 'What's the delay?'

She glanced at the dates. 'No delay – there's a long waiting list for visas.'

'That I can believe. Who can I speak to? Who's in charge?'

She gave him the official's name. Would Mr Kaliski like to make an appointment to see him? But of course. An *early* appointment. She checked her calendar and scratched an entry on it.

'29 June, 10 o'clock. It's the best I can do.'

'June? That's three months away!'

She shrugged, was about to turn to the next supplicant.

'*Now look, I can't wait –*'

A guard materialized from nowhere. 'Is there a problem here?'

Jan looked at the uniform, the gun, the rigid expression in the guard's eyes. Memories of Block 10 rose up, heavy with portent. 'No trouble,' he muttered. 'I'm just leaving.'

On the pavement he stood undecided. He was getting nowhere. Perhaps they never issued visas, just took applications? But in Mamunia's condition how was he to get her out without one? He was reluctant to break the link so newly reforged but perhaps he *should* go himself, come back for her with valid papers? And Lallie could come with him, help him persuade Mamunia ... First he had to get out himself. Every frontier was under communist control; in this world one hand not only washed the other, it helped snap on the handcuffs. The ports ... they were the only chance. Foreign ships came in, they must go out. But the ports were guarded ... it would be possible, if tricky, and what other choice was there?

His mind made up, he headed for the train station. First Zakopane, to say goodbye. Then England, Lallie's warm young arms. His steps quickened crossing Nowy Świat, eager now to get started – and suddenly there was a hand on his arm.

'Jan Kaliski! My God, Jan! What the hell –'

Roman. Roman in Warsaw ... 'What are you doing *here*?'

Roman punched his arm, folded him in a bear hug, punched his arm again, wide face alight with pleasure. 'God, man, but I thought – I never expected – where the hell *were* you, why didn't you write, man?'

'It's a long story. But what about you?'

Roman shook his head. Women! It was Genia. She hadn't been happy in England. 'Homesick – a misery to live with. So I gave in. Now she's sorry – a one-room flat with no hot water and hours in line every day for food.' Two months they'd been back and already she was crying to leave again, but their bridges were burned. 'Burned – hell, they're blown up. Getting *in* here's a hell of a lot easier than getting out. And you, where've you *been*, why didn't you go back for God's sake?'

'As you just said, getting in is easier than getting out. It's a long story ...'

As Jan told him, Roman's face settled first into disquiet, then anxiety, finally into alarm. 'All that time in prison – and we'd thought you'd just ... well, you know, all that trouble with Joe, the arguments, the job ...'

'I'm going back now. I'll get there somehow if I have to swim –'

'Yes, but Lallie – she's had no letters, nothing.'

'But I've written!' *They have lists, Janek, many, many lists.* 'And I'm going back now.'

Roman looked at his feet, at a passing bus, anywhere but at Jan. 'You've been gone a long time, friend. A long time. Nobody waits for ever, *prawda*?'

'She's not –' No, not Lallie.

Roman sighed. 'Joe's sick, very sick – and there's the boy to think about, *prawda*?'

The boy? The boy?

Roman nodded. 'Stefan.'

The passing street cars lurched, blurred, moved to a different rhythm. Stefan, Stefan, Stefan, Stefan. *'I have to go –'*

Roman took his arm, pulled him into the doorway of a shop. 'Think about it first,' he urged. 'She's got nobody but Neil.'

Everything stopped. 'What are you saying?'

'Not what you think. But it's worth thinking about –'

Not when I've a wife and son …

'Nothing's changed for us in England. They don't accept us, never have. Where would you go? Bring her here?' The wide sweep of Roman's arm took in countless women with empty baskets, the bleak look in their eyes as they waited patient as cattle for a bit of meat to put on the family table. *'Joe Wainwright's daughter?'*

The train couldn't get to Zakopane fast enough. Images crowded in. Lallie with a baby, his baby; naming it for Tatuš; Neil and Joe in the wings, the one devoted, the other dominant – but Joe was sick, Roman said. Joe, man of steel, indestructible! It wasn't true, none of it was true …

'It's true,' he told Mamunia. 'You're a grandmother. *Now* will you go to England? I'll come back for you within the year, possibly two, with papers. If you won't go for me, then for your grandson.'

'Who I couldn't talk to. Even Tatuš couldn't teach me the language –'

'But you'll come?'

She closed her eyes. 'We'll see. Only go, go now.' She turned on him the full power of her burning-glass intensity. 'I want you to go. There is nothing for you here.'

Except you. There'll always be you.

He kissed her. Her cheek was cold as marble, not a muscle moving.

After he'd gone she stared for a long time at the closed door. The doctor who visited her soon after had to speak her name twice before she would turn her head to the light. Her expression was still marble, but a glisten of tears ran in all the small tributaries of her cheeks and dropped unheeded to her patiently folded hands.

CHAPTER FORTY-ONE

Ivan had wandered off.

He'd done it before and she wasn't really worried. That russet coat and all-too-friendly expression made him highly recognizable – but it was raining terribly hard and he *was* such an idiot crossing the street.

She was already getting out of the car to look for him when Daddy shouted from the house.

'The vicar was just on the phone. Ivan's gone over there, the silly bugger, says will you pick him up before they all get licked to death?'

She didn't bother to ask which one was the silly bugger; Daddy's opinion of the vicar was on a par with his opinion of the dog. Who has probably tracked mud all over the vicarage carpet, she grumbled as she switched on the windscreen wipers. God, would the rain *never* stop?

Ivan was delighted, as usual, to see her.

So was the vicar, who said she mustn't worry about the rug at all, it would vacuum up just fine after it had dried, and she really must be sure to thank Joe for his donation to the parish fund.

To Ivan's disgust she put him on the back seat, glad now she'd brought the big car. 'You smell of wet dog,' she said, '*naughty* wet dog and I'm very vexed with you. And you're matted!'

Preoccupied with the monumental grooming job waiting for

her when they reached home, she pulled into the old post road just as a new onslaught of rain drummed on the car's roof. It wasn't that she didn't see the coal lorry coming the other way. She saw it's black bulk through the driving rain in plenty of time to stay well on her own side of the road. But Ivan, with his usual exquisite timing, decided on just that moment to make up with her, and she suddenly felt two large russet paws on her shoulders and a pointed snout in front of her face. Her shout of 'Ivan!' was taken for encouragement and he leapt over the seat and scrambled into her lap. She tried to hold the steering and failed. A horn blared, brakes screamed as she fought steering and russet fur and the relentless pink tongue.

There was a jolt, metal crumped on metal, and the sound of splintering wood filled her ears. A heavy door slammed and there was a voice.

'What the bloody hell – pulling afront o' me like that, a second later and you'd be playing a blasted harp! Come on, get out!' A very dirty face was at the windscreen, peering in. 'Are you okay?'

She was shaken but all right, except for a little trickle of blood where her forehead had hit the steering wheel. Thank God she'd been driving slowly. 'Oh, Ivan!' as the trickle of blood was licked off at one swipe.

She climbed out, her legs wobbly under her, and exchanged licences with the other driver. 'I *am* so sorry, it was the dog you see, he –'

'Aye, well,' he muttered, calmer now. 'Are you all right? Shall I call a doctor? Or your family?'

Call Daddy? 'Goodness, no!' As it was she'd have to tell him about this very carefully indeed. 'I'm really fine.'

He pulled her car clear of the ditch and left. It was only then that she remembered what he'd said. *A second later and you'd be playing a blasted harp*! And Stefan with no one but her and Daddy – who'd need one of his pills before she could even tell him she'd driven into a ditch!

She drove home very slowly, planning what to say – if only he wouldn't *worry* so! – and it wasn't until she was almost in the drive that she saw Bob Waithe's black Fiat parked at an odd angle by the front door and Mrs Hodgson standing out in the pouring rain in her apron, no coat or umbrella, nothing but the rain sheeting off her specs and her red hands wringing, wringing ...

Daddy.

Daddy Daddy Daddy – *Touch and go, always will be ...*

'I called the doctor, Lallie, I didn't know what to do ... I took him his tea and he was on the floor –'

Bob Waithe was waiting for her in the hall ... *in the hall ...*

He didn't have to say anything. He had the same look as the constable ... *in the hall* ... '*I'm sorry, Joe,*' he'd said ... Mum ...

'I'm sorry, Lallie.'

Daddy, Daddy – but Bob Waithe was in the way and she tried to push him aside.

'I have to go to him!'

'No –'

'*I have to ...*'

'He said not to let you, love. Don't let her see me like this, he kept saying –'

He was pushing pills on her, and milk, and she felt Mrs Hodgson's arm steering her somewhere.

'Stay with her. I'll wait for Neil,' she heard him say, and a door closed, the light shining off Mrs H's glasses like two searchlights on her ... oh, Daddy, and I wasn't even *here*. You should have waited! If I hadn't gone in the damn ditch, if the dumb dog hadn't ... oh, you should have waited. The house was so *quiet*, so quiet – it'll always be quiet now when Stefan's out – How could she tell him, how –

The searchlights went out and when they came on again they were brown, gentler, and Neil was saying, 'I've called the school, love, they're keeping Stefan till we go and get him –'

Then he was holding her against the grey foundry smock and she was telling him about Ivan and the car and not being here. 'He should have waited ...' her voice rising perilously high.

'He's *been* waiting, love. Ever since he came out of the hospital he's known.'

No! – but of course he had, all that time spent with them, not going back to work, the walks with Stefan, the long hours with her.

'Let's get Stefan, love. He'll be worrying.'

'I – how can I tell him? What can I say?' Her mind was a rat in a trap in a cage in a prison –

'You'll find the words, sweetheart, you'll see.'

Yes. She'd said them before to the same washed-blue eyes. Daddy has to be away, darling – except this time it wasn't his father, it was Gramps, whose lap had always been there, whose arms were always waiting, whose bristly morning chin against his child's cheek was the reassuring start of every day. What kind of words were there?

'Gramps had to go away, darling, we won't see him ...'

But the eyes were older now. Suspicious. 'Is he coming back?' The soft mouth straight, the chin already beginning to crumple. 'Is he coming back, Mummy?'

'No.'

'Like –?'

Then Neil was holding them both, driving them home.

Five days to the funeral, days of Neil never leaving them for a minute. He ran the foundry from the house and he got Bob Waithe's boy to come and take care of the kennels. When he wasn't on the phone he was playing with Stefan, reading to him, rocking him to sleep then sitting with Lallie through the damp, miserable evenings. Whatever would they do without Neil?

The funeral was dreadful. Worse than Mum's. There were so many people – during the war people hadn't had time to go to them all but now all the foundry people came, hundreds of them, their wives and children, neighbours, friends, even a delegation from Backenthorpe dressed in their Sunday best. Condolences poured over her and past her. It didn't help and it didn't hurt. She was frozen, seeing only the little boy at her side and the hole in the moist black earth.

Agnes Armott wanted to come to the house afterwards and Lallie didn't know how to deflect her genteel sympathy. Neil did. Firmly.

'No, Mother. Why don't you take Mrs H to our house and give her a drink? She's worn to a frazzle, poor dear.'

Oh, darling Neil! How did he know she didn't want any of them about when she took Stefan home? Mrs Hodgson was sweet, but so very *bothered*, and Agnes, well –

'If you want to be on your own I can drop you off ...' he said, turning the car into the drive, but Stefan's hand was already tugging at him.

'Come in with us, Uncle Neil. Please?'

Poor little dab ... how tiny he looked, reaching for Neil's hand. A man's hand. It had always been Daddy he reached for, his loving, indulgent Gramps.

Dusk was falling over the quiet street, shadowing its windows but not blinding them from her as the sun sometimes seemed to do. They watched her as they'd always watched, eyes impressively set, gracefully draped, taking in all the events of her life. They'd seen young Joe come up from The Muck with nothing to recommend him but dirt under his fingers and grit in his soul – but they'd seen those fingers smooth a path for a young wife and daughter, had at last respected him for it. They'd seen the war thrust a young stranger on them, the settle and shift of new emotions he'd brought with him. They were tall enough, these windows, to look down on buses driving up from the valley, see the fall of a crippled plane, the lowering of a woman – dear and simple and so pliant as to be almost overlooked – into cold cemetery earth. They'd watched the strange young man come back and go away again, because his war was not yet done, only his seed left behind to mark his journey through Eccles Place. They'd watched the seed grow, flower into his living image, a little boy who gave his love to an old man. Now they'd seen black, pall-bearer shoulders stoop under the burden of the old man's teakwood box, carrying away all she had left of strength ... And now here was Stefan reaching, reaching.

'Please come in with us, Uncle Neil.'

She understood, for his need echoed her own.

Now there was no Gramps to turn to, he was as afraid as she.

In the hall, Daddy's coat still on its hook, his scuffed leather slippers by the umbrella stand, his mail in the slot. The phone bill and an Appeal from the Little Sisters of Something or Other. Seed catalogues and bank statements. And waiting in the living room, the day bed and his pipe stand.

'You can have them moved if you like,' Neil was saying, 'but I thought you'd want to keep them about …'

Yes! Yes, of course she did.

'… and you're both going to sit down while I make you something to drink …'

They sat in the kitchen, Stefan too quiet in her lap, as Neil boiled milk for Ovaltine, kept up a steady stream of talk about nothing at all. And behind it all, the quiet house …

Stefan began to sniffle and then to cry, and she hugged him tighter, the silk of his hair against her aching face. She realized dully that her jaw had been set too long, was tired of holding her face together, but it couldn't seem to let go. And there was Neil stirring milk …

He'll let you use him and use him …

He took care of the mail for a week, then:

'You'll need to pay the gas bill, love.'

'Yes …' But there was Stefan to pick up from school.

'Do you want them to shut it off?'

She frowned. 'They wouldn't do that …'

'Of course they would.'

'I thought … somebody at the foundry took care of all that sort of thing?'

'They always have but they've really plenty to do, you know. It doesn't seem fair to –'

'All right! I'll do it this afternoon.'

In the afternoon it was still raining and the study was so dark, Daddy's desk brooding in the corner, every drawer filled with him.

The first one she opened had the albums in, all the pictures of her since she was a baby, Daddy's captions under every one. A curly-haired Lallie taking her first steps to Mum's outstretched hands: *Stepping Out*. At six, laughing with a gap-toothed mouth: *Is That My Lass?* At nine, on the sands at Morecambe: *That's My Lass!* Her first High School photo, in gym-slip and tie: *What Are They Trying To Do?* At fifteen, in a boat neck with ruffles: *Best Rose of Summer*.

She slammed the drawer shut and hunted for the cheque book, wrote all the cheques Neil said were needed. Then she found his little note. Three words: *Kennels. Pups. Deliver*! And so she drove to Bamford, her mind as blank and featureless as her life.

It was one of those dreary, windless days of early spring, far too cold for the time of year. Old snow still lay in the folds of the hills, and in the valleys winter lingered on in a freezing drizzle, not a new leaf in sight as she drove with one hand on the wheel, the other comforting a crying pup who already missed the warmth of his litter mates.

She hated seeing them go, especially so in this case. The pup was unusually fine, one she would have preferred to keep, and she did not much like his buyer. A coldly efficient man, he would give the dog every care in the world with the possible exception of human affection, but he was an important show-judge she could scarcely have turned down. Giving the soft muzzle one last kiss (she had learned by now not to name each pup the instant it was born), she turned the car for home.

She had not been near Castleton since Jan left and she wasn't sure what now made her take the small detour through its winding lanes, unless it was the weight of cloud and a winter that had lingered past its time. The cottages by the road knew a century of winters and seemed to lean into the hillside, doors and windows fast against the creeping cold. Remote and crumbling on its rise stood the castle, with Cave Dale and Goosehill in tatters of mist around it. She shivered and drove towards the Bull's Head, thinking to stop for coffee, but its familiar steps carried too heavy a load, happier times gone inexplicably wrong, and she found herself steering for Winnats Pass and the enigma of Mam Tor.

What had drawn Jan to walk its wind-quarried rim alone, to come back to her with harebells in his hand and later, so much later, that haunted, driven look in his eyes? Surely not beauty; where was the symmetry in a broken mountain? Not permanence – half its heart was gone, scattered to the winds. Even the limestone outcrop of Winnats had more life, the short turf still green, springy underfoot as she parked and stepped out into a soft, steady drizzle.

She pulled herself up the steep grade, the grass wet and slippery underfoot. Ewes, heavy with lamb and feeding only off the lower slopes, turned wary eyes on her as she passed them to climb higher and higher into the mist, nothing certain but the next step until Mam Tor loomed in front of her, massive and vaguely threatening. Still she walked, tired now, not knowing why she went on except that here was perhaps an answer – but how could she find it when she didn't even know the question!

There was no sound but her breathing and the occasional rattle of a pebble dislodged by the toe of her shoe, no scent but wet earth and things dying unseen.

She reached the top and looked down. Nothing but shifting vapour and random patches of old snow that clung like tufts of white hair around the brooding, broken face of the mountain.

Ten years ago there'd been sun and young lambs grazing. From here they'd looked down on the road to Hope and in their young optimism had marvelled at its name, discovered in it a tremulous symbol. The war ... everything was shifting then, the whole earth moving under its urgent thrust – no time to think, to plan. Even dreams were frantic birds desperate to fly. Young love flowering under the patient eye of sheep, the world all blue and green and rich with promise then, the only shadow a Spitfire, very high and piercingly beautiful. Where had it all gone? Had she been so naive, that young girl who'd wept at its beauty against the clear blue? Gallant, it had looked to her then. Gallant! Could she have been so ignorant, that girl, not to have felt the desperation that flew it? The clinging knowledge that any second might be its last?

Yes she could. Yes she had been.

But there were clouds on her shoulders now, pressing her down.

She searched for the picnic spot they'd used, the shape of the boulder clear in her mind. Squat, it had been, and grey, with moss on its north side and soft grass in its lee, the little cairn of limestone a few feet to the south.

It wasn't here.

But it had to be here, covering the caves and chasms under its crust, all those empty, vaunting caverns, the rushing rivers that knew neither light not season, the stalactites formed drip

400

by slow drip over the centuries.

It was gone. There was no cairn, no boulder in the shape she remembered …'

Heedless of rain and wet grass she threw herself down to the prickly grass and the ground, gritty under her fingers, and sobbed as if her heart was crumbling with the chunk of the mountain's crust. All this time, all this sad empty time he'd been gone she'd hardly cried at all. Now it seemed she couldn't stop.

She cried for his face laughing up at her from the warm summer grass, for the almost forgotten touch of his mouth on hers, for the relief that filled her like a cup as she counted off the thunder of returning Wellingtons and the count was whole. She cried for all the short, shimmering nights when they rejoiced in each other and the miracle that they'd lived another day.

But they were so few, those nights.

And the other nights, Jan my love. Where were you then? I waited for Lalka to come home, for Mum to come home, and you were not there. I waited to tell you there'd be a baby – where were you then? Stefan was born and still you were gone … you were never there, not once in all the long nights you were needed were you there. Now Daddy – my lovely, loving Daddy you didn't even *try* to like – he's gone too.

And where are you, Jan Kaliski, in the longest, emptiest night of all? Lying dead somewhere and no one thinks to tell me? Or snuggled cozy against the body of some young Polish girl who understands your dreams when perhaps I could not? – *because you never told me what they were.*

Where are you?

It was raining hard when she started down the mountain. She felt strangely lighter now, as if accumulated griefs had risen, boiled over like lava, and drained away. She looked up at the mountain one last time. Perhaps, after all, she'd known all the time.

Love and loss came wrapped in the same package.

The rain turned warmer as she neared home. She opened the window and let the soft air of Norton and Eccles Place wash over her.

401

At the house she could hear Mrs Hodgson washing dishes in the kitchen, the bell-like ring of cup against cup, plate against saucer.

It seemed a long time before she could bring herself to ask the question that floated insistently at the top of her mind, and even then then she kept her voice very casual.

'Has Neil called, Mrs H?'

'Aye. He'll be round after dinner, love.'

'Good,' she said softly.

By the time Neil arrived she'd already put Stefan to bed and sent Mrs Hodgson off to the pictures.

'I didn't think it was her night off,' he said, surprised.

'It isn't. I need to talk to you.'

Concern for her was in every feature. 'What's wrong, love? You look ... serious. You're not ill? Stefan ...?'

'He's fine. So am I.'

'Well then?'

She took her coat, hung it next to Daddy's. *Oh Daddy, if only you were here ...* 'There's a drink ready –'

'Wow, I'm really getting the guest treatment tonight.' But he followed her into the sitting-room, accepted a drink.

'So what is it? Tell me.'

She only hesitated for a second. 'It's me. I've not been fair to you, ever. I've used you –'

'No more than I've let you.'

'Let me finish. I've used you because I've needed you. And now Stefan, it's the same story with him. He needs you too.'

'Maybe I like being needed.'

He did, she saw that he did. It wasn't fair and it wasn't enough. For any of them. She took in a hesitant breath as Neil's eyes searched hers, waiting. 'Remember when Stefan climbed that tree on the common and I was so vexed with you?'

The room was suddenly quiet, the insistent tick of Mum's grandfather clock the only sound.

'I remember.' Ice shifted and swirled in Scotch and water.

'You said then you were tired of waiting, that you'd never ask me again.'

'I know.' He was very still.

'So I'm asking *you*. Do you still want us?' She knew the

answer – with Neil she'd always known, but the wonder that filled his eyes, *that* she hadn't quite expected. Nor the sudden caution that followed it. And he didn't touch her, not yet.

'Lallie, are you sure? Because if you're not, if you changed your mind later I don't think I could stand it. If it's only because you're missing Joe –'

'I'll always miss Daddy, but it's not that. Maybe I'm tired of waiting, too.'

'And if Jan came back ...'

'He won't.' The words came out very sure and firm. She could face them now, accept them. 'He won't ever come back.'

'Because he can't or because –'

He was too kind to finish it so she said it for him. 'Can't or won't, the lawyer says it makes no difference. The papers have been drawn up for ages – I've just been too afraid to take the final step.'

'And now you're not?' Very gentle, Neil's voice – but firm, probing, still cautious.

'No. I want to be done with it all, the waiting ... I want to start living again. With you. Married, settled ...'

He touched her cheek, tilted her chin to search her face. 'I can't seem to take it in, love ... you and Stefan –'

'I want him to keep his name, Neil, I do want that.'

She wasn't sure why she insisted on it, hadn't planned to, hadn't thought it through. 'Maybe it's because he's so much like Jan. Do you mind very much? Because if –'

Then he held her, stroked her hair. 'I don't mind anything if I've got you and the boy – what difference does his name make? I couldn't love him any more than I already do ... oh, Lall, it's a miracle. I can't believe it –'

She felt his hands tremble in her hair, pulled his face down to hers, touched his warm, disbelieving lips with her fingertips. 'Believe it,' she said. 'It's true.'

Kissing him, leaning into the circle of his arms, she felt she could lean there forever. The nightmare was over.

'When?' he whispered against her mouth.

'Soon. Very soon, darling.'

It wasn't until next morning, waking to winter sunshine and a new future, that she realized they'd never once used the word 'love'. There'd been no need. Neil knew exactly where he stood and always had. She loved him, but not in the way she'd loved Jan – and judging by the way *that* turned out, perhaps it was no bad thing. But then Stefan came in, small fingers poking gently at her closed eyes.

'Are you waked yet, Mummy?'

'I am now,' she laughed, pulling him in beside her. 'I certainly am.' Hugging the thin, squirming little boy to her she knew that in one respect at least her marriage to Jan Kaliski had been a very good thing indeed.

'Will Uncle Neil be here to watch my riding lesson, d'you think?'

So she told him, very carefully and only just as much as he needed to know.

Blue eyes widened. 'He's going to live here? Right here with us? Every single day for ever and ever and ever …?'

'Yes darling, every single day.'

With Neil Armott, she could say that and mean it. With Neil Armott, the child could depend on it. They both could.

CHAPTER FORTY-TWO

At the port the main problem was not, as he'd expected, the lack of documents and money, though God knew he had none of the first and barely enough of the second – only as many zlotys as Uncle Tadeusz could dig out from behind the root cellar, buried, of course, in a jar. A million times over he wished he'd acted on Joe Wainwright's tip from WWI, but he had not. His leather belt was only that, hardly a commodity worthy of barter.

Food was the greatest need, enough to sustain him until he should somehow take ship. As a legal resident (albeit with a criminal record) he had food coupons, but they were issued in Zakopane and stamped as such. Travellers from another town were required to register with the police. He had not and would not. *Dare not. They keep lists, Janek. They* – and possibly Emil Bura – would know he was at the port, would know why. Better to go hungry. For months he slept in railway sidings, took shelter in disused railway cars, fed off raw carrots and potatoes pilfered from sacks of cargo. He was not alone. There was a desperate little underground in the port area, all looking, like himself, for a way out, but most of them spoke only Polish and their chances were slim compared to his – if ever the right ship dropped anchor. His first opportunity came with the captain of a Finnish vessel headed for Helsinki, but their first stop was Riga, '– no way to hide you at Riga, so sorry. They check very fine, very fine indeed.'

He avoided the dockside bars. According to the underground they were crawling with agents. Instead he haunted the streets, watching for foreign faces rather than foreign uniforms. Uniforms were too conspicuous – *all* uniforms.

By the time he met the Swede, Sven, he'd have sold his soul for a bath, and for a hot meal he'd have thrown his body into the bargain too, not that his body would be an inducement – he doubted he weighed much above 140 lbs now.

'You not look so strong,' the Swede said. 'I need muscle.'

'I can do any work you give me after a few decent meals.' And showers, rasped his flaking skin. Hot, with real soap.

'Where are you going?'

'Manchester.'

'*England?*'

'*Ja.*'

The answer was a blur, a thunderous roar in his brain. Relief and physical weakness made him dizzy. *Don't fall, don't fall down, if you fall down they won't take you* ...

For two days they kept him hidden in the hold, the slosh of bilge water and the pattering of rats for company. But the days were bearable. Each hour brought him closer to Lallie. She was a mother now. Had it changed her much? Would she be bitter? Of course – a young woman to lose so many years, what else must he expect? He would make it up to her somehow ... but the darkness and the steady throb of the engines came laden with doubts too. *Had she waited? Had she waited?* Not like

Roman to be evasive, but he *had* been – and embarrassed. If she'd married Neil, surely he'd have said so. Even supposing she had not, would she still want a husband who'd been so long away, with no word? He'd know soon enough. When she saw his face she wouldn't be able to hide what she felt, not Lallie, and not in the first moment.

The second day, when it was safe, they brought him topside, fed him scrambled eggs and a delectable fish stew with lemon slices floating in it; plum tart and coffee and a bar of Swiss chocolate for dessert. Then the promised shower as hot as he could wish, strong soap and rough, clean towels. After that work, six good weeks of work, tiring but healthy, the sea sluicing away the bitterness of years. He felt fit again, his muscles hard and flexible, his skin brown from sun and wind, his beard and hair long but clean and well brushed. He looked civilized now, Sven said. 'But not like Englishman, yes?' The crew were friendly and the weeks flew by. At night, alone in his bed, his soul was still afraid. He still felt like a fugitive, and perhaps now he always would.

In the years he'd been away Sheffield had undergone a transformation. The shattered old shops from the High Street were rebuilt, their wide new windows filled with goods. Cheerful housewives struggled with shopping bags full to bursting as they darted into coffee shops for elevenses. It was a different world, Lallie's world, a peacetime city without a trace of the war left. The thought of taking her from this to the depressing tedium of life in Poland was preposterous ... but Mamunia, how could he abandon her now?

With something very close to dread he stepped down from the bus into the Wainwright suburb, its redbrick and greystone houses solid and well kept. The bus conductress gave him a long look as the bus pulled away, and he remembered Sven. 'You not look like Englishman, yes?'

The house on Eccles Place was beautiful under a late spring sky, its grounds immaculate, ablaze with tulips and iris, the cherry trees dripping spent blossoms onto the grass. His heart beat faster at the sight of a red tricycle by the back steps and the

Shetland pony in an adjoining field. So they lived here, with Joe! Which meant she wasn't maried to Neil unless – but then, Neil would be perfectly happy to live under Joe Wainwright's roof. They'd all fit together like – like a family. Lallie and Neil and Joe. And the boy.

It took him some moments to gather courage, to lift the brass doorknocker. Don't let it be Joe who answers, the thought of facing Joe, after all this time ... But no one answered. The house was quiet, not even a dog barking.

He walked around to the back door (tradesman's entrance, Joe had rather grandly called it), read the note to Jones the Milk that lay discarded by today's delivery on the porch. Tears gathered in his throat at the sight of Lallie's round, still slightly childish handwriting.

3 pints milk, a dozen eggs – and wish me luck, Jones, we're off to Fannington Dog Show. If Bootsie's around be a lamb and pour her the top off the milk, will you? She's been off her food since the last litter. Thanks – Lall.

He smiled, remembering all her little notes. To the butcher: 'Mrs H wants liver tomorrow, but says you haven't got any, bring chops instead, will you? Liver, ugh!' To the baker: 'A *crusty* white, Mr Flitch, you know how Daddy is ...' You write to them as if they're *friends*, he said once. *But they are*, she'd answered, surprised.

The milk bottle caps were intact so apparently Bootsie hadn't been around. She was now, rubbing her matronly sides against Jan's ankle and weaving figure eights about his feet. In a dream he poured the rich top of the milk into the china saucer and watched her lap. When he left she'd been a skittish kitten. She was now sleek and fat, looked anything but 'off her food'. She finished the milk and looked up expectantly; he obliged, feeling himself slip helplessly back into the past. How many mornings he'd poured milk for this same cat into this same bone-white saucer! He heard Lallie's voice from a long time ago, a breathy little catch in it. 'Mum *did* love that tea-service so, she said it brought summer in the whole year.' He dipped his finger in the milk and touched the painted blue forget-me-nots under its bland surface. Lallie …

But could anything have brought back the passage of time so forcefully as the kennels? Jolly's name had been painted out, as had Silky's before him. Except for Suka the names on the pens were all new to him. Ivan … Salome … Farah … Sharif … Across the street Hodgson's old farmhouse was a picturesque ruin; in the lane the ominous bright yellow of a bulldozer.

Nothing stands still, nothing …

The thought was a troubling one, and he hurried to the bus-stop, trying to remember the way to Fannington Park. The bus was a long time coming, then it crept around the curves, inched up the hills like a diesel-breathing snail. He wanted to get out and push, in a fever now that he'd arrive too late to see her – them – Lallie and the son she'd named for Tatuś.

The park in spring was England at its loveliest. Ducks preened on the pond; daisies starred the lush green of the grass; trees wore their newest, tenderest green. Couples, families, strolled the redbrick walkways, laughing and chatting to each other and to their dogs (of which there were many) and to any passing stranger. But not to Jan, for he kept his head averted, reluctant to enter again into the paradise he'd so often, in that last miserable year here, despised. Again Lallie's voice, singing slightly off key as she scrubbed the kitchen floor at Hempton. 'This demi-paradise, this other Eden.' He'd told her she sounded like a schoolgirl and she'd been quite offended. 'I *learned* it in school, silly! Besides, it's perfectly true.' It had taken marriage to Jan Kaliski, Pole, to show her the other side of Eden, the slobbering Maurice and the poverty of dirty backstreets.

The Fannington Dog Show was in full swing in a far corner of the park. She was there. Somewhere in that milling crowd was his wife – if –

His steps slowed as he approached the stands to hover well back on the fringes of the crowd. Heavily bearded, coat collar up against the breeze and the eyes about him, he was not afraid of being recognized. Around him all was quiet, the spectators almost ridiculously British in their deference and admiration for the spirited, highly-bred dogs that circled the ring one by one, to be led to the judge's stand by their handlers. The dogs being judged were setters but in a far corner of the ring under a clump of willows he could see the needle-noses and plumed tails of Afghans, a dozen or so sheltered from any stray breeze that might ruffle the pampered silk of their coats. A sudden, inexplicable rage shook him. He thought of the prison to which Bura had condemned him, not a bath or a decent scrap of food, and here were dogs treated like princes. Was it the new Poland that was crazy? Or was it this place, smug on its island, blind and deaf to the real world? Myopic in its happy ignorance ...

There was movement near the Afghans, and from a hundred yards away he searched for faces of the handlers, but all were hidden in the new green of the willows.

For a moment an official with ribboned badge blocked his view. It was only as he leaned to look past him that he saw who it was. Neil Armott. But of course Neil would be here, he should have known. Helping with the show, naturally. Being Neil.

Beyond a few extra pounds about his middle he hadn't changed at all. The same pleasant, slightly florid face, the good-natured smile as he directed the handler of a boisterous standard poodle to the registration tent, an elderly woman in tweeds and a hideous stalking cap to the refreshment tent. Just looking at him across the busy show ring you knew Neil Armott was that rare being, a happy man. Contentment radiated from him like spokes from a hub.

As Jan watched, Neil turned in his direction, swept the crowd with a glance that did not pause on Jan. Indeed, it was soon obvious that his eyes searched a much lower level. Then he smiled, waved a clip-board at a slim little boy with silvery hair and very blue eyes, dressed in what was almost the uniform of well-to-do male children from Land's End to John o' Groats. A coat of covert cloth, beige, a wool as fine and smooth as silk, and just short enough to show the bottom half-inch of a pair of short red trews. Dazzling white ankle socks were encased in stout leather shoes with fringed flaps on the front.

The child, peering up into the muzzle of a benign St Bernard, failed to see the waving clip-board.

'Stefan! Stefan!' Neil called.

Mój synku, mój synku …

The words roared in his head, perfect echo of Mamunia opening bright-monkey eyes to the same agonizing joy. The need to run, to gather up his son almost overcame him. The effort to still the impulse left him trembling. First talk with Lallie, find out what the boy knew.

'*Stefan!*' Neil called again, and the child grinned, scratched the St Bernard's chin, and darted off to Neil, wrapping his arm around Neil's solid leg. Jan saw Neil's hand reach down and brush gently at the boy's pale hair as they conversed gravely for a moment or two. Neil reached into his pocket and produced a coin. The boy scampered off and disappeared into the refreshment tent.

Without even knowing what he intended to do Jan followed him, watched him line up at the counter, accept a glass of lemonade, carry it to a long trestle table and insert a straw carefully into the glass. He struggled out of his coat and seated himself. Only then did he take a first, lingering sip.

'The lemonade is good?' Jan stood over him, his own lemonade in evidence. 'May I sit here?'

Opposite him a child's face, slightly narrow, the same face he'd seen in a mirror on Morska Street twenty, thirty years ago. The eyes were very clear, the light bright blue of innocence. The mouth straight. There was intelligence there, and a curious dignity. Not a child one would offer to help to the bathroom, or at table. He took another sip, then licked his lip and pronounced judgment.

'It's a bit sour but I like it. Mrs Cotton makes hers too sweet.'

'Mrs Cotton?'

Blue eyes opened wide, astonished at Jan's ignorance. 'Cotton Primary School of course! Mrs Cotton's my teacher.' He leaned forward and Jan caught the clean-nursery scent of his skin, Lallie's shampoo in his hair. 'Mrs Cotton's got a hair growing out of her chin,' he whispered. 'A black one, this long.' Small hands spread to indicate prodigious length.

'Really that long?' Jan asked, aching. What could he say that would keep this child within reach? 'You don't like her, your teacher?'

410

'Oh, well, I *like* her –' the emphasis was pure Lallie 'but she keeps on calling me Stephen, and it's not right. Gramps called me Stephen but he was my Gramps so it was all right.'

'Your grandfather?'

A shadow flitted across the pink and gold, rather narrow face. 'He died and went up there. But I *wish* Mrs Cotton would call me my proper name. It's only fair.'

'Is it?'

'Daddy Neil says people should call me just what I want them to –'

Children said odd things, didn't they. He didn't mean it the way it sounded. 'Your *daddy* says that?'

He thought for a moment. 'My *one* daddy says that. I've got two, you know,' he said with some pride. 'Nobody at school has two excepting me. Robbie West has none at all – but he's got four uncles. I don't have an uncle now.'

Jan asked about the other daddy. Was he here?

A frown creased the little boy's forehead. 'I don't *think* so … He *was* here but I don't think he's here now, ackshully. He had to go away somewhere.' He guzzled off the last of his lemonade and eyed Jan's glass, still not touched.

Jan forced a smile. 'Do you want it? I'm not thirsty.'

Stefan considered his own empty glass, then Jan's full one. Salivating slightly, he shook his head. Apparently chatting with a stranger was one thing; accepting refreshment was something else. 'No thank you. Mummy says –'

Jan held his breath. 'Your mother is here?'

Again the blue, slightly pitying glance. 'Of course! She's showing Golden Girl and silly old Ivan. Daddy Neil says she can win two events if Ivan behaves. Ivan lollops. I'm not supposed to hug him because he doesn't know his own strength, but sometimes I do – if just Daddy Neil's there.' He scrubbed at his mouth with a handkerchief.

In a dream Jan held out the beige covert-cloth coat as the boy shrugged himself into it and stood, apparently undecided, as if not sure how to take his leave. Then he smiled politely and ducked through the tent flap.

Jan, looking after him, could still feel the fine fabric of the coat and its heavy red lining satiny against the pads of his

411

fingers. *Once there were tailors, Janek ... woollens and silks to the ceiling. And now not a needle – and you thought to bring foreigners to this?* And the boy walking away, secure in his own little world ... and why not? His particular little world *was* secure, safe as the Bank of England – as Joe used to say. Joe's safety had been built on such tenets. And yours? He asked himself. What is your safety built on? In Poland it was built on Mamunia and food coupons, on staying off as many lists as humanly possible. And here? On what would you build safety here? Teaching English to the English? Manhandling ingots in the foundry, or promotions at Neil Armott's pleasure? But there's still South America! his scrabbling mind reminded him, knowing all the time it was far too late for that, probably always had been.

He let himself be absorbed by the crowd and the applause for Jolly's Golden Girl just being announced.

Owned and handled by Kendal Armott. *Kendal?* Lallie! Lallie *Kaliski*! his mind screamed. *Not Armott! But you knew ... you knew before you came. I couldn't know how it would hurt ...*

A honey-coloured descendant of the first Jolly was led into the ring.

By Lallie.

Her stride clean and straight, hair still a dark cloud around a flower face; her whole bearing had that indefinable assurance born of utter financial security, a fine home in the country, the best in cars, shoes like doeskin on long, slender feet. A pale green blouse was tucked into slim, perfectly cut slacks. In her way she was as elegant and patrician as the Afghan now straining at the leash. They both belonged in this world, seemed entitled to affluence by divine right – if you didn't know the right had been purchased by Joe Wainwright's sweat. Hard currency indeed.

He tried to remember her softness, her vulnerability, the sweet breasts he knew were nestled under the green silk, but the years of his own privation got in the way.

He tried to picture her with an empty shopping basket, wedged between the worn, dispirited women in a Warsaw queue. His imagination – *no* imagination – could stretch so far. Or could be so cruel.

And the boy. He remembered the bewildered children in

412

Poland, to whom an orange or a banana was the stuff of dreams … Children in one old sweater over another over another, because enough layers, even if threadbare, brought some kind of warmth.

The judges made a signal for Lallie to approach the stand, and he was pulled back to Fannington Park, to the lush green and the solid security of a people who could afford to indulge in the frivolity of such things as dog shows.

And there was his Lallie walking to the stand, at last facing in his direction.

Her face …

Now at last he saw the change. The features were the same, the colouring as pink and white and fresh as it had always been, the eyes as large and grey – but there was a bruised look in them now, a questioning, as if she wasn't *quite* sure … and the gaiety was gone, her expression subtly altered, as if some artist had stripped off a vibrant rose pink and substituted a pastel instead.

You, he thought. You are the artist.

The judges motioned her to bring the dog closer, walk it again to demonstrate gait.

She paused for a moment, grey eyes searching the crowd. Jan held his breath – but she'd found what she was looking for. Neil and Stefan, standing at the rail.

They each gave her a nod of quiet encouragement and to Jan, watching, it was as if the boy and the man had reached across the show ring and touched her hand.

He turned, walking quickly away, finally finding a deserted bench far from the applause of the ring. Even in the deep pool of his misery the tears that had been dammed up for years were slow to start. He felt them gather, hot and painful, behind his eyes. The beautiful woman and her beautiful child – his and yet not his. And Neil, who'd been good and patient and steadfast – and now had it all.

How could he approach them now, shatter their world, rip open old wounds, bruise again Lallie's already too-bruised spirit? And to what end? What could he offer them to compare with what they had? In England nothing. In Poland queues for bread, waiting-lists for housing, armed police on every corner.

413

But there was Mamunia, locked in her wheelchair, her Poland, her past ... Bitter laughter turned to sobs, to tears scalding his cheeks. So much striving. For nothing, nothing.

He never remembered getting to the docks, the bus and the train and the long walk through dark dockside streets.

When he came to himself he was staring into the window of a little shop and knew there was something important he still must do. Inside, a man and a woman closing up for the night, covering a wheel of cheese with muslin, locking cases of gimcrack jewellery and cigarette lighters. The shop bell rang as he pushed open the door.

'You sell needles?'

'Sixpence a packet. How many?'

'All. Give me all.'

He stuffed them into his pocket next to Lallie's note to Jones the Milk. The woman looked at him strangely as he counted money into her palm through a stinging mist of tears.

Stumbling out into the night he heard her speak.

'Foreigners!' she said. 'There's no understandin' 'em, is there?'

BOOK III

CHAPTER FORTY-THREE

She was happy with Neil, happier than she'd been in a long, long time.

The house had been completely redecorated after the wedding and Mum and Daddy's old room had become hers and Neil's. The room she'd shared with Jan was now Stefan's. It had been Neil's suggestion and she'd been deeply grateful. She didn't think she could have borne, in the beginning, to share the same bed she'd slept in and loved in with Jan.

Neil was so different. Adoring, gentle – even reverent, as if just to cup her breast in his large hand was a privilege so rare, so precious, he was almost speechless with awe. After the momentary awkwardness of friendship blending subtly into the most secret intimacies of lovemaking she found sex with Neil to be a shatteringly earthy experience. Such was his gratitude at her every caress that she found it natural to guide him – so if there were no Catherine wheels spinning crazily into the night, no skyrockets surprising her with starbursts of colour, there was diligence, there was certainty.

Afterwards, in the utter security of his arms, she always knew exactly what he was thinking. That he was the happiest man alive, that surely no one was so blessed as he, with the wife he'd always wanted and the child he loved as much as he'd love his own.

She'd never known what Jan was thinking unless he told her and even then there was that strange centre of reserve that had to do with things she didn't understand – his mother, his country, the crumbling mountain at Castleton. There'd been the sparkling moments and oh! how they'd shone, when just a look from his blue eyes turned her to water, lovely sensuous times when she seemed to exist only for him and by his will, when she'd have gone anywhere, done anything just to stay in his arms and his eyes. But there'd also been the dark moments when she'd feel him next to her but not *with* her, inside her but not *one* with her, other forces tearing at him, pulling him, his loyalties cut into so many parts she'd never been quite sure if she had the lion's share or the leftovers.

With Neil she was sure. To him she was a goddess. His adoration salved her spirit just as surely as his lips stirred desires she'd long suppressed. She needed it all, absorbed every secret glance, responded to every touch of his hands with a hunger that surprised them both.

'I never dreamed you'd be so passionate,' he said over and over again. 'Are you ready, are you sure you're ready?'

'Yes, oh yes!' as his fingers touched secret springs that left her quivering on some moist, breathtaking hilltop. '*Please!*'

'I think I'm in heaven,' he'd say afterwards. 'You're a miracle'.

To Jan she'd been a woman.

To her, he'd been a prince.

Neil was a man, extraordinary in many respects but comfortingly matter-of-fact about the daily routine of running a house. If he wanted them to take in an early movie the very night Mrs Hodgson planned one of her more ambitious dinners he would happily put off the movie for another day. Jan had never understood her need to cater to Daddy and Mrs H as well as just themselves, and she'd racked her brains to compensate for spur-of-the-moment jaunts that nevertheless caused inconvenience, to say nothing of hurt feelings. With Neil there was never a conflict. No longer was she the knot in the household string.

Secure now in the cloistered circle of Neil and Stefan and Mrs Hodgson, confident again in the routines of the leisured, her days threaded through with her beautiful Afghans and their progeny, Lallie Armott was a contented woman. In time she grew to think of Jan with love and not torment, with acceptance and not the bewildered hurt that had earlier tainted her memories of him. Now it was as if their love had been a dream, something that happened a very long time ago to two people breathlessly young and immature.

Real life was Neil, clear and steadfast as Martinswood stream – but mostly life was Stefan.

Equipped with Jan's brooding, intense nature and under Neil's gentle influence Stefan was becoming an extraordinary, complicated child, part prodigy and part puzzle. She worried about him. They no longer had to read to him. He was eight now and could read very well for himself; he absorbed books as if he were blotting paper, with a fervour that seemed almost unnatural to her. Was he going to turn into one of those pale children she sometimes saw at the library, peering through their specs into one heavy tome after another? She tried to temper his enthusiasm and failed. After she forbade books at the breakfast table she'd see his eye running furtively across the fine print of cereal boxes and sauce bottles, his mouth silently trying out the syllables until he couldn't hold the sound in any longer.

'Tamarind, tamarind, tamarind,' he'd chant, as if the word had appeared like magic to his mind. 'What's a tamarind?'

'I don't know,' said Lallie, who didn't. 'No, you may *not* leave the table to look it up!'

One midnight she was drawn by a faint glow which seemed to emanate from somewhere under his eiderdown; he'd fallen asleep with a flashlight and *White Fang*.

She was exasperated. It wasn't as if he did all that well in school. Oh, he did wonderfully in English but he was perilously close to failing science and geometry and was barely scraping through arithmetic.

'What's to be done with him?' she cried to Neil. 'He's going to grow up top-heavy if he goes on like this – and now he's pestering the school to let him take French and Latin!'

Neil set aside his glasses and his paper. 'I'd let him find his own way, love –'

'If he fails at school he won't have any way *to* find … Daddy always swore he'd ruin his eyes with all that reading, even then.'

Neil laughed. 'The only things Joe ever wanted to read were the morning papers and the foundry balance sheet so I don't think *that's* pertinent.'

In the end they struck a bargain. When Stefan made passing grades on everything else they'd get him a language tutor a couple of afternoons a week. Within two months they were scratching around for a tutor and in no time at all they were hearing him read Latin from a primer.

'Remarkable aptitude,' the tutor murmured, pocketing his cheque.

In every other respect he was simply a little boy with a little boy's trials and hobbies. From the ceiling of his room hung a giant model of a Wellington that Neil had helped him make.

'My father flew a bomber exactly like that,' he told visiting friends with pride as Lallie left the room. To Stefan, Neil was still 'Daddy Neil' but Jan was always 'my father'. And she *hated* the plane, hated the black bulk that seemed always about to crash down on her as she dusted and vacuumed, the weight of old anxieties heavy on her shoulders. It wasn't that she discouraged his questions about Jan – they'd decided early on, she and Neil, to tell him the plain facts whenever he asked for them – but he asked very often and sometimes in excrutiating detail.

'Does he have a funny accent like Mr Ryba or does he talk like us?'

'More like us,' she said, pretending not to notice that he invariably spoke of Jan in the present, as if he might one day walk in and surprise them.

'Was my grandmother *very* sick, d'you suppose?'

'I don't know …'

'You're *sure* he speaks French and German and Russian and –'

'I supposed he must …' As time passed, she was no longer sure of anything that concerned Jan …

Sometimes when Neil Armott looked at his wife and Jan Kaliski's son he had to rub a hand across his eyes. That he now shared their lives more intimately than he could ever have imagined seemed so unreal to him that he constantly sought to remind himself – and others – of his changed status.

Photographs of them stood on his desk and their names were forever on his tongue. To his mother or to the staid face of Miss Fitch (who'd been Joe's secretary and was now his) he scarcely let a day go by without sprinkling the names of Lallie and Stefan into the most unlikely of conversations. It amused him to catch himself doing it but it didn't make him stop. Opening the door of Joe Wainwright's old house to find Lallie and Stefan waiting for him was to walk into an Aladdin's cave of riches. Each evening he felt like a man who'd won the sweepstakes without ever having bought a ticket.

The loss of Joe, which could have devastated all of them, became an additional bond. His name came up often, quite naturally, in the house which he'd built and the family he'd nurtured. When Stefan came home with another award for languages Lallie's automatic reaction was: 'Whatever would Daddy say?' When Lallie's best dog took a ribbon at Cruft's their shared exclamation was: 'Joe would be so *proud*!' To Neil, Joe seemed never to have quite left. His personality was still in the house, kept alive by a hundred little traditions Joe had begun and which Neil continued. All except Backen-thorpe.

The first Christmas after Joe died, Lallie had taken Stefan alone. 'You don't mind?' she said. 'It's just that we always did it together, you know, and …' He hadn't minded – well, not much – and when they came home there was a bright fire waiting, and no questions.

Jan Kaliski's name was raised less often, and seldom by Neil. When thoughts of Jan came to him he chased them away with a light touch to Stefan's shoulder or a kiss to Lallie's rose and ivory cheek. In the lying eye of his mind, Jan Kaliski (because he'd disappeared at twenty-seven) never aged. And if the memory of Jan was still blond and blue and forever young to *him*, Neil, how much more so must it be to Lallie, who had loved him? Neil was not, he thought, a fearful man, but for many years something in him cringed at the sight of tall blond young men on a crowded street. At such times he knew without question that were Jan Kaliski to come back into their lives, his own would be blown irrevocably apart.

421

CHAPTER FORTY-FOUR

Poland was still warm, but already the first flocks of swallows were flying south under the hot yellow sky. Storks in their wagon-wheel nests rattled restive wings on farmhouse roofs; by the time he reached Zakopane the storks were rising, gathering for grave, parliamentary deliberations before turning south for North Africa over stubbled fields.

Everything was leaving – or withering, he thought. And I'm coming back to a new life. All his paths seemed to run counter to the prevailing trend, everything he'd ever done just enough out of step to guarantee failure.

The villa was shuttered, its garden overgrown with dandelion and nettles. In a panic he rushed to the convalescent home, sure that this errand was as fruitless as all the rest.

But no. She was there. And improving, they said. He found her in the wheelchair, outdoors. She was under a stand of dusty oaks watching goldfish circle a matted lilypond. In the moment before she saw him he found changes here, too.

Her skin had lost its unhealthy prison pallor. It was warm brown now, and her hair, though silver-white, seemed thicker, was dressed in a bun. The bones of her face were still prominent but the death's-head look was gone and in its place a waiting expression … but for what was she waiting? For death? For him?

Then she saw him. Dark eyes flickered, closed for a moment, then opened wide. She smiled a strange smile, joyful but sad and knowing all at once.

'So,' she said, 'you were too late, eh? You left it too long ... you waited ...'

'I didn't leave it! I got there as soon as I could – it was she who didn't wait long enough.'

She was quiet, dipping her head and plucking at her robe. Then she shrugged. 'Life, it's not so long for anybody, *prawda*?' She reached for his hand and put it to her cheek, warm from the sun. 'Your uncle's dead, *kochany*. A week after you left. Poor Tadeusz – I went to his funeral, they took me in the wheelchair –'

'Oh no ... Mamunia –'

She shrugged again. 'It's all right. I expected it. We should all be so lucky, eh? One minute chopping kindling and the next – poof!'

If he hadn't come back she'd have had nobody, nobody. He gave her the needles and she smiled.

'We're rich again, son. We have the villa – and now needles. I'm ready to move.'

'Will they let you go?'

'They'll not stop me.'

Within a month his life had taken on a routine again.

The villa was not the quiet haven he had expected. True, Mamunia remained confined to her chair, but if her legs were still her tongue was not. The rooms must be aired, the furniture must be polished, the chimneys cleaned before winter. He found work teaching at the local university and, in turn, needed to find someone to care for his mother during the day.

It was she who found the solution. After the others arrived Jan served as a mostly silent spectator to domestic dramas starring his mother and a supporting cast of three. After the chirping, hopeful voices of the young all day in class, he found the constant clash of wills at the villa oddly stimulating.

There was Eva Kapovnik, widow, with a surviving daughter in Łódź and a husband gone to smoke up an Auschwitz chimney.

There was Edek, bachelor, with his bumpy bald head and calcified joints teetering on the brink of senility. 'But he has a soft heart,' Mamunia said.

Panna Mira completed the troika. Spinster. Black eyes, black hair, black humour. Thin as a water reed. At forty, she had a finicky, antique face that seemed to have been drawn in charcoal.

Like Mamunia, all were alumni of the camps – and later of the convalescent home in town.

Jan was never quite sure how he acquired them. One week he and his mother were rattling around the empty villa like two peas in a drum; before he knew it the house was full and Eva, the widow, was doubling up with Mamunia.

Eva had used to visit the villa often – 'Just to check on the old lady, *rozumiesz*?' – and one rainy Wednesday had simply stayed. Mamunia shrugged. 'Let her loose in the kitchen, Janek, she's a cyclone.' Later, Jan had suggested that perhaps Eva might go to her daughter in Łódź. 'But who's to do for me when you're at work?' Mamunia demanded. 'Panna Mira should carry me up to my room, eh? She drops everything she touches. You want me to have a broken back to match my legs?'

Eva stayed.

Edek arrived soon after. Judged at last fit to leave the convalescent home, he had nowhere to go. Mamunia gnawed her lip and whispered with Eva and Panna Mira. 'So he'll come for a day or so, Janek, just until he finds a corner somewhere – have him cut up some wood while he's here.' He cut up all their wood and his swollen knuckles coaxed potatoes and cabbages and onions from the stubborn mountain earth as surely as his goodness buffered the frictions of the women.

Panna Mira – well, to this day she'd never quite moved all her belongings from the home to the villa, just a dress or two, her cringing body, her delusions and her bitterness. She stayed one year, two, then three, but whether she'd be here tomorrow was always in question. She distrusted men, took care never to be alone with Jan or even with Edek, whose 82nd birthday they'd celebrated last Easter. Panna Mira said she'd been raped. In Dachau, in Ravenbruck, in Treblinka –

'You couldn't have been in Treblinka,' Mamunia contradicted, 'or you wouldn't be here now. It was a finishing school.'

Eva cackled but Panna Mira plunged on regardless. 'And

not only by the guards,' she muttered, black eyes wide, spider fingers all atremble, rocking back and forth on a rickety kitchen chair, her arms clasped defensively over the hard little lumps that were her breasts.

Mamunia sighed and rattled her long amber beads against the cane handles of the wheelchair. 'Rape! How long could it take? Half an hour? What's half an hour to wreck your whole life?'

'But I'd kept myself pure,' Panna Mira wailed. 'And then to lose it all at thirty-five!'

'Will you mourn it forever, then?' Mamunia slapped her fingertips against the table once, very sharply. 'What were you saving it for, eh? People lost babies, husbands … if all you lost was your maidenhead, count yourself lucky.'

'I had nothing else!' Panna Mira twisted the ends of her cardigan into two frayed ropes. 'Nothing.'

'Then you didn't have much to lose,' Mamuni said.

Panna Mira let out a quivering sob and stumbled towards her refuge, the verandah, rocking herself into the dusk. The others took up the well-rehearsed litany of Panna Mira's problem. Jan shook his head and tried to tune them out, to wing back the seven hundred miles to Eccles Place and Fannington Park. It was impossible. They could have been dots on another planet. Instead he watched Panna Mira through the steam curling up from his glass of tea.

She was propped against the verandah rail in her usual praying-mantis pose, staring out towards the valley and the rich flat plains beyond. That she'd been physically raped, Jan thought, was questionable; that her entire existence had been violated was beyond doubt. Contemplation of the real past must be painful indeed for such as Panna Mira. Her parents once owned thousands of those fertile acres that ran in a green river to the north. Now they lay limed and buried under the rubble of their Warsaw home. The country estates, once the livelihood of tenant farmers, now lay gasping under the inept supervision of the State. Of all that had been, the land, the high-nosed family, the carriages, the elegant town houses in Warsaw and Paris, only Panna Mira remained – and she with not a shred of humour to carry her through.

Eva, the widow, sipped her tea through a fresh sugar-cube clenched firmly in her front teeth. 'It's not the same without lemon. Imagine, no lemon for the tea.' She nodded at Panna Mira's hostile backbone on the verandah. 'I'll bet she enjoyed it, her little tragedy.'

Mamunia shot her a warning look which took in Jan and Edek, who sat on the stone hearth warming his lumbago. 'Don't be coarse, Eva. Gentlemen are present.'

Eva sniffed. 'Such a virgin! Such a martyr! I still say she enjoyed it – if it ever happened.'

'Make up your mind. You can't have it both ways, *prawda*?'

Eva wiped a drizzle of tea from her chin. 'Who'd want her, a wilting waterweed like that?'

Edek stirred himself, poked the fire and blew into the embers, his white fringe of hair haloed against the flames. 'Poor Panna Mira. Poor, poor Panna Mira.'

Eva rattled her spoon against her glass. At fifty-eight she exuded more vigour from her broad thumbs than Panna Mira seemed to have in her whole, S-shaped body. 'You're too free with your sympathy, Edek. Just like my husband.' With a blunt forefinger she sketched a cross on the firm pillow of her bosom. 'His heart bled for everybody but me. Did I ever tell you? – When they took him to the crematorium he gave the guard his boots? His good boots, can you imagine, that Godlanski in Kalisz made for him the winter before the war – and he smiled at the guard! Yes, smiled at him! The boots were not enough, he had to smile too. Beautiful leather, they were, like gloves on your hand, *rozumiesz*? And he gives them away, just like that.' She snapped her fingers.

'They'd have got them anyway,' Mamunia reminded her.

Edek rubbed his hip to spread the warmth. 'A saint he must have been, a living saint.'

'He was an idiot.' Again Eva sucked at her tea through melting sugar. 'Giving, always giving, *prawda*? Buying his way.' She smiled suddenly, very tight and even. 'Well! So he bought himself a first-class ticket to the ovens, *tak*? I could use them now, those boots.'

'You'd only sell them,' Mamunia said sharply, folding her hands with an air of dismissal. 'It's time you put the bottles in

426

the beds, Eva, then you can help me go up.'

Mamunia persisted in speaking to Eva exactly the way she'd talked to the little live-in housemaids before the war. Eva never seemed to mind or even to notice. She lumbered to her feet now, filled five empty vodka bottles with hot water, wiped them dry on her apron and disappeared towards the bedrooms.

Waiting for the solid thump of her footsteps to recede, Mamunia sat up a little straighter in the wicker wheelchair, aligned her beads and dusted off her pre-war hostess smile.

'Poor Eva,' she said. 'We must be patient with her. She's a peasant and there's no help for it.'

'She works,' Edek put in gently. 'A fine woman, and wonderful with the wash. She darns my socks too – not that I've ever asked her to.'

'If she'd just mend the linens neater,' Mamunia fretted. 'You'd think she sewed with hammer and nails – and if there's one thing we've plenty of it's needles. But I won't hear a word against her – another glass of tea, Edek? Jan? A slice of *babka*? Eva made it but, well, it's not too bad.'

Jan drank his tea and absorbed the by-play of the household. In the beginning it irritated him, this unending push and pull between them all, but as the months, the years passed, he came to believe they needed it, just as they needed sweet Edek to absorb their little spites, arrows shot into the featherbed of his forbearance. They'd all lived through a lot and it was difficult to accept that great suffering had not bestowed great humanity; instead it seemed to have filed sharper points to their angers. And who was he to judge? They seldom mentioned the camps and never whined about them (except for the ritualistic fictions of Panna Mira) but their everyday chatter revealed their lives there better than any catalogue of complaints. Mamunia's thick gold wedding band had bought two slices of bread and a piece of sausage. Her fur coat was bartered for a wafer of scented soap and six small herrings. 'Warm from the smokehouse, Janek, and us with nothing but cabbage slop for months until even Eva – well, you could count her ribs. You'll never know how they tasted, those herrings. In my whole life I never enjoyed food like it. I shared them with Eva (I owed her, you see) and we hid behind the

427

bath-house and stuffed them down our throats before anybody could take them away from us. Animals, *nie?* The juice! It ran off our chins and we laughed and laughed until we almost choked –' They learned to elbow to the front of the line when the soup bucket came round. They learned to fake a semblance of health to be selected for the work parties, because all too often the alternative was the crematorium. 'And even when that butcher rearranged my legs I thought, well, at least I'll get food in the hospital. I didn't of course, the orderlies took it – they hadn't much either. Then Eva got herself assigned to the kitchen and she'd sneak bits of this and bits of that under her apron. I'd have died without her. Sometimes I wanted to but she's a nag, you know, so what could I do?'

After the first difficult year Jan found he enjoyed teaching. The faculty was mostly made up of older teachers but now and then someone close to his own age appeared and friendships were formed. One year there was an affair with a history teacher, Agata, all creamy skin and hair the colour of polished chestnuts. They shared evenings at the theatre, weekends at the river, similar tastes in music and books and an occasional summer week hiking in the mountains, sleeping under a black, pine-pointed sky. But then restive hints to make it permanent crept in, and he drew away. Every woman he met he compared with Lallie, and all suffered by the comparison. There was Basia, a local party official, very pretty when she stopped talking the party line, but she didn't stop often enough.

He avoided looking into the faces of young children, but could not avoid dating events according to his own private calendar. The faculty dining room caught fire the winter Stefan was eight. Gomulka came to power with promises of reform the year Stefan was nine. Edek died the summer Stefan would be ten.

The old man had not been well all winter, and as the days warmed he took to napping on the verandah, lying flat on his back with his hands neatly folded on his chest. 'Practising,' Mamunia said, at which Eva crossed herself and Panna Mira burst into tears. One midday in August Eva took him a glass of buttermilk, only to find that Edek had practised enough. Without his gentling influence the frictions between the women intensified. After one particularly bad Sunday Jan asked his mother why, since she seemed to take no pleasure in their company, she encouraged the two women to stay on.

'You're so impractical,' she said. 'Where would they go? Besides, without them we've too much room. The government would push strangers on us, you know the rule.' Only so many square feet of living space per person and not an inch more. 'And their pensions! Every zloty helps, you'll admit, *prawda*?'

'*Prawda*,' he agreed. With just his salary and Mamunia's pension they'd be in poor straits. With the added pensions of the boarders they all lived better than they could have alone. Panna Mira kept the household books and did the marketing and Jan could only guess what tonight's veal had cost on the black market. And were they all *that* miserable, *that* brutal? Yes, they were. But they were also capable of intense solicitudes.

There were the occasions of Panna Mira's fits, during which her narrow body jerked and writhed until Jan felt the bones must surely snap like dry twigs, and the only thing to do was force a washcloth between her teeth and wait for the spasm to end. When it was over she slept for hours as Mamunia and Eva were moved to action, planning this treat and that for the invalid like elderly children anticipating a party.

Eva would be sent to the farms on Blonski Avenue and ordered not to come back without eggs for Panna Mira's *kolacja*. '... and fresh, mind. Don't let them fob you off with last week's.'

Then Mamunia would fashion little flower 'pretties' for Panna Mira's place at table while Eva, elbow deep in flour, dimpled fists thumping at a ball of dough, rolled out Panna Mira's favourite apple cake. '... you know the poor fool hasn't a shred of meat on her bones.'

The invalid emerged, dazed and drained, to be greeted by a tidal wave of concern.

Had she had a good nap? Did she need a shawl for her shoulders? She must sit here, by the fire. Her room was a Siberia. And she *must* look at the lovely brown eggs Eva had bullied out of the pig man. It would always be mentioned in passing that Eva was doing some washing ... so if Panna Mira had anything she should throw it in the tub. They well knew (how could they not?) that during her fits Panna Mira invariably wet herself and was so ashamed she was known to bundle up the damp underwear and stuff it under her bed.

At such times Jan doubted the sanity of all of them, and certainly his wisdom in leaving the peace of Eccles Place to come to this. He'd been mad, he should have confronted them, that remote, shimmering trio from another world, made them see his need ... But the tortured path of his thought would lose itself in an underbrush of memories and regrets. He'd see children trudging through the Zakopane streets in winter, their faces pinched with cold, and think: It's not so bad after all, their lot. They still laugh, they play – but they had known nothing else, these children. They could no more imagine freedom from want than they could believe St Nicholas came every day. When he tried to see Stefan in their place his own imagination baulked. And Lallie, how could she have understood this house, the women in it? Sometimes he didn't understand them himself, even Mamunia – but he had to admire what he could not understand.

From time to time his mother urged him to marry. 'Find yourself a girl, *kochany* – I'm not going to be here forever. Then what? A lonely old man, such as Tadeusz was? Go to Warsaw, find somebody. Or even here ...'

Sometimes Eva's daughter, who worked in a shoe factory in Łódź, came to visit her mother. In her late twenties, she was short and round and might one day be like Eva, but now she was still pretty, a rose whose petals might soon fall but to whom the blush of youth still clung. She brought little items with her, things difficult to find in a mountain community like Zakopane. A can of syrupy orange juice from the Chinese comrades, shoelaces from Rumania, genuine paprika from their Hungarian brothers – and once, with a blush like a peony, she handed Jan an English magazine.

'How did you get it?' he said. 'They're forbidden –'

'From a student, he had relatives in London, somehow it slipped through.'

'It must have cost you – let me –'

She shook her head, 'My treat,' and blushed again. 'I keep meaning to tell you. Eva, well, I'm grateful you let her stay, otherwise I'd have to take her. She still has the dreams, I suppose?'

'Oh yes, but we're used to them.' He stretched a point to make her feel comfortable. Who could ever get used to Eva's dreams? But they came seldom.

'She's not an easy woman to live with, I know,' her daughter said.

Jan laughed. 'Neither is Mamunia.'

The kitchen was mellow with autumn. Outside the window oaks and beeches dripped gold, and the surrounding hills were on fire with yellow bracken and blood red maples.

In the sudden intimacy of the kitchen he noticed her eyes, the whites startlingly white, the browns deeply brown, moist as melting chocolate. Her eyes, and the lush gloss of the magazine's pages, stirred him. Under his gaze another wave of rose swept her cheeks, made him realize the magazine had been offered less in gratitude than in hope. Well, and why not? There'd been no one since Helena, a brief affair that had faded from his own neglect ...

Eva's daughter was reading him, leaning forward, her lips moist and parted. The slight motion ruffled her hair, releasing the smell of lye soap and a faint underlay of leather. He pictured her stitching shoes at her machine, pushing back her hair with fingers saturated in the oils of pigskin and cowhide. He looked at her eyes again, the benign brown of them, and could not now avoid the suggestion of bovine acceptance in their brown depths.

The moment passed. She seemed to sense his withdrawal and stepped back just as her mother wheeled Mamunia into the kitchen. The two older women seized the magazine, bickering over whose fingers should turn the glossy pages. The articles, in English, interested them not at all. It was the advertisements that held them. The cars – dear god, they were chariots! – the cameras, the watches, shirts so finely woven that cotton seemed to be silk, bottles of rum so golden they eclipsed the autumn pageant outside, shoes of the softest leather –

'Did I ever tell you,' Eva began, 'my husband gave away –'

'Many times,' Mamunia said. 'Look at the crystal! I had a set of goblets like that. Remember, Janek?'

After they'd gone to bed Jan took the magazine to the verandah, a candle flickering in a bottle beside him and the darkening mountains wrapped about his chair.

Page after page of luxury. Once he would have devoured the articles, the news, old as it was. Now, just like the women, he yearned for the riches strewn across the pages like jewels spilled from the pockets of a careless Midas. The bottomless lustre of a black Mercedes, the gold of a Patek-Phillipe against maroon velvet. Ice cubes bobbing and sparkling in a sea of Scotch. Everything shining. Men in fine serge, women in pastel silks. The idea that he had once lived in that world seemed a fantasy. The longer he was away the more dreamlike it had become. Surely he had noticed the pleasure of breaking the seal on a box of Swiss chocolate, the wrappers crackling under his fingers? If so, he could not now remember it. Impossible to believe he'd never noticed the smell of new linen, shirts with the pins still in them, squared and boxed and wrapped in tissue paper? The feathery touch of the cashmere scarf Lallie had given him that first Christmas? He remembered it all now, every luxury, could actually feel in his empty palm the heft of his silver lighter – the guard at the work-camp had taken it away. It was smooth and heavy and cold. Rich.

By contrast, the women on the pages were merely warm. And women were warm everywhere, no less here than there. It was just that their warmth was less and less important, a need to be satisfied as quickly as possible, with a minimum of entanglement.

Needs changed. When tomorrow's bread was as uncertain as next year's crop of wheat, when you couldn't be sure if an old woman's chair would roll even one more season without a new wheel (and where to find one?) well then, the difference between need and desire blurred to meaningless grey. When everything was out of reach, why reach?

He remembered his contempt for Joe Wainwright's avarice, his manic drive to amass. More orders, more steel on hand, more profit. How easy it had been to despise it all, with a full stomach and a warm bed and Lallie to come home to every night. Money grubbers! Nation of shopkeepers! How many times had he hurled the insults at Joe and felt himself puff up with virtue! The hatred that powered him!

And all the time Joe had been right. He'd provided for his own. And he'd won.

CHAPTER FORTY-FIVE

'You want to take *Polish*?' The dean's eyebrows rose.

'Yes.' Stefan spoke quietly, aware as always that he probably seemed very young to the old man opposite. 'It's logical, sir. I'm two years into Russian, which is similar –'

'Yes, but *Polish*! I mean, it's not exactly universal, is it, like French or Latin. You've got German too, but Polish … I mean, what *use* could it be to you?'

'If I get into the BBC foreign department it could be handy.'

'Oh, *them*! Anything's handy *there*!' The dean had the utmost reverence for languages, but very little for their practical use. 'What do your parents say about it?'

'They're agreeable if the department is.'

'It seems too much of a load –'

'I'd like to try, sir.' He tried to keep the pleading out of his voice. 'My father's Polish, you see.'

'Mr Armott? Surely not –'

'No, my *real* father. Neil's my guardian.'

'I see. Well, if they've no objections, I suppose I can arrange it.'

Neil would be pleased, he knew that. As for Mum … she might have some doubts, not that she'd ever say so. It was just that she tended to be a bit skittish when anything to do with her first husband came up. She *didn't* like talking about him no matter how off-hand she was at answering his questions.

It was an old ambition, this, to learn the language of his father, one born in a schoolyard skirmish the year he was twelve. A new boy had come to the grammar school. He was Bill Brunden, a redhead with a domed forehead roomy enough to house genius – but it did not. He saw Stefan's full name on a school list.

'What sort of name's that, then?' he asked the class at large. 'Stefan Kaliski Armott.'

Stefan stepped forward. 'It's *my* name.'

'Foreign, is it?'

'It's Polish.'

'Ah! Your mother was one of *them* then, eh?'

'One of what?'

'My dad says there were a lot of 'em in the war – you know, women that fancied foreigners. Fast pieces, they were –'

It was as far as he got. Stefan, who'd never hit anyone first, felt his fist rise with his anger, and Bill Brunden wasn't expecting it, not in the classroom, with a teacher just outside the door. When he scrambled up he had a split lip and a dribble of blood running off his chin. Stefan expected him to hit back but he didn't. He wiped the blood away and went back to his seat. The lesson was history, and Stefan didn't hear a word of it. His head was pounding with what the boy had said, and with the certain knowledge that it was not over. Stefan had never had a fight before, not a *real* one, and he was frightened. He kept remembering what Neil had told him: Don't fight unless you have to, but if you have to, keep coming. Never let them see you're scared, even if you are.

Bill Brunden was waiting for him behind the privet hedge after school.

'You hit me.'

'That's right.' He made his voice lower, but there was still the bulk of Bill Brunden's shoulders ... 'If you say anything like that again about my mother – or my father – I'll punch you again.'

'Is that a promise?'

'Yes.' *Never let them see you're scared*. But he was, he was.

'All right then, listen to this: Your mother's a whore and your father's a bleeding foreigner. How's that?'

Stefan didn't know what a whore was but he knew the implication. And 'bleeding foreigner' he'd heard before, but only in whispers, never to his face. He sighed and looked again at Bill Brunden's large fists. 'Right, then!' He hit out again and again at the truculent face, which bobbed and weaved and laughed at him. That's what saved him, the laughter. He forgot his fear and kept on coming. At the end of ten minutes he was bruised and bleeding and one of his teeth was loose, but Bill Brunden showed wear, too. They stopped because they were too tired to carry on, and there was no winner.

Neil wanted an explanation of the bruises and Stefan told him the truth. Neil didn't say much, just made sure he disinfected the cuts. 'Better not tell Lallie, all right?'

'Right.'

But that night Neil dug out his father's old log book and its final entry: BREMEN-MISSING, in red ink. They worked back through the book, all the raids of L for Lalka, and when he went to bed Stefan was fiercely glad he'd hit Bill Brunden. After that night he paid special attention to news items about Poland; he cajoled from his mother every detail of his father's last trip – what little she knew. And he spent many hours pondering the old silver cup that had held first his crayons, then pencils, now his pens. He was not sure exactly what made him decide, as he pummelled Bill Brunden's face, that he must sometime learn Polish, but the decision had been made – and now it would happen!

He reached the front steps and threw his coat onto the hall stand.

'Mother! They're letting me enroll! I start next month!'

She wasn't home. There was a note propped against the tea caddy: Gone shopping, darling. Mums.

Restless, filled with his news, he said hello to the dogs and then paced the front walk, a lanky seventeen whose arms always seemed just a fraction too long for his sleeves. A month seemed a long time to wait ... surely there must be Polish books in the house somewhere ... in the attic, that's where they'd be with all the old records and Gramps' golfclubs and dusty old trunks.

It was a treasure house up there! WWII records by the boxful, Gilbert and Sullivan cheek by jowl with Chopin, a group called the Inkspots and a whole dozen Vera Lynns.

435

There were unstrung tennis raquets and his first pair of roller skates, books by the carton, and huge wicker hampers of old clothes and curtains and baby blankets. The inevitable rocking horse and train set.

Lallie came home tired but happy. She *did* so love redecorating and the living room *needed* new curtains for next winter, and surely the chair arms were just a wee bit worn? She hummed as she draped colour swatches on the settee back, pinned more swatches to the grey satin curtains. Stepping back, she gauged the effect. Velvet or brocade this year? Velvet, she decided – but would that old-rose shade be just *too* much red with the burgundy carpet? She'd have asked Alice's opinion (Alice was the housemaid since Mrs H retired) but it was her day off – not that Alice would know, all she ever saw was Stefan, the silly girl. Often now she found herself echoing Daddy's wartime lament. Women made too much in the munition shops – except now it was the dress shops, the restaurants. Time was she could have found somebody *good* to come in, somebody like Mrs H with her deft hand at the stove and plenty of elbow-grease for the furniture. Now she had to be thankful for girls like Alice, who demanded a colour telly in her room and a month off in the summer and who could no more 'fettle' a room than she could boil an egg! All she was really good at was mascara and eyeshadow. And boys. Where *was* Stefan? His coat was in the hall –

The living room door opened slowly and she looked up. She felt the colour drain from her face. Her heart seemed to turn over, then race back twenty-eight years to that first Christmas, to Jan in airforce blue, POLAND on his shoulder and the hall light on his pale hair –

'*Stefan*! What *are* you doing in that uniform? I –'

'I was poking about in the attic looking for – Mother, are you all right?'

She sank down into the settee. 'For a minute I thought you were your father ...' She laughed shakily. 'It was silly of me.'

'I should think so! Why, he must be your age, at least.'

'At least,' she murmured, making herself breathe slowly. All these years, and still the sight of him – no, of Stefan, in *his* clothes ...

He paraded in front of the fire. 'What d'you think? Fits me pretty well, huh? D'you think I look spiffy?'

Spiffy? He looked wonderful, wonderful. 'You smell of mothballs – and the word was 'wizard' then, darling. You look *wizard*.' She *wished* he'd take it off, fold it back in its box where it belonged.

He grinned down at her, the devil in his blue eyes. 'Think it might charm Alice into going to the pictures with me?'

'Alice! I doubt she'd need charming with a uniform, dear. Neil's mother says she's an impudent baggage.'

He laughed at Alice, as she'd known he would. 'Just what Aunt Agnes *would* say.' He folded himself next to her on the settee and the uniform sleeve brushed her bare arm.

She shivered as he dragged a cardboard box onto his knees. 'What on earth have you *got* there?' she said, but she wasn't sure she wanted to know.

'All sorts of things. I'd no *idea* there was so much of my father's stuff up there. Look here! A compass, a prewar map of Poland before the borders changed – and there's this soft stuff in a bag ...'

It was her hair, a little darker then, with no grey in it. She'd cut it herself, in that dreadful flat in Attercliffe ...

The soft mass of it lay in her palm as it had lain in Jan's that day. 'A good reminder,' he'd said – of what he'd brought her to. And afterwards he'd made love to her, desperately and unlovingly, tried to bridge the frightening gap between wartime dreams and peacetime reality. How hard he'd tired to build that bridge all through the last, contentious year before he went to Poland – but how impossible the task. Oil and water ... And how much it hurt, still, to remember it.

'And books,' Stefan was saying. 'In Polish – they're just *exactly* what I need – the dean's letting me take Polish next term.'

'Well, but ... I know you mentioned it but I'd no *idea* you were serious –'

The news greeted Neil the instant he walked in.

437

'He's serious,' she said, an undercurrent in her voice he couldn't quite understand. 'He really means it, he's bound and determined …'

'It's just another language, love. I thought you'd be pleased. There's not many young men these days would care that much.'

'It's not that …'

'Then what?' She really was troubled! Her scent of lavender and lemon blossom reached out to him; he slipped an arm around her shoulders and held her. 'Sweetheart, what harm can it do?'

'I'm just afraid he may be getting … ideas. That maybe Jan's alive somewhere …'

He tilted her face and looked into the clouded grey of her eyes. How beautiful she was still! 'It's always been a possibility, we've known that.'

Her eyes filled. 'I just don't want him waiting and wondering the way I did … it's just too *cruel* –'

'He's a big lad now, love. He can handle things himself.'

'I know …'

He watched her as she made his tea. She had the same concentration she'd had as a girl, aware of each painted flower on each painted cup. Even now, when she was half preoccupied with something else, her long fingers brushed at violets and vines.

He realized again, as he did every day of his life, how very much he loved her and how lucky he was that Jan Kaliski had not come back.

CHAPTER FORTY-SIX

'*Up the chimney*! *Up the chimney*!'

Eva was having a nightmare. They were not quiet, her dreams. Into the peaceful night sounds of the villa – the creak

438

of settling timbers, the rustle and coo of the pigeons in the eaves, the rub of branch on branch in the plum trees – her midnight bellow rent the air.

As usual Jan sprang out of bed, rushed to Mamunia's room and snapped on the light. As usual, Eva's bed was empty, stripped of its feather quilt, while Mamunia, almost buried under Eva and her quilt, made shushing sounds at Jan before turning her attention to the shivering mountain that was Eva.

'Stop the noise, you great fool!' And to Jan: 'Isn't that the trouble with peasants? No control, none whatsoever.'

But her small hands were tender as they stroked Eva's meaty shoulder, as they patted the wide red face. To Jan, the scene always reminded him of Lallie one spring morning, beating off the attack of a brown sparrow who'd been trying, with little success, to feed an enormous cuckoo chick left in her nest. The sparrow, half the size of the chick, had a worm in her beak and was trying desperately to connect the worm with the ravenous maw of the cuckoo. The chick, its beak pointed to heaven, was well out of reach, blindly unaware as the sparrow made one ineffectual jump after another in her effort to inject nourishment into the interloper's gullet. 'Oh, that *idiotic* chick,' Lallie said. 'What *can* it expect with its head way up there!' She ran downstairs with a few bits of meat and her eyebrow tweezers. If the sparrow had been agitated before she went into a frenzy now, dashing at Lallie's head, flapping through the hawthorne bush and Lallie's dark hair as the tweezers deftly poked bits of raw steak into the cuckoo.

Just so did Jan's tiny mother now wave him away.

'Off! Off with you, Janek. Have we no privacy? Can't we even dream in peace.'

Peace was the *last* thing he would have called it, but he went back to bed as he always did, depressed at the knowledge that he could never help them, these women, nearly so well as they could help each other.

Next morning, while Eva made her clatter downstairs, he took up his mother's tea as usual before leaving for work.

'Eva,' he said. 'She was noisy again last night. You're sure she's not too much for you?'

'Eva? Too much?' She gazed her scorn into the pale rose

439

depths of the glass of tea, but Jan thought she looked tired all the same. 'Let me tell you something, *synku*. You don't approve of her, do you? You think she talks her husband down, *tak*? Well, he was a bigger idiot that even *she* thinks he was. He wouldn't have lasted a week at the camp without her. You had to be sharp. He was stupid. A dozen times he almost got both of them baked, let his mouth run away with him, called attention to them, *rozumiesz*? Laughing and toadying to the guards when the best thing to do was melt into the woodwork like the lice, eh?' She scratched at her arm – purely a reflex action, Eva kept the house surgery-clean and had enough energy left over to dig the garden and chop the wood.

'She laughs at him,' Jan said.

Mamunia shrugged. 'Crying is easy, *nie*? It's the Panna Miras who cry – and much good it does them. Eva did what she could *when* she could, but the men's camp was on the other side of the fence. We were at the window when we saw him in line for the ovens. I told her not to look but she wouldn't listen. She's stubborn – well, you know that. And afterwards, not a word out of her for weeks. I've never seen her cry when she's awake, but dreams, they're traitors, *prawda*?' She settled into the pillow, dark, bright-button eyes closed against the light. 'Tatuš used to say that – but you wouldn't remember ...' Her chest, thin under white linen, rose and fell in a slow, fluttering rhythm. Then her eyes flew open, looked to the window. 'It's late. Time you went to work, *nie*?'

It was, but he lingered, disturbed by her pallor and the unusually long speech. 'I've got time,' he said.

'Just remember, then. Eva, she earns her keep, and we'd be in a sorry mess without her. When I think of all those girls we had before the war, poor weakly things that couldn't find the kitchen without a roadmap, I thank God we're –' She stopped, a look of infinite surprise in her dark eyes. 'I'm not ... you're to –'

'Mamunia!'

But her eyes had closed and tea was spilling like pale blood on the pillowcase.

'*Mamunia!*'

The spark was gone, her tongue and her darting eyes finally still.

440

But it was morning. Night was the time to die ...

How long he'd lived with this fear – in the *stalag*; at Eccles Place; on the crumbling rim of Mam Tor; in the work-camp and every day since. Now it was here. The mountain had given up its own, this crippled old woman whose face had been adamantly set towards death because there was nothing left for her in life. Until her son came back into it, gave her a reason to order her household, her faithful Eva, her will. Her loving son, whose coming gave her years she would not otherwise have had and did not, in the beginning, want. But the cost of those years, the terrible, terrible price. Lallie. Stefan. Freedom.

All gone – and now Mamunia was gone too.

He felt a strange calm, looking down at her face on the stained pillow. Always pale, in death her skin had the cream, crinkle-paper look of Uncle Tadeusz's Oriental poppies which still flourished and multiplied behind the villa. But how young she looked, after all, with all the tensions smoothed away, younger by far than the day he'd found her at the convalescent home, her face and her spirit to the wall. He remembered the blaze of joy in her eyes then, and all the ascerbic, invigorating years since, the cutting lash of her tongue that never quite drew blood, not from him ... And all this time he'd thought the years half-wasted.

Stefan. Eighteen now, almost a man. If she could have known her grandson. She'd seldom mentioned him, and when Jan drew his name into conversations (as, in the beginning, he had often done), Mamunia would turn quiet for a long time, black eyes closed, thoughts turned inward. *But dreams, they were traitors, prawda?*

He buried her next to Uncle Tadeusz and sent the bereft Eva to her daughter for a few days with the promise that she could come back later, care for the villa. Panna Mira he sent back to the hospital to battle the avalanche of seizures Mamunia's death had triggered.

He was alone in the old house.

The nights were filled with ghosts, domestic and imported. Mamunia's amber beads dangled from the arm of the wheelchair. Lallie's note to the milkman in its oak frame was yellow with age, the wallpaper behind it a small, bright square in his faded room.

He was almost fifty, with no ties except to the past. Restrictions had eased over the years; he could go anywhere he wanted now, even to England. But as fast as the thought came it faded. Despite all the travel, all the languages Tatuš had drilled into him, he was as Polish as the earth around him. He thought of Kaz's cup, of all the blood they'd spilled to keep this land. And Lallie was middle-aged now. Would she even remember the foreigner who left her to follow an older trail, a man who could not, in the end, renounce the past and its obligations? Of course she would remember – with hurt, with bruised pride, and who could blame her? And Stefan? Surely he was a happy young man, wrapped around with security. What would he want with a father who'd simply 'gone away somewhere'? Was anything left of that golden little boy? Whatever loyalties he had, that son he'd seen but once belonged to his mother and the man who nurtured him, who divided his sorrows and doubled his joys.

When Eva came back to the villa Jan packed his clothes and set off for Warsaw and the translator's job he was offered regularly every year and had just as regularly turned down.

'I'll come back for vacations,' he told Eva at the staion. 'Just keep things ... you know, alive ...'

CHAPTER FORTY-SEVEN

No! It was really *too* bad of Stefan! She uprooted a dandelion with quite unnecessary force. They didn't see him nearly often enough now he was at the BBC – and here he was, proposing to spend his entire summer holiday in Europe, just when Neil had the Lake District cottage booked and all the plans had been made ... and Stefan had always been so *reliable* – surely he wasn't going to change on them now? Not at twenty-five …

'But you've been to Europe,' she protested. 'Lots of times –'

'Not *this* Europe.'

He sat tense in the garden chair, and she felt a strange dread catch at her heart. Surely not that old business of Poland again! She'd thought broadcasting in Polish through the Iron Curtain would satisfy him, would make him feel he was as close as he'd ever get … but they were allowing tourists these days, she knew that. Oh, she should have known …

'I was pottering about in the research files last week. I found something.' He stood up and began to pace the length of the spring flower bed, bright now with jonquil and tulip, humming with bees and the scent of hyacinth. Then he was standing over her, his shadow long on the cement path. 'I came across this translation.'

She stayed on her knees but stopped her weeding, staring instead into the speckled black heart of a scarlet tulip. 'Oh? What was it about?'

'It's not important, Mother. It was the translator's name that jumped out at me –'

No, not again. Another ghost rising …

'*Jan Kaliski*,' he went on in that tight, excited voice. 'Who else could it be?'

Black and scarlet blurred. 'There might be a thousand Kaliskis – maybe it's like Smith or Jones.'

'You know it's not.'

'It could be an old book –'

'I checked the date. It was published last year. I've got the address of the publishing house and everything.'

His voice faded off somewhere, lost in the flood of emotions rushing to engulf her. Jan Kaliski, translator. It wasn't *her* Jan, couldn't be, she wanted to believe that, oh how she wanted to … but Stefan's facts were getting in the way, shifting carefully built defences that had been twenty years in the making. Jan dead she could think of with love and regret; Jan dead had already been mourned and tucked away in that place where only the good memories were allowed in, never the bitter, the wounding, the humiliating. Jan Kaliski alive – well, he'd simply left her, hadn't he? Without a word or a letter … and the wounds she'd thought healed were opening again, stinging again. And this time Stefan was at risk too, open to the same hurt and rejection as she had been. Suppose he found his father, only to be turned away?

'Mother?' He was saying, 'are you listening?'

She sat back on her heels, his shadow long and blurred beside her, his blue eyes looking down at her, full of questions.

'Stefan ... I wish you wouldn't go. Neil's got our whole holiday planned –' She looked up. His face was rigid with determination.

'Neil won't mind. It's more than that, isn't it?'

She shook her head. 'I don't want you to be disappointed, darling, that's all ...' It was more than that, too.

Then he was on his knees beside her, gripping her shoulders. 'I want to *know*, Mother. *I've always wanted to know* ...'

So have I, but not if he's still alive, not if it means he didn't come back because he didn't want me ...

Neil saw the change in her as soon as he walked in. She stood in the middle of the sitting-room staring into an empty grate, and when he kissed the back of her neck there was no quick response, no smile for him.

'Hey, I'm home, love – or hadn't you noticed?'

She turned to him, her eyes too dark. Thunderheads were gathering in their grey depths. 'Oh Neil ...' Her voice quavered on the edge of hysteria, set warning bells to ringing.

'It's Stefan,' she whispered. 'He thinks he's got a line on his father. He's going to Poland –'

Poland.

For a moment he couldn't speak, couldn't think. The word hit him in the chest, stopping his breath, reverberating through every cell in his body. Poland ... Poland ... Safe as houses all these years, his world secure, warmed by this cherished woman ... *his woman* ... and now this. Now, when he'd put it all into the past. Now, when he'd stopped even wondering about Jan Kaliski, stopped worrying that he'd someday walk down the front path and claim his wife, his son. *My* wife! *My* son – or as good as. The Pole, back into his nightmares again. Fear turned to anger, and for the first time in his life he understood Joe's hatred of Jan Kaliski, understood it because he shared it. Lallie's eyes dark with hurt again, Stefan flirting with the same hazard.

'He's going to Poland,' she said again, 'Stefan's going –'

Rage filled him, overflowed into words that could have come from Joe Wainwright, never before from Neil Armott.

'The bloody young fool, what the hell's he thinking about? Poland! He wants his head looked at, he does. What the devil's he up to? He wants a talking-to, upsetting you –'

When Lallie didn't answer he went charging upstairs, burst into Stefan's room without so much as a knock on the door, loomed over him, snatched the travel-guide out of his hand.

'Do you know what you're doing to your mother, eh? Have you thought, you damned fool? Have you considered anybody but yourself –'

Stefan stumbled to his feet, looked at Neil on the same level, mouth set. 'I want to go,' he said quietly. 'I've wanted to for a long time. To find him, to ask him why ...'

'And when you get the answer, what then? How's your mother going to feel then? Answer me that!'

The eyes looking back at him were a man's eyes now, very blue and full of knowledge. 'Are you sure it's just mother you're worried about, Neil?'

That stopped him, cleared the red from his vision, brought Stefan back into focus, this Stefan he'd raised and loved, looking at him now with understanding and quiet persistence.

'Oh, lad ...'

Stefan nodded, put his hand to Neil's shoulder. 'I don't want to hurt you, but I'll never be satisfied until I know, will I?' Then he smiled, his hand tightened. 'You don't have to worry. Mother thinks the sun rises and sets in you. So do I. It's just ...'

Neil sighed. 'Aye. But God, I wish you didn't have to go.'

'I'll come back – and one way or another I'll know. I'll be satisfied. And nothing will have changed for us here, we'll go on as we always have.'

If it were that easy, that simple. The lad was smart enough, sensitive enough, but how could he know all the rough waters that had rolled under a bridge built before he was born?

And when he went back downstairs trouble waited for him

445

there, too. Lallie in the hall, anger in her eyes now instead of hurt, a flush to her cheeks.

'Why did you have to lay into him like that? What he wants – it's only natural, isn't it? To know his own father? Wouldn't you have been the same?'

He looked at her, this woman who was still, to him, the miracle of his life. 'Oh Lall, how can I tell … I *knew* my father, didn't I?'

And didn't like him very much. Maybe when Stefan heard Jan Kaliski's answers he wouldn't like *his* father, either. Which should have cheered him. But something in him, a deep love for this boy he'd raised to a man, made him hope it wouldn't be like that.

After a few awkward days during which Lallie and Neil avoided the subject of his trip whenever possible, a kind of waiting acceptance settled over them, and they gave him their blessing – or said they did, saw him off at the airport with waves and bright smiles that didn't quite fool him.

He knew they were worried, was sure their worry was unfounded. If Jan Kaliski, translator, turned out not to be his father, nothing was lost but a shred of hope. If he *was* … well then, he'd know. The puzzle that had nagged him all his life would be solved. Either the man was a rotter (in which case he was damned lucky to have been raised by Neil Armott instead), or he was a man with a past, with problems no one in England could possibly imagine. Remembering Jan Kaliski's airforce log-book with its neat, laconic entries, all Stefan could know for sure was that the man who'd made those entries was not a coward, was not irresponsible. Why then hadn't he come back? There was a reason, had to be. And he had to know it.

Poland.

He'd read about it, dreamed about it, sent his voice over the airwaves to it a hundred times and more, had thought he knew it. He was wrong.

Where were the dark old buildings and narrow streets? – all

446

the forlorn people he'd heard about?

Such had been his mental picture of Warsaw as he prepared his programme each week, trusting his words to penetrate borders and scramblers and official monitors.

The reality seemed quite different. The hotel was modern, indistinguishable from any new hotel anywhere in Europe. New streets were wide and busy with traffic; pavements were thick with shoppers; women in summer cottons carried full baskets and long loaves of rye bread; at corner kiosks flower-sellers hawked fresh-cut asters and potted geraniums; students overflowed the coffee shops with urgent talk and extravagant gestures.

True, there were multitudes of rules for the tourist and odd, unexpected shortages – where, for instant, could he find a Warsaw phone book? He'd hoped to locate his father's home address, meet him on his own ground rather than appear like a jack-in-the-box at his place of work. There was no phonebook in the room and none, apparently, in the hotel lobby. But it gave him an eerie thrill, just the same, to be asking for it in Polish, here in the city where his father had been born and now presumably lived.

The receptionist gave him a blank look, then a shrug.

'Telephone book?' she said. He might have been asking for the Hope diamond. At length she hauled on a chain. A tattered book appeared and was grudgingly offered – though still attached to the chain. The pages were linty with much thumbing, and the listing for Kaliski (if one existed) was missing, along with what seemed to be about half the book.

He approached the people at the publishing house with caution and in what he knew to be excellent Polish. Still they were cagey. Why did he wish to speak with Mr Kaliski? A *personal* matter? In that case they were sorry – it was not possible to disclose employees' names, *rozumiesz*?

'But I *know* my father works here! I just want to see him.'

Sudden smiles and flurries from the surrounding desks.

'*Pana ojciec?*'

'*Tak*,' he said, leaning across the desk.

Well! If Pan Kaliski was his *father* that was different, *nie?* He was away on vacation now – what a pity! Yes, now they looked closer *of course* he must be the son! Jan was up at his place in Zakopane for a few weeks. No, they didn't have the address but they knew who did! They gave him the address of Roman Kowalewski and assured him he couldn't possibly miss it. He'd be at work right now, of course, but if Stefan went there about four o'clock ...

He couldn't wait.

In the taxi the name Kowalewski nagged at him – yes, he'd seen it in his father's log book. Roman Kowalewski, navigator.

The Kowalewskis lived in an apartment complex the size of a small city, with flower beds and children's swings and a community sandbox. He rang the bell of No 88 and a girl of perhaps nineteen opened the door.

His carefully prepared speech fled.

She was utterly, breathtakingly beautiful! A pointed little face of warm olive tan flushed to rose on exotically high cheekbones. Satiny wings of black hair swept down to a creamy neck in a glossy arrangement of twists and braids. And she was so very tiny! Eyes of a warm dark brown smiled at him. 'Yes?'

He introduced himself and stammered out his errand.

She invited him in and her voice was music, softly modulated but with crisp undertones of intelligence. 'My father will be here soon. He will be happy to see you. I shall make coffee. Do please sit down and wait – your father always likes the green chair when he comes here.'

He settled into the green chair in a daze. *He was here, in Poland, in the very same chair ... and this marvellous girl ...*

Over coffee he discovered she was twenty-two, older than he'd thought, nearer to his own age. She'd just finished medical school and was planning post-graduate studies in pediatrics, probably here '... but in Paris or London if I can arrange it ...'

'You'd *love* London,' he said quickly. 'I have a flat there ...'

She blushed and dipped her head. 'If you prefer we can speak English ... but I'm a little bad at it.'

He was almost sorry when the door flew open and a broad red-cheeked man appeared. *'Where is he?* They called from the publishers – where's – *there you are*! I'd have known you anywhere!'

Stefan stood up. 'I'm –'

'Janek's boy!'

The wide red face looked as if it would never stop smiling, and Stefan was enveloped in a hug that must surely crack his, rib cage.

'You don't remember me, do you?'

Stefan had to admit he did not. It was some five fidgetty minutes before he could come to the point.

'They said my father was away … there's nothing wrong, is there?'

A booming laugh. 'Prison, you mean? No, no, it's not like the old days, thank God – not always, anyway. He's up at the villa in Zakopane.'

'They said you had his address.' But "prison"? What did he mean?

'But of course! No phone up there – a bit isolated, but you'll find it easily. One day's drive, maybe less – I'd drive you myself but I must work tomorrow – oh, what a relief you speak Polish! I never learned English properly. Your father, he always laughed at me. But no, tomorrow I can't go with you. Danuta – you've met my daughter, *nie*? She can drive you. Is that right, Danusiu *kochanie*?'

She blushed as she dusted crumbs off the table into a little tray. 'I'll be happy to.'

Next morning she was waiting for him, that magical Danuta, when he went down to the hotel lobby. Her dress was the colour of sunshine and there was a sprigged kerchief on her hair. Not a trace of makeup but she was beautiful, beautiful! She blushed a little when she saw him and her lashes swept down to crescent her cheeks with darkness.

'I thought you'd want to leave early,' she said, leading him to a small green Fiat – her father's she said, but it smelled of her, of summer and flowers and fresh, bracing air. 'We can stop in Kraków for lunch if you like – I know it very well. I went to medical school there. We can still be in Zakopane before evening.'

As they left Warsaw behind and took the main road south he asked all the typical tourist questions because he couldn't bring himself to ask what he really wanted to know. What was he like, this man who'd fathered him and simply left his mother without a word for more than a quarter century? How would he receive his son? Surely if he'd wanted to see him he'd have come to England? 'Where are we now?' he asked the girl at his side.

Danuta answered readily enough, but from time to time she gave him a searching look from under the long dark lashes. They zoomed through Kielce – 'you can see it's mostly industrial and perhaps we will not stop. You'll want to get on –' Then wheat country, pale gold and rippling in the morning breeze, deeply marked with valleys and mysterious ravines. 'Miechow Hills,' she said, 'but we'll go on ...'

The cobbled streets of Krakow, saturated with history, entranced him, perhaps because Danuta loved the city – *everything* he saw seemed to have sharper edges now – 'See the second window from the left? That's where I lived when I was in med school. See the castle on the hill?' – How could he miss it? It dominated the city – 'It's Wawel. Our kings are buried there. So beautiful, I wish we had more time – but perhaps if you come again to Poland?'

Looking at the lovely, animated face he thought it highly likely he would come again to Poland, no matter how the meeting with his father turned out.

At the Wierzynek in Market Square they ate roast quail with juniper sauce, then small wild strawberries whose flavour was so intense, so exquisite, he promptly ordered more.

'Good. You like them.' She smiled, her teeth very white and even as they bit into a bright red strawberry.

'They're delicious.'

'They're probably from Zakopane. They grow in the mountains.' She gave him a level look over her coffee cup, which he took to be a suggestion.

'Did you know?' he began. 'I've never seen him ... my father.'

She nodded. 'My parents talked for a long time last night after you left – oh, *please* don't mind, they are all old friends, yes? It's a sad story, *nie* – but I'm forgetting you don't know it yet. Better if Pan Janek tells you himself, I think.' She dimpled suddenly and it was like the sun coming out of the clouds. 'I

450

have instructions to leave you alone with him for a long, long time. But you worry I think, when you need not. He will be very happy to see you. Very, very happy.'

Her eyes were so honest, so open, that it was impossible not to take heart. 'How well do you know him, this Pan Janek?' Who also happens to be my stranger-father.

'Almost all my life. In Warsaw he visits with us all the time. We stay at the villa in Zakopane when we go to the skiing, and sometimes in the summer, like now. It's very beautiful there.'

There was one unasked question she had not yet answered, perhaps the most awkward one of all. 'Is he married?'

She covered his hand, her touch soft as rose petals to his heightened senses. 'No. In Warsaw he lives alone. In Zakopane there is Eva, a friend of his mother's. Eva is old, old, but still strong. She takes care of the place.'

He returned the pressure of her hand and asked a question that yesterday wouldn't have mattered at all. 'Do *you* like my father?'

She smiled again, this time into his eyes. 'I love him,' she said simply. 'And he loves me also. He is my godfather. He gives me many gifts, special things that are important to me. Now at last I can give something important to *him*, yes? I take him his son.'

CHAPTER FORTY-EIGHT

On the outskirts of Zakopane Danuta parked the Fiat, produced a book from the glove compartment and settled more deeply into her seat. 'I must study a little. You will follow the path between the two fences.' She dipped her head to the pages and seemed to absorb herself instantly in the intricacies of pediatric medicine.

The villa might have evolved from the hillside, so snugly did it rest in the fold of green. Aspens concealed it from the road;

dark blue spruce sheltered it from the high Tatras, purple in the distance. Under a steeply angled roof the porch was all shadow, the door recessed deep into timbered walls.

The uncertainty Danuta had held at bay came rushing back. His knuckles, tentative on the oak door, produced a hollow rapping. Solid footsteps from inside, the door swinging open, plump hands being dried on a coarse apron. Danute was right. Eva was old indeed.

'*Proszę?*' Brown eyes set in little cushions of fat peered up into his face. There was a quick intake of breath. '*O Bŏze! O Bŏze!*'

Except to call upon God she seemed robbed of speech. Pointing wildly down the long hallway behind her, she threw her apron over her head and scuttled away·through the nearest door. Stefan caught a glimpse of cooking pots and a large hearth, then the door slammed shut.

He'd frightened her. Now what?

For a moment he was tempted to go back, to apologize to Danuta and take the first plane home to Eccles Place, where relationships were set and did not·shift, did not hang on the thread of a stranger's acceptance – a stranger whose life was structured within the narrow confines of an office in Warsaw and this mountain retreat. How would he accept a grown-up son who arrived uninvited, upsetting the balance of years? *He will be happy to see you. Very, very happy.*

Stefan walked quietly down the hall to a glass door and looked out onto a sun-drenched verandah.

A man stood at a table. He was sorting wild mushrooms into little heaps of like species. Stefan could see the back of his head, blond with strong overtones of silver, as he bent to the task. Straightening at last, he picked up first one mushroom and then another, threaded them like pearls on a string, then hung them to dry in the sunlight.

Stefan took a deep breath and opened the door.

From somewhere deep inside the house Jan heard the agitated thump of a cast-iron pot being slammed on the stove. Eva, in one of her moods. He sighed. Sometimes he felt he spent his

452

life humouring the whims and tantrums of the old and infirm. Edek and Mamunia, Panna Mira until she disappeared permanently into the asylum. Now Eva, half the time too old to remember her name, the other half too stubborn to admit the lapse.

He was tired. Perhaps *he* was too old also, at least for this hobby, rising at dawn to search the forest floor for mushrooms, then the long trek home to sort and hang. He found the cathedral quiet of the forest soothing, a green balm that eased him as the city did not – but lately the silence seemed lonelier somehow, as filled with ghosts as the villa itself. It had been a lonely summer … Perhaps he should have asked the Kowalewskis. Roman always restored his spirits, and Danuta was a joy just to look at, to catch her scent, to watch the sun warm her olive skin to ripe apricot. In some small way Danuta filled in for Stefan, and Roman seemed to sense it, to encourage the bond. Yes, he should have invited them for a few days. It was Eva who stopped him. In front of guests she insisted in playing the part of faithful family servant to the hilt; she beat rugs, scrubbed floors, washed windows, baked bread, waited at table – and it was all clearly too much for her. Perhaps at Christmas …

He'd done the morels and was threading the last garland of mushrooms (agarics, they were – it was a spectacularly good summer for them) when he felt another presence, eyes watching him from behind the glass door to the house.

The door opened as he turned.

A young man hesitated on the threshold, squinting in the sudden dazzle of sunlight.

Intense blue eyes met his.

Overhead, the sky seemed to tilt, hang at a crazy angle … The years rolled back and farther back still … *it was himself he was looking at, Jan Kaliski in his mid-twenties, all long bones and narrow hands, pale hair … Jan Kaliski home from the war – he must have looked just so to Lallie …*

The young man was trying to speak.

'Tatuš?'

Father!

This boy called him father! … Stefan … but he was speaking

453

Polish, how could this be? Understanding rushed in and engulfed him, caught at his throat, stung his eyes with sudden salt.

He had learned the language of his father, this son ...

'*Mój synku ... mój synku.*' His own words came to him from a long way off – my son, my son – and he knew at last the elation that swept Mamunia when she opened her eyes to see him standing there. *He was here ...*

Stefan was here. Control began to slip as joy reached out, young arms embraced him. In his son's heartbeat, clear and strong in the still afternoon, the rustle of dead hopes stirred to life.

From the car Danuta saw the two tall figures, black against the late sun, walking across the meadow. They were deep in conversation. As they talked the older man reached out and several times touched his son's sleeve with light, unobtrusive fingers.

She carried the bags, Stefan's and hers, to the house.

Eva was agog. 'A ghost I thought I was looking at. Ayee, Danuta *kochana*, such a shock, eh?' She made lumbering, ineffectual passes between stove and table. 'What on earth shall I give them? There's a borsch cooling in the cellar, maybe with some –'

'They're not hungry, Eva, except for talk. We'll leave them alone.'

A quarter of a century to fill in.

It would be a long walk, she thought.

The first days were days of telling, of many starts and stops, a reluctant trip back through prisons actual and spiritual which only the need and compassion in his son's eyes could have persuaded him to relive. For Stefan he recreated Mamunia, her days in the concentration camp, her legs, her implacable will, then showed him her wheelchair slowly rotting in the shed.

'She must have been really something,' her grandson murmured as he touched the chair's wicker arms.

454

'She was.'

He showed Stefan a book on British dog breeding which charted bloodlines through a listing of kennels, explaining, 'I have access to such things now, because of my job. She's done well, your mother.' My wife.

'You're interested in dog breeding?' Stefan's eyebrows rose and his father forced himself to laugh.

'Not in the least. Here there is no time for such pastimes.' But in its way the book was a comfort, the accomplishments of Jolallie Kennels proof that Lallie was herself again, not the bruised wraith he'd seen that day at the dog show. He told Stefan about the little boy in the refreshment tent – 'I wanted very much to take you both away.'

'And why didn't you?'

'It was too late, Stefan. She was already Mrs Armott, you see, and your grandmother was still here and no way to move her. It was a bad time.'

He closed his eyes – the sun on the veranda suddenly too bright, too cheerful for the question he'd been waiting to ask. Perhaps the boy would think it an intrusion into matters which were no longer his concern – but they *were* his concern, always had been.

'They are happy, your mother and Neil? I've always wondered ...' And I wonder now why I cannot speak her name. Your mother. Neil's wife. Why not Lallie, the name that lived in his thoughts but could not, apparently, come to his tongue?

There was puzzlement on Stefan's face, as if he'd been asked a question whose answer should be quite obvious. 'Why yes, I suppose they must be. They just seem to – well, belong together, you know?'

Oh yes, he'd always known that. Two of a kind. They thought the same thoughts, planned the same plans, dreamed the same English dreams. 'She must have been ... hurt when I did not come back?'

Stefan's face was not quite as open now. He was pressing too hard, too deep, forcing his son to recall emotions best left alone.

'I was too young to know,' he said, his face bleak, with the warmth gone from it. 'I suppose she must have been upset. But there was Neil, and Gramps then.'

He'd been foolish to ask. What could a three-year-old know of mariage and its complexities, of a man's need for pride and a woman's for security? He changed the subject. 'You remember your grandfather, then?'

Stefan's face cleared, filled with pride. 'I certainly do – he used to walk me to kindergarten, you know, made all kinds of plans for me to go into the foundry when I grew up. I suppose he'd be disappointed, if he knew ...'

'You will have sons of your own – perhaps one of *them* –'

Stefan flushed, could not quite stop the swift glance at Danuta who was reading a medical book down in the garden. She looked young and fresh sitting under the knobbly old oak, and Jan felt a swift rush of gratitude towards his god-daughter.

Through all the days of telling Danuta was a discreet shadow in the background, attending their needs and holding Eva firmly in check. At last the telling was done, and now Stefan's eyes turned less often to his father, more and more to the small, pretty girl.

And Jan, seeing their eagerness to escape the villa, invented small errands to town that they must make for him. They were young. Had he and Lallie ever wanted to sit by the hearth with Millie and Joe in the beginning? Never. They'd ached to leave, to be off alone where their every glance need not be veiled, where each touch of the hands was not watched, speculated upon.

The happiness of Danuta and Stefan both pleased and disturbed Jan. True, he now had them both; Danuta, who just to see eased his heart, a reason to buy toys and small garments, as she grew older a pretty scarf and sometimes flowers or books. *And now his son, who'd come looking for him.* The two of them together, in love and so full of optimism, made him feel as if for years he'd been stumbling through a vast desert and had now chanced upon a garden of his own planting. For so long now he'd adored the girl because she'd somehow become a substitute for the boy and now to have them here, under his own roof, seeing the joy they found in each other – it was almost too much.

However, they brought unease also. Would they succeed in bridging the gulf between one culture and another? It seemed so easy to the young, almost inevitable, for they could see no need for bridges. True, they had no Joe Wainwright to battle, that lump of cast iron forged deep in the heart of insular Yorkshire; no Mamunia, as Polish as Kraków's trumpeter – but there were other hazards now. Marriage itself had become a transient state, one to leave at the first tremor of discord. And what about the other state, Poland itself? Despite new freedoms to travel, to communicate, all the old traps lay just under the surface. The gains of recent years could vanish overnight, the curtain come down again, cutting off Poland.

On their last day they told him they planned to marry, Danuta with her pointed little face full of sunshine, Stefan's blue eyes ablaze with dreams and plans for their future.

When they left, taking the life of the villa with them, Jan tasted tears in his throat. Of joy? foreboding? perhaps envy? He didn't know. But the wedding would be soon. They would see him then. He smiled.

Their car was a green dot on the grey snake of road when the possibility struck him, gave new dimension to the shift of his fate.

Would Lallie come for the wedding? Surely it was tempting fate to wish for that also? One stroke of fortune did not presuppose another. But if she came, was it possible she'd also come here, to his home?

He looked about the hall, rich with the smell of apples and furniture polish, still busy with the echoes of old loves and hates. Eva and Panna Mira bickering, the creak of wicker armrests and the rattle of Mamunia's amber beads. Edek's angelic spirit was here, even Eva's dreams – wraithlike things now, since Eva no longer remembered that she'd once been married, let alone what had become of her husband. His own bitterness was here – in the beginning there'd been so *much* of it – and then his acceptance.

If Lallie were to come here (not that she would) how would she see this place? As quaint and foreign, something to chat about at cocktail parties when she was back home? Or a place filled with the past, a past which had robbed her of a future she'd had every right to expect? There was no way to know, but he found himself in his room, reading again a note she'd written to a milkman so many years ago.

CHAPTER FORTY-NINE

Eccles Place laboured under a sultry sun and a tension they were trying to ignore.

Lallie put herself through the motions. She did a dog show or two with disappointing results, picked out new tiles for the downstairs bathroom, watched Neil lose the local golf tournament through sheer indifference, cooked meals for which neither of them had any appetite, and swam endless laps in the pool just behind the rose-garden. And ever second an all too familiar tightrope under her feet, every ring of the phone an alarm, every postal delivery a crisis to be overcome.

She handled it differently now, of course, met the postwoman at the gate with a smile and stood chatting easily about nothing at all before she accepted the daily wad of letters with casual fingers, even pausing then to give the woman a goodbye wave as she pedalled off to the next house. When she felt Neil watching her (did he *have* to watch her all the time?) she was able to toss the bundle unopened onto the hall table and busy herself about the house, humming along with the radio.

Only the façade had changed. Under the assured veneer the same emotions rolled and churned. Three weeks since Stefan left and not a letter or call, not even a wish-you-were-here card.

'Likely he's still looking,' Neil kept saying. 'If there was anything to tell us he'd have written.'

No he wouldn't, not Stef, not if it was that kind of news. Some things can be put in a letter; some have to be worked up to carefully. Instinct told her what the news would be, and after

458

three weeks to prepare herself she was no more ready for it now than when they'd seen him off at the airport. It was not, she told herself bitterly, as if she hadn't had enough practice. Anything to do with Jan Kaliski also had to do with rejection, a feeling she'd known very well, once.

Neil watched his wife more carefully than even she guessed. He saw every small difference and was afraid for her. And for himself. With Stefan's silence stretching between them they hardly talked any more because what was in the front of their minds couldn't be mentioned; it was a Pandora's box that, once opened, might be impossible to close. In the first years of their marriage it had been necessary for her to believe Jan was dead. For pride's sake. And because she needed that belief he'd bolstered it, had even come to believe it himself. And now old wounds were opening again, an uncharacteristic wariness was in her face when they were together – which they seldom were, because she was careful to keep herself busy every second he was home, going from task to task with relentless, terrifying energy. If what she began was left unfinished, as it often was, she seemed not to notice. If he reminded her she'd look surprised for a moment, then recover herself, say snappily that she was getting to it, she was getting to it, and she couldn't be expected to be everywhere at once, could she? A few moments later and she'd be apologizing.

'I *am* sorry dear, I don't know what's wrong with me –'

'It's the weather,' he'd say. 'Just the damn weather.'

They made their dutiful twice-weekly visit to his mother down the street, and Agnes was no help at all.

'Stefan not back yet?' she asked in the querulous voice of the very old. 'I must say it's inconsiderate of him, *quite* inconsiderate.'

Lallie kept mulishly quiet and Neil sighed. Mother had not aged well. Overweening gentility had turned, in recent years, to a waspish bitterness – though what she had to be bitter about he couldn't imagine. She was healthy, had no financial worries such as she'd once had, and had even, by proxy, acquired a grandson – or so she regarded Stefan. And felt free to criticize at will.

'In my day,' she said now. 'in my day one's children were

459

expected to keep in touch. It's little to ask, after all –'

Lallie stood up abruptly, Agnes' bit of embroidery that she'd been expected to admire falling to the floor. 'He'll be back soon, Mrs Armott, and when he is you'll be the first to know. Neil, can we go now? I've things to do …'

His mother pursed her lips. 'Well!' but Lallie was already down the path and in the car. 'I do think, Neil, that Lallie might sometimes bring herself to call me Mother, don't you? Heaven knows I've tried to be one, since Millie passed on. But she's so … prickly.'

He kissed his mother's netted cheek, said 'Later, Mother, all right?' and was off to join Lallie in the car.

'Did you have to snap at her?'

'Yes I did. She's so damned nosey, wants to know every little thing – and when she does know she picks it apart.'

Which was nothing new – but Lallie's reaction was. Aside from refusing to call Agnes 'Mother' she was the dutiful daughter-in-law in every respect. She drove her to the doctor and the dentist, took her to the theatre once a week and the dressmaker when asked, baked her birthday cakes and invited such of Mother's friends who were still alive to decorous little parties at the house. He started the car and remembered, with relief, that tomorrow was Monday. He could escape to the foundry. And that was new, too. The idea that he'd ever want to escape his quiet, well-run house and his still-beautiful wife whom he adored – well, it hurt. The foundry's problems he could face, could deal with. The problem of Jan Kaliski, he could not.

She was at Daddy's old desk making up pedigree charts for the latest litter when she heard Stefan's taxi stop at the gate. Pulling aside velvet curtains, she watched him turn, reach in his pocket to pay the driver, then stand for a moment, looking at the house. She tried to read his face and could not. There was too much in it. Apprehension was there, uncertainty too, but there was something else … an excitement he was trying to suppress. One message she *could* read. The waiting of twenty-five years was over. And for the first time in her son's life she could not make herself go to the door and welcome him home. She sat back at the desk, forced herself to write in the name of Jolallie Kennels with as much care as if she'd been setting a diamond.

She heard him come into the hall, set his cases down so quietly he could have been in church. She heard the kitchen door open, heard him questioning Alice.

'Mum around?'

She'd been right about the excitement. It was in his voice, too. None at all in Alice's.

'Dunno,' she said. 'Nobody tells me nuthin'. You'll be wanting some tea ...'

'No, no.' He sounded vague – so she'd been right about the uncertainty, too. Which left apprehension ... I don't want to know, she thought. It's better not to know.

Then his footsteps in the hall, his hand rattling the doorknob, turning it.

She smelled his aftershave as he stood behind her, felt his hands gently rest on her shoulders.

'I found him,' he said quietly.

Names of innumerable generations of Afghans blurred under her pen, Jolly somewhere among them. Jolly in Little Wood, *Jan's hand on his head, just home from the stalag, so happy to see her ... so happy, so much love ...*

'Mother? Did you hear me?'

So where did it all go?

'Mother? I told you – I found him.'

'I heard you.' And I don't *want* to hear, don't want to know why – The desktop seemed to shift, Stefan's voice seemed to recede ...

'He's just exactly what I expected – here! What on earth ...?' He was bringing her brandy, standing over her as she drank it. She felt blood begin to come back to her face. The room was still again, no chairs and tables shifting, no carpet rising up to meet her. 'Gosh, Mother, you really gave me a turn. I knew it would be a shock, but –'

'So tell me.' Get it over. Tell me who he married, how happy he is, how successful. Why he didn't come back.

'It wasn't hard at all. I went to the publishers of that book, and they sent me to this stranger – well, he was a stranger then – about your age, friendly type, big face, a bit of a pot on him

461

actually, lots of curly black hair. Dad's friend.'

'Roman.'

'How did you know?'

'He was at your christening.'

'He mentioned that, knew me right away. Knew where my father was, and his daughter drove me –'

A daughter? 'So he's married then, your father?' It was what she expected, so why was her heart sinking, dropping through the centre of the earth?

'*No* – Roman's daughter, but I'll come back to her later. My father's not married, there's just this ancient housekeeper – God, I don't know where to start.'

'Why didn't he come back?' That's the place to start because that's the place it all finished.

Stefan hesitated, his fingers working at the cuff of his jacket. 'He did come back, once. But it was too late. Look, let me tell you from the beginning – You have to understand how things were then. They were ... grim, really grim. All that stuff we hear, it's not just propaganda – or it wasn't then, anyway.'

Don't give me politics, not now. 'What happened?'

'They put him in prison almost as soon as he got there.'

'*But he hadn't done anything*!' And already I'm defending him ...

'He didn't have to. Anyway, it was a couple of years before he got out –'

'*Years?*' Years of waiting, watching for mail, half out of her mind, talking to the child in her womb because no one else could possibly know – and all that lonely time he was in prison. Hadn't abandoned her, as Daddy thought, as Neil thought, as even Roman thought. He was locked up, perhaps ill-treated. Relief pushed her deep into the chair, a confused guilt hard on its heels. *Cruel, inhuman to feel relief*, but – 'They didn't hurt him?'

'He didn't talk much about that – ashamed it happened in Poland, I think, but I got a lot of it from Roman. And when they let him go it wasn't much better on the outside. The country was a shambles. Everything we take for granted had simply been blown away – and the new government! He was bitter about that, he said, in the beginning, but then he found his mother –'

And so she heard about Mamunia, her ruined legs, the efforts to get out, the dog show in Fannington Park …

'He was there, and I didn't know …'

'He's still got the note you left for the milkman. He showed me.'

Over twenty years, and he'd kept the note because it was all he had. She remembered her bitterness as she touched his clothes in the wardrobe, the old rancour that gathered again as she thought of it, rancour mixed with shame now – but she hadn't known, couldn't have known. 'Why didn't he *talk* to us that day, why couldn't he –'

'You'd married Neil.'

Ah yes, Neil. Faithful Neil, who'd always been there. And who'd been wonderful, wonderful, remember that …

'He's not bitter about it – he told me to be sure to tell you that. He'd expected it even before he came, and then with Gramps dying –'

'How could he know *that*?'

'Because I told him, in the refreshment tent, this man talking to me …'

'You'd forgotten?'

He nodded, and they were quiet for a long time. 'It was a bad time for him. We must have looked as if we had everything and all he had was his mother, who couldn't – or wouldn't be moved. And we *did* have everything didn't we? Except for Gramps.' Stefan paused. 'He asked me if you were happy.'

'Yes?' Why was she holding her breath?

'Of course, I told him you were.'

He got up, moved restlessly around the small study, picked up a picture of Joe and Lallie at a dog show; hefted an old pipe ashtray made of Blue John stone; riffled the edges of a seed catalogue; pinched out a fading aster from the vase on the mantelpiece. When he spoke next his voice was deeper, perhaps with embarrassment.

'I'm glad I went, Mother, in spite of …' He stopped, started again. 'Look, I should have thought what it would do to you and Neil but I didn't – and even if I had I'd still have gone.'

'I know.' She made an effort to organize her face, put on an understanding smile. 'I'm glad you found him, darling. Neil will be too – and how could it do anything to Neil and me? It hasn't changed anything.' Her voice sounded hollow, even to her.

'No, I suppose not.' His face cleared, and he reached into his pocket. 'I've got some more news for you but now's not the time. I'll wait until Neil gets home for that.'

He went off to find Alice, ask her to make tea, but before he left he laid a small bundle of snapshots on the desk. 'If you want to see them ...'

She was afraid to see them.

She still loved him, had known from the moment Stefan began to speak, from the sudden singing of her blood, the terrible joyous lurch of her heart. No use telling herself she was a middle-aged w~~·~~an – wife – no use at all. Something in her pushed the know~~.~~edge away, wouldn't let her believe it. She felt twenty-one again, yearned to touch him, to see him ...

The pictures on top of the stack were all of Stefan and a girl and she sorted through them with shaking fingers, not even looking because *he* wasn't in them.

One picture. A tall, slim man squinting a little into the sun, smiling at her across a quarter century, the same face – gentler now, some of the intensity washed away – but the same face, the same surge of tenderness in her when she looked into it, the same treacherous, rapturous knowledge that she had no defences against it. Her finger touched the stiff card of the picture and she knew that if his warm, flesh-and-blood face were there she'd melt again into what she'd been before, a young, vulnerable woman who'd been in love.

There was a tap at the door and for a guilty instant she thought it was Neil. She opened a drawer and thrust the snapshot inside – but it was only the kennel-girl come for instructions about the evening feed.

'D'you want me to give Kalat the eggs again?'

'Yes, yes ...'

When the girl had gone Lallie threw on a sweater and headed for the common. Almost time for Neil to come home and she didn't know what to say, didn't want to be there when Stefan told him, was afraid for him to see her face.

Neil took the news with a calm that surprised even himself. 'Your mother knows?' was about all he said.

Stefan looked uneasy. 'I told her. She seemed pleased – said it didn't change anything.'

Neil nodded. Of course she'd say that, she'd want to believe that. Yes, he could be calm. Why not? He'd already faced every possibility a dozen times over. He'd even anticipated, not without fear, the suppressed excitement burning deep in Lallie's eyes when she came in from her walk. Tonight she looked young, young enough to be in love. And Jan Kaliski had been the love of her youth. What was he, Neil Armott, but a distant second accepted only after everything else had slipped away? Then Stefan showed his bundle of snapshots. Like Lallie, Neil riffled through until he came to the one of Jan. As he looked at it a heaviness seemed to settle over him, a depressed knowledge that it was all out of his hands.

'Still a damned good looking chap, don't you think so, Lall?' Trying to sound hearty didn't help either.

He watched her face as he passed her the photograph. She'd already seen it, he could tell. She smiled briefly at it before turning back to the television news – but he knew without question that the instant he left the room she'd pick it up again. Her face was more animated than he'd seen it in years. Her cheeks were flushed in the firelight and there was an aura about her, the mystique of a woman thinking secret, forbidden thoughts.

He left the room acutely conscious of his slight limp and of his foolish efforts to disguise it. As if it mattered. She wouldn't notice him tonight if he sprouted wings and circled the ceiling.

Stefan saved his other news for the dinner table, but he was tired, uneasy with the undercurrents he'd already brought into the house, and let the announcement fall without so much as a word of build-up. Such wonderful news – he'd wanted to give

465

it to them like a gift, but there were too many ripples still eddying around them.

'… so we'll be getting married next month. She'll finish her studies in London so it all works out.'

'Well,' they said together. A pause that lasted a little too long.

'Wonderful news darling,' Lallie said. 'I'm so happy for you – aren't we, Neil?'

'Hell yes – time you settled down, past time. Roman's daughter, you said?'

'Yes. Jan's god-daughter. They're very close.'

Lallie looked at her plate, unwilling for them to see the flash of jealousy she knew was in her eyes. *Very close*.

'You'll love her, Mother, she's … well, you've seen the pictures.'

So they looked at them again, saw the petite girl with honey skin and hair like blackbird's wings around a pointed little face.

'She *is* beautiful,' Lallie said, sounding surprised.

'She's a corker,' Neil said, reverting back to wartime slang.

'Next month, you said?' It was Lallie, stirrings of alarm in her voice. 'Aren't you rushing it a bit?' Foolish question. Had *they* thought they were rushing it, flying home from Castleton to face Daddy who was sitting right in that chair with a list of objections a mile long? Which they'd overcome because they knew (the young always did) that there was no time to waste, not a minute. Mum had understood, was their ally, but Daddy …

'There's nothing to wait for,' Stefan said, speaking carefully now, a question forming in his eyes before it reached his lips. 'The wedding's to be in Warsaw, of course. On the 18th.' He paused, and the ripples began again before he next words were even out of his mouth. He could feel them, see them in his mother's eyes and then Neil's. 'You will come, won't you?'

CHAPTER FIFTY

Eccles Place's long-gone admiral and sundry majors and colonels (retired) had been content to refresh their spirits at Leamington Spa or Harrogate, certainly no farther than Cowes – even there only for the sailing; if they'd thought of the Continent at all it was with faint distaste for one excess or another to which Europeans seemed so regrettably prone. Italians used olive oil and garlic (garlic!); the French were preoccupied with the digestive tract; Scandinavians were too big, too blond, too energetic; the Swiss lavished far too much thought on money and its acquisition; and the Germans – well, less said about *them* the better.

The new breed, accountants and brash young merchants, zoomed off abroad at the hint of a new 'in' resort or a better deal on the latest model Merc. Airports were as familiar to them as Joe Wainwright's Backenthorpe pub had been to him; a holiday wasn't a holiday unless they returned golden brown from the sands of Spain, pink-cheeked and hearty from invigorating runs down the sides of Alps. Stefan took regular ski holidays in Meribel and La Plagne – and even Neil had attended business conferences all over Europe and had twice crossed the Atlantic.

Only Lallie had never been abroad. She'd flown occasionally to Scotland with Neil for the salmon fishing and even more seldom to London for the theatres, but it was always at Neil's urging and she was forever in a fever to get home, back to the security of Eccles Place.

It would be different this time, Neil was sure.

He waited until he caught Stefan alone in the house – not too difficult, since Lallie seemed to be avoiding them both.

'I wish I could make it, I really do. I'd have liked to be at your wedding, but ...'

Stefan looked at first bewildered and then hurt, the event that should have been the highlight of his young life turning into a source of unrest, of silences in this once-happy house.

'But why? I wanted you to *be* there, both of you –'

'I know, but now's not the time. The unions are acting up again and you know what it does to the foundry. I'm sorry.' He looked away, unwilling to meet Stefan's eyes. He was a poor liar and he knew it – but he could no more go to Poland, see Lallie and Jan together again, than –

'Have you told Mother?'

'I'm going to. Now.'

'Do you think she'll come without you?'

Neil sighed. 'Aye, I reckon she will.'

They hadn't discussed it. She was good, these days, at finding urgent reasons not to discuss anything at all. But he knew she'd go. And that she must go alone, even if he had to make her. It was a risk he couldn't avoid. If there was a choice for her to make (of course there was, no use fooling himself) she deserved the chance to make it on her own, without him there to muddy the waters.

He found her on her knees in the attic sorting through an old trunk. He'd made his step loud on the stairs, and slow – but not slow enough to duck the glimpse of airforce blue, the waft of mothballs and old lavender sachets that came at him as she closed the trunk lid; nowhere near slow enough to miss the guilty tide of pure rose that flew to her cheeks when she faced him. God, how defenceless she looked, the strain in her eyes, the softness of her mouth.

'It's about the trip, sweetheart,' he said quietly.

'Oh, there's plenty of time –'

'No there isn't. You'll need a visa and tickets, and there'll be shopping, I expect.'

'We don't *need* anything –'

'Not *we*,' he said carefully. 'You ... I'm not going. Sorry love, but there it is.' He gave her the excuse he'd given Stefan, embroidered it a bit. '... so I just don't see how I can make it. You'll have to go without me.'

She covered it very well, that sudden surge of relief in her eyes, but he'd seen it – and the fear that followed it. *He* was afraid for her, too. He was afraid for himself and even for Jan, for all of them in this too-enduring triangle.

'Perhaps I'd better not go either,' she said. There was no conviction in it, just a questioning, a plea to be persuaded.

'One of us has to go. It's your son's wedding, isn't it? He'll think we don't want her in the family if neither of us show up.'

She turned away from him, straightened a pile of old books and records. 'I'll think about it,' she said, vague again, back in her own thoughts.

She watched him go, caught the heaviness of his step, the droop of his shoulders, and to the excitement that already filled her was added guilt and regret. He'd cleared the path, given his blessing, made the choice hers alone. She saw his goodness, his generosity – but she didn't *want* a choice, was afraid of the hope engulfing her as she again touched the old uniform, pressed her warm cheek to the silver Polish eagle pinned to its breast, cool and hard against her flesh, treacherous memories stirring, reaching for the light, blurring the pull of loves and loyalties – and where did they belong, these loyalties? To Jan, who'd given her a season of rapture, a divided love and – almost incidentally – his son? Or to Neil, who'd given her spring and summer and who'd nurtured Jan's son as his own – and who would give his autumn and winter, too. Whatever she asked Neil would give and feel privileged in the giving. Which made her doubly responsible. Neil's goodness, hers for the asking, had seemed to come so cheaply. *Aye, said Daddy (who'd known the price of everything and counted it as dross beside what he loved). Aye, he said now from wherever he'd gone, price is one thing, cost is another, mi lass ...*

There should be someone she could talk to about it. She'd thought once that she could discuss anything with Neil, but not this. Certainly not Agnes, good God, not Agnes Armott! Not Stefan, already full of his Danuta, already torn between love of Neil and devotion to the ideal of his own father. And Daddy, what would he have said? – as if she didn't know! And Millie, her soft-hearted Mum, who'd been wise in odd, unexpected ways, accepting whatever came and making the best of it, not fighting any of it? Millie would have passed a hand across her apron as she listened, would have thought for a minute or two as she peeled carrots and turnips for the stew. Eventually she would have sighed.

'*What has to be will be.*'

That's what Mum would have said. And that didn't help either. Nothing did.

Neil thought his decision not to go would ease the tension. He was wrong. It stretched like electric wire around the large house and even gave off peripheral sparks as far distant as his mother's sedate little nest.

Agnes, pushing eighty, was determined to maintain some standards in a world which seemed to have none at all. Her disapproving nose had lengthened with the years, allowing her to sniff rather more eloquently at things of which she did not approve, which was a great deal.

'Another foreigner coming into the family – whatever would Joe have to say about that, the poor sensitive soul.'

Neil remembered when his mother denied Joe Wainwright any qualities but vulgarity and avarice, and spoke sharply. 'It's not *your* family, so what are you worried about?'

'Of course it is, by extension. You're the child's guardian –'

'He's a man, and more than capable of making his own decisions –'

'And Lallie, travelling all that way, I mean, how will it *look*?'

'To whom?'

'Well, the neighbours, the vicar ... After all, she *was* married to him, wasn't she?'

The Pole. 'Exactly, that's why –'

'And now she's married to *you*. It doesn't look right, propriety alone ...' Her sniff said it all.

'Nobody gives a tinker's cuss for propriety, Mother. She's going on her own and that's final.'

But Mother was prepared to make the supreme sacrifice.

'One of us ought to be there with her, it seems to me.'

'I hardly think she needs a chaperone and you're *not* well enough to make the trip.' Oh yes she was, never more so. She wanted to go. Neil was tempted – but something in him couldn't interfere with Lallie's new radiance that flickered like a candle flame when she thought no one was watching her. Far better than Agnes he could remember her shadowed times, the waiting at Hempton, the endless games of Monopoly, then the waiting again for Jan to come back from the *stalag*, then more waiting, the girlish trip to the consulate in London ... yes, she'd earned this. 'She'll go alone.'

Yet she was quiet and on edge, this Lallie, and they couldn't seem to talk, not with the old openness. He felt as if he stood under a snowbank with an avalanche on the way.

Each day he saw changes a stranger would never have noticed. Accustomed all her life to vigorous exercise, she now drove herself to the point of exhaustion. When he woke in the mornings, her side of the bed was cold – she was out walking. Instead of their companionable breakfast at the kitchen table she'd give Alice vague instructions what to serve him and escape to the kennels until it was time for him to leave for the foundry. He still got a goodbye kiss on the way out but now there'd be a duster in her hand and a can't-stop-too-much-to-do air about her, and although their lips met she made sure their eyes did not. Home again, she was no longer waiting for him with a smile and a pre-dinner drink. His Martini was in the fridge now, and she was out in the pool, her long body knifing through lap after lap of blue water. Worse, she'd become evasive. Always before, their differences had been quickly aired and quickly forgotten. Now there were long silences and forced conversation in which she clearly monitored every word she uttered.

One morning he was awake when he heard her creep downstairs at dawn. He watched from the window as she strode, head down, through heavy slanting rain and a buffeting wind from the north.

It was enough.

He dressed quickly, pointed the car towards a corner she must eventually cross, and rolled down the window to wait.

She didn't even see the car until he called her name. Then she looked up, surprise quickly covered under a bright, meaningless smile. 'Well! Whatever brings you out so early?'

'You know damned well what. Get in.'

'I'm not done walking yet.'

'For today, you're done.' He threw open the door to the smell of wet earth and summer things dying. 'We've enough problems now, pneumonia doesn't have to be another one. Get in – unless you want me to drag you in.' He knew her pride, saw it do battle with discretion, saw her remember that all up and down the street curtains were being opened to the morning, faces were looking out at the weather. And at them.

She got in, edging well away from him on the wide front seat. 'You forgot your club and loincloth, Tarzan.'

Sarcasm. From Lallie.

'Look love, let's talk, okay?'

'About what?'

'You know about what. About us – and Jan.'

'I don't *want* to talk about it –'

'But you're thinking about it. So am I. I just wish you'd tell me *what* you're thinking.'

She fumbled a cigarette from her pocket and lit it, the pungent smoke a cloud between them. 'I have to go, you do see that?'

'It's me who insisted on it, remember?'

'Perhaps that's what's making it so … difficult. But you see I have to go, you do see?' she persisted.

Had to, yes. *But she wanted to go, that was the devil of it.* It was a canker eating at them, but if they were ever to get back to their old, easy relationship she must go, test the water. 'Lallie, understand me. I'm not quite as giving as you seem to think. Since Stefan came back it's been hell. We haven't been happy – and if we leave things the way they are maybe we'll never be happy again. I know what's likely to happen when you get there, I know I might lose you. But if you don't go, I've lost you anyway.'

She turned to him, her lashes spiked by more, now, than rain. 'Oh Neil, I wish –'

'What? What is it you wish, sweetheart?'
She didn't say. Perhaps she didn't know.

.

CHAPTER FIFTY-ONE

Jan let himself into the hall of his Warsaw apartment, his eyes
gritty with summer dust and endless translations from half a
dozen languages into Polish, obscure papers he sometimes
doubted were of use to anybody. On such days he felt weighted
down with unwanted knowledge of water resources, plant
diseases, the nutritional properties of various vegetables or the
convoluted accounting procedures of state-run businesses. On
such days his work bored him to the bone and it was only the
approaching wedding that gave a spring to his step as he hung
his coat on the hall-tree, slipped a Wieniawski record onto the
turntable and brewed tea for one.

The bedsitter was ridiculously small, shrunk even further by
floor-to-ceiling bookshelves whose contents overflowed every
flat surface, not excluding the floor, but housing was still at a
premium and as a single man this accommodation was all he
could legitimately demand. Its saving grace was the view. From
the front window he looked down into Stare Miasto, the Old
Town which had been entirely demolished in the war and
painstakingly restored now to its seventeenth century elegance,
complete with tile mosaics on its outer walls and narrow,
shadowed alleyways within. Steps were of stone and very
narrow, hollowed with generations of townspeople and these
days the feet of occasional tourists. From his kitchen window
he could look down onto the Vistula in all its moods, coppery
and sluggish now in the hot, windless evening.

In the two weeks since Stefan and Danuta had left him at the
Zakopane villa his spirits had swung from wild, insubstantial
hope to the deadening certainty that the wedding would come
and go, that Lallie would not attend – and afterwards his life

would be the poorer, with even Danuta gone off to London and nothing at all for him here but the daily grind in Warsaw and brief respites at the villa.

Wary of hope or disappointment waiting in unexpected places, he routinely avoided his mail until after his city supper of fruit and cheese (cheese could still be found and in the summer, fruit also.) Meat was hardly worth the effort of lines and the inevitable guilt when, finally at the head of the line, some woman with a manual worker and his five offspring in the background, waited just ahead of him. What was the point, then, of a couple of chops or a roast only a family could appreciate? He'd become, almost by default, a vegetarian. And found it suited him very well.

His social life in town was quiet and unremarkable. There were movies and concerts, small gatherings of office acquaintances, visits to Roman and Genia and, at least twice a month, a duty call on Mrs Adamski. Well into her nineties now, she was ensconced in an old people's home in the Praga district across the river. A busybody all of her life, she now had approximately sixty souls of which to keep track; the task kept her a happy woman. For Jan she was the last link with Morska Street and therefore cherished. Who else remembered Tatuš in his Sunday black strolling towards Łazienki, Mamunia in summer silks on his arm, parasol tapping the pavement while Janek ran on ahead of them? The news that Stefan had appeared at the villa to seek out his father threw her into transports of delight and she had no rest until every last inmate of the home knew the details – a few of which Jan suspected she made up out of whole cloth. Unlike Eva, Mrs Adamski had retained her faculties and fully expected to be at the wedding, was in fact planning her outfit for the occasion. On Jan's last visit to her she was hovering between powder-blue poplin and grey worsted – '... in case it's starting in to winter – you know what autumn's like, Janek, and at my age I have to watch for chills, though I've been down here so long I guess the good Lord's forgotten about me, heh?'

Finishing his tea, washing the single cup and plate, he unlocked his mail slot to find a letter from England. Stefan, of course. Full of dates and wedding plans, brimming over with excitement. The London apartment was being painted for Danuta, he'd arranged all her classes, and there was no way, no way in the world that she could avoid loving London, and if it turned out she was homesick they'd just spend all their vacations in Poland.

It was on page two, in writing rather smaller, less exuberant than the rest, as if Stefan had puzzled over how to say it and opted for formality:

'... Neil sends his regrets. Delighted about the wedding but will be unable to leave the foundry – union problems of some kind. Mother has been persuaded that Eccles Place can exist without her for a couple of weeks and will arrive the day of the wedding ...'

There was more but he couldn't focus on it, could get past nothing beyond the fact that she would be *here*. *In Poland*. *That he would see her again*. In this city, his city. Perhaps even in his Zakopane ...

Suddenly the small apartment couldn't contain him. He wanted to open the window and shout the news down into the square, to take every passer-by by the hand and hold him there until he'd spilled his joy over the city. He called Roman and was immediately sorry. At first the news was simply a question of an extra guest at the reception, another name to be added, where would be the appropriate place to seat her? Jan waited for the significance of her coming to register but it took time. From the beginning they'd been far less concerned with Jan's past suddenly springing to life than they were worried about Danuta's future, Stefan's prospects as her husband, whether they'd get to see their grandchildren. It was natural, Jan knew, and perhaps he was selfish to expect more. But at length Roman sighed gustily, pulled audibly on a cigarette.

'So you'll see her again.'

'It seems that way.'

'And Neil's not coming.'

'No.'

'Well.' Silence hung between them, broken finally by the usual crackle of poor equipment. 'But she's married now.'

As if he needed reminding. 'But she'll be here.'

Another sigh, another crackle. 'Be careful, friend. It's

all a long time ago.'

Hanging up, Jan had the feeling they'd had another similar conversation – also a long time ago. In the mess at Hempton, right after that first Christmas, a red and white scarf between them and Roman warning him of Joe Wainwright. 'He does not love us, I think.' And he'd been right. Then. He was wrong now. No matter how long ago, the old hunger to see Lallie swept him as strong as ever, sent him walking the river bank, marvelling at the new beauty of sunset ripples and marsh grasses black with twilight and later, on the bridge over to Praga, small boats moving down a copper ribbon beneath him. Never had Warsaw been so beautiful.

Even when he found himself on Władysława, standing before the grim, institutional façade of Mrs Adamski's rest home, he found beauty in the fading brick and cracked pavement. And in Mrs Adamski herself, nodding and bobbing first at one inmate and then another before she saw him and hurried over.

'What a thing, what a thing,' she fussed, 'some poor old soul's misplaced her walking stick – if you ask me somebody's taken it, you can trust nobody these days, nobody at all, I was just saying to – oh yes! Guess what, I'm getting my hair done for the wedding, they're a sending a girl up from the shop down the street –' She stopped in sudden fear. 'It's still on, isn't it? They've not called it off or anything?'

'No,' he laughed.

'For a minute I thought, since you don't usually stop in on a weekday – anyway, I thought I might have them give me a rinse, you know? Blue, very likely, what d'you think? And one of the new women's lending me her fur-piece, I don't want to let you down and my, my but don't you look happy tonight? Did they give you a promotion, or what? Not that you don't deserve –'

'My wife is coming for the wedding.' My wife. My wife.

Her small old mouth made an O. 'Well, what a thing! Lalka, her name is –?'

'Lallie.'

'Oh the sweet girl, the dear, dear –'

'A middle-aged girl now, Mrs Adamski.'

'Pooh, middle-aged! Look at me, they called me middle-aged fifty years ago and —' And she was off into a dissertation on ageing which turned to one on romance. 'Never too late, Janek, never too late. Old love never gets rusty, you'll have heard your mother say that I shouldn't wonder —'

He hadn't. Mamunia had less romance in her than any woman he'd ever known, but he was glad to hear Mrs Adamski say it.

Perhaps that's what he'd come for.

CHAPTER FIFTY-TWO

Visa, passport and tickets lay on the dresser. New clothes hung pressed and ready in the wardrobe, softly draped suits in wools and jerseys, blouses of shantung and fine linen, all in muted shades of dove grey and rose and amethyst. A dozen new hairstyles had been tried and rejected; finally she settled for her usual chignon, at the same time resisting the urge to have silver streaks at the temples touched up to blend with the still-dark cloud. The hairdresser, no longer Charles of Merton, cajoled and bullied, said it was a shame to let that one sign of age spoil an otherwise perfect picture.

'I'm going to a wedding, not a honeymoon,' she said crisply, turning back to her sheaf of lists.

There were brisk instructions for the gardener. He should mulch the peonies, tidy up the lilacs, take cuttings off the geraniums for next spring, give the lawns their winter dressings, get tulips in the ground before frost sets in —

'How long d'you say you'll be gone, missus?'

'Two weeks,' she said firmly, 'but no sense letting things get out of hand.'

He slouched off with vague mutterings of the unlikelihood of frost in September — even October.

Her preparations for the care and feeding of Neil were far

477

more elaborate. There were detailed notes of which shirts were to be put out when, which suits could be trusted to local dry cleaners and which must be sent to town. Two weeks worth of orders to butcher and greengrocer and dairy, menus and recipes of what to serve Neil while she was gone – because she just knew Alice's imagination was limited to a can of baked beans and a slice or two of Spam.

Long before she was done eight, Eccles Place could have withstood a three-month siege. Neil, watching all the activity, tried to suppress the thought that it was all an expression of guilt before the fact. He'd seen the night-time ritual of lotions and bathrooms scales and eye-cream grow slightly more protracted and told himself it was quite natural she'd want to look her best for her son's wedding.

'You'll dazzle their eyes out, darling,' he said once. And she would – Jan Kaliski's eyes, anyway. To Neil she seemed far more beautiful than she'd been as a girl; her hips, still slim, were no longer boyish; stomach just as firm but smoothly sculpted now, a marvel of muscle tone and satiny skin. Dressed only in a slip and intense concentration she leaned from the hip to read the bathroom scale and he ached to touch her, press his mouth to smooth shoulders as he'd done a million times. She'd respond, he knew that – but the image of Jan Kaliski was between them always now, could not be blocked out. He told himself he was a fool to let her go alone – as well open a bell jar to let a prized butterfly sense the breeze. But it was out of his hands. The decision, once made, couldn't be undone. She'd never forgive him if he reversed it now.

Her schedule was fine, intentionally so. Stefan left a week early, wedding smile in place and a small package in his hand. For his father, he said – and such was the atmosphere in the house that neither Neil nor Lallie thought to ask what was in it. To the very last minute Stefan begged Lallie to travel with him, to come early so she could help Danuta with the preparations, see something of the city, get to know his father again before the wedding.

She told him no, adding rather sharply that Danuta had a mother to help her and there was in any case plenty to be done at Eccles Place since she'd be away for two whole weeks – why in the world Neil had to get her an excursion ticket she couldn't imagine.

'Two weeks!' she'd said at the time. 'What on earth shall I do with myself in a strange place for two whole –'

'You need the time,' Neil said, looking at her steadily over the thin folder of tickets. 'We've thought about this enough, maybe too much. When you come back it has to be because you're sure, because you want to come.'

Storms gathered in her eyes, impatience and indecision battling doubt and shredded loyalties and the overwhelming desire to please them all: Neil, Jan, Stefan, herself, Joe Wainwright's dogmatic Yorkshire ethic. Twenty years ago she might have stamped her foot and fled upstairs. Now, controlled and mature on the surface, torn within, she smoothed non-existent gloves on her fingers.

'Want to come back? The very idea – *of course* I want to come back.'

But the reservations were left as they were and neither of them mentioned it again.

Everything done and still there were days to fill before she could leave. When Neil left for the foundry she roamed the countryside with camera and film. Perhaps when she *showed* Jan the changes he would see – they'd both see – that the past was truly over.

From the road she took snapshots of the old Hodgson Market Garden; the new owners referred to themselves as 'gentleman farmers' when they dropped into the Three Nuns. The stone farmhouse where Mr Hodgson had stood on bandy legs and roared a welcome to the foreign airman was called a stable these days, though it never saw a bag of feed or heard a whinny except what came from under the hood of a high-powered Porsche or the Volvo runabout. The new house, built where the hen house and Pearl's sty used to be, was an unhappy blend of Georgian grace and rural-cute. The gentleman farmer sold stocks in the city and had much to say about taxes and long-term assets; his wife wore too much face powder and a tight magenta sweater when she walked her

479

schnauzer bitch (her girl-dog, she called it) on the common.

At Hempton the Horse and Rider was now a Bingo parlour. The little cottage by the airfield had been extended, given a thatched roof and leaded windows which looked out on the deserted airfield, on ribbons of moss and grass sketching random patterns in the runway cracks. Thorn bushes had closed the gap in the hedge through which a tall, tired airman had come home to his wife on a hundred misty dawns.

She hesitated a long time before driving to Derbyshire. She'd been right to hesitate. Castleton was unchanged. The ruins of Peveril still raised broken battlements on the hill; as she passed the church a choir was rehearsing 'Sheep May Safely Graze', and dotted swiss still billowed from the windows of the Bull's Head. The day was hot, too perfect, and tourists' cars clotted Winnat's Pass. Families on holiday waited in line to tour underground caves; students lazed on short, springy grass to soak up the last of summer. The broken face of Mam Tor looked down, expressionless as ever, blind to human follies and hopes, blind to its own mass crumbling gritty tears into the valley.

Lallie turned away, pointed her camera towards Hope – but the focus was all wrong, the village too distant, too scattered, the viewfinder too small, too blurred to hold it all.

They were quiet on the drive to Heathrow, Neil apparently calm, intent on the heavy airport traffic; only a flickering pulse in his jaw marked his tension.

Beside him, Lallie kept checking her watch and her flight schedule and the instep of her grey suede shoes.

'We've time, sweetheart, don't worry,' he said, edging past a semi and slipping neatly between a maroon Volkswagon and a black Bentley.

'I know … I'm just wishing I'd taken the earlier plane so I could have been there for the civil thing. As it is, I could even miss the *church* ceremony if the plane's late.'

Neil gave her a tight smile. 'They'd wait for you, love. And the civil ceremony, hell, you'll not have missed much. Government officials and forms to fill out, sign on the dotted line – God! What a start to married life!' He shifted gear and forged ahead. 'Imagine it, though! Stef married –'

'Yes.' She couldn't imagine it, could think of nothing at all but Jan Kaliski waiting for her. If he was ... And Neil left behind at Eccles Place. To wonder. He'd say *something* to her at the airport, how could he help it? But she *wished* he wouldn't, there was nothing *to* say until she came home, and his patient, loving face was just too much, too much. She wanted to be in the plane, away, where he couldn't look at her, couldn't sense that subterranean surge of excitement ...

Then they were at the ticket counter and he didn't say anything much, just gave her a quick hug and a kiss at the barrier, whispered, 'Have a good time, love,' rather huskily in her ear, and hurried off.

His back looked lonely walking away from her down the long corridor and she wanted to run after him, tell him to take her back to Eccles Place and safety, but the grey suede shoes seemed rooted into the air terminal. The steward had to ask for her boarding pass twice before she heard him.

Neil let himself into the empty house. A hint of her perfume still lingered in the hall; her camelhair winter coat hung on its usual hook; on top of the umbrella stand her gardening gloves lay crossed one on another like hands folded and waiting.

Upstairs in their bedroom all was tidy, indefinably empty with no soft pink slippers by the bed, no bottles and jars crowding the top of the dresser. Stooping to smooth a fold of bedspread his fingers encountered silk – a scarf of hyacinth blue she'd forgotten, at the last moment, to pack. He touched it to his lips, tasting her in its soft fragrant silkiness, wondering what in the world he would do with the rest of his life if she came back changed and cold – or perhaps didn't come back at all.

CHAPTER FIFTY-THREE

Warsaw ... Okęcie ... customs sheds ... blank-faced officials
thumbing her passport ... a cavernous waiting-room alive with
travellers ... family groups meeting, laughing, crying,
gesturing, speaking very fast and all at once.

In Polish.

So many years, but the sound of it came back to her as
sharply as if she'd heard it yesterday. Cottage parties at
Hempton, excitable Kaz and saturnine Lech, Ryba's shop with
Henryk and Anna murmuring under rings of sausages and
garlands of dried mushrooms, Froggie on the ground-to-air,
Roman and Genia laughing in the Attercliffe flat. And Jan,
talking in his sleep.

Jan.

Who was waiting for her, walking towards her.

The airport disappeared around her, all its voices stilled as
the colour drained from her face. She was back in Little Wood
seeing a tall stranger come back to her from the war, the same
Jan but indefinably changed – as he was changed now. He was
leaner, honed with living, the lines about his eyes more deeply
etched into the thin tanned face, the eyes themselves a softer,
gentler blue, filled now with uncertainty that echoed her own.
What to say to him? Words to span so many years had never
been coined and it didn't matter anyway because her lips
wouldn't move –

He saw a woman taller than he remembered, more
self-assured, beautiful in maturity, her mouth more subtly

curved, its smile reserved, tentative ... but the delicacy of her lingered in wide grey eyes looking into his.

'You are here.' His voice was soft, too well remembered. The words reached into her heart as his hands reached to touch her face –

– but there was a flash of striped hair-ribbons as a small child darted between them, and the moment was shattered, the airport springing to life around them, loud-speakers booming, children shrieking, his voice in her ear saying her plane had been late, the wedding would be starting and they must hurry, hurry –

His car was a cocoon hurtling them through city streets as they exchanged laboured, formal conversation because twenty-five years now stretched impossibly long between them.

'Your flight was good?'

'It was fine, thank you. How far to the church?'

'A few miles only.'

'So much traffic,' she murmured. 'I hadn't expected –'

'It is our rush-hour.'

'Stefan ...?'

'He is at the church, of course. We expected you might be late.'

They were strangers who looked straight ahead because they could not, somehow, look at each other. The pull of the senses was there, the shock of recognition as his long hands shifted gear, the fragile thread of her fragrance drifting towards him, but emotion was suspended across a deep chasm of time.

The car stopped, he was helping her out, guiding her into the church with a light touch to her elbow, disregarding the turn of heads as the congregation watched their progress to the front pew, subdued whispers behind gloved hands. There was music and candles and a priest. Roman and Genia, only vaguely familiar, nodded to them from the opposite pew. Stefan waited at the altar, flashing them a relieved smile before again turning his attention to the door through which his bride would come.

A foreign bride in a foreign church in a foreign city.

Beside her, a foreign man who'd once been her husband. His sleeve was close to hers, disturbingly close, and she edged

483

away, leafing through a hymn-book she didn't understand. The unreality of it all panicked her and she closed the book and then her eyes in a pretence of prayer.

And Jan, overwhelmed by her nearness, the dream of all the lost years come magically to life, was afraid to look at her, to speak, to touch her hand. She was still a fantasy, as far out of his reach as she'd always been. *Had not always been, no.* Once he'd held her, gloried in her, knew her every breath, shared her every thought. What was she thinking now, this distant dream who was too tantalizingly close? Of her son surely, *his* son, about to be married. Their young and happy son, a mirror image of his father. Their one undeniable link.

And so they gazed at Stefan, unaware that the music suddenly swelled, that candle flames swayed on a breeze from the opening door, that the crowd was stirring in anticipation, that heads were turning, bestowing smiles that knew no time or country upon the small figure in white organdy, upon her mother who was already touching a handkerchief to her eyes, upon her father aglow with pride.

It was not the traditional Polish wedding of folklore, all joyous shouts and striped skirts aswirl, young people dancing. The Kowalewskis and their friends were city people, urbane and restrained, quiet of dress and manner. After the bride passed them by they again turned discreet glances on the English woman, nodded decorously if they caught her eye, and hid their curiosity in their hymnals.

Lallie watched Stefan as the ceremony progressed, could see nothing else, as he and the petite young girl saw only each other. They were rapt, absorbed, his height seeming to lean to her, to protect – but he looked too young, still her little boy. Who was twenty-five, old enough to take a wife. She and Jan had been younger yet and it had not mattered; war's menacing drum was only a distant grumble under the imperative of two people in love, in thrall. Who could forget that irresistible ache *to belong … She* never had, never, it was always there under the surface, drawing her back as surely as the flickering candle-flames behind Stefan's head. Not to her own wedding, no. Before that, before all the rancour with Daddy began, when there were just the two of them in the crowded Christmas church, Aunt June's voice sweet as honey, a benediction on them as their eyes touched and held in candleglow, and after it nothing ever the same ...

He stirred beside her, his hand tentatively reaching for hers.

Fingertips touched, clasped, and broken bonds re-formed, his flesh as warm, as dear as it had ever been, his smile sweet and only a little sadder as he raised her hand to his lips.

'You are here,' he whispered.

The taste of salt was in her throat and tears stung her eyes, tears she couldn't seem to blink away – but what did it matter? What more natural than tears at a wedding?

The rest of the ceremony barely registered. Vows were spoken, Danuta's voice low, Stefan's firm and clear. A bible was read from, rings were slipped on fingers, two young people aglow with the certainty that their whole lives would mirror this moment. How could they know it was hardly ever that easy? For some, it was always out of reach.

Out in the September sunshine of the Warsaw street the mood changed. Gaiety was in the air as well-wishers crowded the church steps to meet the young husband and his beautiful mother, and Lallie must meet Danuta, who reached out to her with warmth. Genia must be kissed, complimented, thanked for giving her such a lovely daughter-in-law. Roman's cheek which the years had widened and rubbed to a ruddy shine, must also be kissed. And there was Jan watching her, loving her, proud of her.

She must change then for the reception so he rushed her to his tiny apartment on the Vistula and unpacked her dress, a soft rose chiffon, and helped her into it, fastened the narrow belt of burgundy suede at her waist, did up a dozen tiny buttons at the back. Something – his lips? – brushed against her hair –'

'They're all waiting –'

'I know,' he murmured.

'And I'm here for two weeks.' Joy bubbled, fizzed, exploded. 'Two whole weeks!'

He bowed, laughing. 'In that case your carriage awaits, Madame.'

An entire quarter century disappeared, lost somewhere in a corsage of gardenias and their breathless rush to the reception, laughing at Mrs Adamski who paced the pavement in her borrowed fur-piece, worried they'd miss the toasts, the fun. '*Oh Boze*, Janek, cutting everything so fine, what a thing if you should miss the reception, eh? Hurry, hurry!'

Roman was effusive, already flushed with champagne as he drew them inside and called to his wife over the music and the dancing crowd and the clink of glasses.

'Genia, come see Lallie. A bloody marvel she looks, as usual. Huh, Jan?'

He smiled. 'She always did.'

Then Roman was reaching for her wrist, putting on the old Maurice act, running smacking kisses up her arm, muttering 'Oh, soft ... Maurice fancies you, Maurice does,' and Jan was frowning at him, drawing her away, and somehow they were dancing, close enough to be disturbing, but circumspect with Stefan watching them from the other side of the room.

'I suppose Neil booked your hotel again?' Jan asked her quietly.

Again? Then she remembered. That first mess party before they were married, Daddy instructing Neil to guard her virtue. Such an old-fashioned word – who used it anymore? Who had it? And no, Neil had not arranged a hotel for her.

'Because if he hasn't – well, we can be in Zakopane in a few hours. The housekeeper's away ...'

She held her breath, panicked again by the implication and the cool pressure of his hand through rose-coloured chiffon.

'Please, Lallie. So many times I have imagined you in my home – it would make me very happy to see you there. It's very beautiful ... perhaps there is snow already.' His mouth was grave, his eyes waiting. If she felt excited and young and romantic all at once, who did it hurt? What did it change? And it was inevitable – she'd known that from the moment Stefan brought his news to Eccles Place.

'How many hours did you say?'

'Before dark, if we drive fast.'

They said their goodbyes to the guests and the Kowalewskis – and to Stefan, who couldn't quite hide his concern. But they were his parents. What could he say? He looked at his watch and then at his mother. 'Now? With Neil's call due any

486

minute? It's been booked for a week ...'

Neil. He could have been on another planet. 'He's calling? Here?' But he hadn't *told* her, or if he had she hadn't heard him.

'If he can get through. To wish us happiness, I suppose.'

Genia was at her elbow, phone in hand, Neil's voice reaching her through static and an obtrusive operator who kept telling him to go ahead, go ahead, that his party was on the line, so that he had to shout everything through a third person. Atrocious as the connection was the tension came through it. How had the wedding gone? Did she need anything? The unions had settled, he could probably come if she needed him ...

'I'm fine,' she said firmly. 'Now I'm here I'm going to have a look around.'

'Yes. So everything's all right? With Jan? He hasn't upset you or anything?'

Upset her? He'd sent her spinning off into the stratosphere but – 'No, everything's fine. I'm handing you over to Stefan and Danuta –'

But Neil was reluctant to break the connection and ran through every detail of her return schedule again. 'I'll be waiting for you, love ...'

Her hands trembled as she passed the phone to Stefan and walked away. Until now she'd never tried to deceive Neil. It didn't come easily. And he hadn't been deceived, either. Beside her, Jan was speaking quietly through the hubbub of wedding guests and music, his eyes very blue, pleading with her, something the old Jan had never done. 'It is hurting you, this visit? I don't want ... but I *do* want you ... very much.' Need was in every angle and plane of his thin face, in his breath warm on her cheek, and she was as helpless as she'd been at twenty, laughing with him and running up to Hodgson's five-acre-field because it was out of sight of the road and the house and they couldn't wait another second to hold, to touch, and there were buttercups in the grass and not a soul in the world but Jan Kaliski and Lallie Wainwright. Lallie Armott now – but her bloodstream didn't believe it, it sang with the old song and the melody was as sweet now as it had ever been.

'Please,' he was saying, 'please, Lallie …'

'We'll leave now,' she said softly.

His shoulders relaxed and he smiled. 'At the villa there is no phone – too far out of town.'

It was early evening and very much colder, the High Tatras massive in the distance, when they arrived. The nearer mountains were blue and lilac smudges under a sky darkening with the first snowfall of the year and already the deep green of spruce was dusted with white.

The villa was another world, remote and quiet, Eva's departing footprints almost erased under the new fall of snow. This was the way he wanted her to see it, to remember it. Isolated, completely separate from their past, no Emil Buras or Joe Wainwrights casting their shadows, no one at all but the two of them.

Eva had lit fires for them, left a dinner in the oven and a babka in the pantry, hot water bottles in the beds. Two beds, he noticed. She'd assumed his mysterious and tentative guest would use Mamunia's old room. He pointed it out to Lallie as he showed her the house.

'She thinks you're sleeping in here.'

He watched her eyes change from light grey to dark, flicker with desire and laughter – but guilt and doubt were in them, too.

'You're more or less my wife,' he reminded her, his lips in her fragrant hair.

'We're dissolutioned or dissolved or annulled,' she said against his mouth, '– or whatever the lawyer called it.'

'Only in England. This house is another country.'

Perhaps that was the trouble. Their whole lives had been lived in other countries, even when they were together at Eccles Place and Hempton.

Downstairs by the wood fire he served her honey wine and watched the firelight on her face give back what the years had taken away. There was softness and clouded hair lightly touched with white, scented still with lavender water and the same shampoo she'd used all her life. The curve of her mouth was full and sweet and he ached to cover it with his own.

'You're thinking I'm old,' she said, covering his eyes with a soft hand.

He shook his head. Other women aged. Lallie matured. Her body, long and elegant as ever, had matured too, her breast slightly heavier in his palm, warm and firm through the soft fabric of her dress. 'I'm thinking I love you.'

Later, in his feather bed with her note to Jones the Milk framed above it and Mamunia's amber beads glowing from the bedpost, his lips tasted all the known hollows of her; his hands lingered over the firm, taut abdomen, stroked the narrow, elegant back. She had never been prudish and was not now. Once committed, their bodies were each other's, to do with as they wanted – and how much they wanted, how long they had waited! His mouth was hungry at her breast, the nipples tight as new rosebuds at his touch; now traversing the satin of her inner thigh as she sighed and shivered, the wind from the Tatras moaning in the chimney as she murmured with pleasure in his bed.

When at last she slept it was to wake again, reach for his hand and imprison it under her cheek. He didn't want to sleep, didn't want to lose a moment of her in this room, this house that had known so much loneliness and was now filled with the two of them.

Through all the long night she woke and slept and woke again, and they talked, remembered old pleasures and avoided old hurts now gentled over with the moss of years. Even their love had softer edges now; young urgency had given way to long kisses punctuated by sighs and quiet laughter.

'You used to be so … impatient,' he whispered.

'I've learned to wait.'

He thought he heard the echo of bitterness, and held his breath. 'I've waited also. I still wait.' His eyes touched hers in the white dawn of the window, embracing the woman and the mountains and the mellow room, but he said no more.

The days passed slowly, every moment tasted to the full, savoured, locked away in memory. They drove high into the mountains, stood on top of a new white world and watched their breath form vapour clouds and merge. They roamed the little tourist shops in town and picked out wooden plates and carved boxes and highland dolls. To take back to Eccles Place, said Lallie. Jan turned away and changed the subject. Their talk was of old times when they first met, were first married – and hardly ever about the present or the long separation in their past. Not at all about the future. She gave him the snapshots she'd taken, showed him all the changes at Eccles Place and Hempton and Attercliffe, but he gave them only a polite glance and set them aside. The picture of Mam Tor he looked at longer, and was quiet for a long time afterwards.

One day he took her to Kraków, showed her the market square and the Clothiers' Hall six centuries old, then Wawel Castle, home and burial place of kings, antique tapestries on the walls, ancient suits of armour and the tattered banners their wearers had carried into battle. 'All this we keep,' he said quietly.

Going home, he asked her to reach into the glove compartment for a small package that seemed to her vaguely familiar – but not from here, not in this setting.

'I have an errand, a family to visit,' he said. 'It's a small detour – you don't mind?'

She minded. They had so little time, the days were passing, would soon be all gone. 'I don't mind.'

'It's Kaz's cup,' he said quietly. 'I asked Stefan to bring it and he remembered.'

She felt its cold hardness under the wrappings. How much it had meant to her once – and how long now since she'd even thought of it. Then Jan was turning the car into a rough rural lane, waiting patiently as a gaggle of geese waddled across it, a black dog harrying them towards a cart-track.

'After Mamunia died I looked for them, Kaz's parents, but of course they were gone, like so much else. There were no brothers so the family name seemed to have disappeared. Then I found a step-sister. Different name of course, older than Kaz would have been, married and with grandchildren now.'

It was a farmhouse, small, crowded with Kaz's step-sister and her daughter, their husbands and the daughter's children, three barefoot stepping-stone boys who looked nothing at all like Kaz, and a small girl who did. Curly hair, impish grin, and a chattering tongue as fast as Kaz's had ever been. The guests were asked to sit, to take tea, Lallie acutely aware that she was too well-dressed, too polished and co-ordinated and perfumed for this rough country kitchen. They were clearly expected; tea glasses were already arranged on an old lace tablecloth; the eyes of the children seemed locked onto a small saffron cake which occupied the centre.

Then the grandmother unwrapped the cup, buffed its acorn-rim with a corner of her apron, crooned over it and rocked herself, a wizened crone who took on new dimension, became a woman who'd once been a carefree girl. Her daughter darted forward to fold mother and cup in a quick, defensive embrace, murmuring comfort into the coiled grey braids. Three little boys and a girl watched, eyes quick as minnows flashing from mother to grandmother to the strangers in their midst. The cup was passed from hand to hand, thumbed and exclaimed over, the grandmother's murmur low and constant in the background. 'Beautiful it was, *nie*? Just imagine, all those years under the root cellar at the Ciechocinek place, more years in another country – ayee, but life can be strange, *prawda*?'

The boys handled it roughly, squabbled over which should hold it. They were rebuked by their mother, who dusted the spotless mantelpiece and set the cup in the middle out of reach of irreverent fingers. But Lallie watched the little girl. She was perhaps five, silent at last, her eyes round with wonder as they rested on the cup, her dimpled hands making unconscious stroking motions on the air.

'I'm sorry,' Jan said when they were once again headed for Zakopane. 'It was out of our way and there is little time.'

'No,' she said quickly. He'd been wise to take her, to make her see. Wise to return Kaz's gift. For that little family it was their past, all of it contained in an empty cup. For Mum it had been the hall clock that came from her grandmother which she wound every day of her life. It was even Daddy's Backenthorpe, going back to it year after year; perhaps he thought he'd gone there to preen his feathers, but it had to be more than that. It was even Jan's mother, whom he'd searched and cared for, not just because he loved her but because she was all that was left from *his* past.

491

Mamunia, that shadowy, alien woman she'd too long resented. She sighed and pulled up her collar as an icy blast from the steppes found its way into the car.

CHAPTER FIFTY-FOUR

Wood-smoke hung heavy in the saloon of the Three Nuns. The publican was polishing glasses as he made sporadic conversation with a couple of locals at their pints of old-and-mild by the oak bar; Neil Armott sat over a light ale and a sandwich at a corner table, his back to the room. He hadn't thought two weeks could be so long. It was endless. A dozen times a day he cursed the quixotic gesture that had driven him to send Lallie off alone. Trouble came to everybody (Joe Wainwright used to say) but only a bloody fool opened the door and invited it in.

So he was a bloody fool.

A heavy hand clapped him on the shoulder. The gentleman-farmer from across the street parked himself and his brandy snifter opposite. Neil groaned. On top of everything, negotiables and stock options with dinner.

'Well! So you have to grab a bite here again, eh? The wife still not back?'

'She's not *due* back yet.' He bit into his sandwich, a slow burn starting between his ribs. Lallie had had Alice dead to rights, too; all the planned and balanced menus were abandoned in the first three days, had descended now to fried eggs and greasy chips or a wedge of pork pie from the corner shop. Without Lallie to keep her in check she spent her days on the phone and her evenings playing records.

The stockbroker-farmer grunted into his snifter. 'A pity we gave 'em the vote, that's my view. Give 'em an inch and they take a mile.'

Neil stood up and pushed his plate away. 'Is it Alice, our

maid, you're talking about? Or my wife?'

The man flushed and blustered and puffed out his cheeks. 'The maid, old chap, what did you think? My God but you're touchy these days –'

Agnes Armott was no better, pursing her lips and snipping a thread from her current bit of embroidery. 'It's a great mistake, this modern business of separate holidays. I'd no more have gone off without your father than I'd ... answer the door in an apron,' that being her epitome of poor judgement. 'The very idea, gallivanting –'

'I wouldn't call a son's wedding "gallivanting", Mother.'

'You should have gone together, then. But no, you're left to eat in public houses and fend for yourself –'

'– I'm hardly helpless –'

'And as for that lazy Alice ...'

He sighed. It wasn't just Alice that made him linger late at the office and take himself off to the Three Nuns as soon as he got home. The fact was, he couldn't stand the house without Lallie in it. Despite the barking from the kennels and Alice's rock records rattling every cup in the china cabinet, the house was a tomb. Its life and soul was still in Poland.

And was happy. Happiness that came clear as glass through all that dreadful talk on the phone. The old chemistry was at work, fizzing, bubbling, out of control, and he was the damn fool who'd mixed the explosive compounds together. As he had in the beginning.

When he went home Alice was asleep in Lallie's favourite chair, an overflowing ashtray beside her and vodka-tonic rings on the coffee table. The din from the stereo competed with the evening news roaring full blast from the telly. He should kick the silly trollop out of Lallie's chair, out of Lallie's house ... But lethargy and self-inflicted wounds kept him quiet. What was the point? The life of the house was out of it and no knowing how much, if any, would come back.

He rubbed the rings from the coffee table and switched off the racket, opened some windows to let out the smoke, and went up to his cold bed.

CHAPTER FIFTY-FIVE

Their days were colder now, and shorter. Jan brought in extra
wood for the fires and warmed the honey wine over a
candleflame before he gave it to her. A frieze of icicles hung
from the eaves and curtains were drawn earlier against the
night. Because he knew her life was not complete without such
things he drove into Zakopane and brought back a pot of small
coral flowers.

'Oh how lovely – impatiens at this altitude!' Then she
frowned. 'They have to be hot-house, darling. Aren't they
terribly … I mean, can you –'

'I have a job, you know – quite a good one.' By current
Polish standards. Perhaps this was the opening he'd been
waiting for, but he was quiet too long and the opening
evaporated in the hiss of the tea kettle. She was attempting –
with no great success – to make English tea from a package
with Chinese characters printed on it. 'It's just so *weak*,' she
muttered, 'no matter what I do it won't come *right*!'

He'd thought of a dozen ways to lead up to it and discarded
them one by one as being either too crass or too cold or too
romantic, too … preposterous. Now time was running out.
Already she glanced more often at her calendar watch and
rechecked the date on her return ticket, afterwards staring out
of the window as if one of the icicles might point to a reprieve.

In less than two weeks of her presence the villa was subtly
changed; cushions in vivid highland weaves of flame and
orange and citron were differently placed – to catch that bit of

494

afternoon sun, she said, and if he had a brass bowl with some of those bronze mums they grew in the Eccles Place greenhouse for the wintertime, well ... She experimented with a string of the mushrooms he'd dried over the summer, soaked them and sliced them and mixed them in a sauce, pronounced them 'really very good. Different of course, a bit stronger than ours, but delicious, just delicious.' But at dinner he couldn't help noticing that her enthusiasm was not matched by her appetite. Perhaps it was the radio he'd turned on for the national news, preceded as always by a few notes of Polonaise.

'I wonder if we could get the BBC,' she said once, 'perhaps we'd hear Stefan –'

'He's on his honeymoon, remember? And the mountains mess up the reception, anyway – but in Warsaw, of course ...'

'Mmm, yes.'

In the end he just asked her.

She was making the bed and remarking, not for the first time, on the wonderful warmth of the goosedown quilt, smoothing its coverlet in exactly the way she'd once touched painted violets on one of Millie's china saucers, her hand absorbing the texture, memorizing it.

And he knew he couldn't bear the thought of her not being here, not walking through these rooms, not turning Mamunia's beads so they caught the light, not resting a slender wrist on the windowsill and peering through the frosty glass every morning ...

'You could stay,' he said quickly. 'I wish you could stay, Lallie.'

She caught her breath, ran her palms down the hips of exquisitely cut slacks, fingered the collar of her lavender silk shirt. 'Ah, wishes,' she sighed, leaning her back against him in the cold light of the morning window, the scent of her hair on his face. 'Two more days,' she whispered.

'It doesn't have to be.' His arms imprisoned her waist, her sweetness. 'We can make a life here. It's possible, now, to live in ... comfort. The system can be ignored. Thousands do it. They are happy.' His fingertips stroked upwards to silk-covered breasts warm to his skin. 'Do you *want* to leave me?'

A sigh that was very close to a sob stirred under his hands. 'Want … I want everything, don't I?'

'But do you want to leave me?' he persisted.

'You know I don't.'

'Then stay. You don't have to go. We could be together.'

'And Neil would be alone.'

'You don't love *him* –'

'Oh but I do, I do – not in the same way, never in – but he's been so *good*.'

'He'd let you go.'

'He already did. He'd give me whatever I wanted even if it killed him. He's so *good*.'

'Good.' He heard the acid in his voice that he was powerless now to dilute, hardly noticing the hot splash of her tears on his arm. 'He's cared for my wife, raised my son. He's stolen half my life. Being good.' He felt her stiffen, try to draw away, and his arms tightened.

'Neil didn't steal anything, you know he didn't. Even this time with you is Neil's gift to me. Could you be that generous?'

That foolish? He knew he couldn't. Between generosity and foolishness was a very fine line, as Joe Wainwright had known well. A line he'd never allowed himself to cross. Neil was not Joe, wouldn't hang on until the bitter end.

'He wouldn't want you to be unhappy.'

She turned to him, her eyes very bright. 'But I'm not. I'm happy here, with you. I'm happy with Neil at home – or I was until all this started. Now I just …'

Her mouth, the curve of it so assured when he'd picked her up at the Warsaw airport, was indefinite again, beginning to have that bruised look he knew too well. It had been there whenever she quarrelled with Joe or with him. He'd seen it for the last time across a show ring in Fannington Park. He'd wept then and wanted to weep again now. To stop himself, to stop her, he crushed her to him and covered the hurt smudge of her mouth with his own, tried to blot out that long-ago voice telling him they were tearing her apart, Jan Kaliski and Joe Wainwright, would always tear her apart … but Joe Wainwright was long dead and still the tearing went on, Neil Armott his trusted deputy. Kind, generous Neil. The tyranny of his goodness.

He tipped up her chin and saw the proof of it. 'We're doing it to you again, aren't we?' smoothing her hair, stroking her chin.

'No, I'm too greedy, I want you and Neil and Eccles Place ...'

But not *this* place, that he'd tried so hard to make perfect for her, that was his refuge against everything. No, it was Eccles Place, always Eccles Place, home. 'It's just a street, a neighbourhood.'

'It's where I belong.' Her gesture took in the looming bulk of the High Tatras in the distance and nearer slopes of spruce overburdened with snow from the east. 'This is beautiful, but it's not mine.'

He made no effort to stop her when she pulled on boots and borrowed his parka, made her way across the white meadow behind the house. He saw her through a haze and it was some time before he realized he'd never seen her walk alone with no one else in the picture, not Joe or Neil or Millie or himself, not even a dog frisking and panting at her heels. Even in his heavy parka she seemed fragile as cut glass; the solid mass of mountains which he'd always seen as benevolent and protective appeared to press her down, threaten and compel this slender woman who belonged in English woodlands, sheltered by centuries of well-being. He suddenly felt very old, the steps to the verandah steeper than yesterday, when he went outside to stand by the railing and wait.

She was right. His love notwithstanding, she would wither here. Not tomorrow or next week but eventually her spirit would shrivel. He could see her next spring, trying to order freesias and being told she'd have to take what came; longing for a 'good cup of tea' and getting whatever the Chinese comrades happened to send; wanting friends and never getting beyond 'how are you' because her thoughts ran on a different course. She was the *Manchester Guardian* and the BBC, sheepdog trials in the Dales in summer, sherry and Dundee cake at Christmas. They – the friends she would try to make – were like himself, careful what they said and to whom, all engaged in the national pastime of watching the government's eternal tightrope walk; one year leaning west, the next prudently tilting to the east. Safer to watch than to participate. As Bura had learned. A brief meteor dazzling the military horizon – a few years later condemned to obscurity in some blind-alley command. And for what? Perhaps even Bura didn't know. For that's how it was here, and how could a Lallie Wainwright ever understand? Wainwright. Except in law her name had never been anything else.

Even from the grave Joe had won. He'd taken care of his own. Lallie would be safe.

He would be alone. But when, since he first left Poland, had he been anything else? It was a long time since he'd thought of leaving again, and much too late now. He'd teased Mamunia, said she was as Polish as Krakow's trumpeter. And she had won too. He was his mother's son.

These things we keep.

This strange snow was unyielding under her feet, no sun yet to soften its crust. Perhaps tomorrow – but tomorrow she should be packing, getting ready to leave, this liquid irresistible yearning as unslaked as the day she'd arrived. She had not lied to him. She *was* happy here, as long as he was within reach, as long as she could touch him, feel his eyes on her, hear his voice. All this time and none of that changed. Let him go into town – or even to the shed for wood, and the emptiness came rushing in. She watched strangers trudge along the street and knew they'd always be strangers, always. If she picked up a vase or a trinket from the dressing table there was nothing familiar in its substance. The chairs in the living room were deep, were comfortable, but who knew who'd chosen them, loved them because of their shape or their texture? Mamunia, whom she'd never known? Uncle Tadeusz? The absent Eva?

It was like being on a wonderful holiday and never wanting it to end – but holidays did end and Eccles Place was always waiting, drawing her back. And how could she think of leaving Neil?

Jan, oh Jan ... a heady and shimmering dream she'd loved more than half her life and still loved, still wanted. Dreams were for dreaming. Eccles Place was where she lived. It would still be warm there, a few fading geraniums where the arbor trapped the sun, where Daddy used to read the evening paper, where Jan Kaliski had listened to Chopin and dreamed his own dreams.

The evening was the perhaps the shortest – and the longest – of her life. The villa was warm in the firelight, the couch deep, his arms comforting. They were very quiet. The words had all been said. He traced her mouth with his fingertips as if committing it to memory, he kissed her eyes and her throat and her hair, and when she felt tears on her face there was no way to tell if they were his or her own.

'Will you come back sometimes?' he asked her once, knowing the answer.

She shook her head, the dark hair brushing his cheek, the clean, familiar scent of it filling his senses.

'Because it's all over for you?' How could it be, when it was still so achingly new to him?

Again her hair touched his cheek. 'Because it will never be over. We can't live on a seesaw.'

'No.'

'Stefan will want you to come and stay with us, I expect.'

And Neil would be there. 'No … I couldn't come.'

Upstairs he watched her prepare for bed, the routine of creams and lotions oddly comforting, a continuation … When she picked up the hairbrush he took it from her.

'Let me.'

He fell into the old rhythm of long, slow strokes. In the darkened room just the steady descent of the silver brush and the luminous glow from her eyes as she watched him through the mirror, the light from a small, shaded lamp reaching only her face, so that it seemed to float, lovely and eternal, just out of his reach.

She reached up at last, drew his face down to hers, and her lips were soft and warm and waiting.

CHAPTER FIFTY-SIX

They didn't kiss goodbye at the airport. There was no need. Their eyes were full of all the kisses they'd ever shared. He bowed his head, touched his lips to her glove, Polish-fashion, and was gone.

In a daze she boarded the plane, let the steward show her to her seat. He was older than most and inclined to be chatty; his voice floated over her head, insubstantial as a cloud.

'... so I'll be back as soon as we're airborne, ma'am.'

The plane roared, lifted, tucked up its wheels and turned her away from Warsaw. Seat-belt signs off, a dozen passengers shuffled up and down the aisle; a blundering toddler wound chocolatey fingers into her skirt; an attendant brought an unwanted drink; the PA system was much too busy; and the woman next to her would not be discouraged from what promised to be a Warsaw-to-London monologue.

She had never been so alone.

Then the chatty steward was hovering, handing her a box wrapped in cellophane, still cool from the fridge.

'Your husband said to be sure you got them first thing, ma'am – heaven knows where he found them this time of year.'

Dewy violets set in leaves of spring green, the fragrance so delicate she had to bathe her face in it to catch their woodland breath. Her husband, the steward said. No telling which one. There was no label on the box saying England or Poland. No note. Just the flowers touching her face with tenderness.

The woman in the next seat leaned closer to peer at the

violets. 'My, they're beautiful,' she said. 'Aren't you the lucky one!'

Lallie opened her eyes to the crowded cabin, to the shrinking world rushing below her. Millions of women in it – the hopeful young, the resigned old. How many of them knew the love of two such men as Jan Kaliski and Neil Armott? Few, she thought, very few.

'Yes,' she said softly. 'I'm very lucky indeed.'